HARRY POTTER

and the Chamber of Secrets

HARRY POTTER

and the Chamber of Secrets

DRACO DORMIENS NUNQUAM TITILLANDUS

J.K. ROWLING

SCHOLASTIC CANADA LTD.

First published in Great Britain in 1998 by
Bloomsbury Publishing Plc, 38 Soho Square, London, W1V 5DF

This edition published by Scholastic Canada Ltd.,
175 Hillmount Road, Markham, Ontario, Canada L6C 1Z7,
by arrangement with Bloomsbury Publishing Plc.
and Raincoast Books

ISBN 0-439-98819-5
School Market Edition

10 9 8 7 6 5 4 3 2 1   0 1 2 3 4 5/0

Printed and bound in Canada

For Séan P. F. Harris,
getaway driver and foulweather friend

— CHAPTER ONE —

The Worst Birthday

Not for the first time, an argument had broken out over breakfast at number four, Privet Drive. Mr Vernon Dursley had been woken in the early hours of the morning by a loud, hooting noise from his nephew Harry's room.

'Third time this week!' he roared across the table. 'If you can't control that owl, it'll have to go!'

Harry tried, yet again, to explain.

'She's *bored*,' he said. 'She's used to flying around outside. If I could just let her out at night ... '

'Do I look stupid?' snarled Uncle Vernon, a bit of fried egg dangling from his bushy moustache. 'I know what'll happen if that owl's let out.'

He exchanged dark looks with his wife, Petunia.

Harry tried to argue back but his words were drowned by a long, loud belch from the Dursleys' son, Dudley.

'I want more bacon.'

'There's more in the frying pan, sweetums,' said Aunt Petunia, turning misty eyes on her massive son. 'We must feed you up while we've got the chance ... I don't like the sound of that school food ...'

'Nonsense, Petunia, I never went hungry when *I* was at Smeltings,' said Uncle Vernon heartily. 'Dudley gets enough, don't you, son?'

Dudley, who was so large his bottom drooped over either side of the kitchen chair, grinned and turned to Harry.

'Pass the frying pan.'

'You've forgotten the magic word,' said Harry irritably.

The effect of this simple sentence on the rest of the family was incredible: Dudley gasped and fell off his chair with a crash that shook the whole kitchen; Mrs Dursley gave a small scream and clapped her hands to her mouth; Mr Dursley jumped to his feet, veins throbbing in his temples.

'I meant "please"!' said Harry quickly. 'I didn't mean –'

'WHAT HAVE I TOLD YOU,' thundered his uncle, spraying spit over the table, 'ABOUT SAYING THE M WORD IN OUR HOUSE?'

'But I –'

'HOW DARE YOU THREATEN DUDLEY!' roared Uncle Vernon, pounding the table with his fist.

'I just –'

'I WARNED YOU! I WILL NOT TOLERATE MENTION OF YOUR ABNORMALITY UNDER THIS ROOF!'

Harry stared from his purple-faced uncle to his pale aunt, who was trying to heave Dudley to his feet.

'All right,' said Harry, '*all right* ...'

Uncle Vernon sat back down, breathing like a winded rhinocerous and watching Harry closely out of the corners of his small, sharp eyes.

Ever since Harry had come home for the summer holidays, Uncle Vernon had been treating him like a bomb that might go off at any moment, because Harry *wasn't* a normal boy. As a matter of fact, he was as not normal as it is possible to be.

Harry Potter was a wizard – a wizard fresh from his first year at Hogwarts School of Witchcraft and Wizardry. And if the Dursleys were unhappy to have him back for the holidays, it was nothing to how Harry felt.

He missed Hogwarts so much it was like having a constant stomach ache. He missed the castle, with its secret passageways and ghosts, his lessons (though perhaps not Snape, the potions master), the post arriving by owl, eating banquets in the Great Hall, sleeping in his four-poster bed in the tower dormitory, visiting the gamekeeper, Hagrid, in his cabin in the grounds next to the forbidden forest and, especially, Quidditch, the most popular sport in the wizarding world (six tall goal-posts, four flying balls and fourteen players on broomsticks).

All Harry's spellbooks, his wand, robes, cauldron and top-of-the-range Nimbus Two Thousand broomstick had been locked in a cupboard under the stairs by Uncle Vernon the instant Harry had come home. What did the Dursleys care if Harry lost his place on the house Quidditch team because he hadn't practised all sum-

mer? What was it to the Dursleys if Harry went back to school
without any of his homework done? The Dursleys were what wizards called Muggles (not a drop of magical blood in their veins)
and as far as they were concerned, having a wizard in the family
was a matter of deepest shame. Uncle Vernon had even padlocked
Harry's owl, Hedwig, inside her cage, to stop her carrying messages to anyone in the wizarding world.

Harry looked nothing like the rest of the family. Uncle Vernon
was large and neckless, with an enormous black moustache; Aunt
Petunia was horse-faced and boney; Dudley was blond, pink and
porky. Harry, on the other hand, was small and skinny, with brilliant green eyes and jet black hair that was always untidy. He wore
round glasses, and on his forehead was a thin, lightning-shaped
scar.

It was this scar that made Harry so particularly unusual, even
for a wizard. This scar was the only hint of Harry's very mysterious past, of the reason he had been left on the Dursleys' doorstep
eleven years before.

At the age of one, Harry had somehow survived a curse from
the greatest dark sorcerer of all time, Lord Voldemort, whose
name most witches and wizards still feared to speak. Harry's parents had died in Voldemort's attack, but Harry had escaped with
his lightning scar, and somehow – nobody understood why –
Voldemort's powers had been destroyed the instant he had failed
to kill Harry.

So Harry had been brought up by his dead mother's sister and
her husband. He had spent ten years with the Dursleys, never
understanding why he kept making odd things happen without
meaning to, believing the Dursleys' story that he had got his scar
in the car crash which had killed his parents.

And then, exactly a year ago, Hogwarts had written to Harry,
and the whole story had come out. Harry had taken up his place
at wizard school, where he and his scar were famous ... but now
the school year was over, and he was back with the Dursleys for
the summer, back to being treated like a dog that had rolled in
something smelly.

The Dursleys hadn't even remembered that today happened to
be Harry's twelfth birthday. Of course, his hopes hadn't been high;
they'd never given him a proper present, let alone a cake – but to
ignore it completely ...

At that moment, Uncle Vernon cleared his throat importantly and said, 'Now, as we all know, today is a very important day.'

Harry looked up, hardly daring to believe it.

'This could well be the day I make the biggest deal of my career,' said Uncle Vernon.

Harry went back to his toast. Of course, he thought bitterly, Uncle Vernon was talking about the stupid dinner party. He'd been talking of nothing else for a fortnight. Some rich builder and his wife were coming to dinner and Uncle Vernon was hoping to get a huge order from him (Uncle Vernon's company made drills).

'I think we should run through the schedule one more time,' said Uncle Vernon. 'We should all be in position at eight o'clock. Petunia, you will be –?'

'In the lounge,' said Aunt Petunia promptly, 'waiting to welcome them graciously to our home.'

'Good, good. And Dudley?'

'I'll be waiting to open the door.' Dudley put on a foul, simpering smile. 'May I take your coats, Mr and Mrs Mason?'

'They'll *love* him!' cried Aunt Petunia rapturously.

'Excellent, Dudley,' said Uncle Vernon. Then he rounded on Harry. 'And *you*?'

'I'll be in my bedroom, making no noise and pretending I'm not there,' said Harry tonelessly.

'Exactly,' said Uncle Vernon nastily. 'I will lead them into the lounge, introduce you, Petunia, and pour them drinks. At eight fifteen –'

'I'll announce dinner,' said Aunt Petunia.

'And Dudley, you'll say –'

'May I take you through to the dining room, Mrs Mason?' said Dudley, offering his fat arm to an invisible woman.

'My perfect little gentleman!' sniffed Aunt Petunia.

'And *you*?' said Uncle Vernon viciously to Harry.

'I'll be in my room, making no noise and pretending I'm not there,' said Harry dully.

'Precisely. Now, we should aim to get in a few good compliments at dinner. Petunia, any ideas?'

'Vernon tells me you're a *wonderful* golfer, Mr Mason ... *Do* tell me where you bought your dress, Mrs Mason ...'

'Perfect ... Dudley?'

'How about: "We had to write an essay about our hero at

school, Mr Mason, and *I* wrote about *you*." '

This was too much for both Aunt Petunia and Harry. Aunt Petunia burst into tears and hugged her son, while Harry ducked under the table so they wouldn't see him laughing.

'And you, boy?'

Harry fought to keep his face straight as he emerged.

'I'll be in my room, making no noise and pretending I'm not there,' he said.

'Too right you will,' said Uncle Vernon forcefully. 'The Masons don't know anything about you and it's going to stay that way. When dinner's over, you take Mrs Mason back to the lounge for coffee, Petunia, and I'll bring the subject round to drills. With any luck, I'll have the deal signed and sealed before the *News at Ten*. We'll be shopping for a holiday home in Majorca this time tomorrow.'

Harry couldn't feel too excited about this. He didn't think the Dursleys would like him any better in Majorca than they did in Privet Drive.

'Right – I'm off into town to pick up the dinner jackets for Dudley and me. And *you*,' he snarled at Harry, 'you stay out of your aunt's way while she's cleaning.'

Harry left through the back door. It was a brilliant, sunny day. He crossed the lawn, slumped down on the garden bench and sang under his breath, 'Happy birthday to me ... happy birthday to me ...'

No cards, no presents, and he would be spending the evening pretending not to exist. He gazed miserably into the hedge. He had never felt so lonely. More than anything else at Hogwarts, more even than playing Quidditch, Harry missed his best friends, Ron Weasley and Hermione Granger. They, however, didn't seem to be missing him at all. Neither of them had written to him all summer, even though Ron had said he was going to ask Harry to come and stay.

Countless times, Harry had been on the point of unlocking Hedwig's cage by magic and sending her to Ron and Hermione with a letter, but it wasn't worth the risk. Under-age wizards weren't allowed to use magic outside school. Harry hadn't told the Dursleys this; he knew it was only their terror that he might turn them all into dung beetles that stopped them locking *him* in the cupboard under the stairs with his wand and broomstick. For the first couple of weeks back, Harry had enjoyed muttering nonsense words under his breath and watching Dudley tearing out of the room as fast as his fat legs would carry him. But the long silence from Ron and Hermione had made Harry feel so cut off from the magical world that even taunting Dudley had lost its appeal – and now Ron and Hermione had forgotten his birthday.

What wouldn't he give now for a message from Hogwarts? From any witch or wizard? He'd almost be glad of a sight of his arch-enemy, Draco Malfoy, just to be sure it hadn't all been a dream ...

Not that his whole year at Hogwarts had been fun. At the very end of last term, Harry had come face-to-face with none other than Lord Voldemort himself. Voldemort might be a ruin of his former self, but he was still terrifying, still cunning, still determined to regain power. Harry had slipped through Voldemort's clutches for a second time, but it had been a narrow escape, and even now, weeks later, Harry kept waking in the night, drenched in cold sweat, wondering where Voldemort was now, remembering his livid face, his wide, mad eyes...

Harry suddenly sat bolt upright on the garden bench. He had been staring absent-mindedly into the hedge – *and the hedge was staring back*. Two enormous green eyes had appeared among the leaves.

Harry jumped to his feet just as a jeering voice floated across the lawn.

'I know what day it is,' sang Dudley, waddling towards him.

The huge eyes blinked and vanished.

'What?' said Harry, not taking his eyes off the spot where they had been.

'I know what day it is,' Dudley repeated, coming right up to him.

'Well done,' said Harry. 'So you've finally learned the days of the week.'

'Today's your *birthday*,' sneered Dudley. 'How come you haven't got any cards? Haven't you even got friends at that freak place?'

'Better not let your mum hear you talking about my school,' said Harry coolly.

Dudley hitched up his trousers, which were slipping down his fat bottom.

'Why're you staring at the hedge?' he said suspiciously.

'I'm trying to decide what would be the best spell to set it on fire,' said Harry.

Dudley stumbled backwards at once, a look of panic on his fat face.

'You c-can't – Dad told you you're not to do m-magic – he said he'll chuck you out of the house – and you haven't got anywhere else to go – you haven't got any *friends* to take you –'

'*Jiggery pokery!*' said Harry in a fierce voice. 'Hocus pocus ... squiggly wiggly ...'

'MUUUUUUM!' howled Dudley, tripping over his feet as he dashed back towards the house. 'MUUUM! He's doing you know what!'

Harry paid dearly for his moment of fun. As neither Dudley nor the hedge was in any way hurt, Aunt Petunia knew he hadn't really done magic, but he still had to duck as she aimed a heavy blow at his head with the soapy frying pan. Then she gave him work to do, with the promise he wouldn't eat again until he'd finished.

While Dudley lolled around watching and eating ice-creams, Harry cleaned the windows, washed the car, mowed the lawn, trimmed the flowerbeds, pruned and watered the roses and re-painted the garden bench. The sun blazed overhead, burning the back of his neck. Harry knew he shouldn't have risen to Dudley's bait, but Dudley had said the very thing Harry had been thinking himself ... maybe he *didn't* have any friends at Hogwarts ...

'Wish they could see famous Harry Potter now,' he thought savagely, as he spread manure on the flowerbeds, his back aching, sweat running down his face.

It was half past seven in the evening when at last, exhausted, he heard Aunt Petunia calling him.

'Get in here! And walk on the newspaper!'

Harry moved gladly into the shade of the gleaming kitchen. On top of the fridge stood tonight's pudding: a huge mound of whipped cream and sugared violets. A joint of roast pork was siz-zling in the oven.

'Eat quickly! The Masons will be here soon!' snapped Aunt Petunia, pointing to two slices of bread and a lump of cheese on the kitchen table. She was already wearing a salmon-pink cocktail dress.

Harry washed his hands and bolted down his pitiful supper. The moment he had finished, Aunt Petunia whisked away his plate. 'Upstairs! Hurry!'

As he passed the door to the living room, Harry caught a glimpse of Uncle Vernon and Dudley in bow ties and dinner jackets. He had only just reached the upstairs landing when the doorbell rang and Uncle Vernon's furious face appeared at the foot of the stairs.

'Remember, boy – one sound ...'

Harry crossed to his bedroom on tiptoe, slipped inside, closed the door and turned to collapse on his bed.

The trouble was, there was already someone sitting on it.

— CHAPTER TWO —

Dobby's Warning

Harry managed not to shout out, but it was a close thing. The little creature on the bed had large, bat-like ears and bulging green eyes the size of tennis balls. Harry knew instantly that this was what had been watching him out of the garden hedge that morning.

As they stared at each other, Harry heard Dudley's voice from the hall.

'May I take your coats, Mr and Mrs Mason?'

The creature slipped off the bed and bowed so low that the end of its long thin nose touched the carpet. Harry noticed that it was wearing what looked like an old pillowcase, with rips for arm- and leg-holes.

'Er – hello,' said Harry nervously.

'Harry Potter!' said the creature, in a high-pitched voice Harry was sure would carry down the stairs. 'So long has Dobby wanted to meet you, sir ... Such an honour it is ...'

'Th-thank you,' said Harry, edging along the wall and sinking into his desk chair, next to Hedwig, who was asleep in her large cage. He wanted to ask, 'What are you?' but thought it would sound too rude, so instead he said, 'Who are you?'

'Dobby, sir. Just Dobby. Dobby the house-elf,' said the creature.

'Oh – really?' said Harry. 'Er – I don't want to be rude or anything, but – this isn't a great time for me to have a house-elf in my bedroom.'

Aunt Petunia's high, false laugh sounded from the living room. The elf hung his head.

'Not that I'm not pleased to meet you,' said Harry quickly, 'but, er, is there any particular reason you're here?'

'Oh, yes, sir,' said Dobby earnestly. 'Dobby has come to tell you, sir ... it is difficult, sir ... Dobby wonders where to begin ...'

'Sit down,' said Harry politely, pointing at the bed.

To his horror, the elf burst into tears – very noisy tears.

'*S-sit down!*' he wailed. '*Never ... never ever ...*'

Harry thought he heard the voices downstairs falter.

'I'm sorry,' he whispered, 'I didn't mean to offend you or anything.'

'Offend Dobby!' choked the elf. 'Dobby has *never* been asked to sit down by a wizard – like an *equal* –'

Harry, trying to say 'Shh!' and look comforting at the same time, ushered Dobby back onto the bed where he sat hiccoughing, looking like a large and very ugly doll. At last he managed to control himself, and sat with his great eyes fixed on Harry in an expression of watery adoration.

'You can't have met many decent wizards,' said Harry, trying to cheer him up.

Dobby shook his head. Then, without warning, he leapt up and started banging his head furiously on the window, shouting, '*Bad* Dobby! *Bad* Dobby!'

'Don't – what are you doing?' Harry hissed, springing up and pulling Dobby back onto the bed. Hedwig had woken up with a particularly loud screech and was beating her wings wildly against the bars of her cage.

'Dobby had to punish himself, sir,' said the elf, who had gone slightly cross-eyed. 'Dobby almost spoke ill of his family, sir ...'

'Your family?'

'The wizard family Dobby serves, sir ... Dobby is a house-elf – bound to serve one house and one family forever ...'

'Do they know you're here?' asked Harry curiously.

Dobby shuddered.

'Oh no, sir, no ... Dobby will have to punish himself most grievously for coming to see you, sir. Dobby will have to shut his ears in the oven door for this. If they ever knew, sir –'

'But won't they notice if you shut your ears in the oven door?'

'Dobby doubts it, sir. Dobby is always having to punish himself for something, sir. They lets Dobby get on with it, sir. Sometimes they reminds me to do extra punishments ...'

'But why don't you leave? Escape?'

'A house-elf must be set free, sir. And the family will never set Dobby free ... Dobby will serve the family until he dies, sir ...'

Harry stared.

'And I thought I was hard-done-by staying here for another four weeks,' he said. 'This makes the Dursleys sound almost human. Can't anyone help you? Can't I?'

Almost at once, Harry wished he hadn't spoken. Dobby dissolved again into wails of gratitude.

'Please,' Harry whispered frantically, 'please be quiet. If the Dursleys hear anything, if they know you're here ...'

'Harry Potter asks if he can help Dobby ... Dobby has heard of your greatness, sir, but of your goodness, Dobby never knew ...'

Harry, who was feeling distinctly hot in the face, said, 'Whatever you've heard about my greatness is a load of rubbish. I'm not even top of my year at Hogwarts, that's Hermione, she –'

But he stopped quickly, because thinking about Hermione was painful.

'Harry Potter is humble and modest,' said Dobby reverently, his orb-like eyes aglow. 'Harry Potter speaks not of his triumph over He Who Must Not Be Named.'

'Voldemort?' said Harry.

Dobby clapped his hands over his bat ears and moaned, 'Ah, speak not the name, sir! Speak not the name!'

'Sorry,' said Harry quickly. 'I know lots of people don't like it – my friend Ron ...'

He stopped again. Thinking about Ron was painful, too.

Dobby leaned towards Harry, his eyes wide as headlamps.

'Dobby heard tell,' he said hoarsely, 'that Harry Potter met the Dark Lord for a second time, just weeks ago ... that Harry Potter escaped *yet again*.'

Harry nodded and Dobby's eyes suddenly shone with tears.

'Ah, sir,' he gasped, dabbing his face with a corner of the grubby pillowcase he was wearing. 'Harry Potter is valiant and bold! He has braved so many dangers already! But Dobby has come to protect Harry Potter, to warn him, even if he *does* have to shut his ears in the oven door later ... *Harry Potter must not go back to Hogwarts*.'

There was a silence broken only by the chink of knives and forks from downstairs and the distant rumble of Uncle Vernon's voice.

'W-what?' Harry stammered. 'But I've got to go back – term starts on September the first. It's all that's keeping me going. You don't know what it's like here. I don't *belong* here. I belong in your world – at Hogwarts.'

'No, no, no,' squeaked Dobby, shaking his head so hard his ears flapped. 'Harry Potter must stay where he is safe. He is too great, too good, to lose. If Harry Potter goes back to Hogwarts, he will be in mortal danger.'

'Why?' said Harry in surprise.

'There is a plot, Harry Potter. A plot to make most terrible things happen at Hogwarts School of Witchcraft and Wizardry this year,' whispered Dobby, suddenly trembling all over. 'Dobby has known it for months, sir. Harry Potter must not put himself in peril. He is too important, sir!'

'What terrible things?' said Harry at once. 'Who's plotting them?'

Dobby made a funny choking noise and then banged his head madly against the wall.

'All right!' cried Harry, grabbing the elf's arm to stop him. 'You can't say, I understand. But why are you warning *me*?' A sudden, unpleasant thought struck him. 'Hang on – this hasn't got anything to do with Vol – sorry – with You Know Who, has it? You could just shake or nod,' he added hastily, as Dobby's head tilted worryingly close to the wall again.

Slowly, Dobby shook his head.

'Not – not *He Who Must Not Be Named*, sir.'

But Dobby's eyes were wide and he seemed to be trying to give Harry a hint. Harry, however, was completely at sea.

'He hasn't got a brother, has he?'

Dobby shook his head, his eyes wider than ever.

'Well then, I can't think who else would have a chance of making horrible things happen at Hogwarts,' said Harry. 'I mean, there's Dumbledore, for one thing – you know who Dumbledore is, don't you?'

Dobby bowed his head.

'Albus Dumbledore is the greatest Headmaster Hogwarts has ever had. Dobby knows it, sir. Dobby has heard Dumbledore's powers rival those of He Who Must Not Be Named at the height of his strength. But sir,' Dobby's voice dropped to an urgent whisper, 'there are powers Dumbledore doesn't ... powers no decent wizard ...'

And before Harry could stop him, Dobby bounded off the bed, seized Harry's desk lamp and started beating himself around the head with ear-splitting yelps.

A sudden silence fell downstairs. Two seconds later Harry, heart thudding madly, heard Uncle Vernon coming into the hall, calling, 'Dudley must have left his television on again, the little tyke!'

'Quick! In the wardrobe!' hissed Harry, stuffing Dobby in, shutting the door and flinging himself onto the bed just as the door handle turned.

'What – the – *devil* – are – you – doing?' said Uncle Vernon through gritted teeth, his face horribly close to Harry's. 'You've just ruined the punchline of my Japanese golfer joke ... one more sound and you'll wish you'd never been born, boy!'

He stomped flat-footed from the room.

Shaking, Harry let Dobby out of the wardrobe.

'See what it's like here?' he said. 'See why I've got to go back to Hogwarts? It's the only place I've got – well, I *think* I've got friends.'

'Friends who don't even *write* to Harry Potter?' said Dobby slyly.

'I expect they've just been – hang on,' said Harry, frowning. 'How do *you* know my friends haven't been writing to me?'

Dobby shuffled his feet.

'Harry Potter mustn't be angry with Dobby – Dobby did it for the best ...'

'*Have you been stopping my letters?*'

'Dobby has them here, sir,' said the elf. Stepping nimbly out of Harry's reach, he pulled a thick wad of envelopes from the inside of the pillowcase he was wearing. Harry could make out Hermione's neat writing, Ron's untidy scrawl and even a scribble that looked as though it was from the Hogwarts gamekeeper, Hagrid.

Dobby blinked anxiously up at Harry.

'Harry Potter mustn't be angry ... Dobby hoped ... if Harry Potter thought his friends had forgotten him ... Harry Potter might not want to go back to school, sir ...'

Harry wasn't listening. He made a grab for the letters, but Dobby jumped out of reach.

'Harry Potter will have them, sir, if he gives Dobby his word that he will not return to Hogwarts. Ah, sir, this is a danger you must not face! Say you won't go back, sir!'

'No,' said Harry angrily. 'Give me my friends' letters!'

'Then Harry Potter leaves Dobby no choice,' said the elf sadly.

Before Harry could move, Dobby had darted to the bedroom door, pulled it open – and sprinted down the stairs.

Mouth dry, stomach lurching, Harry sprang after him, trying not to make a sound. He jumped the last six stairs, landing cat-like on the hall carpet, looking around for Dobby. From the dining room he heard Uncle Vernon saying, '... tell Petunia that very funny story about those American plumbers, Mr Mason, she's been dying to hear ...'

Harry ran up the hall into the kitchen and felt his stomach disappear.

Aunt Petunia's masterpiece of a pudding, the mountain of cream and sugared violets, was floating up near the ceiling. On top of a cupboard in the corner crouched Dobby.

'No,' croaked Harry. 'Please ... they'll kill me ...'

'Harry Potter must say he's not going back to school –'

'Dobby ... please ...'

'Say it, sir ...'

'I can't!'

Dobby gave him a tragic look.

'Then Dobby must do it, sir, for Harry Potter's own good.'

The pudding fell to the floor with a heart-stopping crash. Cream splattered the windows and walls as the dish shattered. With a crack like a whip, Dobby vanished.

There were screams from the dining room and Uncle Vernon burst into the kitchen to find Harry, rigid with shock, covered from head to foot in Aunt Petunia's pudding.

At first, it looked as though Uncle Vernon would manage to gloss the whole thing over ('Just our nephew – very disturbed – meeting strangers upsets him, so we kept him upstairs ...') He shooed the shocked Masons back into the dining room, promised Harry he would flay him to within an inch of his life when the Masons had left, and handed him a mop. Aunt Petunia dug some ice-cream out of the freezer and Harry, still shaking, started scrubbing the kitchen clean.

Uncle Vernon might still have been able to make his deal – if it hadn't been for the owl.

Aunt Petunia was just handing round a box of after-dinner mints when a huge barn owl swooped through the dining room window, dropped a letter on Mrs Mason's head and swooped out again. Mrs Mason screamed like a banshee and ran from the house shouting about lunatics. Mr Mason stayed just long enough to tell the Dursleys that his wife was mortally afraid of birds of all shapes and sizes, and to ask whether this was their idea of a joke.

Harry stood in the kitchen, clutching the mop for support as Uncle Vernon advanced on him, a demonic glint in his tiny eyes.

'Read it!' he hissed evilly, brandishing the letter the owl had delivered. 'Go on – read it!'

Harry took it. It did not contain birthday greetings.

Dear Mr Potter,

We have received intelligence that a Hover Charm was used at your place of residence this evening at twelve minutes past nine.

As you know, under-age wizards are not permitted to perform spells outside school, and further spellwork on your part may lead to expulsion from said school (Decree for the Reasonable Restriction of Under-Age Sorcery, 1875, Paragraph C).

We would also ask you to remember that any magical activity which risks notice by members of the non-magical community (Muggles) is a serious offence, under section 13 of the International Confederation of Warlocks' Statute of Secrecy.

Enjoy your holidays!

Yours sincerely,

Mafalda Hopkirk

Improper Use of Magic Office

Ministry of Magic

Harry looked up from the letter and gulped.

'You didn't tell us you weren't allowed to use magic outside school,' said Uncle Vernon, a mad gleam dancing in his eyes. 'Forgot to mention it ... slipped your mind, I daresay ...'

He was bearing down on Harry like a great bulldog, all his teeth bared. 'Well, I've got news for you, boy ... I'm locking you up ... you're never going back to that school ... never ... and if you try and magic yourself out – they'll expel you!'

And laughing like a maniac, he dragged Harry back upstairs.

Uncle Vernon was as bad as his word. The following morning, he paid a man to fit bars on Harry's window. He himself fitted the cat-flap in the bedroom door, so that small amounts of food could be pushed inside three times a day. They let Harry out to use the bathroom morning and evening. Otherwise, he was locked in his room around the clock.

*

Three days later, the Dursleys were showing no sign of relenting and Harry couldn't see any way out of his situation. He lay on his bed watching the sun sinking behind the bars on the window and wondered miserably what was going to happen to him.

What was the good of magicking himself out of his room if Hogwarts would expel him for doing it? Yet life at Privet Drive had reached an all-time low. Now the Dursleys knew they weren't going to wake up as fruitbats, he had lost his only weapon. Dobby might have saved Harry from horrible happenings at Hogwarts, but the way things were going, he'd probably starve to death anyway.

The cat-flap rattled and Aunt Petunia's hand appeared, pushing a bowl of tinned soup into the room. Harry, whose insides were aching with hunger, jumped off his bed and seized it. The soup was stone cold, but he drank half of it in one gulp. Then he crossed the room to Hedwig's cage and tipped the soggy vegetables at the bottom of the bowl into her empty food tray. She ruffled her feathers and gave him a look of deep disgust.

'It's no good turning your beak up at it, that's all we've got,' said Harry grimly.

He put the empty bowl back on the floor next to the cat-flap and lay back down on the bed, somehow even hungrier than he had been before the soup.

Supposing he was still alive in another four weeks, what would happen if he didn't turn up at Hogwarts? Would someone be sent to see why he hadn't come back? Would they be able to make the Dursleys let him go?

The room was growing dark. Exhausted, stomach rumbling, mind spinning over the same unanswerable questions, Harry fell into an uneasy sleep.

He dreamed that he was on show in a zoo, with a card reading 'Under-age Wizard' attached to his cage. People goggled through the bars at him as he lay, starving and weak, on a bed of straw. He saw Dobby's face in the crowd and shouted out, asking for help, but Dobby called, 'Harry Potter is safe there, sir!' and vanished. Then the Dursleys appeared and Dudley rattled the bars of the cage, laughing at him.

'Stop it,' Harry muttered, as the rattling pounded in his sore head. 'Leave me alone ... cut it out ... I'm trying to sleep ...'

He opened his eyes. Moonlight was shining through the bars on the window. And someone *was* goggling through the bars at him: a freckle-faced, red-haired, long-nosed someone.

Ron Weasley was outside Harry's window.

CHAPTER THREE

The Burrow

'*Ron!*' breathed Harry, creeping to the window and pushing it up so they could talk through the bars. 'Ron, how did you – what the –?'

Harry's mouth fell open as the full impact of what he was seeing hit him. Ron was leaning out of the back window of an old turquoise car, which was parked *in mid-air.* Grinning at Harry from the front seats were Fred and George, Ron's elder twin brothers.

'All right, Harry?'

'What's been going on?' said Ron. 'Why haven't you been answering my letters? I've asked you to stay about twelve times, and then Dad came home and said you'd got an official warning for using magic in front of Muggles ...'

'It wasn't me – and how did he know?'

'He works for the Ministry,' said Ron. 'You *know* we're not supposed to do spells outside school –'

'Bit rich coming from you,' said Harry, staring at the floating car.

'Oh, this doesn't count,' said Ron. 'We're only borrowing this, it's Dad's, *we* didn't enchant it. But doing magic in front of those Muggles you live with ...'

'I told you, I didn't – but it'll take too long to explain now. Look, can you explain to them at Hogwarts that the Dursleys have locked me up and won't let me come back, and obviously I can't magic myself out, because the Ministry'll think that's the second spell I've done in three days, so –'

'Stop gibbering,' said Ron, 'we've come to take you home with us.'

'But you can't magic me out either –'

'We don't need to,' said Ron, jerking his head towards the front seats and grinning. 'You forget who I've got with me.'

'Tie that round the bars,' said Fred, throwing the end of a rope to Harry.

'If the Dursleys wake up, I'm dead,' said Harry, as he tied the rope tightly around a bar and Fred revved up the car.

'Don't worry,' said Fred, 'and stand back.'

Harry moved back into the shadows next to Hedwig, who seemed to have realized how important this was and kept still and silent. The car revved louder and louder and suddenly, with a crunching noise, the bars were pulled clean out of the window as Fred drove straight up in the air – Harry ran back to the window to see the bars dangling a few feet above the ground. Panting, Ron hoisted them up into the car. Harry listened anxiously, but there was no sound from the Dursleys' bedroom.

When the bars were safely in the back seat with Ron, Fred reversed as close as possible to Harry's window.

'Get in,' Ron said.

'But all my Hogwarts stuff ... my wand ... my broomstick ...'

'Where is it?'

'Locked in the cupboard under the stairs, and I can't get out of this room –'

'No problem,' said George from the front passenger seat. 'Out of the way, Harry.'

Fred and George climbed carefully through the window into Harry's room. You had to hand it to them, thought Harry, as George took an ordinary hairpin from his pocket and started to pick the lock.

'A lot of wizards think it's a waste of time, knowing this sort of Muggle trick,' said Fred, 'but we feel they're skills worth learning, even if they are a bit slow.'

There was a small click and the door swung open.

'So – we'll get your trunk – you grab anything you need from your room and hand it out to Ron,' whispered George.

'Watch out for the bottom stair, it creaks,' Harry whispered back, as the twins disappeared onto the dark landing.

Harry dashed around his room, collecting his things together and passing them out of the window to Ron. Then he went to help Fred and George heave his trunk up the stairs. Harry heard Uncle Vernon cough.

At last, panting, they reached the landing, then carried the trunk through Harry's room to the open window. Fred climbed back into the car to pull with Ron, and Harry and George pushed from the bedroom side. Inch by inch, the trunk slid through the window.

Uncle Vernon coughed again.

'A bit more,' panted Fred, who was pulling from inside the car, 'one good push ...'

Harry and George threw their shoulders against the trunk and it slid out of the window into the back seat of the car.

'OK, let's go,' George whispered.

But as Harry climbed onto the window-sill there came a sudden loud screech from behind him, followed immediately by the thunder of Uncle Vernon's voice.

'THAT RUDDY OWL!'

'I've forgotten Hedwig!'

Harry tore back across the room as the landing light clicked on. He snatched up Hedwig's cage, dashed to the window and passed it out to Ron. He was scrambling back onto the chest of drawers when Uncle Vernon hammered on the unlocked door – and it crashed open.

For a split second, Uncle Vernon stood framed in the doorway; then he let out a bellow like an angry bull and dived at Harry, grabbing him by the ankle.

Ron, Fred and George seized Harry's arms and pulled as hard as they could.

'Petunia!' roared Uncle Vernon. 'He's getting away! HE'S GET-TING AWAY!'

The Weasleys gave a gigantic tug and Harry's leg slid out of Uncle Vernon's grasp. As soon as Harry was in the car and had slammed the door shut Ron yelled, 'Put your foot down, Fred!' and the car shot suddenly towards the moon.

Harry couldn't believe it – he was free. He wound down the window, the night air whipping his hair, and looked back at the shrinking rooftops of Privet Drive. Uncle Vernon, Aunt Petunia and Dudley were all hanging, dumbstruck, out of Harry's window.

'See you next summer!' Harry yelled.

The Weasleys roared with laughter and Harry settled back in his seat, grinning from ear to ear.

'Let Hedwig out,' he told Ron, 'she can fly behind us. She hasn't had a chance to stretch her wings for ages.'

George handed the hairpin to Ron and a moment later, Hedwig

had soared joyfully out of the window to glide alongside them like a ghost.

'So – what's the story, Harry?' said Ron impatiently. 'What's been happening?'

Harry told them all about Dobby, the warning he'd given Harry and the fiasco of the violet pudding. There was a long shocked silence when he had finished.

'Very fishy,' said Fred finally.

'Definitely dodgy,' agreed George. 'So he wouldn't even tell you who's supposed to be plotting all this stuff?'

'I don't think he could,' said Harry. 'I told you, every time he got close to letting something slip, he started banging his head against the wall.'

He saw Fred and George look at each other.

'What, you think he was lying to me?' said Harry.

'Well,' said Fred, 'put it this way – house-elves have got power-ful magic of their own, but they can't usually use it without their masters' permission. I reckon old Dobby was sent to stop you coming back to Hogwarts. Someone's idea of a joke. Can you think of anyone at school with a grudge against you?'

'Yes,' said Harry and Ron together, instantly.

'Draco Malfoy,' Harry explained. 'He hates me.'

'Draco Malfoy?' said George, turning round. 'Not Lucius Malfoy's son?'

'Must be, it's not a very common name, is it?' said Harry. 'Why?'

'I've heard Dad talking about him,' said George. 'He was a big supporter of You Know Who.'

'And when You Know Who disappeared,' said Fred, craning around to look at Harry, 'Lucius Malfoy came back saying he'd never meant any of it. Load of dung – Dad reckons he was right in You Know Who's inner circle.'

Harry had heard these rumours about Malfoy's family before, and they didn't surprise him at all. Malfoy made Dudley Dursley look like a kind, thoughtful and sensitive boy.

'I don't know whether the Malfoys own a house-elf ...' said Harry.

'Well, whoever owns him will be an old wizarding family, and they'll be rich,' said Fred.

'Yeah, Mum's always wishing we had a house-elf to do the iron-ing,' said George. 'But all we've got is a lousy old ghoul in the attic and gnomes all over the garden. House-elves come with big old manors and castles and places like that, you wouldn't catch one in our house ...'

Harry was silent. Judging by the fact that Draco Malfoy usually had the best of everything, his family were rolling in wizard gold; he could just see Malfoy strutting around a large manor house. Sending the family servant to stop Harry going back to Hogwarts also sounded exactly like the sort of thing Malfoy would do. Had Harry been stupid to take Dobby seriously?

'I'm glad we came to get you, anyway,' said Ron. 'I was getting really worried when you didn't answer any of my letters. I thought it was Errol's fault at first –'

'Who's Errol?'

'Our owl. He's ancient. It wouldn't be the first time he'd collapsed on a delivery. So then I tried to borrow Hermes –'

'*Who?*'

'The owl Mum and Dad bought Percy when he was made a prefect,' said Fred from the front.

'But Percy wouldn't lend him to me,' said Ron. 'Said he needed him.'

'Percy's been acting very oddly this summer,' said George, frowning. 'And he *has* been sending a lot of letters and spending a load of time shut up in his room ... I mean, there's only so many times you can polish a Prefect badge ... You're driving too far west, Fred,' he added, pointing at a compass on the dashboard. Fred twiddled the steering wheel.

'So, does your Dad know you've got the car?' said Harry, guessing the answer.

'Er, no,' said Ron, 'he had to work tonight. Hopefully we'll be able to get it back in the garage without Mum noticing we flew it.'

'What does your Dad do at the Ministry of Magic, anyway?'

'He works in the most boring department,' said Ron. 'The Misuse of Muggle Artifacts Office.'

'The *what?*'

'It's all to do with bewitching things that are Muggle-made, you know, in case they end up back in a Muggle shop or house. Like, last year, some old witch died and her tea set was sold to an antiques shop. This Muggle woman bought it, took it home and tried to serve her friends tea in it. It was a nightmare – Dad was working overtime for weeks.'

'What happened?'

'The teapot went beserk and squirted boiling tea all over the place and one man ended up in hospital with the sugar tongs clamped to his nose. Dad was going frantic, it's only him and an old warlock called Perkins in the office, and they had to do Memory Charms and all sorts to cover it up ...'

'But your Dad ... this car ...'

Fred laughed. 'Yeah, Dad's mad about everything to do with Muggles, our shed's full of Muggle stuff. He takes it apart, puts spells on it and puts it back together again. If he raided our house he'd have to put himself straight under arrest. It drives Mum mad.'

'That's the main road,' said George, peering down through the windscreen. 'We'll be there in ten minutes ... just as well, it's getting light ...'

A faint pinkish glow was visible along the horizon to the east.

Fred brought the car lower and Harry saw a dark patchwork of fields and clumps of trees.

'We're a little way outside the village,' said George. 'Ottery St Catchpole ...'

Lower and lower went the flying car. The edge of a brilliant red sun was now gleaming through the trees.

'Touchdown!' said Fred as, with a slight bump, they hit the ground. They had landed next to a tumbledown garage in a small yard and Harry looked out for the first time at Ron's house.

It looked as though it had once been a large stone pigsty, but extra rooms had been added here and there until it was several storeys high and so crooked it looked as though it was held up by magic (which, Harry reminded himself, it probably was). Four or five chimneys were perched on top of the red roof. A lopsided sign stuck in the ground near the entrance read 'The Burrow'. Round the front door lay a jumble of wellington boots and a very rusty cauldron. Several fat brown chickens were pecking their way around the yard.

'It's not much,' said Ron.

'It's *brilliant*,' said Harry happily, thinking of Privet Drive.

They got out of the car.

'Now, we'll go upstairs really quietly,' said Fred, 'and wait for Mum to call us for breakfast. Then Ron, you come bounding downstairs going, 'Mum, look who turned up in the night!' and she'll be all pleased to see Harry and no one need ever know we flew the car.'

'Right,' said Ron. 'Come on, Harry, I sleep at the –'

Ron had gone a nasty greenish colour, his eyes fixed on the house. The other three wheeled around.

Mrs Weasley was marching across the yard, scattering chickens, and for a short, plump, kind-faced woman, it was remarkable how much she looked like a sabre-toothed tiger.

'*Ah,*' said Fred.

'Oh dear,' said George.

Mrs Weasley came to a halt in front of them, her hands on her hips, staring from one guilty face to the next. She was wearing a flowered apron with a wand sticking out of the pocket.

'*So,*' she said.

'Morning, Mum,' said George, in what he clearly thought was a jaunty, winning voice.

'Have you any idea how worried I've been?' said Mrs Weasley in a deadly whisper.

'Sorry, Mum, but see, we had to –'

All three of Mrs Weasley's sons were taller than she was, but they cowered as her rage broke over them.

'*Beds empty! No note! Car gone ... could have crashed ... out of my mind with worry ... did you care? ... never, as long as I've lived ... you wait until your father gets home, we never had trouble like this from Bill or Charlie or Percy ...*'

'Perfect Percy,' muttered Fred.

'YOU COULD DO WITH TAKING A LEAF OUT OF PERCY'S BOOK!' yelled Mrs Weasley, prodding a finger in Fred's chest. 'You could have *died,* you could have been *seen,* you could have lost your father his *job* –'

It seemed to go on for hours. Mrs Weasley had shouted herself hoarse before she turned on Harry, who backed away.

'I'm very pleased to see you, Harry, dear,' she said, 'Come in and have some breakfast.'

She turned and walked back into the house and Harry, after a nervous glance at Ron, who nodded encouragingly, followed her.

The kitchen was small and rather cramped. There was a scrubbed wooden table and chairs in the middle and Harry sat down on the edge of his seat, looking around. He had never been in a wizard house before.

The clock on the wall opposite him had only one hand and no numbers at all. Written around the edge were things like 'Time to make tea', 'Time to feed the chickens' and 'You're late'. Books were stacked three deep on the mantelpiece, books with titles like *Charm Your Own Cheese, Enchantment in Baking* and *One Minute Feasts – It's Magic!* And unless Harry's ears were deceiving him, the old radio next to the sink had just announced that coming up was 'Witching Hour, with the popular singing sorceress, Celestina Warbeck'.

Mrs Weasley was clattering around, cooking breakfast a little haphazardly, throwing dirty looks at her sons as she threw sausages into the frying pan. Every now and then she muttered things like 'don't know *what* you were thinking of,' and '*never* would have believed it.'

'I don't blame *you*, dear,' she assured Harry, tipping eight or nine sausages onto his plate. 'Arthur and I have been worried about you, too. Just last night we were saying we'd come and get you ourselves if you hadn't written back to Ron by Friday. But really,' (she was now adding three fried eggs to his plate) 'flying an illegal car halfway across the country – anyone could have seen you –'

She flicked her wand casually at the washing-up in the sink which began to clean itself, clinking gently in the background.

'It was *cloudy*, Mum!' said Fred.

'You keep your mouth closed while you're eating!' Mrs Weasley snapped.

'They were starving him, Mum!' said George.

'And you!' said Mrs Weasley, but it was with a slightly softened expression that she started cutting Harry bread and buttering it for him.

At that moment, there was a diversion in the form of a small, red-headed figure in a long nightdress, who appeared in the kitchen, gave a small squeal, and ran out again.

'Ginny,' said Ron in an undertone to Harry. 'My sister. She's been talking about you all summer.'

'Yeah, she'll be wanting your autograph, Harry,' grinned Fred, but he caught his mother's eye and bent his face over his plate without another word. Nothing more was said until all four plates were clean, which took a surprisingly short time.

'Blimey, I'm tired,' yawned Fred, setting down his knife and fork at last. 'I think I'll go to bed and –'

'You will not,' snapped Mrs Weasley. 'It's your own fault you've been up all night. You're going to de-gnome the garden for me, they're getting completely out of hand again.'

'Oh, Mum –'

'And you two,' she said, glaring at Ron and Fred. 'You can go up to bed, dear,' she added to Harry. 'You didn't ask them to fly that wretched car.'

But Harry, who felt wide awake, said quickly, 'I'll help Ron, I've never seen a de-gnoming –'

'That's very sweet of you, dear, but it's dull work,' said Mrs Weasley. 'Now, let's see what Lockhart's got to say on the subject.'

And she pulled a heavy book from the stack on the mantelpiece. George groaned.

'Mum, we know how to de-gnome a garden.'

Harry looked at the cover of Mrs Weasley's book. Written across it in fancy gold letters were the words: *Gilderoy Lockhart's Guide to Household Pests*. There was a big photograph on the front of a very good-looking wizard with wavy blond hair and bright blue eyes. As always in the wizarding world, the photograph was moving; the wizard, who Harry supposed was Gilderoy Lockhart, kept winking cheekily up at them all. Mrs Weasley beamed down at him.

'Oh, he is marvellous,' she said, 'he knows his household pests, all right, it's a wonderful book ...'

'Mum fancies him,' said Fred, in a very audible whisper.

'Don't be so ridiculous, Fred,' said Mrs Weasley, her cheeks rather pink. 'All right, if you think you know better than Lockhart, you can go and get on with it, and woe betide you if there's a single gnome in that garden when I come out to inspect it.'

Yawning and grumbling, the Weasleys slouched outside with Harry behind them. The garden was large and, in Harry's eyes, exactly what a garden should be. The Dursleys wouldn't have liked it – there were plenty of weeds, and the grass needed cutting – but there were gnarled trees all around the walls, plants Harry had never seen spilling from every flowerbed and a big green pond full of frogs.

'Muggles have garden gnomes too, you know,' Harry told Ron as they crossed the lawn.

'Yeah, I've seen those things they think are gnomes,' said Ron, bent double with his head in a peony bush. 'Like fat little Father Christmases with fishing rods ...'

There was a violent scuffling noise, the peony bush shuddered and Ron straightened up. '*This* is a gnome,' he said grimly.

'Gerroff me! Gerroff me!' squealed the gnome.

It was certainly nothing like Father Christmas. It was small and leathery looking, with a large, knobbly, bald head exactly like a potato. Ron held it at arm's length as it kicked out at him with its horny little feet; he grasped it around the ankles and turned it upside down.

'This is what you have to do,' he said. He raised the gnome above his head ('Gerroff me!') and started to swing it in great circles like a lassoo. Seeing the shocked look on Harry's face, Ron added, 'It doesn't *hurt* them – you've just got to make them really dizzy so they can't find their way back to the gnomeholes.'

He let go of the gnome's ankles: it flew twenty feet into the air and landed with a thud in the field over the hedge.

'Pitiful,' said Fred. 'I bet I can get mine beyond that stump.'

Harry learned quickly not to feel too sorry for the gnomes. He decided just to drop the first one he caught over the hedge, but the gnome, sensing weakness, sank its razor-sharp teeth into Harry's finger and he had a hard job shaking it off until –

'Wow, Harry – that must've been fifty feet ...'

The air was soon thick with flying gnomes.

'See, they're not too bright,' said George, seizing five or six gnomes at once. 'The moment they know the de-gnoming's going on they storm up to have a look. You'd think they'd have learned by now just to stay put.'

Soon, the crowd of gnomes in the field started walking away in a straggling line, their little shoulders hunched.

'They'll be back,' said Ron, as they watched the gnomes disappear into the hedge on the other side of the field. 'They love it here ... Dad's too soft with them, he thinks they're funny ...'

Just then, the front door slammed.

'He's back!' said George. 'Dad's home!'

They hurried through the garden and back into the house.

Mr Weasley was slumped in a kitchen chair with his glasses off and his eyes closed. He was a thin man, going bald, but the little hair he had was as red as any of his children's. He was wearing long green robes which were dusty and travel-worn.

'What a night,' he mumbled, groping for the teapot as they all sat down around him. 'Nine raids. Nine! And old Mundungus Fletcher tried to put a hex on me when I had my back turned ...'

Mr Weasley took a long gulp of tea and sighed.

'Find anything, Dad?' said Fred eagerly.

'All I got were a few shrinking door-keys and a biting kettle,' yawned Mr Weasley. 'There was some pretty nasty stuff that wasn't my department, though. Mortlake was taken away for questioning about some extremely odd ferrets, but that's the Committee on Experimental Charms, thank goodness ...'

'Why would anyone bother making door-keys shrink?' said George.

'Just Muggle-baiting,' sighed Mr Weasley. 'Sell them a key that keeps shrinking to nothing so they can never find it when they need it ... Of course, it's very hard to convict anyone because no Muggle would admit their key keeps shrinking – they'll insist they just keep losing it. Bless them, they'll go to any lengths to ignore magic, even if it's staring them in the face ... but the things our lot have taken to enchanting, you wouldn't believe –'

'LIKE CARS, FOR INSTANCE?'

Mrs Weasley had appeared, holding a long poker like a sword. Mr Weasley's eyes jerked open. He stared guiltily at his wife.

'C-cars, Molly, dear?'

'Yes, Arthur, cars,' said Mrs Weasley, her eyes flashing. 'Imagine a wizard buying a rusty old car and telling his wife all he wanted to do with it was take it apart to see how it worked, while *really* he was enchanting it to make it *fly*.'

Mr Weasley blinked.

'Well, dear, I think you'll find that he would be quite within the law to do that, even if, er, he maybe would have done better to, um, tell his wife the truth ... There's a loophole in the law, you'll find ... as long as he wasn't *intending* to fly the car, the fact that the car *could* fly wouldn't –'

'Arthur Weasley, you made sure there was a loophole when you wrote that law!' shouted Mrs Weasley. 'Just so you could carry on tinkering with all that Muggle rubbish in your shed! And for your information, Harry arrived this morning in the car you weren't intending to fly!'

'Harry?' said Mr Weasley blankly. 'Harry who?'

He looked around, saw Harry and jumped.

'Good Lord, is it Harry Potter? Very pleased to meet you, Ron's told us so much about –'

'*Your sons flew that car to Harry's house and back last night!*' shouted Mrs Weasley. 'What have you got to say about that, eh?'

'Did you really?' said Mr Weasley eagerly. 'Did it go all right? I-I mean,' he faltered, as sparks flew from Mrs Weasley's eyes, 'that-that was very wrong, boys – very wrong indeed ...'

'Let's leave them to it,' Ron muttered to Harry, as Mrs Weasley swelled like a bullfrog. 'Come on, I'll show you my bedroom.'

They slipped out of the kitchen and down a narrow passageway to an uneven staircase, which zigzagged its way up through the house. On the third landing, a door stood ajar. Harry just caught sight of a pair of bright brown eyes staring at him before it closed with a snap.

'Ginny,' said Ron. 'You don't know how weird it is for her to be this shy, she never shuts up normally –'

They climbed two more flights until they reached a door with peeling paint and a small plaque on it, saying 'Ronald's Room'.

Harry stepped in, his head almost touching the sloping ceiling, and blinked. It was like walking into a furnace: nearly everything in Ron's room seemed to be a violent shade of orange: the bed-spread, the walls, even the ceiling. Then Harry realised that Ron had covered nearly every inch of the shabby wallpaper with posters of the same seven witches and wizards, all wearing bright orange robes, carrying broomsticks and waving energetically.

'Your Quidditch team?' said Harry.

'The Chudley Cannons,' said Ron, pointing at the orange bed-spread, which was emblazoned with two giant black Cs and a speeding cannonball. 'Ninth in the league.'

Ron's school spellbooks were stacked untidily in a corner, next to a pile of comics which all seemed to feature *The Adventures of Martin Miggs, the Mad Muggle*. Ron's magic wand was lying on top of a fish tank full of frogspawn on the window-sill, next to his fat grey rat, Scabbers, who was snoozing in a patch of sun.

Harry stepped over a pack of Self-Shuffling playing cards on the floor and looked out of the tiny window. In the field far below he could see a gang of gnomes sneaking one by one back through the Weasleys' hedge. Then he turned to look at Ron, who was watching him almost nervously, as though waiting for his opinion.

'It's a bit small,' said Ron quickly. 'Not like that room you had with the Muggles. And I'm right underneath the ghoul in the attic, he's always banging on the pipes and groaning ...'

But Harry, grinning widely, said, 'This is the best house I've ever been in.'

Ron's ears went pink.

CHAPTER FOUR

At Flourish and Blotts

Life at The Burrow was as different as possible from life in Privet Drive. The Dursleys liked everything neat and ordered; the Weasleys' house burst with the strange and unexpected. Harry got a shock the first time he looked in the mirror over the kitchen mantelpiece and it shouted, '*Tuck your shirt in, scruffy!*' The ghoul in the attic howled and dropped pipes whenever he felt things were getting too quiet and small explosions from Fred and George's bedroom were considered perfectly normal. What Harry found most unusual about life at Ron's, however, wasn't the talking mirror or the clanking ghoul: it was the fact that everybody there seemed to like him.

Mrs Weasley fussed over the state of his socks and tried to force him to eat fourth helpings at every meal. Mr Weasley liked Harry to sit next to him at the dinner table so that he could bombard him with questions about life with Muggles, asking him to explain how things like plugs and the postal service worked.

'*Fascinating!*' he would say, as Harry talked him through using a telephone. '*Ingenious,* really, how many ways Muggles have found of getting along without magic.'

Harry heard from Hogwarts one sunny morning about a week after he had arrived at The Burrow. He and Ron went down to breakfast to find Mr and Mrs Weasley and Ginny already sitting at the kitchen table. The moment she saw Harry, Ginny accidentally knocked her porridge bowl to the floor with a loud clatter. Ginny seemed very prone to knocking things over whenever Harry entered a room. She dived under the table to retrieve the bowl and emerged with her face glowing like the setting sun. Pretending he hadn't noticed this, Harry sat down and took the toast Mrs Weasley offered him.

'Letters from school,' said Mr Weasley, passing Harry and Ron identical envelopes of yellowish parchment, addressed in green ink. 'Dumbledore already knows you're here, Harry – doesn't miss a trick, that man. You two've got them, too,' he added, as Fred and George ambled in, still in their pyjamas.

For a few minutes there was silence as they all read their letters. Harry's told him to catch the Hogwarts Express as usual from King's Cross station on September the first. There was also a list of the new books he'd need for the coming year.

Second year students will require:

> *The Standard Book of Spells, Grade 2* by Miranda Goshawk
> *Break with a Banshee* by Gilderoy Lockhart
> *Gadding with Ghouls* by Gilderoy Lockhart
> *Holidays with Hags* by Gilderoy Lockhart
> *Travels with Trolls* by Gilderoy Lockhart
> *Voyages with Vampires* by Gilderoy Lockhart
> *Wanderings with Werewolves* by Gilderoy Lockhart
> *Year with the Yeti* by Gilderoy Lockhart

Fred, who had finished his own list, peered over at Harry's.

'You've been told to get all Lockhart's books too!' he said. 'The new Defence Against the Dark Arts teacher must be a fan – bet it's a witch.'

At this point, Fred caught his mother's eye and quickly busied himself with the marmalade.

'That lot won't come cheap,' said George, with a quick look at his parents. 'Lockhart's books are really expensive ...'

'Well, we'll manage,' said Mrs Weasley, but she looked worried. 'I expect we'll be able to pick up a lot of Ginny's things second-hand.'

'Oh, are you starting at Hogwarts this year?' Harry asked Ginny.

She nodded, blushing to the roots of her flaming hair, and put her elbow in the butter dish. Fortunately no one saw this except Harry, because just then Ron's elder brother Percy walked in. He was already dressed, his Hogwarts prefect badge pinned to his knitted tank top.

'Morning, all,' said Percy briskly. 'Lovely day.'

He sat down in the only remaining chair but leapt up again almost immediately, pulling from underneath him a moulting, grey feather duster – at least, that was what Harry thought it was, until he saw that it was breathing.

'Errol!' said Ron, taking the limp owl from Percy and extracting a letter from under its wing. '*Finally* – he's got Hermione's answer. I wrote to her saying we were going to try and rescue you from the Dursleys.'

He carried Errol to a perch just inside the back door and tried to stand him on it, but Errol flopped straight off again so Ron lay him on the draining board instead, muttering, 'Pathetic.' Then he ripped open Hermione's letter and read it out loud:

Dear Ron, and Harry if you're there,

I hope everything went all right and that Harry is OK and that you didn't do anything illegal to get him out, Ron, because that would get Harry into trouble, too. I've been really worried and if Harry is all right, will you please let me know at once, but perhaps it would be better if you used a different owl, because I think another delivery might finish your one off.

I'm very busy with school work, of course – 'How *can* she be?' said Ron in horror. 'We're on holiday!' – *and we're going to London next Wednesday to buy my new books. Why don't we meet in Diagon Alley?*

Let me know what's happpening as soon as you can, love from Hermione.

'Well, that fits in nicely, we can go and get all your things then, too,' said Mrs Weasley, starting to clear the table. 'What're you all up to today?'

Harry, Ron, Fred and George were planning to go up the hill to a small paddock the Weasleys owned. It was surrounded by trees that blocked it from view of the village below, meaning that they could practise Quidditch there, as long as they didn't fly too high. They couldn't use real Quidditch balls, which would have been hard to explain if they had escaped and flown away over the village; instead they threw apples for each other to catch. They took it in turns to ride Harry's Nimbus Two Thousand, which was easily the best broom; Ron's old Shooting Star was often outstripped by passing butterflies.

Five minutes later they were marching up the hill, broomsticks over their shoulders. They had asked Percy if he wanted to join them, but he had said he was busy. Harry had only seen Percy at meal-times so far; he stayed shut in his room the rest of the time.

'Wish I knew what he was up to,' said Fred, frowning. 'He's not himself. His exam results came the day before you did; twelve O.W.L.s and he hardly gloated at all.'

'Ordinary Wizarding Levels,' George explained, seeing Harry's puzzled look. 'Bill got twelve too. If we're not careful, we'll have another Head Boy in the family. I don't think I could stand the shame.'

Bill was the oldest Weasley brother. He and the next brother, Charlie, had already left Hogwarts. Harry had never met either of them, but knew that Charlie was in Romania studying dragons and Bill in Egypt working for the wizard's bank, Gringotts.

'Dunno how Mum and Dad are going to afford all our school stuff this year,' said George after a while. 'Five sets of Lockhart books! And Ginny needs robes and a wand and everything ...'

Harry said nothing. He felt a bit awkward. Stored in an underground vault at Gringotts in London was a small fortune that his parents had left him. Of course, it was only in the wizarding world that he had money; you couldn't use Galleons, Sickles and Knuts in Muggle shops. He had never mentioned his Gringotts bank account to the Dursleys; he didn't think their horror of anything connected with magic would stretch to a large pile of gold.

*

Mrs Weasley woke them all early the following Wednesday. After a quick half a dozen bacon sandwiches each, they pulled on their coats and Mrs Weasley took a flowerpot off the kitchen mantelpiece and peered inside.

'We're running low, Arthur,' she sighed. 'We'll have to buy some more today ... ah well, guests first! After you, Harry dear!'

And she offered him the flowerpot.

Harry stared at them all watching him.

'W-what am I supposed to do?' he stammered.

'He's never travelled by Floo powder,' said Ron suddenly. 'Sorry, Harry, I forgot.'

'Never?' said Mr Weasley. 'But how did you get to Diagon Alley to buy your school things last year?'

'I went on the Underground –'

'Really?' said Mr Weasley eagerly. 'Were there *escapators*? How exactly –'

'Not *now*, Arthur,' said Mrs Weasley. 'Floo powder's a lot quicker, dear, but goodness me, if you've never used it before –'

'He'll be all right, Mum,' said Fred. 'Harry, watch us first.'

He took a pinch of glittering powder out of the flowerpot, stepped up to the fire and threw the powder into the flames.

With a roar, the fire turned emerald green and rose higher than Fred, who stepped right into it, shouted, 'Diagon Alley!' and vanished.

'You must speak clearly, dear,' Mrs Weasley told Harry, as George dipped his hand into the flowerpot. 'And mind you get out at the right grate...'

'The right what?' said Harry nervously, as the fire roared and whipped George out of sight too.

'Well, there are an awful lot of wizard fires to choose from, you know, but as long as you've spoken clearly –'

'He'll be fine, Molly, don't fuss,' said Mr Weasley, helping himself to Floo powder too.

'But dear, if he got lost, how would we ever explain to his aunt and uncle?'

'They wouldn't mind,' Harry reassured her. 'Dudley would think it was a brilliant joke if I got lost up a chimney, don't worry about that.'

'Well ... all right ... you go after Arthur,' said Mrs Weasley. 'Now, when you get into the fire, say where you're going –'

'And keep your elbows tucked in,' Ron advised.

'And your eyes shut,' said Mrs Weasley. 'The soot –'

'Don't fidget,' said Ron. 'Or you might well fall out of the wrong fireplace –'

'But don't panic and get out too early, wait until you see Fred and George.'

Trying hard to bear all this in mind, Harry took a pinch of Floo powder and walked to the edge of the fire. He took a deep breath, scattered the powder into the flames and stepped forward; the fire felt like a warm breeze; he opened his mouth and immediately swallowed a lot of hot ash.

'D-Dia-gon Alley,' he coughed.

It felt as though he was being sucked down a giant plug hole. He seemed to be spinning very fast ... the roaring in his ears was deafening ... he tried to keep his eyes open but the whirl of green flames made him feel sick ... something hard knocked his elbow and he tucked it in tightly, still spinning and spinning ... now it felt as though cold hands were slapping his face ... squinting through his glasses he saw a blurred stream of fireplaces and snatched glimpses of the rooms beyond ... his bacon sandwiches were churning inside him ... He closed his eyes again wishing it would stop, and then – he fell, face forward, onto cold stone and felt his glasses shatter.

Dizzy and bruised, covered in soot, he got gingerly to his feet, holding his broken glasses up to his eyes. He was quite alone, but *where* he was, he had no idea. All he could tell was that he was standing in the stone fireplace of what looked like a large, dimly-lit wizard's shop – but nothing in here was ever likely to be on a Hogwarts school list.

A glass case nearby held a withered hand on a cushion, a blood-stained pack of cards and a staring glass eye. Evil-looking masks leered down from the walls, an assortment of human bones lay upon the counter and rusty, spiked instruments hung from the ceiling. Even worse, the dark, narrow street Harry could see through the dusty shop window was definitely not Diagon Alley.

The sooner he got out of here, the better. Nose still stinging where it had hit the hearth, Harry made his way swiftly and silently towards the door, but before he'd got halfway towards it, two people appeared on the other side of the glass – and one of them was the very last person Harry wanted to meet when he was lost, covered in soot and wearing broken glasses: Draco Malfoy.

Harry looked quickly around and spotted a large black cabinet to his left; he shot inside it and pulled the doors to, leaving a small crack to peer through. Seconds later, a bell clanged, and Malfoy stepped into the shop.

The man who followed could only be his father. He had the same pale, pointed face and identical cold grey eyes. Mr Malfoy crossed the shop, looking lazily at the items on display, and rang a bell on the counter before turning to his son and saying, 'Touch nothing, Draco.'

Malfoy, who had reached for the glass eye, said, 'I thought you were going to buy me a present.'

'I said I would buy you a racing broom,' said his father, drumming his fingers on the counter.

'What's the good of that if I'm not on the house team?' said Malfoy, looking sulky and bad-tempered. 'Harry Potter got a

Nimbus Two Thousand last year. Special permission from Dumbledore so he could play for Gryffindor. He's not even that good, it's just because he's *famous*... famous for having a stupid *scar* on his forehead ...'

Malfoy bent down to examine a shelf full of skulls.

'... everyone thinks he's so *smart,* wonderful *Potter* with his *scar* and his *broomstick* –'

'You have told me this at least a dozen times already,' said Mr Malfoy, with a quelling look at his son, 'and I would remind you that it is not – prudent – to appear less than fond of Harry Potter, not when most of our kind regard him as the hero who made the Dark Lord disappear – ah, Mr Borgin.'

A stooping man had appeared behind the counter, smoothing his greasy hair back from his face.

'Mr Malfoy, what a pleasure to see you again,' said Mr Borgin in a voice as oily as his hair. 'Delighted – and young Master Malfoy, too – charmed. How may I be of assistance? I must show you, just in today, and very reasonably priced –'

'I'm not buying today, Mr Borgin, but selling,' said Mr Malfoy.

'Selling?' The smile faded slightly from Mr Borgin's face.

'You have heard, of course, that the Ministry is conducting more raids,' said Mr Malfoy, taking a roll of parchment from his inside pocket and unravelling it for Mr Borgin to read. 'I have a few – ah – items at home that might embarrass me, if the Ministry were to call ...'

Mr Borgin fixed a pair of pince-nez to his nose and looked down the list.

'The Ministry wouldn't presume to trouble you, sir, surely?'

Mr Malfoy's lip curled.

'I have not been visited yet. The name Malfoy still commands a certain respect, yet the Ministry grows ever more meddlesome. There are rumours about a new Muggle Protection Act – no doubt that flea-bitten, Muggle-loving fool Arthur Weasley is behind it –'

Harry felt a hot surge of anger.

'– and as you see, certain of these poisons might make it *appear* –'

'I understand, sir, of course,' said Mr Borgin. 'Let me see ...'

'Can I have *that?*' interrupted Draco, pointing at the withered hand on its cushion.

'Ah, the Hand of Glory!' said Mr Borgin, abandoning Mr Malfoy's list and scurrying over to Draco. 'Insert a candle and it gives light only to the holder! Best friend of thieves and plunderers! Your son has fine taste, sir.'

'I hope my son will amount to more than a thief or a plunderer, Borgin,' said Mr Malfoy coldly and Mr Borgin said quickly, 'No offence, sir, no offence meant –'

'Though if his school marks don't pick up,' said Mr Malfoy, more coldly still, 'that may indeed be all he is fit for.'

'It's not my fault,' retorted Draco. 'The teachers all have favourites, that Hermione Granger –'

'I would have thought you'd be ashamed that a girl of no wizard family beat you in every exam,' snapped Mr Malfoy.

'Ha!' said Harry under his breath, pleased to see Draco looking both abashed and angry.

'It's the same all over,' said Mr Borgin, in his oily voice. 'Wizard blood is counting for less everywhere –'

'Not with me,' said Mr Malfoy, his long nostrils flaring.

'No, sir, nor with me, sir,' said Mr Borgin, with a deep bow.

'In that case, perhaps we can return to my list,' said Mr Malfoy shortly. 'I am in something of a hurry, Borgin, I have important business elsewhere today.'

They started to haggle. Harry watched nervously as Draco drew nearer and nearer to his hiding place, examining the objects for sale. He paused to examine a long coil of hangman's rope and to read, smirking, the card propped on a magnificent necklace of opals: *Caution: Do Not Touch. Cursed – Has Claimed the Lives of Nineteen Muggle Owners to Date.*

Draco turned away and saw the cabinet right in front of him. He walked forward ... he stretched out his hand for the handle ...

'Done,' said Mr Malfoy at the counter. 'Come, Draco!'

Harry wiped his forehead on his sleeve as Draco turned away.

'Good day to you, Mr Borgin, I'll expect you at the manor tomorrow to pick up the goods.'

The moment the door had closed, Mr Borgin dropped his oily manner.

'Good day yourself, *Mister* Malfoy, and if the stories are true, you haven't sold me half of what's hidden in your *manor* ...'

Muttering darkly, Mr Borgin disappeared into a back room. Harry waited for a minute in case he came back, then, quietly as he could, slipped out of the cabinet, past the glass cases and out of the shop door.

Clutching his broken glasses to his face he stared around. He had emerged into a dingy alleyway that seemed to be made up entirely of shops devoted to the dark arts. The one he'd just left, Borgin and Burkes, looked like the largest, but opposite was a nasty window display of shrunken heads, and two doors down, a large cage was alive with gigantic black spiders. Two shabby-looking wizards were watching him from the shadow of a doorway, muttering to each other. Feeling jumpy, Harry set off, trying to hold his glasses on straight and hoping against hope he'd be able to find a way out of there.

An old wooden street sign hanging over a shop selling poisonous candles told him he was in Knockturn Alley. This didn't help, as Harry had never heard of such a place. He supposed he hadn't spoken clearly enough through his mouthful of ashes back in the Weasleys' fire. Trying to stay calm, he wondered what to do.

'Not lost are you, my dear?' said a voice in his ear, making him jump.

An aged witch stood in front of him, holding a tray of what looked horribly like whole human fingernails. She leered at him, showing mossy teeth. Harry backed away.

'I'm fine, thanks,' he said. 'I'm just –'

'HARRY! What d'yeh think yer doin' down there?'

Harry's heart leapt. So did the witch; a load of fingernails cascaded down over her feet and she cursed as the massive form of Hagrid, the Hogwarts gamekeeper, came striding towards them, beetle-black eyes flashing over his great bristling beard.

'Hagrid!' Harry croaked in relief. 'I was lost ... Floo powder ...'

Hagrid seized Harry by the scruff of the neck and pulled him away from the witch, knocking the tray right out of her hands. Her shrieks followed them all the way along the twisting alleyway out into bright sunlight. Harry saw a familiar, snow-white marble building in the distance: Gringotts bank. Hagrid had steered him right into Diagon Alley.

'Yer a mess!' said Hagrid gruffly, brushing soot off Harry so forcefully he nearly knocked him into a barrel of dragon dung outside an apothecary. 'Skulkin' around Knockturn Alley, I dunno – dodgy place, Harry – don' want no one ter see yeh down there –'

'I realised *that*,' said Harry, ducking as Hagrid made to brush him off again. 'I told you, I was lost – what were you doing down there, anyway?'

'*I was lookin' fer a Flesh-Eatin' Slug Repellent,*' growled Hagrid. 'They're ruinin' the school cabbages. Yer not on yer own?'

'I'm staying with the Weasleys but we got separated,' Harry explained. 'I've got to go and find them ...'

They set off together down the street.

'How come yeh never wrote back ter me?' said Hagrid, as Harry jogged alongside him (he had to take three steps to every stride of Hagrid's enormous boots). Harry explained all about Dobby and the Dursleys.

'Ruddy Muggles,' growled Hagrid. 'If I'd've known –'

'Harry! Harry! Over here!'

Harry looked up and saw Hermione Granger standing at the top of the white flight of steps to Gringotts. She ran down to meet them, her bushy brown hair flying behind her.

'What happened to your glasses? Hello, Hagrid ... Oh, it's *wonderful* to see you two again ... Are you coming into Gringotts, Harry?'

'As soon as I've found the Weasleys,' said Harry.

'Yeh won't have long ter wait,' grinned Hagrid.

Harry and Hermione looked around; sprinting up the crowded street were Ron, Fred, George, Percy and Mr Weasley.

'Harry,' Mr Weasley panted. 'We *hoped* you'd only gone one grate too far ...' He mopped his glistening bald patch. 'Molly's frantic – she's coming now.'

'Where did you come out?' Ron asked.

'Knockturn Alley,' said Hagrid grimly.

'*Brilliant!*' said Fred and George together.

'We've never been allowed in,' said Ron enviously.

'I should ruddy well think not,' growled Hagrid.

Mrs Weasley now came galloping into view, her handbag swinging wildly in one hand, Ginny just clinging onto the other.

'Oh, Harry – oh, my dear – you could have been anywhere –'

Gasping for breath she pulled a large clothes brush out of her bag and began sweeping off the soot Hagrid hadn't managed to beat away. Mr Weasley took Harry's glasses, gave them a tap of his wand and returned them, good as new.

'Well, gotta be off,' said Hagrid, who was having his hand wrung by Mrs Weasley ('Knockturn Alley! If you hadn't found him, Hagrid!'). 'See yer at Hogwarts!' And he strode away, head and shoulders taller than anyone else in the packed street.

'Guess who I saw in Borgin and Burkes?' Harry asked Ron and Hermione as they climbed the Gringotts steps. 'Malfoy and his father.'

'Did Lucius Malfoy buy anything?' said Mr Weasley sharply behind them.

'No, he was selling.'

'So he's worried,' said Mr Weasley with grim satisfaction. 'Oh, I'd love to get Lucius Malfoy for something ...'

'You be careful, Arthur,' said Mrs Weasley sharply, as they were ushered into the bank by a bowing goblin at the door. 'That family's trouble, don't go biting off more than you can chew.'

'So you don't think I'm a match for Lucius Malfoy?' said Mr Weasley indignantly, but he was distracted almost at once by the sight of Hermione's parents, who were standing nervously at the counter that ran all along the great marble hall, waiting for Hermione to introduce them.

'But you're *Muggles*!' said Mr Weasley delightedly. 'We must have a drink! What's that you've got there? Oh, you're changing Muggle money. Molly, look!' He pointed excitedly at the ten-pound notes in Mr Granger's hand.

'Meet you back here,' Ron said to Hermione, as the Weasleys and Harry were led off to their underground vaults by another Gringotts goblin.

The vaults were reached by means of small, goblin-driven carts that sped along miniature train-tracks through the bank's underground tunnels. Harry enjoyed the break-neck journey down to the Weasleys' vault, but felt dreadful, far worse than he had in Knockturn Alley, when it was opened. There was a very small pile of silver Sickles inside, and just one gold Galleon. Mrs Weasley felt right into the corners before sweeping the whole lot into her bag. Harry felt even worse when they reached his vault. He tried to block the contents from view as he hastily shoved handfuls of coins into a leather bag.

Back outside on the marble steps, they all separated. Percy muttered vaguely about needing a new quill. Fred and George had spotted their friend from Hogwarts, Lee Jordan. Mrs Weasley and Ginny were going to a second-hand robe shop. Mr Weasley was insisting on taking the Grangers off to the Leaky Cauldron for a drink.

'We'll all meet at Flourish and Blotts in an hour to buy your school books,' said Mrs Weasley, setting off with Ginny. 'And not one step down Knockturn Alley!' she shouted at the twins' retreating backs.

Harry, Ron and Hermione strolled off along the winding, cobbled street. The bag of gold, silver and bronze jangling cheerfully in Harry's pocket was clamouring to be spent, so he bought three large strawberry and peanut butter ice-creams which they slurped happily as they wandered up the alley, examining the fascinating shop windows. Ron gazed longingly at a full set of Chudley Cannon robes in the windows of 'Quality Quidditch Supplies' until Hermione dragged them off to buy ink and parchment next door. In Gambol and Japes Wizarding Joke Shop, they met Fred, George and Lee Jordan, who were stocking up on 'Dr Filibuster's Fabulous Wet-Start, No-Heat Fireworks', and in a tiny junk shop full of broken wands, wonky brass scales and old cloaks covered in potion stains they found Percy, deeply immersed in a small and deeply boring book called *Prefects who Gained Power*.

'*A study of Hogwarts prefects and their later careers,*' Ron read aloud off the back cover. 'That sounds *fascinating* ...'

'Go away,' Percy snapped.

'Course, he's very ambitious, Percy, he's got it all planned out ... he wants to be Minister of Magic ...' Ron told Harry and Hermione in an undertone, as they left Percy to it.

An hour later, they headed for Flourish and Blotts. They were by no means the only ones making their way to the bookshop. As they approached it, they saw to their surprise a large crowd jostling outside the doors, trying to get in. The reason for this was proclaimed by a large banner stretched across the upper windows:

GILDEROY LOCKHART

will be signing copies of his autobiography

MAGICAL ME

today 12.30 – 4.30 pm

'We can actually meet him!' Hermione squealed. 'I mean, he's written almost the whole booklist!'

The crowd seemed to be made up mostly of witches around Mrs Weasley's age. A harrassed-looking wizard stood at the door, saying, 'Calmly, please ladies ... don't push, there ... mind the books, now ...'

Harry, Ron and Hermione squeezed inside. A long queue wound right to the back of the shop, where Gilderoy Lockhart was signing his books. They each grabbed a copy of *Break with a Banshee,* and sneaked up the line to where the rest of the Weasleys were standing with Mr and Mrs Granger.

'Oh, there you are, good,' said Mrs Weasley. She sounded breathless and kept patting her hair. 'We'll be able to see him in a minute ...'

Gilderoy Lockhart came slowly into view, seated at a table surrounded by large pictures of his own face, all winking and flashing dazzlingly white teeth at the crowd. The real Lockhart was wearing robes of forget-me-not blue which exactly matched his eyes; his pointed wizard's hat was set at a jaunty angle on his wavy hair.

A short, irritable looking man was dancing around taking photographs with a large black camera that emitted puffs of purple smoke with every blinding flash.

'Out of the way, there,' he snarled at Ron, moving back to get a better shot. 'This is for the *Daily Prophet.*'

'Big deal,' said Ron, rubbing his foot where the photographer had stepped on it.

Gilderoy Lockhart heard him. He looked up. He saw Ron – and then he saw Harry. He stared. Then he leapt to his feet and positively shouted, 'It *can't* be Harry Potter?'

The crowd parted, whispering excitedly. Lockhart dived forward, seized Harry's arm and pulled him to the front. The crowd burst into applause. Harry's face burned as Lockhart shook his hand for the photographer, who was clicking away madly, wafting thick smoke over the Weasleys.

'Nice big smile, Harry,' said Lockhart, through his own gleaming teeth. 'Together, you and I are worth the front page.'

When he finally let go of Harry's hand, Harry could hardly feel his fingers. He tried to sidle back over to the Weasleys, but Lockhart threw an arm around his shoulders and clamped him tightly to his side.

'Ladies and gentlemen,' he said loudly, waving for quiet. 'What an extraordinary moment this is! The perfect moment for me to make a little announcement I've been sitting on for some time!

'When young Harry here stepped into Flourish and Blotts today, he only wanted to buy my autobiography – which I shall be

happy to present him now, free of charge –' the crowd applauded
again, '– he had *no idea*,' Lockhart continued, giving Harry a little
shake that made his glasses slip to the end of his nose, 'that he
would shortly be getting much, much more than my book,
Magical Me. He and his school fellows will, in fact, be getting the
real, magical me. Yes, ladies and gentlemen, I have great pleasure
and pride in announcing that this September, I will be taking up
the post of Defence Against the Dark Arts teacher at Hogwarts
School of Witchcraft and Wizardry!'

The crowd cheered and clapped and Harry found himself being
presented with the entire works of Gilderoy Lockhart. Staggering
slightly under their weight, he managed to make his way out of
the limelight to the edge of the room, where Ginny was standing
next to her new cauldron.

'You have these,' Harry mumbled to her, tipping the books into
the cauldron. 'I'll buy my own –'

'Bet you loved that, didn't you, Potter?' said a voice Harry had
no trouble recognising. He straightened up and found himself face
to face with Draco Malfoy, who was wearing his usual sneer.

'*Famous* Harry Potter,' said Malfoy. 'Can't even go into a *bookshop* without making the front page.'

'Leave him alone, he didn't want all that!' said Ginny. It was the
first time she had spoken in front of Harry. She was glaring at
Malfoy.

'Potter, you've got yourself a *girlfriend*!' drawled Malfoy. Ginny
went scarlet as Ron and Hermione fought their way over, both
clutching stacks of Lockhart's books.

'Oh, it's you,' said Ron, looking at Malfoy as if he were something unpleasant on the sole of his shoe. 'Bet you're surprised to
see Harry here, eh?'

'Not as surprised as I am to see you in a shop, Weasley,' retorted
Malfoy. 'I suppose your parents will go hungry for a month to pay
for that lot.'

Ron went as red as Ginny. He dropped his books into the cauldron too and started towards Malfoy, but Harry and Hermione
grabbed the back of his jacket.

'Ron!' said Mr Weasley, struggling over with Fred and George.
'What are you doing? It's mad in here, let's go outside.'

'Well, well, well – Arthur Weasley.'

It was Mr Malfoy. He stood with his hand on Draco's shoulder, sneering in just the same way.

'Lucius,' said Mr Weasley, nodding coldly.

'Busy time at the Ministry, I hear,' said Mr Malfoy. 'All those raids ... I hope they're paying you overtime?'

He reached into Ginny's cauldron and extracted, from amidst the glossy Lockhart books, a very old, very battered copy of *A Beginner's Guide to Transfiguration*.

'Obviously not,' he said. 'Dear me, what's the use of being a disgrace to the name of wizard if they don't even pay you well for it?'

Mr Weasley flushed darker than either Ron or Ginny.

'We have a very different idea of what disgraces the name of wizard, Malfoy,' he said.

'Clearly,' said Mr Malfoy, his pale eyes straying to Mr and Mrs Granger, who were watching apprehensively. 'The company you keep, Weasley ... and I thought your family could sink no lower –'

There was a thud of metal as Ginny's cauldron went flying; Mr Weasley had thrown himself at Mr Malfoy, knocking him backwards into a bookshelf. Dozens of heavy spellbooks came thundering down on all their heads; there was a yell of, 'Get him, Dad!' from Fred or George; Mrs Weasley was shrieking, 'No, Arthur, no!'; the crowd stampeded backwards, knocking more shelves over; 'Gentlemen, please – please!' cried the assistant and then, louder than all, 'Break it up, there, gents, break it up –'

Hagrid was wading towards them through the sea of books. In an instant he had pulled Mr Weasley and Mr Malfoy apart. Mr Weasley had a cut lip and Mr Malfoy had been hit in the eye by an *Encyclopaedia of Toadstools*. He was still holding Ginny's old transfiguration book. He thrust it at her, his eyes glittering with malice.

'Here, girl – take your book – it's the best your father can give you –'

Pulling himself out of Hagrid's grip he beckoned to Draco and swept from the shop.

'Yeh should've ignored him, Arthur,' said Hagrid, almost lifting Mr Weasley off his feet as he straightened his robes. 'Rotten ter the core, the whole family, everyone knows that. No Malfoy's worth listenin' ter. Bad blood, that's what it is. Come on now – let's get outta here.'

The assistant looked as though he wanted to stop them leaving, but he barely came up to Hagrid's waist and seemed to think better of it. They hurried up the street, the Grangers shaking with fright and Mrs Weasley beside herself with fury.

'A *fine* example to set to your children ... *brawling* in public ... *what* Gilderoy Lockhart must've thought ...'

'He was pleased,' said Fred. 'Didn't you hear him as we were leaving? He was asking that bloke from the *Daily Prophet* if he'd be able to work the fight into his report – said it was all publicity.'

But it was a subdued group who headed back to the fireside in the Leaky Cauldron, where Harry, the Weasleys and all their shopping would be travelling back to The Burrow using Floo powder. They said goodbye to the Grangers, who were leaving the pub for the Muggle street on the other side. Mr Weasley started to ask them how bus stops worked, but stopped quickly at the look on Mrs Weasley's face.

Harry took off his glasses and put them safely in his pocket before helping himself to Floo powder. It definitely wasn't his favourite way to travel.

— CHAPTER FIVE —

The Whomping Willow

The end of the summer holidays came too quickly for Harry's liking. He was looking forward to getting back to Hogwarts, but his month at The Burrow had been the happiest of his life. It was difficult not to feel jealous of Ron when he thought of the Dursleys and the sort of welcome he could expect next time he turned up in Privet Drive.

On their last evening, Mrs Weasley conjured up a sumptuous dinner which included all of Harry's favourite things, ending with a mouthwatering treacle pudding. Fred and George rounded off the evening with a display of Filibuster fireworks; they filled the kitchen with red and blue stars that bounced from ceiling to wall for at least half an hour. Then it was time for a last mug of hot chocolate and bed.

It took a long while to get started next morning. They were up at cock-crow, but somehow they still seemed to have a great deal to do. Mrs Weasley dashed about in a bad mood looking for spare socks and quills, people kept colliding on the stairs, half-dressed with bits of toast in their hands, and Mr Weasley nearly broke his neck, tripping over a stray chicken as he crossed the yard carrying Ginny's trunk to the car.

Harry couldn't see how eight people, six large trunks, two owls and a rat were going to fit into one small Ford Anglia. He had reckoned, of course, without the special features which Mr Weasley had added.

'Not a word to Molly,' he whispered to Harry as he opened the boot and showed him how it had been magically expanded so that the trunks fitted easily.

When at last they were all in the car, Mrs Weasley glanced into the back seat, where Harry, Ron, Fred, George and Percy were all sitting comfortably side by side, and said, 'Muggles *do* know more than we give them credit for, don't they?' She and Ginny got into the front seat, which had been stretched so that it resembled a park bench. 'I mean, you'd never know it was this roomy from the outside, would you?'

Mr Weasley started up the engine and they trundled out of the yard, Harry turning back for a last look at the house. He barely had time to wonder when he'd see it again when they were back: George had forgotten his box of Filibuster fireworks. Five minutes after that, they skidded to a halt in the yard so that Fred could run in for his broomstick. They had almost reached the motorway when Ginny shrieked that she'd left her diary. By the time she had clambered back into the car, they were running very late, and tempers were running high.

Mr Weasley glanced at his watch and then at his wife.

'Molly, dear –'

'*No*, Arthur.'

'No one would see. This little button here is an Invisibility Booster I installed – that'd get us up in the air – then we fly above the clouds. We'd be there in ten minutes and no one would be any the wiser ...'

'I said *no*, Arthur, not in broad daylight.'

They reached King's Cross at a quarter to eleven. Mr Weasley dashed across the road to get trolleys for their trunks and they all hurried into the station.

Harry had caught the Hogwarts Express the previous year. The tricky bit was getting onto platform nine and three quarters, which wasn't visible to the Muggle eye. What you had to do was walk through the solid barrier dividing platforms nine and ten. It didn't hurt, but it had to be done carefully so that none of the Muggles noticed you vanishing.

'Percy first,' said Mrs Weasley, looking nervously at the clock overhead, which showed they had only five minutes to disappear casually through the barrier.

Percy strode briskly forward and vanished. Mr Weasley went next, Fred and George followed.

'I'll take Ginny and you two come right after us,' Mrs Weasley told Harry and Ron, grabbing Ginny's hand and setting off. In the blink of an eye they were gone.

'Let's go together, we've only got a minute,' Ron said to Harry.

Harry made sure that Hedwig's cage was safely wedged on top

of his trunk and wheeled his trolley about to face the barrier. He felt perfectly confident; this wasn't nearly as uncomfortable as using Floo powder. Both of them bent low over the handles of their trolleys and walked purposefully towards the barrier, gathering speed. A few feet away from it, they broke into a run and –
CRASH.

Both trolleys hit the barrier and bounced backwards. Ron's trunk fell off with a loud thump, Harry was knocked off his feet, and Hedwig's cage bounced onto the shiny floor and she rolled away, shrieking indignantly. People all around them stared and a guard nearby yelled, 'What in blazes d'you think you're doing?'

'Lost control of the trolley,' Harry gasped, clutching his ribs as he got up. Ron ran to pick up Hedwig, who was causing such a scene that there was a lot of muttering about cruelty to animals from the surrounding crowd.

'Why can't we get through?' Harry hissed to Ron.

'I dunno –'

Ron looked wildly around. A dozen curious people were still watching them.

'We're going to miss the train,' Ron whispered. 'I don't understand why the gateway's sealed itself ...'

Harry looked up at the giant clock with a sickening feeling in the pit of his stomach. Ten seconds ... nine seconds ...

He wheeled his trolley forward cautiously until it was right against the barrier, and pushed with all his might. The metal remained solid.

Three seconds ... two seconds ... one second ...

'It's gone,' said Ron, sounding stunned. 'The train's left. What if Mum and Dad can't get back through to us? Have you got any Muggle money?'

Harry gave a hollow laugh. 'The Dursleys haven't given me pocket money for about six years.'

Ron pressed his ear to the cold barrier.

'Can't hear a thing,' he said tensely. 'What're we going to do? I don't know how long it'll take Mum and Dad to get back to us.'

They looked around. People were still watching them, mainly because of Hedwig's continuing screeches.

'I think we'd better go and wait by the car,' said Harry. 'We're attracting too much atten –'

'Harry!' said Ron, his eyes gleaming. 'The car!'

'What about it?'

'We can fly the car to Hogwarts!'

'But I thought –'

'We're stuck, right? And we've got to get to school, haven't we? And even under-age wizards are allowed to use magic if it's a real emergency, section nineteen or something of the Restriction of Thingy ...'

Harry's feeling of panic turned suddenly to excitement.

'Can you fly it?'

'No problem,' said Ron, wheeling his trolley around to face the exit. 'C'mon, let's go, if we hurry we'll be able to follow the Hogwarts Express.'

And they marched off through the crowd of curious Muggles, out of the station and back into the side road where the old Ford Anglia was parked.

Ron unlocked the cavernous boot with a series of taps from his wand. They heaved their trunks back in, put Hedwig on the back seat and got into the front.

'Check no one's watching,' said Ron, starting the ignition with another tap of his wand. Harry stuck his head out of the window: traffic was rumbling along the main road ahead, but their street was empty.

'OK,' he said.

Ron pressed a tiny silver button on the dashboard. The car around them vanished – and so did they. Harry could feel the seat vibrating beneath him, hear the engine, feel his hands on his knees and his glasses on his nose, but for all he could see, he had become a pair of eyeballs, floating a few feet above the ground in a dingy street full of parked cars.

'Let's go,' said Ron's voice from his right.

The ground and the dirty buildings on either side fell away, dropping out of sight as the car rose; in seconds, the whole of London lay, smoky and glittering, below them.

Then there was a popping noise and the car, Harry and Ron reappeared.

'Uh oh,' said Ron, jabbing at the Invisibility Booster. 'It's faulty –'

Both of them pummelled it. The car vanished. Then it flickered back again.

'Hold on!' Ron yelled, and he slammed his foot on the accelerator; they shot straight into the low woolly clouds and everything turned dull and foggy.

'Now what?' said Harry, blinking at the solid mass of cloud pressing in on them from all sides.

'We need to see the train to know what direction to go in,' said Ron.

'Dip back down again – quickly –'

They dropped back beneath the clouds and twisted around in their seats, squinting at the ground –

'I can see it!' Harry yelled. 'Right ahead – there!'

The Hogwarts Express was streaking along below them like a scarlet snake.

'Due north,' said Ron, checking the compass on the dashboard. 'OK, we'll just have to check on it every half an hour or so. Hold on ...' And they shot up through the clouds. A minute later, they burst out into a blaze of sunlight.

It was a different world. The wheels of the car skimmed the sea of fluffy cloud, the sky a bright, endless blue under the blinding white sun.

'All we've got to worry about now are aeroplanes,' said Ron.

They looked at each other and started to laugh; for a long time, they couldn't stop.

It was as though they had been plunged into a fabulous dream. This, thought Harry, was surely the only way to travel: past swirls and turrets of snowy cloud, in a car full of hot, bright sunlight, with a fat pack of toffees in the glove compartment, and the prospect of seeing Fred and George's jealous faces when they landed smoothly and spectacularly on the sweeping lawn in front of Hogwarts castle.

They made regular checks on the train as they flew further and further north, each dip beneath the clouds showing them a different view. London was soon far behind them, replaced by neat green fields which gave way in turn to wide, purplish moors, villages with tiny toy churches and a great city alive with cars like multi-coloured ants.

Several uneventful hours later, however, Harry had to admit that some of the fun was wearing off. The toffees had made them extremely thirsty and they had nothing to drink. He and Ron had pulled off their jumpers, but Harry's T-shirt was sticking to the back of his seat and his glasses kept sliding down to the end of his sweaty nose. He had stopped noticing the fantastic cloud shapes now, and was thinking longingly of the train miles below, where you could buy ice-cold pumpkin juice from a trolley pushed by a plump witch. *Why* hadn't they been able to get onto platform nine and three quarters?

'Can't be much further, can it?' croaked Ron, hours later still, as the sun started to sink into their floor of cloud, staining it a deep pink. 'Ready for another check on the train?'

It was still right below them, winding its way past a snow-capped mountain. It was much darker beneath the canopy of clouds.

Ron put his foot on the accelerator and drove them upwards again, but as he did so, the engine began to whine.

Harry and Ron exchanged nervous glances.

'It's probably just tired,' said Ron. 'It's never been this far before ...'

And they both pretended not to notice the whining growing louder and louder as the sky became steadily darker. Stars were blossoming in the blackness. Harry pulled his jumper back on, trying to ignore the way the windscreen wipers were now waving feebly, as though in protest.

'Not far,' said Ron, more to the car than to Harry, 'not far now,' and he patted the dashboard nervously.

When they flew back beneath the clouds a little while later, they had to squint through the darkness for a landmark they knew.

'*There!*' Harry shouted, making Ron and Hedwig jump. 'Straight ahead!'

Silhouetted on the dark horizon, high on the cliff over the lake, stood the many turrets and towers of Hogwarts castle.

But the car had begun to shudder and was losing speed.

'Come on,' Ron said cajolingly, giving the steering wheel a little shake, 'nearly there, come on –'

The engine groaned. Narrow jets of steam were issuing from under the bonnet. Harry found himself gripping the edges of his seat very hard as they flew towards the lake.

The car gave a nasty wobble. Glancing out of his window, Harry saw the smooth, black, glassy surface of the water, a mile below. Ron's knuckles were white on the steering wheel. The car wobbled again.

'Come *on*,' Ron muttered.

They were over the lake ... the castle was right ahead ... Ron put his foot down.

There was a loud clunk, a splutter, and the engine died completely.

'Uh oh,' said Ron, into the silence.

The nose of the car dropped. They were falling, gathering speed, heading straight for the solid castle wall.

'*Noooooo!*' Ron yelled, swinging the steering wheel around; they missed the dark stone wall by inches as the car turned in a great arc, soaring over the dark greenhouses, then the vegetable patch and then out over the black lawns, losing height all the time.

Ron let go of the steering wheel completely and pulled his wand out of his back pocket.

'STOP! STOP!' he yelled, whacking the dashboard and the windscreen, but they were still plummeting, the ground flying up towards them ...

'MIND THAT TREE!' Harry bellowed, lunging for the steering wheel, but too late –

CRUNCH.

With an ear-splitting bang of metal on wood, they hit the thick tree trunk and dropped to the ground with a heavy jolt. Steam was billowing from under the crumpled bonnet; Hedwig was shrieking in terror, a golf-ball sized lump was throbbing on Harry's head where he had hit the windscreen, and to his right, Ron let out a low, despairing groan.

'Are you OK?' Harry said urgently.

'My wand,' said Ron, in a shaky voice. 'Look at my wand.'

It had snapped, almost in two; the tip was dangling limply, held on by a few splinters.

Harry opened his mouth to say he was sure they'd be able to mend it up at the school, but he never even got started. At that very moment, something hit his side of the car with the force of a charging bull, sending him lurching sideways into Ron, just as an equally heavy blow hit the roof.

'What's happen –?'

Ron gasped, staring through the windscreen, and Harry looked around just in time to see a branch as thick as a python smash into it. The tree they had hit was attacking them. Its trunk was bent almost double, and its gnarled boughs were pummelling every inch of the car it could reach.

'Aaargh!' said Ron, as another twisted limb punched a large dent into his door; the windscreen was now trembling under a hail of blows from knuckle-like twigs and a branch as thick as a battering ram was pounding furiously on the roof, which seemed to be caving in –

'Run for it!' Ron shouted, throwing his full weight against his door, but next second he had been knocked backwards into Harry's lap by a vicious upper cut from another branch.

'We're done for!' he moaned, as the ceiling sagged, but suddenly the floor of the car was vibrating – the engine had re-started.

'*Reverse!*' Harry yelled, and the car shot backwards. The tree was still trying to hit them; they could hear its roots creaking as it almost ripped itself up, lashing out at them as they sped out of reach.

'That,' panted Ron, 'was close. Well done, car.'

The car, however, had reached the end of its tether. With two smart clunks, the doors flew open and Harry felt his seat tip sideways: next thing he knew he was sprawled on the damp ground. Loud thuds told him that the car was ejecting their luggage from the boot. Hedwig's cage flew through the air and burst open; she rose out of it with a loud, angry screech and sped off towards the castle without a backwards look. Then, dented, scratched and steaming, the car rumbled off into the darkness, its rear lights blazing angrily.

'Come back!' Ron yelled after it, brandishing his broken wand. 'Dad'll kill me!'

But the car disappeared from view with one last snort from its exhaust.

'Can you *believe* our luck?' said Ron miserably, bending down to pick up Scabbers the rat. 'Of all the trees we could've hit, we had to get one that hits back.'

He glanced over his shoulder at the ancient tree, which was still flailing its branches threateningly.

'Come on,' said Harry wearily, 'we'd better get up to the school ...'

It wasn't at all the triumphant arrival they had pictured. Stiff, cold and bruised, they seized the ends of their trunks and began dragging them up the grassy slope, towards the great oak front doors.

'I think the feast's already started,' said Ron, dropping his trunk at the foot of the front steps and crossing quietly to look through a brightly lit window. 'Hey, Harry, come and look – it's the Sorting!'

Harry hurried over and together, he and Ron peered in at the Great Hall.

Innumerable candles were hovering in mid-air over four long, crowded tables, making the golden plates and goblets sparkle. Overhead, the bewitched ceiling which always mirrored the sky outside, sparkled with stars.

Through the forest of pointed black Hogwarts hats, Harry saw a long line of scared-looking first years filing into the Hall. Ginny was amongst them, easily visible because of her vivid Weasley hair. Meanwhile, Professor McGonagall, a bespectacled witch with her hair in a tight bun, was placing the famous Hogwarts Sorting Hat on a stool before the newcomers.

Every year, this aged old hat, patched, frayed and dirty, sorted new students into the four Hogwarts houses (Gryffindor, Hufflepuff, Ravenclaw and Slytherin). Harry well remembered putting it on, exactly one year ago, and waiting, petrified, for its decision as it muttered aloud in his ear. For a few horrible seconds he had feared that the hat was going to put him in Slytherin, the house which had turned out more dark witches and wizards than any other – but he had ended up in Gryffindor, along with Ron, Hermione and the rest of the Weasleys. Last term, Harry and Ron had helped Gryffindor win the House Championship, beating Slytherin for the first time in seven years.

A very small, mousey-haired boy had been called forward to place the hat on his head. Harry's eyes wandered past him to where Professor Dumbledore, the headmaster, sat watching the Sorting from the staff table, his long silver beard and half-moon glasses shining brightly in the candlelight. Several seats along, Harry saw Gilderoy Lockhart, dressed in robes of aquamarine. And there at the end was Hagrid, huge and hairy, drinking deeply from his goblet.

'Hang on ...' Harry muttered to Ron. 'There's an empty chair at the staff table ... Where's Snape?'

Professor Severus Snape was Harry's least favourite teacher. Harry also happened to be Snape's least favourite student. Cruel, sarcastic and disliked by everybody except the students from his own house (Slytherin), Snape taught Potions.

'Maybe he's ill!' said Ron hopefully.

'Maybe he's *left*,' said Harry, 'because he missed out on the Defence Against Dark Arts job *again!*'

'Or he might have been *sacked!*' said Ron enthusiastically. 'I mean, everyone hates him –'

'Or maybe,' said a very cold voice right behind them, 'he's waiting to hear why you two didn't arrive on the school train.'

Harry spun around. There, his black robes rippling in a cold breeze, stood Severus Snape. He was a thin man with sallow skin, a hooked nose and greasy, shoulder-length black hair, and at this moment, he was smiling in a way that told Harry he and Ron were in very deep trouble.

'Follow me,' said Snape.

Not daring even to look at each other, Harry and Ron followed Snape up the steps into the vast, echoing entrance hall, which was lit with flaming torches. A delicious smell of food was wafting from the Great Hall, but Snape led them away from the warmth and light, down a narrow stone staircase that led into the dungeons.

'In!' he said, opening a door halfway down the cold passageway and pointing.

They entered Snape's office, shivering. The shadowy walls were lined with shelves of large glass jars, in which floated all manner of revolting things Harry didn't really want to know the name of at the moment. The fireplace was dark and empty. Snape closed the door and turned to look at them.

'So,' he said softly, 'the train isn't good enough for the famous Harry Potter and his faithful sidekick Weasley. Wanted to arrive with a *bang,* did we, boys?'

'No, sir, it was the barrier at King's Cross, it –'

'Silence!' said Snape coldly. 'What have you done with the car?'

Ron gulped. This wasn't the first time Snape had given Harry the impression of being able to read minds. But a moment later, he understood, as Snape unrolled today's issue of the *Evening Prophet.*

'You were seen,' he hissed, showing them the headline: FLYING FORD ANGLIA MYSTIFIES MUGGLES. He began to read aloud. 'Two Muggles in London, convinced they saw an old car flying over the Post Office tower ... at noon in Norfolk, Mrs Hetty Bayliss, while hanging out her washing ... Mr Angus Fleet, of Peebles, reported to police ... six or seven Muggles in all. I believe *your* father works in the Misuse of Muggle Artefacts Office?' he said, looking up at Ron and smiling still more nastily. 'Dear, dear ... his own son ...'

Harry felt as though he'd just been walloped in the stomach by one of the mad tree's larger branches. If anyone found out Mr Weasley had bewitched the car ... he hadn't thought of that ...

'I noticed, in my search of the park, that considerable damage seems to have been done to a very valuable Whomping Willow,' Snape went on.

'That tree did more damage to *us* than we —' Ron blurted out.

'*Silence!*' snapped Snape again. 'Most unfortunately, you are not in my House and the decision to expel you does not rest with me. I shall go and fetch the people who *do* have that happy power. You will wait here.'

Harry and Ron stared at each other, white-faced. Harry didn't feel hungry any more. He now felt extremely sick. He tried not to look at a large, slimy something suspended in green liquid on a shelf behind Snape's desk. If Snape had gone to fetch Professor McGonagall, head of Gryffindor house, they were hardly any better off. She might be fairer than Snape, but she was still extremely strict.

Ten minutes later, Snape returned, and sure enough it was Professor McGonagall who accompanied him. Harry had seen Professor McGonagall angry on several occasions, but either he had forgotten just how thin her mouth could go, or he had never seen her this angry before. She raised her wand the moment she entered. Harry and Ron both flinched, but she merely pointed it at the empty fireplace, where flames suddenly erupted.

'Sit,' she said, and they both backed into chairs by the fire.

'Explain,' she said, her glasses glinting ominously.

Ron launched into the story, starting with the barrier at the station refusing to let them through.

'... so we had no choice, Professor, we couldn't get on the train.'

'Why didn't you send us a letter by owl? I believe *you* have an owl?' Professor McGonagall said coldly to Harry.

Harry gaped at her. Now she said it, that seemed the obvious thing to have done.

'I — I didn't think —'

'That,' said Professor McGonagall, 'is obvious.'

There was a knock on the office door and Snape, now looking

happier than ever, opened it. There stood the headmaster, Professor Dumbledore.

Harry's whole body went numb. Dumbledore was looking unusually grave. He stared down his very crooked nose at them and Harry suddenly found himself wishing he and Ron were still being beaten up by the Whomping Willow.

There was a long silence. Then Dumbledore said, 'Please explain why you did this.'

It would have been better if he had shouted. Harry hated the disappointment in his voice. For some reason, he was unable to look Dumbledore in the eyes, and spoke instead to his knees. He told Dumbledore everything except that Mr Weasley owned the bewitched car, making it sound as though he and Ron had happened to find a flying car parked outside the station. He knew Dumbledore would see through this at once, but Dumbledore asked no questions about the car. When Harry had finished, he merely continued to peer at them through his spectacles.

'We'll go and get our stuff,' said Ron in a hopeless sort of voice.

'What are you talking about, Weasley?' barked Professor McGonagall.

'Well, you're expelling us, aren't you?' said Ron.

Harry looked quickly at Dumbledore.

'Not today, Mr Weasley,' said Dumbledore. 'But I must impress upon both of you the seriousness of what you have done. I will be writing to both your families tonight. I must also warn you that if you do anything like this again, I will have no choice but to expel you.'

Snape looked as though Christmas had been cancelled. He cleared his throat and said, 'Professor Dumbledore, these boys have flouted the Decree for the Restriction of Under-age Wizardry, caused serious damage to an old and valuable tree ... surely acts of this nature ...'

'It will be for Professor McGonagall to decide on these boys' punishments, Severus,' said Dumbledore calmly. 'They are in her House and are therefore her responsibility.' He turned to Professor McGonagall. 'I must go back to the feast, Minerva, I've got to give out a few notices. Come, Severus, there's a delicious-looking custard tart I want to sample.'

Snape shot a look of pure venom at Harry and Ron as he allowed himself to be swept out of his office, leaving them alone with Professor McGonagall, who was still eyeing them like a wrathful eagle.

'You'd better get along to the hospital wing, Weasley, you're bleeding.'

'Not much,' said Ron, hastily wiping the cut over his eye with his sleeve. 'Professor, I wanted to watch my sister being Sorted –'

'The Sorting Ceremony is over,' said Professor McGonagall. 'Your sister is also in Gryffindor.'

'Oh, good,' said Ron.

'And speaking of Gryffindor –' Professor McGonagall said sharply, but Harry cut in: 'Professor, when we took the car, term hadn't started, so – so Gryffindor shouldn't really have points taken from it, should it?' he finished, watching her anxiously.

Professor McGonagall gave him a piercing look, but he was sure she had almost smiled. Her mouth looked less thin, anyway.

'I will not take any points from Gryffindor,' she said, and Harry's heart lightened considerably. 'But you will both get a detention.'

It was better than Harry had expected. As for Dumbledore's writing to the Dursleys, that was nothing. Harry knew perfectly well they'd just be disappointed that the Whomping Willow hadn't squashed him flat.

Professor McGonagall raised her wand again and pointed it at Snape's desk. A large plate of sandwiches, two silver goblets and a jug of iced pumpkin juice appeared with a pop.

'You will eat in here and then go straight up to your dormitory,' she said. 'I must also return to the feast.'

When the door had closed behind her, Ron let out a long, low whistle.

'I thought we'd had it,' he said, grabbing a sandwich.

'So did I,' said Harry, taking one too.

'Can you believe our luck, though?' said Ron thickly through a mouthful of chicken and ham. 'Fred and *George* must've flown that car five or six times and no Muggle ever saw *them*.' He swallowed and took another huge bite. '*Why* couldn't we get through the barrier?'

Harry shrugged. 'We'll have to watch our step from now on, though,' he said, taking a grateful swig of pumpkin juice. 'Wish we could've gone up to the feast ...'

'She didn't want us showing off,' said Ron sagely. 'Doesn't want people to think it's clever, arriving by flying car.'

When they had eaten as many sandwiches as they could (the plate kept re-filling itself) they rose and left the office, treading the familiar path to Gryffindor tower. The castle was quiet; it seemed that the feast was over. They walked past muttering portraits and creaking suits of armour, and climbed narrow flights of stone stairs, until at last they reached the passage where the secret entrance to Gryffindor tower was hidden, behind an oil painting of a very fat woman in a pink silk dress.

'Password?' she said, as they approached.

'Er –' said Harry.

They didn't know the new year's password, not having met a Gryffindor prefect yet, but help came almost immediately; they heard hurrying feet behind them and turned to see Hermione dashing towards them.

'*There* you are! Where have you *been*? The most *ridiculous* rumours – someone said you'd been expelled for crashing a flying *car*.'

'Well, we haven't been expelled,' Harry assured her.

'You're not telling me you *did* fly here?' said Hermione, sounding almost as severe as Professor McGonagall.

'Skip the lecture,' said Ron impatiently, 'and tell us the new password.'

'It's "wattlebird",' said Hermione impatiently, 'but that's not the point –'

Her words were cut short, however, as the portrait of the fat lady swung open and there was a sudden storm of clapping. It looked as though the whole of Gryffindor house was still awake, packed into the circular common room, standing on the lopsided tables and squashy armchairs, waiting for them to arrive. Arms reached through the portrait hole to pull Harry and Ron inside, leaving Hermione to scramble in after them.

'Brilliant!' yelled Lee Jordan. 'Inspired! What an entrance! Flying a car right into the Whomping Willow, people'll be talking about that one for years!'

'Good on you,' said a fifth year Harry had never spoken to; someone was patting him on the back as though he'd just won a marathon. Fred and George pushed their way to the front of the crowd and said together, 'Why couldn't you've called us back, eh?' Ron was scarlet in the face, grinning embarrassedly, but Harry could see one person who didn't look happy at all. Percy was visible over the heads of some excited first years, and he seemed to be trying to get near enough to start telling them off. Harry nudged Ron in the ribs and nodded in Percy's direction. Ron got the point at once.

'Got to get upstairs – bit tired,' he said, and the two of them started pushing their way towards the door on the other side of the room, which led to a spiral staircase and the dormitories.

'Night,' Harry called back to Hermione, who was wearing a scowl just like Percy's.

They managed to get to the other side of the common room, still having their backs slapped, and gained the peace of the staircase. They hurried up it, right to the top, and at last reached the door of their old dormitory, which now had a sign on it saying 'second years'. They entered the familiar, circular room, with its five four-posters hung with red velvet and its high, narrow windows. Their trunks had been brought up for them and placed at the ends of their beds.

Ron grinned guiltily at Harry.

'I know I shouldn't've enjoyed that or anything, but –'

The dormitory door flew open and in came the other second year Gryffindor boys, Seamus Finnigan, Dean Thomas and Neville Longbottom.

'*Unbelievable!*' beamed Seamus.

'Cool,' said Dean.

'Amazing,' said Neville, awestruck.

Harry couldn't help it. He grinned, too.

— CHAPTER SIX —

Gilderoy Lockhart

The next day, however, Harry barely grinned once. Things started to go downhill from breakfast in the Great Hall. The four long house tables were laden with tureens of porridge, plates of kippers, mountains of toast and dishes of eggs and bacon, beneath the enchanted ceiling (today, a dull, cloudy grey). Harry and Ron sat down at the Gryffindor table next to Hermione, who had her copy of *Voyages with Vampires* propped open against a milk jug. There was a slight stiffness in the way she said 'Morning' which told Harry that she was still disapproving of the way they had arrived. Neville Longbottom, on the other hand, greeted them cheerfully. Neville was a round-faced and accident-prone boy with the worst memory of anyone Harry had ever met.

'Post's due any minute – I think Gran's sending on a few things I forgot.'

Harry had only just started his porridge when, sure enough, there was a rushing sound overhead and a hundred or so owls streamed in, circling the hall and dropping letters and packages into the chattering crowd. A big, lumpy parcel bounced off Neville's head and a second later, something large and grey fell into Hermione's jug, spraying them all with milk and feathers.

'*Errol!*' said Ron, pulling the bedraggled owl out by the feet. Errol slumped, unconscious, onto the table, his legs in the air and a damp red envelope in his beak.

'Oh no –' Ron gasped.

'It's all right, he's still alive,' said Hermione, prodding Errol gently with the tip of her finger.

'It's not that – it's *that*.'

Ron was pointing at the red envelope. It looked quite ordinary to Harry, but Ron and Neville were both looking at it as though they expected it to explode.

'What's the matter?' said Harry.

'She's – she's sent me a Howler,' said Ron faintly.

'You'd better open it, Ron,' said Neville, in a timid whisper. 'It'll be worse if you don't. My Gran sent me one once, and I ignored it and – ' he gulped, 'it was horrible.'

Harry looked from their petrified faces to the red envelope.

'What's a Howler?' he said.

But Ron's whole attention was fixed on the letter, which had begun to smoke at the corners.

'Open it,' Neville urged. 'It'll all be over in a few minutes ...'

Ron stretched out a shaking hand, eased the envelope from Errol's beak and slit it open. Neville stuffed his fingers in his ears. A split second later, Harry knew why. He thought for a moment it *had* exploded; a roar of sound filled the huge hall, shaking dust from the ceiling.

' ... *STEALING THE CAR, I WOULDN'T HAVE BEEN SUR-PRISED IF THEY'D EXPELLED YOU, YOU WAIT TILL I GET HOLD OF YOU, I DON'T SUPPOSE YOU STOPPED TO THINK WHAT YOUR FATHER AND I WENT THROUGH WHEN WE SAW IT HAD GONE ...*'

Mrs Weasley's yells, a hundred times louder than usual, made the plates and spoons rattle on the table, and echoed deafeningly off the stone walls. People throughout the hall were swivelling around to see who had received the Howler and Ron sank so low in his chair that only his crimson forehead could be seen.

' ... *LETTER FROM DUMBLEDORE LAST NIGHT, I THOUGHT YOUR FATHER WOULD DIE OF SHAME, WE DIDN'T BRING YOU UP TO BEHAVE LIKE THIS, YOU AND HARRY COULD BOTH HAVE DIED ...*'

Harry had been wondering when his name was going to crop up. He tried very hard to look as though he couldn't hear the voice that was making his eardrums throb.

' ... *ABSOLUTELY DISGUSTED, YOUR FATHER'S FACING AN ENQUIRY AT WORK, IT'S ENTIRELY YOUR FAULT AND IF YOU PUT ANOTHER TOE OUT OF LINE WE'LL BRING YOU STRAIGHT BACK HOME.*'

A ringing silence fell. The red envelope, which had dropped from Ron's hand, burst into flames and curled into ashes. Harry and Ron sat stunned, as though a tidal wave had just passed over them. A few people laughed and gradually, a babble of talk broke out again.

Hermione closed *Voyages with Vampires* and looked down at the top of Ron's head.

'Well, I don't know what you expected, Ron, but you –'

'Don't tell me I deserved it,' snapped Ron.

Harry pushed his porridge away. His insides were burning with guilt. Mr Weasley was facing an enquiry at work. After all Mr and Mrs Weasley had done for him over the summer ...

But he had no time to dwell on this; Professor McGonagall was moving along the Gryffindor table, handing out timetables. Harry took his, and saw that they had double Herbology with the Hufflepuffs first.

Harry, Ron and Hermione left the castle together, crossed the vegetable patch and made for the greenhouses, where the magical plants were kept. At least the Howler had done one good thing: Hermione seemed to think they had now been punished enough and was being perfectly friendly again.

As they neared the greenhouses they saw the rest of the class standing outside, waiting for Professor Sprout. Harry, Ron and Hermione had only just joined them when she came striding into view across the lawn, accompanied by Gilderoy Lockhart. Professor Sprout's arms were full of bandages, and with another twinge of guilt, Harry spotted the Whomping Willow in the distance, several of its branches now in slings.

Professor Sprout was a squat little witch who wore a patched hat over her flyaway hair; there was usually a large amount of earth on her clothes and her fingernails would have made Aunt Petunia faint. Gilderoy Lockhart, however, was immaculate in sweeping robes of turquoise, his golden hair shining under a perfectly positioned turquoise hat with gold trimming.

'Oh, hello there!' Lockhart called, beaming around at the assembled students. 'Just been showing Professor Sprout the right way to doctor a Whomping Willow! But I don't want you running away with the idea that I'm better at Herbology than she is! I just happen to have met several of these exotic plants on my travels ...'

'Greenhouse Three today, chaps!' said Professor Sprout, who was looking distinctly disgruntled, not at all her usual cheerful self.

There was a murmur of interest. They had only ever worked in Greenhouse One before – Greenhouse Three housed far more interesting and dangerous plants. Professor Sprout took a large key from her belt and unlocked the door. Harry caught a whiff of damp earth and fertilizer, mingling with the heavy perfume of some giant, umbrella-sized flowers dangling from the ceiling. He was about to follow Ron and Hermione inside when Lockhart's hand shot out.

'Harry! I've been wanting a word – you don't mind if he's a couple of minutes late, do you, Professor Sprout?'

Judging by Professor Sprout's scowl, she did mind, but Lockhart said, 'That's the ticket,' and closed the greenhouse door in her face.

'Harry,' said Lockhart, his large white teeth gleaming in the sunlight as he shook his head. 'Harry, Harry, Harry.'

Completely nonplussed, Harry said nothing.

'When I heard – well, of course, it was all my fault. Could have kicked myself.'

Harry had no idea what he was talking about. He was about to say so when Lockhart went on, 'Don't know when I've been more shocked. Flying a car to Hogwarts! Well, of course, I knew at once why you'd done it. Stood out a mile. Harry, Harry, *Harry*.'

It was remarkable how he could show every one of those brilliant teeth even when he wasn't talking.

'Gave you a taste for publicity, didn't I?' said Lockhart. 'Gave you the *bug*. You got onto the front page of the paper with me and you couldn't wait to do it again.'

'Oh – no, Professor, see –'

'Harry, Harry, Harry,' said Lockhart, reaching out and grasping his shoulder. '*I understand*. Natural to want a bit more once you've had that first taste – and I blame myself for giving you that, because it was bound to go to your head – but see here, young man, you can't start *flying cars* to try and get yourself noticed. Just calm down, all right? Plenty of time for all that when you're older. Yes, yes, I know what you're thinking! "It's all right for him, he's an internationally famous wizard already!" But when I was twelve, I was just as much of a nobody as you are now. In fact, I'd say I was even more of a nobody! I mean, a few people have heard of you, haven't they? All that business with He Who Must Not Be Named!' He glanced at the lightning scar on Harry's forehead. 'I know, I know, it's not quite as good as winning *Witch Weekly*'s Most-Charming-Smile Award five times in a row, as I have – but it's a *start,* Harry, it's a *start.*'

He gave Harry a hearty wink and strode off. Harry stood stunned for a few seconds, then, remembering he was supposed to be in the greenhouse, he opened the door and slid inside.

Professor Sprout was standing behind a trestle bench in the centre of the greenhouse. About twenty pairs of different coloured earmuffs were lying on the bench. When Harry had taken his place between Ron and Hermione, she said, 'We'll be re-potting Mandrakes today. Now, who can tell me the properties of the Mandrake?'

To nobody's surprise, Hermione's hand was first into the air.

'Mandrake, or Mandragora, is a powerful restorative,' said Hermione, sounding as usual as though she had swallowed the textbook. 'It is used to return people who have been transfigured or cursed to their original state.'

'Excellent. Ten points to Gryffindor,' said Professor Sprout. 'The Mandrake forms an essential part of most antidotes. It is also, however, dangerous. Who can tell me why?'

Hermione's hand narrowly missed Harry's glasses as it shot up again.

'The cry of the Mandrake is fatal to anyone who hears it,' she said promptly.

'Precisely. Take another ten points,' said Professor Sprout. 'Now, the Mandrakes we have here are still very young.'

She pointed to a row of deep trays as she spoke and everyone shuffled forward for a better look. A hundred or so tufty little plants, purplish green in colour, were growing there in rows. They looked quite unremarkable to Harry, who didn't have the slightest idea what Hermione meant by the 'cry' of the Mandrake.

'Everyone take a pair of earmuffs,' said Professor Sprout.

There was a scramble as everyone tried to seize a pair that wasn't pink and fluffy.

'When I tell you to put them on, make sure your ears are *completely* covered,' said Professor Sprout. 'When it is safe to remove them, I will give you the thumbs up. Right – earmuffs *on.*'

Harry snapped the earmuffs over his ears. They shut out sound completely. Professor Sprout put a pink fluffy pair over her own ears, rolled up the sleeves of her robes, grasped one of the tufty plants firmly, and pulled hard.

Harry let out a gasp of surprise that no one could hear.

Instead of roots, a small, muddy and extremely ugly baby popped out of the earth. The leaves were growing right out of his head. He had pale green, mottled skin, and was clearly bawling at the top of his lungs.

Professor Sprout took a large plant pot from under the table and plunged the Mandrake into it, burying him in dark, damp compost until only the tufted leaves were visible. Professor Sprout dusted off her hands, gave them all the thumbs up and removed her own earmuffs.

'As our Mandrakes are only seedlings, their cries won't kill yet,' she said calmly, as though she'd just done nothing more exciting than water a begonia. 'However, they *will* knock you out for several hours, and as I'm sure none of you want to miss your first day back, make sure your earmuffs are securely in place while you work. I will attract your attention when it is time to pack up.

'Four to a tray – there is a large supply of pots here – compost in the sacks over there – and be careful of the Venemous Tentacula, it's teething.'

She gave a sharp slap to a spiky, dark red plant as she spoke, making it draw in the long feelers that had been inching sneakily over her shoulder.

Harry, Ron and Hermione were joined at their tray by a curly haired Hufflepuff boy Harry knew by sight, but had never spoken to.

'Justin Finch-Fletchley,' he said brightly, shaking Harry by the hand. 'Know who you are, of course, the famous Harry Potter ... and you're Hermione Granger – always top in everything ...' (Hermione beamed as she had her hand shaken too) 'and Ron Weasley. Wasn't that your flying car?'

Ron didn't smile. The Howler was obviously still on his mind.

'That Lockhart's something, isn't he?' said Justin happily, as they began filling their plant pots with dragon dung compost. 'Awfully brave chap. Have you read his books? I'd have died of fear if I'd been cornered in a telephone box by a werewolf, but he stayed cool and – zap – just *fantastic*.

'My name was down for Eton, you know, I can't tell you how glad I am I came here instead. Of course, mother was slightly disappointed, but since I made her read Lockhart's books I think she's begun to see how useful it'll be to have a fully trained wizard in the family ...'

After that they didn't have much chance to talk. Their earmuffs were back on and they needed to concentrate on the Mandrakes. Professor Sprout had made it look extremely easy, but it wasn't. The Mandrakes didn't like coming out of the earth, but didn't seem to want to go back into it either. They squirmed, kicked, flailed their sharp little fists and gnashed their teeth; Harry spent ten whole minutes trying to squash a particularly fat one into a pot.

By the end of the class, Harry, like everyone else, was sweaty, aching and covered in earth. They traipsed back to the castle for a quick wash and then the Gryffindors hurried off to Transfiguration.

Professor McGonagall's classes were always hard work, but today was especially difficult. Everything Harry had learned last year seemed to have leaked out of his head during the summer. He was supposed to be turning a beetle into a button, but all he managed to do was give his beetle a lot of exercise as it scuttled over the desk top avoiding his wand.

Ron was having far worse problems. He had patched up his wand with some borrowed Spellotape, but it seemed to be damaged beyond repair. It kept crackling and sparking at odd moments, and every time Ron tried to transfigure his beetle it engulfed him in thick grey smoke which smelled of rotten eggs. Unable to see what he was doing, Ron accidentally squashed his beetle with his elbow and had to ask for a new one. Professor McGonagall wasn't pleased.

Harry was relieved to hear the lunch bell. His brain felt like a wrung sponge. Everyone filed out of the classroom except him and Ron, who was whacking his wand furiously on the desk.

'Stupid ... useless ... thing ...'

'Write home for another one,' Harry suggested, as the wand let off a volley of bangs like a firecracker.

'Oh yeah, and get another Howler back,' said Ron, stuffing the now hissing wand into his bag. '*It's your own fault your wand got snapped –*'

They went down to lunch, where Ron's mood was not improved by Hermione showing them the handful of perfect coat buttons she had produced in Transfiguration.

'What've we got this afternoon?' said Harry, hastily changing the subject.

'Defence Against the Dark Arts,' said Hermione at once.

'*Why*,' demanded Ron, seizing her timetable, 'have you outlined all Lockhart's lessons in little hearts?'

Hermione snatched the timetable back, flushing furiously.

They finished lunch and went outside into the overcast court-yard. Hermione sat down on a stone step and buried her nose in *Voyages with Vampires* again. Harry and Ron stood talking about Quidditch for several minutes before Harry became aware that he was being closely watched. Looking up, he saw the very small, mousey-haired boy he'd seen trying on the Sorting Hat last night, staring at Harry as though transfixed. He was clutching what looked like an ordinary Muggle camera, and the moment Harry looked at him, he went bright red.

'All right, Harry? I'm – I'm Colin Creevey,' he said breathlessly, taking a tentative step forward. 'I'm in Gryffindor, too. D'you think – would it be all right if – can I have a picture?' he said, raising the camera hopefully.

'A picture?' Harry repeated blankly.

'So I can prove I've met you,' said Colin Creevey eagerly, edging further forwards. 'I know all about you. Everyone's told me. About how you survived when You Know Who tried to kill you and how he disappeared and everything and how you've still got a light-ning scar on your forehead,' (his eyes raked Harry's hairline) 'and a boy in my dormitory said if I develop the film in the right potion, the pictures'll *move*.' Colin drew a great shuddering breath of excitement and said, 'It's *brilliant* here, isn't it? I never knew all the odd stuff I could do was magic till I got the letter from Hogwarts. My dad's a milkman, he couldn't believe it either. So I'm taking loads of pictures to send home to him. And it'd be real-ly good if I had one of you –' he looked imploringly at Harry, '– maybe your friend could take it and I could stand next to you? And then, could you sign it?'

'*Signed photos?* You're giving out *signed photos*, Potter?'

Loud and scathing, Draco Malfoy's voice echoed around the courtyard. He had stopped right behind Colin, flanked, as he always was at Hogwarts, by his large and thuggish cronies, Crabbe and Goyle.

'Everyone queue up!' Malfoy roared to the crowd. 'Harry Potter's giving out signed photos!'

'No, I'm not,' said Harry angrily, his fists clenching. 'Shut up, Malfoy.'

'You're just jealous,' piped up Colin, whose entire body was about as thick as Crabbe's neck.

'*Jealous*?' said Malfoy, who didn't need to shout any more; half the courtyard was listening in. 'Of what? I don't want a foul scar right across my head, thanks. I don't think getting your head cut open makes you that special, myself.'

Crabbe and Goyle were sniggering stupidly.

'Eat slugs, Malfoy,' said Ron angrily. Crabbe stopped laughing and started rubbing his conker-like knuckles in a menacing way.

'Be careful, Weasley,' sneered Malfoy. 'You don't want to start any trouble or your Mummy'll have to come and take you away from school.' He put on a shrill, piercing voice. '*If you put another toe out of line —*'

A knot of Slytherin fifth years nearby laughed loudly at this.

'Weasley would like a signed photo, Potter,' smirked Malfoy. 'It'd be worth more than his family's whole house.'

Ron whipped out his Spellotaped wand, but Hermione shut *Voyages with Vampires* with a snap and whispered, 'Look out!'

'What's all this, what's all this?' Gilderoy Lockhart was striding towards them, his turquoise robes swirling behind him. 'Who's giving out signed photos?'

Harry started to speak but he was cut short as Lockhart flung an arm around his shoulders and thundered jovially, 'Shouldn't have asked! We meet again, Harry!'

Pinned to Lockhart's side and burning with humiliation, Harry saw Malfoy slide smirking back into the crowd.

'Come on then, Mr Creevey,' said Lockhart, beaming at Colin. 'A double portrait, can't say fairer than that, and we'll *both* sign it for you.'

Colin fumbled for his camera and took the picture as the bell rang behind them, signalling the start of afternoon classes.

'Off you go, move along there,' Lockhart called to the crowd, and he set off back to the castle with Harry, who was wishing he knew a good vanishing spell, still clasped to his side.

'A word to the wise, Harry,' said Lockhart paternally as they entered the building through a side door. 'I covered up for you back there with young Creevey – if he was photographing me, too, your schoolfellows won't think you're setting yourself up so much ...'

Deaf to Harry's stammers, Lockhart swept him down a corridor lined with staring students and up a staircase.

'Let me just say that handing out signed pictures at this stage of your career isn't sensible – looks a tad bigheaded, Harry, to be frank. There may well come a time when, like me, you'll need to keep a stack handy wherever you go, but –' he gave a little chortle, 'I don't think you're quite there yet.'

They had reached Lockhart's classroom and he let Harry go at last. Harry yanked his robes straight and headed for a seat at the very back of the class, where he busied himself with piling all seven of Lockhart's books in front of him, so that he could avoid looking at the real thing.

The rest of the class came clattering in and Ron and Hermione sat down on either side of Harry.

'You could've fried an egg on your face' said Ron. 'You'd better hope Creevey doesn't meet Ginny, they'll be starting a Harry Potter fan club.'

'Shut up,' snapped Harry. The last thing he needed was for Lockhart to hear the phrase 'Harry Potter fan club'.

When the whole class was seated, Lockhart cleared his throat loudly and silence fell. He reached forward, picked up Neville Longbottom's copy of *Travels with Trolls* and held it up to show his own, winking portrait on the front.

'Me,' he said, pointing at it and winking as well, 'Gilderoy Lockhart, Order of Merlin, third class, Honorary Member of the Dark Force Defence League and five times winner of *Witch Weekly's* Most-Charming-Smile Award – but I don't talk about that. I didn't get rid of the Bandon banshee by *smiling* at her!'

He waited for them to laugh; a few people smiled weakly.

'I see you've all bought a complete set of my books – well done. I thought we'd start today with a little quiz. Nothing to worry about – just to check how well you've read them, how much you've taken in ...'

When he had handed out the test papers he returned to the front of the class and said, 'You have thirty minutes. Start – *now!*'

Harry looked down at his paper and read:

1. *What is Gilderoy Lockhart's favourite colour?*
2. *What is Gilderoy Lockhart's secret ambition?*
3. *What, in your opinion, is Gilderoy Lockhart's greatest achievement to date?*

On and on it went, over three sides of paper, right down to:

54. *When is Gilderoy Lockhart's birthday, and what would his ideal gift be?*

Half an hour later, Lockhart collected in the papers and rifled through them in front of the class.

'Tut, tut – hardly any of you remembered that my favourite colour is lilac. I say so in *Year with a Yeti*. And a few of you need to read *Weekend with a Werewolf* more carefully – I clearly state in chapter twelve that my ideal birthday gift would be harmony between all magic and non-magic peoples – though I wouldn't say no to a large bottle of Ogden's Old Firewhisky!'

He gave them another roguish wink. Ron was now staring at Lockhart with an expression of disbelief on his face; Seamus Finnigan and Dean Thomas, who were sitting in front, were shaking with silent laughter. Hermione, on the other hand, was listening to Lockhart with rapt attention, and gave a start when he mentioned her name.

'... but Miss Hermione Granger knew my secret ambition is to rid the world of evil and market my own range of hair-care potions – good girl! In fact –' he flipped her paper over, 'full marks! Where is Miss Hermione Granger?'

Hermione raised a trembling hand.

'Excellent!' beamed Lockhart, 'quite excellent! Take ten points for Gryffindor! And so, to business ...'

He bent down behind his desk and lifted a large, covered cage onto it.

'Now – be warned! It is my job to arm you against the foulest creatures known to wizardkind! You may find yourselves facing your worst fears in this room. Know only that no harm can befall you whilst I am here. All I ask is that you remain calm.'

In spite of himself, Harry leaned around his pile of books for a better look at the cage. Lockhart placed a hand on the cover. Dean and Seamus had stopped laughing now. Neville was cowering in his front row seat.

'I must ask you not to scream,' said Lockhart in a low voice. 'It might provoke them.'

As the whole class held its breath, Lockhart whipped off the cover.

'Yes,' he said dramatically. *'Freshly caught Cornish pixies.'*

Seamus Finnigan couldn't control himself. He let out a snort of laughter which even Lockhart couldn't mistake for a scream of terror.

'Yes?' he smiled at Seamus.

'Well, they're not – they're not very – *dangerous,* are they?' Seamus choked.

'Don't be so sure!' said Lockhart, waggling a finger annoyingly at Seamus. 'Devilish tricky little blighters they can be!'

The pixies were electric blue and about eight inches high, with pointed faces and voices so shrill it was like listening to a lot of budgies arguing. The moment the cover had been removed, they had started jabbering and rocketing around, rattling the bars and pulling bizarre faces at the people nearest them.

'Right then,' Lockhart said loudly. 'Let's see what you make of them!' And he opened the cage.

It was pandemonium. The pixies shot in every direction like rockets. Two of them seized Neville by the ears and lifted him into the air. Several shot straight through the window, showering the back row with broken glass. The rest proceeded to wreck the classroom more effectively than a rampaging rhino. They grabbed ink bottles and sprayed the class with them, shredded books and papers, tore pictures from the walls, upended the waste bin, grabbed bags and books and threw them out of the smashed window; within minutes, half the class was sheltering under desks and Neville was swinging from the candelabra in the ceiling.

'Come on now, round them up, round them up, they're only pixies ...' Lockhart shouted.

He rolled up his sleeves, brandished his wand and bellowed, *'Peskipiksi Pesternomi!'*

It had absolutely no effect; one of the pixies seized Lockhart's wand and threw it out of the window too. Lockhart gulped and dived under his own desk, narrowly avoiding being squashed by Neville, who fell a second later as the candelabra gave way.

The bell rang and there was a mad rush towards the exit. In the relative calm that followed, Lockhart straightened up, caught sight of Harry, Ron and Hermione, who were almost at the door, and said, 'Well, I'll ask you three to just nip the rest of them back into their cage.' He swept past them and shut the door quickly behind him.

'Can you *believe* him?' roared Ron, as one of the remaining pixies bit him painfully on the ear.

'He just wants to give us some hands-on experience,' said
Hermione, immobilising two pixies at once with a clever Freezing
Charm and stuffing them back into their cage.

'*Hands on?*' said Harry, who was trying to grab a pixie dancing
out of reach with its tongue out. 'Hermione, he didn't have a clue
what he was doing.'

'Rubbish,' said Hermione. 'You've read his books – look at all
those amazing things he's done ...'

'He *says* he's done,' Ron muttered.

CHAPTER SEVEN

Mudbloods and Murmurs

Harry spent a lot of time over the next few days dodging out of sight whenever he saw Gilderoy Lockhart coming down a corridor. Harder to avoid was Colin Creevey, who seemed to have memorised Harry's timetable. Nothing seemed to give Colin a bigger thrill than to say, 'All right, Harry?' six or seven times a day and hear, 'Hullo, Colin,' back, however exasperated Harry sounded when he said it.

Hedwig was still angry with Harry about the disastrous car journey and Ron's wand was still malfunctioning, surpassing itself on Friday morning by shooting out of Ron's hand in Charms and hitting tiny old Professor Flitwick squarely between the eyes, creating a large, throbbing green boil where it had struck. So with one thing and another, Harry was quite glad to reach the weekend. He, Ron and Hermione were planning to visit Hagrid on Saturday morning. Harry, however, was shaken awake several hours earlier than he would have liked by Oliver Wood, Captain of the Gryffindor Quidditch team.

'Whassamatter?' said Harry groggily.

'Quidditch practice!' said Wood. 'Come on!'

Harry squinted at the window. There was a thin mist hanging across the pink and gold sky. Now he was awake, he couldn't understand how he could have slept through the racket the birds were making.

'Oliver,' Harry croaked, 'it's the crack of dawn.'

'Exactly,' said Wood. He was a tall and burly sixth year and at the moment, his eyes were gleaming with a mad enthusiasm. 'It's part of our new training programme. Come on, grab your broom and let's go,' said Wood heartily. 'None of the other teams have started training yet, we're going to be first off the mark this year ...'

Yawning and shivering slightly, Harry climbed out of bed and tried to find his Quidditch robes.

'Good man,' said Wood. 'Meet you on the pitch in fifteen minutes.'

When he'd found his scarlet team robes and pulled on his cloak for warmth, Harry scribbled a note to Ron explaining where he'd gone and went down the spiral staircase to the common room, his Nimbus Two Thousand on his shoulder. He had just reached the portrait hole when there was a clatter behind him and Colin Creevey came dashing down the spiral staircase, his camera swinging madly around his neck and something clutched in his hand.

'I heard someone saying your name on the stairs, Harry! Look what I've got here! I've had it developed, I wanted to show you –'

Harry looked bemusedly at the photograph Colin was brandishing under his nose.

A moving, black and white Lockhart was tugging hard on an arm Harry recognised as his own. He was pleased to see that his photographic self was putting up a good fight and refusing to be dragged into view. As Harry watched, Lockhart gave up and slumped, panting, against the white edge of the picture.

'Will you sign it?' said Colin eagerly.

'No,' said Harry flatly, glancing around to check that the room was really deserted. 'Sorry, Colin, I'm in a hurry – Quidditch practice.'

He climbed through the portrait hole.

'Oh wow! Wait for me! I've never watched a Quidditch game before!'

Colin scrambled through the hole after him.

'It'll be really boring,' Harry said quickly, but Colin ignored him, his face shining with excitement.

'You were the youngest house player in a hundred years, weren't you, Harry? Weren't you?' said Colin, trotting alongside him. 'You must be brilliant. I've never flown. Is it easy? Is that your own broom? Is that the best one there is?'

Harry didn't know how to get rid of him. It was like having an extremely talkative shadow.

'I don't really understand Quidditch,' said Colin breathlessly. 'Is it true there are four balls? And two of them fly round trying to knock people off their brooms?'

'Yes,' said Harry heavily, resigned to explaining the complicated rules of Quidditch. 'They're called Bludgers. There are two Beaters on each team who carry clubs to beat the Bludgers away from their side. Fred and George Weasley are the Gryffindor Beaters.'

'And what are the other balls for?' Colin asked, tripping down a couple of steps because he was gazing open-mouthed at Harry.

'Well, the Quaffle – that's the biggish red one – is the one that scores goals. Three Chasers on each team throw the Quaffle to each other and try and get it through the goalposts at the end of the pitch – they're three long poles with hoops on the end.'

'And the fourth ball –'

'– is the Golden Snitch,' said Harry, 'and it's very small, very fast and difficult to catch. But that's what the Seeker's got to do, because a game of Quidditch doesn't end until the Snitch has been caught. And whichever team's Seeker gets the Snitch earns his team an extra hundred and fifty points.'

'And you're Gryffindor Seeker, aren't you?' said Colin in awe.

'Yes,' said Harry, as they left the castle and started across the dew drenched grass. 'And there's the Keeper, too. He guards the goalposts. That's it, really.'

But Colin didn't stop questioning Harry all the way down the sloping lawns to the Quidditch pitch, and Harry only shook him off when he reached the changing rooms. Colin called after him in a piping voice, 'I'll go and get a good seat, Harry!' and hurried off to the stands.

The rest of the Gryffindor team were already in the changing room. Wood was the only person who looked truly awake. Fred and George Weasley were sitting, puffy-eyed and tousle-haired, next to fourth year Alicia Spinnet, who seemed to be nodding off against the wall behind her. Her fellow Chasers, Katie Bell and Angelina Johnson, were yawning side by side opposite them.

'There you are, Harry, what kept you?' said Wood briskly. 'Now, I wanted a quick talk with you all before we actually get onto the pitch, because I spent the summer devising a whole new training programme, which I really think will make all the difference ...'

Wood was holding up a large diagram of a Quidditch pitch, on which were drawn many lines, arrows and crosses in different coloured inks. He took out his wand, tapped the board and the arrows began to wiggle over the diagram like caterpillars. As Wood launched into a speech about his new tactics, Fred Weasley's head drooped right on to Alicia Spinnet's shoulder and he began to snore.

The first board took nearly twenty minutes to explain, but there was another board under that, and a third under that one. Harry sank into a stupor as Wood droned on and on.

'So,' said Wood, at long last, jerking Harry from a wistful fantasy about what he could be eating for breakfast at this very moment up at the castle, 'is that clear? Any questions?'

'I've got a question, Oliver,' said George, who had woken with a start. 'Why couldn't you have told us all this yesterday when we were awake?'

Wood wasn't pleased.

'Now, listen here, you lot,' he said, glowering at them all, 'we should have won the Quidditch cup last year. We're easily the best team. But unfortunately, owing to circumstances beyond our control ...'

Harry shifted guiltily in his seat. He had been unconscious in the hospital wing for the final match of the previous year, meaning that Gryffindor had been a player short and had suffered their worst defeat in three hundred years.

Wood took a moment to regain control of himself. Their last defeat was clearly still torturing him.

'So this year, we train harder than ever before ... OK, let's go and put our new theories into practice!' Wood shouted, seizing his broomstick and leading the way out of the changing rooms. Stiff-legged and still yawning, his team followed.

They had been in the changing room so long that the sun was up properly now, although remnants of mist hung over the grass in the stadium. As Harry walked onto the pitch, he saw Ron and Hermione sitting in the stands.

'Aren't you finished yet?' called Ron incredulously.

'Haven't even started,' said Harry, looking jealously at the toast and marmalade Ron and Hermione had brought out of the Great Hall. 'Wood's been teaching us new moves.'

He mounted his broomstick and kicked at the ground, soaring up into the air. The cool morning air whipped his face, waking him far more effectively than Wood's long talk. It felt wonderful to be back on the Quidditch pitch. He soared right around the stadium at full speed, racing Fred and George.

'What's that funny clicking noise?' called Fred, as they hurtled around the corner.

Harry looked into the stands. Colin was sitting in one of the highest seats, his camera raised, taking picture after picture, the sound strangely magnified in the deserted stadium.

'Look this way, Harry! This way!' he cried shrilly.

'Who's that?' said Fred.

'No idea,' Harry lied, putting on a spurt of speed that took him as far away as possible from Colin.

'What's going on?' said Wood, frowning, as he skimmed through the air towards them. 'Why's that first year taking pictures? I don't like it. He could be a Slytherin spy, trying to find out about our new training programme.'

'He's in Gryffindor,' said Harry quickly.

'And the Slytherins don't need a spy, Oliver,' said George.

'What makes you say that?' said Wood testily.

'Because they're here in person,' said George, pointing.

Several people in green robes were walking onto the pitch, broomsticks in their hands.

'I don't believe it!' Wood hissed in outrage. 'I booked the pitch for today! We'll see about this!'

Wood shot towards the ground, landing rather harder than he meant to in his anger, staggering slightly as he dismounted. Harry, Fred and George followed.

'Flint!' Wood bellowed at the Slytherin Captain. 'This is our practice time! We got up specially! You can clear off now!'

Marcus Flint was even larger than Wood. He had a look of troll-ish cunning on his face as he replied, 'Plenty of room for all of us, Wood.'

Angelina, Alicia and Katie had come over, too. There were no girls on the Slytherin team – who stood shoulder to shoulder, facing the Gryffindors, leering to a man.

'But I booked the pitch!' said Wood, positively spitting with rage. 'I booked it!'

'Ah,' said Flint, 'but I've got a specially signed note here from Professor Snape. *I, Professor S. Snape, give the Slytherin team permission to practise today on the Quidditch pitch owing to the need to train their new Seeker.*'

'You've got a new Seeker?' said Wood, distracted. 'Where?'

And from behind the six large figures before them came a seventh, smaller boy, smirking all over his pale, pointed face. It was Draco Malfoy.

'Aren't you Lucius Malfoy's son?' said Fred, looking at Malfoy with dislike.

'Funny you should mention Draco's father,' said Flint, as the whole Slytherin team smiled still more broadly. 'Let me show you the generous gift he's made to the Slytherin team.'

All seven of them held out their broomsticks. Seven highly polished, brand new handles and seven sets of fine gold lettering spelling the words 'Nimbus Two Thousand and One' gleamed under the Gryffindors' noses in the early morning sun.

'Very latest model. Only came out last month,' said Flint carelessly, flicking a speck of dust from the end of his own. 'I believe it outstrips the old Two Thousand series by a considerable amount. As for the old Cleansweeps,' he smiled nastily at Fred and George, who were both clutching Cleansweep Fives, 'sweeps the board with them.'

None of the Gryffindor team could think of anything to say for a moment. Malfoy was smirking so broadly his cold eyes were reduced to slits.

'Oh look,' said Flint. 'A pitch invasion.'

Ron and Hermione were crossing the grass to see what was going on.

'What's happening?' Ron asked Harry. 'Why aren't you playing? And what's *he* doing here?'

He was looking at Malfoy, taking in his Slytherin Quidditch robes.

'I'm the new Slytherin seeker, Weasley,' said Malfoy, smugly. 'Everyone's just been admiring the brooms my father's bought our team.'

Ron gaped, open-mouthed, at the seven superb broomsticks in front of him.

'Good, aren't they?' said Malfoy smoothly. 'But perhaps the Gryffindor team will be able to raise some gold and get new brooms too. You could raffle off those Cleansweep Fives, I expect a museum would bid for them.'

The Slytherin team howled with laughter.

'At least no one on the Gryffindor team had to *buy* their way in,' said Hermione sharply. '*They* got in on pure talent.'

The smug look on Malfoy's face flickered.

'No one asked your opinion, you filthy little Mudblood,' he spat.

Harry knew at once that Malfoy had said something really bad because there was an instant uproar at his words. Flint had to dive in front of Malfoy to stop Fred and George jumping on him, Alicia shrieked, 'How dare you!' and Ron plunged his hand into his robes, pulled out his wand, yelling, 'You'll pay for that one, Malfoy!' and pointed it furiously under Flint's arm at Malfoy's face.

A loud bang echoed around the stadium and a jet of green light shot out of the wrong end of Ron's wand, hitting him in the stomach and sending him reeling backwards on to the grass.

'Ron! Ron! Are you all right?' squealed Hermione.

Ron opened his mouth to speak, but no words came out. Instead he gave an almighty belch and several slugs dribbled out of his mouth on to his lap.

The Slytherin team were paralysed with laughter. Flint was doubled up, hanging on to his new broomstick for support. Malfoy was on all fours, banging the ground with his fist. The Gryffindors were gathered around Ron, who kept belching large, glistening slugs. Nobody seemed to want to touch him.

'We'd better get him to Hagrid's, it's nearest,' said Harry to Hermione, who nodded bravely, and the pair of them pulled Ron up by the arms.

'What happened, Harry? What happened? Is he ill? But you can cure him, can't you?' Colin had run down from his seat and was now dancing alongside them as they left the pitch. Ron gave a huge heave and more slugs dribbled down his front.

'Oooh,' said Colin, fascinated and raising his camera. 'Can you hold him still, Harry?'

'Get out of the way, Colin!' said Harry angrily. He and Hermione supported Ron out of the stadium and across the grounds towards the edge of the forest.

'Nearly there, Ron,' said Hermione, as the gamekeeper's cabin came into view. 'You'll be all right in a minute ... almost there ...'

They were within twenty feet of Hagrid's house when the front door opened, but it wasn't Hagrid who emerged. Gilderoy Lockhart, wearing robes of palest mauve today, came striding out.

'Quick, behind here,' Harry hissed, dragging Ron behind a nearby bush. Hermione followed, somewhat reluctantly.

'It's a simple matter if you know what you're doing!' Lockhart was saying loudly to Hagrid. 'If you need help, you know where I

am! I'll let you have a copy of my book – I'm surprised you
haven't already got one. I'll sign one tonight and send it over.
Well, goodbye!' And he strode away towards the castle.

Harry waited until Lockhart was out of sight, then pulled Ron
out of the bush and up to Hagrid's front door. They knocked
urgently.

Hagrid appeared at once, looking very grumpy, but his expression brightened when he saw who it was.

'Bin wonderin' when you'd come ter see me – come in, come in
– thought you mighta bin Professor Lockhart back again.'

Harry and Hermione supported Ron over the threshold, into
the one-roomed cabin, which had an enormous bed in one corner,
a fire crackling merrily in the other. Hagrid didn't seem perturbed
by Ron's slug problem, which Harry hastily explained as he lowered Ron into a chair.

'Better out than in,' he said cheerfully, plonking a large copper
basin in front of him. 'Get 'em all up, Ron.'

'I don't think there's anything to do except wait for it to stop,'
said Hermione anxiously, watching Ron bend over the basin.
'That's a difficult curse to work at the best of times, but with a
broken wand ...'

Hagrid was bustling around making them tea. His boarhound,
Fang, was slobbering over Harry.

'What did Lockhart want with you, Hagrid?' Harry asked,
scratching Fang's ears.

'Givin' me advice on gettin' kelpies out of a well,' growled
Hagrid, moving a half-plucked rooster off his scrubbed table and
setting down the teapot. 'Like I don' know. An' bangin' on about
some Banshee he banished. If one word of it was true, I'll eat my
kettle.'

It was most unlike Hagrid to criticise a Hogwarts teacher and
Harry looked at him in surprise. Hermione, however, said in a
voice somewhat higher than usual, 'I think you're being a bit
unfair. Professor Dumbledore obviously thought he was the best
man for the job –'

'He was the *on'y* man for the job,' said Hagrid, offering them a
plate of treacle fudge, while Ron coughed squelchily into his
basin. 'An' I mean the *on'y* one. Gettin' very difficult ter find anyone fer the Dark Arts job. People aren't too keen ter take it on,
see. They're startin' ter think it's jinxed. No one's lasted long fer a

while now. So tell me,' said Hagrid, jerking his head at Ron, 'who was he tryin' ter curse?'

'Malfoy called Hermione something. It must've been really bad, because everyone went mad.'

'It *was* bad,' said Ron hoarsely, emerging over the table top looking pale and sweaty. 'Malfoy called her "Mudblood", Hagrid —'

Ron dived out of sight again as a fresh wave of slugs made their appearance. Hagrid looked outraged.

'He didn'!' he growled at Hermione.

'He did,' she said. 'But I don't know what it means. I could tell it was really rude, of course ...'

'It's about the most insulting thing he could think of,' gasped Ron, coming back up. 'Mudblood's a really foul name for someone who was Muggle-born — you know, non-magic parents. There are some wizards — like Malfoy's family — who think they're better than everyone else because they're what people call pure-blood.' He gave a small burp, and a single slug fell into his outstretched hand. He threw it into the basin and continued, 'I mean, the rest of us know it doesn't make any difference at all. Look at Neville Longbottom — he's pure-blood and he can hardly stand a cauldron the right way up.'

'An' they haven't invented a spell our Hermione can't do,' said Hagrid proudly, making Hermione go a brilliant shade of magenta.

'It's a disgusting thing to call someone,' said Ron, wiping his sweaty brow with a shaking hand. 'Dirty blood, see. Common blood. It's mad. Most wizards these days are half-blood anyway. If we hadn't married Muggles we'd've died out.'

He retched and ducked out of sight again.

'Well, I don' blame yeh fer tryin' ter curse him, Ron,' said Hagrid loudly over the thuds of more slugs hitting the basin. 'Bu' maybe it was a good thing yer wand backfired. 'Spect Lucius Malfoy would've come marchin' up ter school if yeh'd cursed his son. Least yer not in trouble.'

Harry would have pointed out that trouble didn't come much worse than having slugs pouring out of your mouth, but he couldn't; Hagrid's treacle toffee had cemented his jaws together.

'Harry,' said Hagrid suddenly, as though struck by a sudden thought, 'gotta bone ter pick with yeh. I've heard you've bin givin' out signed photos. How come I haven't got one?'

Furious, Harry wrenched his teeth apart.

'I have *not* been giving out signed photos,' he said hotly. 'If Lockhart's still putting that about –'

But then he saw that Hagrid was laughing.

'I'm on'y jokin',' he said, patting Harry genially on the back and sending him face first into the table. 'I knew yeh hadn't really. I told Lockhart yeh didn' need teh. Yer more famous than him without tryin'.'

'Bet he didn't like that,' said Harry, sitting up and rubbing his chin.

'Don' think he did,' said Hagrid, his eyes twinkling. 'An' then I told him I'd never read one o' his books an' he decided ter go. Treacle toffee, Ron?' he added, as Ron re-appeared.

'No thanks,' said Ron weakly. 'Better not risk it.'

'Come an' see what I've bin growin',' said Hagrid, as Harry and Hermione finished the last of their tea.

In the small vegetable patch behind Hagrid's house were a dozen of the largest pumpkins Harry had ever seen. Each was the size of a large boulder.

'Gettin' on well, aren't they?' said Hagrid happily. 'Fer the Hallowe'en feast ... should be big enough by then.'

'What've you been feeding them?' said Harry.

Hagrid looked over his shoulder to check that they were alone.

'Well, I've bin givin' them – you know – a bit o' help.'

Harry noticed Hagrid's flowery pink umbrella leaning against the back wall of the cabin. Harry had had reason to believe before now that this umbrella was not all it looked; in fact, he had the strong impression that Hagrid's old school wand was concealed inside it. Hagrid wasn't supposed to use magic. He had been expelled from Hogwarts in his third year, but Harry had never found out why – any mention of the matter and Hagrid would clear his throat loudly and become mysteriously deaf until the subject was changed.

'An Engorgement Charm, I suppose?' said Hermione, halfway between disapproval and amusement. 'Well, you've done a good job on them.'

'That's what yer little sister said,' said Hagrid, nodding at Ron. 'Met her jus' yesterday.' Hagrid looked sideways at Harry, his beard twitching. 'Said she was jus' lookin' round the grounds, but I reckon she was hopin' she might run inter someone else at my house.' He winked at Harry. 'If yeh ask me, *she* wouldn' say no ter a signed –'

'Oh, shut up,' said Harry. Ron snorted with laughter and the ground was sprayed with slugs.

'Watch it!' Hagrid roared, pulling Ron away from his precious pumpkins.

It was nearly lunchtime and as Harry had only had one bit of treacle fudge since dawn, he was keen to go back to school to eat. They said goodbye to Hagrid and walked back up to the castle, Ron hiccoughing occasionally, but only bringing up two, very small slugs.

They had barely set foot in the cool Entrance Hall when a voice rang out. 'There you are, Potter, Weasley.' Professor McGonagall was walking towards them, looking stern. 'You will both do your detentions this evening.'

'What are we doing, Professor?' said Ron, nervously suppressing a burp.

'*You* will be polishing the silver in the trophy room with Mr Filch,' said Professor McGonagall. 'And no magic, Weasley – elbow grease.'

Ron gulped. Argus Filch, the caretaker, was loathed by every student in the school.

'And you, Potter, will be helping Professor Lockhart answer his fan mail,' said Professor McGonagall.

'Oh no – can't I go and do the trophy room too?' said Harry desperately.

'Certainly not,' said Professor McGonagall, raising her eyebrows. 'Professor Lockhart requested you particularly. Eight o'clock sharp, both of you.'

Harry and Ron slouched into the Great Hall in states of deepest gloom, Hermione behind them, wearing a *well-you-did-break-school-rules* sort of expression. Harry didn't fancy his shepherd's pie as much as he'd thought. Both he and Ron felt they'd got the worse deal.

'Filch'll have me there all night,' said Ron heavily. 'No magic! There must be about a hundred cups in that room. I'm no good at Muggle cleaning.'

'I'd swap any time,' said Harry hollowly. 'I've had loads of practice with the Dursleys. Answering Lockhart's fan mail ... he'll be a nightmare ...'

Saturday afternoon seemed to melt away, and in what seemed like no time, it was five minutes to eight, and Harry was dragging his feet along the second floor corridor to Lockhart's office. He gritted his teeth and knocked.

The door flew open at once. Lockhart beamed down at him.

'Ah, here's the scallywag!' he said. 'Come in, Harry, come in.'

Shining brightly on the walls by the light of many candles were countless framed photographs of Lockhart. He had even signed a few of them. Another large pile lay on his desk.

'You can address the envelopes!' Lockhart told Harry, as though this was a huge treat. 'This first one's to Gladys Gudgeon, bless her – huge fan of mine.'

The minutes snailed by. Harry let Lockhart's voice wash over him, occasionally saying, 'Mmm' and 'Right' and 'Yeah'. Now and then he caught a phrase like, 'Fame's a fickle friend, Harry,' or 'Celebrity is as celebrity does, remember that.'

The candles burned lower and lower, making the light dance over the many moving faces of Lockhart watching him. Harry moved his aching hand over what felt like the thousandth envelope, writing out Veronica Smethley's address. It must be nearly time to leave, Harry thought miserably, please let it be nearly time ...

And then he heard something – something quite apart from the spitting of the dying candles and Lockhart's prattle about his fans.

It was a voice, a voice to chill the bone-marrow, a voice of breath-taking, ice-cold venom.

'*Come ... come to me ... let me rip you ... let me tear you ... let me kill you ...*'

Harry gave a huge jump and a large lilac blot appeared on Veronica Smethley's street.

'*What?*' he said loudly.

'I know!' said Lockhart. 'Six solid months at the top of the best-seller list! Broke all records!'

'No,' said Harry frantically. 'That voice!'

'Sorry?' said Lockhart, looking puzzled. 'What voice?'

'That – that voice that said – didn't you hear it?'

Lockhart was looking at Harry in high astonishment.

'What *are* you talking about, Harry? Perhaps you're getting a little drowsy? Great Scott – look at the time! We've been here nearly four hours! I'd never have believed it – the time's flown, hasn't it?'

Harry didn't answer. He was straining his ears to hear the voice again, but there was no sound now except for Lockhart telling him he mustn't expect a treat like this every time he got detention. Feeling dazed, Harry left.

It was so late that the Gryffindor common room was almost empty. Harry went straight up to the dormitory. Ron wasn't back yet. Harry pulled on his pyjamas, got into bed and waited. Half an hour later, Ron arrived, nursing his right arm and bringing a strong smell of polish into the darkened room.

'My muscles have all seized up,' he groaned, sinking on his bed. 'Fourteen times he made me buff up that Quidditch cup before he was satisfied. And then I had another slug attack all over a Special Award for Services to the School. Took ages to shift the slime ... How was it with Lockhart?'

Keeping his voice low so as not to wake Neville, Dean and Seamus, Harry told Ron exactly what he had heard.

'And Lockhart said he couldn't hear it?' said Ron. Harry could see him frowning in the moonlight. 'D'you think he was lying? But I don't get it – even someone invisible would've had to open the door.'

'I know,' said Harry, lying back in his four poster and staring at the canopy above him. 'I don't get it either.'

CHAPTER EIGHT

The Deathday Party

October arrived, spreading a damp chill over the grounds and into the castle. Madam Pomfrey, the matron, was kept busy by a sudden spate of colds among the staff and students. Her Pepperup potion worked instantly, though it left the drinker smoking at the ears for several hours afterwards. Ginny Weasley, who had been looking peaky, was bullied into taking some by Percy. The steam pouring from under her vivid hair gave the impression that her whole head was on fire.

Raindrops the size of bullets thundered on the castle windows for days on end; the lake rose, the flowerbeds turned into muddy streams and Hagrid's pumpkins swelled to the size of garden sheds. Oliver Wood's enthusiasm for regular training sessions, however, was not dampened, which was why Harry was to be found, late one stormy Saturday afternoon a few days before Hallowe'en, returning to Gryffindor tower, drenched to the skin and splattered with mud.

Even aside from the rain and wind it hadn't been a happy practice session. Fred and George, who had been spying on the Slytherin team, had seen for themselves the speed of those new Nimbus Two Thousand and Ones. They reported that the Slytherin team were no more than seven greenish blurs, shooting through the air like jump-jets.

As Harry squelched along the deserted corridor he came across somebody who looked just as preoccupied as he was. Nearly Headless Nick, the ghost of Gryffindor Tower, was staring morosely out of a window, muttering under his breath, '... don't fulfil their requirements ... half an inch, if that ...'

'Hello, Nick,' said Harry.

'Hello, hello,' said Nearly Headless Nick, starting and looking round. He wore a dashing, plumed hat on his long curly hair, and a tunic with a ruff, which concealed the fact that his neck was almost completely severed. He was pale as smoke, and Harry could see right through him to the dark sky and torrential rain outside.

'You look troubled, young Potter,' said Nick, folding a transparent letter as he spoke and tucking it inside his doublet.

'So do you,' said Harry.

'Ah,' Nearly Headless Nick waved an elegant hand, 'a matter of no importance ... it's not as though I really wanted to join ... thought I'd apply, but apparently I "don't fulfil requirements".'

In spite of his airy tone, there was a look of great bitterness on his face.

'But you would think, wouldn't you,' he erupted suddenly, pulling the letter back out of his pocket, 'that getting hit forty-five times in the neck with a blunt axe would qualify you to join the Headless Hunt?'

'Oh – yes,' said Harry, who was obviously supposed to agree.

'I mean, nobody wishes more than I do that it had all been quick and clean, and my head had come off properly, I mean, it would have saved me a great deal of pain and ridicule. However ...' Nearly Headless Nick shook his letter open and read furiously,

'*We can only accept huntsmen whose heads have parted company with their bodies. You will appreciate that it would be impossible otherwise for members to participate in hunt activities such as Horseback Head-Juggling and Head Polo. It is with the greatest regret, therefore, that I must inform you that you do not fulfil our requirements. With very best wishes, Sir Patrick Delaney-Podmore.*'

Fuming, Nearly Headless Nick stuffed the letter away.

'Half an inch of skin and sinew holding my neck on, Harry! Most people would think that's good and beheaded, but oh no, it's not enough for Sir Properly Decapitated-Podmore.'

Nearly Headless Nick took several deep breaths and then said, in a far calmer tone, 'So – what's bothering you? Anything I can do?'

'No,' said Harry. 'Not unless you know where we can get seven free Nimbus Two Thousand and Ones for our match against Sly –'

The rest of Harry's sentence was drowned by a high pitched mewing from somewhere near his ankles. He looked down and found himself gazing into a pair of lamp-like yellow eyes. It was Mrs Norris, the skeletal grey cat who was used by the caretaker,

Argus Filch, as a sort of deputy in his endless battle against students.

'You'd better get out of here, Harry,' said Nick quickly. 'Filch isn't in a good mood. He's got flu and some third years accidentally plastered frog brains all over the ceiling in dungeon five; he's been cleaning all morning, and if he sees you dripping mud all over the place ...'

'Right,' said Harry, backing away from the accusing stare of Mrs Norris, but not quickly enough. Drawn to the spot by the mysterious power that seemed to connect him with his foul cat, Argus Filch burst suddenly through a tapestry to Harry's right, wheezing and looking wildly about for the rule-breaker. There was a thick tartan scarf bound around his head, and his nose was unusually purple.

'Filth!' he shouted, his jowls aquiver, his eyes popping alarmingly as he pointed at the muddy puddle that had dripped from Harry's Quidditch robes. 'Mess and muck everywhere! I've had enough of it, I tell you! Follow me, Potter!'

So Harry waved a gloomy goodbye to Nearly Headless Nick, and followed Filch back downstairs, doubling the number of muddy footprints on the floor.

Harry had never been inside Filch's office before; it was a place most students avoided. The room was dingy and windowless, lit by a single oil-lamp dangling from the low ceiling. A faint smell of fried fish lingered about the place. Wooden filing cabinets stood around the walls; from their labels, Harry could see that they contained details of every pupil Filch had ever punished. Fred and George Weasley had an entire drawer to themselves. A highly polished collection of chains and manacles hung on the wall behind Filch's desk. It was common knowledge that he was always begging Dumbledore to let him suspend students by their ankles from the ceiling.

Filch grabbed a quill from a pot on his desk and began shuffling around looking for parchment.

'Dung,' he muttered furiously, 'great sizzling dragon bogies ... frog brains ... rat intestines ... I've had enough of it ... make an *example* ... where's the form ... yes ...'

He retrieved a large roll of parchment from his desk drawer and stretched it out in front of him, dipping his long black quill into the ink pot.

'*Name* ... Harry Potter. *Crime* ...'

'It was only a bit of mud!' said Harry.

'It's only a bit of mud to you, boy, but to me it's an extra hour scrubbing!' shouted Filch, a drip shivering unpleasantly at the end of his bulbous nose. '*Crime* ... befouling the castle ... *suggested sentence* ...'

Dabbing at his streaming nose, Filch squinted unpleasantly at Harry who waited with bated breath for his sentence to fall.

But as Filch lowered his quill, there was a great BANG! on the ceiling of the office which made the oil lamp rattle.

'PEEVES!' Filch roared, flinging down his quill in a transport of rage. 'I'll have you this time, I'll have you!'

And without a backwards glance at Harry, Filch ran flat-footed from the office, Mrs Norris streaking alongside him.

Peeves was the school poltergeist, a grinning, airborne menace who lived to cause havoc and distress. Harry didn't much like Peeves, but couldn't help feeling grateful for his timing. Hopefully, whatever Peeves had done (and it sounded as though he'd wrecked something very big this time) would distract Filch from Harry.

Thinking that he should probably wait for Filch to come back, Harry sank into a moth-eaten chair next to the desk. There was only one thing on it apart from his half-completed form: a large, glossy, purple envelope with silver lettering on the front. With a quick glance at the door to check that Filch wasn't on his way back, Harry picked up the envelope and read:

KWIKSPELL
A Correspondence Course in
Beginners' Magic

Intrigued, Harry flicked the envelope open and pulled out the sheaf of parchment inside. More curly silver writing on the front page said:

Feel out of step in the world of modern magic? Find yourself making excuses not to perform simple spells? Ever been taunted for your woeful wandwork?
There is an answer!

Kwikspell is an all-new, fail-safe, quick-result, easy-learn
course. Hundreds of witches and wizards have benefited
from the Kwikspell method!

Madam Z. Nettles of Topsham writes:

'I had no memory for incantations and my potions were
a family joke! Now, after a Kwikspell course, I am
the centre of attention at parties and friends beg
for the recipe of my Scintillation Solution!'

Warlock D. J. Prod of Didsbury says:

'My wife used to sneer at my feeble charms but one
month into your fabulous Kwikspell course I
succeeded in turning her into a yak! Thank you,
Kwikspell!'

Fascinated, Harry thumbed through the rest of the envelope's
contents. Why on earth did Filch want a Kwikspell course? Did
this mean he wasn't a proper wizard? Harry was just reading
'Lesson One: Holding Your Wand (Some Useful Tips)' when shuffling footsteps outside told him Filch was coming back. Stuffing
the parchment back into the envelope. Harry threw it back onto
the desk just as the door opened.

Filch was looking triumphant.

'That vanishing cabinet was extremely valuable!' he was saying
gleefully to Mrs Norris. 'We'll have Peeves out this time, my sweet.'

His eyes fell on Harry and then darted to the Kwikspell envelope which, Harry realised too late, was lying two feet away from
where it had started.

Filch's pasty face went brick red. Harry braced himself for a
tidal wave of fury. Filch hobbled across to his desk, snatched up
the envelope and threw it into a drawer.

'Have you – did you read –?' he spluttered.

'No,' Harry lied quickly.

Filch's knobbly hands were twisting together.

'If I thought you'd read my private ... not that it's mine ... for a
friend ... be that as it may ... however ...'

Harry was staring at him, alarmed; Filch had never looked
madder. His eyes were popping, a tic was going in one of his
pouchy cheeks and the tartan scarf didn't help.

'Very well ... go ... and don't breathe a word ... not that ... however, if you didn't read ... go now, I have to write up Peeves' report ... go ...'

Amazed at his luck, Harry sped out of the office, up the corridor and back upstairs. To escape from Filch's office without punishment was probably some kind of school record.

'Harry! Harry! Did it work?'

Nearly Headless Nick came gliding out of a classroom. Behind him, Harry could see the wreckage of a large black and gold cabinet which appeared to have been dropped from a great height.

'I persuaded Peeves to crash it right over Filch's office,' said Nick eagerly. 'Thought it might distract him –'

'Was that you?' said Harry gratefully. 'Yeah, it worked, I didn't even get detention. Thanks, Nick!'

They set off up the corridor together. Nearly Headless Nick, Harry noticed, was still holding Sir Patrick's rejection letter.

'I wish there was something I could do for you about the Headless Hunt,' Harry said.

Nearly Headless Nick stopped in his tracks and Harry walked right through him. He wished he hadn't; it was like stepping through an icy shower.

'But there *is* something you could do for me,' said Nick excitedly. 'Harry – would I be asking too much – but no, you wouldn't want –'

'What is it?' said Harry.

'Well, this Hallowe'en will be my five hundredth deathday,' said Nearly Headless Nick, drawing himself up and looking dignified.

'Oh,' said Harry, not sure whether he should look sorry or happy about this. 'Right.'

'I'm holding a party down in one of the roomier dungeons. Friends will be coming from all over the country. It would be such an *honour* if you would attend. Mr Weasley and Miss Granger would be most welcome too, of course – but I daresay you'd rather go to the school feast?' He watched Harry on tenterhooks.

'No,' said Harry quickly, 'I'll come –'

'My dear boy! Harry Potter, at my Deathday Party! And,' he hesitated, looking excited, 'do you think you could *possibly* mention to Sir Patrick how *very* frightening and impressive you find me?'

'Of – of course,' said Harry.

Nearly Headless Nick beamed at him.

*

'A Deathday Party?' said Hermione keenly, when Harry had changed at last and joined her and Ron in the common room. 'I bet there aren't many living people who can say they've been to one of those – it'll be fascinating!'

'Why would anyone want to celebrate the day they died?' said Ron, who was halfway through his Potions homework and grumpy. 'Sounds dead depressing to me ...'

Rain was still lashing the windows, which were now inky black, but inside, all looked bright and cheerful. The firelight glowed over the countless squashy armchairs where people sat reading, talking, doing homework or, in the case of Fred and George Weasley, trying to find out what would happen if you fed a Filibuster Firework to a Salamander. Fred had 'rescued' the brilliant orange, fire-dwelling lizard from a Care of Magical Creatures class and it was now smouldering gently on a table surrounded by a knot of curious people.

Harry was on the point of telling Ron and Hermione about Filch and the Kwikspell course when the Salamander suddenly whizzed into the air, emitting loud sparks and bangs as it whirled wildly round the room. The sight of Percy bellowing himself hoarse at Fred and George, the spectacular display of tangerine stars showering from the Salamander's mouth, and its escape into the fire, with accompanying explosions, drove both Filch and the Kwikspell envelope from Harry's mind.

*

By the time Hallowe'en arrived, Harry was regretting his rash promise to go to the Deathday Party. The rest of the school were happily anticipating their Hallowe'en feast; the Great Hall had been decorated with the usual live bats, Hagrid's vast pumpkins had been carved into lanterns large enough for three men to sit in and there were rumours that Dumbledore had booked a troupe of dancing skeletons for the entertainment.

'A promise is a promise,' Hermione reminded Harry bossily. 'You *said* you'd go to the Deathday party.'

So at seven o'clock, Harry, Ron and Hermione walked straight past the doorway to the packed Great Hall, which was glittering invitingly with gold plates and candles, and directed their steps instead towards the dungeons.

The passageway leading to Nearly Headless Nick's party had been lined with candles too, though the effect was far from cheerful: these were long, thin, jet-black tapers, all burning bright blue, casting a dim, ghostly light even over their own living faces. The temperature dropped with every step they took. As Harry shivered and drew his robes tightly around him, he heard what sounded like a thousand fingernails scraping an enormous blackboard.

'Is that supposed to be *music*?' Ron whispered. They turned a corner and saw Nearly Headless Nick standing at a doorway hung with black velvet drapes.

'My dear friends,' he said mournfully, 'welcome, welcome ... so pleased you could come ...'

He swept off his plumed hat and bowed them inside.

It was an incredible sight. The dungeon was full of hundreds of pearly-white, translucent people, mostly drifting around a crowded dance floor, waltzing to the dreadful, quavering sound of thirty musical saws, played by an orchestra on a black-draped platform. A chandelier overhead blazed midnight blue with a thousand more black candles. Their breath rose in a mist before them; it was like stepping into a freezer.

'Shall we have a look around?' Harry suggested, wanting to warm up his feet.

'Careful not to walk through anyone,' said Ron nervously, and they set off around the edge of the dance floor. They passed a group of gloomy nuns, a ragged man wearing chains, and the Fat Friar, a cheerful Hufflepuff ghost, who was talking to a knight with an arrow sticking out of his forehead. Harry wasn't surprised to see that the Bloody Baron, a gaunt, staring Slytherin ghost covered in silver bloodstains, was being given a wide berth by the other ghosts.

'Oh no,' said Hermione, stopping abruptly. 'Turn back, turn back, I don't want to talk to Moaning Myrtle –'

'Who?' said Harry, as they backtracked quickly.

'She haunts the girls' toilet on the first floor,' said Hermione.

'She haunts a *toilet*?'

'Yes. It's been out of order all year because she keeps having tantrums and flooding the place. I never went in there anyway if I could avoid it, it's awful trying to go to the loo with her wailing at you –'

'Look, food!' said Ron.

On the other side of the dungeon was a long table, also covered in black velvet. They approached it eagerly, but next moment had stopped in their tracks, horrified. The smell was quite disgusting. Large, rotten fish were laid on handsome silver platters; cakes, burned charcoal black, were heaped on salvers; there was a great maggoty haggis, a slab of cheese covered in furry green mould and, in pride of place, an enormous grey cake in the shape of a tombstone, with tar-like icing forming the words,

Sir Nicholas de Mimsy-Porpington
died 31st October, 1492

Harry watched, amazed, as a portly ghost approached the table, crouched low and walked through it, his mouth held wide so that it passed through one of the stinking salmon.

'Can you taste it if you walk though it?' Harry asked him.

'Almost,' said the ghost sadly, and he drifted away.

'I expect they've let it rot to give it a stronger flavour,' said Hermione knowledgably, pinching her nose and leaning closer to look at the putrid haggis.

'Can we move, I feel sick,' said Ron.

They had barely turned around, however, when a little man swooped suddenly from under the table and came to a halt in mid-air before them.

'Hello, Peeves,' said Harry cautiously.

Unlike the ghosts around them, Peeves the poltergeist was the very reverse of pale and transparent. He was wearing a bright orange party hat, a revolving bow tie and a broad grin on his wide, wicked face.

'Nibbles?' he said sweetly, offering them a bowl of peanuts covered in fungus.

'No thanks,' said Hermione.

'Heard you talking about poor Myrtle,' said Peeves, his eyes dancing. '*Rude* you was about poor Myrtle.' He took a deep breath and bellowed, 'OY! MYRTLE!'

'Oh, no, Peeves, don't tell her what I said, she'll be really upset,' Hermione whispered frantically. 'I didn't mean it, I don't mind her – er, hello, Myrtle.'

The squat ghost of a girl had glided over. She had the glummest face Harry had ever seen, half-hidden behind lank hair and thick, pearly spectacles.

'What?' she said sulkily.

'How are you, Myrtle?' said Hermione, in a falsely bright voice. 'It's nice to see you out of the toilet.'

Myrtle sniffed.

'Miss Granger was just talking about you –' said Peeves slyly in Myrtle's ear.

'Just saying – saying – how nice you look tonight,' said Hermione, glaring at Peeves.

Myrtle eyed Hermione suspiciously.

'You're making fun of me,' she said, silver tears welling rapidly in her small, see-through eyes.

'No – honestly – didn't I just say how nice Myrtle's looking?' said Hermione, nudging Harry and Ron painfully in the ribs.

'Oh, yeah ...'

'She did ...'

'Don't lie to me,' Myrtle gasped, tears now flooding down her face, while Peeves chuckled happily over her shoulder. 'D'you think I don't know what people call me behind my back? Fat Myrtle! Ugly Myrtle! Miserable, moaning, moping Myrtle!'

'You've missed out "spotty",' Peeves hissed in her ear.

Moaning Myrtle burst into anguished sobs and fled from the dungeon. Peeves shot after her, pelting her with mouldy peanuts, yelling, 'Spotty! Spotty!'

'Oh, dear,' said Hermione sadly.

Nearly Headless Nick now drifted towards them through the crowd.

'Enjoying yourselves?'

'Oh, yes,' they lied.

'Not a bad turnout,' said Nearly Headless Nick proudly. 'The Wailing Widow came all the way up from Kent ... It's nearly time for my speech, I'd better go and warn the orchestra ...'

The orchestra, however, stopped playing at that very moment. They, and everyone else in the dungeon, fell silent, looking around in excitement, as a hunting horn sounded.

'Oh, here we go,' said Nearly Headless Nick bitterly.

Through the dungeon wall burst a dozen ghost horses, each ridden by a headless horseman. The assembly clapped wildly; Harry started to clap too, but stopped quickly at the sight of Nick's face.

The horses galloped into the middle of the dance floor and halted, rearing and plunging; a large ghost at the front, whose bearded head was under his arm, blowing the horn, leapt down, lifted his head high in the air so he could see over the crowd (everyone laughed) and strode over to Nearly Headless Nick, squashing his head back onto his neck.

'Nick!' he roared. 'How are you? Head still hanging in there?'

He gave a hearty guffaw and clapped Nearly Headless Nick on the shoulder.

'Welcome, Patrick,' said Nick stiffly.

'Live 'uns!' said Sir Patrick, spotting Harry, Ron and Hermione and giving a huge, fake jump of astonishment, so that his head fell off again (the crowd howled with laughter).

'Very amusing,' said Nearly Headless Nick darkly.

'Don't mind Nick!' shouted Sir Patrick's head from the floor. 'Still upset we won't let him join the Hunt! But I mean to say – look at the fellow –'

'I think,' said Harry hurriedly, at a meaningful look from Nick, 'Nick's very – frightening and – er –'

'Ha!' yelled Sir Patrick's head. 'Bet he asked you to say that!'

'If I could have everyone's attention, it's time for my speech!' said Nearly Headless Nick loudly, striding towards the podium and climbing into an icy blue spotlight.

'My late lamented lords, ladies and gentlemen, it is my great sorrow ...'

But nobody heard much more. Sir Patrick and the rest of the Headless Hunt had just started a game of Head Hockey and the crowd were turning to watch. Nearly Headless Nick tried vainly to recapture his audience, but gave up as Sir Patrick's head went sailing past him to loud cheers.

Harry was very cold by now, not to mention hungry.

'I can't stand much more of this,' Ron muttered, his teeth chattering, as the orchestra ground back into action and the ghosts swept back onto the dance floor.

'Let's go,' Harry agreed.

They backed towards the door, nodding and beaming at anyone who looked at them, and a minute later were hurrying back up the passageway full of black candles.

'Pudding might not be finished yet,' said Ron hopefully, leading the way towards the steps to the Entrance Hall.

And then Harry heard it.

'... *rip ... tear ... kill ...*'

It was the same voice, the same cold, murderous voice he had heard in Lockhart's office.

He stumbled to a halt, clutching at the stone wall, listening with all his might, looking around, squinting up and down the dimly lit passageway.

'Harry, what're you –?'

'It's that voice again – shut up a minute –'

'... *soo hungry ... for so long ...*'

'Listen!' said Harry urgently, and Ron and Hermione froze, watching him.

'... *kill ... time to kill ...*'

The voice was growing fainter. Harry was sure it was moving away – moving upwards. A mixture of fear and excitement gripped him as he stared at the dark ceiling; how could it be moving upwards? Was it a phantom, to whom stone ceilings didn't matter?

'This way,' he shouted, and he began to run, up the stairs, into the Entrance Hall. It was no good hoping to hear anything here, the babble of talk from the Hallowe'en Feast was echoing out of the Great Hall. Harry sprinted up the marble staircase to the first floor, Ron and Hermione clattering behind him.

'Harry, what are we –'

'SHH!'

Harry strained his ears. Distantly, from the floor above, and growing fainter still, he heard the voice: '... *I smell blood ... I SMELL BLOOD!*'

His stomach lurched. 'It's going to kill someone!' he shouted, and ignoring Ron and Hermione's bewildered faces, he ran up the next flight of steps three at a time, trying to listen over his own pounding footsteps.

Harry hurtled around the whole of the second floor, Ron and Hermione panting behind him, not stopping until they turned a corner into the last, deserted passage.

'Harry, *what* was that all about?' said Ron, wiping sweat off his face. 'I couldn't hear anything ...'

But Hermione gave a sudden gasp, pointing down the corridor.

'*Look!*'

Something was shining on the wall ahead. They approached, slowly, squinting through the darkness. Foot high words had been daubed on the wall between two windows, shimmering in the light cast by the flaming torches.

THE CHAMBER OF SECRETS HAS BEEN OPENED.
ENEMIES OF THE HEIR, BEWARE.

'What's that thing – hanging underneath?' said Ron, a slight quiver in his voice.

As they edged nearer, Harry almost slipped over: there was a large puddle of water on the floor. Ron and Hermione grabbed him, and they inched towards the message, eyes fixed on a dark shadow beneath it. All three of them realised what it was at once, and leapt backwards with a splash.

Mrs Norris, the caretaker's cat, was hanging by her tail from the torch bracket. She was stiff as a board, her eyes wide and staring.

For a few seconds, they didn't move. Then Ron said, 'Let's get out of here.'

'Shouldn't we try and help –' Harry began awkwardly.

'Trust me,' said Ron. 'We don't want to be found here.'

But it was too late. A rumble, as though of distant thunder, told them that the Feast had just ended. From either end of the corridor where they stood came the sound of hundreds of feet climbing the stairs, and the loud, happy talk of well-fed people; next moment, students were crashing into the passage from both ends.

The chatter, the bustle, the noise died suddenly as the people in front spotted the hanging cat. Harry, Ron and Hermione stood alone, in the middle of the corridor, as silence fell among the mass of students, pressing forward to see the grisly sight.

Then someone shouted through the quiet.

'Enemies of the Heir, beware! You'll be next, Mudbloods!'

It was Draco Malfoy. He had pushed to the front of the crowd, his cold eyes alive, his usually bloodless face flushed, as he grinned at the sight of the hanging, immobile cat.

— CHAPTER NINE —

The Writing on the Wall

'What's going on here? What's going on?'

Attracted no doubt by Malfoy's shout, Argus Filch came shouldering his way through the crowd. Then he saw Mrs Norris and fell back, clutching his face in horror.

'My cat! My cat! What's happened to Mrs Norris?' he shrieked.

And his popping eyes fell on Harry.

'*You!*' he screeched, '*You!* You've murdered my cat! You've killed her! I'll kill you! I'll –'

'*Argus!*'

Dumbledore had arrived on the scene, followed by a number of other teachers. In seconds, he had swept past Harry, Ron and Hermione and detached Mrs Norris from the torch bracket.

'Come with me, Argus,' he said to Filch. 'You too, Mr Potter, Mr Weasley, Miss Granger.'

Lockhart stepped forward eagerly.

'My office is nearest, Headmaster – just upstairs – please feel free –'

'Thank you, Gilderoy,' said Dumbledore.

The silent crowd parted to let them pass. Lockhart, looking excited and important, hurried after Dumbledore; so did Professors McGonagall and Snape.

As they entered Lockhart's darkened office there was a flurry of movement across the walls; Harry saw several of the Lockharts in the pictures dodging out of sight, their hair in rollers. The real Lockhart lit the candles on his desk and stood back. Dumbledore lay Mrs Norris on the polished surface and began to examine her. Harry, Ron and Hermione exchanged tense looks and sank into chairs outside the pool of candlelight, watching.

The tip of Dumbledore's long, crooked nose was barely an inch from Mrs Norris's fur. He was looking at her closely through his

half-moon spectacles, his long fingers gently prodding and poking. Professor McGonagall was bent almost as close, her eyes nar-
rowed. Snape loomed behind them, half in shadow, wearing a
most peculiar expression: it was as though he was trying hard not
to smile. And Lockhart was hovering around all of them, making
suggestions.

'It was definitely a curse that killed her – probably the
Transmogrifian Torture. I've seen it used many times, so unlucky I
wasn't there, I know the very counter-curse that would have saved
her ...'

Lockhart's comments were punctuated by Filch's dry, racking
sobs. He was slumped in a chair by the desk, unable to look at
Mrs Norris, his face in his hands. Much as he detested Filch,
Harry couldn't help feeling a bit sorry for him, though not nearly
as sorry as he felt for himself. If Dumbledore believed Filch, he
would be expelled for sure.

Dumbledore was now muttering strange words under his
breath and tapping Mrs Norris with his wand, but nothing happened: she continued to look as though she had been recently
stuffed.

'... I remember something very similar happening in
Ouagadogou,' said Lockhart, 'a series of attacks, the full story's in
my autobiography. I was able to provide the townsfolk with various amulets which cleared the matter up at once ...'

The photographs of Lockhart on the walls were all nodding in
agreement as he talked. One of them had forgotten to remove his
hairnet.

At last Dumbledore straightened up.

'She's not dead, Argus,' he said softly.

Lockhart stopped abruptly in the middle of counting the number of murders he had prevented.

'Not dead?' choked Filch, looking through his fingers at Mrs
Norris. 'But why's she all – all stiff and frozen?'

'She has been Petrified,' said Dumbledore ('Ah! I thought so!'
said Lockhart). 'But how, I cannot say ...'

'Ask *him*!' shrieked Filch, turning his blotched and tear-stained
face to Harry.

'No second year could have done this,' said Dumbledore firmly.
'It would take Dark Magic of the most advanced –'

'He did it, he did it!' Filch spat, his pouchy face purpling. 'You saw what he wrote on the wall! He found – in my office – he knows I'm a – I'm a –' Filch's face worked horribly. 'He knows I'm a Squib!' he finished.

'I never *touched* Mrs Norris!' Harry said loudly, uncomfortably aware of everyone looking at him, including all the Lockharts on the walls. 'And I don't even know what a Squib *is*.'

'Rubbish!' snarled Filch. 'He saw my Kwikspell letter!'

'If I might speak, Headmaster,' said Snape from the shadows, and Harry's sense of forboding increased; he was sure nothing Snape had to say was going to do him any good.

'Potter and his friends may have simply been in the wrong place at the wrong time,' he said, a slight sneer curling his mouth as though he doubted it, 'but we do have a set of suspicious circumstances here. Why were they in the upstairs corridor at all? Why weren't they at the Hallowe'en feast?'

Harry, Ron and Hermione all launched into an explanation about the Deathday party, '... there were hundreds of ghosts, they'll tell you we were there –'

'But why not join the feast afterwards?' said Snape, his black eyes glittering in the candlelight. 'Why go up to that corridor?'

Ron and Hermione looked at Harry.

'Because – because –' Harry said, his heart thumping very fast; something told him it would sound very far-fetched if he told them he had been led there by a bodiless voice no one but he could hear, 'because we were tired and wanted to go to bed,' he said.

'Without any supper?' said Snape, a triumphant smile flickering across his gaunt face. 'I didn't think ghosts provided food fit for living people at their parties.'

'We weren't hungry,' said Ron loudly, as his stomach gave a huge rumble.

Snape's nasty smile widened.

'I suggest, Headmaster, that Potter is not being entirely truthful,' he said. 'It might be a good idea if he were deprived of certain privileges until he is ready to tell us the whole story. I personally feel he should be taken off the Gryffindor Quidditch team until he is ready to be honest.'

'Really, Severus,' said Professor McGonagall sharply, 'I see no reason to stop the boy playing Quidditch. This cat wasn't hit over the head with a broomstick. There is no evidence at all that Potter has done anything wrong.'

Dumbledore was giving Harry a searching look. His twinkling light blue gaze made Harry feel as though he was being X-rayed.

'Innocent until proven guilty, Severus,' he said firmly.

Snape looked furious. So did Filch.

'My cat has been Petrified!' he shrieked, his eyes popping. 'I want to see some *punishment*!'

'We will be able to cure her, Argus,' said Dumbledore patiently. 'Madam Sprout recently managed to procure some Mandrakes. As soon as they have reached their full size, I will have a potion made which will revive Mrs Norris.'

'I'll make it,' Lockhart butted in. 'I must have done it a hundred times, I could whip up a Mandrake Restorative Draught in my sleep –'

'Excuse me,' said Snape icily, 'but I believe I am the Potions master at this school.'

There was a very awkward pause.

'You may go,' Dumbledore said to Harry, Ron and Hermione.

They went, as quickly as they could without actually running. When they were a floor up from Lockhart's office, they turned into an empty classroom and closed the door quietly behind them. Harry squinted at his friends' darkened faces.

'D'you think I should have told them about that voice I heard?'

'No,' said Ron, without hesitation. 'Hearing voices no one else can hear isn't a good sign, even in the wizarding world.'

Something in Ron's voice made Harry ask, 'You do believe me, don't you?'

'Course I do,' said Ron quickly. 'But – you must admit it's weird ...'

'I know it's weird,' said Harry. 'The whole thing's weird. What was that writing on the wall about? *The Chamber has been Opened* ... what's that supposed to mean?'

'You know, it rings a sort of bell,' said Ron slowly. 'I think some-one told me a story about a secret chamber at Hogwarts once ... might've been Bill ...'

'And what on earth's a Squib?' said Harry.

To his surprise, Ron stifled a snigger.

'Well – it's not funny really – but as it's Filch ...' he said. 'A Squib is someone who was born into a wizarding family but hasn't got any magic powers. Kind of the opposite of Muggle-born wizards, but Squibs are quite unusual. If Filch's trying to learn magic from a Kwikspell course, I reckon he must be a Squib. It would explain a lot. Like why he hates students so much.' Ron gave a satisfied smile. 'He's bitter.'

A clock chimed somewhere.

'Midnight,' said Harry. 'We'd better get to bed before Snape comes along and tries to frame us for something else.'

*

For a few days, the school could talk of little but the attack on Mrs Norris. Filch kept it fresh in everyone's minds by pacing the spot where she had been attacked, as though he thought the attacker might come back. Harry had seen him scrubbing the message on the wall with 'Mrs Skower's All-Purpose Magical Mess Remover', but to no effect; the words still gleamed as brightly as ever on the stone. When Filch wasn't guarding the scene of the crime, he was skulking red-eyed through the corridors, lunging out at unsuspecting students and trying to put them in detention for things like 'breathing loudly' and 'looking happy'.

Ginny Weasley seemed very disturbed by Mrs Norris' fate. According to Ron, she was a great cat-lover.

'But you hadn't really got to know Mrs Norris,' Ron told her bracingly. 'Honestly, we're much better off without her.' Ginny's lip trembled. 'Stuff like this doesn't often happen at Hogwarts,' Ron assured her. 'They'll catch the nutter who did it and have him out of here in no time. I just hope he's got time to Petrify Filch before he's expelled. I'm only joking –' Ron added hastily, as Ginny blanched.

The attack had also had an effect on Hermione. It was quite usual for Hermione to spend a lot of time reading, but she was now doing almost nothing else. Nor could Harry and Ron get much response from her when they asked what she was up to, and not until the following Wednesday did they find out.

Harry had been held back in Potions, where Snape had made him stay behind to scrape tubeworms off the desks. After a hurried lunch, he went upstairs to meet Ron in the library, and saw Justin Finch-Fletchley, the Hufflepuff boy from Herbology, coming towards him. Harry had just opened his mouth to say hello when Justin caught sight of him, turned abruptly and sped off in the opposite direction.

Harry found Ron at the back of the library, measuring his

History of Magic homework. Professor Binns had asked for a three foot long composition on 'The Medieval Assembly of European Wizards'.

'I don't believe it, I'm still eight inches short ...' said Ron furiously, letting go of his parchment which sprang back into a roll, 'and Hermione's done four feet seven inches and her writing's *tiny*.'

'Where is she?' asked Harry, grabbing the tape measure and unrolling his own homework.

'Somewhere over there,' said Ron, pointing along the shelves, 'looking for another book. I think she's trying to read the whole library before Christmas.'

Harry told Ron about Justin Finch-Fletchley running away from him.

'Dunno why you care, I thought he was a bit of an idiot,' said Ron, scribbling away, making his writing as large as possible. 'All that rubbish about Lockhart being so great –'

Hermione emerged from between the bookshelves. She looked irritable and at last seemed ready to talk to them.

'*All* the copies of *Hogwarts: A History* have been taken out,' she said, sitting down next to Harry and Ron. 'And there's a two week waiting list. I *wish* I hadn't left my copy at home, but I couldn't fit it in my trunk with all the Lockhart books.'

'Why do you want it?' said Harry.

'The same reason everyone else wants it,' said Hermione, 'to read up on the legend of the Chamber of Secrets.'

'What's that?' said Harry quickly.

'That's just it. I can't remember,' said Hermione, biting her lip. 'And I can't find the story anywhere else –'

'Hermione, let me read your composition,' said Ron desperately, checking his watch.

'No, I won't,' said Hermione, suddenly severe. 'You've had ten days to finish it.'

'I only need another two inches, go on ...'

The bell rang. Ron and Hermione led the way to History of Magic, bickering.

History of Magic was the dullest subject on their timetable. Professor Binns, who taught it, was their only ghost teacher, and the most exciting thing that ever happened in his classes was his entering the room through the blackboard. Ancient and shrivelled, many people said he hadn't noticed he was dead. He had simply got up to teach one day and left his body behind him in an armchair in front of the staff room fire; his routine had not varied in the slightest since.

Today was as boring as ever. Professor Binns opened his notes and began to read in a flat drone like an old vacuum cleaner until nearly everyone in the class was in a deep stupor, occasionally coming round long enough to copy down a name or date, then falling asleep again. He had been speaking for half an hour when something happened that had never happened before. Hermione put up her hand.

Professor Binns, glancing up in the middle of a deadly dull lecture on the International Warlock Convention of 1289, looked amazed.

'Miss – er –?'

'Granger, Professor. I was wondering if you could tell us anything about the Chamber of Secrets,' said Hermione in a clear voice.

Dean Thomas, who had been sitting with his mouth hanging open, gazing out of the window, jerked out of his trance; Lavender Brown's head came up off her arms and Neville's elbow slipped off his desk.

Professor Binns blinked.

'My subject is History of Magic,' he said in his dry, wheezy voice. 'I deal with *facts,* Miss Granger, not myths and legends.' He cleared his throat with a small noise like chalk snapping and continued, 'In September of that year, a sub-committee of Sardinian sorcerers –'

He stuttered to a halt. Hermione's hand was waving in the air again.

'Miss Grant?'

'Please, sir, don't legends always have a basis in fact?'

Professor Binns was looking at her in such amazement, Harry was sure no student had ever interrupted him before, alive or dead.

'Well,' said Professor Binns slowly, 'yes, one could argue that, I suppose.' He peered at Hermione as though he had never seen a student properly before. 'However, the legend of which you speak is such a very *sensational,* even *ludicrous* tale ...'

But the whole class was now hanging on Professor Binns' every word. He looked dimly at them all, every face turned to his. Harry could tell he was completely thrown by such an unusual show of interest.

'Oh, very well,' he said slowly. 'Let me see ... the Chamber of Secrets ...

'You all know, of course, that Hogwarts was founded over a thousand years ago – the precise date is uncertain – by the four greatest witches and wizards of the age. The four school houses are named after them: Godric Gryffindor, Helga Hufflepuff, Rowena Ravenclaw and Salazar Slytherin. They built this castle together, far from prying Muggle eyes, for it was an age when magic was feared by common people and witches and wizards suffered much persecution.'

He paused, gazed blearily around the room, and continued, 'For a few years, the founders worked in harmony together, seeking out youngsters who showed signs of magic and bringing them to the castle to be educated. But then disagreements sprang up between them. A rift began to grow between Slytherin and the others. Slytherin wished to be more *selective* about the students admitted to Hogwarts. He believed that magical learning should be kept within all-magic families. He disliked taking students of Muggle parentage, believing them to be untrustworthy. After a while, there was a serious argument on the subject between Slytherin and Gryffindor, and Slytherin left the school.'

Professor Binns paused again, pursing his lips, looking like a wrinkled old tortoise.

'Reliable historical sources tell us this much,' he said, 'but these honest facts have been obscured by the fanciful legend of the Chamber of Secrets. The story goes that Slytherin had built a hidden chamber in the castle, of which the other founders knew nothing.

'Slytherin, according to the legend, sealed the Chamber of Secrets so that none would be able to open it until his own true heir arrived at the school. The heir alone would be able to unseal the Chamber of Secrets, unleash the horror within, and use it to purge the school of all who were unworthy to study magic.'

There was silence as he finished telling the story, but it wasn't the usual, sleepy silence that filled Professor Binns' classes. There was unease in the air as everyone continued to watch him, hoping for more. Professor Binns looked faintly annoyed.

'The whole thing is arrant nonsense, of course,' he said. 'Naturally, the school has been searched for evidence of such a chamber, many times, by the most learned witches and wizards. It does not exist. A tale told to frighten the gullible.'

Hermione's hand was back in the air.

'Sir – what exactly do you mean by the 'horror within' the Chamber?'

'That is believed to be some sort of monster, which the heir of Slytherin alone can control,' said Professor Binns in his dry, reedy voice.

The class exchanged nervous looks.

'I tell you, the thing does not exist,' said Professor Binns, shuffling his notes. 'There is no Chamber and no monster.'

'But, sir,' said Seamus Finnigan, 'if the Chamber can only be opened by Slytherin's true heir, no one else *would* be able to find it, would they?'

'Nonsense, O'Flaherty,' said Professor Binns in an aggravated tone. 'If a long succession of Hogwarts headmasters and headmistresses haven't found the thing –'

'But, Professor,' piped up Parvati Patil, 'you'd probably have to use Dark Magic to open it –'

'Just because a wizard *doesn't* use Dark Magic, doesn't mean he *can't*, Miss Patil,' snapped Professor Binns. 'I repeat, if the likes of Dumbledore –'

'But maybe you've got to be related to Slytherin, so Dumbledore couldn't –' began Dean Thomas, but Professor Binns had had enough.

'That will do,' he said sharply. 'It is a myth! It does not exist! There is not a shred of evidence that Slytherin ever built so much as a secret broom cupboard! I regret telling you such a foolish story! We will return, if you please, to *history,* to solid, believable, verifiable *fact!*'

And within five minutes, the class had sunk back into its usual torpor.

*

'I always knew Salazar Slytherin was a twisted old loony,' Ron told Harry and Hermione, as they fought their way through the teeming corridors at the end of the lesson to drop off their bags before dinner. 'But I never knew he started all this pure-blood stuff. I wouldn't be in his house if you paid me. Honestly, if the Sorting Hat had tried to put me in Slytherin, I'd've got the train straight back home ...'

Hermione nodded fervently, but Harry didn't say anything. His stomach had just dropped unpleasantly.

Harry had never told Ron and Hermione that the Sorting Hat had seriously considered putting *him* in Slytherin. He could remember, as though it was yesterday, the small voice that had spoken in his ear when he'd placed the hat on his head a year before.

'*You could be great, you know, it's all here in your head, and Slytherin would help you on the way to greatness, no doubt about that ...*'

But Harry, who had already heard of Slytherin house's reputation for turning out dark wizards, had thought desperately, 'Not Slytherin!' and the hat had said, '*Oh, well, if you're sure ... better be Gryffindor ...*'

As they were shunted along in the throng, Colin Creevy went past.

'Hiya, Harry!'

'Hullo, Colin,' said Harry automatically.

'Harry – Harry – a boy in my class has been saying you're –'

But Colin was so small he couldn't fight against the tide of people bearing him towards the Great Hall; they heard him squeak, 'See you, Harry!' and he was gone.

'What's a boy in his class saying about you?' Hermione wondered.

'That I'm Slytherin's heir, I expect,' said Harry, his stomach dropping another inch or so, as he suddenly remembered the way Justin Finch-Fletchley had run away from him at lunchtime.

'People here'll believe anything,' said Ron in disgust.

The crowd thinned and they were able to climb the next staircase without difficulty.

'D'you *really* think there's a Chamber of Secrets?' Ron asked Hermione.

'I don't know,' she said, frowning. 'Dumbledore couldn't cure Mrs Norris, and that makes me think that whatever attacked her might not be – well – human.'

As she spoke, they turned a corner and found themselves at the end of the very corridor where the attack had happened. They stopped and looked. The scene was just as it had been that night, except that there was no stiff cat hanging from the torch bracket, and an empty chair stood against the wall bearing the message

'The Chamber has been Opened.'

'That's where Filch has been keeping guard,' Ron muttered.

They looked at each other. The corridor was deserted.

'Can't hurt to have a poke around,' said Harry, dropping his bag and getting to his hands and knees so that he could crawl along, searching for clues.

'Scorch marks!' he said. 'Here – and here –'

'Come and look at this!' said Hermione. 'This is funny ...'

Harry got up and crossed to the window next to the message on the wall. Hermione was pointing at the topmost pane, where around twenty spiders were scuttling, apparently fighting to get through a small crack in the glass. A long, silvery thread was dangling like a rope, as though they had all climbed it in their hurry to get outside.

'Have you ever seen spiders act like that?' said Hermione wonderingly.

'No,' said Harry, 'have you, Ron? Ron?'

He looked over his shoulder. Ron was standing well back, and seemed to be fighting the impulse to run.

'What's up?' said Harry.

'I – don't – like – spiders,' said Ron tensely.

'I never knew that,' said Hermione, looking at Ron in surprise. 'You've used spiders in potions loads of times ...'

'I don't mind them dead,' said Ron, who was carefully looking anywhere but at the window, 'I just don't like the way they move ...'

Hermione giggled.

'It's not funny,' said Ron, fiercely. 'If you must know, when I was three, Fred turned my – my teddy bear into a dirty great spider because I broke his toy broomstick. You wouldn't like them either if you'd been holding your bear and suddenly it had too many legs and ...'

He broke off, shuddering. Hermione was obviously still trying not to laugh. Feeling they had better get off the subject, Harry said, 'Remember all that water on the floor? Where did that come from? Someone's mopped it up.'

'It was about here,' said Ron, recovering himself to walk a few paces past Filch's chair and pointing. 'Level with this door.'

He reached for the brass doorknob but suddenly withdrew his hand as though he'd been burned.

'What's the matter?' said Harry.

'Can't go in there,' said Ron gruffly, 'that's a girls' toilet.'

'Oh, Ron, there won't be anyone in there,' said Hermione, standing up and coming over. 'That's Moaning Myrtle's place. Come on, let's have a look.'

And ignoring the large 'Out of Order' sign, she opened the door.

It was the gloomiest, most depressing bathroom Harry had ever set foot in. Under a large, cracked and spotted mirror were a row of chipped, stone sinks. The floor was damp and reflected the dull light given off by the stubs of a few candles, burning low in their holders; the wooden doors to the cubicles were flaking and scratched and one of them was dangling off its hinges.

Hermione put her fingers to her lips and set off towards the end cubicle. When she reached it she said, 'Hello, Myrtle, how are you?'

Harry and Ron went to look. Moaning Myrtle was floating on the cistern of the toilet, picking a spot on her chin.

'This is a *girls'* bathroom,' she said, eyeing Ron and Harry suspiciously. '*They're* not girls.'

'No,' Hermione agreed. 'I just wanted to show them how – er – nice it is in here.'

She waved vaguely at the dirty old mirror and the damp floor.

'Ask her if she saw anything,' Harry mouthed at Hermione.

'What are you whispering?' said Myrtle, staring at him.

'Nothing,' said Harry quickly. 'We wanted to ask –'

'I wish people would stop talking behind my back!' said Myrtle, in a voice choked with tears. 'I *do* have feelings, you know, even if I *am* dead.'

'Myrtle, no one wants to upset you,' said Hermione. 'Harry only –'

'No one wants to upset me! That's a good one!' howled Myrtle. 'My life was nothing but misery at this place and now people come along ruining my death!'

'We wanted to ask you if you'd seen anything funny lately,' said Hermione quickly, 'because a cat was attacked right outside your front door on Hallowe'en.'

'Did you see anyone near here that night?' said Harry.

'I wasn't paying attention,' said Myrtle dramatically. 'Peeves upset me so much I came in here and tried to *kill* myself. Then, of course, I remembered that I'm – that I'm –'

'Already dead,' said Ron helpfully.

Myrtle gave a tragic sob, rose up in the air, turned over and dived head first into the toilet, splashing water all over them and vanishing from sight; from the direction of her muffled sobs, she had come to rest somewhere in the U-bend.

Harry and Ron stood with their mouths open, but Hermione shrugged wearily and said, 'Honestly, that was almost cheerful for Myrtle ... come on, let's go.'

Harry had barely closed the door on Myrtle's gurgling sobs when a loud voice made all three of them jump.

'RON!'

Percy Weasley had stopped dead at the head of the stairs, prefect badge agleam, an expression of complete shock on his face.

'That's a *girls'* bathroom!' he gasped. 'What were *you* –?'

'Just having a look around,' Ron shrugged. 'Clues, you know ...'

Percy swelled in a manner that reminded Harry forcefully of Mrs Weasley.

'Get – away – from – there –' he said, striding towards them and starting to chivvy them along, flapping his arms. 'Don't you *care* what this looks like? Coming back here while everyone's at dinner ...'

'Why shouldn't we be here?' said Ron hotly, stopping short and glaring at Percy. 'Listen, we never laid a finger on that cat!'

'That's what I told Ginny,' said Percy fiercely, 'but she still seems to think you're going to be expelled; I've never seen her so upset, crying her eyes out. You might think of *her*, all the first years are thoroughly over-excited by this business –'

'*You* don't care about Ginny,' said Ron, whose ears were reddening now. '*You're* just worried I'm going to mess up your chances of being Head Boy.'

'Five points from Gryffindor!' Percy said tersely, fingering his prefect badge. 'And I hope it teaches you a lesson! No more *detective work*, or I'll write to Mum!'

And he strode off, the back of his neck as red as Ron's ears.

*

Harry, Ron and Hermione chose seats as far as possible from Percy in the common room that night. Ron was still in a very bad temper and kept blotting his Charms homework. When he reached absently for his wand to remove the smudges, it ignited the parchment. Fuming almost as much as his homework, Ron slammed *The Standard Book of Spells, Grade 2* shut. To Harry's surprise,

Hermione followed suit.

'Who can it be, though?' she said in a quiet voice, as though continuing a conversation they had just been having. 'Who'd *want* all the Squibs and Muggle-borns out of Hogwarts?'

'Let's think,' said Ron in mock puzzlement. 'Who do we know who thinks Muggle-borns are scum?'

He looked at Hermione. Hermione looked back, unconvinced.

'If you're talking about Malfoy –'

'Of course I am!' said Ron. 'You heard him: *"You'll be next, Mudbloods!"* Come on, you've only got to look as his foul rat face to know it's him –'

'Malfoy, the Heir of Slytherin?' said Hermione sceptically.

'Look at his family,' said Harry, closing his books, too. 'The whole lot of them have been in Slytherin, he's always boasting about it. They could easily be Slytherin's descendants. His father's definitely evil enough.'

'They could've had the key to the Chamber of Secrets for centuries!' said Ron. 'Handing it down, father to son ...'

'Well,' said Hermione cautiously, 'I suppose it's possible ...'

'But how do we prove it?' said Harry darkly.

'There might be a way,' said Hermione slowly, dropping her voice still further with a quick glance across the room at Percy. 'Of course, it would be difficult. And dangerous, very dangerous. We'd be breaking about fifty school rules, I expect.'

'If, in a month or so, you feel like explaining, you will let us know, won't you?' said Ron irritably.

'All right,' said Hermione coldly. 'What we'd need to do is to get inside the Slytherin common room and ask Malfoy a few questions without him realising it's us.'

'But that's impossible,' Harry said, as Ron laughed.

'No, it's not,' said Hermione. 'All we'd need would be some Polyjuice Potion.'

'What's that?' said Ron and Harry together.

'Snape mentioned it in class a few weeks ago –'

'D'you think we've got nothing better to do in Potions than listen to Snape?' muttered Ron.

'It transforms you into somebody else. Think about it! We could change into three of the Slytherins. No one would know it was us. Malfoy would probably tell us anything. He's probably boasting about it in the Slytherin common room right now, if only we could hear him.'

'This Polyjuice stuff sounds a bit dodgy to me,' said Ron, frowning. 'What if we were stuck looking like three of the Slytherins forever?'

'It wears off after a while,' said Hermione, waving her hand impatiently, 'but getting hold of the recipe will be very difficult. Snape said it was in a book called *Moste Potente Potions* and it's bound to be in the Restricted Section of the library.'

There was only one way to get out a book from the Restricted Section: you needed a signed note of permission from a teacher.

'Hard to see why we'd want the book, really,' said Ron, 'if we weren't going to try and make one of the potions.'

'I think,' said Hermione, 'that if we made it sound as though we were just interested in the theory, we might stand a chance ...'

'Oh, come on, no teacher's going to fall for that,' said Ron. 'They'd have to be really thick ...'

CHAPTER TEN

The Rogue Bludger

Since the disastrous episode of the pixies, Professor Lockhart had not brought live creatures to class. Instead, he read passages from his books to them, and sometimes re-enacted some of the more dramatic bits. He usually picked Harry to help him with these reconstructions; so far, Harry had been forced to play a simple Transylvanian villager whom Lockhart had cured of a Babbling Curse, a yeti with a head-cold and a vampire who had been unable to eat anything except lettuce since Lockhart had dealt with him.

Harry was hauled to the front of the class during their very next Defence Against the Dark Arts lesson, this time acting a werewolf. If he hadn't had a very good reason for keeping Lockhart in a good mood, he would have refused to do it.

'Nice loud howl, Harry – exactly – and then, if you'll believe it, I pounced – like this – *slammed* him to the floor – thus – with one hand, I managed to hold him down – with my other, I put my wand to his throat – I then screwed up my remaining strength and performed the immensely complex Homorphus Charm – he let out a piteous moan – go on, Harry – higher than that – good – the fur vanished – the fangs shrank – and he turned back into a man. Simple, yet effective – and another village will remember me forever as the hero who delivered them from the monthly terror of werewolf attacks.'

The bell rang and Lockhart got to his feet.

'Homework: compose a poem about my defeat of the Wagga Wagga werewolf! Signed copies of *Magical Me* to the author of the best one!'

The class began to leave. Harry returned to the back of the room, where Ron and Hermione were waiting.

'Ready?' Harry muttered.

'Wait till everyone's gone,' said Hermione nervously. 'All right ...'

She approached Lockhart's desk, a piece of paper clutched tightly in her hand, Harry and Ron right behind her.

'Er – Professor Lockhart?' Hermione stammered. 'I wanted to – to get this book out of the library. Just for background reading.' She held out the piece of paper, her hand shaking slightly. 'But the thing is, it's in the Restricted Section of the library, so I need a teacher to sign for it – I'm sure it would help me understand what you say in *Gadding with Ghouls* about slow-acting venoms ...'

'Ah, *Gadding with Ghouls*!' said Lockhart, taking the note from Hermione and smiling widely at her. 'Possibly my very favourite book. You enjoyed it?'

'Oh, yes,' said Hermione eagerly. 'So clever, the way you trapped that last one with the tea-strainer ...'

'Well, I'm sure no one will mind me giving the best student in the year a little extra help,' said Lockhart warmly, and he pulled out an enormous peacock quill. 'Yes, nice, isn't it?' he said, mis-reading the revolted look on Ron's face. 'I usually save it for book-signings.'

He scrawled an enormous loopy signature on the note and handed it back to Hermione.

'So, Harry,' said Lockhart, while Hermione folded the note with fumbling fingers and slipped it into her bag, 'tomorrow's the first Quidditch match of the season, I believe? Gryffindor against Slytherin, is it not? I hear you're a useful player. I was a Seeker too. I was asked to try for the National Squad, but preferred to dedicate my life to the eradication of the Dark Forces. Still, if ever you feel the need for a little private training, don't hesitate to ask. Always happy to pass on my expertise to less able players ...'

Harry made an indistinct noise in his throat and then hurried off after Ron and Hermione.

'I don't believe it,' he said, as the three of them examined the signature on the note, 'He didn't even *look* at the book we wanted.'

'That's because he's a brainless git,' said Ron. 'But who cares, we've got what we needed.'

'He is *not* a brainless git,' said Hermione shrilly, as they half ran towards the library.

'Just because he said you were the best student in the year ...'

They dropped their voices as they entered the muffled stillness of the library.

Madam Pince, the librarian, was a thin, irritable woman who looked like an underfed vulture.

'*Moste Potente Potions*?' she repeated suspiciously, trying to take the note from Hermione; but Hermione wouldn't let go.

'I was wondering if I could keep it,' she said breathlessly.

'Oh, come on,' said Ron, wrenching it from her grasp and thrusting it at Madam Pince. 'We'll get you another autograph. Lockhart'll sign anything if it stands still long enough.'

Madam Pince held the note up to the light, as though determined to detect a forgery, but it passed the test. She stalked away between the lofty shelves and returned several minutes later carrying a large and mouldy-looking book. Hermione put it carefully into her bag and they left, trying not to walk too quickly or look too guilty.

Five minutes later, they were barricaded in Moaning Myrtle's out-of-order bathroom once again. Hermione had overridden Ron's objections by pointing out that it was the last place anyone in their right minds would go, so they were guaranteed some privacy. Moaning Myrtle was crying noisily in her cubicle, but they were ignoring her, and she them.

Hermione opened *Moste Potente Potions* carefully, and the three of them bent over the damp-spotted pages. It was clear from a glance why it belonged in the Restricted Section. Some of the potions had effects almost too gruesome to think about, and there were some very unpleasant illustrations, which included a man who seemed to have been turned inside out and a witch sprouting several extra pairs of arms out of her head.

'Here it is,' said Hermione excitedly, as she found the page headed *The Polyjuice Potion*. It was decorated with drawings of people halfway through transforming into other people. Harry sincerely hoped the artist had imagined the looks of intense pain on their faces.

'This is the most complicated potion I've ever seen,' said Hermione, as they scanned the recipe. 'Lacewing flies, leeches, fluxweed and knotgrass,' she murmured, running her finger down the list of ingredients. 'Well, they're easy enough, they're in the student store-cupboard, we can help ourselves. Oooh, look, powdered horn of a Bicorn – don't know where we're going to get that ... Shredded skin of a Boomslang – that'll be tricky too – and of course a bit of whoever we want to change into.'

'Excuse me?' said Ron sharply. 'What d'you mean, a bit of who-ever we're changing into? I'm drinking *nothing* with Crabbe's toe-nails in it ...'

Hermione continued as though she hadn't heard him.

'We don't have to worry about that yet, though, because we add those bits last ...'

Ron turned, speechless, to Harry, who had another worry.

'D'you realise how much we're going to have to steal, Hermione? Shredded skin of Boomslang, that's definitely not in the students' cupboard. What're we going to do, break into Snape's private stores? I don't know if this is a good idea ...'

Hermione shut the book with a snap.

'Well, if you two are going to chicken out, fine,' she said. There were bright pink patches on her cheeks and her eyes were brighter than usual. '*I* don't want to break rules, you know. *I* think threatening Muggle-borns is far worse than brewing up a difficult potion. But if you don't want to find out if it's Malfoy, I'll go straight to Madam Pince now and hand the book back in ...'

'I never thought I'd see the day when you'd be persuading us to break rules,' said Ron. 'All right, we'll do it. But not toenails, OK?'

'How long will it take to make, anyway?' said Harry, as Hermione, looking happier, opened the book again.

'Well, as the fluxweed has got to be picked at the full moon and the lacewings have got to be stewed for twenty-one days ... I'd say it'd be ready in about a month, if we can get all the ingredients.'

'A month?' said Ron. 'Malfoy could have attacked half the Muggle-borns in the school by then!' But Hermione's eyes nar-rowed dangerously again, and he added swiftly, 'But it's the best plan we've got, so full steam ahead, I say.'

However, while Hermione was checking the coast was clear for them to leave the bathroom, Ron muttered to Harry, 'It'll be a lot less hassle if you can just knock Malfoy off his broom tomorrow.'

*

Harry woke early on Saturday morning and lay for a while think-ing about the coming Quidditch match. He was nervous, mainly at the thought of what Wood would say if Gryffindor lost, but also at the idea of facing a team mounted on the fastest racing brooms gold could buy. He had never wanted to beat Slytherin so badly. After half an hour of lying there with his insides churning, he got up, dressed, and went down to breakfast early, where he found the rest of the Gryffindor team huddled at the long, empty table, all looking uptight and not speaking much.

As eleven o'clock approached, the whole school started to make its way down to the Quidditch stadium. It was a muggy sort of day with a hint of thunder in the air. Ron and Hermione came hurrying over to wish Harry good luck as he entered the changing rooms. The team pulled on their scarlet Gryffindor robes, then sat down to listen to Wood's usual pre-match pep talk.

'Slytherin have better brooms than us,' he began, 'no point denying it. But we've got better *people* on our brooms. We've trained harder than they have, we've been flying in all weathers –' ('Too true,' muttered George Weasley. 'I haven't been properly dry since August') '– and we're going to make them rue the day they let that little bit of slime, Malfoy, buy his way onto their team.'

Chest heaving with emotion, Wood turned to Harry.

'It'll be down to you, Harry, to show them that a Seeker has to have something more than a rich father. Get to that Snitch before Malfoy or die trying, Harry, because we've got to win today, we've got to.'

'So no pressure, Harry,' said Fred, winking at him.

As they walked out onto the pitch, a roar of noise greeted them; mainly cheers, because Ravenclaw and Hufflepuff were anxious to see Slytherin beaten, but the Slytherins in the crowd made their boos and hisses heard too. Madam Hooch, the Quidditch teacher, asked Flint and Wood to shake hands, which they did, giving each other threatening stares and gripping rather harder than was necessary.

'On my whistle,' said Madam Hooch, 'three ... two ... one ...'

With a roar from the crowd to speed them upwards, the four-teen players rose towards the leaden sky. Harry flew higher than any of them, squinting around for the Snitch.

'All right there, Scarhead?' yelled Malfoy, shooting underneath him as though to show off the speed of his broom.

Harry had no time to reply. At that very moment, a heavy black Bludger came pelting towards him; he avoided it so narrowly that he felt it ruffle his hair as it passed.

'Close one, Harry!' said George, streaking past him with his club in his hand, ready to knock the Bludger back towards a Slytherin. Harry saw George give the Bludger a powerful whack in the direction of Adrian Pucey, but the Bludger changed direction in mid-air and shot straight for Harry again.

Harry dropped quickly to avoid it, and George managed to hit it hard towards Malfoy. Once again, the Bludger swerved like a boomerang and shot at Harry's head.

Harry put on a burst of speed and zoomed towards the other end of the pitch. He could hear the Bludger whistling along behind him. What was going on? Bludgers never concentrated on one player like this, it was their job to try and unseat as many people as possible ...

Fred Weasley was waiting for the Bludger at the other end. Harry ducked as Fred swung at the Bludger with all his might; the Bludger was knocked off course.

'That's done it!' Fred yelled happily, but he was wrong; as though it was magnetically attracted towards Harry, the Bludger pelted after him once more and Harry was forced to fly off at full speed.

It had started to rain; Harry felt heavy drops fall onto his face, splattering onto his glasses. He didn't have a clue what was going on in the rest of the game until he heard Lee Jordan, who was commentating, say, 'Slytherin lead, sixty points to zero.'

The Slytherins' superior brooms were clearly doing their jobs, and meanwhile the mad Bludger was doing all it could to knock Harry out of the air. Fred and George were now flying so close to him on either side that Harry could see nothing at all except their flailing arms and had no chance to look for the Snitch, let alone catch it.

'Someone's – tampered – with – this – Bludger –' Fred grunted, swinging his bat with all his might at it as it launched a new attack on Harry.

'We need time out,' said George, trying to signal to Wood and stop the Bludger breaking Harry's nose at the same time.

Wood had obviously got the message. Madam Hooch's whistle rang out and Harry, Fred and George dived for the ground, still trying to avoid the mad Bludger.

'What's going on?' said Wood, as the Gryffindor team huddled together, while Slytherins in the crowd jeered. 'We're being flattened. Fred, George, where were you when that Bludger stopped Angelina scoring?'

'We were twenty feet above her, stopping the other Bludger

murdering Harry, Oliver,' said George angrily. 'Someone's fixed it – it won't leave Harry alone, it hasn't gone for anyone else all game. The Slytherins must have done something to it.'

'But the Bludgers have been locked in Madam Hooch's office since our last practice, and there was nothing wrong with them then ...' said Wood, anxiously.

Madam Hooch was walking towards them. Over her shoulder, Harry could see the Slytherin team jeering and pointing in his direction.

'Listen,' said Harry, as she came nearer and nearer, 'with you two flying round me all the time the only way I'm going to catch the Snitch is if it flies up my sleeve,' said Harry. 'Go back to the rest of the team and let me deal with the rogue one.'

'Don't be thick,' said Fred. 'It'll take your head off.'

Wood was looking from Harry to the Weasleys.

'Oliver, this is mad,' said Alicia Spinnet angrily. 'You can't let Harry deal with that thing on his own. Let's ask for an enquiry –'

'If we stop now, we'll have to forfeit the match!' said Harry. 'And we're not losing to Slytherin just because of a mad Bludger! Come on, Oliver, tell them to leave me alone!'

'This is all your fault,' George said angrily to Wood. '"Get the Snitch or die trying," – what a stupid thing to tell him!'

Madam Hooch had joined them.

'Ready to resume play?' she asked Wood.

Wood looked at the determined look on Harry's face.

'All right,' he said. 'Fred, George, you heard Harry – leave him alone and let him deal with the Bludger on his own.'

The rain was falling more heavily now. On Madam Hooch's whistle, Harry kicked hard into the air and heard the tell-tale whoosh of the Bludger behind him. Higher and higher Harry climbed. He looped and swooped, spiralled, zig-zagged and rolled. Slightly dizzy, he nevertheless kept his eyes wide open. Rain was speckling his glasses and ran up his nostrils as he hung upside down, avoiding another fierce dive from the Bludger. He could hear laughter from the crowd; he knew he must look very stupid, but the rogue Bludger was heavy and couldn't change direction as quickly as he could. He began a kind of roller-coaster ride around the edges of the stadium, squinting through the silver sheets of rain to the Gryffindor goal-posts, where Adrian Pucey was trying to get past Wood ...

A whistling in Harry's ear told him the Bludger had just missed him again; he turned right over and sped in the opposite direction.

'Training for the ballet, Potter?' yelled Malfoy, as Harry was forced to do a stupid kind of twirl in mid-air to dodge the Bludger. Off Harry fled, the Bludger trailing a few feet behind him: and then, glaring back at Malfoy in hatred, he saw it, *the Golden Snitch*. It was hovering inches above Malfoy's left ear – and Malfoy, busy laughing at Harry, hadn't seen it.

For an agonising moment, Harry hung in mid-air, not daring to speed towards Malfoy in case he looked up and saw the Snitch.

WHAM!

He had stayed still a second too long. The Bludger had hit him at last, smashed into his elbow, and Harry felt his arm break. Dimly, dazed by the searing pain in his arm, he slid sideways on his rain-drenched broom, one knee still crooked over it, his right arm dangling useless at his side. The Bludger came pelting back for a second attack, this time aiming at his face. Harry swerved out of the way, one idea firmly lodged in his numb brain: *get to Malfoy*.

Through a haze of rain and pain he dived for the shimmering, sneering face below him and saw its eyes widen with fear: Malfoy thought Harry was attacking him.

'What the –' he gasped, careering out of Harry's way.

Harry took his remaining hand off his broom and made a wild snatch; he felt his fingers close on the cold Snitch but was now only gripping the broom with his legs and there was a yell from the crowd below as he headed straight for the ground, trying hard not to pass out.

With a splattering thud he hit the mud and rolled off his broom. His arm was hanging at a very strange angle. Riddled with pain, he heard, as though from a distance, a good deal of whistling and shouting. He focused on the Snitch clutched in his good hand.

'Aha,' he said vaguely, 'we've won.'

And he fainted.

He came round, rain falling on his face, still lying on the pitch, with someone leaning over him. He saw a glitter of teeth.

'Oh no, not you,' he moaned.

'Doesn't know what he's saying,' said Lockhart loudly, to the anxious crowd of Gryffindors pressing around them. 'Not to worry, Harry. I'm about to fix your arm.'

'*No!*' said Harry. 'I'll keep it like this, thanks ...'

He tried to sit up, but the pain was terrible. He heard a familiar clicking noise nearby.

'I don't want a photo of this, Colin,' he said loudly.

'Lie back, Harry,' said Lockhart soothingly. 'It's a simple charm I've used countless times.'

'Why can't I just go to the hospital wing?' said Harry through clenched teeth.

'He should really, Professor,' said a muddy Wood, who couldn't help grinning even though his Seeker was injured. 'Great capture, Harry, really spectacular, your best yet, I'd say.'

Through the thicket of legs around him, Harry spotted Fred and George Weasley, wrestling the rogue Bludger into a box. It was still putting up a terrific fight.

'Stand back,' said Lockhart, who was rolling up his jade-green sleeves.

'No – don't –' said Harry weakly, but Lockhart was twirling his wand and a second later had directed it straight at Harry's arm.

A strange and unpleasant sensation started at Harry's shoulder and spread all the way down to his fingertips. It felt as though his arm was being deflated. He didn't dare look at what was happening. He had shut his eyes, his face turned away from his arm, but his worst fears were realised as the people above him gasped and Colin Creevey began clicking away madly. His arm didn't hurt any more – but nor did it feel remotely like an arm.

'Ah,' said Lockhart. 'Yes. Well, that can sometimes happen. But the point is, the bones are no longer broken. That's the thing to bear in mind. So, Harry, just toddle up to the Hospital Wing – ah, Mr Weasley, Miss Granger, would you escort him? – and Madam Pomfrey will be able to – er – tidy you up a bit.'

As Harry got to his feet, he felt strangely lopsided. Taking a deep breath he looked down at his right side. What he saw nearly made him pass out again.

Poking out of the end of his robes was what looked like a thick, flesh-coloured rubber glove. He tried to move his fingers. Nothing happened.

Lockhart hadn't mended Harry's bones. He had removed them.

*

Madam Pomfrey wasn't at all pleased.

'You should have come straight to me!' she raged, holding up the sad, limp remainder of what, half an hour before, had been a working arm. 'I can mend bones in a second – but growing them back –'

'You will be able to, won't you?' said Harry desperately.

'I'll be able to, certainly, but it will be painful,' said Madam Pomfrey grimly, throwing Harry a pair of pyjamas. 'You'll have to stay the night ...'

Hermione waited outside the curtain drawn around Harry's bed while Ron helped him into his pyjamas. It took a while to stuff the rubbery, boneless arm into a sleeve.

'How can you stick up for Lockhart now, Hermione, eh?' Ron called through the curtain as he pulled Harry's limp fingers through the cuff. 'If Harry had wanted de-boning he would have asked.'

'Anyone can make a mistake,' said Hermione, 'And it doesn't hurt any more, does it, Harry?'

'No,' said Harry, 'but it doesn't do anything else, either.'

As he swung himself onto the bed, his arm flapped pointlessly.

Hermione and Madam Pomfrey came around the curtain. Madam Pomfrey was holding a large bottle of something labelled 'Skele-Gro'.

'You're in for a rough night,' she said, pouring out a steaming beakerful and handing it to him. 'Regrowing bones is a nasty business.'

So was taking the Skele-Gro. It burned Harry's mouth and throat as it went down, making him cough and splutter. Still tut-tutting about dangerous sports and inept teachers, Madam Pomfrey retreated, leaving Ron and Hermione to help Harry gulp down some water.

'We won, though,' said Ron, a grin breaking across his face. 'That was some catch you made. Malfoy's face ... he looked ready to kill!'

'I want to know how he fixed that Bludger,' said Hermione darkly.

'We can add that to the list of questions we'll ask him when we've taken the Polyjuice Potion,' said Harry, sinking back onto his pillows. 'I hope it tastes better than this stuff ...'

'If it's got bits of Slytherins in it? You've got to be joking,' said Ron.

The door of the hospital wing burst open at that moment. Filthy and soaking wet, the rest of the Gryffindor team had arrived to see Harry.

'Unbelievable flying, Harry,' said George. 'I've just seen Marcus Flint yelling at Malfoy. Something about having the Snitch on top of his head and not noticing. Malfoy didn't seem too happy.'

They had brought cakes, sweets and bottles of pumpkin juice; they gathered around Harry's bed and were just getting started on what promised to be a good party when Madam Pomfrey came storming over, shouting, 'This boy needs rest, he's got thirty-three bones to regrow! Out! OUT!'

And Harry was left alone, with nothing to distract him from the stabbing pains in his limp arm.

*

Hours and hours later, Harry woke quite suddenly in the pitch blackness and gave a small yelp of pain: his arm now felt full of large splinters. For a second, he thought it was that which had woken him. Then, with a thrill of horror, he realised that someone was sponging his forehead in the dark.

'Get off!' he said loudly, and then, '*Dobby!*'

The house elf's goggling tennis-ball eyes were peering at Harry through the darkness. A single tear was running down his long, pointed nose.

'Harry Potter came back to school,' he whispered miserably. 'Dobby warned and warned Harry Potter. Ah sir, why didn't you heed Dobby? Why didn't Harry Potter go back home when he missed the train?'

Harry heaved himself up on his pillows and pushed Dobby's sponge away.

'What're you doing here?' he said. 'And how did you know I missed the train?'

Dobby's lip trembled and Harry was seized by a sudden suspicion.

'It was *you*!' he said slowly. '*You* stopped the barrier letting us through!'

'Indeed yes, sir,' said Dobby, nodding his head vigorously, ears flapping. 'Dobby hid and watched for Harry Potter and sealed the gateway and Dobby had to iron his hands afterwards –' he showed Harry ten, long, bandaged fingers, '– but Dobby didn't care, sir, for he thought Harry Potter was safe, and *never* did Dobby dream that

Harry Potter would get to school another way!'

He was rocking backwards and forwards, shaking his ugly head.

'Dobby was so shocked when he heard Harry Potter was back at Hogwarts, he let his master's dinner burn! Such a flogging Dobby never had, sir ...'

Harry slumped back onto his pillows.

'You nearly got Ron and me expelled,' he said fiercely. 'You'd better clear off before my bones come back, Dobby, or I might strangle you.'

Dobby smiled weakly.

'Dobby is used to death threats, sir. Dobby gets them five times a day at home.'

He blew his nose on a corner of the filthy pillowcase he wore, looking so pathetic that Harry felt his anger ebb away in spite of himself.

'Why d'you wear that thing, Dobby?' he asked curiously.

'This, sir?' said Dobby, plucking at the pillowcase. ''Tis a mark of the house-elf's enslavement, sir. Dobby can only be freed if his masters present him with clothes, sir. The family is careful not to pass Dobby even a sock, sir, for then he would be free to leave their house forever.'

Dobby mopped his bulging eyes and said suddenly, 'Harry Potter *must* go home! Dobby thought his Bludger would be enough to make –'

'*Your* Bludger?' said Harry, anger rising once more. 'What d'you mean, *your* Bludger? *You* made that Bludger try and kill me?'

'Not kill you, sir, never kill you!' said Dobby, shocked. 'Dobby wants to save Harry Potter's life! Better sent home, grievously injured, than remain here, sir! Dobby only wanted Harry Potter hurt enough to be sent home!'

'Oh, is that all?' said Harry angrily. 'I don't suppose you're going to tell me *why* you wanted me sent home in pieces?'

'Ah, if Harry Potter only knew!' Dobby groaned, more tears dripping onto his ragged pillowcase. 'If he knew what he means to us, to the lowly, the enslaved, us dregs of the magical world! Dobby remembers how it was when He Who Must Not Be Named was at the height of his powers, sir! We house-elfs were treated like vermin, sir! Of course, Dobby is still treated like that, sir,' he admitted, drying his face on the pillowcase. 'But mostly, sir, life has improved for my kind since you triumphed over He Who Must Not Be Named. Harry Potter survived, and the Dark Lord's power was broken, and it was a new dawn, sir, and Harry Potter shone like a beacon of hope for those of us who thought the Dark days would never end, sir ... And now, at Hogwarts, terrible things are to happen, are perhaps happening already, and Dobby cannot let Harry Potter stay here now that history is to repeat itself, now that the Chamber of Secrets is open once more –'

Dobby froze, horror-struck, then grabbed Harry's water jug from his bedside table and cracked it over his own head, toppling out of sight. A second later, he crawled back onto the bed, cross-eyed, muttering, 'Bad Dobby, very bad Dobby ...'

'So there *is* a Chamber of Secrets?' Harry whispered. 'And – did you say it's been opened *before*? *Tell* me, Dobby!'

He seized the elf's bony wrist as Dobby's hand inched towards the water jug. 'But I'm not Muggle-born – how can I be in danger from the Chamber?'

'Ah, sir, ask no more, ask no more of poor Dobby,' stammered the elf, his eyes huge in the dark. 'Dark deeds are planned in this place, but Harry Potter must not be here when they happen. Go home, Harry Potter. Go home. Harry Potter must not meddle in this, sir, 'tis too dangerous –'

'Who is it, Dobby?' Harry said, keeping a firm hold on Dobby's wrist to stop him hitting himself with the water jug again. 'Who's opened it? Who opened it last time?'

'Dobby can't, sir, Dobby can't, Dobby mustn't tell!' squealed the elf. 'Go home, Harry Potter, go home!'

'I'm not going anywhere!' said Harry fiercely. 'One of my best friends is Muggle-born, she'll be first in line if the Chamber really has been opened –'

'Harry Potter risks his own life for his friends!' moaned Dobby, in a kind of miserable ecstasy. 'So noble! So valiant! But he must save himself, he must, Harry Potter must not –'

Dobby suddenly froze, his bat ears quivering. Harry heard it too. There were footsteps coming down the passageway outside.

'Dobby must go!' breathed the elf, terrified; there was a loud crack, and Harry's fist was suddenly clenched on thin air. He slumped back into bed, his eyes on the dark doorway to the hospital wing as the footsteps drew nearer.

Next moment, Dumbledore was backing into the dormitory,

wearing a long woolly dressing gown and a nightcap. He was carrying one end of what looked like a statue. Professor McGonagall appeared a second later, carrying its feet. Together, they heaved it onto a bed.

'Get Madam Pomfrey,' whispered Dumbledore, and Professor McGonagall hurried past the end of Harry's bed out of sight. Harry lay quite still, pretending to be asleep. He heard urgent voices, and then Professor McGonagall swept back into view, closely followed by Madam Pomfrey, who was pulling a cardigan on over her nightdress. He heard a sharp intake of breath.

'What happened?' Madam Pomfrey whispered to Dumbledore, bending over the statue on the bed.

'Another attack,' said Dumbledore. 'Minerva found him on the stairs.'

'There was a bunch of grapes next to him,' said Professor McGonagall. 'We think he was trying to sneak up here to visit Potter.'

Harry's stomach gave a horrible lurch. Slowly and carefully, he raised himself a few inches so he could look at the statue on the bed. A ray of moonlight lay across its staring face.

It was Colin Creevey. His eyes were wide and his hands were stuck up in front of him, holding his camera.

'Petrified?' whispered Madam Pomfrey.

'Yes,' said Professor McGonagall. 'But I shudder to think ... If Albus hadn't been on the way downstairs for hot chocolate, who knows what might have ...'

The three of them stared down at Colin. Then Dumbledore leaned forward and prised the camera out of Colin's rigid grip.

'You don't think he managed to get a picture of his attacker?' said Professor McGonagall eagerly.

Dumbledore didn't answer. He prised open the back of the camera.

'Good gracious!' said Madam Pomfrey.

A jet of steam had hissed out of the camera. Harry, three beds away, caught the acrid smell of burnt plastic.

'Melted,' said Madam Pomfrey wonderingly, 'all melted ...'

'What does this *mean*, Albus?' Professor McGonagall asked urgently.

'It means,' said Dumbledore, 'that the Chamber of Secrets is indeed open again.'

Madam Pomfrey clapped a hand to her mouth. Professor McGonagall stared at Dumbledore.

'But Albus ... surely ... *who*?'

'The question is not *who*,' said Dumbledore, his eyes on Colin. 'The question is, *how* ...'

And from what Harry could see of Professor McGonagall's shadowy face, she didn't understand this any better than he did.

CHAPTER ELEVEN

The Duelling Club

Harry woke up on Sunday morning to find the dormitory blazing with winter sunlight and his arm re-boned but very stiff. He sat up quickly and looked over at Colin's bed, but it had been blocked from view by the high curtains Harry had changed behind yesterday. Seeing that he was awake, Madam Pomfrey came bustling over with a breakfast tray and then began bending and stretching his arm and fingers.

'All in order,' she said, as he clumsily fed himself porridge left-handed. 'When you've finished eating, you may leave.'

Harry dressed as quickly as he could and hurried off to Gryffindor tower, desperate to tell Ron and Hermione about Colin and Dobby, but they weren't there. Harry left to look for them, wondering where they could have got to and feeling slightly hurt that they weren't interested in whether he had his bones back or not.

As Harry passed the library, Percy Weasley strolled out of it, looking in far better spirits than last time they'd met.

'Oh, hello, Harry,' he said. 'Excellent flying yesterday, really excellent. Gryffindor have just taken the lead for the House Cup – you earned fifty points!'

'You haven't seen Ron or Hermione, have you?' said Harry.

'No, I haven't,' said Percy, his smile fading. 'I hope Ron's not in another *girls' toilet* ...'

Harry forced a laugh, watched Percy out of sight and then headed straight for Moaning Myrtle's bathroom. He couldn't see why Ron and Hermione would be in there again, but after making sure that neither Filch nor any prefects were around, he opened the door and heard their voices coming from a locked cubicle.

'It's me,' he said, closing the door behind him. There was a clunk, a splash and a gasp from within the cubicle and he saw

Hermione's eye peering through the keyhole.

'*Harry!*' she said. 'You gave us such a fright. Come in – how's your arm?'

'Fine,' said Harry, squeezing into the cubicle. An old cauldron was perched on the toilet, and a crackling from under the rim told Harry they had lit a fire beneath it. Conjuring up portable, waterproof fires was a speciality of Hermione's.

'We'd've come to meet you, but we decided to get started on the Polyjuice Potion,' Ron explained, as Harry, with difficulty, locked the cubicle again. 'We've decided this is the safest place to hide it.'

Harry started to tell them about Colin, but Hermione interrupted. 'We already know, we heard Professor McGonagall telling Professor Flitwick this morning. That's why we decided we'd better get going –'

'The sooner we get a confession out of Malfoy, the better,' snarled Ron. 'D'you know what I think? He was in such a foul temper after the Quidditch match, he took it out on Colin.'

'There's something else,' said Harry, watching Hermione tearing bundles of knotgrass and throwing them into the potion. 'Dobby came to visit me in the middle of the night.'

Ron and Hermione looked up, amazed. Harry told them everything Dobby had told him – or hadn't told him. Ron and Hermione listened with their mouths open.

'The Chamber of Secrets has been opened *before*?' said Hermione.

'This settles it,' said Ron in a triumphant voice. 'Lucius Malfoy must've opened the Chamber when he was at school here and now he's told dear old Draco how to do it. It's obvious. Wish Dobby'd told you what kind of monster's in there, though. I want to know how come nobody's noticed it sneaking round the school.'

'Maybe it can make itself invisible,' said Hermione, prodding leeches to the bottom of the cauldron. 'Or maybe it can disguise itself – pretend to be a suit of armour or something. I've read about Chameleon Ghouls ...'

'You read too much, Hermione,' said Ron, pouring dead lacewings on top of the leeches. He crumpled up the empty lacewing bag and looked round at Harry.

'So Dobby stopped us getting on the train and broke your arm ...' He shook his head. 'You know what, Harry? If he doesn't stop trying to save your life he's going to kill you.'

*

The news that Colin Creevey had been attacked and was now lying as though dead in the hospital wing had spread through the entire school by Monday morning. The air was suddenly thick with rumour and suspicion. The first years were now moving around the castle in tight-knit groups, as though scared they would be attacked if they ventured forth alone.

Ginny Weasley, who sat next to Colin Creevey in Charms, was distraught, but Harry felt that Fred and George were going the wrong way about cheering her up. They were taking it in turns to cover themselves with fur or boils and jump out at her from behind statues. They only stopped when Percy, apoplectic with rage, told them he was going to write to Mrs Weasley and tell her Ginny was having nightmares.

Meanwhile, hidden from the teachers, a roaring trade in talismans, amulets and other protective devices was sweeping the school. Neville Longbottom bought a large, evil-smelling green onion, a pointed purple crystal and a rotting newt-tail before the other Gryffindor boys pointed out that he was in no danger: he was a pure-blood, and therefore unlikely to be attacked.

'They went for Filch first,' Neville said, his round face fearful, 'and everyone knows I'm almost a Squib.'

*

In the second week of December Professor McGonagall came around as usual, collecting names of those who would be staying at school for Christmas. Harry, Ron and Hermione signed her list; they had heard that Malfoy was staying, which struck them as very suspicious. The holidays would be the perfect time to use the Polyjuice Potion and try to worm a confession out of him.

Unfortunately, the potion was only half-finished. They still needed the Bicorn horn and the Boomslang skin, and the only place they were going to get them was from Snape's private stores. Harry privately felt he'd rather face Slytherin's legendary monster than have Snape catch him robbing his office.

'What we need,' said Hermione briskly, as Thursday afternoon's double Potions lesson loomed nearer, 'is a diversion. Then one of us can sneak into Snape's office and take what we need.'

Harry and Ron looked at her nervously.

'I think I'd better do the actual stealing,' Hermione continued, in a matter of fact tone. 'You two will be expelled if you get in any more trouble, and I've got a clean record. So all you need to do is cause enough mayhem to keep Snape busy for five minutes or so.'

Harry smiled feebly. Deliberately causing mayhem in Snape's Potions class was about as safe as poking a sleeping dragon in the eye.

Potions lessons took place in one of the large dungeons. Thursday afternoon's lesson proceeded in the usual way. Twenty cauldrons stood steaming between the wooden desks, on which stood brass scales and jars of ingredients. Snape prowled through the fumes, making waspish remarks about the Gryffindors' work while the Slytherins sniggered appreciatively. Draco Malfoy, who was Snape's favourite student, kept flicking puffer-fish eyes at Ron and Harry, who knew that if they retaliated they would get detention faster than you could say 'unfair'.

Harry's Swelling Solution was far too runny, but he had his mind on more important things. He was waiting for Hermione's signal, and he hardly listened as Snape paused to sneer at his watery potion. When Snape turned and walked off to bully Neville, Hermione caught Harry's eye and nodded.

Harry ducked swiftly down behind his cauldron, pulled one of Fred's Filibuster fireworks out of his pocket and gave it a quick prod with his wand. The firework began to fizz and sputter. Knowing he had only seconds, Harry straightened up, took aim, and lobbed it into the air; it landed right on target in Goyle's cauldron.

Goyle's potion exploded, showering the whole class. People shrieked as splashes of the Swelling Solution hit them. Malfoy got a faceful and his nose began to swell like a balloon; Goyle blundered around, his hands over his eyes, which had explanded to the size of dinner plates, while Snape was trying to restore calm and find out what had happened. Through the confusion, Harry saw Hermione slip quietly out of the door.

'Silence! SILENCE!' Snape roared. 'Anyone who has been splashed, come here for a Deflating Draft. When I find out who did this ...'

Harry tried not to laugh as he watched Malfoy hurry forward, his head drooping with the weight of a nose like a small melon. As half the class lumbered up to Snape's desk, some weighed down with arms like clubs, others unable to talk through gigantic puffed-up lips, Harry saw Hermione slide back into the dungeon, the front of her robes bulging.

When everyone had taken a swig of antidote and the various swellings had subsided, Snape swept over to Goyle's cauldron and scooped out the twisted black remains of the firework. There was a sudden hush.

'If I ever find out who threw this,' Snape whispered, 'I shall *make sure* that person is expelled.'

Harry arranged his face into what he hoped was a puzzled expression. Snape was looking right at him, and the bell which rang ten minutes later could not have been more welcome.

'He knew it was me,' Harry told Ron and Hermione, as they hurried back to Moaning Myrtle's bathroom. 'I could tell.'

Hermione threw the new ingredients into the cauldron and began to stir feverishly.

'It'll be ready in a fortnight,' she said happily.

'Snape can't prove it was you,' said Ron reassuringly to Harry. 'What can he do?'

'Knowing Snape, something foul,' said Harry, as the potion frothed and bubbled.

*

A week later, Harry, Ron and Hermione were walking across the Entrance Hall when they saw a small knot of people gathered around the notice board, reading a piece of parchment that had just been pinned up. Seamus Finnigan and Dean Thomas beckoned them over, looking excited.

'They're starting a Duelling Club!' said Seamus. 'First meeting tonight! I wouldn't mind duelling lessons, they might come in handy one of these days ...'

'What, you reckon Slytherin's monster can duel?' said Ron, but he too read the sign with interest.

'Could be useful,' he said to Harry and Hermione as they went into dinner. 'Shall we go?'

Harry and Hermione were all for it, so at eight o'clock that evening they hurried back to the Great Hall. The long dining tables had vanished and a golden stage had appeared along one wall, lit by thousands of candles floating overhead. The ceiling was velvety black once more and most of the school seemed to be packed beneath it, all carrying their wands and looking excited.

'I wonder who'll be teaching us?' said Hermione, as they edged into the chattering crowd. 'Someone told me Flitwick was a duelling champion when he was young, maybe it'll be him.'

'As long as it's not –' Harry began, but he ended on a groan: Gilderoy Lockhart was walking onto the stage, resplendent in robes of deep plum and accompanied by none other than Snape, wearing his usual black.

Lockhart waved an arm for silence and called, 'Gather round, gather round! Can everyone see me? Can you all hear me? Excellent!

'Now, Professor Dumbledore has granted me permission to start this little duelling club, to train you all up in case you ever need to defend yourselves as I myself have done on countless occasions – for full details, see my published works.

'Let me introduce my assistant Professor Snape,' said Lockhart, flashing a wide smile. 'He tells me he knows a tiny little bit about duelling himself and has sportingly agreed to help me with a short demonstration before we begin. Now, I don't want any of you youngsters to worry – you'll still have your Potions master when I'm through with him, never fear!'

'Wouldn't it be good if they finished each other off?' Ron muttered in Harry's ear.

Snape's upper lip was curling. Harry wondered why Lockhart was still smiling; if Snape had been looking at *him* like that he'd have been running as fast as he could in the opposite direction.

Lockhart and Snape turned to face each other and bowed; at least, Lockhart did, with much twirling of his hands, whereas Snape jerked his head irritably. Then they raised their wands like swords in front of them.

'As you see, we are holding our wands in the accepted combative position,' Lockhart told the silent crowd. 'On the count of three, we will cast our first spells. Neither of us will be aiming to kill, of course.'

'I wouldn't bet on that,' Harry murmured, watching Snape baring his teeth.

'One – two – three –'

Both of them swung their wands up and over their shoulders. Snape cried: '*Expelliarmus!*' There was a dazzling flash of scarlet light and Lockhart was blasted off his feet: he flew backwards off the stage, smashed into the wall and slid down it to sprawl on the floor.

Malfoy and some of the other Slytherins cheered. Hermione was dancing on tip-toes. 'Do you think he's all right?' she squealed through her fingers.

'Who cares?' said Harry and Ron together.

Lockhart was getting unsteadily to his feet. His hat had fallen off and his wavy hair was standing on end.

'Well, there you have it!' he said, tottering back onto the platform. 'That was a Disarming Charm – as you see, I've lost my wand – ah, thank you, Miss Brown. Yes, an excellent idea to show them that, Professor Snape, but if you don't mind my saying so, it was very obvious what you were about to do. If I had wanted to stop you it would have been only too easy. However, I felt it would be instructive to let them see ...'

Snape was looking murderous. Possibly Lockhart had noticed, because he said, 'Enough demonstrating! I'm going to come amongst you now and put you all into pairs. Professor Snape, if you'd like to help me ...'

They moved through the crowd, matching up partners. Lockhart teamed Neville with Justin Finch-Fletchley, but Snape reached Harry and Ron first.

'Time to split up the dream team, I think,' he sneered. 'Weasley, you can partner Finnigan. Potter –'

Harry moved automatically towards Hermione.

'I don't think so,' said Snape, smiling coldly. 'Mr Malfoy, come over here. Let's see what you make of the famous Potter. And you, Miss Granger – you can partner Miss Bulstrode.'

Malfoy strutted over, smirking. Behind him walked a Slytherin girl who reminded Harry of a picture he'd seen in *Holidays with Hags*. She was large and square and her heavy jaw jutted aggressively. Hermione gave her a weak smile which she did not return.

'Face your partners!' called Lockhart, back on the platform, 'and bow!'

Harry and Malfoy barely inclined their heads, not taking their eyes off each other.

'Wands at the ready!' shouted Lockhart. 'When I count to three, cast your charms to disarm your opponent – *only* to disarm them – we don't want any accidents. One ... two ... three ...'

Harry swung his wand over his shoulder, but Malfoy had already started on 'two': his spell hit Harry so hard he felt as though he'd been hit over the head with a saucepan. He stumbled, but everything still seemed to be working, and wasting no more time, Harry pointed his wand straight at Malfoy and shouted, '*Rictusempra!*'

A jet of silver light hit Malfoy in the stomach and he doubled up, wheezing.

'*I said disarm only!*' Lockhart shouted in alarm over the heads of the battling crowd, as Malfoy sank to his knees; Harry had hit him with a Tickling Charm, and he could barely move for laughing. Harry hung back, with a vague feeling it would be unsporting to bewitch Malfoy while he was on the floor, but this was a mistake. Gasping for breath, Malfoy pointed his wand at Harry's knees, choked, '*Tarantallegra!*' and next second Harry's legs had begun to jerk around out of his control in a kind of quickstep.

'Stop! Stop!' screamed Lockhart, but Snape took charge.

'*Finite Incantatem!*' he shouted; Harry's feet stopped dancing, Malfoy stopped laughing and they were able to look up.

A haze of greenish smoke was hovering over the scene. Both Neville and Justin were lying on the floor, panting; Ron was holding up an ashen-faced Seamus, apologising for whatever his broken wand had done; but Hermione and Millicent Bulstrode were still moving; Millicent had Hermione in a headlock and Hermione was whimpering in pain. Both their wands lay forgotten on the floor. Harry leapt forward and pulled Millicent off. It was difficult, she was a lot bigger than he was.

'Dear, dear,' said Lockhart, skittering through the crowd, looking at the aftermath of the duels. 'Up you get, Macmillan ... careful there, Miss Fawcett ... pinch it hard, it'll stop bleeding in a second, Boot ...

'I think I'd better teach you how to *block* unfriendly spells,' said Lockhart, standing flustered in the midst of the hall. He glanced at Snape, whose black eyes glinted, and looked quickly away. 'Let's have a volunteer pair – Longbottom and Finch-Fletchley, how about you?'

'A bad idea, Professor Lockhart,' said Snape, gliding over like a large and malevolant bat. 'Longbottom causes devastation with the simplest spells. We'll be sending what's left of Finch-Fletchley up to the hospital wing in a matchbox.' Neville's round pink face went pinker. 'How about Malfoy and Potter?' said Snape with a twisted smile.

'Excellent idea!' said Lockhart, gesturing Harry and Malfoy into the middle of the hall as the crowd backed away to give them room.

'Now, Harry,' said Lockhart, 'when Draco points his wand at

you, you do *this*.'

He raised his own wand, attempted a complicated sort of wiggling action and dropped it. Snape smirked as Lockhart quickly picked it up, saying, 'Whoops – my wand is a little over-excited.'

Snape moved closer to Malfoy, bent down and whispered something in his ear. Malfoy smirked too. Harry looked nervously up at Lockhart and said, 'Professor, could you show me that blocking thing again?'

'Scared?' muttered Malfoy, so that Lockhart couldn't hear him.

'You wish,' said Harry out of the corner of his mouth.

Lockhart cuffed Harry merrily on the shoulder. 'Just do what I did, Harry!'

'What, drop my wand?'

But Lockhart wasn't listening.

'Three – two – one – go!' he shouted.

Malfoy raised his wand quickly and bellowed, '*Serpensortia!*'

The end of his wand exploded. Harry watched, aghast, as a long black snake shot out of it, fell heavily onto the floor between them and raised itself, ready to strike. There were screams as the crowd backed swiftly away, clearing the floor.

'Don't move, Potter,' said Snape lazily, clearly enjoying the sight of Harry standing motionless, eye to eye with the angry snake. 'I'll get rid of it ...'

'Allow me!' shouted Lockhart. He brandished his wand at the snake and there was a loud bang; the snake, instead of vanishing, flew ten feet into the air and fell back to the floor with a loud smack. Enraged, hissing furiously, it slithered straight towards Justin Finch-Fletchley and raised itself again, fangs exposed, poised to strike.

Harry wasn't sure what made him do it. He wasn't even aware of deciding to do it. All he knew was that his legs were carrying him forward as though he was on castors and that he had shouted stupidly at the snake, 'Leave him!' And miraculously – inexplicably – the snake slumped to the floor, docile as a thick black garden hose, its eyes now on Harry. Harry felt the fear drain out of him. He knew the snake wouldn't attack anyone now, though how he knew it, he couldn't have explained.

He looked up at Justin, grinning, expecting to see Justin looking relieved, or puzzled, or even grateful – but certainly not angry and scared.

'What do you think you're playing at?' he shouted, and before Harry could say anything, Justin had turned and stormed out of the hall.

Snape stepped forward, waved his wand and the snake vanished in a small puff of black smoke. Snape, too, was looking at Harry in an unexpected way: it was a shrewd and calculating look, and Harry didn't like it. He was also dimly aware of an ominous muttering all around the walls. Then he felt a tugging on the back of his robes.

'Come on,' said Ron's voice in his ear. 'Move – come *on* ...'

Ron steered him out of the hall, Hermione hurrying alongside them. As they went through the doors, the people on either side drew away as though they were frightened of catching something. Harry didn't have a clue what was going on, and neither Ron nor Hermione explained anything until they had dragged him all the way up to the empty Gryffindor common room. Then Ron pushed Harry into an armchair and said, 'You're a Parselmouth. Why didn't you tell us?'

'I'm a what?' said Harry.

'*A Parselmouth*!' said Ron. 'You can talk to snakes!'

'I know,' said Harry. 'I mean, that's only the second time I've ever done it. I accidentally set a boa constrictor on my cousin Dudley at the zoo once – long story – but it was telling me it had never seen Brazil and I sort of set it free without meaning to. That was before I knew I was a wizard ...'

'A boa constrictor told you it had never seen Brazil?' Ron repeated faintly.

'So?' said Harry. 'I bet loads of people here can do it.'

'Oh no they can't,' said Ron. 'It's not a very common gift. Harry, this is bad.'

'What's bad?' said Harry, starting to feel quite angry. 'What's wrong with everyone? Listen, if I hadn't told that snake not to attack Justin –'

'Oh, that's what you said to it?'

'What d'you mean? You were there ... you heard me.'

'I heard you speaking Parseltongue,' said Ron, 'snake language. You could have been saying anything. No wonder Justin panicked, you sounded like you were egging the snake on or something. It was creepy, you know.'

Harry gaped at him.

'I spoke a different language? But – I didn't realise – how can I speak a language without knowing I can speak it?'

Ron shook his head. Both he and Hermione were looking as though someone had died. Harry couldn't see what was so terrible.

'D'you want to tell me what's wrong with stopping a dirty great snake biting Justin's head off?' he said. 'What does it matter *how* I did it as long as Justin doesn't have to join the Headless Hunt?'

'It matters,' said Hermione, speaking at last in a hushed voice, 'because being able to talk to snakes was what Salazar Slytherin was famous for. That's why the symbol of Slytherin house is a serpent.'

Harry's mouth fell open.

'Exactly,' said Ron. 'And now the whole school's going to think you're his great-great-great-great-grandson or something ...'

'But I'm not,' said Harry, with a panic he couldn't quite explain.

'You'll find that hard to prove,' said Hermione. 'He lived about a thousand years ago; for all we know, you could be.'

*

Harry lay awake for hours that night. Through a gap in the hangings round his four-poster he watched snow starting to drift past the tower window, and wondered.

Could he be a descendant of Salazar Slytherin? He didn't know anything about his father's family, after all. The Dursleys had always forbidden questions about his wizarding relatives.

Quietly, Harry tried to say something in Parseltongue. The words wouldn't come. It seemed he had to be face to face with a snake to do it.

'But I'm in *Gryffindor*,' Harry thought. 'The Sorting Hat wouldn't have put me in here if I had Slytherin blood ...'

'*Ah*,' said a nasty little voice in his brain, 'But the Sorting Hat *wanted* to put you in Slytherin, don't you remember?'

Harry turned over. He'd see Justin next day in Herbology and he'd explain that he'd been calling the snake off, not egging it on, which (he thought angrily, pumelling his pillow) any fool should have realised.

*

By next morning, however, the snow that had begun in the night had turned into a blizzard so thick that the last Herbology lesson of term was cancelled: Professor Sprout wanted to fit socks and scarves on the Mandrakes, a tricky operation she would entrust to no one else, now that it was so important for the Mandrakes to grow quickly and revive Mrs Norris and Colin Creevey.

Harry fretted about this next to the fire in the Gryffindor common room, while Ron and Hermione used their lesson off to play a game of wizard chess.

'For heaven's sake, Harry,' said Hermione, exasperated, as one of Ron's bishops wrestled her knight off his horse and dragged him off the board. 'Go and *find* Justin if it's so important to you.'

So Harry got up and left through the Portrait hole, wondering where Justin might be.

The castle was darker than it usually was in daytime, because of the thick, swirling grey snow at every window. Shivering, Harry walked past classrooms where lessons were taking place, catching snatches of what was happening within. Professor McGonagall was shouting at someone who, by the sound of it, had turned his friend into a badger. Resisting the urge to take a look, Harry walked on by, thinking that Justin might be using his free lesson to catch up on some work, and deciding to check the library first.

A group of the Hufflepuffs who should have been in Herbology were indeed sitting at the back of the library, but they didn't seem to be working. Between the long lines of high bookshelves, Harry could see that their heads were close together and they were having what looked like an absorbing conversation. He couldn't see whether Justin was among them. He was walking towards them when something of what they were saying met his ears, and he paused to listen, hidden in the Invisibility section.

'So anyway,' a stout boy was saying, 'I told Justin to hide up in our dormitory. I mean to say, if Potter's marked him down as his next victim, it's best if he keeps a low profile for a while. Of course, Justin's been waiting for something like this to happen ever since he let slip to Potter he was Muggle-born. Justin actually *told* him he'd been down for Eton. That's not the kind of thing you bandy about with Slytherin's heir on the loose, is it?'

'You definitely think it *is* Potter, then, Ernie?' said a girl with blonde pigtails anxiously.

'Hannah,' said the stout boy solemnly, 'he's a Parselmouth. Everyone knows that's the mark of a dark wizard. Have you ever heard of a decent one who could talk to snakes? They called

Slytherin himself Serpent-tongue.'

There was some heavy murmuring at this, and Ernie went on, 'Remember what was written on the wall? *Enemies of the Heir Beware*. Potter had some sort of run-in with Filch. Next thing we know, Filch's cat's attacked. That first year, Creevey, was annoying Potter at the Quidditch match, taking pictures of him while he was lying in the mud. Next thing we know, Creevey's been attacked.'

'He always seems so nice, though,' said Hannah uncertainly, 'and, well, he's the one who made You Know Who disappear. He can't be all bad, can he?'

Ernie lowered his voice mysteriously, the Hufflepuffs bent closer, and Harry edged nearer so that he could catch Ernie's words.

'No one knows how he survived that attack by You Know Who. I mean to say, he was only a baby when it happened. He should have been blasted into smithereens. Only a really powerful Dark Wizard could have survived a curse like that.' He dropped his voice until it was barely more than a whisper, and said, '*That's* probably why You Know Who wanted to kill him in the first place. Didn't want another Dark Lord *competing* with him. I wonder what other powers Potter's been hiding?'

Harry couldn't take any more. Clearing his throat loudly, he stepped out from behind the bookshelves. If he hadn't been feeling so angry, he would have found the sight that greeted him funny: every one of the Hufflepuffs looked as though they had been Petrified by the sight of him, and the colour was draining out of Ernie's face.

'Hello,' said Harry. 'I'm looking for Justin Finch-Fletchley.'

The Hufflepuffs' worst fears had clearly been confirmed. They all looked fearfully at Ernie.

'What do you want with him?' said Ernie, in a quavering voice.

'I wanted to tell him what really happened with that snake at the Duelling Club,' said Harry.

Ernie bit his white lips and then, taking a deep breath, said, 'We were all there. We saw what happened.'

'Then you noticed that after I spoke to it, the snake backed off?' said Harry.

'All I saw,' said Ernie stubbornly, though he was trembling as he spoke, 'was you speaking Parseltongue and chasing the snake towards Justin.'

'I didn't chase it at him!' Harry said, his voice shaking with anger. 'It didn't even *touch* him!'

'It was a very near miss,' said Ernie. 'And in case you're getting ideas,' he added hastily, 'I might tell you that you can trace my family back through nine generations of witches and warlocks and my blood's as pure as anyone's, so –'

'I don't care what sort of blood you've got!' said Harry fiercely. 'Why would I want to attack Muggle-borns?'

'I've heard you hate those Muggles you live with,' said Ernie swiftly.

'It's not possible to live with the Dursleys and not hate them,' said Harry. 'I'd like to see you try it.'

He turned on his heel and stormed out of the library, earning himself a reproving glare from Madam Pince, who was polishing the gilded cover of a large spellbook.

Harry blundered up the corridor, barely noticing where he was going, he was in such a fury. The result was that he walked into something very large and solid, which knocked him backwards onto the floor.

'Oh, hullo, Hagrid,' Harry said, looking up.

Hagrid's face was entirely hidden by a woolly, snow-covered balaclava, but it couldn't possibly be anyone else, as he filled most of the corridor in his moleskin overcoat. A dead rooster was hanging from one of his massive, gloved hands.

'All righ', Harry?' he said, pulling up the balaclava so he could speak. 'Why aren't yeh in class?'

'Cancelled,' said Harry, getting up. 'What're you doing in here?'

Hagrid held up the limp rooster.

'Second one killed this term,' he explained. 'It's either foxes or a Blood-Suckin' Bugbear, an' I need the headmaster's permission ter put a charm round the hen-coop.'

He peered more closely at Harry from under his thick, snow-flecked eyebrows.

'Yeh sure yeh're all righ'? Yeh look all hot an' bothered.'

Harry couldn't bring himself to repeat what Ernie and the rest of the Hufflepuffs had been saying about him.

'It's nothing,' he said. 'I'd better get going, Hagrid, it's Transfiguration next and I've got to pick up my books.'

He walked off, his mind still full of what Ernie had said about him.

'Justin's been waiting for something like this to happen ever since he let slip to Potter he was Muggle-born ...'

Harry stamped up the stairs and turned along another corridor, which was particularly dark; the torches had been extinguished by a strong, icy draught which was blowing through a loose window pane. He was halfway down the passage when he tripped head-long over something lying on the floor.

He turned to squint at what he'd fallen over, and felt as though his stomach had dissolved.

Justin Finch-Fletchley was lying on the floor, rigid and cold, a look of shock frozen on his face, his eyes staring blankly at the ceiling. And that wasn't all. Next to him was another figure, the strangest sight Harry had ever seen.

It was Nearly Headless Nick, no longer pearly-white and transparent, but black and smoky, floating immobile and horizontal, six inches off the floor. His head was half off and his face wore an expression of shock identical to Justin's.

Harry got to his feet, his breathing fast and shallow, his heart doing a kind of drum-roll against his ribs. He looked wildly up and down the deserted corridor and saw a line of spiders scuttling as fast as they could away from the bodies. The only sounds were the muffled voices of teachers from the classes on either side.

He could run, and no one would ever know he had been there. But he couldn't just leave them lying here ... he had to get help. Would anyone believe he hadn't had anything to do with this?

As he stood there, panicking, a door right next to him opened with a bang. Peeves the poltergeist came shooting out.

'Why, it's potty wee Potter!' cackled Peeves, knocking Harry's glasses askew as he bounced past him. 'What's Potter up to? Why's Potter lurking –'

Peeves stopped, halfway through a mid-air somersault. Upside down, he spotted Justin and Nearly Headless Nick. He flipped the right way up, filled his lungs and, before Harry could stop him, screamed, 'ATTACK! ATTACK! ANOTHER ATTACK! NO MORTAL OR GHOST IS SAFE! RUN FOR YOUR LIVES! ATTAAAACK!'

Crash – crash – crash: door after door flew open along the corridor and people flooded out. For several long minutes, there was a scene of such confusion that Justin was in danger of being squashed and people kept standing in Nearly Headless Nick.

Harry found himself pinned against the wall as the teachers shouted for quiet. Professor McGonagall came running, followed by her own class, one of whom still had black and white striped hair. She used her wand to set off a loud bang, which restored silence, and ordered everyone back into their classes. No sooner had the scene cleared somewhat than Ernie the Hufflepuff arrived, panting, on the scene.

'*Caught in the act!*' Ernie yelled, his face stark white, pointing his finger dramatically at Harry.

'That will do, Macmillan!' said Professor McGonagall sharply.

Peeves was bobbing overhead, now grinning wickedly, surveying the scene; Peeves always loved chaos. As the teachers bent over Justin and Nearly Headless Nick, examining them, Peeves broke into song:

'*Oh Potter, you rotter, oh what have you done,*
You're killing off students, you think it's good fun –'

'That's enough Peeves!' barked Professor McGonagall, and Peeves zoomed away backwards, with his tongue out at Harry.

Justin was carried up to the hospital wing by Professor Flitwick and Professor Sinistra of the Astronomy department, but nobody seemed to know what to do for Nearly Headless Nick. In the end, Professor McGonagall conjured a large fan out of thin air, which she gave to Ernie with instructions to waft Nearly Headless Nick up the stairs. This Ernie did, fanning Nick along like a silent black hovercraft. This left Harry and Professor McGonagall alone together.

'This way, Potter,' she said.

'Professor,' said Harry at once, 'I swear I didn't –'

'This is out of my hands, Potter,' said Professor McGonagall curtly.

They marched in silence around a corner and she stopped before a large and extremely ugly stone gargoyle.

'Sherbert lemon!' she said. This was evidently a password, because the gargoyle sprang suddenly to life, and hopped aside as the wall behind him split in two. Even full of dread for what was coming, Harry couldn't fail to be amazed. Behind the wall was a spiral staircase which was moving smoothly upwards, like an escalator. As he and Professor McGonagall stepped onto it, Harry heard the wall thud closed behind them. They rose upwards in circles, higher and higher, until at last, slightly dizzy, Harry could see a gleaming oak door ahead, with a brass knocker in the shape of a griffon.

He knew where he was being taken. This must be where Dumbledore lived.

— CHAPTER TWELVE —

The Polyjuice Potion

They stepped off the stone staircase at the top and Professor McGonagall rapped on the door. It opened silently and they entered. Professor McGonagall told Harry to wait, and left him there, alone.

Harry looked around. One thing was certain: of all the teachers' offices Harry had visited so far this year, Dumbledore's was by far the most interesting. If he hadn't been scared out of his wits that he was about to be thrown out of school, he would have been very pleased to have a chance to look around it.

It was a large and beautiful circular room, full of funny little noises. A number of curious silver instruments stood on spindle-legged tables, whirring and emitting little puffs of smoke. The walls were covered with portraits of old headmasters and mistresses, all of whom were snoozing gently in their frames. There was also an enormous, claw-footed desk, and, sitting on a shelf behind it, a shabby, tattered wizard's hat – the *Sorting Hat*.

Harry hesitated. He cast a wary eye around the sleeping witches and wizards on the walls. Surely it couldn't hurt if he took the hat down and tried it on again? Just to see ... just to make sure it *had* put him in the right house.

He walked quietly around the desk, lifted the hat from its shelf, and lowered it slowly onto his head. It was much too large and slipped down over his eyes, just as it had done the last time he'd put it on. Harry stared at the black inside of the hat, waiting. Then a small voice said in his ear, 'Bee in your bonnet, Harry Potter?'

'Er, yes,' Harry muttered. 'Er – sorry to bother you – I wanted to ask –'

'You've been wondering whether I put you in the right house,' said the hat smartly. 'Yes ... you were particularly difficult to place. But I stand by what I said before –' Harry's heart leapt '– you *would* have done well in Slytherin.'

Harry's stomach plummeted. He grabbed the point of the hat and pulled it off. It hung limply in his hand, grubby and faded. Harry pushed it back onto its shelf, feeling sick.

'You're wrong,' he said aloud to the still and silent hat. It didn't move. Harry backed away, watching it. Then a strange, gagging noise behind him made him wheel around.

He wasn't alone after all. Standing on a golden perch behind the door was a decrepit-looking bird which resembled a half-plucked turkey. Harry stared at it and the bird looked balefully back, making its gagging noise again. Harry thought it looked very ill. Its eyes were dull and, even as Harry watched, a couple more feathers fell out of its tail.

Harry was just thinking that all he needed was for Dumbledore's pet bird to die while he was alone in the office with it, when the bird burst into flames.

Harry yelled in shock and backed away into the desk. He looked feverishly around in case there was a glass of water somewhere, but couldn't see one. The bird, meanwhile, had become a fireball; it gave one loud shriek and next second there was nothing but a smouldering pile of ash on the floor.

The office door opened. Dumbledore came in, looking very sombre.

'Professor,' Harry gasped, 'your bird – I couldn't do anything – he just caught fire –'

To Harry's astonishment, Dumbledore smiled.

'About time, too,' he said. 'He's been looking dreadful for days, I've been telling him to get a move on.'

He chuckled at the stunned look on Harry's face.

'Fawkes is a phoenix, Harry. Phoenixes burst into flame when it is time for them to die and are reborn from the ashes. Watch him ...'

Harry looked down in time to see a tiny, wrinkled, new-born bird poke its head out of the ashes. It was quite as ugly as the old one.

'It's a shame you had to see him on a Burning Day,' said Dumbledore, seating himself behind his desk. 'He's really very handsome most of the time: wonderful red and gold plumage. Fascinating creatures, phoenixes. They can carry immensely heavy loads, their tears have healing powers and they make highly *faithful* pets.'

In the shock of Fawkes catching fire, Harry had forgotten what he was there for, but it all came back to him as Dumbledore settled himself in the high-backed chair behind the desk and fixed Harry with his penetrating, light blue stare.

Before Dumbledore could speak another word, however, the door of the office flew open with an almighty bang and Hagrid burst in, a wild look in his eyes, his balaclava perched on top of his shaggy black head and the dead rooster still swinging from his hand.

'It wasn' Harry, Professor Dumbledore!' said Hagrid urgently. 'I was talkin' ter him *seconds* before that kid was found, he never had time, sir ...'

Dumbledore tried to say something, but Hagrid went ranting on, waving the rooster around in his agitation, sending feathers everywhere.

'... It can't've bin him, I'll swear it in front o' the Ministry o' Magic if I have to ...'

'Hagrid, I –'

'... Yeh've got the wrong boy, sir, I *know* Harry never –'

'*Hagrid!*' said Dumbledore loudly. 'I do *not* think that Harry attacked those people.'

'Oh,' said Hagrid, the rooster falling limply at his side. 'Right. I'll wait outside then, Headmaster.'

And he stomped out looking embarrassed.

'You don't think it was me, Professor?' Harry repeated hopefully, as Dumbledore brushed rooster feathers off his desk.

'No, Harry, I don't,' said Dumbledore, though his face was sombre again. 'But I still want to talk to you.'

Harry waited nervously while Dumbledore considered him, the tips of his long fingers together.

'I must ask you, Harry, whether there is anything you'd like to tell me,' he said gently. 'Anything at all.'

Harry didn't know what to say. He thought of Malfoy shouting, 'You'll be next, Mudbloods!' and of the Polyjuice potion, simmering away in Moaning Myrtle's bathroom. Then he thought of the disembodied voice he had heard twice and remembered what Ron had said: '*Hearing voices no one else can hear isn't a good sign, even in the wizarding world.*' He thought, too, about what everyone was saying about him, and his growing dread that he was somehow connected with Salazar Slytherin ...

'No,' said Harry, 'there isn't anything, Professor.'

*

The double attack on Justin and Nearly Headless Nick turned what had hitherto been nervousness into real panic. Curiously, it was Nearly Headless Nick's fate that seemed to worry people most. What could possibly do that to a ghost, people asked each other; what terrible power could harm someone who was already dead? There was almost a stampede to book seats on the Hogwarts Express so that students could go home for Christmas.

'At this rate, we'll be the only ones left,' Ron told Harry and Hermione. 'Us, Malfoy, Crabbe and Goyle. What a jolly holiday it's going to be.'

Crabbe and Goyle, who always did whatever Malfoy did, had signed up to stay over the holidays too. But Harry was glad that most people were leaving. He was tired of people skirting around him in the corridors, as though he was about to sprout fangs or spit poison; tired of all the muttering, pointing and hissing as he passed.

Fred and George, however, found all this very funny. They went out of their way to march ahead of Harry down the corridors, shouting, 'Make way for the Heir of Slytherin, seriously evil wizard coming through ...'

Percy was deeply disapproving of this behaviour.

'It is *not* a laughing matter,' he said coldly.

'Oh, get out of the way, Percy,' said Fred. 'Harry's in a hurry.'

'Yeah, he's nipping off to the Chamber of Secrets for a cup of tea with his fanged servant,' said George, chortling.

Ginny didn't find it amusing either.

'Oh, *don't*,' she wailed every time Fred asked Harry loudly who he was planning to attack next, or George pretended to ward Harry off with a large clove of garlic when they met.

Harry didn't mind; it made him feel better that Fred and George, at least, thought the idea of his being Slytherin's heir was quite ludicrous. But their antics seemed to be aggravating Draco Malfoy, who looked increasingly sour each time he saw them at it.

'It's because he's *bursting* to say it's really him,' said Ron knowingly. 'You know how he hates anyone beating him at anything, and you're getting all the credit for his dirty work.'

'Not for long,' said Hermione in a satisfied tone. 'The Polyjuice

Potion's nearly ready. We'll be getting the truth out of him any day now.'

*

At last the term ended, and a silence deep as the snow on the grounds descended on the castle. Harry found it peaceful, rather than gloomy, and enjoyed the fact that he, Hermione and the Weasleys had the run of Gryffindor tower, which meant they could play Exploding Snap loudly without bothering anyone, and practise duelling in private. Fred, George and Ginny had chosen to stay at school rather than visit Bill in Egypt with Mr and Mrs Weasley. Percy, who disapproved of what he termed their childish behaviour, didn't spend much time in the Gryffindor common room. He had already told them pompously that *he* was only staying over Christmas because it was his duty as a prefect to support the teachers during this troubled time.

Christmas morning dawned, cold and white. Harry and Ron, the only ones left in their dormitory, were woken very early by Hermione, who burst in, fully dressed and carrying presents for them both.

'Wake up,' she said loudly, pulling back the curtains at the window.

'Hermione – you're not supposed to be in here,' said Ron, shielding his eyes against the light.

'Merry Christmas to you, too,' said Hermione, throwing him his present. 'I've been up for nearly an hour, adding more lacewings to the potion. It's ready.'

Harry sat up, suddenly wide awake.

'Are you sure?'

'Positive,' said Hermione, shifting Scabbers the rat so that she could sit down on the end of his four-poster. 'If we're going to do it, I say it should be tonight.'

At that moment, Hedwig swooped into the room, carrying a very small package in her beak.

'Hello,' said Harry happily, as she landed on his bed, 'are you speaking to me again?'

She nibbled his ear in an affectionate sort of way, which was a far better present than the one which she had brought him, which turned out to be from the Dursleys. They had sent Harry a toothpick and a note telling him to find out whether he'd be able to stay at Hogwarts for the summer holidays, too.

The rest of Harry's Christmas presents were far more satisfactory. Hagrid had sent him a large tin of treacle fudge, which Harry decided to soften by the fire before eating; Ron had given him a book called *Flying with the Cannons*, a book of interesting facts about his favourite Quidditch team; and Hermione had bought him a luxury eagle-feather quill. Harry opened the last present to find a new, hand-knitted jumper from Mrs Weasley and a large plum cake. He put up her card with a fresh surge of guilt, thinking about Mr Weasley's car, which hadn't been seen since its crash with the Whomping Willow, and the bout of rule-breaking he and Ron were planning next.

*

No one, not even someone dreading taking Polyjuice Potion later, could fail to enjoy Christmas dinner at Hogwarts.

The Great Hall looked magnificent. Not only were there a dozen frost-covered Christmas trees and thick streamers of holly and mistletoe criss-crossing the ceiling, but enchanted snow was falling, warm and dry, from the ceiling. Dumbledore led them in a few of his favourite carols, Hagrid booming more and more loudly with every goblet of eggnog he consumed. Percy, who hadn't noticed that Fred had bewitched his Prefect badge so that it now read 'Pinhead', kept asking them all what they were sniggering at. Harry didn't even care that Draco Malfoy was making loud, snide remarks about his new jumper from the Slytherin table. With a bit of luck, Malfoy would be getting his come-uppance in a few hours' time.

Harry and Ron had barely finished their third helpings of Christmas pudding when Hermione ushered them out of the hall to finalise their plans for the evening.

'We still need a bit of the people you're changing into,' said Hermione matter-of-factly, as though she was sending them to the supermarket for washing-powder. 'And obviously, it'll be best if you can get something of Crabbe and Goyle's; they're Malfoy's best friends, he'll tell them anything. And we also need to make sure the real Crabbe and Goyle can't burst in on us while we're interrogating him.

'I've got it all worked out,' she went on smoothly, ignoring Harry and Ron's stupefied faces. She held up two plump chocolate cakes. 'I've filled these with a simple Sleeping Draught. All you have to do is make sure Crabbe and Goyle find them. You know how greedy they are, they're bound to eat them. Once they're asleep, pull out a few of their hairs and hide them in a broom cupboard.'

Harry and Ron looked incredulously at each other.

'Hermione, I don't think –'

'That could go seriously wrong –'

But Hermione had a steely glint in her eye not unlike the one Professor McGonagall sometimes had.

'The potion will be useless without Crabbe and Goyle's hair,' she said sternly. 'You do *want* to investigate Malfoy, don't you?'

'Oh, all right, all right,' said Harry. 'But what about you? Whose hair are you ripping out?'

'I've already got mine!' said Hermione brightly, pulling a tiny bottle out of her pocket and showing them the single hair inside it. 'Remember Millicent Bulstrode wrestling with me at the Duelling Club? She left this on my robes when she was trying to strangle me! And she's gone home for Christmas – so I'll just have to tell the Slytherins I've decided to come back.'

When Hermione had bustled off to check on the Polyjuice Potion again, Ron turned to Harry with a doom-laden expression.

'Have you ever heard of a plan where so many things could go wrong?'

*

But to Harry and Ron's utter amazement, stage one of the operation went just as smoothly as Hermione had said. They lurked in the deserted Entrance Hall after Christmas tea, waiting for Crabbe and Goyle who had remained alone at the Slytherin table, shovelling down fourth helpings of trifle. Harry had perched the chocolate cakes on the end of the bannisters. When they spotted Crabbe and Goyle coming out of the Great Hall, Harry and Ron hid quickly behind a suit of armour next to the front door.

'How thick can you get?' Ron whispered ecstatically, as Crabbe gleefully pointed out the cakes to Goyle and grabbed them. Grinning stupidly, they stuffed the cakes whole into their large mouths. For a moment, both of them chewed greedily, looks of triumph on their faces. Then, without the smallest change of expression, they both keeled over backwards onto the floor.

Much the most difficult bit was hiding them in the cupboard across the hall. Once they were safely stowed amongst the buckets and mops, Harry yanked out a couple of the bristles that covered

Goyle's forehead and Ron pulled out several of Crabbe's hairs. They also stole their shoes, because their own were far too small for Crabbe and Goyle-sized feet. Then, still stunned at what they had just done, they sprinted up to Moaning Myrtle's bathroom.

They could hardly see for the thick black smoke issuing from the cubicle in which Hermione was stirring the cauldron. Pulling their robes up over their faces, Harry and Ron knocked softly on the door.

'Hermione?'

They heard the scrape of the lock and Hermione emerged, shiny-faced and looking anxious. Behind her they heard the *gloop gloop* of the bubbling, treacle-thick potion. Three glass tumblers stood ready on the toilet seat.

'Did you get them?' Hermione asked breathlessly.

Harry showed her Goyle's hair.

'Good. And I sneaked these spare robes out of the laundry,' Hermione said, holding up a small sack. 'You'll need bigger sizes once you're Crabbe and Goyle.'

The three of them stared into the cauldron. Close up, the potion looked like thick, dark mud, bubbling sluggishly.

'I'm sure I've done everything right,' said Hermione, nervously re-reading the splotched page of *Moste Potente Potions*. 'It looks like the book says it should ... Once we've drunk it, we'll have exactly an hour before we change back into ourselves.'

'Now what?' Ron whispered.

'We separate it into three glasses and add the hairs.'

Hermione ladled large dollops of the potion into each of the glasses. Then, her hand trembling, she shook Millicent Bulstrode's hair out of its bottle into the first glass.

The potion hissed loudly like a boiling kettle and frothed madly. A second later, it had turned a sick sort of yellow.

'Urgh – essence of Millicent Bulstrode,' said Ron, eyeing it with loathing. 'Bet it tastes disgusting.'

'Add yours, then,' said Hermione.

Harry dropped Goyle's hair into the middle glass and Ron put Crabbe's into the last one. Both glasses hissed and frothed: Goyle's turned the khaki colour of a bogey, Crabbe's a dark, murky brown.

'Hang on,' said Harry, as Ron and Hermione reached for their glasses. 'We'd better not all drink them in here: once we turn into

Crabbe and Goyle we won't fit. And Millicent Bulstrode's no pixie.'

'Good thinking,' said Ron, unlocking the door. 'We'll take separate cubicles.'

Careful not to spill a drop of his Polyjuice potion, Harry slipped into the middle cubicle.

'Ready?' he called.

'Ready,' came Ron and Hermione's voices.

'One ... two ... three ...'

Pinching his nose, Harry drank the potion down in two large gulps. It tasted like overcooked cabbage.

Immediately, his insides started writhing as though he'd just swallowed live snakes – doubled up, he wondered whether he was going to be sick – then a burning sensation spread rapidly from his stomach to the very ends of his fingers and toes. Next, bringing him gasping to all fours, came a horrible melting feeling, as the skin all over his body bubbled like hot wax, and before his eyes, his hands began to grow, the fingers thickened, the nails broadened and the knuckles were bulging like bolts. His shoulders stretched painfully and a prickling on his forehead told him that hair was creeping down towards his eyebrows; his robes ripped as his chest expanded like a barrel bursting its hoops; his feet were agony in shoes four sizes too small ...

As suddenly as it had started, everything stopped. Harry lay face down on the cold stone floor, listening to Myrtle gurgling morosely in the end toilet. With difficulty, he kicked off his shoes and stood up. So this was what it felt like, being Goyle. His large hand trembling, he pulled off his old robes, which were hanging a foot above his ankles, pulled on the spare ones and laced up Goyle's boat-like shoes. He reached up to brush his hair out of his eyes and met only the short growth of wiry bristles, low on his forehead. Then he realised that his glasses were clouding his eyes, because Goyle obviously didn't need them. He took them off and called, 'Are you two OK?' Goyle's low rasp of a voice issued from his mouth.

'Yeah,' came the deep grunt of Crabbe from his right.

Harry unlocked his door and stepped in front of the cracked mirror. Goyle stared back at him out of dull, deepset eyes. Harry scratched his ear. So did Goyle.

Ron's door opened. They stared at each other. Except that he looked pale and shocked, Ron was indistinguishable from Crabbe, from the pudding-basin haircut to the long, gorilla arms.

'This is unbelievable,' said Ron, approaching the mirror and prodding Crabbe's flat nose. '*Unbelievable.*'

'We'd better get going,' said Harry, loosening the watch that was cutting into Goyle's thick wrist. 'We've still got to find out where the Slytherin common room is, I only hope we can find someone to follow ...'

Ron, who had been gazing at Harry, said, 'You don't know how bizarre it is to see Goyle *thinking.*' He banged on Hermione's door. 'C'mon, we need to go ...'

A high-pitched voice answered him. 'I – I don't think I'm going to come after all. You go on without me.'

'Hermione, we know Millicent Bulstrode's ugly, no one's going to know it's you.'

'No – really – I don't think I'll come. You two hurry up, you're wasting time.'

Harry looked at Ron, bewildered.

'*That* looks more like Goyle,' said Ron. 'That's how he looks every time a teacher asks him a question.'

'Hermione, are you OK?' said Harry through the door.

'Fine – I'm fine ... Go on –'

Harry looked at his watch. Five of their precious sixty minutes had already passed.

'We'll meet you back here, all right?' he said.

Harry and Ron opened the door of the bathroom carefully, checked that the coast was clear and set off.

'Don't swing your arms like that,' Harry muttered to Ron.

'Eh?'

'Crabbe holds them sort of stiff ...'

'How's this?'

'Yeah, that's better.'

They went down the marble staircase. All they needed now was a Slytherin who they could follow to the Slytherin common room, but there was nobody around.

'Any ideas?' muttered Harry.

'The Slytherins always come up to breakfast from over there,' said Ron, nodding at the entrance to the dungeons. The words had barely left his mouth when a girl with long curly hair emerged from the entrance.

'Excuse me,' said Ron, hurrying up to her, 'we've forgotten the way to our common room.'

'I beg your pardon?' said the girl stiffly. '*Our* common room? *I'm* a Ravenclaw.'

She walked away, looking suspiciously back at them.

Harry and Ron hurried down the stone steps into the darkness, their footsteps echoing particularly loudly as Crabbe and Goyle's huge feet hit the floor, feeling that this wasn't going to be as easy as they had hoped.

The labyrinthine passages were deserted. They walked deeper and deeper under the school, constantly checking their watches to see how much time they had left. After a quarter of an hour, just when they were getting desperate, they heard a sudden movement ahead.

'Ha!' said Ron excitedly. 'There's one of them now!'

The figure was emerging from a side room. As they hurried nearer, however, their hearts sank. It wasn't a Slytherin, it was Percy.

'What're you doing down here?' said Ron in surprise.

Percy looked affronted.

'That,' he said stiffly, 'is none of your business. It's Crabbe, isn't it?'

'Wh – oh, yeah,' said Ron.

'Well, get off to your dormitories,' said Percy sternly. 'It's not safe to go wandering around dark corridors these days.'

'*You* are,' Ron pointed out.

'I,' said Percy, drawing himself up, 'am a prefect. Nothing's about to attack *me*.'

A voice suddenly echoed behind Harry and Ron. Draco Malfoy was strolling towards them, and for the first time in his life, Harry was pleased to see him.

'There you are,' he drawled, looking at them. 'Have you two been pigging out in the Great Hall all this time? I've been looking for you, I want to show you something really funny.'

Malfoy glanced witheringly at Percy.

'And what're you doing down here, Weasley?' he sneered.

Percy looked outraged.

'You want to show a bit more respect to a school prefect!' he said. 'I don't like your attitude!'

Malfoy sneered and motioned Harry and Ron to follow him. Harry almost said something apologetic to Percy but caught himself just in time. He and Ron hurried after Malfoy, who said as they turned into the next passage, 'That Peter Weasley –'

'Percy,' Ron corrected him automatically.

'Whatever,' said Malfoy. 'I've noticed him sneaking around a lot lately. And I bet I know what he's up to. He thinks he's going to catch Slytherin's heir single-handed.'

He gave a short, derisive laugh. Harry and Ron exchanged excited looks.

Malfoy paused by a stretch of bare, damp stone wall.

'What's the new password again?' he said to Harry.

'Er –' said Harry.

'Oh yeah – *pure-blood*!' said Malfoy, not listening, and a stone door concealed in the wall slid open. Malfoy marched through it and Harry and Ron followed him.

The Slytherin common room was a long, low underground room with rough stone walls and ceiling, from which round, greenish lamps were hanging on chains. A fire was crackling under an elaborately carved mantelpiece ahead of them, and several Slytherins were silhouetted around it in carved chairs.

'Wait here,' said Malfoy to Harry and Ron, motioning them to a pair of empty chairs set back from the fire. 'I'll go and get it – my father's just sent it to me –'

Wondering what Malfoy was going to show them, Harry and Ron sat down, doing their best to look at home.

Malfoy came back a minute later, holding what looked like a newspaper cutting. He thrust it under Ron's nose.

'That'll give you a laugh,' he said.

Harry saw Ron's eyes widen in shock. He read the cutting quickly, gave a very forced laugh and handed it to Harry.

It had been clipped out of the *Daily Prophet*, and it said:

ENQUIRY AT THE MINISTRY OF MAGIC

Arthur Weasley, Head of the Misuse of Muggle Artefacts Office, was today fined fifty Galleons for bewitching a Muggle car.

Mr Lucius Malfoy, a governor of Hogwarts School of Witchcraft and Wizardry, where the enchanted car crashed earlier this year, called today for Mr Weasley's resignation.

'Weasley has brought the Ministry into disrepute,' Mr Malfoy told our reporter. 'He is clearly unfit to draw up our

*laws and his ridiculous Muggle Protection Act should be scrapped
immediately.'*

*Mr Weasley was unavailable for comment, although his
wife told reporters to clear off or she'd set the family ghoul
on them.*

'Well?' said Malfoy impatiently, as Harry handed the cutting
back to him. 'Don't you think it's funny?'

'Ha, ha,' said Harry bleakly.

'Arthur Weasley loves Muggles so much he should snap his
wand in half and go and join them,' said Malfoy scornfully. 'You'd
never know the Weasleys were pure-bloods, the way they behave.'

Ron's – or rather, Crabbe's – face was contorted with fury.

'What's up with you, Crabbe?' snapped Malfoy.

'Stomach ache,' Ron grunted.

'Well, go up to the hospital wing and give all those Mudbloods
a kick from me,' said Malfoy, snickering. 'You know, I'm surprised
the *Daily Prophet* hasn't reported all these attacks yet,' he went on
thoughtfully. 'I suppose Dumbledore's trying to hush it all up.
He'll be sacked if it doesn't stop soon. Father's always said
Dumbledore's the worst thing that's ever happened to this place.
He loves Muggle-borns. A decent headmaster would never've let
slime like that Creevey in.'

Malfoy started taking pictures with an imaginary camera and
did a cruel but accurate impression of Colin: 'Potter, can I have
your picture, Potter? Can I have your autograph? Can I lick your
shoes, please, Potter?'

He dropped his hands and looked at Harry and Ron.

'What's the *matter* with you two?'

Far too late, Harry and Ron forced themselves to laugh, but
Malfoy seemed satisfied; perhaps Crabbe and Goyle were always
slow on the uptake.

'Saint Potter, the Mudbloods' friend,' said Malfoy slowly. 'He's
another one with no proper wizard feeling, or he wouldn't go
around with that jumped up Granger Mudblood. And people
think *he's* Slytherin's heir!'

Harry and Ron waited with bated breath: Malfoy was surely
seconds away from telling them it was him. But then –

'I *wish* I knew who it *is*,' said Malfoy petulantly. 'I could help
them.'

Ron's jaw dropped so that Crabbe's face looked even more gormless than usual. Fortunately, Malfoy didn't notice, and Harry, thinking fast, said, 'You must have some idea who's behind it all ...'

'You know I haven't, Goyle, how many times do I have to tell you?' snapped Malfoy. 'And father won't tell me *anything* about the last time the Chamber was opened, either. Of course, it was fifty years ago, so it was before his time, but he knows all about it, and he says that it was all kept quiet and it'll look suspicious if I know too much about it. But I know one thing: last time the Chamber of Secrets was opened, a Mudblood *died*. So I bet it's a matter of time before one of them's killed this time ... I hope it's Granger,' he said with relish.

Ron was clenching Crabbe's gigantic fists. Feeling that it would be a bit of a give-away if Ron punched Malfoy, Harry shot him a warning look and said, 'D'you know if the person who opened the Chamber last time was caught?'

'Oh, yeah ... whoever it was was expelled,' said Malfoy. 'They're probably still in Azkaban.'

'Azkaban?' said Harry, puzzled.

'Azkaban – *the wizard prison,* Goyle,' said Malfoy, looking at him in disbelief. 'Honestly, if you were any slower, you'd be going backwards.'

He shifted restlessly in his chair and said, 'Father says to keep my head down and let the heir of Slytherin get on with it. He says the school needs ridding of all the Mudblood filth, but not to get mixed up in it. Of course, he's got a lot on his plate at the moment. You know the Ministry of Magic raided our Manor last week?'

Harry tried to force Goyle's dull face into a look of concern.

'Yeah ...' said Malfoy. 'Luckily, they didn't find much. Father's got some *very* valuable Dark Arts stuff. But luckily, we've got our own secret chamber under the drawing room floor –'

'Ho!' said Ron.

Malfoy looked at him. So did Harry. Ron blushed. Even his hair was turning red. His nose was also slowly lengthening – their hour was up. Ron was turning back into himself, and from the look of horror he was suddenly giving Harry, he must be, too.

They both jumped to their feet.

'Medicine for my stomach,' Ron grunted, and without further

ado they sprinted the length of the Slytherin common room, hurled themselves at the stone wall and dashed up the passage, hoping against hope that Malfoy hadn't noticed anything. Harry could feel his feet slipping around in Goyle's huge shoes and had to hoist up his robes as he shrank; they crashed up the steps into the dark entrance hall, which was full of a muffled pounding coming from the cupboard where they'd locked Crabbe and Goyle. Leaving their shoes outside the cupboard door, they sprinted in their socks up the marble staircase towards Moaning Myrtle's bathroom.

'Well, it wasn't a complete waste of time,' Ron panted, closing the bathroom door behind them. 'I know we still haven't found out who's doing the attacks, but I'm going to write to Dad tomorrow and tell him to check under the Malfoys' drawing room.'

Harry checked his face in the cracked mirror. He was back to normal. He put his glasses on as Ron hammered on the door of Hermione's cubicle.

'Hermione, come out, we've got loads to tell you –'

'Go away!' Hermione squeaked.

Harry and Ron looked at each other.

'What's the matter?' said Ron. 'You must be back to normal by now, we are ...'

But Moaning Myrtle glided suddenly through the cubicle door. Harry had never seen her looking so happy.

'Ooooooh, wait til you see,' she said. 'It's *awful*!'

They heard the lock slide back and Hermione emerged, sobbing, her robes pulled up over her head.

'What's up?' said Ron uncertainly. 'Have you still got Millicent's nose or something?'

Hermione let her robes fall and Ron backed into the sink.

Her face was covered in black fur. Her eyes had gone yellow and there were long pointed ears poking through her hair.

'It was a c-cat hair!' she howled. 'M-Millicent Bulstrode m-must have a cat! And the p-potion isn't supposed to be used for animal transformations!'

'Uh oh,' said Ron.

'You'll be teased something *dreadful*,' said Myrtle happily.

'It's OK, Hermione,' said Harry quickly. 'We'll take you up to the hospital wing. Madam Pomfrey never asks too many questions ...'

It took a long time to persuade Hermione to leave the bath-room. Moaning Myrtle sped them on their way with a hearty guffaw.

'Wait till everyone finds out you've got a *tail*!'

CHAPTER THIRTEEN

The Very Secret Diary

Hermione remained in the hospital wing for several weeks. There was a flurry of rumour about her disappearance when the rest of the school arrived back from their Christmas holidays, because of course everyone thought that she had been attacked. So many students filed past the hospital wing trying to catch a glimpse of her that Madam Pomfrey took out her curtains again and placed them around Hermione's bed, to spare her the shame of being seen with a furry face.

Harry and Ron went to visit her every evening. When the new term started, they brought her each day's homework.

'If I'd sprouted whiskers, I'd take a break from work,' said Ron, tipping a stack of books onto Hermione's bedside table one evening.

'Don't be silly, Ron, I've got to keep up,' said Hermione briskly. Her spirits were greatly improved by the fact that all the hair had gone from her face and her eyes were turning slowly back to brown. 'I don't suppose you've got any new leads?' she added in a whisper, so that Madam Pomfrey couldn't hear her.

'Nothing,' said Harry gloomily.

'I was so *sure* it was Malfoy,' said Ron, for about the hundredth time.

'What's that?' asked Harry, pointing to something gold sticking out from under Hermione's pillow.

'Just a Get Well card,' said Hermione hastily, trying to poke it out of sight, but Ron was too quick for her. He pulled it out, flicked it open and read aloud:

'*To Miss Granger, wishing you a speedy recovery, from your concerned teacher, Professor Gilderoy Lockhart, Order of Merlin Third Class, Honorary Member of the Dark Force Defence League and five times winner of* Witch Weekly's *Most-Charming-Smile Award.*'

Ron looked up at Hermione, disgusted.

'You sleep with this under your *pillow*?'

But Hermione was spared answering by Madam Pomfrey sweeping over with her evening dose of medicine.

'Is Lockhart the smarmiest bloke you've ever met, or what?' Ron said to Harry as they left the dormitory and started up the stairs towards Gryffindor tower. Snape had given them so much homework, Harry thought he was likely to be in the sixth year before he finished it. Ron was just saying he wished he had asked Hermione how many rat tails you were supposed to add to a Hair Raising potion, when an angry outburst from the floor above reached their ears.

'That's Filch,' Harry muttered, as they hurried up the stairs and paused, out of sight, listening hard.

'You don't think someone else's been attacked?' said Ron tensely.

They stood still, their heads inclined towards Filch's voice, which sounded quite hysterical.

'*... even more work for me! Mopping all night, like I haven't got enough to do! No, this is the final straw, I'm going to Dumbledore ...*'

His footsteps receded and they heard a distant door slam.

They poked their heads around the corner. Filch had clearly been manning his usual look-out post: they were once again on the spot where Mrs Norris had been attacked. They saw at a glance what Filch had been shouting about. A great flood of water stretched over half the corridor, and it looked as though it was still seeping from under the door of Moaning Myrtle's bathroom. Now Filch had stopped shouting, they could hear Myrtle's wails echoing off the bathroom walls.

'*Now* what's up with her?' said Ron.

'Let's go and see,' said Harry, and holding their robes over their ankles they stepped through the great wash of water to the door bearing its Out Of Order sign, ignored it as always, and entered.

Moaning Myrtle was crying, if possible, louder and harder than ever before. She seemed to be hiding down her usual toilet. It was dark in the bathroom, because the candles had been extinguished in the great rush of water that had left both walls and floor soaking wet.

'What's up, Myrtle?' said Harry.

'Who's that?' glugged Myrtle miserably. 'Come to throw something else at me?'

Harry waded across to her cubicle and said, 'Why would I throw something at you?'

'Don't ask me,' Myrtle shouted, emerging with a wave of yet more water, which splashed onto the already sopping floor. 'Here I am, minding my own business, and someone thinks it's funny to throw a book at me ...'

'But it can't hurt you if someone throws something at you,' said Harry, reasonably. 'I mean, it'd just go right through you, wouldn't it?'

He had said the wrong thing. Myrtle puffed herself up and shrieked, 'Let's all throw books at Myrtle, because *she* can't feel it! Ten points if you can get it through her stomach! Fifty points if it goes through her head! Well, ha ha ha! What a lovely game, I *don't* think!'

'Who threw it at you, anyway?' asked Harry.

'*I* don't know ... I was just sitting in the U-bend, thinking about death, and it fell right through the top of my head,' said Myrtle, glaring at them. 'It's over there, it got washed out.'

Harry and Ron looked under the sink, where Myrtle was pointing. A small, thin book lay there. It had a shabby black cover and was as wet as everything else in the bathroom. Harry stepped forward to pick it up, but Ron suddenly flung out an arm to hold him back.

'What?' said Harry.

'Are you mad?' said Ron. 'It could be dangerous.'

'*Dangerous?*' said Harry, laughing. 'Come off it, how could it be dangerous?'

'You'd be surprised,' said Ron, who was looking apprehensively at the book. 'Some of the books the Ministry's confiscated – Dad's told me – there was one that burned your eyes out. And everyone who read *Sonnets of a Sorcerer* spoke in limericks for the rest of their lives. And some old witch in Bath had a book that you could *never stop reading*! You just had to wander around with your nose in it, trying to do everything one-handed. And –'

'All right, I've got the point,' said Harry.

The little book lay on the floor, nondescript and soggy.

'Well, we won't find out unless we look at it,' he said, and he ducked round Ron and picked it off the floor.

Harry saw at once that it was a diary, and the faded year on the cover told him it was fifty years old. He opened it eagerly. On the first page he could just make out the name 'T. M. Riddle' in smudged ink.

'Hang on,' said Ron, who had approached cautiously and was looking over Harry's shoulder. 'I know that name ... T. M. Riddle got an award for special services to the school fifty years ago.'

'How on earth d'you know that?' said Harry in amazement.

'Because Filch made me polish his shield about fifty times in detention,' said Ron resentfully. 'That was the one I burped slugs all over. If you'd wiped slime off a name for an hour, you'd remember it, too.'

Harry peeled the wet pages apart. They were completely blank. There wasn't the faintest trace of writing on any of them, not even 'Auntie Mabel's birthday', or 'dentist, half past three'.

'He never wrote in it,' said Harry, disappointed.

'I wonder why someone wanted to flush it away?' said Ron curiously.

Harry turned to the back cover of the book and saw the printed name of a newsagents in Vauxhall Road, London.

'He must've been Muggle-born,' said Harry thoughtfully, 'to have bought a diary from Vauxhall Road ...'

'Well, it's not much use to you,' said Ron. He dropped his voice. 'Fifty points if you can get it through Myrtle's nose.'

Harry, however, pocketed it.

*

Hermione left the hospital wing, de-whiskered, tail-less and fur-free, at the beginning of February. On her first evening back in Gryffindor Tower, Harry showed her T. M. Riddle's diary and told her the story of how they had found it.

'Oooh, it might have hidden powers,' said Hermione enthusiastically, taking the diary and looking at it closely.

'If it has, it's hiding them very well,' said Ron. 'Maybe it's shy. I don't know why you don't chuck it, Harry.'

'I wish I knew why someone *did* try to chuck it,' said Harry. 'I wouldn't mind knowing how Riddle got an award for special services to Hogwarts, either.'

'Could've been anything,' said Ron. 'Maybe he got thirty O.W.Ls or saved a teacher from the giant squid. Maybe he murdered Myrtle, that would've done everyone a favour ...'

But Harry could tell from the arrested look on Hermione's face that she was thinking what he was thinking.

'What?' said Ron, looking from one to the other.

'Well, the Chamber of Secrets was opened fifty years ago, wasn't it?' he said. 'That's what Malfoy said.'

'Yeah ...' said Ron slowly.

'And *this diary* is fifty years old,' said Hermione, tapping it excitedly.

'So?'

'Oh, Ron, wake up,' snapped Hermione. 'We know the person who opened the Chamber last time was expelled *fifty years ago*. We know T. M. Riddle got an award for special services to the school *fifty years ago*. Well, what if Riddle got his special award for *catching the Heir of Slytherin*? His diary would probably tell us everything: where the Chamber is, and how to open it, and what sort of creature lives in it. The person who's behind the attacks this time wouldn't want that lying around, would they?'

'That's a *brilliant* theory, Hermione,' said Ron, 'with just one tiny little flaw. *There's nothing written in his diary*.'

But Hermione was pulling her wand out of her bag.

'It might be invisible ink!' she whispered.

She tapped the diary three times and said, '*Aparecium!*'

Nothing happened. Undaunted, Hermione shoved her hand back into her bag and pulled out what appeared to be a bright red eraser.

'It's a Revealer, I got it in Diagon Alley,' she said.

She rubbed hard on 'January the first'. Nothing happened.

'I'm telling you, there's nothing to find in there,' said Ron. 'Riddle just got a diary for Christmas and couldn't be bothered filling it in.'

*

Harry couldn't explain, even to himself, why he didn't just throw Riddle's diary away. The fact was that even though he *knew* the diary was blank, he kept absent-mindedly picking it up and turning the pages, as though it was a story he wanted to finish. And while Harry was sure he had never heard the name T. M. Riddle before, it still seemed to mean something to him, almost as though Riddle was a friend he'd had when he was very small, and half-forgotten. But this was absurd. He'd never had friends before Hogwarts, Dudley had made sure of that.

Nevertheless, Harry was determined to find out more about

Riddle, so next day at break, he headed for the trophy-room to examine Riddle's special award, accompanied by an interested Hermione and a thoroughly unconvinced Ron, who told them he'd seen enough of the trophy-room to last him a lifetime.

Riddle's burnished gold shield was tucked away in a corner cabinet. It didn't carry details of why it had been given to him ('Good thing too, or it'd be even bigger and I'd still be polishing it,' said Ron). However, they did find Riddle's name on an old Medal for Magical Merit, and on a list of old Head Boys.

'He sounds like Percy,' said Ron, wrinkling his nose in disgust. 'Prefect, Head Boy – probably top of every class.'

'You say that like it's a bad thing,' said Hermione, in a slightly hurt voice.

*

The sun had now begun to shine weakly on Hogwarts again. Inside the castle, the mood had grown more hopeful. There had been no more attacks since those on Justin and Nearly Headless Nick, and Madam Pomfrey was pleased to report that the Mandrakes were becoming moody and secretive, meaning that they were fast leaving childhood.

'The moment their acne clears up, they'll be ready for repotting again,' Harry heard her telling Filch kindly one afternoon. 'And after that, it won't be long until we're cutting them up and stewing them. You'll have Mrs Norris back in no time.'

Perhaps the heir of Slytherin had lost his or her nerve, thought Harry. It must be getting riskier and riskier to open the Chamber of Secrets, with the school so alert and suspicious. Perhaps the monster, whatever it was, was even now settling itself down to hibernate for another fifty years ...

Ernie Macmillan of Hufflepuff didn't take this cheerful view. He was still convinced that Harry was the guilty one, that he had 'given himself away' at the Duelling Club. Peeves wasn't helping matters: he kept popping up in the crowded corridors singing 'Oh Potter, you rotter ...,' now with a dance-routine to match.

Gilderoy Lockhart seemed to think he himself had made the attacks stop. Harry overheard him telling Professor McGonagall so while the Gryffindors were lining up for Transfiguration.

'I don't think there'll be any more trouble, Minerva,' he said, tapping his nose knowingly and winking. 'I think the Chamber has been locked for good this time. The culprit must have known it was only a matter of time before I caught them. Rather sensible to stop now, before I came down hard on them.

'You know, what the school needs now is a morale-booster. Wash away the memories of last term! I won't say any more just now, but I think I know just the thing ...'

He tapped his nose again and strode off.

Lockhart's idea of a morale-booster became clear at breakfast time on February the fourteenth. Harry hadn't had much sleep because of a late-running Quidditch practice the night before, and he hurried down to the Great Hall slightly late. He thought, for a moment, that he'd walked through the wrong doors.

The walls were all covered with large, lurid pink flowers. Worse still, heart-shaped confetti was falling from the pale blue ceiling. Harry went over to the Gryffindor table, where Ron was sitting looking sickened, and Hermione seemed to have come over rather giggly.

'What's going on?' Harry asked them, sitting down, and wiping confetti off his bacon.

Ron pointed to the teachers' table, apparently too disgusted to speak. Lockhart, wearing lurid pink robes to match the decorations, was waving for silence. The teachers on either side of him were looking stony-faced. From where he sat, Harry could see a muscle going in Professor McGonagall's cheek. Snape looked as though someone had just fed him a large beaker of Skele-Gro.

'Happy Valentine's Day!' Lockhart shouted. 'And may I thank the forty-six people who have so far sent me cards! Yes, I have taken the liberty of arranging this little surprise for you all – and it doesn't end here!'

Lockhart clapped his hands and through the doors to the Entrance Hall marched a dozen surly-looking dwarfs. Not just any dwarfs, however. Lockhart had them all wearing golden wings and carrying harps.

'My friendly, card-carrying cupids!' beamed Lockhart. 'They will be roving around the school today delivering your Valentines! And the fun doesn't stop here! I'm sure my colleagues will want to enter into the spirit of the occasion! Why not ask Professor Snape to show you how to whip up a Love Potion! And while you're at it, Professor Flitwick knows more about Entrancing Enchantments than any wizard I've ever met, the sly old dog!'

Professor Flitwick buried his face in his hands. Snape was looking as though the first person to ask him for a Love Potion would be force-fed poison.

'Please, Hermione, tell me you weren't one of the forty-six,' said Ron, as they left the Great Hall for their first lesson. Hermione suddenly became very interested in searching her bag for her timetable and didn't answer.

All day long, the dwarfs kept barging into their classes to deliver Valentines, to the annoyance of the teachers, and late that afternoon, as the Gryffindors were walking upstairs for Charms, one of them caught up with Harry.

'Oy, you! 'Arry Potter!' shouted a particularly grim-looking dwarf, elbowing people out of the way to get to Harry.

Hot all over at the thought of being given a Valentine in front of a queue of first years, which happened to include Ginny Weasley, Harry tried to escape. The dwarf, however, cut his way through the crowd by kicking people's shins, and reached him before he'd gone two paces.

'I've got a musical message to deliver to 'Arry Potter in person,' he said, twanging his harp in a threatening sort of way.

'Not here,' Harry hissed, trying to escape.

'Stay still!' grunted the dwarf, grabbing hold of Harry's bag and pulling him back.

'Let me go!' Harry snarled, tugging.

With a loud ripping noise, his bag split in two. His books, wand, parchment and quill spilled onto the floor and his ink bottle smashed over the lot.

Harry scrambled around, trying to pick it all up before the dwarf started singing, causing something of a hold-up in the corridor.

'What's going on here?' came the cold, drawling voice of Draco Malfoy. Harry started stuffing everything feverishly into his ripped bag, desperate to get away before Malfoy could hear his musical Valentine.

'What's all this commotion?' said another familiar voice, as Percy Weasley arrived.

Losing his head, Harry tried to make a run for it, but the dwarf seized him around the knees and brought him crashing to the floor.

'Right,' he said, sitting on Harry's ankles, 'here is your singing Valentine:

'*His eyes are as green as a fresh pickled toad,*
His hair is as dark as a blackboard.
I wish he was mine, he's really divine,
The hero who conquered the Dark Lord.'

Harry would have given all the gold in Gringotts to evaporate on the spot. Trying valiantly to laugh along with everyone else, he got up, his feet numb from the weight of the dwarf, as Percy Weasley did his best to disperse the crowd, some of whom were crying with mirth.

'Off you go, off you go, the bell rang five minutes ago, off to class, now,' he said, shooing some of the younger students away. '*And* you, Malfoy.'

Harry, glancing over, saw Malfoy stoop and snatch up something. Leering, he showed it to Crabbe and Goyle, and Harry realised that he'd got Riddle's diary.

'Give that back,' said Harry quietly.

'Wonder what Potter's written in this?' said Malfoy, who obviously hadn't noticed the year on the cover, and thought he had Harry's own diary. A hush fell over the onlookers. Ginny was staring from the diary to Harry, looking terrified.

'Hand it over, Malfoy,' said Percy sternly.

'When I've had a look,' said Malfoy, waving the diary tauntingly at Harry.

Percy said, 'As a school Prefect –', but Harry had lost his temper. He pulled out his wand and shouted, '*Expelliarmus!*' and just as Snape had disarmed Lockhart, so Malfoy found the diary shooting out of his hand into the air. Ron, grinning broadly, caught it.

'Harry!' said Percy loudly. 'No magic in the corridors. I'll have to report this, you know!'

But Harry didn't care, he'd got one over on Malfoy, and that was worth five points from Gryffindor any day. Malfoy was looking furious, and as Ginny passed him to enter her classroom, he yelled spitefully after her, 'I don't think Potter liked your Valentine much!'

Ginny covered her face with her hands and ran into class. Snarling, Ron pulled out his wand, too, but Harry pulled him away. Ron didn't need to spend the whole of Charms belching slugs.

It wasn't until they had reached Professor Flitwick's class that Harry noticed something rather odd about Riddle's diary. All his other books were drenched in scarlet ink. The diary, however, was as clean as it had been before the ink bottle had smashed all over it. He tried to point this out to Ron, but Ron was having trouble with his wand again; large purple bubbles were blossoming out of the end, and he wasn't much interested in anything else.

*

Harry went to bed before anyone else in his dormitory that night. This was partly because he didn't think he could stand Fred and George singing, '*His eyes are as green as a fresh pickled toad*', one more time, and partly because he wanted to examine Riddle's diary again, and knew that Ron thought he was wasting his time.

Harry sat on his four-poster and flicked through the blank pages, not one of which had a trace of scarlet ink on it. Then he pulled a new bottle out of his bedside cabinet, dipped his quill into it, and dropped a blot onto the first page of the diary.

The ink shone brightly on the paper for a second and then, as though it was being sucked into the page, vanished. Excited, Harry loaded up his quill a second time and wrote, 'My name is Harry Potter.'

The words shone momentarily on the page and they too sank without trace. Then, at last, something happened.

Oozing back out of the page, in his very own ink, came words Harry had never written.

'*Hello, Harry Potter. My name is Tom Riddle. How did you come by my diary?*'

These words, too, faded away, but not before Harry had started to scribble back.

'Someone tried to flush it down a toilet.'

He waited eagerly for Riddle's reply.

'*Lucky that I recorded my memories in some more lasting way than ink. But I always knew that there would be those who would not want this diary read.*'

'What do you mean?' Harry scrawled, blotting the page in his excitement.

'*I mean that this diary holds memories of terrible things. Things which were covered up. Things which happened at Hogwarts School of Witchcraft and Wizardry.*'

'That's where I am now,' Harry wrote quickly. 'I'm at Hogwarts, and horrible stuff's been happening. Do you know anything about the Chamber of Secrets?'

His heart was hammering. Riddle's reply came quickly, his writing becoming untidier, as though he was hurrying to tell all he knew.

'*Of course I know about the Chamber of Secrets. In my day, they told us it was a legend, that it did not exist. But this was a lie. In my fifth year, the Chamber was opened and the monster attacked several students, finally killing one. I caught the person who'd opened the Chamber and he was expelled. But the Headmaster, Professor Dippet, ashamed that such a thing had happened at Hogwarts, forbade me to tell the truth. A story was given out that the girl had died in a freak accident. They gave me a nice, shiny, engraved trophy for my trouble and warned me to keep my mouth shut. But I knew it could happen again. The monster lived on, and the one who had the power to release it was not imprisoned.*'

Harry nearly upset his ink bottle in his hurry to write back.

'It's happening again now. There have been three attacks and no one seems to know who's behind them. Who was it last time?'

'*I can show you, if you like,*' came Riddle's reply. '*You don't have to take my word for it. I can take you inside my memory of the night when I caught him.*'

Harry hesitated, his quill suspended over the diary. What did Riddle mean? How could he be taken inside somebody else's memory? He glanced nervously at the door to the dormitory, which was growing dark. When he looked back at the diary, he saw fresh words forming.

'*Let me show you.*'

Harry paused for a fraction of a second and then wrote two letters.

'OK.'

The pages of the diary began to blow as though caught in a high wind, stopping halfway through the month of June. Mouth hanging open, Harry saw that the little square for June the thirteenth seemed to have turned into a miniscule television screen. His hands trembling slightly, he raised the book to press his eye against the little window, and before he knew what was happening, he was tilting forwards; the window was widening, he felt his body leave his bed and he was pitched headfirst through the opening in the page, into a whirl of colour and shadow.

He felt his feet hit solid ground, and stood, shaking, as the blurred shapes around him came suddenly into focus.

He knew immediately where he was. This circular room with the sleeping portraits was Dumbledore's office – but it wasn't Dumbledore who was sitting behind the desk. A wizened, frail-looking wizard, bald except for a few wisps of white hair, was reading a letter by candlelight. Harry had never seen this man before.

'I'm sorry,' he said shakily, 'I didn't mean to butt in ...'

But the wizard didn't look up. He continued to read, frowning slightly. Harry drew nearer to his desk and stammered, 'Er – I'll just go, shall I?'

Still the wizard ignored him. He didn't seem even to have heard him. Thinking that the wizard might be deaf, Harry raised his voice.

'Sorry I disturbed you, I'll go now,' he half-shouted.

The wizard folded up the letter with a sigh, stood up, walked past Harry without glancing at him and went to draw the curtains at his window.

The sky outside the window was ruby-red; it seemed to be sunset. The wizard went back to the desk, sat down and twiddled his thumbs, watching the door.

Harry looked around the office. No Fawkes the phoenix; no whirring silver contraptions. This was Hogwarts as Riddle had known it, meaning that this unknown wizard was Headmaster, not Dumbledore, and he, Harry, was little more than a phantom, completely invisible to the people of fifty years ago.

There was a knock on the office door.

'Enter,' said the old wizard in a feeble voice.

A boy of about sixteen entered, taking off his pointed hat. A silver prefect's badge was glinting on his chest. He was much taller than Harry, but he, too, had jet black hair.

'Ah, Riddle,' said the Headmaster.

'You wanted to see me, Professor Dippet?' said Riddle. He looked nervous.

'Sit down,' said Dippet. 'I've just been reading the letter you sent me.'

'Oh,' said Riddle. He sat down, gripping his hands together very tightly.

'My dear boy,' said Dippet kindly, 'I cannot possibly let you stay at school over the summer. Surely you want to go home for the holidays?'

'No,' said Riddle at once, 'I'd much rather stay at Hogwarts than go back to that – to that –'

'You live in a Muggle orphanage during the holidays, I believe?' said Dippet curiously.

'Yes, sir,' said Riddle, reddening slightly.

'You are Muggle-born?'

'Half-blood, sir,' said Riddle. 'Muggle father, witch mother.'

'And are both your parents –?'

'My mother died just after I was born, sir. They told me at the orphanage she lived just long enough to name me: Tom after my father, Marvolo after my grandfather.'

Dippet clucked his tongue sympathetically.

'The thing is, Tom,' he sighed, 'special arrangements might have been made for you, but in the current circumstances ...'

'You mean all these attacks, sir?' said Riddle, and Harry's heart leapt, and he moved closer, scared of missing anything.

'Precisely,' said the headmaster. 'My dear boy, you must see how foolish it would be of me to allow you to remain at the castle when term ends. Particularly in the light of the recent tragedy ... the death of that poor little girl ... You will be safer by far at your orphanage. As a matter of fact, the Ministry of Magic is even now talking about closing the school. We are no nearer locating the – er – source of all this unpleasantness ...'

Riddle's eyes had widened.

'Sir – if the person was caught ... If it all stopped ...'

'What do you mean?' said Dippet, with a squeak in his voice, sitting up in his chair. 'Riddle, do you mean you know something about these attacks?'

'No, sir,' said Riddle quickly.

But Harry was sure it was the same sort of 'no' that he himself had given Dumbledore.

Dippet sank back, looking faintly disappointed.

'You may go, Tom ...'

Riddle slid off his chair and stumped out of the room. Harry followed him.

Down the moving spiral staircase they went, emerging next to the gargoyle in the darkening corridor. Riddle stopped, and so did Harry, watching him. Harry could tell that Riddle was doing some serious thinking. He was biting his lip, his forehead furrowed.

Then, as though he had suddenly reached a decision, he hurried off, Harry gliding noiselessly behind him. They didn't see another person until they reached the Entrance Hall, when a tall wizard with long, sweeping auburn hair and beard called to Riddle from the marble staircase.

'What are you doing, wandering around this late, Tom?'

Harry gaped at the wizard. He was none other than a fifty-year-younger Dumbledore.

'I had to see the Headmaster, sir,' said Riddle.

'Well, hurry off to bed,' said Dumbledore, giving Riddle exactly the kind of penetrating stare Harry knew so well. 'Best not to roam the corridors these days. Not since ...'

He sighed heavily, bade Riddle goodnight and strode off. Riddle watched him out of sight and then, moving quickly, headed straight down the stone steps to the dungeons, with Harry in hot pursuit.

But to Harry's disappointment, Riddle led him not into a hidden passageway or a secret tunnel but the very dungeon in which Harry had Potions with Snape. The torches hadn't been lit, and when Riddle pushed the door almost closed, Harry could only just see Riddle, standing stock-still by the door, watching the passage outside.

It felt to Harry that they were there for at least an hour. All he could see was the figure of Riddle at the door, staring through the crack, waiting like a statue. And just when Harry had stopped feeling expectant and tense, and started wishing he could return to the present, he heard something move beyond the door.

Someone was creeping along the passage. He heard whoever it was pass the dungeon where he and Riddle were hidden. Riddle, quiet as a shadow, edged through the door and followed, Harry tiptoeing behind him, forgetting that he couldn't be heard.

For perhaps five minutes they followed the footsteps, until Riddle stopped suddenly, his head inclined in the direction of new noises. Harry heard a door creak open, and then someone speaking in a hoarse whisper.

'C'mon ... gotta get yeh outta here ... c'mon now ... in the box ...'

There was something familiar about that voice.

Riddle suddenly jumped around the corner. Harry stepped out behind him. He could see the dark outline of a huge boy who was crouching in front of an open door, a very large box next to it.

'Evening, Rubeus,' said Riddle sharply.

The boy slammed the door shut and stood up.

'What yer doin' down here, Tom?'

Riddle stepped closer.

'It's all over,' he said. 'I'm going to have to turn you in, Rubeus. They're talking about closing Hogwarts if the attacks don't stop.'

'What d'yeh –'

'I don't think you meant to kill anyone. But monsters don't make good pets. I suppose you just let it out for exercise and –'

'It never killed no one!' said the large boy, backing against the closed door. From behind him, Harry could hear a funny rustling and clicking.

'Come on, Rubeus,' said Riddle, moving yet closer. 'The dead girl's parents will be here tomorrow. The least Hogwarts can do is make sure that the thing that killed their daughter is slaughtered ...'

'It wasn' him!' roared the boy, his voice echoing in the dark passage. 'He wouldn'! He never!'

'Stand aside,' said Riddle, drawing out his wand.

His spell lit the corridor with a sudden flaming light. The door behind the large boy flew open with such force it knocked him into the wall opposite. And out of it came something that made Harry let out a long, piercing scream no one but he seemed to hear.

A vast, low-slung, hairy body and a tangle of black legs; a gleam of many eyes and a pair of razor-sharp pincers – Riddle raised his wand again, but he was too late. The thing bowled him over as it scuttled away, tearing up the corridor and out of sight. Riddle scrambled to his feet, looking after it; he raised his wand, but the huge boy leapt on him, seized his wand and threw him back down, yelling, 'NOOOOOOO!'

The scene whirled, the darkness became complete, Harry felt himself falling and with a crash, he landed spread-eagled on his four-poster in the Gryffindor dormitory, Riddle's diary lying open on his stomach.

Before he had had time to regain his breath, the dormitory door opened and Ron came in.

'There you are,' he said.

Harry sat up. He was sweating and shaking.

'What's up?' said Ron, looking at him with concern.

'It was Hagrid, Ron. Hagrid opened the Chamber of Secrets fifty years ago.'

CHAPTER FOURTEEN

Cornelius Fudge

Harry, Ron and Hermione had always known that Hagrid had an unfortunate liking for large and monstrous creatures. During their first year at Hogwarts he had tried to raise a dragon in his little wooden house, and it would be a long time before they forgot the giant, three-headed dog he'd christened 'Fluffy'. And if, as a boy, Hagrid had heard that a monster was hidden somewhere in the castle, Harry was sure he'd have gone to any lengths for a glimpse of it. He'd probably thought it was a shame that the monster had been cooped up so long, and thought it deserved the chance to stretch its many legs; Harry could just imagine the thirteen-year-old Hagrid trying to fit a lead and collar on it. But he was equally certain that Hagrid would never have meant to kill anybody.

Harry half wished he hadn't found out how to work Riddle's diary. Again and again Ron and Hermione made him recount what he'd seen, until he was heartily sick of telling them and sick of the long, circular conversations that followed.

'Riddle *might* have got the wrong person,' said Hermione. 'Maybe it was some other monster that was attacking people ...'

'How many monsters d'you think this place can hold?' Ron asked dully.

'We always knew Hagrid had been expelled,' said Harry miserably. 'And the attacks must've stopped after Hagrid was kicked out. Otherwise, Riddle wouldn't have got his award.'

Ron tried a different tack.

'Riddle *does* sound like Percy – who asked him to grass on Hagrid, anyway?'

'But the monster had *killed* someone, Ron,' said Hermione.

'And Riddle was going to go back to some Muggle orphanage if they closed Hogwarts,' said Harry. 'I don't blame him for wanting to stay here ...'

Ron bit his lip, then said tentatively, 'You met Hagrid down Knockturn Alley, didn't you, Harry?'

'He was buying a flesh-eating slug repellant,' said Harry quickly.

The three of them fell silent. After a long pause, Hermione voiced the knottiest question of all in a hesitant voice: 'Do you think we should go and *ask* Hagrid about it all?'

'That'd be a cheerful visit,' said Ron. 'Hello, Hagrid, tell us, have you been setting anything mad and hairy loose in the castle lately?'

In the end, they decided that they wouldn't say anything to Hagrid unless there was another attack, and as more and more days went by with no whisper from the disembodied voice, they became hopeful that they would never need to talk to him about why he had been expelled. It was now nearly four months since Justin and Nearly Headless Nick had been Petrified, and nearly everybody seemed to think that the attacker, whoever it was, had retired for good. Peeves had finally got bored of his 'Oh Potter, you rotter' song, Ernie Macmillan asked Harry quite politely to pass a bucket of leaping toadstools in Herbology one day, and in March several of the Mandrakes threw a loud and raucous party in Greenhouse Three. This made Professor Sprout very happy.

'The moment they start trying to move into each other's pots, we'll know they're fully mature,' she told Harry. 'Then we'll be able to revive those poor people in the hospital wing.'

*

The second years were given something new to think about during their Easter holidays. The time had come to choose their subjects for the third year, a matter that Hermione, at least, took very seriously.

'It could affect our whole future,' she told Harry and Ron, as they pored over lists of new subjects, marking them with ticks.

'I just want to give up Potions,' said Harry.

'We can't,' said Ron gloomily. 'We keep all our old subjects, or I'd've ditched Defence Against the Dark Arts.'

'But that's very important!' said Hermione, shocked.

'Not the way Lockhart teaches it,' said Ron. 'I haven't learned anything from him except not to set pixies loose.'

Neville Longbottom had been sent letters from all the witches and wizards in his family, all giving him different advice on what to choose. Confused and worried, he sat reading the subject lists with his tongue poking out, asking people whether they thought Arithmancy sounded more difficult than the study of Ancient Runes. Dean Thomas, who, like Harry, had grown up with Muggles, ended up closing his eyes and jabbing his wand at the list, then picking the subjects it landed on. Hermione took nobody's advice but signed up for everything.

Harry smiled grimly to himself at the thought of what Uncle Vernon and Aunt Petunia would say if he tried to discuss his career in wizardry with them. Not that he didn't get any guidance: Percy Weasley was eager to share his experience.

'Depends where you want to *go*, Harry,' he said. 'It's never too early to think about the future, so I'd recommend Divination. People say Muggle Studies is a soft option, but I personally think wizards should have a thorough understanding of the non-magical community, particularly if they're thinking of working in close contact with them – look at my father, he has to deal with Muggle business all the time. My brother Charlie was always more of an outdoor type, so he went for Care of Magical Creatures. Play to your strengths, Harry.'

But the only thing Harry felt he was really good at was Quidditch. In the end, he chose the same new subjects as Ron, feeling that if he was rubbish at them, at least he'd have someone friendly to help him.

*

Gryffindor's next Quidditch match would be against Hufflepuff. Wood was insisting on team practices every night after dinner, so that Harry barely had time for anything but Quidditch and home-work. However, the training sessions were getting better, or at least drier, and the evening before Saturday's match, he went up to his dormitory to drop off his broomstick feeling Gryffindor's chances for the Quidditch cup had never been better.

But his cheerful mood didn't last long. At the top of the stairs to the dormitory, he met Neville Longbottom, who was looking frantic.

'Harry – I don't know who did it. I just found –'

Watching Harry fearfully, Neville pushed open the door.

The contents of Harry's trunk had been thrown everywhere. His cloak lay ripped on the floor. The bedclothes had been pulled off his four-poster and the drawer had been pulled out of his bedside cabinet, the contents strewn over the mattress.

Harry walked over to the bed, open-mouthed, treading on a few loose pages of *Travels with Trolls*.

As he and Neville pulled the blankets back onto his bed, Ron, Dean and Seamus came in. Dean swore loudly.

'What happened, Harry?'

'No idea,' said Harry. But Ron was examining Harry's robes. All the pockets were hanging out.

'Someone's been looking for something,' said Ron. 'Is there anything missing?'

Harry started to pick up all his things and throw them into his trunk. It was only as he threw the last of the Lockhart books back into it that he realised what wasn't there.

'Riddle's diary's gone,' he said in an undertone to Ron.

'*What?*'

Harry jerked his head towards the dormitory door and Ron followed him out. They hurried back down to the Gryffindor common room, which was half-empty, and joined Hermione, who was sitting alone, reading a book called *Ancient Runes Made Easy*.

Hermione looked aghast at the news.

'But – only a Gryffindor could have stolen – nobody else knows our password ...'

'Exactly,' said Harry.

*

They woke next day to brilliant sunshine and a light, refreshing breeze.

'Perfect Quidditch conditions!' said Wood enthusiastically at the Gryffindor table, loading the team's plates with scrambled eggs. 'Harry, buck up there, you need a decent breakfast.'

Harry had been staring down the packed Gryffindor table, wondering if the new owner of Riddle's diary was right in front of his eyes. Hermione had been urging him to report the robbery, but Harry didn't like the idea. He'd have to tell a teacher all about the diary and how many people knew why Hagrid had been expelled fifty years ago? He didn't want to be the one who brought it all up again.

As he left the Great Hall with Ron and Hermione to go and collect his Quidditch things, another, very serious worry was added to Harry's growing list. He had just set foot on the marble staircase when he heard it yet again: '*Kill this time ... let me rip ... tear ...*'

He shouted aloud and Ron and Hermione both jumped away

from him in alarm.

'The voice!' said Harry, looking over his shoulder. 'I just heard it again – didn't you?'

Ron shook his head, wide-eyed. Hermione, however, clapped a hand to her forehead.

'Harry – I think I've just understood something! I've got to go to the library!'

And she sprinted away, up the stairs.

'*What* does she understand?' said Harry distractedly, still looking around, trying to tell where the voice had come from.

'Loads more than I do,' said Ron, shaking his head.

'But why's she got to go to the library?'

'Because that's what Hermione does,' said Ron, shrugging. 'When in doubt, go to the library.'

Harry stood, irresolute, trying to catch the voice again, but people were now emerging from the Great Hall behind him, talking loudly, exiting through the front doors on their way to the Quidditch pitch.

'You'd better get moving,' said Ron. 'It's nearly eleven – the match.'

Harry raced up to Gryffindor tower, collected his Nimbus Two Thousand and joined the large crowd swarming across the grounds, but his mind was still in the castle, along with the bodiless voice, and as he pulled on his scarlet robes in the changing room, his only comfort was that everyone was now outside to watch the game.

The teams walked onto the pitch to tumultuous applause. Oliver Wood took off for a warm-up flight around the goal-posts, Madam Hooch released the balls. The Hufflepuffs, who played in canary yellow, were standing in a huddle, having a last minute discussion of tactics.

Harry was just mounting his broom when Professor McGonagall came half-marching, half-running across the pitch, carrying an enormous purple megaphone.

Harry's heart dropped like a stone.

'This match has been cancelled,' Professor McGonagall called through the megaphone, addressing the packed stadium. There were boos and shouts. Oliver Wood, looking devastated, landed and ran towards Professor McGonagall without getting off his broomstick.

'But Professor!' he shouted. 'We've got to play ... the cup ... *Gryffindor* ...'

Professor McGonagall ignored him and continued to shout through her megaphone: 'All students are to make their way back to the house common rooms, where their Heads of Houses will give them further information. As quickly as you can, please!'

Then she lowered the megaphone and beckoned Harry over to her.

'Potter, I think you'd better come with me ...'

Wondering how she could possibly suspect him this time, Harry saw Ron detach himself from the complaining crowd; he came running up to them as they set off towards the castle. To Harry's surprise, Professor McGonagall didn't object.

'Yes, perhaps you'd better come too, Weasley.'

Some of the students swarming around them were grumbling about the match being cancelled, others looked worried. Harry and Ron followed Professor McGonagall back into the school and up the marble staircase. But they weren't taken to anybody's office this time.

'This will be a bit of a shock,' said Professor McGonagall in a surprisingly gentle voice as they approached the hospital wing. 'There has been another attack ... another *double* attack.'

Harry's insides did a horrible somersault. Professor McGonagall pushed the door open and he and Ron entered.

Madam Pomfrey was bending over a fifth year girl with long curly hair. Harry recognised her as the Ravenclaw they'd accidentally asked for directions to the Slytherin common room. And on the bed next to her was –

'*Hermione!*' Ron groaned.

Hermione lay utterly still, her eyes open and glassy.

'They were found near the library,' said Professor McGonagall. 'I don't suppose either of you can explain this? It was on the floor next to them ...'

She was holding up a small, circular mirror.

Harry and Ron shook their heads, both staring at Hermione.

'I will escort you back to Gryffindor Tower,' said Professor McGonagall heavily. 'I need to address the students in any case.'

*

'All students will return to their house common rooms by six o'clock in the evening. No student is to leave the dormitories after that time. You will be escorted to each lesson by a teacher. No student is to use the bathroom unaccompanied by a teacher. All further Quidditch training and matches are to be postponed. There will be no more evening activities.'

The Gryffindors packed inside the common room listened to Professor McGonagall in silence. She rolled up the parchment from which she had been reading and said in a somewhat choked voice, 'I need hardly add that I have rarely been so distressed. It is likely that the school will be closed unless the culprit behind these attacks is caught. I would urge anyone who thinks they might know anything about them to come forward.'

She climbed somewhat awkwardly out of the portrait hole, and the Gryffindors began talking immediately.

'That's two Gryffindors down, not counting a Gryffindor ghost, one Ravenclaw and one Hufflepuff,' said the Weasley twins' friend Lee Jordan, counting on his fingers. 'Haven't *any* of the teachers noticed that the Slytherins are all safe? Isn't it *obvious* all this stuff's coming from Slytherin? The *heir* of Slytherin, the *monster* of Slytherin – why don't they just chuck all the Slytherins out?' he roared, to nods and scattered applause.

Percy Weasley was sitting in a chair behind Lee, but for once he didn't seem keen to make his views heard. He was looking pale and stunned.

'Percy's in shock,' George told Harry quietly. 'That Ravenclaw girl – Penelope Clearwater – she's a prefect. I don't think he thought the monster would dare attack a *prefect*.'

But Harry was only half-listening. He didn't seem to be able to get rid of the picture of Hermione, lying on the hospital bed as though carved out of stone. And if the culprit wasn't caught soon, he was looking at a lifetime back with the Dursleys. Tom Riddle had turned Hagrid in because he was faced with the prospect of a Muggle orphanage if the school closed. Harry now knew exactly how he had felt.

'What're we going to do?' said Ron quietly in Harry's ear. 'D'you think they suspect Hagrid?'

'We've got to go and talk to him,' said Harry, making up his mind. 'I can't believe it's him this time, but if he set the monster loose last time he'll know how to get inside the Chamber of Secrets, and that's a start.'

'But McGonagall said we've got to stay in our tower unless we're in class –'

'I think,' said Harry, more quietly still, 'it's time to get my dad's old cloak out again.'

*

Harry had inherited just one thing from his father: a long and silvery Invisibility Cloak. It was their only chance of sneaking out of the school to visit Hagrid without anyone knowing about it. They went to bed at the usual time, waited until Neville, Dean and Seamus had stopped discussing the Chamber of Secrets and finally fallen asleep, then got up, dressed again, and threw the cloak over themselves.

The journey through the dark and deserted castle corridors wasn't enjoyable. Harry, who had wandered the castle at night several times before, had never seen it so crowded after sunset. Teachers, prefects and ghosts were marching the corridors in pairs, staring around for any unusual activity. Their Invisibility Cloak didn't stop them making any noise, and there was a particularly tense moment when Ron stubbed his toe only yards from the spot where Snape stood standing guard. Thankfully, Snape sneezed at almost exactly the moment Ron swore. It was with relief that they reached the oak front doors and eased them open.

It was a clear, starry night. They hurried towards the lit windows of Hagrid's house, and pulled off the cloak only when they were right outside his front door.

Seconds after they had knocked, Hagrid flung it open. They found themselves face to face with him aiming a crossbow at them, Fang the boarhound barking loudly behind him.

'Oh,' he said, lowering the weapon and staring at them. 'What're you two doin' here?'

'What's that for?' said Harry, pointing at the crossbow as they stepped inside.

'Nothin' ... nothin',' Hagrid muttered. 'I've bin expectin' ... doesn' matter ... Sit down ... I'll make tea ...'

He hardly seemed to know what he was doing. He nearly extinguished the fire, spilling water from the kettle on it, and then smashed the teapot with a nervous jerk of his massive hand.

'Are you OK, Hagrid?' said Harry. 'Did you hear about Hermione?'

'Oh, I heard, all righ',' said Hagrid, a slight break in his voice.

He kept glancing nervously at the windows. He poured them both large mugs of boiling water (he had forgotten to add tea bags) and was just putting a slab of fruitcake on a plate, when there was a loud knock on the door.

Hagrid dropped the fruitcake. Harry and Ron exchanged panic-stricken looks, then threw the Invisibility Cloak back over themselves and retreated into a corner. Hagrid checked that they were hidden, seized his crossbow and flung open his door once more.

'Good evening, Hagrid.'

It was Dumbledore. He entered, looking deadly serious, and was followed by a second, very odd-looking man.

The stranger was a short, portly man with rumpled grey hair and an anxious expression. He was wearing a strange mixture of clothes: a pin-striped suit, a scarlet tie, a long black cloak and pointed purple boots. Under his arm he carried a lime-green bowler.

'That's Dad's boss!' Ron breathed. 'Cornelius Fudge, the Minister of Magic!'

Harry elbowed Ron hard to make him shut up.

Hagrid had gone pale and sweaty. He dropped into one of his chairs and looked from Dumbledore to Cornelius Fudge.

'Bad business, Hagrid,' said Fudge, in rather clipped tones. 'Very bad business. Had to come. Four attacks on Muggle-borns. Things've gone far enough. Ministry's got to act.'

'I never,' said Hagrid, looking imploringly at Dumbledore, 'you know I never, Professor Dumbledore, sir ...'

'I want it understood, Cornelius, that Hagrid has my full confidence,' said Dumbledore, frowning at Fudge.

'Look, Albus,' said Fudge, uncomfortably. 'Hagrid's record's against him. Ministry's got to do something – the school governors have been in touch.'

'Yet again, Cornelius, I tell you that taking Hagrid away will not help in the slightest,' said Dumbledore. His blue eyes were full of a fire Harry had never seen before.

'Look at it from my point of view,' said Fudge, fidgeting with his bowler. 'I'm under a lot of pressure. Got to be seen to be doing something. If it turns out it wasn't Hagrid, he'll be back and no more said. But I've got to take him. Got to. Wouldn't be doing my duty –'

'Take me?' said Hagrid, who was trembling. 'Take me where?'

'For a short stretch only,' said Fudge, not meeting Hagrid's eyes. 'Not a punishment, Hagrid, more a precaution. If someone else is caught, you'll be let out with a full apology ...'

'Not Azkaban?' croaked Hagrid.

Before Fudge could answer, there was another loud rap on the door.

Dumbledore answered it. It was Harry's turn for an elbow in the ribs: he'd let out an audible gasp.

Mr Lucius Malfoy strode into Hagrid's hut, swathed in a long black travelling cloak, smiling a cold and satisfied smile. Fang started to growl.

'Already here, Fudge,' he said approvingly. 'Good, good ...'

'What're you doin' here?' said Hagrid furiously. 'Get outta my house!'

'My dear man, please believe me, I have no pleasure at all in being inside your – er – d'you call this a house?' said Lucius Malfoy, sneering as he looked around the small cabin. 'I simply called at the school and was told that the Headmaster was here.'

'And what exactly did you want with me, Lucius?' said Dumbledore. He spoke politely, but the fire was still blazing in his blue eyes.

'*Dreadful* thing, Dumbledore,' said Mr Malfoy lazily, taking out a long roll of parchment, 'but the governors feel it's time for you to step aside. This is an Order of Suspension – you'll find all twelve signatures on it. I'm afraid we feel you're losing your touch. How many attacks have there been now? Two more this afternoon, wasn't it? At this rate, there'll be no Muggle-borns left at Hogwarts, and we all know what an *awful* loss that would be to the school.'

'Oh, now, see here, Lucius,' said Fudge, looking alarmed, 'Dumbledore suspended ... no, no ... last thing we want just now ...'

'The appointment – or suspension – of the Headmaster is a matter for the governors, Fudge,' said Mr Malfoy smoothly. 'And as Dumbledore has failed to stop these attacks ...'

'Now look, Lucius, if *Dumbledore* can't stop them –' said Fudge, whose upper lip was sweating now, 'I mean to say, who *can*?'

'That remains to be seen,' said Mr Malfoy, with a nasty smile. 'But as all twelve of us have voted ...'

Hagrid leapt to his feet, his shaggy black head grazing the ceiling.

'An' how many did yeh have ter threaten an' blackmail before they agreed, Malfoy, eh?' he roared.

'Dear, dear, you know, that temper of yours will lead you into trouble one of these days, Hagrid,' said Mr Malfoy. 'I would advise you not to shout at the Azkaban guards like that. They won't like it at all.'

'Yeh can' take Dumbledore!' yelled Hagrid, making Fang the boarhound cower and whimper in his basket. 'Take him away, an' the Muggle-borns won' stand a chance! There'll be killin's next!'

'Calm yourself, Hagrid,' said Dumbledore sharply. He looked at Lucius Malfoy.

'If the governors want my removal, Lucius, I shall of course step aside.'

'But –' stuttered Fudge.

'*No!*' growled Hagrid.

Dumbledore had not taken his bright blue eyes off Lucius Malfoy's cold grey ones.

'However,' said Dumbledore, speaking very slowly and clearly, so that none of them could miss a word, 'you will find that I will only *truly* have left this school when none here are loyal to me. You will also find that help will always be given at Hogwarts to those who ask for it.'

For a second, Harry was almost sure Dumbledore's eyes flickered towards the corner where he and Ron stood hidden.

'Admirable sentiments,' said Malfoy, bowing. 'We shall all miss your – er – highly individual way of running things, Albus, and only hope that your successor will manage to prevent any – ah – "*killin's*".'

He strode to the cabin door, opened it and bowed Dumbledore out. Fudge, fiddling with his bowler, waited for Hagrid to go ahead of him, but Hagrid stood his ground, took a deep breath and said carefully, 'If anyone wanted ter find out some *stuff,* all they'd have ter do would be ter follow the *spiders*. That'd lead 'em right! That's all I'm sayin'.'

Fudge stared at him in amazement.

'All right, I'm comin',' said Hagrid, pulling on his moleskin overcoat. But as he was about to follow Fudge through the door, he stopped again and said loudly, 'An' someone'll need ter feed Fang while I'm away.'

The door banged shut and Ron pulled the Invisibility Cloak off.

'We're in trouble now,' he said hoarsely. 'No Dumbledore. They might as well close the school tonight. There'll be an attack a day with him gone.'

Fang started howling, scratching at the closed door.

— CHAPTER FIFTEEN —

Aragog

Summer was creeping over the grounds around the castle; sky and lake alike turned periwinkle blue and flowers large as cabbages burst into bloom in the greenhouses. But with no Hagrid visible from the castle windows, striding the grounds with Fang at his heels, the scene didn't look right to Harry; no better, in fact, than the inside of the castle, where things were so horribly wrong.

Harry and Ron had tried to visit Hermione, but visitors were now barred from the hospital wing.

'We're taking no more chances,' Madam Pomfrey told them severely through a crack in the hospital door. 'No, I'm sorry, there's every chance the attacker might come back to finish these people off ...'

With Dumbledore gone, fear had spread as never before, so that the sun warming the castle walls outside seemed to stop at the mullioned windows. There was barely a face to be seen in the school that didn't look worried and tense, and any laughter that rang through the corridors sounded shrill and unnatural and was quickly stifled.

Harry constantly repeated Dumbledore's final words to himself. *'I will only truly have left this school when none here are loyal to me ... Help will always be given at Hogwarts to those who ask for it.'* But what good were these words? Who exactly were they supposed to ask for help, when everyone was just as confused and scared as they were?

Hagrid's hint about the spiders was far easier to understand – the trouble was, there didn't seem to be a single spider left in the castle to follow. Harry looked everywhere he went, helped (rather reluctantly) by Ron. They were hampered, of course, by the fact that they weren't allowed to wander off on their own, but had to move around the castle in a pack with the other Gryffindors. Most

of their fellow students seemed glad that they were being shep-
herded from class to class by teachers, but Harry found it very irk-
some.

One person, however, seemed to be thoroughly enjoying the
atmosphere of terror and suspicion. Draco Malfoy was strutting
around the school as though he had just been appointed Head
Boy. Harry didn't realise what he was so pleased about until the
Potions lesson about a fortnight after Dumbledore and Hagrid had
left, when, sitting right behind Malfoy, Harry overheard him gloat-
ing to Crabbe and Goyle.

'I always thought Father might be the one who got rid of
Dumbledore,' he said, not troubling to keep his voice down. 'I
told you he thinks Dumbledore's the worst Headmaster the
school's ever had. Maybe we'll get a decent Headmaster now.
Someone who won't *want* the Chamber of Secrets closed.
McGonagall won't last long, she's only filling in ...'

Snape swept past Harry, making no comment about Hermione's
empty seat and cauldron.

'Sir,' said Malfoy loudly. 'Sir, why don't *you* apply for the
Headmaster's job?'

'Now, now, Malfoy,' said Snape, though he couldn't suppress a
thin-lipped smile. 'Professor Dumbledore has only been suspended by the governors. I daresay he'll be back with us soon enough.'

'Yeah, right,' said Malfoy, smirking. 'I expect you'd have Father's
vote, sir, if you wanted to apply for the job. *I'll* tell Father you're
the best teacher here, sir ...'

Snape smirked as he swept off around the dungeon, fortunately
not spotting Seamus Finnigan, who was pretending to vomit into
his cauldron.

'I'm quite surprised the Mudbloods haven't all packed their
bags by now,' Malfoy went on. 'Bet you five Galleons the next one
dies. Pity it wasn't Granger ...'

The bell rang at that moment, which was lucky; at Malfoy's last
words, Ron had leapt off his stool, and in the scramble to collect
bags and books, his attempts to reach Malfoy went unnoticed.

'Let me at him,' Ron growled, as Harry and Dean hung onto his
arms. 'I don't care, I don't need my wand, I'm going to kill him
with my bare hands –'

'Hurry up, I've got to take you all to Herbology,' barked Snape
over the class's heads, and off they went, crocodile fashion, with

Harry, Ron and Dean bringing up the rear, Ron still trying to get loose. It was only safe to let go of him when Snape had seen them out of the castle, and they were making their way across the vegetable patch towards the greenhouses.

The Herbology class was very subdued; there were now two missing from their number, Justin and Hermione.

Professor Sprout set them all to work pruning the Abyssinian Shrivelfigs. Harry went to tip an armful of withered stalks onto the compost heap and found himself face to face with Ernie Macmillan. Ernie took a deep breath and said, very formally, 'I just want to say, Harry, that I'm sorry I ever suspected you. I know you'd never attack Hermione Granger, and I apologise for all the stuff I said. We're all in the same boat now, and, well –'

He held out a pudgy hand, and Harry shook it.

Ernie and his friend Hannah came to work at the same Shrivelfig as Harry and Ron.

'That Draco Malfoy character,' said Ernie, breaking off dead twigs, 'he seems very pleased about all this, doesn't he? D'you know, I think *he* might be Slytherin's heir.'

'That's clever of you,' said Ron, who didn't seem to have forgiven Ernie as readily as Harry.

'Do *you* think it's Malfoy, Harry?' Ernie asked.

'No,' said Harry, so firmly that Ernie and Hannah stared.

A second later, Harry spotted something that made him hit Ron over the hand with his pruning shears.

'*Ouch!* What're you –'

Harry was pointing at the ground a few feet away. Several large spiders were scurrying across the earth.

'Oh, yeah,' said Ron, trying, and failing, to look pleased. 'But we can't follow them now ...'

Ernie and Hannah were listening curiously.

Harry watched the spiders running away.

'Looks like they're heading for the forbidden forest ...'

And Ron looked even unhappier about that.

At the end of the lesson Professor Snape escorted the class to their Defence Against the Dark Arts lesson. Harry and Ron lagged behind the others so they could talk out of earshot.

'We'll have to use the Invisibility Cloak again,' Harry told Ron. 'We can take Fang with us. He's used to going into the forest with Hagrid, he might be some help.'

'Right,' said Ron, who was twirling his wand nervously in his fingers. 'Er – aren't there – aren't there supposed to be werewolves in the Forest?' he added, as they took their usual places at the back of Lockhart's classroom.

Preferring not to answer that question, Harry said, 'There are good things in there, too. The centaurs are all right, and the unicorns.'

Ron had never been into the Forbidden Forest before. Harry had entered it only once, and had hoped never to do so again.

Lockhart bounded into the room and the class stared at him. Every other teacher in the place was looking grimmer than usual, but Lockhart appeared nothing short of buoyant.

'Come now,' he cried, beaming around him, 'why all these long faces?'

People swapped exasperated looks, but nobody answered.

'Don't you people realise,' said Lockhart, speaking slowly, as though they were all a bit dim, 'the danger has passed! The culprit has been taken away.'

'Says who?' said Dean Thomas loudly.

'My dear young man, the Minister of Magic wouldn't have taken Hagrid if he hadn't been one hundred per cent sure that he was guilty,' said Lockhart, in the tone of someone explaining that one and one made two.

'Oh, yes he would,' said Ron, even more loudly than Dean.

'I flatter myself I know a *touch* more about Hagrid's arrest than you do, Mr Weasley,' said Lockhart in a self-satisfied tone.

Ron started to say that he didn't think so, somehow, but stopped in mid-sentence when Harry kicked him hard under the desk.

'We weren't there, remember?' Harry muttered.

But Lockhart's disgusting cheeriness, his hints that he had always thought Hagrid was no good, his confidence that the whole business was now at an end, irritated Harry so much that he yearned to throw *Gadding with Ghouls* right in Lockhart's stupid face. Instead he contented himself with scrawling a note to Ron: '*Let's do it tonight.*'

Ron read the message, swallowed hard and looked sideways at the empty seat usually filled by Hermione. The sight seemed to stiffen his resolve, and he nodded.

*

The Gryffindor common room was always very crowded these days, because from six o'clock onwards, the Gryffindors had nowhere else to go. They also had plenty to talk about, with the result that the common room often didn't empty until past midnight.

Harry went to get the Invisibility Cloak out of his trunk right after dinner, and spent the evening sitting on it, waiting for the room to clear. Fred and George challenged Harry and Ron to a few games of Exploding Snap and Ginny sat watching them, very subdued in Hermione's usual chair. Harry and Ron kept losing on purpose, trying to finish the games quickly, but even so, it was well past midnight when Fred, George and Ginny finally went to bed.

Harry and Ron waited for the distant sounds of two dormitory doors closing before seizing the cloak, throwing it over themselves, and climbing through the portrait hole.

It was another difficult journey through the castle, dodging all the teachers. At last they reached the Entrance Hall, slid back the lock on the oak front doors, squeezed between them, trying to stop any creaking, and stepped out into the moonlit grounds.

''Course,' said Ron abruptly, as they strode across the black grass, 'we might get to the forest and find there's nothing to follow. Those spiders might not've been going there at all. I know it looked like they were moving in that sort of general direction, but ...'

His voice trailed away hopefully.

They reached Hagrid's house, sad and sorry looking with its blank windows. When Harry pushed the door open, Fang went mad with joy at the sight of them. Worried he might wake everyone at the castle with his deep, booming barks, they hastily fed him treacle fudge from a tin on the mantelpiece, which glued his teeth together.

Harry left the Invisibility Cloak on Hagrid's table. There would be no need for it in the pitch dark forest.

'C'mon, Fang, we're going for a walk,' said Harry, patting his leg, and Fang bounded happily out of the house behind them, dashed to the edge of the forest and lifted his leg against a large sycamore tree.

Harry took out his wand, murmured, '*Lumos!*' and a tiny light appeared at the end of it, just enough to let them watch the path for signs of spiders.

'Good thinking,' said Ron. 'I'd light mine too, but you know – it'd probably blow up or something ...'

Harry tapped Ron on the shoulder, pointing at the grass. Two solitary spiders were hurrying away from the wandlight into the shade of the trees.

'OK,' Ron sighed, as though resigned to the worst, 'I'm ready. Let's go.'

So, with Fang scampering around them, sniffing tree roots and leaves, they entered the forest. By the glow of Harry's wand, they followed the steady trickle of spiders moving along the path. They walked for about twenty minutes, not speaking, listening hard for noises other than breaking twigs and rustling leaves. Then, when the trees had become thicker than ever, so that the stars overhead were no longer visible, and Harry's wand shone alone in the sea of dark, they saw their spider guides leaving the path.

Harry paused, trying to see where the spiders were going, but everything outside his little sphere of light was pitch black. He had never been this deep into the forest before. He could vividly remember Hagrid advising him not to leave the forest path last time he'd been in here. But Hagrid was miles away now, probably sitting in a cell in Azkaban, and he had also said to follow the spiders.

Something wet touched Harry's hand and he jumped backwards, crushing Ron's foot, but it was only Fang's nose.

'What d'you reckon?' Harry said to Ron, whose eyes he could just make out, reflecting the light from his wand.

'We've come this far,' said Ron.

So they followed the darting shadows of the spiders into the trees. They couldn't move very quickly now; there were tree roots and stumps in their way, barely visible in the near blackness. Harry could feel Fang's hot breath on his hand. More than once, they had to stop, so that Harry could crouch down and find the spiders in the wandlight.

They walked for what seemed like at least half an hour, their robes snagging on low-slung branches and brambles. After a while, they noticed that the ground seemed to be sloping downwards, though the trees were as thick as ever.

Then Fang suddenly let loose a great, echoing bark, making both Harry and Ron jump out of their skins.

'What?' said Ron loudly, looking around into the pitch dark, and gripping Harry's elbow very hard.

'There's something moving over there,' Harry breathed. 'Listen ... Sounds like something big.'

They listened. Some distance to their right, the something big was snapping branches as it carved a path through the trees.

'Oh no,' said Ron. 'Oh no, oh no, oh –'

'Shut up,' said Harry frantically. 'It'll hear you.'

'Hear *me*?' said Ron in an unnaturally high voice. 'It's already heard Fang!'

The darkness seemed to be pressing on their eyeballs as they stood, terrified, waiting. There was a strange rumbling noise and then silence.

'What d'you think it's doing?' said Harry.

'Probably getting ready to pounce,' said Ron.

They waited, shivering, hardly daring to move.

'D'you think it's gone?' Harry whispered.

'Dunno –'

Then, to their right, came a sudden blaze of light, so bright in the darkness that both of them flung up their hands to shield their eyes. Fang yelped and tried to run, but got lodged in a tangle of thorns and yelped even louder.

'Harry!' Ron shouted, his voice breaking with relief. 'Harry, it's our car!'

'*What?*'

'Come on!'

Harry blundered after Ron towards the light, stumbling and tripping, and a moment later they had emerged into a clearing.

Mr Weasley's car was standing, empty, in the middle of a circle of thick trees under a roof of dense branches, its headlamps ablaze. As Ron walked, open-mouthed, towards it, it moved slowly towards him, exactly like a large, turquoise dog greeting its owner.

'It's been here all the time!' said Ron delightedly, walking around the car. 'Look at it. The forest's turned it wild ...'

The wings of the car were scratched and smeared with mud. Apparently it had taken to trundling around the forest on its own. Fang didn't seem at all keen on it; he kept close to Harry, who could feel him quivering. His breathing slowing down again, Harry stuffed his wand back into his robes.

'And we thought it was going to attack us!' said Ron, leaning against the car and patting it. 'I wondered where it had gone!'

Harry squinted around on the floodlit ground for signs of more spiders, but they had all scuttled away from the glare of the head-lights.

'We've lost the trail,' he said. 'C'mon, let's go and find them.'

Ron didn't speak. He didn't move. His eyes were fixed on a point some ten feet above the forest floor, right behind Harry. His face was livid with terror.

Harry didn't even have time to turn around. There was a loud clicking noise and suddenly he felt something long and hairy seize him around the middle and lift him off the ground, so that he was hanging face down. Struggling, terrified, he heard more clicking, and saw Ron's legs leave the ground too, heard Fang whimpering and howling – next moment, he was being swept away into the dark trees.

Head hanging, Harry saw that what had hold of him was marching on six immensely long, hairy legs, the front two clutch-ing him tightly below a pair of shining black pincers. Behind him, he could hear another of the creatures, no doubt carrying Ron. They were moving into the very heart of the forest. Harry could hear Fang fighting to free himself from a third monster, whining loudly, but Harry couldn't have yelled even if he had wanted to; he seemed to have left his voice back with the car in the clearing.

He never knew how long he was in the creature's clutches; he only knew that the darkness suddenly lifted enough for him to see that the leaf-strewn ground was now swarming with spiders. Craning his neck sideways, he realised that they had reached the rim of a vast hollow, a hollow which had been cleared of trees, so that the stars shone brightly onto the worst scene he had ever clapped eyes upon.

Spiders. Not tiny spiders like those surging over the leaves below. Spiders the size of carthorses, eight-eyed, eight-legged, black, hairy, gigantic. The massive specimen that was carrying Harry made its way down the steep slope, towards a misty domed web in the very centre of the hollow, while its fellows closed in all around it, clicking their pincers excitedly at the sight of its load.

Harry fell to the ground on all fours as the spider released him. Ron and Fang thudded down next to him. Fang wasn't howling any more, but cowering silently on the spot. Ron looked exactly like Harry felt. His mouth was stretched wide in a kind of silent scream and his eyes were popping.

Harry suddenly realized that the spider which had dropped him was saying something. It had been hard to tell, because he clicked his pincers with every word he spoke.

'Aragog!' it called. 'Aragog!'

And from the middle of the misty domed web, a spider the size of a small elephant emerged, very slowly. There was grey in the black of his body and legs, and each of the eyes on his ugly, pincered head was milky white. He was blind.

'What is it?' he said, clicking his pincers rapidly.

'Men,' clicked the spider who had caught Harry.

'Is it Hagrid?' said Aragog, moving closer, his eight milky eyes wandering vaguely.

'Strangers,' clicked the spider who had brought Ron.

'Kill them,' clicked Aragog fretfully. 'I was sleeping ...'

'We're friends of Hagrid's,' Harry shouted. His heart seemed to have left his chest to pound in his throat.

Click, click, click went the pincers of the spiders all around the hollow.

Aragog paused.

'Hagrid has never sent men into our hollow before,' he said slowly.

'Hagrid's in trouble,' said Harry, breathing very fast. 'That's why we've come.'

'In trouble?' said the aged spider, and Harry thought he heard concern beneath the clicking pincers. 'But why has he sent you?'

Harry thought of getting to his feet, but decided against it; he didn't think his legs would support him. So he spoke from the ground, as calmly as he could.

'They think, up at the school, that Hagrid's been setting a – a – something on students. They've taken him to Azkaban.'

Aragog clicked his pincers furiously, and all around the hollow the sound was echoed by the crowd of spiders; it was like applause, except applause didn't usually make Harry feel sick with fear.

'But that was years ago,' said Aragog fretfully. 'Years and years ago. I remember it well. That's why they made him leave the school. They believed that *I* was the monster that dwells in what they call the Chamber of Secrets. They thought that Hagrid had opened the Chamber and set me free.'

'And you ... you didn't come from the Chamber of Secrets?' said Harry, who could feel cold sweat on his forehead.

'I!' said Aragog, clicking angrily. 'I was not born in the castle. I come from a distant land. A traveller gave me to Hagrid when I was an egg. Hagrid was only a boy, but he cared for me, hidden in a cupboard in the castle, feeding me on scraps from the table. Hagrid is my good friend, and a good man. When I was discovered, and blamed for the death of a girl, he protected me. I have lived here in the forest ever since, where Hagrid still visits me. He even found me a wife, Mosag, and you see how our family has grown, all through Hagrid's goodness ...'

Harry summoned what remained of his courage.

'So you never – never attacked anyone?'

'Never,' croaked the old spider. 'It would have been my instinct, but from respect of Hagrid, I never harmed a human. The body of the girl who was killed was discovered in a bathroom. I never saw any part of the castle but the cupboard in which I grew up. Our kind like the dark and the quiet ...'

'But then ... Do you know what *did* kill that girl?' said Harry. 'Because whatever it is, it's back and attacking people again –'

His words were drowned by a loud outbreak of clicking and the rustling of many long legs shifting angrily; large black shapes shifted all around him.

'The thing that lives in the castle,' said Aragog, 'is an ancient creature we spiders fear above all others. Well do I remember how I pleaded with Hagrid to let me go, when I sensed the beast moving about the school.'

'What is it?' said Harry urgently.

More loud clicking, more rustling; the spiders seemed to be closing in.

'We do not speak of it!' said Aragog fiercely. 'We do not name it! I never even told Hagrid the name of that dread creature, though he asked me, many times.'

Harry didn't want to press the subject, not with the spiders pressing closer on all sides. Aragog seemed to be tired of talking. He was backing slowly into his domed web, but his fellow spiders continued to inch slowly towards Harry and Ron.

'We'll just go, then,' Harry called desperately to Aragog, hearing leaves rustling behind him.

'Go?' said Aragog slowly. 'I think not ...'

'But – but –'

'My sons and daughters do not harm Hagrid, on my command. But I cannot deny them fresh meat, when it wanders so willingly into our midst. Goodbye, friend of Hagrid.'

Harry spun around. Feet away, towering above him, was a solid wall of spiders, clicking, their many eyes gleaming in their ugly black heads ...

Even as he reached for his wand, Harry knew it was no good, there were too many of them, but as he tried to stand, ready to die fighting, a loud, long note sounded, and a blaze of light flamed through the hollow.

Mr Weasley's car was thundering down the slope, headlamps glaring, its horn screeching, knocking spiders aside; several were thrown onto their backs, their endless legs waving in the air. The car screeched to a halt in front of Harry and Ron and the doors flew open.

'Get Fang!' Harry yelled, diving into the front seat; Ron seized the boarhound round the middle and threw him, yelping, into the back of the car. The doors slammed shut. Ron didn't touch the accelerator but the car didn't need him; the engine roared and they were off, hitting more spiders. They sped up the slope, out of the hollow, and they were soon crashing through the forest, branches whipping the windows as the car wound its way cleverly through the widest gaps, following a path it obviously knew.

Harry looked sideways at Ron. His mouth was still open in the silent scream, but his eyes weren't popping any more.

'Are you OK?'

Ron stared straight ahead, unable to speak.

They smashed their way through the undergrowth, Fang howling loudly in the back seat, and Harry saw the wing mirror snap off as they squeezed past a large oak. After ten noisy, rocky minutes, the trees thinned, and Harry could again see patches of sky.

The car stopped so suddenly that they were nearly thrown into the windscreen. They had reached the edge of the forest. Fang flung himself at the window in his anxiety to get out and when Harry opened the door, he shot off through the trees to Hagrid's house, tail between his legs. Harry got out too and after a minute or so, Ron seemed to regain the feeling in his limbs and followed, still stiff-necked and staring. Harry gave the car a grateful pat as it reversed back into the forest and disappeared from view.

Harry went back into Hagrid's cabin to get the Invisibility Cloak. Fang was trembling under a blanket in his basket. When Harry got outside again, he found Ron being violently sick in the pumpkin patch.

'Follow the spiders,' said Ron weakly, wiping his mouth on his sleeve. 'I'll never forgive Hagrid. We're lucky to be alive.'

'I bet he thought Aragog wouldn't hurt friends of his,' said Harry.

'That's exactly Hagrid's problem!' said Ron, thumping the wall of the cabin. 'He always thinks monsters aren't as bad as they're made out, and look where it's got him! A cell in Azkaban!' He was shivering uncontrollably now. 'What was the point of sending us in there? What have we found out, I'd like to know?'

'That Hagrid never opened the Chamber of Secrets,' said Harry, throwing the cloak over Ron and prodding him in the arm to make him walk. 'He was innocent.'

Ron gave a loud snort. Evidently, hatching Aragog out in a cupboard wasn't his idea of being innocent.

As the castle loomed nearer Harry twitched the cloak to make sure their feet were hidden, then pushed the creaking front doors ajar. They walked carefully back across the Entrance Hall and up the marble staircase, holding their breath as they passed corridors where watchful sentries were walking. At last they reached the safety of the Gryffindor common room, where the fire had burned itself into glowing ash. They took off the cloak and climbed the winding staircase to their dormitory.

Ron fell onto his bed without bothering to get undressed. Harry, however, didn't feel very sleepy. He sat on the edge of his four-poster, thinking hard about everything Aragog had said.

The creature that was lurking somewhere in the castle, he thought, sounded like a sort of monster Voldemort – even other monsters didn't want to name it. But he and Ron were no closer to finding out what it was, or how it Petrified its victims. Even Hagrid had never known what was in the Chamber of Secrets.

Harry swung his legs up onto his bed and leaned back against his pillows, watching the moon glinting at him through the tower window.

He couldn't see what else they could do. They had hit dead ends everywhere. Riddle had caught the wrong person, the heir of

Slytherin had got off, and no one could tell whether it was the same person, or a different one, who had opened the Chamber this time. There was nobody else to ask. Harry lay down, still thinking about what Aragog said.

He was becoming drowsy when what seemed like their very last hope occurred to him and he suddenly sat bolt upright.

'Ron,' he hissed through the dark. 'Ron!'

Ron woke with a yelp like Fang's, stared wildly around and saw Harry.

'Ron – that girl who died. Aragog said she was found in a bath-room,' said Harry, ignoring Neville's snuffling snores from the corner. 'What if she never left the bathroom? What if she's still there?'

Ron rubbed his eyes, frowning through the moonlight. And then he understood.

'You *don't* think – not *Moaning Myrtle*?'

CHAPTER SIXTEEN

The Chamber of Secrets

'All those times we were in that bathroom, and she was just three toilets away,' said Ron bitterly at breakfast next day, 'and we could've asked her, and now ...'

It had been hard enough trying to look for spiders. Escaping their teachers long enough to sneak into a girls' bathroom, the girls' bathroom, moreover, right next to the scene of the first attack, was going to be almost impossible.

But something happened in their first lesson, Transfiguration, which drove the Chamber of Secrets out of their minds for the first time in weeks. Ten minutes into the class, Professor McGonagall told them that their exams would start on the first of June, one week from today.

'*Exams?*' howled Seamus Finnigan. 'We're still getting *exams?*'

There was a loud bang behind Harry as Neville Longbottom's wand slipped, vanishing one of the legs on his desk. Professor McGonagall restored it with a wave of her own wand, and turned, frowning, to Seamus.

'The whole point of keeping the school open at this time is for you to receive your education,' she said sternly. 'The exams will therefore take place as usual, and I trust you are all revising hard.'

Revising hard! It had never occurred to Harry that there would be exams with the castle in this state. There was a great deal of mutinous muttering around the room, which made Professor McGonagall scowl even more darkly.

'Professor Dumbledore's instructions were to keep the school running as normally as possible,' she said. 'And that, I need hardly point out, means finding out how much you have learned this year.'

Harry looked down at the pair of white rabbits he was supposed to be turning into slippers. What had he learned so far this year? He couldn't seem to think of anything that would be useful in an exam.

Ron looked as though he'd been just been told he had to go and live in the Forbidden Forest.

'Can you imagine me taking exams with this?' he asked Harry, holding up his wand, which had just started whistling loudly.

*

Three days before their first exam, Professor McGonagall made another announcement at breakfast.

'I have good news,' she said, and the Great Hall, instead of falling silent, erupted.

'Dumbledore's coming back!' several people yelled joyfully.

'You've caught the Heir of Slytherin!' squealed a girl on the Ravenclaw table.

'Quidditch matches are back on!' roared Wood excitedly.

When the hubbub had subsided, Professor McGonagall said, 'Professor Sprout has informed me that the Mandrakes are ready for cutting at last. Tonight, we will be able to revive those people who have been Petrified. I need hardly remind you all that one of them may well be able to tell us who, or what, attacked them. I am hopeful that this dreadful year will end with our catching the culprit.'

There was an explosion of cheering. Harry looked over at the Slytherin table and wasn't at all surprised to see that Draco Malfoy hadn't joined in. Ron, however, was looking happier than he'd looked in days.

'It won't matter that we never asked Myrtle, then!' he said to Harry. 'Hermione'll probably have all the answers when they wake her up! Mind you, she'll go mad when she finds out we've got exams in three days' time. She hasn't revised. It might be kinder to leave her where she is till they're over.'

Just then, Ginny Weasley came over and sat down next to Ron. She looked tense and nervous, and Harry noticed that her hands were twisting in her lap.

'What's up?' said Ron, helping himself to more porridge.

Ginny didn't say anything, but glanced up and down the Gryffindor table with a scared look on her face that reminded Harry of someone, though he couldn't think who.

'Spit it out,' said Ron, watching her.

Harry suddenly realized who Ginny looked like. She was rock-

ing backwards and forwards slightly in her chair, exactly like
Dobby did when he was teetering on the edge of revealing forbidden information.

'I've got to tell you something,' Ginny mumbled, carefully not
looking at Harry.

'What is it?' said Harry.

Ginny looked as though she couldn't find the right words.

'*What?*' said Ron.

Ginny opened her mouth, but no sound came out. Harry
leaned forward and spoke quietly, so that only Ginny and Ron
could hear him.

'Is it something about the Chamber of Secrets? Have you seen
something? Someone acting oddly?'

Ginny drew a deep breath and at that precise moment, Percy
Weasley appeared, looking tired and wan.

'If you've finished eating, I'll take that seat, Ginny. I'm starving,
I've only just come off patrol duty.'

Ginny jumped up as though her chair had just been electrified,
gave Percy a fleeting, frightened look, and scarpered away. Percy
sat down and grabbed a mug from the centre of the table.

'Percy!' said Ron angrily. 'She was just about to tell us something important!'

Halfway through a gulp of tea, Percy choked.

'What sort of thing?' he said, coughing.

'I just asked her if she'd seen anything odd, and she started to
say –'

'Oh – that – that's nothing to do with the Chamber of Secrets,'
said Percy at once.

'How do you know?' said Ron, his eyebrows raised.

'Well, er, if you must know, Ginny, er, walked in on me the
other day when I was – well, never mind – the point is, she spotted me doing something and I, um, I asked her not to mention it
to anybody. I must say, I did think she'd keep her word. It's nothing, really, I'd just rather –'

Harry had never seen Percy look so uncomfortable.

'What were you doing, Percy?' said Ron, grinning. 'Go on, tell
us, we won't laugh.'

Percy didn't smile back.

'Pass me those rolls, Harry, I'm starving.'

*

Harry knew the whole mystery might be solved tomorrow without their help, but he wasn't about to pass up a chance to speak to Myrtle if it turned up – and to his delight it did, mid-morning, when they were being led to History of Magic by Gilderoy Lockhart.

Lockhart, who had so often assured them that all danger had passed, only to be proved wrong straightaway, was now wholeheartedly convinced that it was hardly worth the trouble to see them safely down the corridors. His hair wasn't as sleek as usual; it seemed he had been up most of the night, patrolling the fourth floor.

'Mark my words,' he said, ushering them around a corner, 'the first words out of those poor Petrified people's mouths will be "*it was Hagrid*." Frankly, I'm astounded Professor McGonagall thinks all these security measures are necessary.'

'I agree, sir,' said Harry, making Ron drop his books in surprise.

'Thank you, Harry,' said Lockhart graciously, while they waited for a long line of Hufflepuffs to pass. 'I mean, we teachers have quite enough to be getting on with, without walking students to classes and standing guard all night ...'

'That's right,' said Ron, catching on. 'Why don't you leave us here, sir, we've only got one more corridor to go.'

'You know, Weasley, I think I will,' said Lockhart. 'I really should go and prepare my next class.'

And he hurried off.

'Prepare his class,' Ron sneered after him. 'Gone to curl his hair, more like.'

They let the rest of the Gryffindors draw ahead of them, then darted down a side passage and hurried off towards Moaning Myrtle's bathroom. But just as they were congratulating each other on their brilliant scheme ...

'Potter! Weasley! What are you doing?'

It was Professor McGonagall, and her mouth was the thinnest of thin lines.

'We were – we were –' Ron stammered, 'we were going to – to go and see –'

'Hermione,' said Harry. Ron and Professor McGonagall both looked at him.

'We haven't seen her for ages, Professor,' Harry went on hurriedly, treading on Ron's foot, 'and we thought we'd sneak into the hospital wing, you know, and tell her the Mandrakes are nearly ready and, er, not to worry.'

Professor McGonagall was still staring at him, and for a moment, Harry thought she was going to explode, but when she spoke, it was in a strangely croaky voice.

'Of course,' she said, and Harry, amazed, saw a tear glistening in her beady eye. 'Of course, I realise this has all been hardest on the friends of those who have been ... I quite understand. Yes, Potter, of course you may visit Miss Granger. I will inform Professor Binns where you've gone. Tell Madam Pomfrey I have given my permission.'

Harry and Ron walked away, hardly daring to believe that they'd avoided detention. As they turned the corner, they distinctly heard Professor McGonagall blow her nose.

'That,' said Ron fervently, 'was the best story you've ever come up with.'

They had no choice now but to go to the hospital wing and tell Madam Pomfrey that they had Professor McGonagall's permission to visit Hermione.

Madam Pomfrey let them in, but reluctantly.

'There's just no *point* talking to a Petrified person,' she said, and they had to admit she was right when they'd taken their seats next to Hermione. It was plain that Hermione didn't have the faintest inkling that she had visitors, and that they might just as well tell her bedside cabinet not to worry for all the good it would do.

'Wonder if she did see the attacker, though?' said Ron, looking sadly at Hermione's rigid face. 'Because if he sneaked up on them all, no one'll ever know ...'

But Harry wasn't looking at Hermione's face. He was more interested in her right hand. It lay clenched on top of her blankets, and bending closer, he saw that a piece of paper was scrunched inside her fist.

Making sure that Madam Pomfrey was nowhere near, he pointed this out to Ron.

'Try and get it out,' Ron whispered, shifting his chair so that he blocked Harry from Madam Pomfrey's view.

It was no easy task. Hermione's hand was clamped so tightly around the paper that Harry was sure he was going to tear it. While Ron kept watch he tugged and twisted, and at last, after several tense minutes, the paper came free.

It was a page torn from a very old library book. Harry smoothed it out eagerly and Ron leant close to read it too.

Of the many fearsome beasts and monsters that roam our land, there is none more curious or more deadly than the Basilisk, known also as the King of Serpents. This snake, which may reach gigantic size, and live many hundreds of years, is born from a chicken's egg, hatched beneath a toad. Its methods of killing are most wondrous, for aside from its deadly and venomous fangs, the Basilisk has a murderous stare, and all who are fixed with the beam of its eye shall suffer instant death. Spiders flee before the Basilisk, for it is their mortal enemy, and the Basilisk flees only from the crowing of the rooster, which is fatal to it.

And beneath this, a single word had been written, in a hand Harry recognised as Hermione's. *Pipes.*

It was as though somebody had just flicked a light on in his brain.

'Ron,' he breathed, 'this is it. This is the answer. The monster in the Chamber's a *Basilisk* – a giant serpent! *That's* why I've been hearing that voice all over the place, and nobody else has heard it. It's because I understand Parseltongue ...'

Harry looked up at the beds around him.

'The Basilisk kills people by looking at them. But no one's died – because no one looked it straight in the eye. Colin saw it through his camera. The Basilisk burned up all the film inside it, but Colin just got Petrified. Justin ... Justin must've seen the Basilisk through Nearly Headless Nick! Nick got the full blast of it, but he couldn't die *again* ... and Hermione and that Ravenclaw prefect were found with a mirror next to them. Hermione had just realised the monster was a Basilisk. I bet you anything she warned the first person she met to look round corners with a mirror first! And that girl pulled out her mirror – and –'

Ron's jaw had dropped.

'And Mrs Norris?' he whispered eagerly.

Harry thought hard, picturing the scene on the night of Hallowe'en.

'The water ...' he said slowly, 'the flood from Moaning Myrtle's bathroom. I bet you Mrs Norris only saw the reflection ...'

He scanned the page in his hand eagerly. The more he looked at it, the more it made sense.

'*The crowing of the rooster is fatal to it!*' he read aloud. 'Hagrid's roosters were killed! The Heir of Slytherin didn't want one anywhere near the castle once the Chamber was opened! *Spiders flee before it!* It all fits!'

'But how's the Basilisk been getting around the place?' said Ron. 'A dirty great snake ... Someone would've seen ...'

Harry, however, pointed at the word Hermione had scribbled at the foot of the page.

'Pipes,' he said. 'Pipes ... Ron, it's been using the plumbing. I've been hearing that voice inside the walls ...'

Ron suddenly grabbed Harry's arm.

'The entrance to the Chamber of Secrets!' he said hoarsely. 'What if it's a bathroom? What if it's in –'

'– *Moaning Myrtle's bathroom*,' said Harry.

They sat there, excitement coursing through them, hardly able to believe it.

'This means,' said Harry, 'I can't be the only Parselmouth in the school. The Heir of Slytherin's one too. That's how they've been controlling the Basilisk.'

'What're we going to do?' said Ron, whose eyes were flashing. 'Shall we go straight to McGonagall?'

'Let's go to the staff room,' said Harry, jumping up. 'She'll be there in ten minutes, it's nearly break.'

They ran downstairs. Not wanting to be discovered hanging around in another corridor, they went straight into the deserted staff room. It was a large, panelled room full of dark wooden chairs. Harry and Ron paced around it, too excited to sit down.

But the bell to signal break never came.

Instead, echoing through the corridors came Professor McGonagall's voice, magically magnified.

'*All students to return to their house dormitories at once. All teachers return to the staff room. Immediately, please.*'

Harry wheeled around to stare at Ron.

'Not another attack? Not now?'

'What'll we do?' said Ron, aghast. 'Go back to the dormitory?'

'No,' said Harry, glancing around. There was an ugly sort of wardrobe to his left, full of the teachers' cloaks. 'In here. Let's hear what it's all about. Then we can tell them what we've found out.'

They hid themselves inside it, listening to the rumbling of hundreds of people moving overhead, and the staff room door banging open. From between the musty folds of the cloaks, they watched the teachers filtering into the room. Some of them were looking puzzled, others downright scared. Then Professor McGonagall arrived.

'It has happened,' she told the silent staff room. 'A student has been taken by the monster. Right into the Chamber itself.'

Professor Flitwick let out a squeal. Professor Sprout clapped her hands over her mouth. Snape gripped the back of a chair very hard and said, 'How can you be sure?'

'The Heir of Slytherin,' said Professor McGonagall, who was very white, 'left another message. Right underneath the first one. *Her skeleton will lie in the Chamber forever.*'

Professor Flitwick burst into tears.

'Who is it?' said Madam Hooch, who had sunk, weak-kneed into a chair. 'Which student?'

'Ginny Weasley,' said Professor McGonagall.

Harry felt Ron slide silently down onto the wardrobe floor beside him.

'We shall have to send all the students home tomorrow,' said Professor McGonagall. 'This is the end of Hogwarts. Dumbledore always said ...'

The staff room door banged open again. For one wild moment, Harry was sure it would be Dumbledore. But it was Lockhart, and he was beaming.

'So sorry – dozed off – what have I missed?'

He didn't seem to notice that the other teachers were looking at him with something remarkably like hatred. Snape stepped forward.

'Just the man,' he said. 'The very man. A girl has been snatched by the monster, Lockhart. Taken into the Chamber of Secrets itself. Your moment has come at last.'

Lockhart blanched.

'That's right, Gilderoy,' chipped in Professor Sprout. 'Weren't you saying just last night that you've known all along where the entrance to the Chamber of Secrets is?'

'I – well, I –' spluttered Lockhart.

'Yes, didn't you tell me you were sure you knew what was inside it?' piped up Professor Flitwick.

'D-did I? I don't recall ...'

'I certainly remember you saying you were sorry you hadn't had a crack at the monster before Hagrid was arrested,' said Snape. 'Didn't you say that the whole affair had been bungled, and that you should have been given a free rein from the first?'

Lockhart stared around at his stony-faced colleagues.

'I ... I really never ... You may have misunderstood ...'

'We'll leave it to you, then, Gilderoy,' said Professor McGonagall. 'Tonight will be an excellent time to do it. We'll make sure everyone's out of your way. You'll be able to tackle the monster all by youself. A free rein at last.'

Lockhart gazed desperately around him, but nobody came to the rescue. He didn't look remotely handsome any more. His lip was trembling, and in the absence of his usually toothy grin he looked weak-chinned and weedy.

'V-very well,' he said. 'I'll – I'll be in my office, getting – getting ready.'

And he left the room.

'Right,' said Professor McGonagall, whose nostrils were flared, 'that's got *him* out from under our feet. The Heads of Houses should go and inform their students what has happened. Tell them the Hogwarts Express will take them home first thing tomorrow. Will the rest of you please make sure no students have been left outside their dormitories.'

The teachers rose, and left one by one.

*

It was probably the worst day of Harry's entire life. He, Ron, Fred and George sat together in a corner of the Gryffindor common room, unable to say anything to each other. Percy wasn't there. He had gone to send an owl to Mr and Mrs Weasley, then shut himself up in his dormitory.

No afternoon ever lasted as long as that one, nor had Gryffindor tower ever been so crowded, yet so quiet. Near sunset, Fred and George went up to bed, unable to sit there any longer.

'She knew something, Harry,' said Ron, speaking for the first time since they had entered the wardrobe in the staff room. 'That's why she was taken. It wasn't some stupid thing about Percy at all. She'd found out something about the Chamber of Secrets. That must be why she was –' Ron rubbed his eyes frantically. 'I mean, she was a pure-blood. There can't be any other reason.'

Harry could see the sun sinking, blood-red, below the skyline. This was the worst he had ever felt. If only there was something they could do. Anything.

'Harry,' said Ron, 'd'you think there's any chance at all she's not – you know –'

Harry didn't know what to say. He couldn't see how Ginny could still be alive.

'D'you know what?' said Ron, 'I think we should go and see Lockhart. Tell him what we know. He's going to try and get into the Chamber. We can tell him where we think it is, and tell him it's a Basilisk in there.'

Because Harry couldn't think of anything else to do, and because he wanted to be doing something, he agreed. The Gryffindors around them were so miserable, and felt so sorry for the Weasleys, that nobody tried to stop them as they got up, crossed the room, and left through the portrait hole.

Darkness was falling as they walked down to Lockhart's office. There seemed to be a lot of activity going on inside it. They could hear scraping, thumps and hurried footsteps.

Harry knocked and there was a sudden silence from inside. Then the door opened the tiniest crack and they saw one of Lockhart's eyes peering through it.

'Oh ... Mr Potter ... Mr Weasley ...' he said, opening the door a mite wider. 'I'm rather busy at the moment. If you would be quick ...'

'Professor, we've got some information for you,' said Harry. 'We think it'll help you.'

'Er – well – it's not terribly –' The side of Lockhart's face that they could see looked very uncomfortable. 'I mean – well – all right.'

He opened the door and they entered.

His office had been almost completely stripped. Two large trunks stood open on the floor. Robes, jade-green, lilac, midnight blue, had been hastily folded into one of them; books were jumbled untidily into the other. The photographs that had covered the walls were now crammed into boxes on the desk.

'Are you going somewhere?' said Harry.

'Er, well, yes,' said Lockhart, ripping a life-size poster of himself from the back of the door as he spoke, and starting to roll it up. 'Urgent call ... unavoidable ... got to go ...'

'What about my sister?' said Ron jerkily.

'Well, as to that – most unfortunate,' said Lockhart, avoiding their eyes as he wrenched open a drawer and started emptying the contents into a bag. 'No one regrets more than I –'

'You're the Defence Against the Dark Arts teacher!' said Harry. 'You can't go now! Not with all the Dark stuff going on here!'

'Well, I must say ... when I took the job ...' Lockhart muttered, now piling socks on top of his robes, 'nothing in the job description ... didn't expect ...'

'You mean you're *running away*?' said Harry disbelievingly. 'After all that stuff you did in your books?'

'Books can be misleading,' said Lockhart delicately.

'You wrote them!' Harry shouted.

'My dear boy,' said Lockhart, straightening up and frowning at Harry. 'Do use your common sense. My books wouldn't have sold half as well if people didn't think *I'd* done all those things. No one wants to read about some ugly old Armenian warlock, even if he did save a village from werewolves. He'd look dreadful on the front cover. No dress sense at all. And the witch who banished the Bandon Banshee had a hare lip. I mean, come on ...'

'So you've just been taking credit for what a load of other people have done?' said Harry incredulously.

'Harry, Harry,' said Lockhart, shaking his head impatiently, 'it's not nearly as simple as that. There was work involved. I had to track these people down. Ask them exactly how they managed to do what they did. Then I had to put a Memory Charm on them so they wouldn't remember doing it. If there's one thing I pride myself on, it's my Memory Charms. No, it's been a lot of work, Harry. It's not all book-signings and publicity photos, you know. You want fame, you have to be prepared for a long hard slog.'

He banged the lids of his trunks shut and locked them.

'Let's see,' he said. 'I think that's everything. Yes. Only one thing left.'

He pulled out his wand and turned to them.

'Awfully sorry, boys, but I'll have to put a Memory Charm on you now. Can't have you blabbing my secrets all over the place. I'd never sell another book ...'

Harry reached his wand just in time. Lockhart had barely raised his, when Harry bellowed, '*Expelliarmus!*'

Lockhart was blasted backwards, falling over his trunk. His wand flew high into the air; Ron caught it, and flung it out of the open window.

'Shouldn't have let Professor Snape teach us that one,' said Harry furiously, kicking Lockhart's trunk aside. Lockhart was looking up at him, weedy once more. Harry was still pointing his wand at him.

'What d'you want me to do?' said Lockhart weakly. 'I don't know where the Chamber of Secrets is. There's nothing I can do.'

'You're in luck,' said Harry, forcing Lockhart to his feet at wandpoint. 'We think *we* know where it is. *And* what's inside it. Let's go.'

They marched Lockhart out of his office and down the nearest stairs, along the dark corridor where the messages shone on the wall, to the door of Moaning Myrtle's bathroom.

They sent Lockhart in first. Harry was pleased to see that he was shaking.

Moaning Myrtle was sitting on the cistern of the end toilet.

'Oh, it's you,' she said, when she saw Harry. 'What do you want this time?'

'To ask you how you died,' said Harry.

Myrtle's whole aspect changed at once. She looked as though she had never been asked such a flattering question.

'Ooooh, it was dreadful,' she said with relish. 'It happened right in here. I died in this very cubicle. I remember it so well. I'd hidden because Olive Hornby was teasing me about my glasses. The door was locked, and I was crying, and then I heard somebody come in. They said something funny. A different language, I think it must have been. Anyway, what really got me was that it was a *boy* speaking. So I unlocked the door, to tell him to go and use his own toilet, and then –' Myrtle swelled importantly, her face shining, 'I *died*.'

'How?' said Harry.

'No idea,' said Myrtle in hushed tones. 'I just remember seeing a pair of great big yellow eyes. My whole body sort of seized up, and then I was floating away ...' She looked dreamily at Harry. 'And then I came back again. I was determined to haunt Olive Hornby, you see. Oh, she was sorry she'd ever laughed at my glasses.'

'Where exactly did you see the eyes?' said Harry.

'Somewhere there,' said Myrtle, pointing vaguely towards the sink in front of her toilet.

Harry and Ron hurried over to it. Lockhart was standing well back, a look of utter terror on his face.

It looked like an ordinary sink. They examined every inch of it, inside and out, including the pipes below. And then Harry saw it: scratched on the side of one of the copper taps was a tiny snake.

'That tap's never worked,' said Myrtle brightly, as he tried to turn it.

'Harry,' said Ron, 'say something. Something in Parseltongue.'

'But –' Harry thought hard. The only times he'd ever managed to speak Parseltongue were when he'd been faced with a real snake. He stared hard at the tiny engraving, trying to imagine it was real.

'Open up,' he said.

He looked at Ron, who shook his head.

'English,' he said.

Harry looked back at the snake, willing himself to believe it was alive. If he moved his head, the candlelight made it look as though it was moving.

'Open up,' he said.

Except that the words weren't what he heard; a strange hissing had escaped him, and at once the tap glowed with a brilliant white light and began to spin. Next second, the sink began to move. The sink, in fact, sank, right out of sight, leaving a large pipe exposed, a pipe wide enough for a man to slide into.

Harry heard Ron gasp and looked up again. He had made up his mind what he was going to do.

'I'm going down there,' he said.

He couldn't not go, not now they had found the entrance to the Chamber, not if there was even the faintest, slimmest, wildest chance that Ginny might be alive.

'Me too,' said Ron.

There was a pause.

'Well, you hardly seem to need me,' said Lockhart, with a shadow of his old smile. 'I'll just –'

He put his hand on the door knob, but Ron and Harry both pointed their wands at him.

'You can go first,' Ron snarled.

White-faced and wandless, Lockhart approached the opening.

'Boys,' he said, his voice feeble, 'boys, what good will it do?'

Harry jabbed him in the back with his wand. Lockhart slid his legs into the pipe.

'I really don't think –' he started to say, but Ron gave him a push, and he slid out of sight. Harry followed quickly. He lowered himself slowly into the pipe, then let go.

It was like rushing down an endless, slimy, dark slide. He could see more pipes branching off in all directions, but none as large as theirs, which twisted and turned, sloping steeply downwards, and he knew that he was falling deeper below the school than even the dungeons. Behind him he could hear Ron, thudding slightly at the curves.

And then, just as he had begun to worry about what would happen when he hit the ground, the pipe levelled out, and he shot out of the end with a wet thud, landing on the damp floor of a dark stone tunnel, large enough to stand in. Lockhart was getting to his feet a little way away, covered in slime and white as a ghost. Harry stood aside as Ron came whizzing out of the pipe, too.

'We must be miles under the school,' said Harry, his voice echoing in the black tunnel.

'Under the lake, probably,' said Ron, squinting around at the dark, slimy walls.

All three of them turned to stare into the darkness ahead.

'*Lumos!*' Harry muttered to his wand and it lit again. 'C'mon,' he said to Ron and Lockhart, and off they went, their footsteps slapping loudly on the wet floor.

The tunnel was so dark that they could only see a little distance ahead. Their shadows on the wet walls looked monstrous in the wandlight.

'Remember,' Harry said quietly, as they walked cautiously forward, 'any sign of movement, close your eyes straight away ...'

But the tunnel was quiet as the grave, and the first unexpected sound they heard was a loud *crunch* as Ron stepped on what turned out to be a rat's skull. Harry lowered his wand to look at the floor and saw that it was littered with small animal bones. Trying very hard not to imagine what Ginny might look like if they found her, Harry led the way forward, round a dark bend in the tunnel.

'Harry, there's something up there ...' said Ron hoarsely,

grabbing Harry's shoulder.

They froze, watching. Harry could just see the outline of something huge and curved, lying right across the tunnel. It wasn't moving.

'Maybe it's asleep,' he breathed, glancing back at the other two. Lockhart's hands were pressed over his eyes. Harry turned back to look at the thing, his heart beating so fast it hurt.

Very slowly, his eyes as narrow as he could make them and still see, Harry edged forward, his wand held high.

The light slid over a gigantic snake skin, of a vivid, poisonous green, lying curled and empty across the tunnel floor. The creature that had shed it must have been twenty feet long at least.

'Blimey,' said Ron weakly.

There was a sudden movement behind them. Gilderoy Lockhart's knees had given way.

'Get up,' said Ron sharply, pointing his wand at Lockhart.

Lockhart got to his feet – then he dived at Ron, knocking him to the ground.

Harry jumped forward, but too late. Lockhart was straightening up, panting, Ron's wand in his hand and a gleaming smile back on his face.

'The adventure ends here, boys!' he said. 'I shall take a bit of this skin back up to the school, tell them I was too late to save the girl, and that you two *tragically* lost your minds at the sight of her mangled body. Say goodbye to your memories!'

He raised Ron's Spellotaped wand high over his head and yelled, '*Obliviate!*'

The wand exploded with the force of a small bomb. Harry flung his arms over his head and ran, slipping over the coils of snakeskin, out of the way of great chunks of tunnel ceiling which were thundering to the floor. Next moment, he was standing alone, gazing at a solid wall of broken rock.

'Ron!' he shouted. 'Are you OK? Ron!'

'I'm here!' came Ron's muffled voice from behind the rockfall. 'I'm OK. This git's not, though – he got blasted by the wand.'

There was a dull thud and a loud 'ow!' It sounded as though Ron had just kicked Lockhart in the shins.

'What now?' Ron's voice said, sounding desperate. 'We can't get through. It'll take ages ...'

Harry looked up at the tunnel ceiling. Huge cracks had

appeared in it. He had never tried to break apart anything as large as these rocks by magic, and now didn't seem a good moment to try – what if the whole tunnel caved in?

There was another thud and another 'ow!' from behind the rocks. They were wasting time. Ginny had already been in the Chamber of Secrets for hours. Harry knew there was only one thing to do.

'Wait there,' he called to Ron. 'Wait with Lockhart. I'll go on. If I'm not back in an hour ...'

There was a very pregnant pause.

'I'll try and shift some of this rock,' said Ron, who seemed to be trying to keep his voice steady. 'So you can – can get back through. And, Harry –'

'See you in a bit,' said Harry, trying to inject some confidence into his shaking voice.

And he set off alone past the giant snake skin.

Soon the distant noise of Ron straining to shift the rocks was gone. The tunnel turned and turned again. Every nerve in Harry's body was tingling unpleasantly. He wanted the tunnel to end, yet dreaded what he'd find when it did. And then, at last, as he crept around yet another bend, he saw a solid wall ahead on which two entwined serpents were carved, their eyes set with great, glinting emeralds.

Harry approached, his throat very dry. There was no need to pretend these stone snakes were real, their eyes looked strangely alive.

He could guess what he had to do. He cleared his throat, and the emerald eyes seemed to flicker.

'*Open*,' said Harry, in a low, faint hiss.

The serpents parted as the wall cracked open, the halves slid smoothly out of sight, and Harry, shaking from head to foot, walked inside.

CHAPTER SEVENTEEN

The Heir of Slytherin

He was standing at the end of a very long, dimly lit chamber. Towering stone pillars entwined with more carved serpents rose to support a ceiling lost in darkness, casting long black shadows through the odd, greenish gloom that filled the place.

His heart beating very fast, Harry stood listening to the chill silence. Could the Basilisk be lurking in a shadowy corner, behind a pillar? And where was Ginny?

He pulled out his wand and moved forward between the serpentine columns. Every careful footstep echoed loudly off the shadowy walls. He kept his eyes narrowed, ready to clamp them shut at the smallest sign of movement. The hollow eye sockets of the stone snakes seemed to be following him. More than once, with a jolt of the stomach, he thought he saw one stir.

Then, as he drew level with the last pair of pillars, a statue high as the Chamber itself loomed into view, standing against the back wall.

Harry had to crane his neck to look up into the giant face above: it was ancient and monkey-like, with a long thin beard that fell almost to the bottom of the wizard's sweeping stone robes, where two enormous grey feet stood on the smooth chamber floor. And between the feet, face down, lay a small, black-robed figure with flaming red hair.

'*Ginny!*' Harry muttered, sprinting to her and dropping to his knees. 'Ginny! Don't be dead! Please don't be dead!' He flung his wand aside, grabbed Ginny's shoulders and turned her over. Her face was white as marble, and as cold, yet her eyes were closed, so she wasn't Petrified. But then she must be ...

'Ginny, please wake up,' Harry muttered desperately, shaking her. Ginny's head lolled hopelessly from side to side.

'She won't wake,' said a soft voice.

Harry jumped and spun around on his knees.

A tall, black-haired boy was leaning against the nearest pillar, watching. He was strangely blurred around the edges, as though Harry was looking at him through a misted window. But there was no mistaking him.

'Tom – *Tom Riddle?*'

Riddle nodded, not taking his eyes off Harry's face.

'What d'you mean, she won't wake?' Harry said desperately. 'She's not – she's not –?'

'She's still alive,' said Riddle. 'But only just.'

Harry stared at him. Tom Riddle had been at Hogwarts fifty years ago, yet here he stood, a weird, misty light shining about him, not a day older than sixteen.

'Are you a ghost?' Harry said uncertainly.

'A memory,' said Riddle quietly. 'Preserved in a diary for fifty years.'

He pointed towards the floor near the statue's giant toes. Lying open there was the little black diary Harry had found in Moaning Myrtle's bathroom. For a second, Harry wondered how it had got there – but there were more pressing matters to deal with.

'You've got to help me, Tom,' Harry said, raising Ginny's head again. 'We've got to get her out of here. There's a Basilisk ... I don't know where it is, but it could be along any moment. Please, help me ...'

Riddle didn't move. Harry, sweating, managed to hoist Ginny half off the floor, and bent to pick up his wand again.

But his wand had gone.

'Did you see –?'

He looked up. Riddle was still watching him – twirling Harry's wand between his long fingers.

'Thanks,' said Harry, stretching out his hand for it.

A smile curled the corners of Riddle's mouth. He continued to stare at Harry, twirling the wand idly.

'Listen,' said Harry urgently, his knees sagging with Ginny's dead weight, '*we've got to go!* If the Basilisk comes ...'

'It won't come until it is called,' said Riddle calmly.

Harry lowered Ginny back onto the floor, unable to hold her up any longer.

'What d'you mean?' he said. 'Look, give me my wand, I might need it.'

Riddle's smile broadened.

'You won't be needing it,' he said.

Harry stared at him.

'What d'you mean, I won't be –?'

'I've waited a long time for this, Harry Potter,' said Riddle. 'For the chance to see you. To speak to you.'

'Look,' said Harry, losing patience, 'I don't think you get it. We're in the *Chamber of Secrets*. We can talk later.'

'We're going to talk now,' said Riddle, still smiling broadly, and he pocketed Harry's wand.

Harry stared at him. There was something very funny going on here.

'How did Ginny get like this?' he asked slowly.

'Well, that's an interesting question,' said Riddle pleasantly. 'And quite a long story. I suppose the real reason Ginny Weasley's like this is because she opened her heart and spilled all her secrets to an invisible stranger.'

'What are you talking about?' said Harry.

'The diary,' said Riddle. '*My* diary. Little Ginny's been writing in it for months and months, telling me all her pitiful worries and woes: how her brothers *tease* her, how she had to come to school with second-hand robes and books, how –' Riddle's eyes glinted '– how she didn't think famous, good, great Harry Potter would *ever* like her ...'

All the time he spoke, Riddle's eyes never left Harry's face. There was an almost hungry look in them.

'It's very *boring*, having to listen to the silly little troubles of an eleven-year-old girl,' he went on. 'But I was patient. I wrote back, I was sympathetic, I was kind. Ginny simply *loved* me. *No one's ever understood me like you, Tom ... I'm so glad I've got this diary to confide in ... It's like having a friend I can carry round in my pocket ...*'

Riddle laughed, a high, cold laugh that didn't suit him. It made the hairs stand up on the back of Harry's neck.

'If I say it myself, Harry, I've always been able to charm the people I needed. So Ginny poured out her soul to me, and her soul happened to be exactly what I wanted. I grew stronger and stronger on a diet of her deepest fears, her darkest secrets. I grew powerful, far more powerful than little Miss Weasley. Powerful enough to start feeding Miss Weasley a few of *my* secrets, to start pouring a little of *my* soul back into *her* ...'

'What d'you mean?' said Harry, whose mouth had gone very dry.

'Haven't you guessed yet, Harry Potter?' said Riddle softly. 'Ginny Weasley opened the Chamber of Secrets. She strangled the school roosters and daubed threatening messages on the walls. She set the Serpent of Slytherin on four Mudbloods, and the Squib's cat.'

'No,' Harry whispered.

'Yes,' said Riddle, calmly. 'Of course, she didn't *know* what she was doing at first. It was very amusing. I wish you could have seen her new diary entries ... Far more interesting, they became ... *Dear Tom,*' he recited, watching Harry's horrified face, '*I think I'm losing my memory. There are rooster feathers all over my robes and I don't know how they got there. Dear Tom, I can't remember what I did on the night of Hallowe'en, but a cat was attacked and I've got paint all down my front. Dear Tom, Percy keeps telling me I'm pale and I'm not myself. I think he suspects me ... There was another attack today and I don't know where I was. Tom, what am I going to do? I think I'm going mad ... I think I'm the one attacking everyone, Tom!*'

Harry's fists were clenched, the nails digging deep into his palms.

'It took a very long time for stupid little Ginny to stop trusting her diary,' said Riddle. 'But she finally became suspicious and tried to dispose of it. And that's where *you* came in, Harry. You found it, and I couldn't have been more delighted. Of all the people who could have picked it up, it was *you*, the very person I was most anxious to meet ...'

'And why did you want to meet me?' said Harry. Anger was coursing through him and it was an effort to keep his voice steady.

'Well, you see, Ginny told me all about you, Harry,' said Riddle. 'Your whole *fascinating* history.' His eyes roved over the lightning scar on Harry's forehead, and his expression grew hungrier. 'I knew I must find out more about you, talk to you, meet you if I could. So I decided to show you my famous capture of that great oaf, Hagrid, to gain your trust.'

'Hagrid's my friend,' said Harry, his voice now shaking. 'And you framed him, didn't you? I thought you made a mistake, but –'

Riddle laughed his high laugh again.

'It was my word against Hagrid's, Harry. Well, you can imagine how it looked to old Armando Dippet. On the one hand, Tom

Riddle, poor but brilliant, parentless but so *brave*, school prefect, model student; on the other hand, big, blundering Hagrid, in trouble every other week, trying to raise werewolf cubs under his bed, sneaking off to the forbidden forest to wrestle trolls. But I admit, even *I* was surprised how well the plan worked. I thought *someone* must realise that Hagrid couldn't possibly be the Heir of Slytherin. It had taken *me* five whole years to find out everything I could about the Chamber of Secrets and discover the secret entrance ... as though Hagrid had the brains, or the power!

'Only the Transfiguration teacher, Dumbledore, seemed to think Hagrid was innocent. He persuaded Dippet to keep Hagrid and train him as gamekeeper. Yes, I think Dumbledore might have guessed. Dumbledore never seemed to like me as much as the other teachers did ...'

'I bet Dumbledore saw right through you,' said Harry, his teeth gritted.

'Well, he certainly kept an annoyingly close watch on me after Hagrid was expelled,' said Riddle carelessly. 'I knew it wouldn't be safe to open the Chamber again while I was still at school. But I wasn't going to waste those long years I'd spent searching for it. I decided to leave behind a diary, preserving my sixteen-year-old self in its pages, so that one day, with luck, I would be able to lead another in my footsteps, and finish Salazar Slytherin's noble work.'

'Well, you haven't finished it,' said Harry triumphantly. 'No one's died this time, not even the cat. In a few hours the Mandrake Draught will be ready and everyone who was Petrified will be all right again.'

'Haven't I already told you,' said Riddle quietly, 'that killing Mudbloods doesn't matter to me any more? For many months now, my new target has been – *you.*'

Harry stared at him.

'Imagine how angry I was when the next time my diary was opened, it was Ginny who was writing to me, not you. She saw you with the diary, you see, and panicked. What if you found out how to work it, and I repeated all her secrets to you? What if, even worse, I told you who'd been strangling roosters? So the foolish little brat waited until your dormitory was deserted and stole it back. But I knew what I must do. It was clear to me that you were on the trail of Slytherin's heir. From everything Ginny had told me about you, I knew you would go to any lengths to solve the mystery – particularly if one of your best friends was attacked. And Ginny had told me the whole school was buzzing because you could speak Parseltongue ...

'So I made Ginny write her own farewell on the wall and come down here to wait. She struggled and cried and became *very* boring. But there isn't much life left in her: she put too much into the diary, into me. Enough to let me leave its pages at last. I have been waiting for you to appear since we arrived here. I knew you'd come. I have many questions for you, Harry Potter.'

'Like what?' Harry spat, fists still clenched.

'Well,' said Riddle, smiling pleasantly, 'how is it that a baby with no extraordinary magical talent managed to defeat the greatest wizard of all time? How did *you* escape with nothing but a scar, while Lord Voldemort's powers were destroyed?'

There was an odd red gleam in his hungry eyes now.

'Why do you care how I escaped?' said Harry slowly. 'Voldemort was after your time.'

'Voldemort,' said Riddle softly, 'is my past, present and future, Harry Potter ...'

He pulled Harry's wand from his pocket and began to trace it through the air, writing three shimmering words:

TOM MARVOLO RIDDLE

Then he waved the wand once, and the letters of his name re-arranged themselves:

I AM LORD VOLDEMORT

'You see?' he whispered. 'It was a name I was already using at Hogwarts, to my most intimate friends only, of course. You think I was going to use my filthy Muggle father's name forever? I, in whose veins runs the blood of Salazar Slytherin himself, through my mother's side? I, keep the name of a foul, common Muggle, who abandoned me even before I was born, just because he found out his wife was a witch? No, Harry. I fashioned myself a new name, a name I knew wizards everywhere would one day fear to speak, when I had become the greatest sorcerer in the world!'

Harry's brain seemed to have jammed. He stared numbly at Riddle, at the orphaned boy who had grown up to murder Harry's own parents, and so many others ... At last he forced himself to speak.

'You're not,' he said, his quiet voice full of hatred.

'Not what?' snapped Riddle.

'Not the greatest sorcerer in the world,' said Harry, breathing fast. 'Sorry to disappoint you, and all that, but the greatest wizard in the world is Albus Dumbledore. Everyone says so. Even when you were strong, you didn't dare try and take over at Hogwarts. Dumbledore saw through you when you were at school and he still frightens you now, wherever you're hiding these days.'

The smile had gone from Riddle's face, to be replaced by a very ugly look.

'Dumbledore's been driven out of this castle by the mere *memory* of me!' he hissed.

'He's not as gone as you might think!' Harry retorted. He was speaking at random, wanting to scare Riddle, wishing rather than believing it to be true.

Riddle opened his mouth, but froze.

Music was coming from somewhere. Riddle whirled around to stare down the empty chamber. The music was growing louder. It was eerie, spine-tingling, unearthly; it lifted the hair on Harry's scalp and made his heart feel as though it was swelling to twice its normal size. Then, as the music reached such a pitch that Harry felt it vibrating inside his own ribs, flames erupted at the top of the nearest pillar.

A crimson bird the size of a swan had appeared, piping its weird music to the vaulted ceiling. It had a glittering golden tail as long as a peacock's and gleaming golden talons, which were gripping a ragged bundle.

A second later, the bird was flying straight at Harry. It dropped the ragged thing it was carrying at his feet, then landed heavily on his shoulder. As it folded its great wings, Harry looked up and saw it had a long, sharp golden beak and beady black eyes.

The bird stopped singing. It sat still and warm next to Harry's cheek, gazing steadily at Riddle.

'That's a phoenix ...' said Riddle, staring shrewdly back at it.

'*Fawkes?*' Harry breathed, and he felt the bird's golden claws squeeze his shoulder gently.

'And *that* –' said Riddle, now eyeing the ragged thing that Fawkes had dropped, 'that's the old school Sorting Hat.'

So it was. Patched, frayed and dirty, the hat lay motionless at Harry's feet.

Riddle began to laugh again. He laughed so hard that the dark chamber rang with it, as though ten Riddles were laughing at once.

'This is what Dumbledore sends his defender! A songbird and an old hat! Do you feel brave, Harry Potter? Do you feel safe now?'

Harry didn't answer. He might not see what use Fawkes or the Sorting Hat were, but he was no longer alone, and he waited with mounting courage for Riddle to stop laughing.

'To business, Harry,' said Riddle, still smiling broadly. 'Twice – in *your* past, in *my* future – we have met. And twice I failed to kill you. *How did you survive?* Tell me everything. The longer you talk,' he added softly, 'the longer you stay alive.'

Harry was thinking fast, weighing his chances. Riddle had the wand. He, Harry, had Fawkes and the Sorting Hat, neither of which would be much good in a duel. It looked bad, all right. But the longer Riddle stood there, the more life was dwindling out of Ginny ... and in the meantime, Harry noticed suddenly, Riddle's outline was becoming clearer, more solid. If it had to be a fight between him and Riddle, better sooner than later.

'No one knows why you lost your powers when you attacked me,' said Harry abruptly. 'I don't know myself. But I know why you couldn't *kill* me. Because my mother died to save me. My common *Muggle-born* mother,' he added, shaking with suppressed rage. 'She stopped you killing me. And I've seen the real you, I saw you last year. You're a wreck. You're barely alive. That's where all your power got you. You're in hiding. You're ugly, you're foul!'

Riddle's face contorted. Then he forced it into an awful smile.

'So. Your mother died to save you. Yes, that's a powerful counter-charm. I can see now – there is nothing special about you, after all. I wondered, you see. Because there are strange likenesses between us, Harry Potter. Even you must have noticed. Both half-bloods, orphans, raised by Muggles. Probably the only two Parselmouths to come to Hogwarts since the great Slytherin himself. We even *look* something alike ... But after all, it was merely a lucky chance that saved you from me. That's all I wanted to know.'

Harry stood, tense, waiting for Riddle to raise his wand. But Riddle's twisted smile was widening again.

'Now, Harry, I'm going to teach you a little lesson. Let's match the powers of Lord Voldemort, Heir of Salazar Slytherin, against famous Harry Potter, and the best weapons Dumbledore can give him.'

He cast an amused eye over Fawkes and the Sorting Hat, then walked away. Harry, fear spreading up his numb legs, watched Riddle stop between the high pillars and look up into the stone face of Slytherin, high above him in the half-darkness. Riddle opened his mouth wide and hissed – but Harry understood what he was saying.

'*Speak to me, Slytherin, greatest of the Hogwarts Four.*'

Harry wheeled around to look up at the statue, Fawkes swaying on his shoulder.

Slytherin's gigantic stone face was moving. Horrorstruck, Harry saw his mouth opening, wider and wider, to make a huge black hole.

And something was stirring inside the statue's mouth. Something was slithering up from its depths.

Harry backed away until he hit the dark Chamber wall, and as he shut his eyes tight he felt Fawkes' wing sweep his cheek as he took flight. Harry wanted to shout, 'Don't leave me!' but what chance did a phoenix have against the king of serpents?

Something huge hit the stone floor of the chamber, Harry felt it shudder. He knew what was happening, he could sense it, could almost see the giant serpent uncoiling itself from Slytherin's mouth. Then he heard Riddle's hissing voice: '*Kill him.*'

The Basilisk was moving towards Harry, he could hear its heavy body slithering ponderously across the dusty floor. Eyes still tightly shut, Harry began to run blindly sideways, his hands outstretched, feeling his way. Riddle was laughing ...

Harry tripped. He fell hard onto the stone and tasted blood. The serpent was barely feet from him, he could hear it coming.

There was a loud, explosive spitting sound right above him and then something heavy hit Harry so hard that he was smashed against the wall. Waiting for fangs to sink through his body he heard more mad hissing, something thrashing wildly off the pillars.

He couldn't help it. He opened his eyes wide enough to squint at what was going on.

The enormous serpent, bright, poisonous green, thick as an oak trunk, had raised itself high in the air and its great blunt head was weaving drunkenly between the pillars. As Harry trembled, ready to close his eyes if it turned, he saw what had distracted the snake.

Fawkes was soaring around its head, and the Basilisk was

snapping furiously at him with fangs long and thin as sabres.

Fawkes dived. His long golden beak sank out of sight and a sudden shower of dark blood spattered the floor. The snake's tail thrashed, narrowly missing Harry, and before Harry could shut his eyes, it turned. Harry looked straight into its face, and saw that its eyes, both its great bulbous yellow eyes, had been punctured by the phoenix; blood was streaming to the floor and the snake was spitting in agony.

'No!' Harry heard Riddle screaming. 'Leave the bird! Leave the bird! The boy is behind you! You can still smell him! Kill him!'

The blinded serpent swayed, confused, still deadly. Fawkes was circling its head, piping his eerie song, jabbing here and there at the Basilisk's scaly nose as the blood poured from its ruined eyes.

'Help me, help me,' Harry muttered wildly, 'someone, anyone!'

The snake's tail whipped across the floor again. Harry ducked. Something soft hit his face.

The Basilisk had swept the Sorting Hat into Harry's arms. Harry seized it. It was all he had left, his only chance. He rammed it onto his head and threw himself flat onto the floor as the Basilisk's tail swung over him again.

'Help me ... help me ...' Harry thought, his eyes screwed tight under the hat. 'Please help me!'

There was no answering voice. Instead, the hat contracted, as though an invisible hand was squeezing it very tightly.

Something very hard and heavy thudded onto the top of Harry's head, almost knocking him out. Stars winking in front of his eyes, he grabbed the top of the hat to pull it off and felt something long and hard beneath it.

A gleaming silver sword had appeared inside the hat, its handle glittering with rubies the size of eggs.

'Kill the boy! Leave the bird! The boy is behind you! Sniff – smell him!'

Harry was on his feet, ready. The Basilisk's head was falling, its body coiling around, hitting pillars as it twisted to face him. He could see the vast, bloody eye sockets, see the mouth stretching wide, wide enough to swallow him whole, lined with fangs long as his sword, thin, glittering, venomous ...

It lunged blindly. Harry dodged and it hit the Chamber wall. It lunged again, and its forked tongue lashed Harry's side. He raised the sword in both his hands.

The Basilisk lunged again, and this time its aim was true. Harry threw his whole weight behind the sword and drove it to the hilt into the roof of the serpent's mouth.

But as warm blood drenched Harry's arms, he felt a searing pain just above his elbow. One long, poisonous fang was sinking deeper and deeper into his arm and it splintered as the Basilisk keeled over sideways and fell, twitching, to the floor.

Harry slid down the wall. He gripped the fang that was spreading poison through his body and wrenched it out of his arm. But he knew it was too late. White hot pain was spreading slowly and steadily from the wound. Even as he dropped the fang and watched his own blood soaking his robes, his vision went foggy. The chamber was dissolving in a whirl of dull colour.

A patch of scarlet swam past and Harry heard a soft clatter of claws beside him.

'Fawkes,' said Harry thickly. 'You were brilliant, Fawkes ...' He felt the bird lay its beautiful head on the spot where the serpent's fang had pierced him.

He could hear echoing footsteps and then a dark shadow moved in front of him.

'You're dead, Harry Potter,' said Riddle's voice above him. 'Dead. Even Dumbledore's bird knows it. Do you see what he's doing, Potter? He's crying.'

Harry blinked. Fawke's head slid in and out of focus. Thick, pearly tears were trickling down the glossy feathers.

'I'm going to sit here and watch you die, Harry Potter. Take your time. I'm in no hurry.'

Harry felt drowsy. Everything around him seemed to be spinning.

'So ends the famous Harry Potter,' said Riddle's distant voice. 'Alone in the Chamber of Secrets, forsaken by his friends, defeated at last by the Dark Lord he so unwisely challenged. You'll be back with your dear Mudblood mother soon, Harry ... She bought you twelve years of borrowed time ... but Lord Voldemort got you in the end, as you knew he must.'

If this is dying, thought Harry, it's not so bad. Even the pain was leaving him ...

But was this dying? Instead of going black, the Chamber seemed to be coming back into focus. Harry gave his head a little shake and there was Fawkes, still resting his head on Harry's arm.

A pearly patch of tears was shining all around the wound – except that there *was* no wound.

'Get away, bird,' said Riddle's voice suddenly. 'Get away from him. I said, *get away!*'

Harry raised his head. Riddle was pointing Harry's wand at Fawkes; there was a bang like a gun and Fawkes took flight again in a whirl of gold and scarlet.

'Phoenix tears ...' said Riddle quietly, staring at Harry's arm. 'Of course ... healing powers ... I forgot ...'

He looked into Harry's face. 'But it makes no difference. In fact, I prefer it this way. Just you and me, Harry Potter ... you and me ...'

He raised the wand.

Then, in a rush of wings, Fawkes soared back overhead and something fell into Harry's lap – *the diary*.

For a split second, both Harry and Riddle, wand still raised, stared at it. Then, without thinking, without considering, as though he had meant to do it all along, Harry seized the Basilisk fang on the floor next to him and plunged it straight into the heart of the book.

There was a long, dreadful, piercing scream. Ink spurted out of the diary in torrents, streaming over Harry's hands, flooding the floor. Riddle was writhing and twisting, screaming and flailing and then ...

He had gone. Harry's wand fell to the floor with a clatter and there was silence. Silence except for the steady *drip drip* of ink still oozing from the diary. The Basilisk venom had burned a sizzling hole right through it.

Shaking all over, Harry pulled himself up. His head was spinning as though he'd just travelled miles by Floo powder. Slowly, he gathered together his wand and the Sorting Hat, and, with a huge tug, retrieved the glittering sword from the roof of the Basilisk's mouth.

Then came a faint moan from the end of the Chamber. Ginny was stirring. As Harry hurried towards her, she sat up. Her bemused eyes travelled from the huge form of the dead Basilisk, over Harry, in his blood-soaked robes, then to the diary in his hand. She drew a great, shuddering gasp and tears began to pour down her face.

'Harry – oh, Harry – I tried to tell you at b-breakfast, but I c-*couldn't* say it in front of Percy. It was *me*, Harry – but I – I s-swear I d-didn't mean to – R-Riddle made me, he t-took me over – and – *how* did you kill that – that thing? W-where's Riddle? The last thing I r-remember is him coming out of the diary –'

'It's all right,' said Harry, holding up the diary, and showing Ginny the fang hole, 'Riddle's finished. Look! Him *and* the Basilisk. C'mon, Ginny, let's get out of here –'

'I'm going to be expelled!' Ginny wept, as Harry helped her awkwardly to her feet. 'I've looked forward to coming to Hogwarts ever since B-Bill came and n-now I'll have to leave and – *w-what'll Mum and Dad say?*'

Fawkes was waiting for them, hovering in the Chamber entrance. Harry urged Ginny forward; they stepped over the motionless coils of the dead Basilisk, through the echoing gloom and back into the tunnel. Harry heard the stone doors close behind them with a soft hiss.

After a few minutes' progress up the dark tunnel, a distant sound of slowly shifting rock reached Harry's ears.

'Ron!' Harry yelled, speeding up. 'Ginny's OK! I've got her!'

He heard Ron give a strangled cheer and they turned the next bend to see his eager face staring through the sizeable gap he had managed to make in the rock fall.

'*Ginny!*' Ron thrust an arm through the gap in the rock to pull her through first. 'You're alive! I don't believe it! What happened?'

He tried to hug her but Ginny held him off, sobbing.

'But you're okay, Ginny,' said Ron, beaming at her. 'It's over now, it's – where did that bird come from?'

Fawkes had swooped through the gap after Ginny.

'He's Dumbledore's,' said Harry, squeezing through himself.

'And how come you've got a *sword*?' said Ron, gaping at the glittering weapon in Harry's hand.

'I'll explain when we get out of here,' said Harry, with a side-ways glance at Ginny.

'But –'

'Later,' Harry said quickly. He didn't think it was a good idea to tell Ron yet who'd been opening the Chamber, not in front of Ginny, anyway. 'Where's Lockhart?'

'Back there,' said Ron, grinning and jerking his head up the tunnel towards the pipe. 'He's in a bad way. Come and see.'

Led by Fawkes, whose wide scarlet wings emitted a soft golden glow in the darkness, they walked all the way back to the mouth of the pipe. Gilderoy Lockhart was sitting there, humming placid-ly to himself.

'His memory's gone,' said Ron. 'The Memory Charm backfired. Hit him instead of us. Hasn't got a clue who he is, or where he is, or who we are. I told him to come and wait here. He's a danger to himself.'

Lockhart peered good-naturedly up at them all.

'Hello,' he said. 'Odd sort of place, this, isn't it? Do you live here?'

'No,' said Ron, raising his eyebrows at Harry.

Harry bent down and looked up the long, dark pipe.

'Have you thought how we're going to get back up this?' he said to Ron.

Ron shook his head, but Fawkes the phoenix had swooped past Harry and was now fluttering in front of him, his beady eyes bright in the dark. He was waving his long golden tail feathers. Harry looked uncertainly at him.

'He looks like he wants you to grab hold ...' said Ron, looking perplexed. 'But you're much too heavy for a bird to pull up there.'

'Fawkes,' said Harry, 'isn't an ordinary bird.' He turned quickly to the others. 'We've got to hold on to each other. Ginny, grab Ron's hand. Professor Lockhart –'

'He means you,' said Ron sharply to Lockhart.

'You hold Ginny's other hand.'

Harry tucked the sword and the Sorting Hat into his belt, Ron took hold of the back of Harry's robes, and Harry reached out and took hold of Fawkes' strangely hot tail feathers.

An extraordinary lightness seemed to spread through his whole body and next second, with a whoosh, they were flying upwards through the pipe. Harry could hear Lockhart dangling below him, saying, 'Amazing! Amazing! This is just like magic!' The chill air was whipping through Harry's hair, and before he'd stopped enjoying the ride, it was over – all four of them were hitting the wet floor of Moaning Myrtle's floor, and as Lockhart straightened his hat, the sink that hid the pipe was sliding back into place.

Myrtle goggled at them.

'You're alive,' she said blankly to Harry.

'There's no need to sound so disappointed,' he said grimly, wiping flecks of blood and slime off his glasses.

'Oh, well ... I'd just been thinking. If you had died, you'd have been welcome to share my toilet,' said Myrtle, blushing silver.

'Urgh!' said Ron, as they left the bathroom for the dark, deserted corridor outside. 'Harry! I think Myrtle's got *fond* of you! You've got competition, Ginny!'

But tears were still flooding silently down Ginny's face.

'Where now?' said Ron, with an anxious look at Ginny. Harry pointed.

Fawkes was leading the way, glowing gold along the corridor. They strode after him, and moments later, found themselves outside Professor McGonagall's office.

Harry knocked and pushed the door open.

CHAPTER EIGHTEEN

Dobby's Reward

For a moment, there was silence as Harry, Ron, Ginny and Lockhart stood in the doorway, covered in muck and slime and (in Harry's case) blood. Then there was a scream.

'*Ginny!*'

It was Mrs Weasley, who had been sitting crying in front of the fire. She leapt to her feet, closely followed by Mr Weasley, and both of them flung themselves on their daughter.

Harry, however, was looking past them. Professor Dumbledore was standing by the mantelpiece, beaming, next to Professor McGonagall, who was taking great, steadying gasps, clutching her chest. Fawkes went whooshing past Harry's ear and settled on Dumbledore's shoulder, just as Harry found himself and Ron being swept into Mrs Weasley's tight embrace.

'You saved her! You saved her! *How* did you do it?'

'I think we'd all like to know that,' said Professor McGonagall weakly.

Mrs Weasley let go of Harry, who hesitated for a moment, then walked over to the desk and laid upon it the Sorting Hat, the ruby-encrusted sword and what remained of Riddle's diary.

Then he started telling them everything. For nearly a quarter of an hour he spoke into the rapt silence: he told them about hearing the disembodied voice, how Hermione had finally realized that he was hearing a Basilisk in the pipes; how he and Ron had followed the spiders into the forest, that Aragog had told them where the last victim of the Basilisk had died; how he had guessed that Moaning Myrtle had been the victim, and that the entrance to the Chamber of Secrets might be in her bathroom ...

'Very well,' Professor McGonagall prompted him, as he paused, 'so you found out where the entrance was – breaking a hundred school rules into pieces along the way, I might add – but how on *earth* did you all get out of there alive, Potter?'

So Harry, his voice now growing hoarse from all this talking, told them about Fawkes' timely arrival and about the Sorting Hat giving him the sword. But then he faltered. He had so far avoided mentioning Riddle's diary – or Ginny. She was standing with her head against Mrs Weasley's shoulder, and tears were still coursing silently down her cheeks. What if they expelled her? Harry thought in panic. Riddle's diary didn't work any more ... How could they prove it had been he who'd made her do it all?

Instinctively, Harry looked at Dumbledore, who smiled faintly, the firelight glancing off his half-moon spectacles.

'What interests *me* most,' said Dumbledore gently, 'is how Lord Voldemort managed to enchant Ginny, when my sources tell me he is currently in hiding in the forests of Albania.'

Relief – warm, sweeping, glorious relief – swept over Harry.

'W-what's that?' said Mr Weasley in a stunned voice. '*You Know Who*? En-enchant *Ginny*? But Ginny's not ... Ginny hasn't been ... has she?'

'It was this diary,' said Harry quickly, picking it up and showing it to Dumbledore. 'Riddle wrote it when he was sixteen.'

Dumbledore took the diary from Harry and peered keenly down his long, crooked nose at its burnt and soggy pages.

'Brilliant,' he said softly. 'Of course, he was probably the most brilliant student Hogwarts has ever seen.' He turned around to the Weasleys, who were looking utterly bewildered.

'Very few people know that Lord Voldemort was once called Tom Riddle. I taught him myself, fifty years ago, at Hogwarts. He disappeared after leaving the school ... travelled far and wide ... sank so deeply into the Dark Arts, consorted with the very worst of our kind, underwent so many dangerous, magical transform-ations, that when he resurfaced as Lord Voldemort, he was barely recognisable. Hardly anyone connected Lord Voldemort with the clever, handsome boy who was once Head Boy here.'

'But Ginny,' said Mrs Weasley, 'what's our Ginny got to do with – with – *him*?'

'His d-diary!' Ginny sobbed. 'I've b-been writing in it, and he's been w-writing back all year –'

'*Ginny!*' said Mr Weasley, flabbergasted. 'Haven't I taught you *anything*? What have I always told you? Never trust anything that can think for itself *if you can't see where it keeps its brain*. Why didn't you show the diary to me, or your mother? A suspicious object like that, it was *clearly* full of dark magic!'

'I d-didn't know,' sobbed Ginny. 'I found it inside one of the books Mum got me. I th-thought someone had just left it in there and forgotten about it ...'

'Miss Weasley should go up to the hospital wing straight away,' Dumbledore interrupted in a firm voice. 'This has been a terrible ordeal for her. There will be no punishment. Older and wiser wizards than she have been hoodwinked by Lord Voldemort.' He strode over to the door and opened it. 'Bed rest and perhaps a large, steaming mug of hot chocolate. I always find that cheers me up,' he added, twinkling kindly down at her. 'You will find that Madam Pomfrey is still awake. She's just giving out Mandrake juice – I daresay the Basilisk's victims will be waking up any moment.'

'So Hermione's OK!' said Ron brightly.

'There has been no lasting harm done,' said Dumbledore.

Mrs Weasley led Ginny out, and Mr Weasley followed, still looking deeply shaken.

'You know, Minerva,' Professor Dumbledore said thoughtfully to Professor McGonagall, 'I think all this merits a good *feast*. Might I ask you to go and alert the kitchens?'

'Right,' said Professor McGonagall crisply, also moving to the door. 'I'll leave you to deal with Potter and Weasley, shall I?'

'Certainly,' said Dumbledore.

She left, and Harry and Ron gazed uncertainly at Dumbledore. What exactly had Professor McGonagall meant, *deal* with them? Surely – *surely* – they weren't about to be punished?

'I seem to remember telling you both that I would have to expel you if you broke any more school rules,' said Dumbledore.

Ron opened his mouth in horror.

'Which goes to show that the best of us must sometimes eat our words,' Dumbledore went on, smiling. 'You will both receive Special Awards for Services to the School and – let me see – yes, I think two hundred points apiece for Gryffindor.'

Ron went as brightly pink as Lockhart's Valentine flowers and closed his mouth again.

'But one of us seems to be keeping mightily quiet about his part in this dangerous adventure,' Dumbledore added. 'Why so modest, Gilderoy?'

Harry gave a start. He had completely forgotten about Lockhart.

He turned and saw that Lockhart was standing in a corner of the room, still wearing his vague smile. When Dumbledore addressed him, Lockhart looked over his shoulder to see who he was talking to.

'Professor Dumbledore,' Ron said quickly, 'there was an accident down in the Chamber of Secrets. Professor Lockhart –'

'Am I a Professor?' said Lockhart in mild surprise. 'Goodness. I expect I was hopeless, was I?'

'He tried to do a Memory Charm and the wand backfired,' Ron explained quietly to Dumbledore.

'Dear me,' said Dumbledore, shaking his head, his long silver moustache quivering. 'Impaled upon your own sword, Gilderoy!'

'Sword?' said Lockhart dimly. 'Haven't got a sword. That boy has, though.' He pointed at Harry. 'He'll lend you one.'

'Would you mind taking Professor Lockhart up to the hospital wing, too?' Dumbledore said to Ron. 'I'd like a few more words with Harry ...'

Lockhart ambled out. Ron cast a curious look back at Dumbledore and Harry as he closed the door.

Dumbledore crossed to one of the chairs by the fire.

'Sit down, Harry,' he said, and Harry sat, feeling unaccountably nervous.

'First of all, Harry, I want to thank you,' said Dumbledore, eyes twinkling again. 'You must have shown me real loyalty down in the Chamber. Nothing but that could have called Fawkes to you.'

He stroked the phoenix, which had fluttered down onto his knee. Harry grinned awkwardly as Dumbledore watched him.

'And so you met Tom Riddle,' said Dumbledore thoughtfully. 'I imagine he was *most* interested in you ...'

Suddenly, something that was nagging at Harry came tumbling out of his mouth.

'Professor Dumbledore ... Riddle said I'm like him. Strange like-nesses, he said ...'

'*Did* he, now?' said Dumbledore, looking thoughtfully under his thick silver eyebrows at Harry. 'And what do you think, Harry?'

'I don't think I'm like him!' said Harry, more loudly than he'd intended. 'I mean, I'm – I'm in *Gryffindor,* I'm ...'

But he fell silent, a lurking doubt resurfacing in his mind.

'Professor,' he started again after a moment, 'the Sorting Hat told me I'd – I'd have done well in Slytherin. Everyone thought I was Slytherin's heir for a while ... because I can speak Parseltongue ...'

'You can speak Parseltongue, Harry,' said Dumbledore calmly, 'because Lord Voldemort – who is the last remaining ancestor of Salazar Slytherin – can speak Parseltongue. Unless I'm much mistaken, he transferred some of his own powers to you the night he gave you that scar. Not something he intended to do, I'm sure ...'

'Voldemort put a bit of himself in *me*?' Harry said, thunderstruck.

'It certainly seems so.'

'So I *should* be in Slytherin,' Harry said, looking desperately into Dumbledore's face. 'The Sorting Hat could see Slytherin's power in me, and it –'

'Put you in Gryffindor,' said Dumbledore calmly. 'Listen to me, Harry. You happen to have many qualities Salazar Slytherin prized in his hand-picked students. His own very rare gift, Parseltongue ... resourcefulness ... determination ... a certain disregard for rules,' he added, his moustache quivering again. 'Yet the Sorting Hat placed you in Gryffindor. You know why that was. Think.'

'It only put me in Gryffindor,' said Harry in a defeated voice, 'because I asked not to go in Slytherin ...'

'*Exactly*,' said Dumbledore, beaming once more. 'Which makes you very *different* from Tom Riddle. It is our choices, Harry, that show what we truly are, far more than our abilities.' Harry sat motionless in his chair, stunned. 'If you want proof, Harry, that you belong in Gryffindor, I suggest you look more closely at *this*.'

Dumbledore reached across to Professor McGonagall's desk, picked up the blood-stained silver sword and handed it to Harry. Dully, Harry turned it over, the rubies blazing in the firelight. And then he saw the name engraved just below the hilt.

Godric Gryffindor.

'Only a true Gryffindor could have pulled that out of the hat, Harry,' said Dumbledore simply.

For a minute, neither of them spoke. Then Dumbledore pulled open one of the drawers in Professor McGonagall's desk, and took out a quill and a bottle of ink.

'What you need, Harry, is some food and sleep. I suggest you go down to the feast, while I write to Azkaban – we need our gamekeeper back. And I must draft an advertisement for the *Daily*

Prophet too,' he added thoughtfully. 'We'll be needing a new Defence Against the Dark Arts teacher. Dear me, we do seem to run through them, don't we?'

Harry got up and crossed to the door. He had just reached for the handle, however, when the door burst open so violently that it bounced back off the wall.

Lucius Malfoy stood there, fury in his face. And cowering under his arm, heavily wrapped in bandages, was *Dobby*.

'Good evening, Lucius,' said Dumbledore pleasantly.

Mr Malfoy almost knocked Harry over as he swept into the room. Dobby went scurrying in after him, crouching at the hem of his cloak, a look of abject terror on his face.

'So!' said Lucius Malfoy, his cold eyes fixed on Dumbledore. 'You've come back. The governors suspended you, but you still saw fit to return to Hogwarts.'

'Well, you see, Lucius,' said Dumbledore, smiling serenely, 'the other eleven governors contacted me today. It was something like being caught in a hailstorm of owls, to tell the truth. They'd heard that Arthur Weasley's daughter had been killed and wanted me back here at once. They seemed to think I was the best man for the job after all. Very strange tales they told me, too. Several of them seemed to think that you had threatened to curse their families if they didn't agree to suspend me in the first place.'

Mr Malfoy went even paler than usual, but his eyes were still slits of fury.

'So – have you stopped the attacks yet?' he sneered. 'Have you caught the culprit?'

'We have,' said Dumbledore, with a smile.

'*Well?*' said Mr Malfoy sharply. 'Who is it?'

'The same person as last time, Lucius,' said Dumbledore. 'But this time, Lord Voldemort was acting through somebody else. By means of this diary.'

He held up the small black book with the large hole through the centre, watching Mr Malfoy closely. Harry, however, was watching Dobby.

The elf was doing something very odd. His great eyes fixed meaningfully on Harry, he kept pointing at the diary, then at Mr Malfoy, and then hitting himself hard on the head with his fist.

'I see ...' said Mr Malfoy slowly to Dumbledore.

'A clever plan,' said Dumbledore in a level voice, still staring Mr

Malfoy straight in the eye. 'Because if Harry here –' Mr Malfoy shot Harry a swift, sharp look, 'and his friend Ron hadn't discovered this book, why – Ginny Weasley might have taken all the blame. No one would ever have been able to prove she hadn't acted of her own free will ...'

Mr Malfoy said nothing. His face was suddenly mask-like.

'And imagine,' Dumbledore went on, 'what might have happened then ... The Weasleys are one of our most prominent pure-blood families. Imagine the effect on Arthur Weasley and his Muggle Protection Act, if his own daughter was discovered attacking and killing Muggle-borns. Very fortunate the diary was discovered, and Riddle's memories wiped from it. Who knows what the consequences might have been otherwise ...'

Mr Malfoy forced himself to speak.

'Very fortunate,' he said stiffly.

And still, behind his back, Dobby was pointing, first to the diary, then to Lucius Malfoy, then punching himself in the head.

And Harry suddenly understood. He nodded at Dobby, and Dobby backed into a corner, now twisting his ears in punishment.

'Don't you want to know how Ginny got hold of that diary, Mr Malfoy?' said Harry.

Lucius Malfoy rounded on him.

'How should I know how the stupid little girl got hold of it?' he said.

'Because you gave it to her,' said Harry. 'In Flourish and Blotts. You picked up her old Transfiguration book, and slipped the diary inside it, didn't you?'

He saw Mr Malfoy's white hands clench and unclench.

'Prove it,' he hissed.

'Oh, no one will be able to do that,' said Dumbledore, smiling at Harry. 'Not now Riddle has vanished from the book. On the other hand, I would advise you, Lucius, not to go giving out any more of Lord Voldemort's old school things. If any more of them find their way into innocent hands, I think Arthur Weasley, for one, will make sure they are traced back to you ...'

Lucius Malfoy stood for a moment, and Harry distinctly saw his right hand twitch as though he was longing to reach for his wand. Instead, he turned to his house-elf.

'We're going, Dobby!'

He wrenched open the door and as the elf came hurrying up to him, he kicked him right through it. They could hear Dobby squealing with pain all the way along the corridor. Harry stood for a moment, thinking hard. Then it came to him.

'Professor Dumbledore,' he said hurriedly, 'can I give that diary *back* to Mr Malfoy, please?'

'Certainly, Harry,' said Dumbledore calmly. 'But hurry. The feast, remember.'

Harry grabbed the diary and dashed out of the office. He could hear Dobby's squeals of pain receding around the corner. Quickly, wondering if this plan could possibly work, Harry took off one of his shoes, pulled off his slimy, filthy sock, and stuffed the diary into it. Then he ran down the dark corridor.

He caught up with them at the top of the stairs.

'Mr Malfoy,' he gasped, skidding to a halt, 'I've got something for you.'

And he forced the smelly sock into Lucius Malfoy's hand.

'What the –?'

Mr Malfoy ripped the sock off the diary, threw it aside, then looked furiously from the ruined book to Harry.

'You'll meet the same sticky end as your parents one of these days, Harry Potter,' he said softly. 'They were meddlesome fools, too.'

He turned to go.

'Come, Dobby. I said, *come*!'

But Dobby didn't move. He was holding up Harry's disgusting, slimy sock, and looking at it as though it were a priceless treasure.

'Master has given Dobby a sock,' said the elf in wonderment. 'Master gave it to Dobby.'

'What's that?' spat Mr Malfoy. 'What did you say?'

'Dobby has got a sock,' said Dobby in disbelief. 'Master threw it, and Dobby caught it, and Dobby – Dobby is *free*.'

Lucius Malfoy stood frozen, staring at the elf. Then he lunged at Harry.

'You've lost me my servant, boy!'

But Dobby shouted, 'You shall not harm Harry Potter!'

There was a loud bang, and Mr Malfoy was thrown backwards. He crashed down the stairs, three at a time, landing in a crumpled heap on the landing below. He got up, his face livid, and pulled out his wand, but Dobby raised a long threatening finger.

'You shall go now,' he said fiercely, pointing down at Mr Malfoy.

'You shall not touch Harry Potter. You shall go now.'

Lucius Malfoy had no choice. With a last, incensed stare at the pair of them, he swung his cloak around him and hurried out of sight.

'Harry Potter freed Dobby!' said the elf shrilly, gazing up at Harry, moonlight from the nearest window reflected in his orb-like eyes. 'Harry Potter set Dobby free!'

'Least I could do, Dobby,' said Harry, grinning. 'Just promise never to try and save my life again.'

The elf's ugly brown face split suddenly into a wide, toothy smile.

'I've just got one question, Dobby,' said Harry, as Dobby pulled on Harry's sock with shaking hands. 'You told me all this had nothing to do with He Who Must Not Be Named, remember? Well –'

'It was a clue, sir,' said Dobby, his eyes widening, as though this was obvious. 'Dobby was giving you a clue. The Dark Lord, before he changed his name, could be freely named, you see?'

'Right,' said Harry weakly. 'Well, I'd better go. There's a feast, and my friend Hermione should be awake by now ...'

Dobby threw his arms around Harry's middle and hugged him.

'Harry Potter is greater by far than Dobby knew!' he sobbed. 'Farewell, Harry Potter!'

And with a final loud crack, Dobby disappeared.

*

Harry had been to several Hogwarts feasts, but never one quite like this. Everybody was in their pyjamas, and the celebrations lasted all night. Harry didn't know whether the best bit was Hermione running towards him, screaming, 'You solved it! You solved it!' or Justin hurrying over from the Hufflepuff table to wring his hand and apologise endlessly for suspecting him, or Hagrid turning up at half past three, cuffing Harry and Ron so hard on the shoulders that they were knocked into their plates of trifle, or his and Ron's four hundred points for Gryffindor securing the House Cup for the second year running, or Professor McGonagall standing up to tell them all that the exams had been cancelled as a school treat ('Oh, *no!*' said Hermione), or Dumbledore announcing that, unfortunately, Professor Lockhart would be unable to return next year, owing to the fact that he needed to go away and get his memory back. Quite a few of the teachers joined in the cheering that greeted this news.

'Shame,' said Ron, helping himself to a jam doughnut. 'He was starting to grow on me.'

*

The rest of the summer term passed in a haze of blazing sunshine. Hogwarts was back to normal, with only a few, small differences: Defence Against the Dark Arts classes were cancelled ('but we've had plenty of practice at that anyway,' Ron told a disgruntled Hermione) and Lucius Malfoy had been sacked as a school governor. Draco was no longer strutting around the school as though he owned the place. On the contrary, he looked resentful and sulky. On the other hand, Ginny Weasley was perfectly happy again.

Too soon, it was time for the journey home on the Hogwarts Express. Harry, Ron, Hermione, Fred, George and Ginny got a compartment to themselves. They made the most of the last few hours in which they were allowed to do magic before the holidays. They played Exploding Snap, set off the very last of Fred and George's Filibuster Fireworks, and practised disarming each other by magic. Harry was getting very good at it.

They were almost at King's Cross when Harry remembered something.

'Ginny – what did you see Percy doing, that he didn't want you to tell anyone?'

'Oh, that,' said Ginny, giggling. 'Well – Percy's got a *girlfriend*.'

Fred dropped a stack of books on George's head.

'*What?*'

'It's that Ravenclaw prefect, Penelope Clearwater,' said Ginny. 'That's who he was writing to all last summer. He's been meeting her all over the school in secret. I walked in on them kissing in an empty classroom one day. He was so upset when she was – you know – attacked. You won't tease him, will you?' she added anxiously.

'Wouldn't dream of it,' said Fred, who was looking as if his birthday had come early.

'Definitely not,' said George, sniggering.

The Hogwarts Express slowed and finally stopped.

Harry pulled out his quill and a bit of parchment and turned to Ron and Hermione.

'This is called a telephone number,' he told Ron, scribbling it twice, tearing the parchment in two and handing it to them. 'I told your Dad how to use a telephone last summer, he'll know. Call me at the Dursleys, OK? I can't stand another two months with only Dudley to talk to ...'

'Your Aunt and Uncle will be proud, though, won't they?' said Hermione, as they got off the train and joined the crowd thronging towards the enchanted barrier. 'When they hear what you did this year?'

'Proud?' said Harry. 'Are you mad? All those times I could've died, and I didn't manage it? They'll be furious ...'

And together they walked back through the gateway to the Muggle world.

Stars and Planets

The Most Complete Guide to the Stars,
Planets, Galaxies, and the Solar System

Fully Revised and Expanded Edition

Ian Ridpath

Illustrated by
Wil Tirion

Princeton University Press
Princeton and Oxford

Acknowledgements and sources

This book is the result of an unusual collaboration between an author and an illustrator in different countries, united by their common fascination with the sky. International cooperation of another kind is apparent in the photographic illustrations in this book, which are the result of the efforts of professional and amateur astronomers from many nations. Such awesome images rank with the most enduring works of art produced by humankind. It is fitting that the observatories concerned have made their results so readily available. The urge to study the sky transcends national boundaries, and so it should. The skies are open to us all.

The authors would like to thank those whose photographs are used in this book, in particular the staff of the National Optical Astronomy Observatory, Tucson, Arizona. Pictures are credited individually where they appear. The photographic Moon maps are courtesy Mark Rosiek and the U.S. Geological Survey, Flagstaff, Arizona. Dimensions of formations are from the list by Ewen Whitaker in *Norton's Star Atlas*, 19th and 20th editions.

The following publications have been consulted extensively during the preparation of this book: *The Hipparcos and Tycho Catalogues* by M. Perryman *et al.* (European Space Agency, Noordwijk); *The Millennium Star Atlas* by R.W. Sinnott and M. Perryman (European Space Agency; and Sky Publishing Corp., Cambridge, Mass.); *Sky Atlas 2000.0* (2nd edition) by Wil Tirion and R.W. Sinnott (Sky Publishing Corp.; and Cambridge University Press, Cambridge, England); *Sky Catalogue 2000.0*, Vols 1 and 2 (Sky Publishing Corp. and Cambridge University Press); *The Bright Star Catalogue*, 4th edition, by Dorrit Hoffleit (Yale University Observatory); the Washington Double Star Catalogue (online edition); *Burnham's Celestial Handbook* by Robert Burnham, Jr (Dover, New York; Constable, London); *Sky & Telescope* magazine (Cambridge, Mass.). Further details of the origin and mythology of the constellations may be found in *Star Tales* by Ian Ridpath (Lutterworth, Cambridge). For more on the meanings of individual star names see *A Dictionary of Modern Star Names* by Paul Kunitzsch and Tim Smart (Sky Publishing, Cambridge, Mass.).

We thank Peter Gill for commenting on the proofs of this fourth edition, and we remain grateful for the continuing support of our editors at HarperCollins.

I.R., W.T.
http://www.ianridpath.com/
http://www.wil-tirion.com/

Published in North America by Princeton University Press, 41 William Street, Princeton, New Jersey 08540

In the United Kingdom, published by HarperCollins Publishers

First published in 1984 as *Collins Pocket Guide Stars and Planets*. This revised fourth edition published in 2007.

Library of Congress Control Number 2007930251
ISBN: 978-0-691-13556-4

press.princeton.edu

Design: Emma Jern
Typesetting and layout: Ian Ridpath

Colour reproduction by Colourscan, Singapore
Printed and bound by Printing Express, Hong Kong

10 9 8 7 6 5 4 3 2 1

CONTENTS

SECTION I

INTRODUCTION

The night sky is one of the most beautiful sights in nature. Yet many people remain lost among the jostling crowd of stars, and are baffled by the progressively changing appearance of the sky from hour to hour and from season to season. The charts and descriptions in this book will guide you to the most splendid celestial sights, many of them within the range of simple optical equipment such as binoculars, and all accessible with an average-sized telescope of the type used by amateur astronomers.

It must be emphasized that you do not need a telescope to take up stargazing. Use the charts in this book to find your way among the stars first with your own eyes, and then with the aid of binoculars, which bring the stars more readily into view. Binoculars are a worthwhile investment, being relatively cheap, easy to carry and useful for many purposes other than stargazing.

Stars and planets

In the night sky, stars appear to the naked eye as spiky, twinkling lights. Those stars near the horizon seem to flash and change colour. The twinkling and flashing effects are due not to the stars themselves but to the Earth's atmosphere: turbulent air currents cause the stars' light to dance around. The steadiness of the atmosphere is referred to as the *seeing*. Steady air means good seeing. The spikiness of star images is due to optical effects in the observer's eye. In reality, stars are spheres of gas similar to our own Sun, emitting their own heat and light.

Stars come in various sizes, from giants to dwarfs, and in a range of colours according to their temperature. At first glance all stars appear white, but more careful inspection reveals that certain ones are somewhat orange, notably Betelgeuse, Antares, Aldebaran and Arcturus, while others such as Rigel, Spica

and Vega have a bluish tinge. Binoculars bring out the colours more readily than the naked eye does. Section II of this book, starting on page 267, explains more fully the different types of star that exist.

By contrast, planets are cold bodies that shine by reflecting the Sun's light. They too are described in more detail in Section II, from page 304 onwards. The planets are constantly on the move as they orbit the Sun. Four of them can be easily seen with the naked eye: Venus, Mars, Jupiter and Saturn. Venus, the brightest of all, appears as a dazzling object in the evening or morning sky. Charts showing the positions of Mars, Jupiter and Saturn for a 5-year period can be found on the HarperCollins website: www.collins.co.uk/starsandplanets

About 2000 stars are visible to the naked eye on a clear, dark night, but you will not need to learn them all. Start by identifying the brightest stars and major constellations, and use these as signposts to the fainter, less prominent stars and constellations. Once you know the main features of the night sky, you will never again be lost among the stars.

Constellations

The sky is divided into 88 sections known as constellations which astronomers use as a convenient way of locating and naming celestial objects. Most of the stars in a constellation have no real connection with one another at all; they may lie at vastly differing distances from Earth, and form a pattern simply by chance. Incidentally, when astronomers talk of an object being 'in' a given constellation they mean that it lies in that particular area of sky.

Some constellations are easier to recognize than others, such as the magnificent Orion or the distinctive Cassiopeia and Crux. Others are faint and obscure, such as Lynx

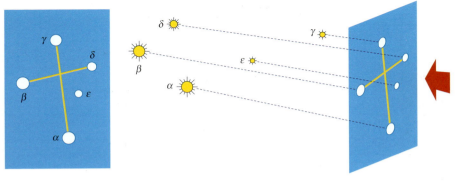

Constellations: Stars in a constellation are usually unrelated to one another. Above, the stars of Crux, the Southern Cross, are shown as they appear from Earth, left, and as they actually lie in space, right. (Wil Tirion)

and Telescopium. Whether large or small, bright or faint, each constellation is given a separate chart and description in this book.

The main constellations were devised at the dawn of history by Middle Eastern peoples who fancied that they could see a likeness to certain fabled creatures and mythological heroes among the stars. Of particular importance were the 12 constellations of the zodiac, through which the Sun passes during its yearly path around the heavens. However, it should be realized that the astrological 'signs' of the zodiac are not the same as the modern astronomical constellations, even though they share the same names.

Our modern system of constellations derives from a catalogue of 48 compiled by the Greek astronomer Ptolemy in AD 150. This list was expanded by navigators and celestial map-makers, notably the Dutchmen Pieter Dirkszoon Keyser (c. 1540–96) and Frederick de Houtman (1571–1627), the Pole Johannes Hevelius (see page 166) and the Frenchman Nicolas Louis de Lacaille (see page 216).

Keyser and de Houtman introduced 12 new constellations, and Lacaille 14, in parts of the southern sky not visible from Medi-

terranean regions; Hevelius and others invented constellations to fill in the gaps between the figures recognized by the Greeks. The whole process sounds rather arbitrary, and indeed it was. A number of the newly devised patterns fell into disuse, leaving a total of 88 constellations that were officially adopted by the International Astronomical Union, astronomy's governing body, in 1922 (see the table on pages 8–9).

As well as the officially recognized constellations, you can find other patterns among the stars called *asterisms*. An asterism can be composed of stars belonging to one or more constellations. Well-known examples are the Plough or Big Dipper (part of Ursa Major), the Square of Pegasus, the Sickle of Leo and the Teapot of Sagittarius.

Star names

The main stars in each constellation are labelled with a letter of the Greek alphabet, the brightest star usually (but not always!) being termed α (alpha). Notable exceptions in which the stars marked β (beta) are in fact the brightest include the constellations Orion and Gemini. The entire Greek alphabet is given in the table on page 10.

Particularly confusing are the southern constellations Vela and Puppis, which were once joined with Carina to make the extensive figure of Argo Navis, the ship of the

THE 88 CONSTELLATIONS

Name	Genitive	Abbrevn.	Area (square degs.)	Order of size	Origin*
Andromeda	Andromedae	And	722	19	1
Antlia	Antliae	Ant	239	62	6
Apus	Apodis	Aps	206	67	3
Aquarius	Aquarii	Aqr	980	10	1
Aquila	Aquilae	Aql	652	22	1
Ara	Arae	Ara	237	63	1
Aries	Arietis	Ari	441	39	1
Auriga	Aurigae	Aur	657	21	1
Boötes	Boötis	Boo	907	13	1
Caelum	Caeli	Cae	125	81	6
Camelopardalis	Camelopardalis	Cam	757	18	4
Cancer	Cancri	Cnc	506	31	1
Canes Venatici	Canum Venaticorum	CVn	465	38	5
Canis Major	Canis Majoris	CMa	380	43	1
Canis Minor	Canis Minoris	CMi	183	71	1
Capricornus	Capricorni	Cap	414	40	1
Carina	Carinae	Car	494	34	6
Cassiopeia	Cassiopeiae	Cas	598	25	1
Centaurus	Centauri	Cen	1060	9	1
Cepheus	Cephei	Cep	588	27	1
Cetus	Ceti	Cet	1231	4	1
Chamaeleon	Chamaeleontis	Cha	132	79	3
Circinus	Circini	Cir	93	85	6
Columba	Columbae	Col	270	54	4
Coma Berenices	Comae Berenices	Com	386	42	2
Corona Australis	Coronae Australis	CrA	128	80	1
Corona Borealis	Coronae Borealis	CrB	179	73	1
Corvus	Corvi	Crv	184	70	1
Crater	Crateris	Crt	282	53	1
Crux	Crucis	Cru	68	88	4
Cygnus	Cygni	Cyg	804	16	1
Delphinus	Delphini	Del	189	69	1
Dorado	Doradus	Dor	179	72	3
Draco	Draconis	Dra	1083	8	1
Equuleus	Equulei	Equ	72	87	1
Eridanus	Eridani	Eri	1138	6	1
Fornax	Fornacis	For	398	41	6
Gemini	Geminorum	Gem	514	30	1
Grus	Gruis	Gru	366	45	3
Hercules	Herculis	Her	1225	5	1
Horologium	Horologii	Hor	249	58	6
Hydra	Hydrae	Hya	1303	1	1
Hydrus	Hydri	Hyi	243	61	3
Indus	Indi	Ind	294	49	3
Lacerta	Lacertae	Lac	201	68	5
Leo	Leonis	Leo	947	12	1
Leo Minor	Leonis Minoris	LMi	232	64	5
Lepus	Leporis	Lep	290	51	1

Name	Genitive	Abbrevn.	Area (square degs.)	Order of size	Origin*
Libra	Librae	Lib	538	29	1
Lupus	Lupi	Lup	334	46	1
Lynx	Lyncis	Lyn	545	28	5
Lyra	Lyrae	Lyr	286	52	1
Mensa	Mensae	Men	153	75	6
Microscopium	Microscopii	Mic	210	66	6
Monoceros	Monocerotis	Mon	482	35	4
Musca	Muscae	Mus	138	77	3
Norma	Normae	Nor	165	74	6
Octans	Octantis	Oct	291	50	6
Ophiuchus	Ophiuchi	Oph	948	11	1
Orion	Orionis	Ori	594	26	1
Pavo	Pavonis	Pav	378	44	3
Pegasus	Pegasi	Peg	1121	7	1
Perseus	Persei	Per	615	24	1
Phoenix	Phoenicis	Phe	469	37	3
Pictor	Pictoris	Pic	247	59	6
Pisces	Piscium	Psc	889	14	1
Piscis Austrinus	Piscis Austrini	PsA	245	60	1
Puppis	Puppis	Pup	673	20	6
Pyxis	Pyxidis	Pyx	221	65	6
Reticulum	Reticuli	Ret	114	82	6
Sagitta	Sagittae	Sge	80	86	1
Sagittarius	Sagittarii	Sgr	867	15	1
Scorpius	Scorpii	Sco	497	33	1
Sculptor	Sculptoris	Scl	475	36	6
Scutum	Scuti	Sct	109	84	5
Serpens	Serpentis	Ser	637	23	1
Sextans	Sextantis	Sex	314	47	5
Taurus	Tauri	Tau	797	17	1
Telescopium	Telescopii	Tel	252	57	6
Triangulum	Trianguli	Tri	132	78	1
Triangulum Australe	Trianguli Australis	TrA	110	83	3
Tucana	Tucanae	Tuc	295	48	3
Ursa Major	Ursae Majoris	UMa	1280	3	1
Ursa Minor	Ursae Minoris	UMi	256	56	1
Vela	Velorum	Vel	500	32	6
Virgo	Virginis	Vir	1294	2	1
Volans	Volantis	Vol	141	76	3
Vulpecula	Vulpeculae	Vul	268	55	5

* Origin:
1   One of the original 48 Greek constellations listed by Ptolemy. The Greek figure of Argo Navis has since been divided into Carina, Puppis and Vela.
2   Considered by the Greeks as part of Leo; made separate by Gerardus Mercator in 1551.
3   The 12 southern constellations of Pieter Dirkszoon Keyser and Frederick de Houtman, *c.* 1600.
4   Four constellations added by Petrus Plancius.
5   Seven constellations of Johannes Hevelius.
6   The 14 southern constellations of Nicolas Louis de Lacaille, who also divided the Greeks' Argo Navis into Carina, Puppis and Vela.

Argonauts. As a result of Argo's subsequent trisection, neither Vela nor Puppis possesses stars labelled α or β, and there are gaps in the sequence of Greek letters in Carina as well.

The system of labelling stars with Greek letters was introduced by Johann Bayer (see page 246), so these designations are often known as Bayer letters. The genitive (possessive) case of the constellation's name is always used when referring to a star within it; hence Canis Major, for instance, becomes Canis Majoris, and the name α Canis Majoris means 'the star α in Canis Major'. All constellation names have standard three-letter abbreviations; for instance, the abbreviated form of Canis Major is CMa.

In heavily populated constellations, where Greek letters ran out, fainter stars were assigned Roman letters, both lower-case and capital, such as l Carinae, P Cygni and L Puppis. An additional system of identifying stars is that of Flamsteed numbers, originating from their order in a star catalogue drawn up by England's first Astronomer Royal, John Flamsteed (1646–1719). Examples are 61 Cygni and 70 Ophiuchi (see also page 178).

Before 1930, there were no officially recognized constellation boundaries; some constellations overlapped, and some stars were shared between constellations. In that year, the International Astronomical Union published definitive boundaries for all constellations. In the process, certain stars allocated by the Bayer and Flamsteed systems to one constellation found themselves transferred to a neighbour, leading to gaps in the sequence of letters and numbers.

Prominent stars also have proper names by which they are commonly known. For example, α Canis Majoris, the brightest star in the sky, is better known as Sirius. Stars' proper names originate from several sources. Some, such as Sirius, Castor and Pollux, date back to ancient Greek times. Many others, such as Aldebaran, are of Arabic origin. Still others were added more recently by European astronomers who borrowed Arabic words in

THE GREEK ALPHABET			
α	alpha	ξ	xi
β	beta	o	omicron
γ	gamma	π	pi
δ	delta		
ε	epsilon	ρ	rho
ζ	zeta	σ	sigma
η	eta	τ	tau
θ or ϑ	theta	υ	upsilon
ι	iota		
κ	kappa	φ or ϕ	phi
λ	lambda	χ	chi
μ	mu	ψ	psi
ν	nu	ω	omega

corrupted form; an example is Betelgeuse, which in its current form is meaningless in Arabic. To add to the confusion, spelling of names can vary from list to list, and some stars have more than one proper name. For the maps in this book we have adopted the names used by the *Millennium Star Atlas* (European Space Agency and Sky Publishing Corp., 1997).

Star clusters, nebulae and galaxies have a different system of identification. The most prominent of them are given numbers prefixed by the letter M from a catalogue compiled in the late 18th century by the French astronomer Charles Messier (1730–1817). For example, M1 is the Crab Nebula and M31 the Andromeda Galaxy.

Messier's catalogue contained 103 objects. A few more were added later by other astronomers, bringing the total to 110. A far more comprehensive listing, containing many thousands of objects, is the *New General Catalogue* (NGC) compiled by J.L.E. Dreyer (1852–1926), with two supplements called the *Index Catalogues* (IC).

Messier numbers and NGC/IC numbers remain in use by astronomers, and both systems are used in this book. On the charts, such objects are labelled with their Messier number if they have one, or otherwise by their NGC number (without the 'NGC' prefix) or IC number (prefixed 'I').

Star brightness

Stars appear of different brightnesses in the sky, for two reasons. Firstly, they give out different amounts of light. But also, and just as importantly, they lie at vastly differing distances. Hence, a modest star that is quite close to us can appear brighter than a tremendously powerful star that is a long way away.

Astronomers call a star's brightness its *magnitude*. The magnitude scale was introduced by the Greek astronomer Hipparchus in 129 BC. Hipparchus divided the naked-eye stars into six classes of brightness, from 1st magnitude (the brightest stars) to 6th magnitude (the faintest visible to the naked eye). In his day there was no means of measuring star brightness precisely, so this rough classification sufficed. But with the coming of technology it became possible to measure a star's brightness to a fraction of a magnitude.

In 1856 the English astronomer Norman Pogson (1829–91) put the magnitude scale on a precise mathematical footing by defining a star of magnitude 1 as being exactly 100 times brighter than a star of magnitude 6. Since, on this scale, a difference of five magnitudes corresponds to a brightness difference of 100 times, a step of one magnitude is equal to a brightness difference of just over 2.5 times (the fifth root of 100).

Objects more than 250 times brighter than 6th magnitude are given negative (minus) magnitudes. For example, Sirius, the brightest star in the sky, is of magnitude −1.44. At the other end of the scale, stars fainter than magnitude 6 are given progressively larger positive magnitudes. The faintest objects detected by telescopes on Earth are around magnitude 27.

Any object of magnitude 1.49 or brighter is said to be of first magnitude; objects from 1.50 to 2.49 are termed second magnitude; and so on. The magnitude system may sound confusing at first, but it works well in practice and has the advantage that it can be extended indefinitely in both directions, to the very bright and the very faint.

When used without further qualification, the term 'magnitude' refers to how bright a star appears to us in the sky; strictly, this is the star's *apparent magnitude*. But because the distance of a star affects how bright it appears, the apparent magnitude bears little relation to its actual light output, or *absolute magnitude*.

A star's absolute magnitude is defined as the brightness it would appear to have if it were at a standard distance from us of 10 parsecs (32.6 light years). The origin of the parsec is explained on page 13. The table below shows the apparent and absolute magnitudes of the ten brightest stars visible

THE TEN BRIGHTEST STARS AS SEEN FROM EARTH				
Star name	Constellation	Apparent magnitude	Absolute magnitude	Distance (l.y.)
Sirius	Canis Major	−1.44	+1.45	8.60
Canopus	Carina	−0.62	−5.53	313
Rigil Kentaurus	Centaurus	−0.28	+4.07	4.39
Arcturus	Boötes	−0.05	−0.31	36.7
Vega	Lyra	+0.03	+0.58	25.3
Capella	Auriga	+0.08	−0.48	42.2
Rigel	Orion	+0.18	−6.69	773
Procyon	Canis Minor	+0.40	+2.68	11.4
Achernar	Eridanus	+0.45	−2.77	144
Betelgeuse	Orion	+0.45	−5.14	427

in the night sky. Astronomers calculate the absolute magnitude from knowledge of the star's nature and its distance.

Absolute magnitude is a good way of comparing the intrinsic brightness of stars. For instance, our daytime star the Sun has an apparent magnitude of −26.7, but an absolute magnitude of 4.8 (when no sign is given the magnitude is understood to be positive). Deneb (α Cygni) has an apparent magnitude of 1.3, but an absolute magnitude of −8.7. From comparison of these absolute magnitudes we deduce that Deneb gives out over 250,000 times as much light as the Sun and hence is one of the most luminous stars known, even though there is nothing at first sight to mark it out as extraordinary.

A number of stars actually vary in their light output, for various reasons, and are a favourite subject for study by amateur astronomers. The nature of such so-called variable stars is discussed on pages 284–287.

Star distances

In the Universe, distances are so huge that astronomers have abandoned the puny kilometre (km) and have invented their own units. Most familiar of these is the *light year* (l.y.), the distance that a beam of light travels in one year. Light moves at the fastest known speed in the Universe, 299,792.5 km per second. A light year is equivalent to 9.46 million million km.

On average, stars are several light years apart. For instance, the closest star to the Sun, Proxima Centauri (actually a member of the α Centauri triple system), is 4.2 light years away. Sirius is 8.6 l.y. away and Deneb over 3000 l.y. away.

The distance of the nearest stars can be found directly in the following way. A star's position is measured accurately when the Earth is on one side of the Sun, and then remeasured six months later when the Earth has moved around its orbit to the other side of the Sun. When viewed from two widely differing points in space in this way, a nearby star will appear to have shifted slightly in position with respect to more distant stars (see diagram on the facing page).

This effect is known as parallax, and applies to any object viewed from two vantage points against a fixed background, such as a tree against the horizon. A star's parallax shift is so small that under normal circumstances it is unnoticeable – in the case of Proxima Centauri, which has the greatest parallax shift of any star, the amount is about the same as the width of a small coin seen at a distance of 2 km. Once the star's parallax shift has been measured, a simple calculation reveals how far away it is.

THE TEN CLOSEST STARS TO EARTH				
Star name	Constellation	Apparent magnitude	Absolute magnitude	Distance (l.y.)
Proxima Centauri	Centaurus	11.05	15.45	4.22
α Centauri A	Centaurus	−0.01	4.34	4.39
α Centauri B	Centaurus	1.35	5.70	4.39
Barnard's Star	Ophiuchus	9.54	13.24	5.94
Wolf 359	Leo	13.54	16.57	7.8
Lalande 21185	Ursa Major	7.49	10.46	8.31
Sirius A	Canis Major	−1.44	1.45	8.60
Sirius B	Canis Major	8.44	11.33	8.60
UV Ceti A	Cetus	12.52	15.42	8.7
UV Ceti B	Cetus	12.96	15.82	8.7

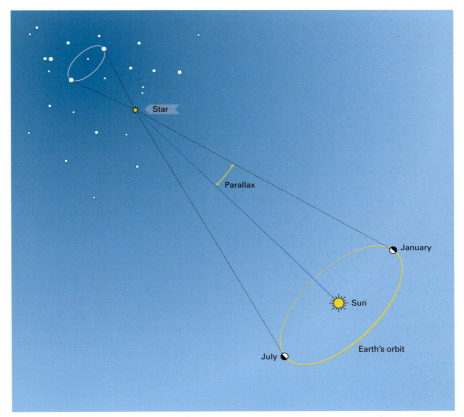

Labels on image: Star, Parallax, January, Sun, July, Earth's orbit

An object close enough to us to show a parallax shift of 1″ (one second of arc) would, in the jargon of astronomers, be said to lie at a distance of one *parsec*, equivalent to 3.26 light years. In practice, no star is this close; the parallax of Proxima Centauri is 0″.77. Astronomers frequently use parsecs in preference to light years because of the ease of converting parallax into distance: a star's distance in parsecs is simply the inverse of its parallax in seconds of arc. For example, a star 2 parsecs away has a parallax of 0″.5, 4 parsecs away its parallax is 0″.25, and so on.

The farther away a star is, the smaller its parallax. Beyond about 50 light years a star's parallax becomes too small to be measured

Parallax: As the Earth moves around its orbit, so a nearby star appears to change in position against the celestial background. The shift in position is known as the star's parallax. The nearer the star is to us, the greater its parallax. Here, the amount of parallax is exaggerated for clarity. (Wil Tirion)

accurately by telescopes on Earth. Before the launch of the European Space Agency's astrometry satellite Hipparcos in 1989, astronomers had been able to establish reliable parallaxes for fewer than 1000 stars from Earth; from space, Hipparcos has increased the number of reliable parallaxes to over 100,000.

For stars that are too distant to have had their parallax measured even by Hipparcos, astronomers first of all estimate the star's absolute magnitude by studying the spectrum of its light. They then compare this estimated absolute magnitude with the observed apparent magnitude to determine the star's distance. The distance obtained in this way is open to considerable error, and the values quoted in various books and catalogues often differ widely as a result.

Distances of stars given in this book are all expressed in light years. Like the star magnitudes, they are taken from *The Hipparcos Catalogue* (European Space Agency, 1997). Most of these distances are accurate to better than 10 per cent, with the uncertainties tending to become greater for the more distant stars.

Star positions

To determine positions of objects in the sky, astronomers use a system of coordinates similar to latitude and longitude on Earth. The celestial equivalent of latitude is called *declination* and the equivalent of longitude is called *right ascension*. Declination is measured in degrees, minutes and seconds (abbreviated °, ′ and ″) of arc from 0° on the celestial equator to 90° at the celestial poles. The celestial poles lie exactly above the Earth's poles, while the celestial equator is the projection onto the sky of the Earth's equator.

Right ascension is measured in hours, minutes and seconds (abbreviated h, m and s), from 0h to 24h. The 0h line of right ascension, the celestial equivalent of the Greenwich meridian, is defined as the point where the Sun crosses the celestial equator on its way into the northern hemisphere each year. Technically, this point is known as the *vernal* (or spring) *equinox*.

Ecliptic: As the Earth moves along its orbit, the Sun is seen in different directions against the star background. The Sun's path against the stars is known as the ecliptic. The constellations that the Sun passes in front of during the year are known as the constellations of the zodiac. Below, the Sun's apparent motion through Gemini, Cancer and Leo is shown. (Wil Tirion)

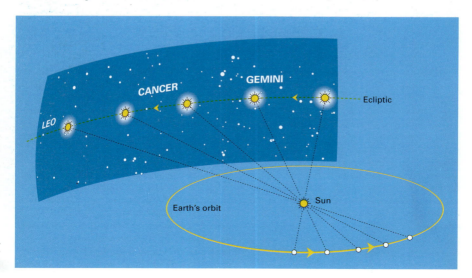

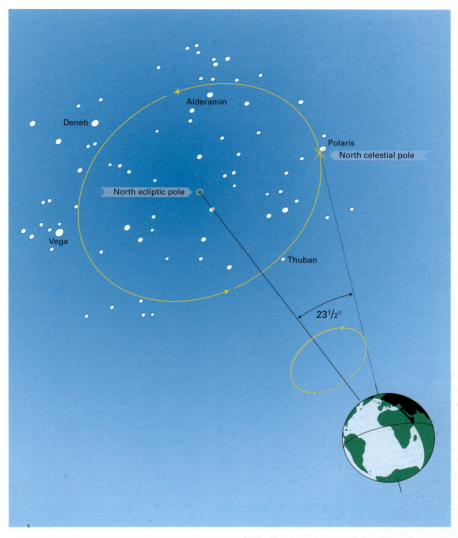

Precession: The Earth is very slowly wobbling in space like a tilted spinning top, a movement known as precession. As a consequence, the celestial poles trace out a complete circle on the sky every 26,000 years. Only the path of the north celestial pole is shown here, but the effect applies to the south pole as well. (Wil Tirion)

The Sun's path around the sky each year is known as the *ecliptic*. This path is inclined at 23½° to the celestial equator, because that is the angle at which the Earth's axis is inclined to the vertical. The most northerly and southerly points that the Sun reaches in the sky each year are called the *solstices*, and they lie 23½° north and south of the celestial equator. If the Earth's axis were directly upright with respect to its orbit around the Sun, then the celestial equator and ecliptic would coincide. We would then have no seasons, for the Sun would always remain directly above the Earth's equator.

One additional effect that becomes important over long periods of time is that the Earth is slowly wobbling on its axis, like a spinning top. The axis remains inclined at an angle of 23½°, but the position in the sky to which the north and south poles of the Earth are pointing moves slowly. This wobbling of the Earth in space is termed *precession*.

As a result of precession, the Earth's north and south poles describe a large circle on the sky, taking 26,000 years to return to their starting places (see the diagram on page 15). Hence the positions of the celestial poles are always changing, albeit imperceptibly, as are the two points at which the Sun's path (the ecliptic) cuts the celestial equator.

As an example of the effects caused by precession, Polaris will not always be the Pole Star. Although Polaris currently lies less than 1° from the celestial pole, that is just a matter of chance. In 11,000 years' time the north celestial pole will lie near Vega in the constellation Lyra, having moved through Cepheus and Cygnus in the interim. Similarly, the vernal equinox, which lay in Aries between 1865 BC and 67 BC, now lies in Pisces and in AD 2597 will have reached Aquarius.

The effect of precession means that the coordinates of all celestial objects – the catalogued positions of stars, galaxies, and even constellation boundaries – are continually drifting. Astronomers draw up catalogues and star charts for a standard reference date, or *epoch*, commonly chosen to be the start or middle of a century. The epoch of the star positions in this book is the year 2000. For most general purposes, precession does not introduce a noticeable error until after about 50 years, so the charts in this book will be usable without amendment until halfway through the 21st century.

Proper motions

All the stars visible in the sky are members of a vast wheeling mass of stars called the Galaxy. Those stars visible to the naked eye are among the nearest to us in the Galaxy. More distant stars in the Galaxy crowd together in a hazy band called the Milky Way, which can be seen arching across the sky on dark nights.

The Sun and the other stars are all orbiting the centre of the Galaxy; the Sun takes about 250 million years to complete one orbit. Other stars move at different speeds, like cars in different lanes on a highway. As a result, stars are all very slowly changing their positions relative to one another.

Such stellar movement, termed *proper motion*, is so slight that it is undetectable to the naked eye even over a human lifetime, but it can be measured through telescopes. As with many other aspects of stellar positions, our knowledge of proper motions has been radically improved by the Hipparcos satellite.

If ancient Greek astronomers could be transported 2000 years forward in time to the present day, they would notice little difference in the sky, with the exception of Arcturus, a fast-moving bright star, which has drifted more than two Moon diameters from its position then. Over very long periods of time the proper motions of stars considerably distort the shapes of all constellations. The diagrams on the facing page show some examples of how proper motions will alter some familiar patterns.

An additional long-term effect of stellar motions is to change the apparent magnitudes of stars as they move towards us or away. For example, Sirius will brighten by 20 per cent over the next 60,000 years as its

Proper motions: Three familiar star patterns as they appear today, at left of diagram, and as they will appear in 100,000 years' time, right. The changes in appearance are due to the proper motions of the stars. (Wil Tirion)

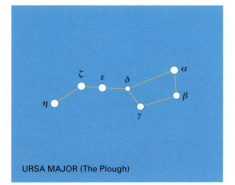

URSA MAJOR (The Plough)

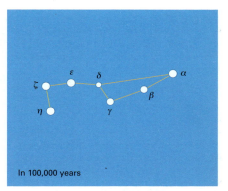

In 100,000 years

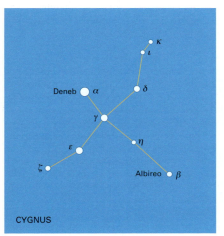

CYGNUS

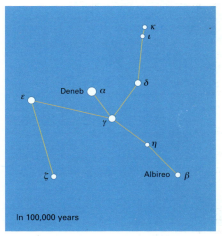

In 100,000 years

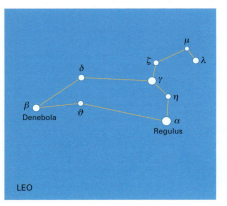

LEO

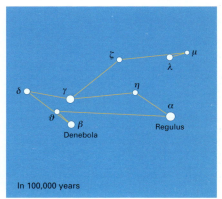

In 100,000 years

distance shrinks by 0.8 light years. Then, as it moves away again, it will be superseded as the brightest star in the sky by Vega, which will peak at magnitude −0.8 nearly 300,000 years from now.

Appearance of the sky

Three factors affect the appearance of the sky: the time of night, the time of year and your latitude on Earth. Firstly, let's consider the effect of latitude.

At one of the Earth's poles, latitude 90°, an observer would see the celestial pole directly overhead (at the *zenith*), and as the Earth turned all stars would circle around the celestial pole without rising or setting (see the top diagram on the facing page).

At the other extreme, an observer stationed exactly on the Earth's equator, latitude 0°, would see the celestial equator directly overhead, as shown in the middle diagram opposite. The north and south celestial poles would lie on the north and south horizons respectively, and every part of the sky would be visible at one time or another. All stars would rise in the east and set in the west as the Earth rotated.

For most observers, the real sky appears somewhere between these two extremes: the celestial pole is at some intermediate altitude between horizon and zenith, and the stars closest to it circle around it without setting (they are said to be *circumpolar*) while the rest of the stars rise and set.

The exact angle of the celestial pole above the horizon depends on the observer's latitude. For someone at latitude 50° north, for instance, the north celestial pole is 50° above the northern horizon (bottom diagram opposite). As another example, if you were at latitude 30° south, the south celestial pole would be 30° above the southern horizon. In other words, the altitude of the celestial pole above the horizon is exactly equal to your latitude, a fact long recognized by navigators.

As the Earth turns, completing one 360° rotation every 24 hours, the stars march across the heavens at the rate of 15° per hour. Therefore the appearance of the sky changes with the time of night. An added complication is that the Earth is also orbiting the Sun each year, so the constellations on show change with the seasons.

For example, a constellation such as Orion, splendidly seen in December and January, will be in the daytime sky six months later and hence will then be invisible. The maps on pages 26–73 will help you find out which stars are on view each month of the year, wherever you are on Earth.

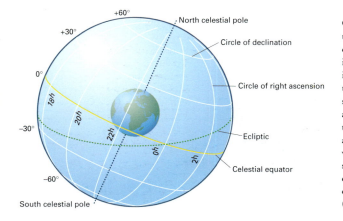

Celestial sphere: To understand celestial coordinates and motions, it helps to think of objects in the sky as lying on a transparent sphere surrounding the Earth, as shown in the diagram on the left. Right ascension and declination can be visualized as circles on this sphere, along with the celestial equator and the ecliptic.
(Wil Tirion)

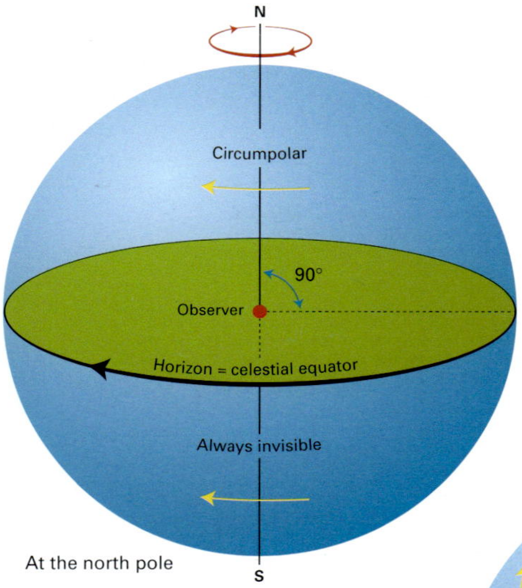

N

Circumpolar

90°

Observer

Horizon = celestial equator

Always invisible

At the north pole

S

The changing appearance of the sky as seen from different latitudes on Earth.

Left: For an observer at the Earth's pole, only one half of the sky is ever visible, the other half being permanently below the horizon.

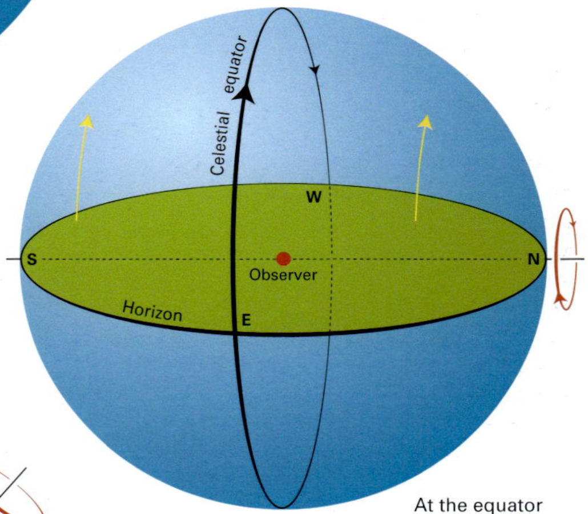

Celestial equator

W

Observer

S

N

Horizon

E

At the equator

Right: At the equator, by contrast, all the sky is visible; as the Earth rotates, stars appear to rise in the east and set in the west.

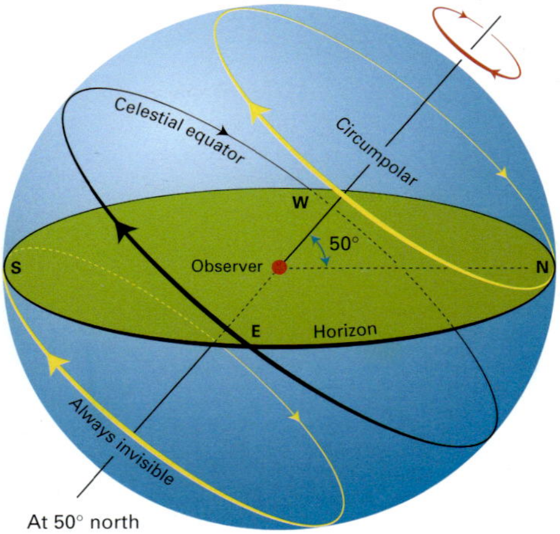

Celestial equator

Circumpolar

W

Observer

50°

S

N

E   Horizon

Always invisible

At 50° north

Left: At intermediate latitudes, the situation is between the two extremes. Part of the sky is always above the horizon (the part marked 'Circumpolar'), but an equal part is always below the horizon and hence is invisible. Stars between these two regions rise and set during the night. (Wil Tirion)

THE STAR CHARTS

The hemisphere charts

On the following four pages are charts showing the complete northern and southern hemispheres of the sky. As well as the main stars of each hemisphere, the charts depict the hazy band of the Milky Way; the dashed red line is the ecliptic, the Sun's path in the heavens. When planets are visible, they will be found near the ecliptic.

Around the rim of each chart are listed the months of the year, to help you find which constellations are best placed at about 10 p.m. local time each month, or 11 p.m. when daylight-saving time (DST, or summer time) is in operation.

Observers in mid-northern latitudes should take the northern hemisphere chart and turn it so that the month of observation is at the bottom. The chart will show the sky that is visible when you face due south that evening. Rotate the chart 15° anticlockwise for each hour after 10 p.m., and turn it clockwise for each hour before 10 p.m.

Observers in mid-southern latitudes should take the southern hemisphere chart and turn it so that the month of observation is at the bottom. The chart will then show the stars as they appear when you are facing due north. Turn the chart 15° clockwise for each hour after 10 p.m., and 15° anticlockwise for each hour before.

In all cases above, for 10 p.m. read 11 p.m. when daylight-saving time, DST, is in operation. Up-to-date information on the application of DST worldwide can be found on the following website:
http://webexhibits.org/daylightsaving/

Spinning Earth: Star trails over the dome of the William Herschel Telescope on La Palma in the Canary Islands, created as the Earth rotated during a time exposure. The bright star near the centre is Polaris. (Nik Szymanek)

The monthly charts

Next comes a series of maps showing the sky as it appears when facing north or south at 10 p.m. (11 p.m. daylight-saving time) in mid-month from various latitudes. The first set of maps is for use in the northern hemisphere from latitudes 60° to 10° north; the second set is for use from the equator to 50° south. (They will also be usable for about 10° either side of this range without significant error.) Curved lines on each map depict the horizon for each latitude. Taking these monthly charts in conjunction with those of the complete celestial hemispheres, you should be able to identify the stars in the sky no matter where you are on Earth.

The constellation charts

The centrepiece of this book, starting on page 74, consists of individual charts of each constellation accompanied by descriptions of the brightest stars and main objects of interest. All stars within each constellation down to magnitude 6.0 are shown, with the sizes of the symbols graded in half-magnitude steps, plus the most prominent examples of what are termed *deep-sky objects* (star clusters, nebulae and galaxies). The total number of stars shown is about 5000.

All constellation maps are to the same scale, with the exception of the rambling Hydra, the largest constellation of all, which is drawn to a significantly smaller scale to fit the page. Areas of particular interest in certain constellations, such as the Hyades and Pleiades clusters in Taurus, and the Orion Nebula, are shown to a larger scale in special detail charts.

We hope that the charts and descriptions in this book will serve as trusty companions for many nights of exploration under the stars. Good stargazing!

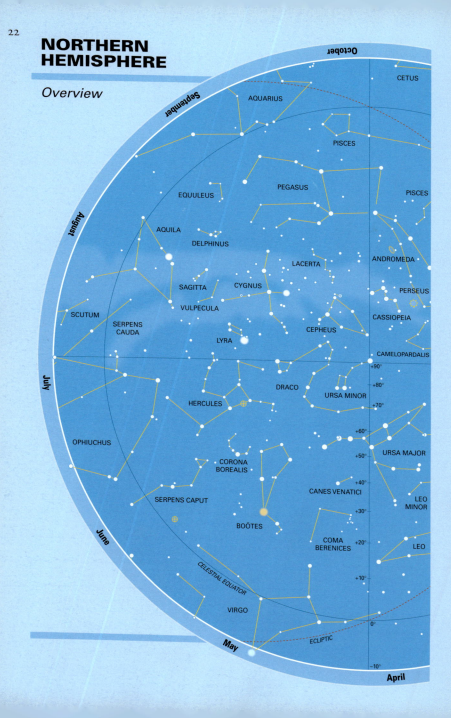

NORTHERN HEMISPHERE

Overview

October

September

August

July

June

May

April

CETUS

AQUARIUS

PISCES

PISCES

EQUULEUS

PEGASUS

ANDROMEDA

AQUILA

DELPHINUS

LACERTA

PERSEUS

SAGITTA

CYGNUS

CEPHEUS

CASSIOPEIA

SCUTUM

SERPENS
CAUDA

VULPECULA

CAMELOPARDALIS

LYRA

+90°

DRACO

URSA MINOR

+80°

+70°

HERCULES

+60°

URSA MAJOR

OPHIUCHUS

+50°

CORONA
BOREALIS

CANES VENATICI

+40°

LEO
MINOR

SERPENS CAPUT

+30°

BOÖTES

COMA
BERENICES

+20°

LEO

+10°

CELESTIAL EQUATOR

0°

VIRGO

ECLIPTIC

−10°

NORTHERN HEMISPHERE

Overview

October

November

December

January

February

March

April

CELESTIAL EQUATOR

ECLIPTIC

CETUS

PISCES

PEGASUS

LACERTA

ARIES

TRIANGULUM

ANDROMEDA

ERIDANUS

TAURUS

CASSIOPEIA

PERSEUS

CEPHEUS

CAMELOPARDALIS

AURIGA

ORION

+90°
+80°
+70°
+60°
+50°
+40°
+30°
+20°
+10°
0°
−10°

LYNX

GEMINI

URSA MINOR

DRACO

URSA MAJOR

CANIS MINOR

CANES VENATICI

LEO MINOR

CANCER

MONOCEROS

COMA BERENICES

LEO

HYDRA

VIRGO

SEXTANS

Galaxy
Bright nebula
Globular cluster
Open cluster

Magnitudes: >0   0   1   2   3   4   5   var.

SOUTHERN HEMISPHERE

Overview

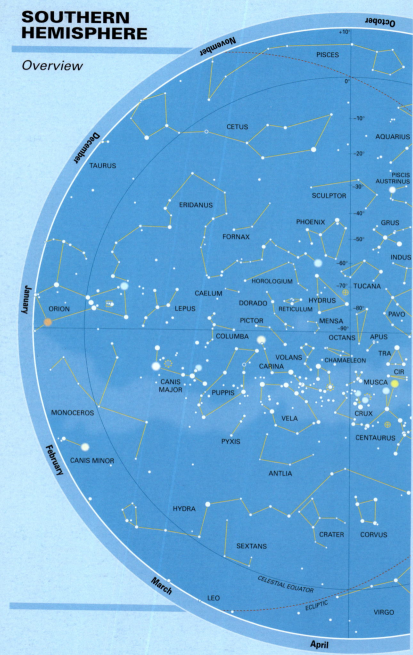

October

November

December

PISCES

+10°

0°

CETUS

−10°

AQUARIUS

−20°

TAURUS

SCULPTOR

−30°

PISCIS
AUSTRINUS

ERIDANUS

PHOENIX

−40°

GRUS

FORNAX

−50°

INDUS

−60°

HOROLOGIUM

TUCANA

January

CAELUM

−70°

HYDRUS

DORADO

ORION

LEPUS

RETICULUM

−80°

PAVO

PICTOR

MENSA

−90°

COLUMBA

OCTANS

APUS

VOLANS

CHAMAELEON

TRA

CARINA

CIR

MUSCA

CANIS
MAJOR

PUPPIS

CRUX

MONOCEROS

VELA

CENTAURUS

February

PYXIS

CANIS MINOR

ANTLIA

HYDRA

CRATER

CORVUS

SEXTANS

CELESTIAL EQUATOR

March

LEO

ECLIPTIC

VIRGO

April

SOUTHERN HEMISPHERE

Overview

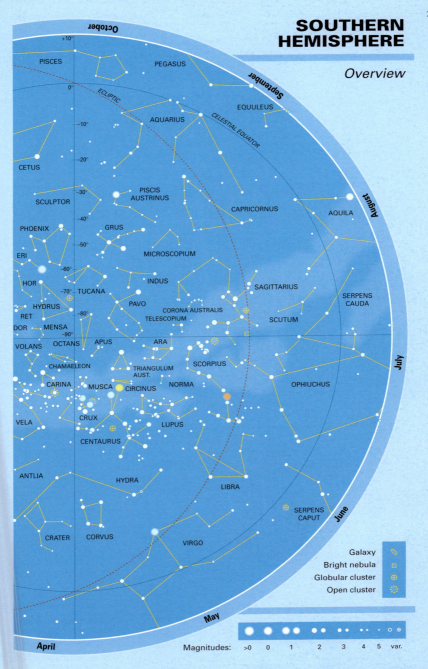

October

PISCES

PEGASUS

September

0°

ECLIPTIC

+10°

EQUULEUS

AQUARIUS

CELESTIAL EQUATOR

–10°

–20°

CETUS

PISCIS
AUSTRINUS

CAPRICORNUS

–30°

SCULPTOR

AQUILA

August

–40°

PHOENIX

GRUS

ERI

–50°

MICROSCOPIUM

HOR

–60°

INDUS

TUCANA

SAGITTARIUS

SERPENS
CAUDA

–70°

PAVO

HYDRUS

RET

–80°

CORONA AUSTRALIS

SCUTUM

July

DOR

MENSA

TELESCOPIUM

–90°

VOLANS

OCTANS

APUS

ARA

CHAMAELEON

TRIANGULUM
AUST.

SCORPIUS

OPHIUCHUS

CARINA

MUSCA

CIRCINUS

NORMA

VELA

CRUX

LUPUS

CENTAURUS

ANTLIA

HYDRA

LIBRA

SERPENS
CAPUT

June

CRATER

CORVUS

VIRGO

May

April

Galaxy
Bright nebula
Globular cluster
Open cluster

Magnitudes: >0   0   1   2   3   4   5   var.

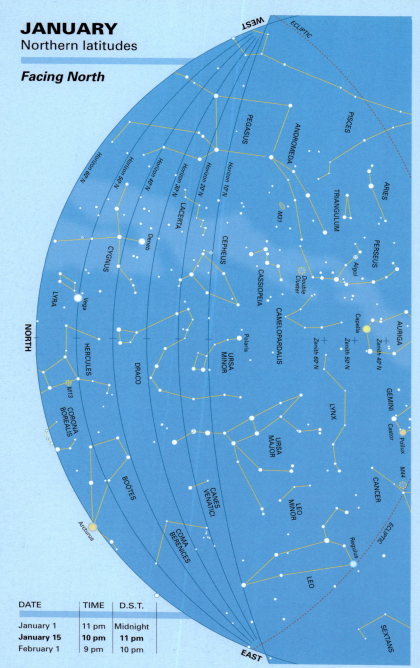

26

JANUARY
Northern latitudes

Facing North

WEST

ECLIPTIC

PEGASUS

ANDROMEDA

PISCES

ARIES

TRIANGULUM

M31

PERSEUS

Algol

Double Cluster

CEPHEUS

CASSIOPEIA

Deneb

Horizon 10°N
Horizon 20°N
Horizon 30°N
Horizon 40°N
Horizon 50°N
Horizon 60°N
Horizon 80°N

LACERTA

CYGNUS

CAMELOPARDALIS

Capella

AURIGA

Zenith 40°N
Zenith 50°N
Zenith 60°N

GEMINI

Castor
Pollux

M44

LYRA

Vega

NORTH

Polaris

URSA
MINOR

LYNX

HERCULES

DRACO

M13

CORONA
BOREALIS

URSA
MAJOR

LEO
MINOR

CANCER

BOÖTES

CANES
VENATICI

Regulus

COMA
BERENICES

Arcturus

LEO

ECLIPTIC

SEXTANS

EAST

DATE	TIME	D.S.T.
January 1	11 pm	Midnight
January 15	**10 pm**	**11 pm**
February 1	9 pm	10 pm

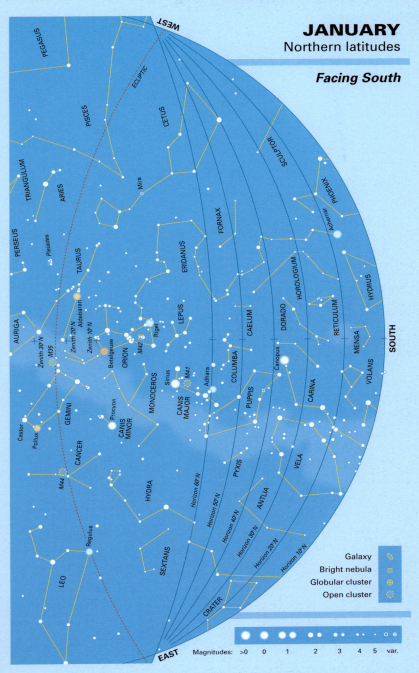

JANUARY
Northern latitudes

Facing South

WEST

PEGASUS

PISCES

CETUS

ECLIPTIC

SCULPTOR

TRIANGULUM

ARIES

Mira

PHOENIX

PERSEUS

Pleiades

FORNAX

Achernar

TAURUS

ERIDANUS

HOROLOGIUM

HYDRUS

Aldebaran

Zenith 20° N

Zenith 10° N

LEPUS

CAELUM

DORADO

RETICULUM

MENSA

SOUTH

AURIGA

Zenith 30° N

M35

Betelgeuse

ORION

Rigel

M42

COLUMBA

CANOPUS

CARINA

VOLANS

Castor

GEMINI

Procyon

MONOCEROS

Sirius

CANIS MAJOR

M41

Adhara

PUPPIS

VELA

Pollux

CANIS MINOR

CANCER

PYXIS

ANTLIA

M44

HYDRA

Horizon 60° N

Horizon 50° N

Horizon 40° N

Horizon 30° N

Horizon 20° N

Horizon 10° N

Regulus

SEXTANS

LEO

CRATER

EAST

Galaxy
Bright nebula
Globular cluster
Open cluster

Magnitudes: >0   0   1   2   3   4   5   var.

JANUARY
Southern latitudes

Facing North

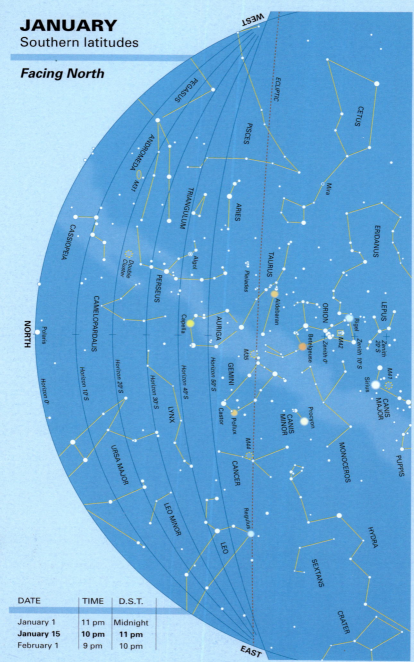

WEST

ECLIPTIC

PEGASUS

ANDROMEDA

M31

CASSIOPEIA

CETUS

PISCES

TRIANGULUM

ARIES

Double Cluster

Algol

PERSEUS

ERIDANUS

Mira

TAURUS

Pleiades

CAMELOPARDALIS

Aldebaran

LEPUS

ORION

Rigel

Zenith 10°S

Zenith 20°S

Zenith 0°

M42

NORTH

Polaris

Capella

AURIGA

M35

Betelgeuse

M41

Sirius

CANIS MAJOR

Horizon 0°

Horizon 10°S

Horizon 20°S

Horizon 30°S

Horizon 40°S

Horizon 50°S

GEMINI

CANIS MINOR

Procyon

PUPPIS

LYNX

Castor

Pollux

MONOCEROS

URSA MAJOR

M44

CANCER

LEO MINOR

Regulus

HYDRA

LEO

SEXTANS

CRATER

EAST

DATE	TIME	D.S.T.
January 1	11 pm	Midnight
January 15	**10 pm**	**11 pm**
February 1	9 pm	10 pm

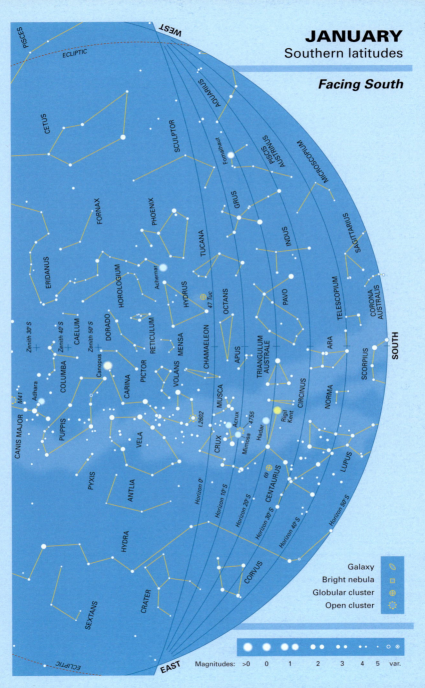

JANUARY
Southern latitudes

Facing South

WEST

PISCES

ECLIPTIC

CETUS

SCULPTOR

AQUARIUS

Fomalhaut

PISCIS AUSTRINUS

MICROSCOPIUM

FORNAX

PHOENIX

GRUS

INDUS

SAGITTARIUS

ERIDANUS

HOROLOGIUM

Achernar

HYDRUS

TUCANA

47 Tuc

OCTANS

PAVO

TELESCOPIUM

CORONA AUSTRALIS

Zenith 30°S

CAELUM

Zenith 40°S

RETICULUM

Zenith 50°S

DORADO

MENSA

CHAMAELEON

APUS

TRIANGULUM AUSTRALE

ARA

SOUTH

CANIS MAJOR

M41

Adhara

COLUMBA

Canopus

PICTOR

VOLANS

MUSCA

4755

CIRCINUS

SCORPIUS

Zenith 50°S

CARINA

I.2602

Acrux

Rigil Kent

NORMA

PUPPIS

VELA

CRUX

Mimosa

Hadar

CENTAURUS

LUPUS

PYXIS

ANTLIA

Horizon 0°

Horizon 10°S

Horizon 20°S

Horizon 30°S

Horizon 40°S

Horizon 50°S

HYDRA

CORVUS

SEXTANS

CRATER

ECLIPTIC

EAST

Galaxy
Bright nebula
Globular cluster
Open cluster

Magnitudes: >0   0   1   2   3   4   5   var.

FEBRUARY
Northern latitudes

Facing North

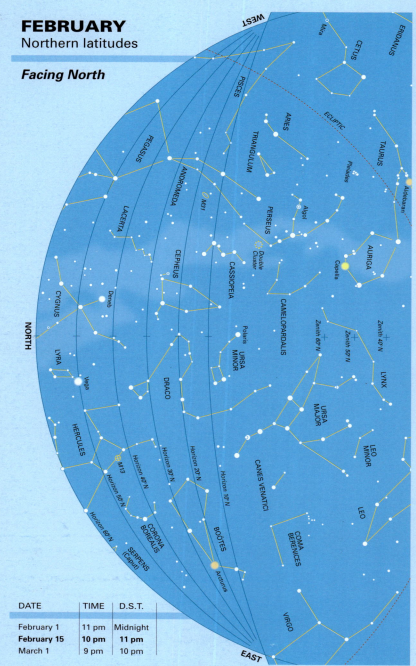

WEST

Mira

CETUS

ERIDANUS

PISCES

ECLIPTIC

ARIES

TRIANGULUM

TAURUS

Pleiades

PEGASUS

ANDROMEDA

M31

PERSEUS

Algol

Double
Cluster

AURIGA

Capella

LACERTA

CEPHEUS

CASSIOPEIA

CAMELOPARDALIS

Zenith 40° N

Zenith 50° N

Zenith 60° N

LYNX

CYGNUS

Deneb

Polaris

URSA
MINOR

NORTH

LYRA

Vega

DRACO

URSA
MAJOR

LEO
MINOR

HERCULES

Horizon 20° N

Horizon 30° N

CANES VENATICI

LEO

M13

Horizon 40° N

Horizon 10° N

Horizon 50° N

CORONA
BOREALIS

BOÖTES

COMA
BERENICES

Horizon 60° N

SERPENS
(Caput)

Arcturus

VIRGO

EAST

DATE	TIME	D.S.T.
February 1	11 pm	Midnight
February 15	**10 pm**	**11 pm**
March 1	9 pm	10 pm

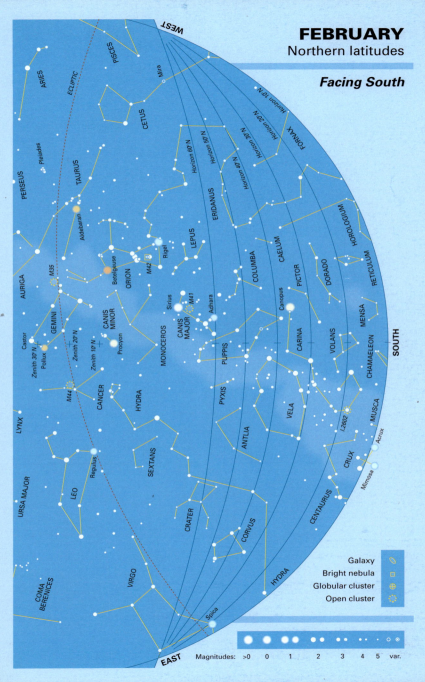

FEBRUARY
Northern latitudes

Facing South

Galaxy
Bright nebula
Globular cluster
Open cluster

Magnitudes: >0 0 1 2 3 4 5 var.

WEST

SOUTH

EAST

PISCES
ARIES
Mira
CETUS
ECLIPTIC
PERSEUS
Pleiades
TAURUS
Aldebaran
AURIGA
M35
GEMINI
Castor
Pollux
Zenith 30 N
Zenith 20 N
Zenith 10 N
Betelgeuse
ORION
M42
Rigel
LEPUS
ERIDANUS
Horizon 60 N
Horizon 50 N
Horizon 40 N
Horizon 30 N
Horizon 20 N
Horizon 10 N
FORNAX
HOROLOGIUM
RETICULUM
CAELUM
COLUMBA
PICTOR
DORADO
MENSA
CANIS MINOR
Procyon
Sirius
M41
CANIS MAJOR
Adhara
MONOCEROS
PUPPIS
PYXIS
Canopus
CARINA
VOLANS
CHAMAELEON
MUSCA
Acrux
Mimosa
CRUX
I.2602
VELA
CENTAURUS
ANTLIA
M44
CANCER
HYDRA
LYNX
URSA MAJOR
LEO
Regulus
SEXTANS
CRATER
CORVUS
HYDRA
VIRGO
COMA BERENICES
Spica

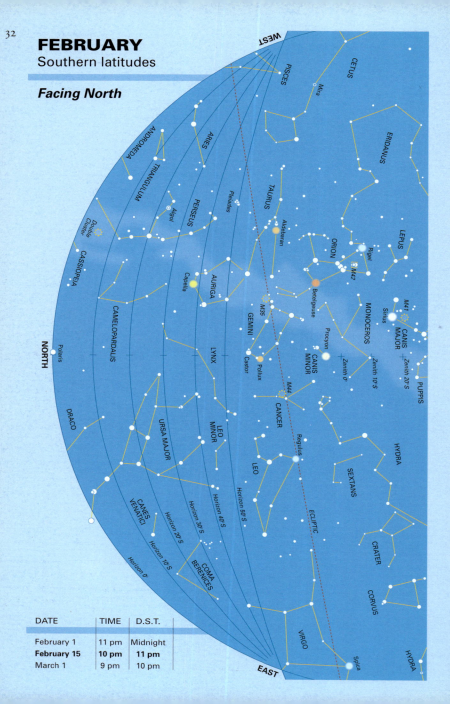

32

FEBRUARY
Southern latitudes

Facing North

WEST

PISCES

CETUS

Mira

ERIDANUS

ANDROMEDA

ARIES

TRIANGULUM

Pleiades

TAURUS

Algol

PERSEUS

Aldebaran

ORION

LEPUS

Rigel

Double Cluster

CASSIOPEIA

Capella

AURIGA

M42

Betelgeuse

MONOCEROS

M41

Sirius

CANIS MAJOR

M35

GEMINI

CAMELOPARDALIS

LYNX

Procyon

CANIS MINOR

Zenith 0°

Zenith 10°S

Zenith 20°S

PUPPIS

NORTH

Polaris

Castor

Pollux

M44

DRACO

CANCER

URSA MAJOR

LEO MINOR

Regulus

LEO

HYDRA

SEXTANS

CANES VENATICI

Horizon 50°S

Horizon 40°S

Horizon 30°S

Horizon 20°S

COMA BERENICES

Horizon 10°S

CRATER

Horizon 0°

CORVUS

ECLIPTIC

VIRGO

Spica

HYDRA

EAST

DATE	TIME	D.S.T.
February 1	11 pm	Midnight
February 15	**10 pm**	**11 pm**
March 1	9 pm	10 pm

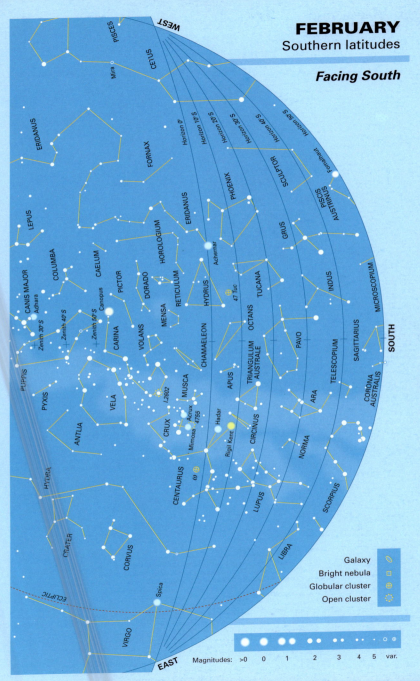

FEBRUARY
Southern latitudes

Facing South

WEST

EAST

SOUTH

PISCES
CETUS
Mira
ERIDANUS
FORNAX
Horizon 0°
Horizon 10° S
Horizon 20° S
Horizon 30° S
Horizon 40° S
Horizon 50° S
Horizon 90° S
Fomalhaut
PHOENIX
Achernar
SCULPTOR
PISCIS AUSTRINUS
GRUS
LEPUS
COLUMBA
CAELUM
PICTOR
DORADO
HOROLOGIUM
RETICULUM
ERIDANUS
HYDRUS
47 Tuc
MENSA
TUCANA
INDUS
MICROSCOPIUM
CANIS MAJOR
Adhara
Canopus
Zenith 30° S
Zenith 40° S
Zenith 50° S
CARINA
VOLANS
CHAMAELEON
OCTANS
OCTANS
PAVO
SAGITTARIUS
PUPPIS
PYXIS
VELA
L2602
MUSCA
APUS
TRIANGULUM AUSTRALE
TELESCOPIUM
CORONA AUSTRALIS
ANTLIA
CRUX
Acrux
4755
Mimosa
Hadar
Rigil Kent
CIRCINUS
NORMA
ARA
HYDRA
CENTAURUS
ω
LUPUS
SCORPIUS
CRATER
CORVUS
LIBRA
ECLIPTIC
Spica
VIRGO

Galaxy
Bright nebula
Globular cluster
Open cluster

Magnitudes: >0 0 1 2 3 4 5 var.

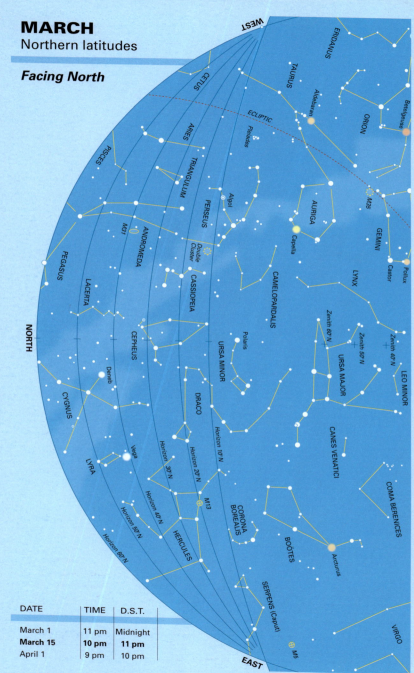

MARCH
Northern latitudes

Facing North

WEST

ERIDANUS

TAURUS

Aldebaran

ORION

Betelgeuse

CETUS

ECLIPTIC

Pleiades

ARIES

GEMINI

M35

AURIGA

Castor

Pollux

TRIANGULUM

Algol

Capella

PERSEUS

Double
Cluster

M31

LYNX

ANDROMEDA

CASSIOPEIA

CAMELOPARDALIS

PEGASUS

Zenith 60° N

Zenith 50° N

Zenith 40° N

LEO MINOR

LACERTA

Polaris

URSA MINOR

URSA MAJOR

CEPHEUS

NORTH

DRACO

CANES VENATICI

Deneb

CYGNUS

Horizon 10° N

Horizon 20° N

COMA BERENICES

Vega

Horizon 30° N

LYRA

Horizon 40° N

M13

CORONA
BOREALIS

BOÖTES

Horizon 50° N

HERCULES

Arcturus

Horizon 60° N

SERPENS (Caput)

VIRGO

M5

EAST

DATE	TIME	D.S.T.
March 1	11 pm	Midnight
March 15	**10 pm**	**11 pm**
April 1	9 pm	10 pm

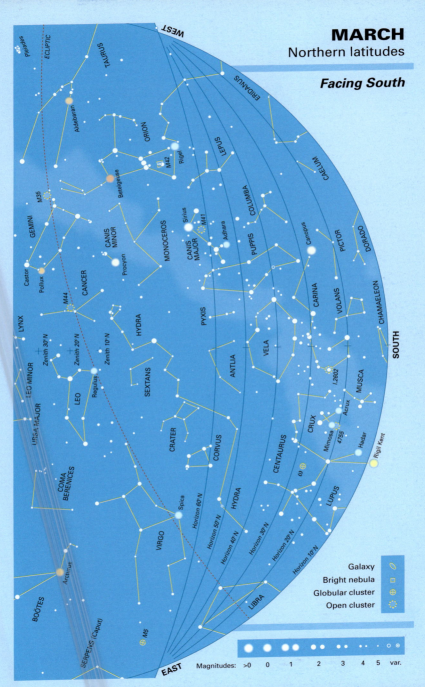

MARCH
Northern latitudes

Facing South

Galaxy
Bright nebula
Globular cluster
Open cluster

Magnitudes: >0 0 1 2 3 4 5 var.

MARCH
Southern latitudes

Facing North

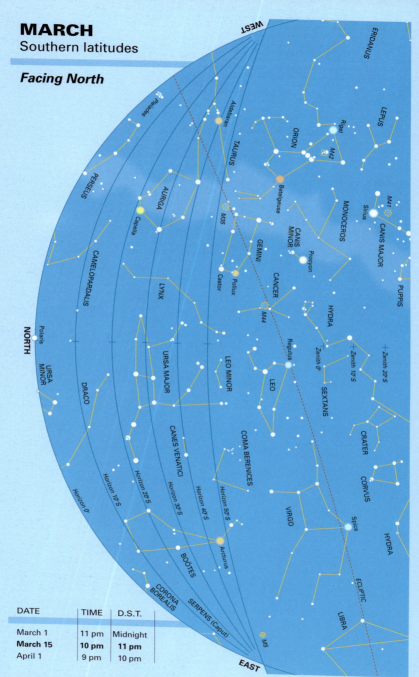

WEST

ERIDANUS

LEPUS

Pleiades

Aldebaran

TAURUS

ORION

Rigel

M42

Betelgeuse

PERSEUS

AURIGA

Capella

M35

GEMINI

CANIS
MINOR

MONOCEROS

Sirius

M41

CANIS MAJOR

PUPPIS

CAMELOPARDALIS

LYNX

Castor

Pollux

CANCER

Procyon

M44

HYDRA

NORTH

Polaris

URSA
MINOR

DRACO

URSA MAJOR

LEO MINOR

LEO

Regulus

Zenith 0°

Zenith 10° S

Zenith 20° S

SEXTANS

CRATER

CANES VENATICI

COMA BERENICES

CORVUS

Horizon 0°

Horizon 10° S

Horizon 20° S

Horizon 30° S

Horizon 40° S

Horizon 50° S

VIRGO

Spica

HYDRA

BOÖTES

Arcturus

ECLIPTIC

CORONA
BOREALIS

SERPENS (Caput)

LIBRA

M5

EAST

DATE	TIME	D.S.T.
March 1	11 pm	Midnight
March 15	**10 pm**	**11 pm**
April 1	9 pm	10 pm

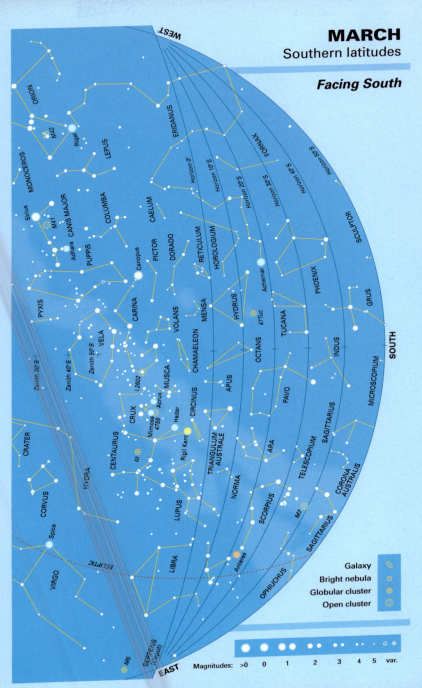

MARCH
Southern latitudes

Facing South

WEST

ORION

MONOCEROS

M42

Rigel

LEPUS

ERIDANUS

Horizon 0°

Horizon 10° S

Horizon 20° S

PHOENIX

Horizon 30° S

Horizon 40° S

Horizon 50° S

SCULPTOR

Sirius

M41

CANIS MAJOR

COLUMBA

CAELUM

Adhara

PUPPIS

PICTOR

DORADO

RETICULUM

HOROLOGIUM

Achernar

GRUS

Canopus

PYXIS

CARINA

VELA

VOLANS

MENSA

HYDRUS

47 Tuc

TUCANA

INDUS

SOUTH

Zenith 30° S

Zenith 40° S

Zenith 50° S

I.2602

MUSCA

CHAMAELEON

APUS

OCTANS

PAVO

MICROSCOPIUM

CRUX

Acrux

CIRCINUS

TRIANGULUM AUSTRALE

SAGITTARIUS

CRATER

CENTAURUS

Mimosa 4755

Hadar

ω

Rigil Kent

NORMA

ARA

TELESCOPIUM

CORONA AUSTRALIS

HYDRA

CORVUS

LUPUS

SCORPIUS

M7

SAGITTARIUS

Spica

VIRGO

LIBRA

Antares

OPHIUCHUS

ECLIPTIC

SERPENS (Caput)

M5

EAST

Galaxy

Bright nebula

Globular cluster

Open cluster

Magnitudes: >0   0   1   2   3   4   5   var.

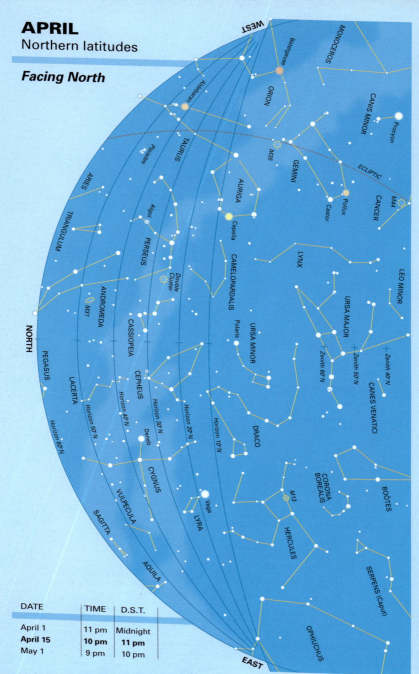

38

APRIL
Northern latitudes

Facing North

WEST

Betelgeuse

MONOCEROS

ORION

Aldebaran

CANIS MINOR

Procyon

Pleiades

TAURUS

M35

GEMINI

CANCER

ECLIPTIC

M44

ARIES

AURIGA

Pollux

Castor

TRIANGULUM

Algol

PERSEUS

Capella

CAMELOPARDALIS

LYNX

LEO MINOR

ANDROMEDA

Double
Cluster

URSA MAJOR

Zenith 40° N

M31

Polaris

Zenith 50° N

CANES VENATICI

NORTH

CASSIOPEIA

URSA MINOR

Zenith 60° N

PEGASUS

CEPHEUS

Horizon 50° N

Horizon 40° N

Horizon 30° N

Horizon 20° N

Horizon 10° N

DRACO

LACERTA

Deneb

Horizon 60° N

CYGNUS

CORONA
BOREALIS

BOÖTES

VULPECULA

Vega

M13

LYRA

HERCULES

SAGITTA

SERPENS (Caput)

AQUILA

OPHIUCHUS

DATE	TIME	D.S.T.
April 1	11 pm	Midnight
April 15	**10 pm**	**11 pm**
May 1	9 pm	10 pm

EAST

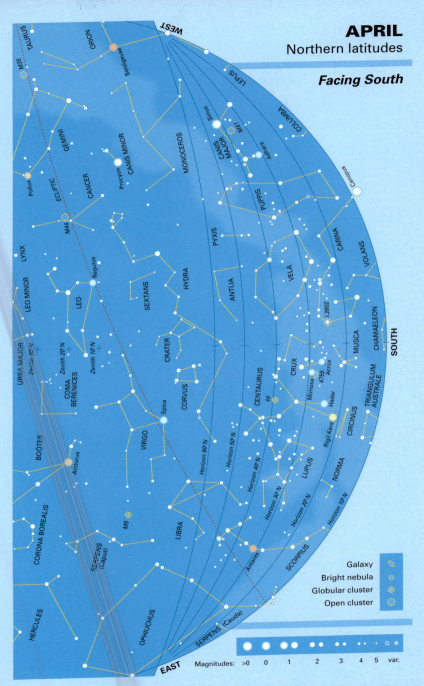

APRIL
Northern latitudes

Facing South

WEST

TAURUS
M35
ORION
Betelgeuse
GEMINI
Pollux
ECLIPTIC
CANCER
M44
LYNX
LEO MINOR
Regulus
URSA MAJOR
Zenith 30° N
Zenith 20° N
Zenith 10° N
LEO
COMA BERENICES
BOÖTES
Arcturus
CORONA BOREALIS
SERPENS (Caput)
M5
HERCULES
OPHIUCHUS

LEPUS
Sirius
M41
CANIS MAJOR
Adhara
COLUMBA
CANIS MINOR
Procyon
MONOCEROS
PUPPIS
CANOPUS
PYXIS
HYDRA
SEXTANS
ANTLIA
VELA
CARINA
VOLANS
CRATER
CORVUS
Spica
VIRGO
CENTAURUS
ω
CRUX
4755
Mimosa
Acrux
Hadar
Rigil Kent
IC2602
MUSCA
CHAMAELEON
TRIANGULUM AUSTRALE
SOUTH
CIRCINUS
LUPUS
NORMA
LIBRA
Antares
SCORPIUS
SERPENS (Cauda)

Horizon 60° N
Horizon 50° N
Horizon 40° N
Horizon 30° N
Horizon 20° N
Horizon 10° N

EAST

Galaxy
Bright nebula
Globular cluster
Open cluster

Magnitudes: >0   0   1   2   3   4   5   var.

APRIL
Southern latitudes

Facing North

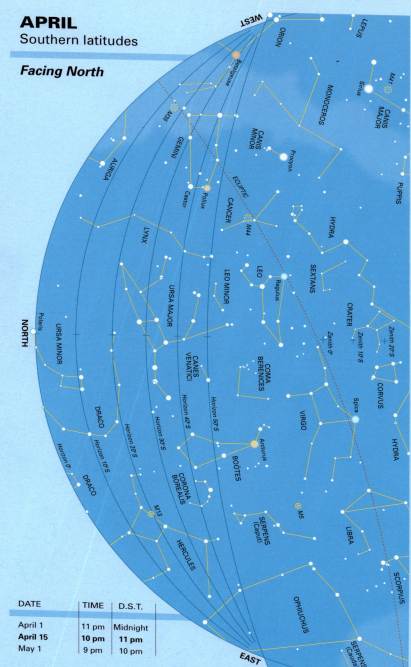

WEST

ORION

LEPUS

Betelgeuse

Sirius

M41

CANIS MAJOR

MONCEROS

M35

Procyon

PUPPIS

AURIGA

GEMINI

CANIS MINOR

Castor

Pollux

ECLIPTIC

CANCER

M44

HYDRA

LYNX

LEO MINOR

LEO

Regulus

SEXTANS

CRATER

Zenith 10°S

Zenith 20°S

URSA MAJOR

Zenith 0°

Polaris

NORTH

URSA MINOR

CANES VENATICI

COMA BERENICES

CORVUS

Spica

Horizon 40°S

Horizon 50°S

VIRGO

HYDRA

DRACO

Horizon 20°S

Horizon 30°S

Arcturus

BOÖTES

Horizon 10°S

Horizon 0°

DRACO

CORONA BOREALIS

M13

SERPENS (Caput)

M5

LIBRA

HERCULES

SCORPIUS

OPHIUCHUS

SERPENS (Cauda)

EAST

DATE	TIME	D.S.T.
April 1	11 pm	Midnight
April 15	**10 pm**	**11 pm**
May 1	9 pm	10 pm

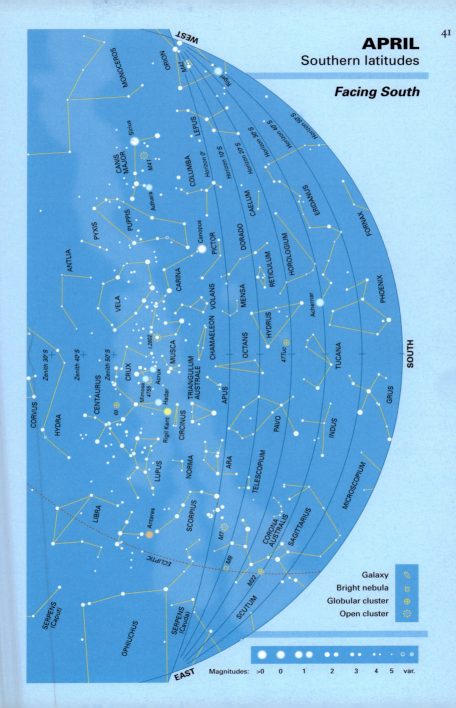

APRIL

Southern latitudes

Facing South

41

Galaxy
Bright nebula
Globular cluster
Open cluster

Magnitudes: >0 0 1 2 3 4 5 var.

WEST

EAST

SOUTH

MONOCEROS
ORION
M42
Rigel
LEPUS
COLUMBA
Horizon 0°S
Horizon 10°S
Horizon 20°S
Horizon 30°S
Horizon 40°S
Horizon 50°S
Sirius
CANIS MAJOR
M41
Adhara
PUPPIS
PYXIS
ANTLIA
Canopus
PICTOR
CARINA
CAELUM
DORADO
RETICULUM
HOROLOGIUM
ERIDANUS
FORNAX
PHOENIX
Achernar
VELA
VOLANS
CHAMAELEON
MENSA
HYDRUS
OCTANS
47Tuc
TUCANA
Zenith 30°S
Zenith 40°S
Zenith 50°S
I.2602
4755
Mimosa
CRUX
Acrux
MUSCA
TRIANGULUM AUSTRALE
APUS
PAVO
GRUS
INDUS
MICROSCOPIUM
CORVUS
HYDRA
CENTAURUS
ω
Rigil Kent
Hadar
CIRCINUS
NORMA
ARA
TELESCOPIUM
SAGITTARIUS
CORONA AUSTRALIS
LIBRA
LUPUS
Antares
SCORPIUS
M7
M8
M22
SCUTUM
ECLIPTIC
SERPENS (Caput)
OPHIUCHUS
SERPENS (Cauda)

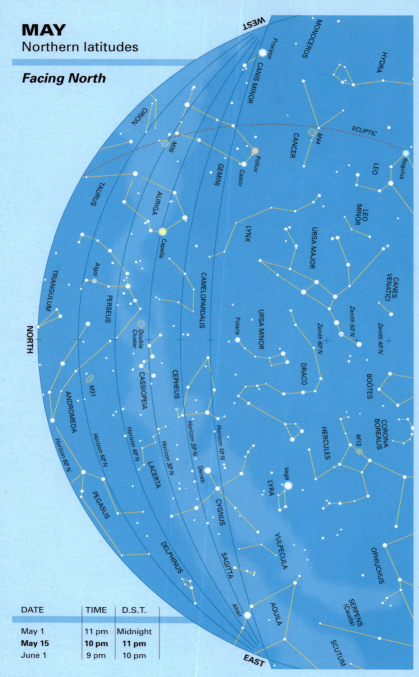

42

MAY
Northern latitudes

Facing North

WEST

MONOCEROS

HYDRA

Procyon

CANIS MINOR

ORION

ECLIPTIC

CANCER

M44

LEO

Regulus

GEMINI

Pollux

Castor

TAURUS

AURIGA

LYNX

LEO MINOR

Capella

URSA MAJOR

CANES VENATICI

TRIANGULUM

Algol

CAMELOPARDALIS

Zenith 50° N

Zenith 40° N

Polaris

Zenith 60° N

PERSEUS

URSA MINOR

Double Cluster

BOÖTES

NORTH

M31

CASSIOPEIA

CEPHEUS

DRACO

CORONA BOREALIS

ANDROMEDA

LACERTA

HERCULES

M13

Horizon 60° N

Horizon 50° N

Horizon 40° N

Horizon 30° N

Horizon 20° N

Horizon 10° N

Deneb

Vega

PEGASUS

CYGNUS

LYRA

DELPHINUS

VULPECULA

OPHIUCHUS

SAGITTA

AQUILA

SERPENS (Cauda)

Altair

SCUTUM

EAST

DATE	TIME	D.S.T.
May 1	11 pm	Midnight
May 15	**10 pm**	**11 pm**
June 1	9 pm	10 pm

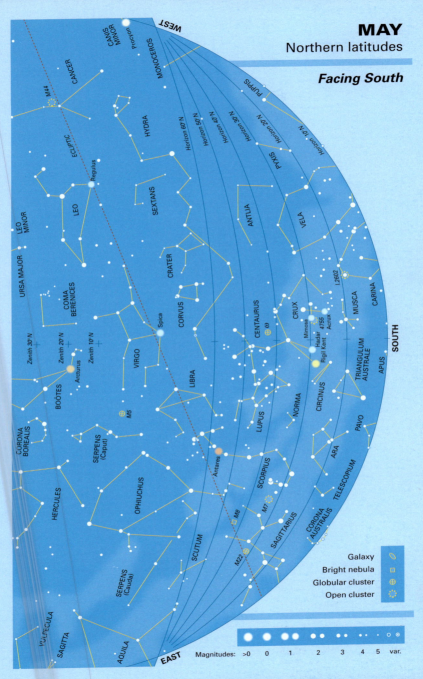

MAY
Northern latitudes

Facing South

WEST

CANIS MINOR
Procyon
CANCER
M44
MONOCEROS
LEO
Regulus
LEO MINOR
URSA MAJOR
COMA BERENICES
ECLIPTIC
HYDRA
SEXTANS
CRATER
CORVUS
Spica
VIRGO
Zenith 30°N
Zenith 20°N
Zenith 10°N
Arcturus
BOÖTES
LIBRA
M5
CORONA BOREALIS
SERPENS (Caput)
HERCULES
OPHIUCHUS
Antares
SCUTUM
SERPENS (Cauda)
VULPECULA
SAGITTA
AQUILA
EAST

PUPPIS
Horizon 60°N
Horizon 50°N
Horizon 40°N
Horizon 30°N
Horizon 20°N
Horizon 10°N
PYXIS
ANTLIA
VELA
CENTAURUS
ω
CRUX
Mimosa
Acrux
4755
Hadar
Rigil Kent
NORMA
CIRCINUS
LUPUS
MUSCA
CARINA
I.2602
TRIANGULUM AUSTRALE
APUS
SOUTH
PAVO
ARA
TELESCOPIUM
SCORPIUS
M7
SAGITTARIUS
M8
CORONA AUSTRALIS
M22

Galaxy
Bright nebula
Globular cluster
Open cluster

Magnitudes: >0 0 1 2 3 4 5 var.

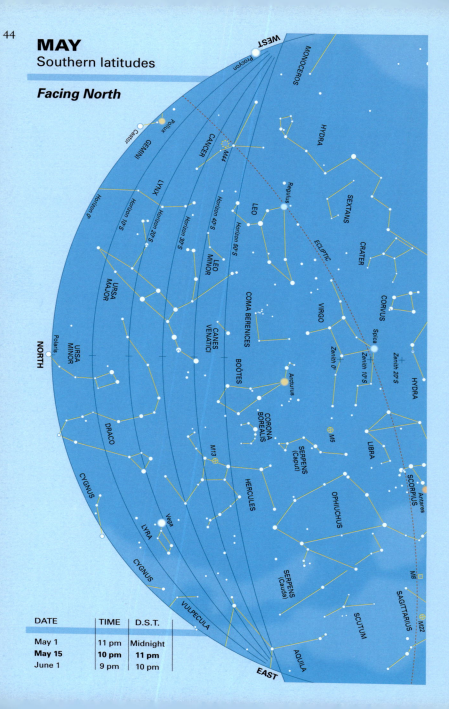

44

MAY
Southern latitudes

Facing North

WEST

NORTH

EAST

MONOCEROS

Procyon

Castor

Pollux

GEMINI

CANCER

M44

LYNX

Horizon 0°

Horizon 10°S

Horizon 20°S

Horizon 30°S

Horizon 40°S

Horizon 50°S

Horizon 60°S

LEO MINOR

LEO

Regulus

HYDRA

SEXTANS

CRATER

ECLIPTIC

URSA MAJOR

COMA BERENICES

CANES VENATICI

VIRGO

CORVUS

Spica

Zenith 0°

Zenith 10°S

Zenith 20°S

HYDRA

Polaris

URSA MINOR

BOÖTES

Arcturus

CORONA BOREALIS

M5

LIBRA

DRACO

SERPENS (Caput)

M13

OPHIUCHUS

Antares

SCORPIUS

CYGNUS

HERCULES

Vega

LYRA

CYGNUS

SERPENS (Cauda)

M8

SAGITTARIUS

M22

VULPECULA

SCUTUM

AQUILA

DATE	TIME	D.S.T.
May 1	11 pm	Midnight
May 15	**10 pm**	**11 pm**
June 1	9 pm	10 pm

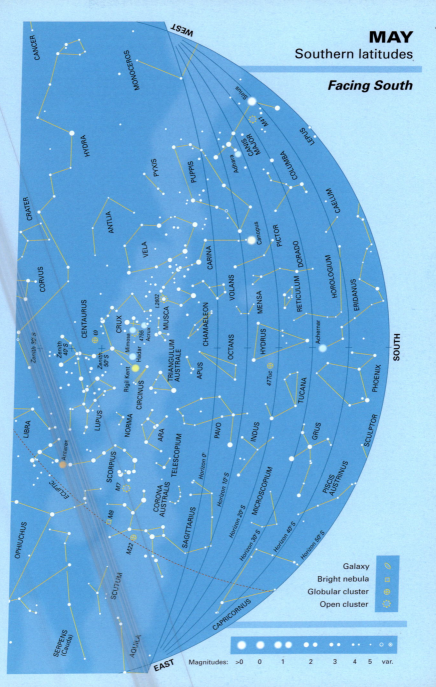

MAY
Southern latitudes

Facing South

WEST

CANCER

MONOCEROS

HYDRA

Sirius
M41

CANIS MAJOR
Adhara
LEPUS
COLUMBA
CAELUM

CRATER

ANTLIA

PYXIS
PUPPIS

VELA

CARINA
Canopus
PICTOR
DORADO
HOROLOGIUM
ERIDANUS

CORVUS

CENTAURUS
ω
CRUX
Mimosa
4755
Acrux
Hadar
λ2602
MUSCA
VOLANS
CHAMAELEON
MENSA
RETICULUM
Achernar

Zenith 30° S
Zenith 40° S
Zenith 50° S
Rigil Kent
CIRCINUS
TRIANGULUM AUSTRALE
APUS
OCTANS
HYDRUS
47Tuc
TUCANA
PHOENIX

SOUTH

LIBRA

LUPUS
NORMA
ARA
TELESCOPIUM
PAVO
INDUS
GRUS
SCULPTOR

Antares
ECLIPTIC
SCORPIUS
M7
M8
CORONA AUSTRALIS
SAGITTARIUS
Horizon 0°
Horizon 10° S
Horizon 20° S
MICROSCOPIUM
Horizon 30° S
Horizon 40° S
PISCIS AUSTRINUS
Horizon 50° S

OPHIUCHUS

M22

SCUTUM

SERPENS (Cauda)

AQUILA

CAPRICORNUS

EAST

Galaxy
Bright nebula
Globular cluster
Open cluster

Magnitudes: >0   0   1   2   3   4   5   var.

JUNE
Northern latitudes

Facing North

WEST

SEXTANS

ECLIPTIC

Regulus

LEO

CANCER

M44

LEO MINOR

COMA BERENICES

Pollux

Castor

GEMINI

LYNX

URSA MAJOR

CANES VENATICI

BOÖTES

Horizon 60° N

Horizon 50° N

Horizon 40° N

Horizon 30° N

Horizon 20° N

Horizon 10° N

TAURUS

AURIGA

Capella

CAMELOPARDALIS

URSA MINOR

Zenith 60° N

Zenith 50° N

Zenith 40° N

M13

HERCULES

NORTH

PERSEUS

Polaris

DRACO

Algol

Double Cluster

CASSIOPEIA

CEPHEUS

Vega

LYRA

TRIANGULUM

M31

ANDROMEDA

Deneb

VULPECULA

PISCES

LACERTA

CYGNUS

SAGITTA

DELPHINUS

Altair

PEGASUS

AQUILA

EQUULEUS

EAST

DATE	TIME	D.S.T.
June 1	11 pm	Midnight
June 15	**10 pm**	**11 pm**
July 1	9 pm	10 pm

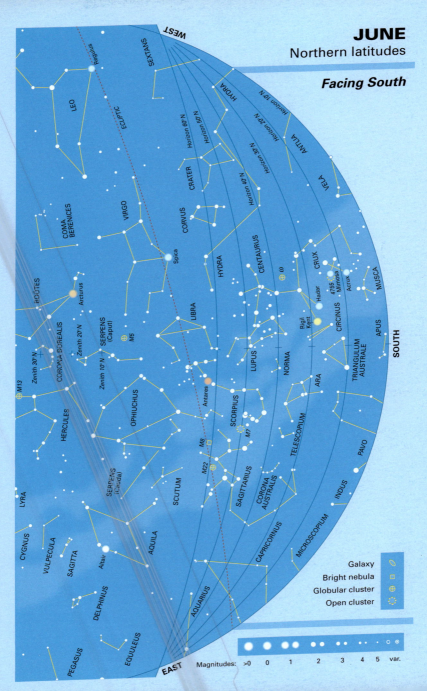

JUNE
Northern latitudes

Facing South

47

WEST

SEXTANS

LEO

Regulus

ECLIPTIC

HYDRA

Horizon 60° N
Horizon 50° N
Horizon 20° N
Horizon 10° N

ANTLIA

CRATER

Horizon 30° N

VELA

Horizon 40° N

COMA
BERENICES

VIRGO

CORVUS

HYDRA

CENTAURUS

CRUX

MUSCA

Spica

4755
Mimosa
Acrux

ω

BOÖTES

Arcturus

LIBRA

Hadar

CIRCINUS

APUS

SOUTH

SERPENS
(Caput)

M5

Rigil
Kent

CORONA BOREALIS

Zenith 30° N
Zenith 20° N
Zenith 10° N

M13

Antares

LUPUS

NORMA

TRIANGULUM
AUSTRALE

HERCULES

OPHIUCHUS

SCORPIUS

ARA

TELESCOPIUM

M7

M8

PAVO

SERPENS
(Cauda)

M22

SAGITTARIUS

CORONA
AUSTRALIS

INDUS

LYRA

SCUTUM

CYGNUS

VULPECULA

AQUILA

CAPRICORNUS

MICROSCOPIUM

SAGITTA

Altair

DELPHINUS

AQUARIUS

Galaxy
Bright nebula
Globular cluster
Open cluster

PEGASUS

EQUULEUS

EAST

Magnitudes: >0   0   1   2   3   4   5   var.

48

JUNE
Southern latitudes

Facing North

WEST

NORTH

EAST

DATE	TIME	D.S.T.
June 1	11 pm	Midnight
June 15	**10 pm**	**11 pm**
July 1	9 pm	10 pm

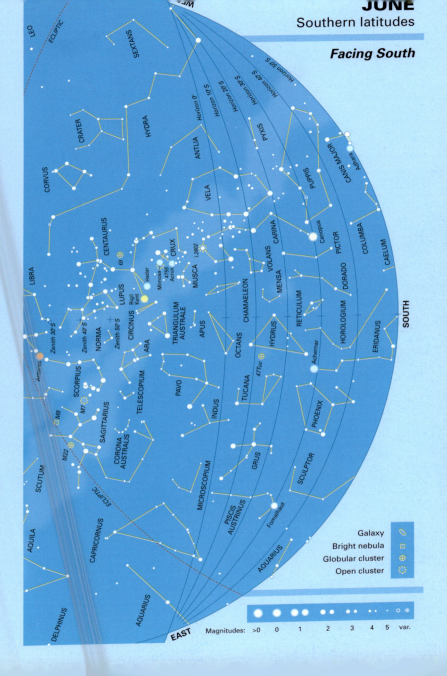

LEO

ECLIPTIC

SEXTANS

CRATER

HYDRA

Horizon 0°S
Horizon 10°S
Horizon 20°S
Horizon 30°S
Horizon 40°S
Horizon 50°S

ANTLIA

CORVUS

VELA

PYXIS

PUPPIS

CANIS MAJOR

Adhara

CENTAURUS

CRUX

Mimosa
4755
Acrux

MUSCA

L2602

CARINA

Canopus

PICTOR

COLUMBA

CAELUM

Hadar

VOLANS

LIBRA

LUPUS

ω

Rigil
Kent

MENSA

DORADO

ω

CIRCINUS

TRIANGULUM
AUSTRALE

CHAMAELEON

RETICULUM

HOROLOGIUM

Zenith 30°S

NORMA

Zenith 40°S

Zenith 50°S

ARA

APUS

OCTANS

HYDRUS

Achernar

ERIDANUS

SOUTH

Antares

SCORPIUS

M7

47Tuc ⊕

PAVO

TUCANA

PHOENIX

M8

SAGITTARIUS

TELESCOPIUM

INDUS

GRUS

SCULPTOR

M22 ⊕

CORONA
AUSTRALIS

SCUTUM

MICROSCOPIUM

AQUILA

ECLIPTIC

CAPRICORNUS

PISCIS
AUSTRINUS

Fomalhaut

DELPHINUS

AQUARIUS

EAST

50

JULY
Northern latitudes

Facing North

WEST

ECLIPTIC

VIRGO

COMA BERENICES

CANES VENATICI

BOÖTES

CORONA BOREALIS

Arcturus

HERCULES

M13

LEO

Regulus

CANCER

LEO MINOR

URSA MAJOR

LYNX

DRACO

URSA MINOR

Polaris

Zenith 60 N

Zenith 50 N

Zenith 40 N

Vega

LYRA

CYGNUS

Pollux

Castor

GEMINI

Horizon 60 N

Horizon 50 N

Horizon 40 N

Horizon 30 N

Horizon 20 N

Horizon 10 N

CAMELOPARDALIS

CEPHEUS

Denab

NORTH

AURIGA

Capella

Double Cluster

Algol

LACERTA

DELPHINUS

CASSIOPEIA

PERSEUS

EQUULEUS

TRIANGULUM

M31

ANDROMEDA

PEGASUS

ARIES

PISCES

PISCES

AQUARIUS

EAST

DATE	TIME	D.S.T.
July 1	11 pm	Midnight
July 15	**10 pm**	**11 pm**
August 1	9 pm	10 pm

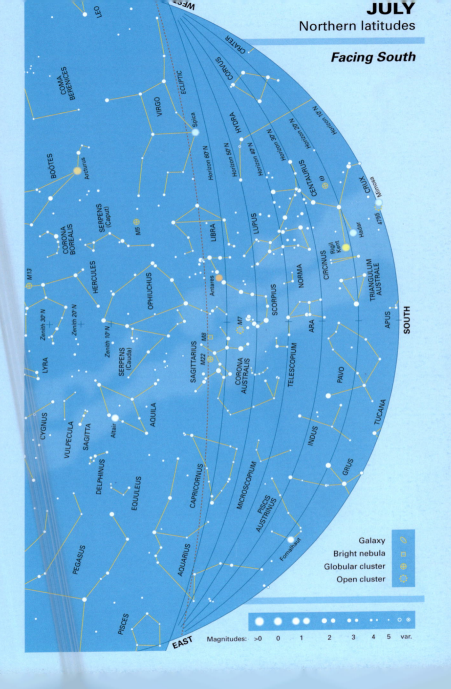

JULY
Northern latitudes

Facing South

WEST

LEO

COMA
BERENICES

CRATER

CORVUS

VIRGO

ECLIPTIC

HYDRA

Spica

Horizon 60° N

BOÖTES

Arcturus

Horizon 50° N

Horizon 40° N

CENTAURUS

ω

Horizon 30° N

Horizon 20° N

Horizon 10° N

CRUX

Mimosa

4755

SERPENS
(Caput)

CORONA
BOREALIS

M5

LIBRA

LUPUS

Hadar

Rigil
Kent

TRIANGULUM
AUSTRALE

HERCULES

OPHIUCHUS

CIRCINUS

NORMA

M13

Zenith 30° N

Zenith 20° N

SCORPIUS

ARA

APUS

SOUTH

Antares

Zenith 10° N

M7

SERPENS
(Cauda)

M8

SAGITTARIUS

M22

CORONA
AUSTRALIS

TELESCOPIUM

PAVO

LYRA

CYGNUS

VULPECULA

SAGITTA

Altair

AQUILA

INDUS

TUCANA

DELPHINUS

EQUULEUS

CAPRICORNUS

MICROSCOPIUM

GRUS

PEGASUS

AQUARIUS

PISCIS
AUSTRINUS

Fomalhaut

Galaxy

Bright nebula

Globular cluster

Open cluster

PISCES

EAST

Magnitudes: >0   0   1   2   3   4   5   var.

52

JULY
Southern latitudes

Facing North

WEST

NORTH

EAST

CRATER

CORVUS

HYDRA

LIBRA

SCORPIUS

Antares

SAGITTARIUS

CAPRICORNUS

ECLIPTIC

AQUARIUS

PISCES

EQUULEUS

DELPHINUS

SAGITTA

AQUILA

Altair

SCUTUM

M22

M8

SERPENS
(Cauda)

OPHIUCHUS

Zenith 20°S

Zenith
10°S

Zenith 0°

SERPENS
(Caput)

M5

Spica

VIRGO

LEO

COMA
BERENICES

CANES
VENATICI

Horizon 0°
Horizon 10°S
Horizon 20°S
Horizon 30°S
Horizon 40°S
Horizon 50°S

Arcturus

BOÖTES

CORONA
BOREALIS

M13

HERCULES

Vega

LYRA

CYGNUS

Deneb

VULPECULA

PEGASUS

URSA
MAJOR

URSA
MINOR

Polaris

DRACO

CEPHEUS

LACERTA

DATE	TIME	D.S.T.
July 1	11 pm	Midnight
July 15	**10 pm**	**11 pm**
August 1	9 pm	10 pm

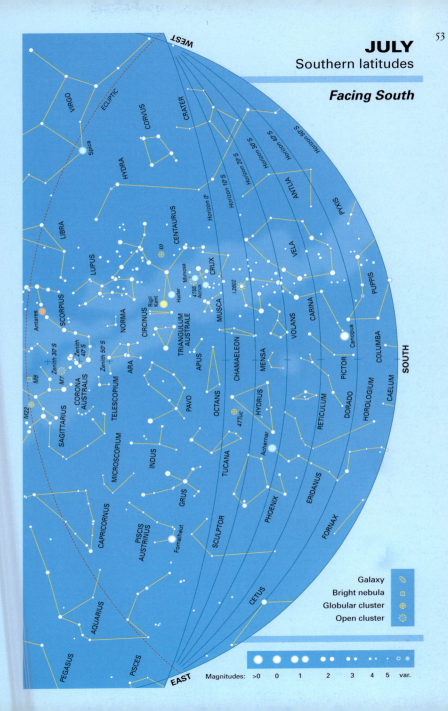

Facing South

WEST

VIRGO

ECLIPTIC

CORVUS

CRATER

Spica

HYDRA

Horizon 50° S

Horizon 40° S

Horizon 30° S

Horizon 20° S

Horizon 10° S

Horizon 0°

LIBRA

CENTAURUS

ANTLIA

PYXIS

LUPUS

CRUX

ω

VELA

Mimosa

Hadar

4755

Acrux

I 2602

MUSCA

PUPPIS

SCORPIUS

Antares

Rigil
Kent

CIRCINUS

NORMA

TRIANGULUM
AUSTRALE

APUS

CHAMAELEON

MENSA

VOLANS

CARINA

Canopus

SOUTH

Zenith 30° S

Zenith 40° S

Zenith 50° S

M7

ARA

TELESCOPIUM

PAVO

HYDRUS

PICTOR

COLUMBA

CAELUM

M8

CORONA
AUSTRALIS

OCTANS

47 Tuc

DORADO

HOROLOGIUM

M22

MICROSCOPIUM

INDUS

Achernar

RETICULUM

SAGITTARIUS

TUCANA

ERIDANUS

GRUS

PHOENIX

FORNAX

CAPRICORNUS

PISCIS
AUSTRINUS

Fomalhaut

SCULPTOR

AQUARIUS

CETUS

PEGASUS

PISCES

EAST

Galaxy		⬯
Bright nebula		⊡
Globular cluster		⊕
Open cluster		⊙

Magnitudes: >0   0   1   2   3   4   5   var.

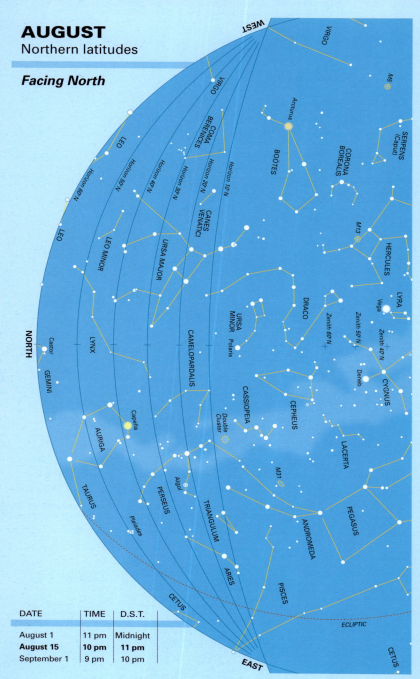

54

AUGUST
Northern latitudes

Facing North

WEST

VIRGO

M5

SERPENS (Caput)

VIRGO

COMA BERENICES

Arcturus

BOÖTES

CORONA BOREALIS

M13

HERCULES

LEO

Horizon 60° N

Horizon 50° N

Horizon 40° N

Horizon 30° N

Horizon 20° N

Horizon 10° N

CANES VENATICI

LYRA

Vega

DRACO

LEO

LEO MINOR

URSA MAJOR

URSA MINOR

Polaris

Zenith 60° N

Zenith 50° N

Zenith 40° N

Deneb

CYGNUS

NORTH

Castor

LYNX

CAMELOPARDALIS

CASSIOPEIA

CEPHEUS

LACERTA

GEMINI

Capella

Double Cluster

M31

AURIGA

Algol

PEGASUS

TAURUS

PERSEUS

ANDROMEDA

Pleiades

TRIANGULUM

ARIES

PISCES

CETUS

CETUS

ECLIPTIC

EAST

DATE	TIME	D.S.T.
August 1	11 pm	Midnight
August 15	**10 pm**	**11 pm**
September 1	9 pm	10 pm

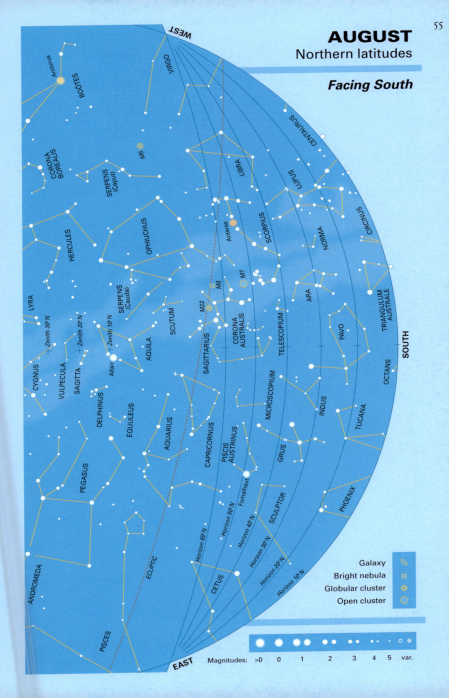

AUGUST
Northern latitudes

Facing South

WEST

Arcturus
BOÖTES
VIRGO
CORONA BOREALIS
SERPENS (Caput)
M5
HERCULES
OPHIUCHUS
CENTAURUS
LIBRA
SCORPIUS
LUPUS
NORMA
Antares
CIRCINUS
LYRA
CORONA BOREALIS
SERPENS (Cauda)
SCUTUM
M8
M7
ARA
TRIANGULUM AUSTRALE
CYGNUS
VULPECULA
SAGITTA
Zenith 30°N
Zenith 20°N
Zenith 10°N
AQUILA
Altair
M22
SAGITTARIUS
CORONA AUSTRALIS
TELESCOPIUM
PAVO
SOUTH
OCTANS
DELPHINUS
EQUULEUS
AQUARIUS
CAPRICORNUS
PISCIS AUSTRINUS
MICROSCOPIUM
GRUS
INDUS
TUCANA
PEGASUS
Fomalhaut
SCULPTOR
PHOENIX
Horizon 60°N
Horizon 50°N
Horizon 40°N
Horizon 30°N
Horizon 20°N
Horizon 10°N
ANDROMEDA
CETUS
ECLIPTIC
PISCES
EAST

Galaxy
Bright nebula
Globular cluster
Open cluster

Magnitudes: >0   0   1   2   3   4   5   var.

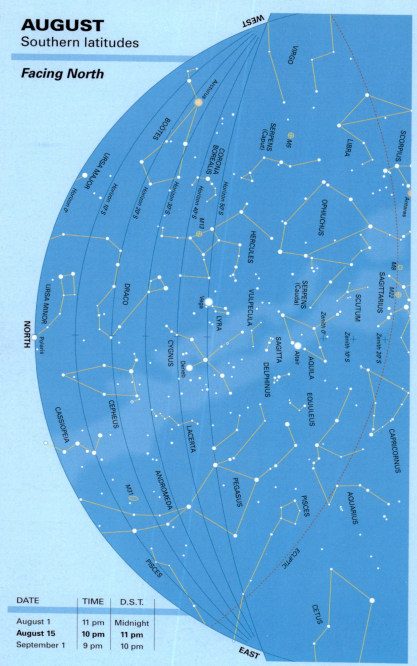

56

AUGUST
Southern latitudes

Facing North

WEST

VIRGO

Arcturus

BOÖTES

SERPENS
(Caput)

M5

LIBRA

SCORPIUS

URSA MAJOR

CORONA
BOREALIS

Antares

Horizon 0°

Horizon 10°S

Horizon 20°S

Horizon 30°S

Horizon 40°S

Horizon 50°S

M13

OPHIUCHUS

M8

DRACO

HERCULES

SERPENS
(Cauda)

SAGITTARIUS

M22

URSA MINOR

Vega

VULPECULA

SCUTUM

Zenith 20°S

NORTH

Polaris

LYRA

SAGITTA

Zenith 0°

Zenith 10°S

CYGNUS

AQUILA

Altair

Deneb

DELPHINUS

EQUULEUS

CASSIOPEIA

CEPHEUS

LACERTA

PEGASUS

PISCES

CAPRICORNUS

M31

ANDROMEDA

AQUARIUS

PISCES

ECLIPTIC

CETUS

EAST

DATE	TIME	D.S.T.
August 1	11 pm	Midnight
August 15	**10 pm**	**11 pm**
September 1	9 pm	10 pm

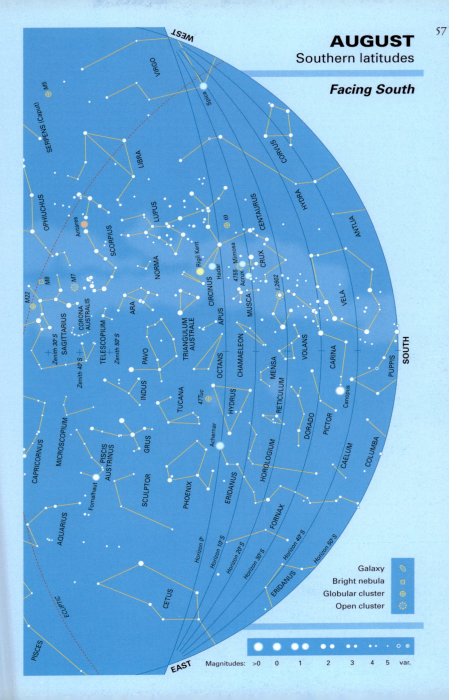

AUGUST
Southern latitudes

Facing South

WEST

SERPENS (Caput)

⊕ M5

VIRGO

Spica

LIBRA

CORVUS

OPHIUCHUS

LUPUS

HYDRA

Antares

SCORPIUS

CENTAURUS

ANTLIA

NORMA

Rigil Kent

ω

4755 Mimosa

CRUX

Hadar

Acrux

MUSCA

I 2602

VELA

M8

M7

ARA

CIRCINUS

APUS

M22

CORONA AUSTRALIS

TELESCOPIUM

TRIANGULUM AUSTRALE

CHAMAELEON

VOLANS

CARINA

SAGITTARIUS

Zenith 30° S

PAVO

OCTANS

MENSA

PUPPIS

SOUTH

Zenith 40° S

Zenith 50° S

INDUS

TUCANA

47 Tuc ⊕

HYDRUS

RETICULUM

DORADO

PICTOR

Canopus

CAPRICORNUS

MICROSCOPIUM

GRUS

Achernar

HOROLOGIUM

CAELUM

COLUMBA

Fomalhaut

PISCIS AUSTRINUS

SCULPTOR

PHOENIX

ERIDANUS

FORNAX

AQUARIUS

ERIDANUS

ECLIPTIC

Horizon 0° S

Horizon 10° S

Horizon 20° S

Horizon 30° S

Horizon 40° S

Horizon 50° S

CETUS

Galaxy	⬭
Bright nebula	◻
Globular cluster	⊕
Open cluster	✳

PISCES

EAST

Magnitudes: >0   0   1   2   3   4   5   var.

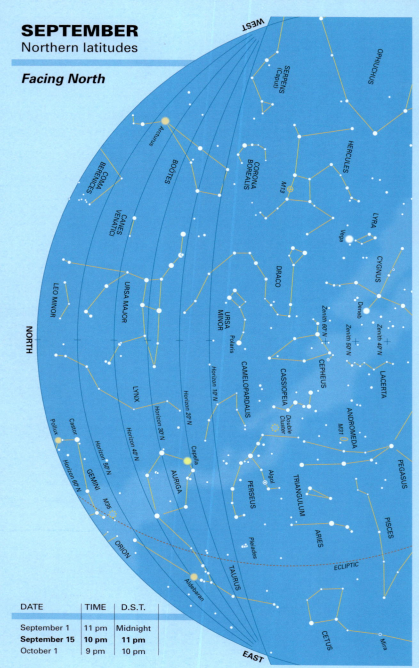

58

SEPTEMBER
Northern latitudes

Facing North

WEST

OPHIUCHUS

SERPENS
(Caput)

HERCULES

Arcturus

BOÖTES

CORONA
BOREALIS

M13

LYRA

COMA
BERENICES

Vega

CYGNUS

CANES
VENATICI

Deneb

DRACO

Zenith 60° N

Zenith 40° N

LEO MINOR

URSA
MAJOR

URSA
MINOR

Zenith 50° N

LACERTA

NORTH

Polaris

Horizon 10° N

CEPHEUS

Horizon 20° N

CAMELOPARDALIS

CASSIOPEIA

LYNX

Horizon 30° N

ANDROMEDA

M31

Double
Cluster

Horizon 40° N

Castor

Pollux

Horizon 50° N

Capella

PEGASUS

Algol

AURIGA

PERSEUS

TRIANGULUM

Horizon 60° N

GEMINI

PISCES

M35

Pleiades

ARIES

ORION

ECLIPTIC

TAURUS

Aldebaran

CETUS

Mira

EAST

DATE	TIME	D.S.T.
September 1	11 pm	Midnight
September 15	**10 pm**	**11 pm**
October 1	9 pm	10 pm

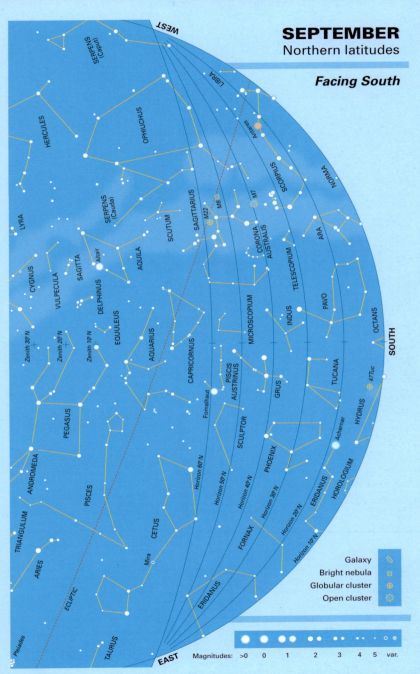

59

SEPTEMBER
Northern latitudes

Facing South

WEST

SERPENS (Caput)
HERCULES
OPHIUCHUS
LIBRA
Antares
SCORPIUS
NORMA
LYRA
SERPENS (Cauda)
SCUTUM
SAGITTARIUS
M8
M22
M7
CORONA AUSTRALIS
ARA
TELESCOPIUM
CYGNUS
VULPECULA
SAGITTA
Altair
AQUILA
DELPHINUS
MICROSCOPIUM
INDUS
PAVO
OCTANS
EQUULEUS
Zenith 30° N
Zenith 20° N
Zenith 10° N
AQUARIUS
CAPRICORNUS
PISCIS AUSTRINUS
GRUS
TUCANA
47 Tuc
SOUTH
PEGASUS
Fomalhaut
SCULPTOR
PHOENIX
HYDRUS
Achernar
ANDROMEDA
TRIANGULUM
PISCES
Horizon 60° N
Horizon 50° N
Horizon 40° N
Horizon 30° N
Horizon 20° N
ERIDANUS
HOROLOGIUM
ARIES
CETUS
Mira
FORNAX
Horizon 10° N
ECLIPTIC
ERIDANUS
Pleiades
TAURUS
EAST

	Galaxy
	Bright nebula
	Globular cluster
	Open cluster

Magnitudes: >0 0 1 2 3 4 5 var.

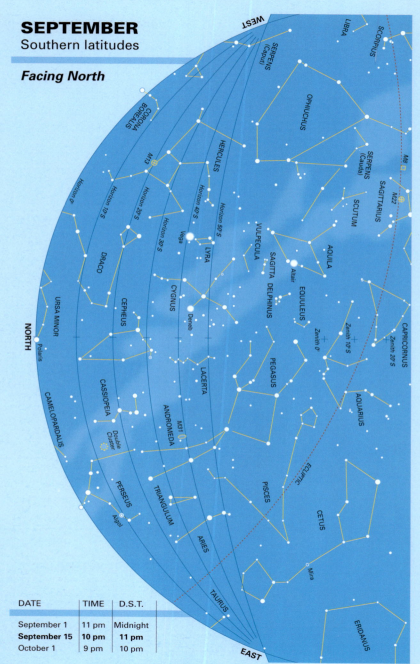

60

SEPTEMBER
Southern latitudes

Facing North

WEST

NORTH

EAST

DATE	TIME	D.S.T.
September 1	11 pm	Midnight
September 15	**10 pm**	**11 pm**
October 1	9 pm	10 pm

LIBRA

SCORPIUS

SERPENS (Caput)

OPHIUCHUS

SERPENS (Cauda)

M8

SAGITTARIUS

M22

SCUTUM

AQUILA

Altair

CORONA BOREALIS

M13

HERCULES

Horizon 0°

Horizon 10°S

Horizon 20°S

Horizon 30°S

Horizon 40°S

Horizon 50°S

Vega

LYRA

VULPECULA

SAGITTA

DELPHINUS

EQUULEUS

CAPRICORNUS

DRACO

CYGNUS

Deneb

Zenith 0°

Zenith 10°S

Zenith 20°S

URSA MINOR

Polaris

CEPHEUS

LACERTA

PEGASUS

AQUARIUS

CAMELOPARDALIS

CASSIOPEIA

Double Cluster

ANDROMEDA

M31

PISCES

CETUS

ECLIPTIC

PERSEUS

Algol

TRIANGULUM

ARIES

Mira

TAURUS

ERIDANUS

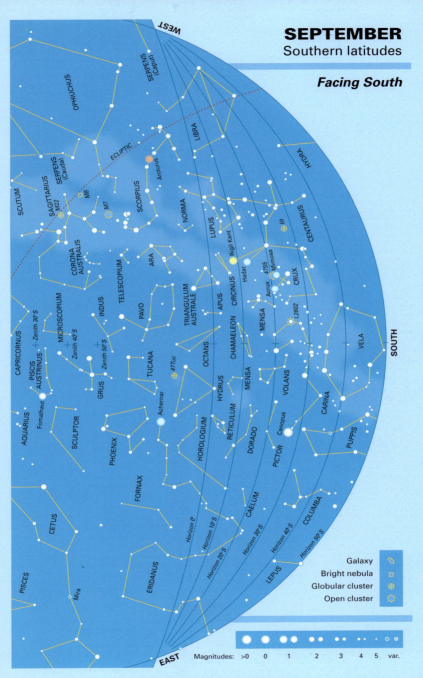

SEPTEMBER
Southern latitudes

Facing South

WEST

EAST

SOUTH

OPHIUCHUS
SERPENS (Caput)
SCUTUM
SERPENS (Cauda)
SAGITTARIUS
M22
M8
M7
CORONA AUSTRALIS
SCORPIUS
ECLIPTIC
Arcturus
LIBRA
NORMA
LUPUS
CENTAURUS
HYDRA
Rigil Kent
Hadar
4755
Mimosa
Acrux
CRUX
Omega
CIRCINUS
APUS
TRIANGULUM AUSTRALE
ARA
TELESCOPIUM
PAVO
CHAMAELEON
MENSA
I.2602
CARINA
VELA
TUCANA
47Tuc
OCTANS
HYDRUS
MENSA
VOLANS
Zenith 30°S
Zenith 40°S
Zenith 50°S
MICROSCOPIUM
INDUS
CAPRICORNUS
PISCIS AUSTRINUS
Fomalhaut
GRUS
Achernar
PHOENIX
RETICULUM
DORADO
PICTOR
Canopus
PUPPIS
AQUARIUS
SCULPTOR
HOROLOGIUM
CAELUM
COLUMBA
FORNAX
CETUS
ERIDANUS
LEPUS
PISCES
Mira

Horizon 0°
Horizon 10°S
Horizon 20°S
Horizon 30°S
Horizon 40°S
Horizon 50°S

Galaxy
Bright nebula
Globular cluster
Open cluster

Magnitudes: >0 0 1 2 3 4 5 var.

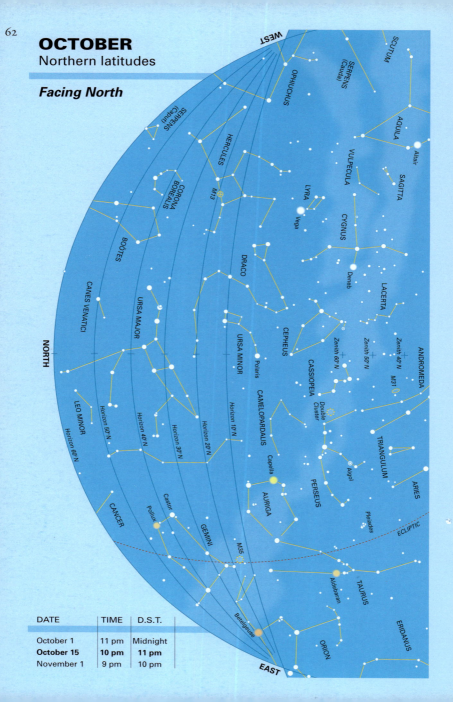

62

OCTOBER
Northern latitudes

Facing North

WEST

NORTH

EAST

Horizon 60 N

Horizon 50 N

Horizon 40 N

Horizon 30 N

Horizon 20 N

Horizon 10 N

Zenith 40 N

Zenith 50 N

Zenith 60 N

ECLIPTIC

SCUTUM

SERPENS (Cauda)

AQUILA

SAGITTA

Altair

VULPECULA

LYRA

Vega

CYGNUS

Deneb

LACERTA

ANDROMEDA

M31

Double Cluster

TRIANGULUM

Algol

ARIES

PERSEUS

Pleiades

CASSIOPEIA

CEPHEUS

CAMELOPARDALIS

AURIGA

Capella

Castor

Pollux

GEMINI

M35

TAURUS

Aldebaran

Betelgeuse

ORION

ERIDANUS

CANCER

LEO MINOR

CANES VENATICI

URSA MAJOR

URSA MINOR

Polaris

DRACO

HERCULES

M13

SERPENS (Caput)

OPHIUCHUS

BOÖTES

CORONA BOREALIS

DATE	TIME	D.S.T.
October 1	11 pm	Midnight
October 15	**10 pm**	**11 pm**
November 1	9 pm	10 pm

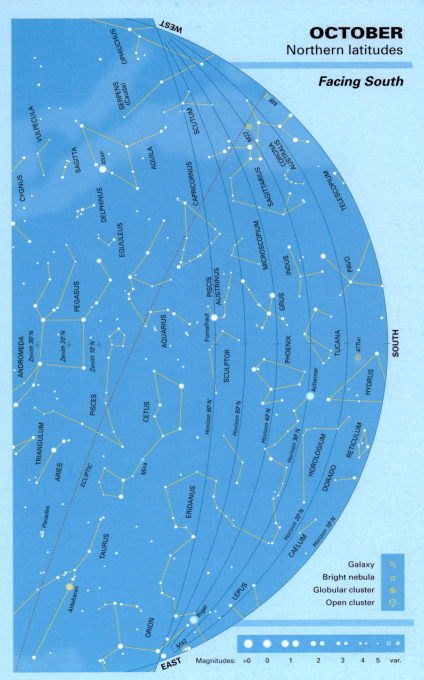

OCTOBER
Northern latitudes

Facing South

WEST

OPHIUCHUS

SERPENS (Cauda)

VULPECULA

SCUTUM

M8

CORONA AUSTRALIS

M22

SAGITTA

CYGNUS

AQUILA

Altair

CAPRICORNUS

SAGITTARIUS

TELESCOPIUM

DELPHINUS

MICROSCOPIUM

EQUULEUS

INDUS

PAVO

PEGASUS

PISCIS AUSTRINUS

GRUS

Zenith 30° N

Fomalhaut

PHOENIX

TUCANA

47 Tuc

SOUTH

Zenith 20° N

ANDROMEDA

Zenith 10° N

AQUARIUS

Achernar

HYDRUS

PISCES

SCULPTOR

Horizon 60° N

CETUS

Horizon 50° N

TRIANGULUM

Horizon 40° N

RETICULUM

ARIES

Horizon 30° N

HOROLOGIUM

ECLIPTIC

Mira

DORADO

Horizon 20° N

Pleiades

ERIDANUS

CAELUM

Horizon 10° N

TAURUS

Aldebaran

	Galaxy
	Bright nebula
	Globular cluster
	Open cluster

LEPUS

ORION

Rigel

M42

EAST

Magnitudes: >0   0   1   2   3   4   5 var.

OCTOBER
Southern latitudes

Facing North

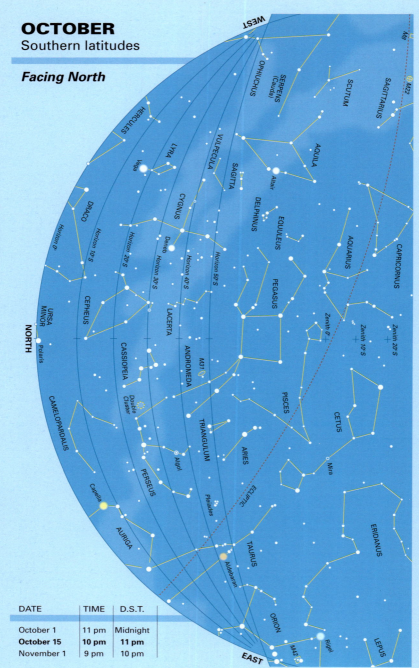

WEST

OPHIUCHUS

SERPENS
(Cauda)

SCUTUM

SAGITTARIUS

M8

M22

HERCULES

LYRA

VULPECULA

AQUILA

Vega

SAGITTA

Altair

DRACO

CYGNUS

DELPHINUS

Deneb

EQUULEUS

Horizon 0°

Horizon 10°S

Horizon 20°S

Horizon 30°S

Horizon 40°S

Horizon 50°S

AQUARIUS

CAPRICORNUS

PEGASUS

Zenith 0°

Zenith 10°S

Zenith 20°S

URSA
MINOR

CEPHEUS

LACERTA

CASSIOPEIA

ANDROMEDA

M31

PISCES

CETUS

NORTH

Polaris

Double
Cluster

TRIANGULUM

ARIES

Mira

ECLIPTIC

CAMELOPARDALIS

PERSEUS

Algol

Pleiades

ERIDANUS

Capella

AURIGA

TAURUS

Aldebaran

ORION

LEPUS

M42

Rigel

EAST

DATE	TIME	D.S.T.
October 1	11 pm	Midnight
October 15	**10 pm**	**11 pm**
November 1	9 pm	10 pm

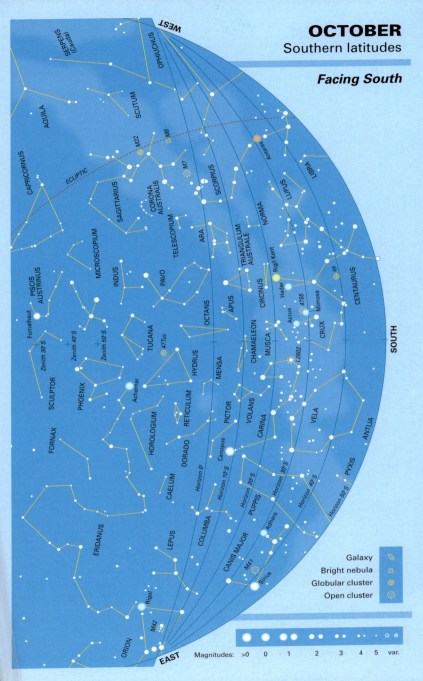

OCTOBER
Southern latitudes

Facing South

WEST

SERPENS (Cauda)
OPHIUCHUS
SCUTUM
AQUILA
CAPRICORNUS
ECLIPTIC
M22
M8
M7
SAGITTARIUS
CORONA AUSTRALIS
SCORPIUS
Antares
LIBRA
LUPUS
NORMA
MICROSCOPIUM
TELESCOPIUM
ARA
TRIANGULUM AUSTRALE
Rigil Kent
INDUS
PAVO
APUS
CIRCINUS
Hadar
4755
Mimosa
CENTAURUS
PISCIS AUSTRINUS
Fomalhaut
OCTANS
Acrux
CRUX
ω
Zenith 30 S
Zenith 40 S
Zenith 50 S
TUCANA
47Tuc
HYDRUS
MENSA
CHAMAELEON
MUSCA
I.2602
SCULPTOR
PHOENIX
Achernar
HOROLOGIUM
RETICULUM
PICTOR
VOLANS
VELA
FORNAX
DORADO
CAELUM
Canopus
CARINA
ANTLIA
ERIDANUS
Horizon 0
Horizon 10 S
COLUMBA
Horizon 20 S
PUPPIS
Horizon 30 S
Horizon 40 S
PYXIS
Horizon 50 S
Horizon 60 S
LEPUS
CANIS MAJOR
Adhara
M41
Sirius
Rigel
ORION
M42
SOUTH

EAST

Galaxy
Bright nebula
Globular cluster
Open cluster

Magnitudes: >0   0   1   2   3   4   5   var.

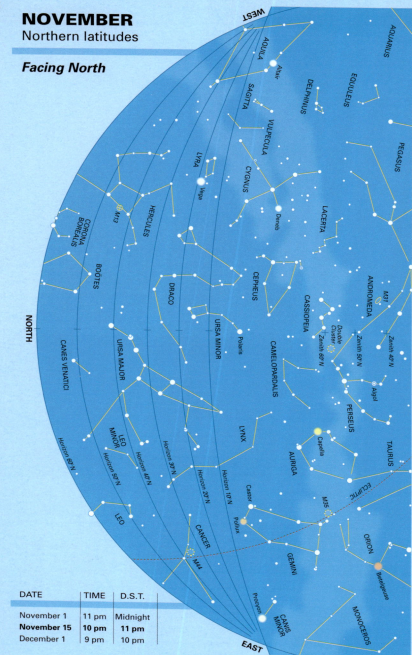

NOVEMBER
Northern latitudes

Facing North

WEST

AQUARIUS

AQUILA
Altair

EQUULEUS

DELPHINUS

PEGASUS

SAGITTA

VULPECULA

CYGNUS

LYRA
Vega

LACERTA

Deneb

M13

HERCULES

ANDROMEDA

M31

CORONA BOREALIS

CEPHEUS

Zenith 40° N

BOÖTES

DRACO

CASSIOPEIA

Double Cluster

Zenith 50° N

Zenith 60° N

Algol

NORTH

URSA MINOR

Polaris

CAMELOPARDALIS

PERSEUS

CANES VENATICI

URSA MAJOR

LYNX

Capella

TAURUS

LEO MINOR

AURIGA

ECLIPTIC

Horizon 60° N

Horizon 50° N

Horizon 40° N

Horizon 30° N

Horizon 20° N

Horizon 10° N

Castor

Pollux

M35

LEO

CANCER

GEMINI

ORION

M44

Procyon

Betelgeuse

CANIS MINOR

MONOCEROS

EAST

DATE	TIME	D.S.T.
November 1	11 pm	Midnight
November 15	**10 pm**	**11 pm**
December 1	9 pm	10 pm

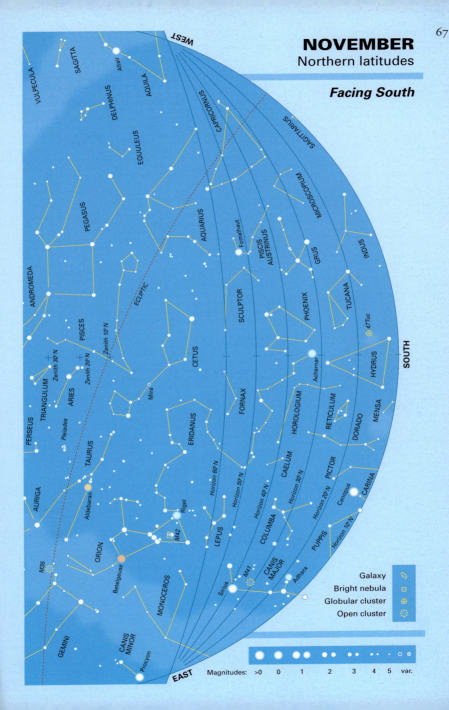

NOVEMBER
Northern latitudes

Facing South

WEST

VULPECULA

SAGITTA

Altair

AQUILA

DELPHINUS

EQUULEUS

PEGASUS

ANDROMEDA

PERSEUS

TRIANGULUM

Zenith 30°N

Pleiades

ARIES

Zenith 20°N

PISCES

Zenith 10°N

ECLIPTIC

AQUARIUS

CAPRICORNUS

SAGITTARIUS

MICROSCOPIUM

Fomalhaut

PISCIS AUSTRINUS

GRUS

INDUS

PHOENIX

TUCANA

47Tuc

SOUTH

CETUS

SCULPTOR

Mira

FORNAX

Achernar

HYDRUS

HOROLOGIUM

RETICULUM

DORADO

MENSA

TAURUS

Aldebaran

ERIDANUS

CAELUM

Horizon 30°N

PICTOR

CARINA

AURIGA

Rigel

Horizon 60°N

Horizon 60°N

Horizon 40°N

COLUMBA

Horizon 20°N

Canopus

M42

ORION

M43

LEPUS

Horizon 10°N

M35

Betelgeuse

PUPPIS

MONOCEROS

Sirius

M41

CANIS MAJOR

Adhara

GEMINI

CANIS MINOR

Procyon

EAST

Galaxy

Bright nebula

Globular cluster

Open cluster

Magnitudes: >0   0   1   2   3   4   5 var.

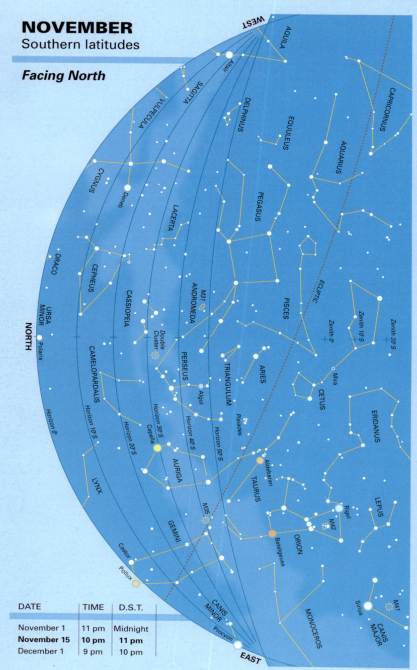

68

NOVEMBER
Southern latitudes

Facing North

WEST

EAST

NORTH

AQUILA
Altair
SAGITTA
VULPECULA
DELPHINUS
EQUULEUS
AQUARIUS
CAPRICORNUS
CYGNUS
Deneb
LACERTA
PEGASUS
ECLIPTIC
DRACO
CEPHEUS
CASSIOPEIA
ANDROMEDA
M31
PISCES
Zenith 0
Mira
Zenith 10°S
Zenith 20°S
URSA MINOR
Polaris
CAMELOPARDALIS
Double Cluster
PERSEUS
TRIANGULUM
ARIES
CETUS
ERIDANUS
Algol
Pleiades
Horizon 0°
Horizon 10°S
Horizon 20°S
Horizon 30°S
Horizon 40°S
Horizon 50°S
Capella
LYNX
AURIGA
Aldebaran
TAURUS
LEPUS
Rigel
M42
Castor
GEMINI
M35
ORION
Pollux
Betelgeuse
CANIS MINOR
Procyon
MONOCEROS
Sirius
M41
CANIS MAJOR

DATE	TIME	D.S.T.
November 1	11 pm	Midnight
November 15	**10 pm**	**11 pm**
December 1	9 pm	10 pm

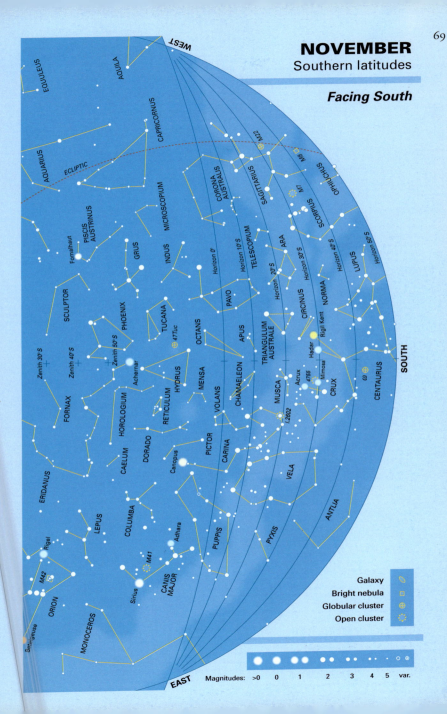

NOVEMBER
Southern latitudes

Facing South

DECEMBER
Northern latitudes

Facing North

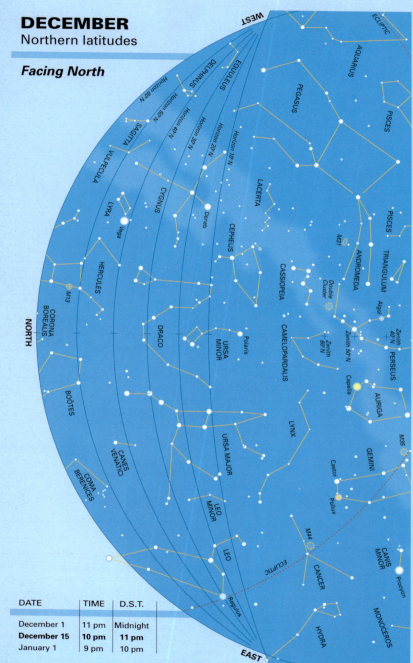

DATE	TIME	D.S.T.
December 1	11 pm	Midnight
December 15	**10 pm**	**11 pm**
January 1	9 pm	10 pm

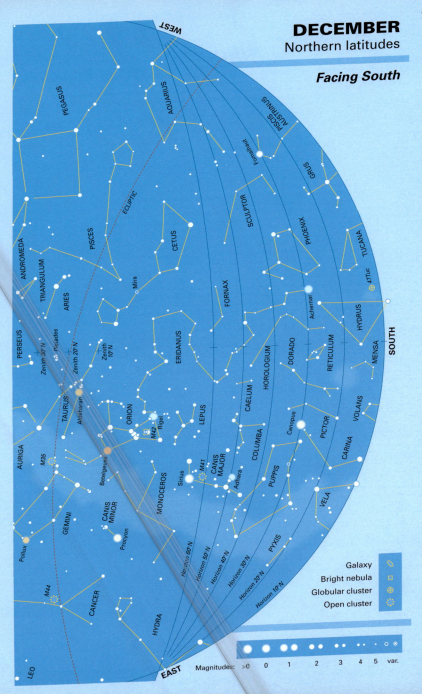

DECEMBER
Northern latitudes

Facing South

WEST

PEGASUS

AQUARIUS

PISCIS AUSTRINUS

Fomalhaut

GRUS

ANDROMEDA

TRIANGULUM

ARIES

PISCES

ECLIPTIC

Mira

CETUS

SCULPTOR

PHOENIX

TUCANA

47 Tuc

FORNAX

Achernar

HYDRUS

PERSEUS

Pleiades

Zenith 30 N

Zenith 20 N

Zenith 10 N

ERIDANUS

HOROLOGIUM

DORADO

RETICULUM

MENSA

SOUTH

TAURUS

Aldebaran

ORION

M42

Rigel

LEPUS

CAELUM

COLUMBA

Canopus

PICTOR

VOLANS

CARINA

AURIGA

M35

Betelgeuse

Sirius

M41

CANIS MAJOR

Adhara

PUPPIS

VELA

MONOCEROS

Horizon 60 N

Horizon 50 N

Horizon 40 N

Horizon 30 N

Horizon 20 N

Horizon 10 N

GEMINI

CANIS MINOR

Procyon

PYXIS

Pollux

M44

CANCER

HYDRA

LEO

EAST

Galaxy
Bright nebula
Globular cluster
Open cluster

Magnitudes: >0 0 1 2 3 4 5 var.

DECEMBER
Southern latitudes

Facing North

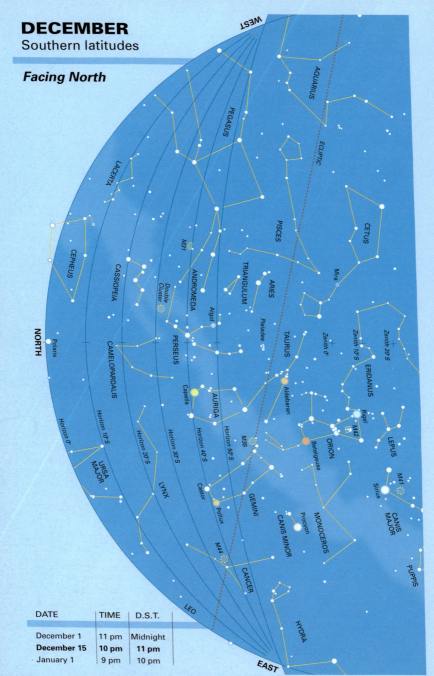

WEST

AQUARIUS

PEGASUS

ECLIPTIC

LACERTA

PISCES

CETUS

CEPHEUS

CASSIOPEIA

M31

ANDROMEDA

TRIANGULUM

ARIES

Mira

Double Cluster

Algol

Pleiades

TAURUS

Zenith 0°

Zenith 10°S

Zenith 20°S

ERIDANUS

NORTH

Polaris

CAMELOPARDALIS

PERSEUS

Capella

AURIGA

Aldebaran

Rigel

M42

LEPUS

Horizon 0°

Horizon 10°S

Horizon 20°S

Horizon 30°S

Horizon 40°S

Horizon 50°S

M35

ORION

Betelgeuse

M41

Sirius

URSA MAJOR

LYNX

Castor

Pollux

GEMINI

CANIS MINOR

Procyon

MONOCEROS

CANIS MAJOR

PUPPIS

M44

CANCER

LEO

HYDRA

EAST

DATE	TIME	D.S.T.
December 1	11 pm	Midnight
December 15	**10 pm**	**11 pm**
January 1	9 pm	10 pm

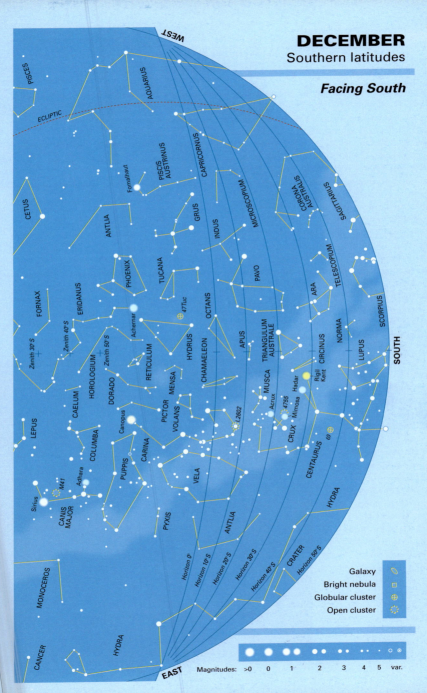

DECEMBER
Southern latitudes

Facing South

WEST

PISCES

AQUARIUS

ECLIPTIC

PISCIS AUSTRINUS

CAPRICORNUS

Fomalhaut

CETUS

GRUS

MICROSCOPIUM

CORONA AUSTRALIS

SAGITTARIUS

ANTLIA

INDUS

PAVO

TELESCOPIUM

PHOENIX

TUCANA

OCTANS

ARA

SCORPIUS

FORNAX

ERIDANUS

47Tuc

APUS

TRIANGULUM AUSTRALE

NORMA

Zenith 30 S

Zenith 40 S

Achernar

HYDRUS

CHAMAELEON

MUSCA

CIRCINUS

LUPUS

SOUTH

RETICULUM

Zenith 50 S

HOROLOGIUM

DORADO

MENSA

Rigil Kent

CAELUM

PICTOR

VOLANS

4755

Hadar

Acrux

Mimosa

CRUX

CENTAURUS

ω

LEPUS

COLUMBA

Canopus

CARINA

C2602

VELA

Sirius

M41

Adhara

PUPPIS

ANTLIA

CANIS MAJOR

PYXIS

CRATER

HYDRA

MONOCEROS

Horizon 0

Horizon 10 S

Horizon 20 S

Horizon 30 S

Horizon 40 S

Horizon 50 S

CANCER

HYDRA

EAST

Galaxy
Bright nebula
Globular cluster
Open cluster

Magnitudes: >0   0   1   2   3   4   5   var.

Andromeda

Andromeda represents the daughter of Queen Cassiopeia who was chained to a rock as a sacrifice to the sea monster Cetus until saved by Perseus, whom she subsequently married. The constellation originated in ancient times. Despite its fame, Andromeda is not particularly striking: its brightest stars are only 2nd magnitude. Its most prominent feature is a crooked line of four stars extending from the Square of Pegasus; the first of these stars marks a corner of the Square, although it is actually part of Andromeda. This star, known both as Alpheratz and Sirrah, marks the head of the chained Andromeda; another star in the line, Mirach, represents her waist and a third, Almaak, is her chained foot. The most celebrated object in the constellation is the Andromeda Galaxy, M31, a spiral galaxy like our own Milky Way; it is the most distant object visible to the naked eye. Two stars leading from Mirach, β (beta) Andromedae, act as a guide to it.

α (alpha) Andromedae, 0h 08m +29°.1, (Alpheratz or Sirrah), mag. 2.1, is a blue-white star 97 l.y. away.

β (beta) And, 1h 10m +35°.6, (Mirach), mag. 2.1, is a red giant 199 l.y. away.

γ (gamma) And, 2h 04m +42°.3, (Almaak or Almach), 355 l.y. away, is an outstanding triple star. Its two brightest components, of mags. 2.3 and 4.8, form one of the finest pairs for small telescopes: their colours are orange and blue. The fainter, blue star also has a close 6th-mag. blue-white companion that orbits it every 64 years. This fainter pair is closest around the year 2015 and is unresolvable by amateur telescopes for several years either side.

▶

M31, the Andromeda Galaxy, is a magnificent spiral visible to the naked eye, with two smaller companion galaxies that can be seen in small telescopes: M32, superimposed on one of the spiral arms just below centre, and the larger but fainter M110 to the upper right. The full Moon has been added to the same scale to give an impression of the Andromeda spiral's full extent. (Galaxy image: Bill Schoening, Vanessa Harvey/REU program/ NOAO/AURA/NSF)

Andromeda · And · Andromedae

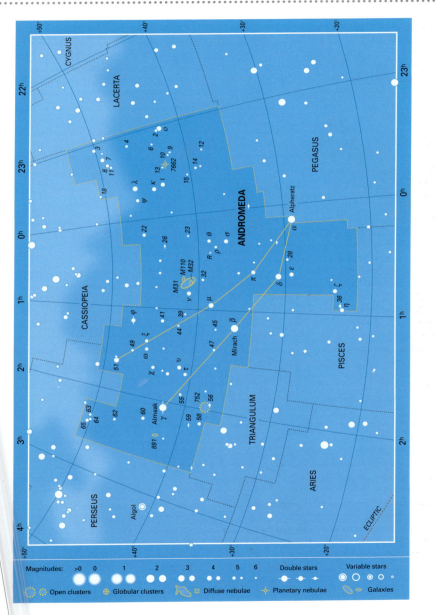

Magnitudes: >0 0 1 2 3 4 5 6   Double stars   Variable stars

Open clusters   Globular clusters   Diffuse nebulae   Planetary nebulae   Galaxies

δ (delta) And, 0h 39m +30°.9, mag. 3.3, is an orange giant 101 l.y. away.

μ (mu) And, 0h 57m +38°.5, mag. 3.9, is a white star 136 l.y. away.

π (pi) And, 0h 37m +33°.7, 660 l.y. away, is a blue-white star of mag. 4.3 with a mag. 8.9 companion visible in small telescopes.

υ (upsilon) And, 1h 37m, +41°.4, mag. 4.1, is a yellow-white main-sequence star 44 l.y. away. Astronomers have found that it is accompanied by three planets, the first known multi-planet system around a star other than our own Sun.

56 And, 1h 56m +37°.3, is a yellow giant star of mag. 5.7, 320 l.y. away, with an orange giant companion, mag. 5.9 and 990 l.y. away, easily split in binoculars. The two stars are found near the star cluster NGC 752 but are actually closer to us.

M31 (NGC 224), 0h 43m +41°.3, the Andromeda Galaxy, is a spiral galaxy 2.5 million l.y. away. It is visible to the naked eye as an elliptical fuzzy patch, and becomes more prominent when seen through binoculars or a telescope with low magnification (too high a power reduces the contrast and renders the fainter parts of the galaxy less visible). Dark lanes can be seen in the spiral arms surrounding the nucleus. But the full extent of the galaxy becomes apparent only on long-exposure photographs (visual observers see just its brightest, central portion). If the entire Andromeda Galaxy were bright enough to be seen by the naked eye, it would appear five or six times the diameter of the full Moon, as demonstrated in the composite image on page 74. M31 is accompanied by two small satellite galaxies, the equivalents of our Magellanic Clouds but both elliptical rather than irregular in shape. The brighter of these, M32 (NGC 221), is visible in small telescopes as a fuzzy, 8th-mag. star-like glow ½° south of M31's core. The second companion, M110 (also known as NGC 205), is larger but visually more elusive, and over 1° northwest of M31.

NGC 752, 1h 58m +37°.7, is a widely spread cluster of about 60 stars of 9th mag. and fainter, 1200 l.y. away, visible in binoculars and easily resolved in telescopes.

NGC 7662, 23h 26m +42°.6, is one of the brightest and easiest planetary nebulae to see with a small telescope. At low powers it appears as a fuzzy, 9th-mag. blue-green star, but magnifications of ×100 or so reveal its slightly elliptical disk. Larger apertures show a central hole; the central star is a difficult object for amateur telescopes. NGC 7662 lies about 4000 l.y. away.

Antlia – The Air Pump

An obscure southern constellation introduced on a map published in 1756 by the French astronomer Nicolas Louis de Lacaille to commemorate the air pump invented by the French physicist Denis Papin. Lacaille, the first person to map the naked-eye stars in the southern skies completely (see page 216), introduced 14 new constellations to fill gaps between existing ones. Most of these new figures are unremarkable, as is Antlia.

α (alpha) Antliae, 10h 27m −31°.1, mag. 4.3, the constellation's brightest star, is an orange giant 366 l.y. distant.

δ (delta) Ant, 10h 30m −30°.6, 481 l.y. away, is a blue-white star of mag. 5.6 with a mag. 9.6 companion visible in small telescopes.

ζ¹ ζ² (zeta¹ zeta²) Ant, 9h 31m −31°.9, 373 l.y. away, is a wide pair of stars of mags. 5.8 and 5.9, visible in binoculars. Small telescopes show that ζ¹ Ant is itself double, with components of mags. 6.2 and 7.0.

▶

Antlia · Ant · Antliae

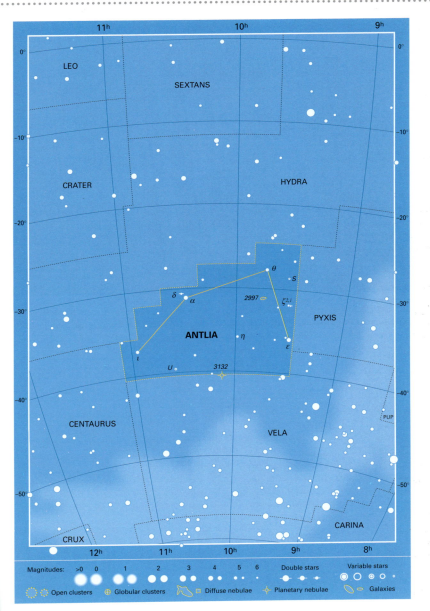

Magnitudes: >0 0 1 2 3 4 5 6   Double stars   Variable stars

Open clusters   Globular clusters   Diffuse nebulae   Planetary nebulae   Galaxies

NGC 2997: Knots of young blue stars and pink gas as well as lanes of dark dust are visible in the curling arms of this handsome 9th-magnitude spiral galaxy in central Antlia, presented virtually face-on to us. Moderate-sized amateur telescopes are required to see it. (M. Bessell, R. Sutherland and M. Buxton, RSAA – Australian National University)

Apus – The Bird of Paradise

A faint constellation near the south celestial pole, one of the 12 new figures introduced in the 1590s by the Dutch navigators Pieter Dirkszoon Keyser and Frederick de Hout-man during voyages to the southern hemi-sphere. This one represents the bird of paradise, native to New Guinea.

α (alpha) Apodis, 14h 48m −79°.0, mag. 3.8, is an orange giant star 411 l.y. away.

β (beta) Aps, 16h 43m −77°.5, mag. 4.2, is an orange giant 158 l.y. away.

γ (gamma) Aps, 16h 33m −78°.9, mag. 3.9, is an orange giant 160 l.y. away.

δ¹ δ² (delta¹ delta²) Aps, 16h 20m −78°.7, is a naked-eye or binocular pair of red and orange giant stars of mags. 4.7 and 5.3, 765 and 663 l.y. away.

θ (theta) Aps, 14h 05m −76°.8, 328 l.y. away, is a red giant that varies semi-regularly between 5th and 7th mags. every 4 months or so.

Apus · Aps · Apodis

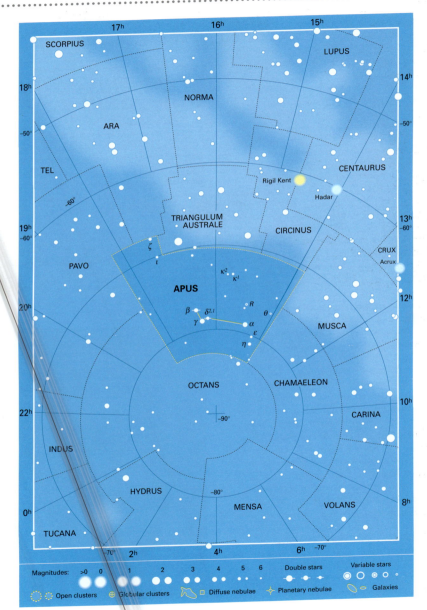

Aquarius – The Water Carrier

Aquarius is one of the most ancient constellations. The Babylonians saw in this area of sky the figure of a man pouring water from a jar. In Greek mythology the constellation represents Ganymede, a shepherd boy carried off by Zeus to Mount Olympus, where he became wine-waiter to the gods.

The most prominent part of Aquarius is the Y-shaped asterism of four stars representing the Water Jar itself, centred on the star ζ (zeta) Aquarii. Aquarius is in an area of 'watery' constellations that includes Pisces, Cetus and Capricornus. The Sun is within the boundaries of Aquarius from late February to early March. Aquarius will one day contain the vernal equinox, the point at which the Sun crosses into the northern celestial hemisphere each year. This astronomically important point, from which the coordinate of right ascension is measured, will move into Aquarius from neighbouring Pisces in AD 2597 because of the effect of precession. Hence the so-called Age of Aquarius is a long way off yet.

Three main meteor showers radiate from Aquarius each year. The first, the Eta Aquarids, is the richest, reaching a maximum of 35 meteors per hour around May 5–6. The Delta Aquarids have a double radiant: the southerly one produces about 20 meteors per hour around July 29, while the northerly radiant (which is actually near the Circlet of Pisces) peaks at about 10 an hour on August 6. A weaker stream, the Iota Aquarids, produces a maximum of 8 meteors per hour, also on August 6. Each shower is named after the bright star closest to its radiant.

α (alpha) Aquarii, 22h 06m −0°.3, (Sadalmelik, from the Arabic for 'the lucky stars of the king'), mag. 2.9, is a yellow supergiant 760 l.y. away.

β (beta) Aqr, 21h 32m −5°.6, (Sadalsuud, from the Arabic for 'luckiest of the lucky stars'), mag. 2.9, is a yellow supergiant 610 l.y. away.

γ (gamma) Aqr, 22h 22m −1°.4, (Sadachbia), mag. 3.9, is a blue-white star 158 l.y. away.

δ (delta) Aqr, 22h 55m −15°.8, (Skat), mag. 3.3, is a blue-white star 160 l.y. away.

ε (epsilon) Aqr, 20h 48m −9°.5, (Albali), mag. 3.8, is a blue-white star 102 l.y. away.

ζ (zeta) Aqr, 22h 29m −0°.0, 103 l.y. away, is a celebrated binary consisting of twin white stars of mags. 4.3 and 4.5 orbiting each other every 590 years. The two stars are gradually moving apart as seen from Earth and hence are becoming increasingly easy to divide in small telescopes. ▶

NGC 7009 is popularly known as the Saturn Nebula because of the faint 'handles' either side of it, like Saturn's rings, that can be seen through large telescopes and in photographs. The name Saturn Nebula was given to it in the 19th century by Lord Rosse. (SAAO)

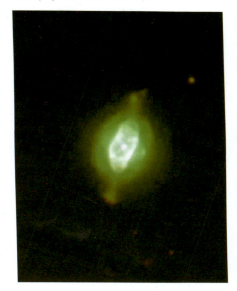

Aquarius · Aqr · Aquarii

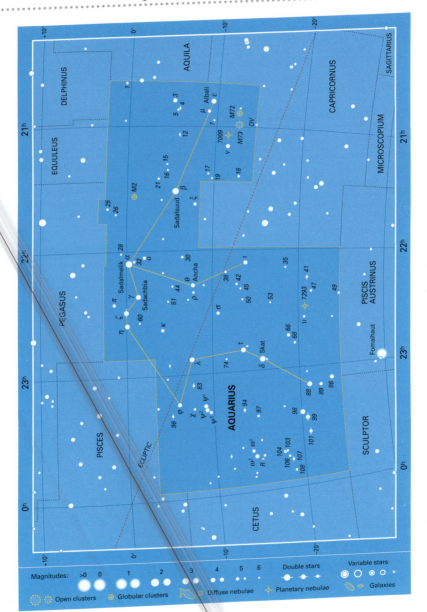

Magnitudes: >0 0 1 2 3 4 5 6 Double stars Variable stars

Open clusters · Globular clusters · Diffuse nebulae · Planetary nebulae · Galaxies

M2 (NGC 7089), 21h 34m −0°.8, is a mag. 6.5 globular cluster easily visible in binoculars or small telescopes, but requiring 100 mm aperture to resolve the brightest individual stars. This rich and highly concentrated globular lies 37,000 l.y. away.

M72 (NGC 6981), 20h 54m −12°.5, is a 9th-mag. globular cluster 56,000 l.y. away, much smaller and less impressive than M2.

NGC 7009, 21h 04m −11°.4, is a famous planetary nebula, 3000 l.y. away, known as the Saturn Nebula because of its resemblance to that planet when seen in large telescopes (see the photograph on page 80). But in most amateur telescopes, of 75 mm aperture or more, it appears as merely an 8th-mag. blue-green ellipse of similar apparent size to the globe of Saturn. Its central star is of mag. 11.5.

NGC 7293, 22h 30m −20°.8, is the nearest planetary nebula to the Sun, about 700 l.y. away, and is commonly known as the Helix Nebula. It is the largest planetary nebula in apparent size, covering ¼° of sky, half the apparent size of the Moon. Its popular name arises because on early photographs it appeared to consist of two overlapping turns of a spiral, although that

NGC 7293, the Helix Nebula, appears as a colourful ring on photographs, but visually is only a pale grey disk. (Nik Szymanek)

structure is less apparent on modern colour images which instead emphasize its ring shape (see the photograph above). Despite its size the Helix Nebula is quite faint and is best found with binoculars or very low power on a telescope, when it appears as a circular misty patch, not as impressive as its large size would suggest.

Aquila – The Eagle

A constellation dating from ancient times, representing the bird that in Greek mythology carried the thunderbolts of Zeus. According to Greek myth, Zeus sent an eagle (or, in a variant of the tale, turned himself into an eagle) to abduct the shepherd boy Ganymede, represented in the sky by the neighbouring constellation of Aquarius.

Aquila's brightest star, Altair, forms one corner of a giant stellar triangle (known in the northern hemisphere as the Summer Triangle) that is completed by Deneb in Cygnus and Vega in Lyra. The name Altair comes from the Arabic *al-nasr al-tair*,

meaning 'the flying eagle'. Two fainter stars, β (beta) and γ (gamma) Aquilae, stand like sentinels either side of it; these are called Alshain and Tarazed, both from the Persian *shahin-i tarazu*, a translation of an Arabic name meaning 'the balance' which referred jointly to these two stars and Altair. Aquila lies in the Milky Way and contains rich starfields, particularly towards Scutum in the south. It is an abundant area for novae.

α (alpha) Aquilae, 19h 51m +8°.9, (Altair, 'the flying eagle'), mag. 0.76, is a white star 17 l.y. away, among the closest naked-eye stars to us.   ▶

Aquila · Aql · Aquilae

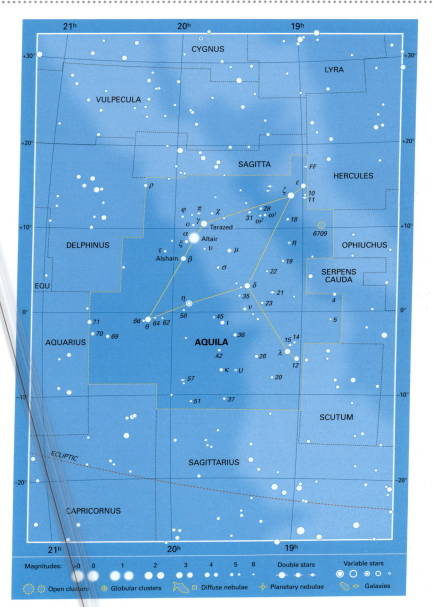

Magnitudes: <0 0 1 2 3 4 5 6   Double stars   Variable stars

Open clusters   ⊕ Globular clusters   Diffuse nebulae   Planetary nebulae   Galaxies

β (beta) Aql, 19h 55m +6°.4, (Alshain), mag. 3.7, is a yellow star 45 l.y. away.

γ (gamma) Aql, 19h 46m +10°.6, (Tarazed), mag. 2.7, is an orange giant star 460 l.y. away.

ζ (zeta) Aql, 19h 05m +13°.9, mag. 3.0, is a blue-white star 83 l.y. away.

η (eta) Aql, 19h 52m +1°.0, a yellow-white super-giant 1200 l.y. away, is one of the brightest Cepheid variable stars. Its brightness ranges from mag. 3.5 to 4.4 with a period of 7.2 days.

15 Aql, 19h 05m −4°.0, is an orange giant star of mag. 5.4, 325 l.y. away, with a purplish mag. 7.0 companion, 550 l.y. away, easily visible in small telescopes.

57 Aql, 19h 55m −8°.2, is an easy double for small telescopes, consisting of a bluish star of mag. 5.7 with a mag. 6.5 companion, both about 350 l.y. away.

R Aql, 19h 06m +8°.2, 690 l.y. away, is a red giant variable of Mira type, about 400 times the diameter of the Sun, ranging from 6th to 12th mag. every 9 months or so.

FF Aql, 18h 58m +17°.4, is a yellow-white super-giant Cepheid variable that ranges from mag. 5.2 to 5.7 every 4.5 days. It lies about 2500 l.y. away.

NGC 6709, 18h 52m +10°.3, is a loosely scattered cluster of some 40 stars of mags. 9 to 11, about 3000 l.y. away.

Ara – The Altar

This constellation, although faint and relatively little-known, originated with the Greeks, who visualized it as the altar on which the gods of Olympus swore an oath of allegiance before their war against the Titans, who at that time ruled the Universe. After their victory, the Olympian gods divided up the Universe between them. Zeus, the greatest of them all, was allotted the sky and placed the altar of the gods among the stars in lasting memory of their victory. Old star atlases depict Ara as the altar on which Centaurus, the centaur, is about to sacrifice Lupus, the wolf. Ara lies in a rich part of the Milky Way, south of Scorpius.

α (alpha) Arae, 17h 32m −49°.9, mag. 2.8, is a blue-white star 242 l.y. away.

β (beta) Ara, 17h 25m −55°.5, mag. 2.8, is an orange supergiant 600 l.y. away.

γ (gamma) Ara, 17h 25m −56°.4, mag. 3.3, is a blue supergiant 1140 l.y. away.

δ (delta) Ara, 17h 31m −60°.7, mag. 3.6, is a blue-white star 187 l.y. away.

ζ (zeta) Ara, 16h 59m −56°.0, mag. 3.1, is an orange giant star 574 l.y. away.

NGC 6193, 16h 41m −48°.8, is a 5th-mag. open cluster of about 30 stars 4200 l.y. away, about half the apparent size of the full Moon. The brightest member is a blue-white star of mag. 5.6 which small telescopes show has a companion of mag. 6.9. Around the cluster is an irregularly shaped patch of faint nebulosity, NGC 6188, which shows up well only on photographs.

NGC 6397, 17h 41m −53°.7, is a 6th-mag. globular cluster that appears as a fuzzy star through binoculars; under good conditions it is visible to the naked eye. Small telescopes resolve the brightest stars in its outer regions, which extend across at least half the apparent diameter of the full Moon. It is one of the closer globulars to us, 10,500 l.y. away.

Ara · Ara · Arae

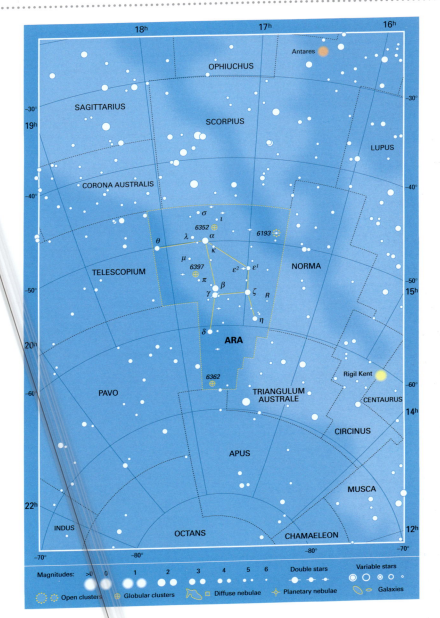

OPHIUCHUS

Antares

SAGITTARIUS

-30°

SCORPIUS

19ʰ

LUPUS

CORONA AUSTRALIS

-40°

σ   ι

6352

θ   λ   α   6193

μ   κ

NORMA

6397   ε² ε¹

TELESCOPIUM

π

β

γ   ζ   R

-50°   η   15ʰ

δ

ARA

20ʰ

Rigil Kent

6362

PAVO   -60°

TRIANGULUM
AUSTRALE

CENTAURUS

14ʰ

CIRCINUS

APUS

MUSCA

22ʰ

12ʰ

INDUS   OCTANS   CHAMAELEON

-70°   -80°   -80°   -70°

Magnitudes: >0   0   1   2   3   4   5   6   Double stars   Variable stars

Open clusters   Globular clusters   Diffuse nebulae   Planetary nebulae   Galaxies

Aries – The Ram

A constellation lying between Taurus and Andromeda, whose origin dates back to ancient times. Aries represents the ram of Greek legend whose golden fleece was sought by Jason and the Argonauts. Despite its faintness, Aries has assumed great importance in astronomy because, over 2000 years ago, it contained the point where the Sun passes from south to north across the celestial equator each year. This point, the vernal equinox, is still sometimes known as the First Point of Aries, although it no longer lies in Aries, having moved into neighbouring Pisces in 67 BC as a result of the slow wobble of the Earth in space known as precession. It is now headed for Aquarius (see diagram below). Currently, the Sun passes through Aries from late April to mid-May.

α (alpha) Arietis, 2h 07m +23°.5, (Hamal, from the Arabic for 'lamb'), mag. 2.0, is an orange giant star 66 l.y. away.

β (beta) Ari, 1h 55m +20°.8, (Sheratan, from the Arabic for 'two'), mag. 2.6, is a blue-white star 60 l.y. away.

γ (gamma) Ari, 1h 54m +19°.3, (Mesartim), 204 l.y. away, is a striking double consisting of twin white stars of mags. 4.7 and 4.6, clearly visible through small telescopes even under low magnification.

ε (epsilon) Ari, 2h 59m +21°.3, 290 l.y. away, is a challenging double star for apertures of 100 mm or more. High magnification reveals a tight pair of white stars of mags. 5.2 and 5.5.

λ (lambda) Ari, 1h 58m +23°.6, 133 l.y. away, is a white star of mag. 4.8 with a yellow mag. 7.3 companion visible in small telescopes or even good binoculars.

π (pi) Ari, 2h 49m +17°.5, 600 l.y. away, is a blue-white star of mag. 5.3, with a close mag. 8.5 companion, difficult to distinguish in the smallest telescopes.

Movement of the so-called First Point of Aries over 800 years. At present it lies in Pisces and is approaching Aquarius. (Wil Tirion)

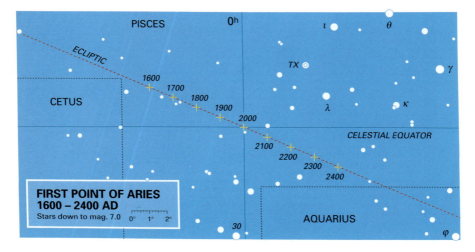

Aries · Ari · Arietis

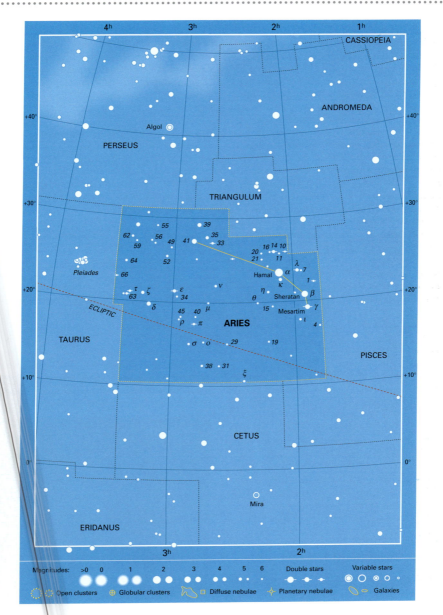

CASSIOPEIA

ANDROMEDA

PERSEUS

Algol

TRIANGULUM

55

62   56   49   41
59
64   52
Pleiades
66

τ   ζ   ε
63   ν
δ   34
45 40   μ
ρ   π

σ   ο   29
38   31
ξ

39
35
33
20 16 14 10
21   11
λ
Hamal   α   7
κ   1
η
θ   β
Sheratan   γ
15   Mesartim   ι
4

ARIES

19

TAURUS

ECLIPTIC

PISCES

CETUS

Mira

ERIDANUS

Magnitudes: >0   0   1   2   3   4   5 6   Double stars   Variable stars

Open clusters   Globular clusters   Diffuse nebulae   Planetary nebulae   Galaxies

Auriga – The Charioteer

A large and prominent constellation, usually identified by the ancient Greeks as Erichthonius, a legendary king of Athens and a skilled charioteer. Auriga's leading star is Capella, sixth-brightest in the whole sky and the most northerly first-magnitude star. In legend this star represented the she-goat Amaltheia which suckled the infant Zeus; the stars ζ (zeta) and η (eta) Aurigae are supposedly her kids and were visualized as being carried in the charioteer's arms. The star marking the charioteer's foot was originally shared with Taurus the Bull, but it is now assigned exclusively to Taurus as β (beta) Tauri. However, it once bore the alternative designation of γ (gamma) Aurigae and is shown on the chart to complete the classical figure.

α (alpha) Aurigae, 5h 17m +46°.0, (Capella, 'she-goat'), mag. 0.08, lies 42 l.y. away. It is a spectroscopic binary, consisting of two yellow giant stars orbiting every 104 days, although they do not eclipse each other.

β (beta) Aur, 6h 00m +44°.9, (Menkalinan, 'shoulder of the charioteer'), 82 l.y. away, is an eclipsing variable of mag. 1.9 consisting of two blue-white stars that orbit every 3.96 days, causing two dips in brightness of 0.1 mag. on each orbit.

ε (epsilon) Aur, 5h 02m +43°.6, a white supergiant about 2000 l.y. away, is an eclipsing binary of exceptionally long period. Normally it appears at mag. 3.0, but every 27 years it sinks to mag. 3.8 as it is eclipsed by a dark companion, remaining at minimum for a year. One theory is that ε Aurigae's companion is a binary star enveloped in a disk of matter. Its next eclipse starts in late 2009.

ζ (zeta) Aur, 5h 02m +41°.1, 790 l.y. away, is a famous eclipsing binary of contrasting stars: an orange giant orbited every 972 days by a smaller blue companion. During eclipses, ζ Aurigae's brightness drops from mag. 3.7 to 4.0.

θ (theta) Aur, 6h 00m +37°.2, 173 l.y. away, is a blue-white star of mag. 2.6. It has a yellowish companion of mag. 7.1 which, because of its closeness and relative faintness, needs at least 100 mm aperture and high magnification to distinguish. This is a tough double for steady nights.

ψ¹ (psi¹) Aur, 6h 25m +49°.3, is a variable orange supergiant that ranges between mags. 4.8 and 5.7 with no set period. Its distance is uncertain.

4 Aur, 4h 59m +37°.9, 159 l.y. away, is a double star of mags. 5.0 and 8.1, divisible through small telescopes.

14 Aur, 5h 15m +32°.7, 270 l.y. away, is a white star of mag. 5.0 with a mag. 7.9 companion, 82 l.y. away, split in small telescopes.

RT Aurigae, 6h 29m +30°.5, a yellow-white supergiant, is a Cepheid variable ranging between mag. 5.0 and 5.8 every 3.7 days. It lies about 1600 l.y. away.

►

M36 is the most prominent of the three Messier clusters in Auriga when viewed through small instruments. It displays crooked chains of stars and a triangular centre. (Peter Wienerroither)

Auriga · Aur · Aurigae

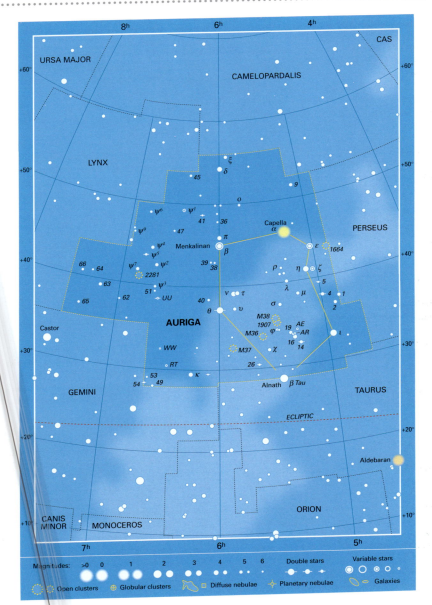

Magnitudes: >0   0   1   2   3   4   5   6   Double stars   Variable stars

Open clusters   Globular clusters   Diffuse nebulae   Planetary nebulae   Galaxies

UU Aur, 6h 37m +38°.4, is a semi-regular variable, ranging between 5th and 7th mags. with a rough period of 234 days. It is a giant star appearing deep red in colour, around 2000 l.y. away.

M36 (NGC 1960), 5h 36m +34°.1, is a small, bright open cluster of about 60 stars, visible in binoculars and resolvable into stars in small telescopes (see the picture on the previous page). It appears about one-third the diameter of the full Moon and is the most prominent of Auriga's three Messier clusters. M36 lies 3900 l.y. away.

M37 (NGC 2099), 5h 52m +33°.5, is the largest and richest of the three Messier clusters in Auriga, containing about 150 stars. In binoculars the cluster appears as a hazy, unresolved patch about

half the diameter of the full Moon, but a 100-mm telescope resolves it into a sparkling field of faint stardust, with a brighter orange star at the centre. It lies 4200 l.y. away.

M38 (NGC 1912), 5h 29m +35°.8, is a large, scattered cluster of about 100 faint stars, visible in binoculars, with a noticeable cross-shape when seen through a telescope. Its distance is 3900 l.y. Half a degree south of it lies the small fuzzy blob of NGC 1907, a much smaller and fainter cluster 4200 l.y. away.

NGC 2281, 6h 49m +41°.1, is a binocular cluster of about 30 stars, 1500 l.y. away. Through a telescope the stars appear to be arranged in a crescent, with four brighter stars forming a diamond shape.

Boötes – The Herdsman

An ancient constellation, representing a herdsman driving a bear (Ursa Major) around the sky; the herdsman is often depicted holding the leash of the hunting dogs, Canes Venatici. The name of the constellation's brightest star, Arcturus, actually means 'bear-keeper' in Greek. In Greek mythology Boötes represents Arcas, the son of Zeus and the nymph Callisto (neighbouring Ursa Major represents Callisto herself, who was turned into a bear by Zeus's jealous wife Hera).

Arcturus is the brightest star in the northern half of the sky, and is easily identified: the curving handle of the Big Dipper or Plough points to it. Arcturus forms the base of a large 'Y' shape completed by ε (epsilon) Boötis, γ (gamma) Boötis and α (alpha) Coronae Borealis. The other stars of the constellation are much fainter than Arcturus, but include many doubles of interest.

The year's most abundant meteor shower, the Quadrantids, radiates from the northern

part of Boötes, an area of sky that was once occupied by the now-abandoned constellation of Quadrans Muralis, the Mural Quadrant (hence the shower's name). The Quadrantid meteors reach a peak of about 100 per hour on January 3–4 each year, although they are not as bright as other rich showers such as the Perseids and Geminids.

α (alpha) Boötis, 14h 16m +19°.2, (Arcturus), mag. −0.05, is the fourth-brightest star in the entire sky. It is an orange giant, about 27 times the diameter of the Sun, lying 37 l.y. away; its ruddy colour is noticeable to the naked eye, and is more striking with optical aid. Arcturus has a mass similar to our Sun's, and it is believed that the Sun will swell up to become a red giant like Arcturus 5000 million years from now.

β (beta) Boo, 15h 02m +40°.4, (Nekkar, corrupted from the Arabic for 'ox-driver', referring to the whole constellation), mag. 3.5, is a yellow giant 219 l.y. away.

▶

Boötes · Boo · Boötis

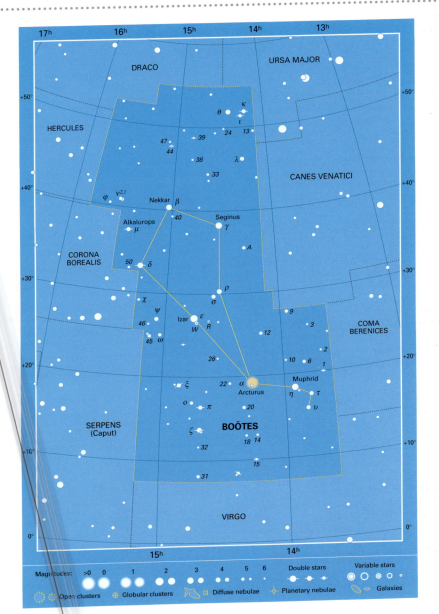

γ (gamma) Boo, 14h 32m +38°.3, (Seginus), mag. 3.0, is a white star 85 l.y. away.

δ (delta) Boo, 15h 16m +33°.3, mag. 3.5, is a yellow giant 117 l.y. away. It has a wide binocular companion of mag. 7.8.

ε (epsilon) Boo, 14h 45m +27°.1, (Izar, 'girdle' or 'loincloth'), 210 l.y. away, is a celebrated double star: an orange giant primary of mag. 2.5 with a blue main-sequence companion of mag. 4.6. This close double of contrasting colours requires a telescope of at least 75 mm at ×100 power or more, because the bright primary tends to overwhelm its fainter companion; but its appearance when split has led to the alternative name Pulcherrima, meaning 'most beautiful'.

ι (iota) Boo, 14h 16m +51°.4, 97 l.y. away, is a wide double star of mags. 4.8 and 7.5.

κ (kappa) Boo, 14h 13m +51°.8, is an easy double star for small telescopes, consisting of unrelated components of mags. 4.5 and 6.6, distances 155 and 196 l.y.

μ (mu) Boo, 15h 24m +37°.4, (Alkalurops, 'club' or 'staff'), 121 l.y. distant, is an attractive triple star. To the naked eye it appears as a blue-white star of mag. 4.3, but binoculars reveal a wide companion of mag. 6.5. Telescopes of 75 mm aperture with high magnification show that this companion actually consists of two close stars of mags. 7.0 and 7.6; they orbit each other every 260 years.

ν¹ ν² (nu¹ nu²) Boo, 15h 31m +40°.8, is an unrelated binocular duo: ν¹ is an orange giant of mag. 5.0, 870 l.y. distant, while ν² is a white star also of mag. 5.0, 430 l.y. away.

π (pi) Boo, 14h 41m +16°.4, 317 l.y. away, is a double star with blue-white components of mags. 4.9 and 5.8, visible in small telescopes.

ξ (xi) Boo, 14h 51m +19°.1, 22 l.y. away, is a showpiece double for small telescopes, consisting of yellow and orange stars of mags. 4.7 and 7.0, orbiting each other every 150 years.

44 Boo, 15h 04m +47°.7, 42 l.y. away, is a complex double–variable star. To the naked eye it appears as a yellow star of mag. 4.8. In fact, it is a binary of mags. 5.3 and 6.1 orbiting every 206 years. Until the year 2011 the two can be split in apertures of 100 mm, but thereafter they will become more difficult as they move together until, around their closest in 2019–20, they will be indivisible in amateur telescopes. The fainter star is itself an eclipsing binary with a period of 6.4 hours and a range of 0.6 mag.

Caelum – The Chisel

An obscure, almost irrelevant constellation at the foot of Eridanus, representing a pair of engraving tools, or burins. It was one of the figures representing instruments of the arts and sciences introduced in the 1750s by the French astronomer Nicolas Louis de Lacaille during his mapping of the southern sky.

α (alpha) Caeli, 4h 41m −41°.9, mag. 4.4, is a white main-sequence star 66 l.y. away.

β (beta) Cae, 4h 42m −37°.1, mag. 5.0, is a white star 90 l.y. away.

γ (gamma) Cae, 5h 04m −35°.5, mag. 4.6, is an orange giant 185 l.y. away. It has a close mag. 8.1 companion, difficult to see in the smallest apertures because of the brightness contrast.

δ (delta) Cae, 4h 31m −45°.0, mag. 5.1, is a blue-white star 710 l.y. away.

Caelum · Cae · Caeli

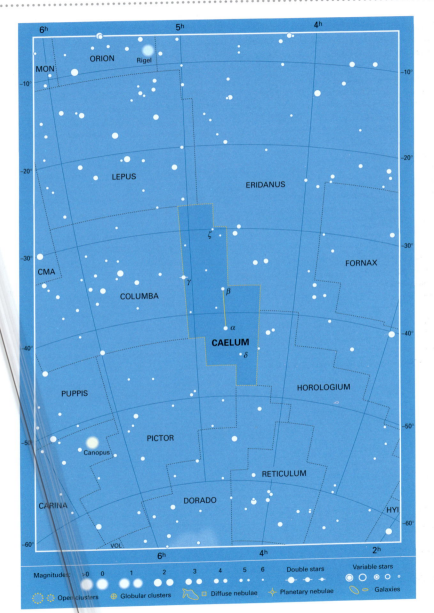

Camelopardalis – The Giraffe

A faint and obscure constellation of the north polar region of the sky, sometimes written as Camelopardus, an obsolete variant of the name. It was invented in 1613 by the Dutch theologian and astronomer Petrus Plancius. The German astronomer Jacob Bartsch wrote that it represented the camel on which Rebecca rode into Canaan for her marriage to Isaac. But Camelopardalis is a giraffe not a camel, so its true meaning remains unclear.

α (alpha) Camelopardalis, 4h 54m +66°.3, mag. 4.3, is a highly luminous blue supergiant star approximately 5000 l.y. away, exceptionally distant for a naked-eye star.

β (beta) Cam, 5h 03m +60°.4, at mag. 4.0 the brightest star in the constellation, is a yellow supergiant 1000 l.y. distant. It has a wide mag. 8.6 companion star visible in small telescopes or even good binoculars.

11 Cam, 5h 06m +59°.0, mag. 5.2, forms an easy binocular pairing with 12 Cam, mag. 6.1. Both lie at a similar distance, about 650 l.y., but are too widely separated to be a genuine double.

Σ 1694 (Struve 1694), 12h 49m +83°.4, 300 l.y. away, is a pair of blue-white stars, mags. 5.4 and 5.9, easily split in small telescopes. In some old catalogues the star was listed as 32 Cam.

NGC 1502, 4h 08m +62°.3, is a small 6th-mag. open star cluster with about 45 members visible in binoculars or a small telescope, somewhat triangular in shape and with an easy 7th-mag. double star at its centre. It lies 3000 l.y. away. Note a chain of 15 or more stars called Kemble's Cascade which runs for 2½° from NGC 1502 towards Cassiopeia, parallel to the Milky Way (see illustration below). The brightest star in the chain is of 5th magnitude, about halfway along.

NGC 2403, 7h 37m +65°.6, is an 8th-mag. spiral galaxy ¼° long, visible as an elliptical glow in a 100-mm telescope. It lies about 12 million l.y. away.

Kemble's Cascade is a chain of faint stars visible in binoculars and small telescopes near the open cluster NGC 1502. (Wil Tirion)

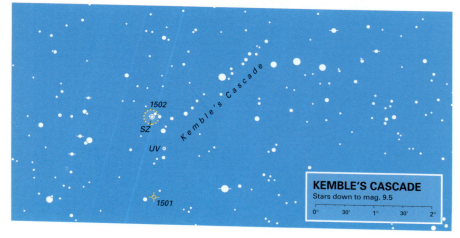

Camelopardalis · Cam · Camelopardalis

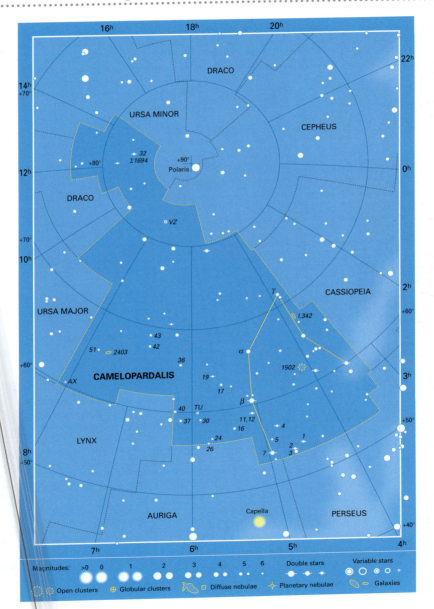

DRACO

URSA MINOR

32
Σ1694

+80°

+90°
Polaris

CEPHEUS

DRACO

VZ

CASSIOPEIA

γ

l.342

URSA MAJOR

43
51   42
2403

1502

CAMELOPARDALIS

AX

α

19
36
17

β

40   TU
37   30
11,12
16
4

24
5   1
26
2
3
7

LYNX

AURIGA

Capella

PERSEUS

Magnitudes: >0   0   1   2   3   4   5   6   Double stars   Variable stars

○ Open clusters   ⊕ Globular clusters   Diffuse nebulae   Planetary nebulae   Galaxies

Cancer – The Crab

Cancer represents the crab that attacked Hercules when he was fighting the multi-headed Hydra; the luckless crab was crushed underfoot by mighty Hercules but was subsequently elevated to the heavens.

In ancient times, the Sun reached its most northerly point in the sky each year while it was in Cancer. The date on which the Sun is farthest north of the Earth's equator, on or around June 21, is the northern summer solstice; on this day the Sun appears overhead at noon at latitude 23½° north on Earth. This latitude came to be known as the Tropic of Cancer, a name it retains today even though, because of the effect of precession, the Sun now lies in the constellation of Taurus on that date.

With only two stars brighter than mag. 4.0, Cancer is the faintest of the 12 constellations of the zodiac, but it nevertheless contains much of interest, notably the star cluster Praesepe, the Manger. Praesepe is flanked by a pair of 4th- and 5th-magnitude stars, Asellus Borealis and Asellus Australis, the northern and southern donkeys, visualized as feeding at the stellar manger.

α (alpha) Cancri, 8h 58m +11°.9, (Acubens, 'the claw'), mag. 4.3, is a white star 174 l.y. away. It has a 12th-mag. companion visible with telescopes of 75 mm aperture and over.

β (beta) Cnc, 8h 17m +9°.2, mag. 3.5, an orange giant 290 l.y. away, is the brightest star in the constellation.

γ (gamma) Cnc, 8h 43m +21°.5, (Asellus Borealis, 'northern donkey'), mag. 4.7, is a white star 158 l.y. away.

δ (delta) Cnc, 8h 45m +18°.2, (Asellus Australis, 'southern donkey'), mag. 3.9, is an orange giant star 136 l.y. away.

ζ (zeta) Cnc, 8h 12m +17°.6, 83 l.y. away, is an interesting multiple star. A small telescope reveals two yellow stars of mags. 5.0 and 6.2; they form a genuine binary with an estimated orbital period of 1100 years. Larger telescopes split the brighter component into a tight binary of mags. 5.6 and 6.0, orbital period 59.5 years. These two stars are currently moving apart; at their widest, around the year 2018, 100 mm should be sufficient to split them, but 150 mm will be needed before about 2010.

ι (iota) Cnc, 8h 47m +28°.8, 298 l.y. away, is a yellow giant of mag. 4.0 with a blue-white mag. 6.6 companion just visible in binoculars, or easily seen through a small telescope.

M44 (NGC 2632), 8h 40m +20°.0, Praesepe ('manger'), commonly called the Beehive Cluster, is a swarm of about 50 stars of 6th mag. and fainter, visible as a misty patch to the naked eye and best seen through binoculars. The brightest member of this open cluster, ε (epsilon) Cancri, is mag. 6.3. Praesepe sprawls over 1½° of sky, three times the apparent diameter of the Moon. The distance to the cluster's centre is 577 l.y. according to the Hipparcos measurements.

M67 (NGC 2682), 8h 50m +11°.8, is a smaller and denser open cluster than M44, visible as a Moon-sized misty ellipse in binoculars or small telescopes. Apertures of at least 75 mm are needed to resolve the brightest of its 200 or so individual stars, which are of 10th mag. and fainter. It lies 2500 l.y. away.

Cancer · Cnc · Cancri

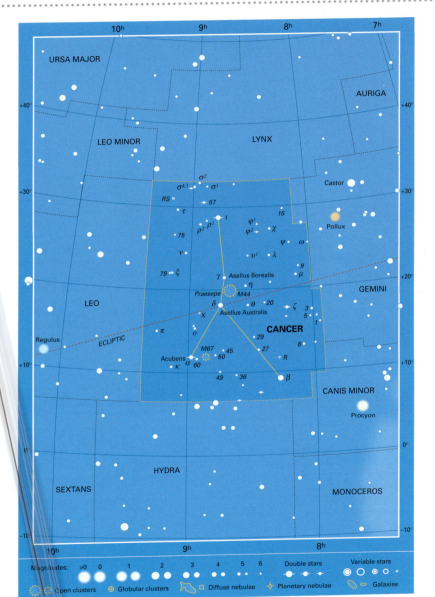

Canes Venatici – The Hunting Dogs

A constellation introduced in 1687 by the Polish astronomer Johannes Hevelius, consisting of a sprinkling of faint stars below Ursa Major. It represents two dogs, Asterion ('little star') and Chara ('joy'), held on a leash by neighbouring Boötes as they pursue the Great Bear around the pole. Canes Venatici contains numerous galaxies, the most famous being M51, the Whirlpool, a beautiful face-on spiral (pictured on page 290). It was the first galaxy in which spiral form was detected, by Lord Rosse in 1845 with his 72-inch (1.8-m) reflector at Birr Castle, Ireland.

α (alpha) Canum Venaticorum, 12h 56m +38°.3, is popularly called Cor Caroli, meaning 'Charles's heart', a reference to the executed King Charles I of England; it is reputed, doubtless apocryphally, to have shone particularly brightly in 1660 on the arrival of Charles II in England at the Restoration of the monarchy. It is a double star of mags. 2.9 and 5.6, easily split in small telescopes. Both stars are white, but various observers have reported subtle shades of colour in them when viewed through a telescope. The brighter star is the standard example of a rare class of stars with strong and variable magnetic fields; its brightness fluctuates slightly but not enough to be noticeable to the eye. Cor Caroli is 110 l.y. away.

β (beta) CVn, 12h 34m +41°.4, (Chara, 'joy'), mag. 4.2, is the only other star of any prominence in the constellation. It is a yellow main-sequence star similar to the Sun, 27 l.y. away.

Y CVn, 12h 45m +45°.4, 710 l.y. away, is a semi-regular variable supergiant of deep red colour sometimes known as La Superba. Its range is about mag. 5.0 to 6.5 and its period is approximately 160 days.

M3 (NGC 5272), 13h 42m +28°.4, is a rich globular cluster located midway between Cor Caroli and Arcturus, regarded as one of the finest globulars in the northern sky. At 6th mag. it is on the naked-eye limit, but can be picked up easily as a hazy star in binoculars or a small telescope; a 6th-mag. star nearby acts as a guide. In small telescopes the cluster appears as a condensed ball of light with a faint outer halo. Apertures of 100 mm or more are needed to resolve individual stars in its outer regions. M3 is 32,000 l.y. away.

M51 (NGC 5194), 13h 30m +47°.2, the Whirlpool Galaxy, is an 8th-mag. spiral galaxy about 26 million l.y. away with a smaller satellite galaxy, NGC 5195, apparently lying at the end of one of its arms; in reality, this companion lies slightly behind M51, having brushed past it some time in the past 100 million years or so. The Whirlpool can be seen in binoculars, appearing elongated. It is disappointing in small telescopes, which show a faint milky radiance around the starlike nuclei of the galaxy and its satellite; apertures of at least 250 mm are needed to see the spiral arms well. Nevertheless, M51 is well worth hunting for on clear, dark nights. (For a photograph of M51 and NGC 5195 see page 290.)

M63 (NGC 5055), 13h 16m +42°.0, is a 9th-mag. spiral galaxy visible in small telescopes as an elliptical haze with a somewhat mottled texture. It is popularly known as the Sunflower Galaxy because of its appearance in large instruments.

M94 (NGC 4736), 12h 51m +41°.1, is a compact spiral galaxy presented nearly face-on. In amateur telescopes it looks like an 8th-mag. comet, with a fuzzy star-like nucleus surrounded by an elliptical halo. M94 is about 15 million l.y. away.

Canes Venatici · CVn · Canum Venaticorum

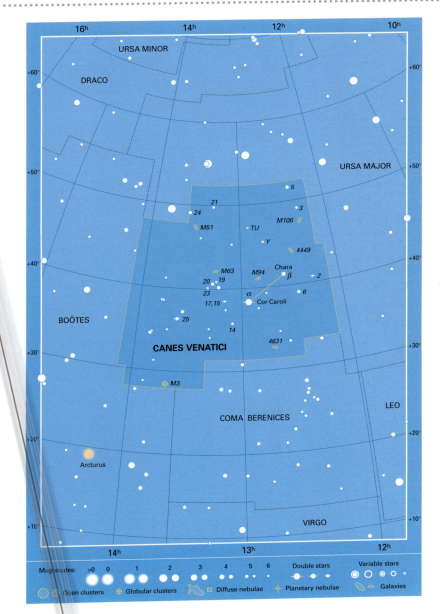

Canis Major – The Greater Dog

An ancient constellation, representing one of the two dogs (the other being Canis Minor) following at the heels of Orion. In other Greek legends it was identified as Laelaps, a dog so swift that no prey could outrun it. Laelaps was sent in pursuit of a fox that could never be caught. The chase would have continued for eternity had not Zeus plucked up the dog and placed it in the sky as Canis Major, although without the fox.

Canis Major contains many brilliant stars, making it one of the most prominent constellations; its leading star, Sirius, is the brightest star in the entire sky as seen from Earth. Sirius features in many legends, and the ancient Egyptians based their calendar on its yearly motion around the sky.

α (alpha) Canis Majoris, 6h 45m −16°.7, (Sirius, from the Greek meaning 'searing' or 'scorching'), mag. −1.44, is a brilliant white star 8.6 l.y. away, one of the Sun's closest neighbours; the Hipparcos satellite detected variability of 0.1 mag. or so in its brightness. It has a white dwarf companion of mag. 8.4 that orbits it every 50 years. The brilliance of Sirius overpowers this white dwarf so that even when the two stars are at their greatest separation, as between the years 2020 and 2025, telescopes of 200 mm aperture or more and steady atmospheric conditions are required to see it. The two were last at their closest in 1993.

β (beta) CMa, 6h 23m −18°.0, (Mirzam, 'the announcer', i.e. of Sirius), mag. 2.0, is a blue giant 500 l.y. away. It is a pulsating star whose variations, of a few hundredths of a magnitude every 6 hours, are undetectable to the naked eye.

δ (delta) CMa, 7h 08m −26°.4, (Wezen, 'the weight'), mag. 1.8, is a white supergiant star 1800 l.y. away.

ε (epsilon) CMa, 6h 59m −29°.0, (Adhara, 'the virgins'), mag. 1.5, is a blue giant 430 l.y. away. It has a mag. 7.4 companion which is difficult to see in small telescopes because of the glare from the primary.

η (eta) CMa, 7h 24m −29°.3, (Aludra), mag. 2.4, is a blue supergiant about 3200 l.y. away.

μ (mu) CMa, 6h 56m −14°.0, mag. 5.0, is a yellow giant about 900 l.y. away with a close 7th-mag. blue-white companion difficult to pick up in the smallest apertures because of the magnitude contrast.

ν¹ (nu¹) CMa, 6h 36m −18°.7, mag. 5.7, is a yellow giant 278 l.y. away with a mag. 8.1 companion, visible in small telescopes.

UW CMa, 7h 19m −24°.6, is an eclipsing binary of β (beta) Lyrae type that varies between mags. 4.8 and 5.3 in 4.4 days. It lies about 3000 l.y. away.

M41 (NGC 2287), 6h 47m −20°.7, is a large and bright open cluster of about 80 stars, easily visible through binoculars or a small telescope and, with a total magnitude of 4.5, detectable by the naked eye under good conditions – it was known to the ancient Greeks. A low-power view in a small telescope shows the individual stars grouped in bunches and curves, covering an area of sky equivalent to the apparent diameter of the Moon. The brightest stars in the cluster are 7th-mag. orange giants. M41 is 2100 l.y. away.

NGC 2362, 7h 19m −25°.0, is a compact cluster surrounding the mag. 4.4 blue supergiant star τ (tau) Canis Majoris, which is a genuine member. Small telescopes show about 60 stars in the cluster, which lies some 5200 l.y. away.

Canis Major · CMa · Canis Majoris

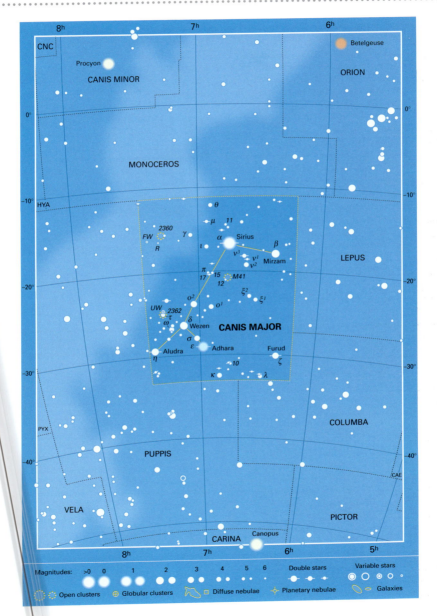

Canis Minor – The Lesser Dog

The second of the two dogs of Orion, the other being Canis Major. In one Greek legend, the constellation represents Maera, dog of Icarius, the man who was first taught to make wine by the god Dionysus. When some shepherds drank the wine they became intoxicated. Suspecting that Icarius had poisoned them they killed him. Maera the dog ran howling to Icarius's daughter Erigone and led her to her father's body. Both Erigone and the dog took their own lives where Icarius lay. Zeus placed their images among the stars as a reminder of the tragic affair. In this story, Icarius is identified with the constellation Boötes, Erigone is Virgo and Maera is Canis Minor.

Apart from its leading star Procyon, which is the eighth-brightest star in the sky, there are few objects of importance in Canis Minor. Procyon forms a prominent equilateral triangle with the bright stars Sirius (in Canis Major) and Betelgeuse (in Orion).

α (alpha) Canis Minoris, 7h 39m +5°.2, (Procyon, from the Greek meaning 'preceding the dog', referring to its rising before Sirius), mag. 0.40, is a yellow-white star 11.4 l.y. away, and therefore among the nearest stars to the Sun. Like Sirius, Procyon has a white dwarf companion, but this star, of mag. 10.7, is even more difficult to see than the companion of Sirius, requiring the use of large professional telescopes. Procyon's companion orbits it every 41 years.

β (beta) CMi, 7h 27m +8°.3, (Gomeisa), mag. 2.9, is a blue-white main-sequence star 170 l.y. away.

White dwarfs

By a remarkable coincidence both Sirius and Procyon, the brightest stars in Canis Major and Canis Minor respectively, are accompanied by tiny, faint stars known as white dwarfs. The existence of these companion stars was predicted in 1844 by the German astronomer Friedrich Wilhelm Bessel (1784–1846), who detected a slight wobble in the proper motions (*page 16*) of Sirius and Procyon. Bessel realized that this wobble was most probably caused by the presence of unseen companions orbiting around the visible stars.

The companion of Sirius, called Sirius B, was first seen in 1862 by the American astronomer Alvan G. Clark using a 47-cm (18½-inch) refractor, while the companion to Procyon (Procyon B) was first seen in 1896 by John M. Schaeberle with the 91-cm (36-inch) refractor at Lick Observatory.

But not until 1915 did astronomers realize the truly extraordinary nature of these stars. Observations showed that Sirius B was very hot, very small and very dense. In fact Sirius B has the mass of the Sun packed into a sphere less than 1 per cent of the Sun's diameter (that is, their diameter is about the same as that of the Earth). The resulting density of Sirius B is over 100,000 times that of water.

We now know that a white dwarf is a star at the end of its life; it is the shrunken remnant of a once-proud star like the Sun whose central nuclear fires have burnt out. The cause of the immense densities of white dwarfs is the inexorable pull of gravity, which squeezes the electrons of the dying star as closely together as is physically possible.

Canis Minor · CMi · Canis Minoris

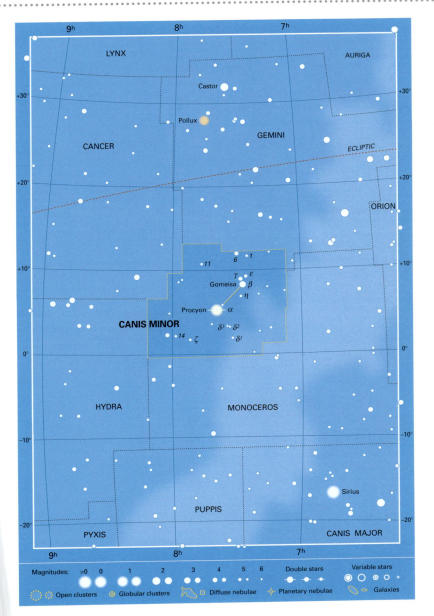

Capricornus – The Sea Goat

Capricornus is depicted as a goat with a fish's tail. Amphibious creatures feature prominently in ancient legends, and the origin of Capricornus certainly dates back to ancient times. In Greek legend, the constellation represented the goat-headed god Pan who jumped into a river to escape the approach of the monster Typhon, turning his lower half into a fish.

Before about 130 BC the Sun lay in Capricornus when it reached its farthest point south of the equator each year; this point, known as the northern winter solstice, currently occurs on December 21 or 22 (the date can vary from year to year). The latitude on Earth at which the Sun appears overhead at noon on that date, 23½° south, became known as the Tropic of Capricorn. Because of precession, the northern winter solstice has since moved from Capricornus into the neighbouring constellation Sagittarius (and will reach Ophiuchus in the year 2269), but the Tropic of Capricorn retains its name.

Capricornus is the smallest constellation of the zodiac. The Sun is within its boundaries from late January to mid-February.

α^1 α^2 (alpha^1 alpha^2) Capricorni, 20h 18m −12°.5, (Algedi or Giedi, both from the Arabic meaning 'the kid' in reference to the constellation as a whole) is a multiple star, consisting of an unrelated yellow supergiant of mag. 4.3 and a yellow giant of mag. 3.6, 690 and 109 l.y. away respectively, visible separately with the naked eye or binoculars. Telescopes reveal that each star is itself double. The fainter of the pair, α^1, has a wide mag. 9.2 companion visible in small telescopes; α^2 has its own companion of mag. 11. Telescopes of at least 100 mm aperture show that this faint companion is itself composed of two 11th-mag. stars. α Capricorni is therefore a fascinating hybrid system.

β (beta) Cap, 20h 21m −14°.8, (Dabih, from the Arabic meaning 'the lucky stars of the slaughterer'), 340 l.y. away, is a golden-yellow giant star of mag. 3.1 with a wide, blue-white companion of mag. 6.1, visible through binoculars or small telescopes.

γ (gamma) Cap, 21h 40m −16°.7, (Nashira), mag. 3.7, is a white giant star 139 l.y. away.

δ (delta) Cap, 21h 47m −16°.1, (Deneb Algedi, 'the kid's tail'), mag. 2.9, is the brightest star in the constellation. It is an eclipsing binary of β (beta) Lyrae type, varying by a barely perceptible 0.2 mag. over 24.5 hours. It lies 39 l.y. away.

π (pi) Cap, 20h 27m −18°.2, 670 l.y. away, is a blue-white star of mag. 5.1 with a close mag. 8.3 companion visible with a small telescope.

M30 (NGC 7099), 21h 40m −23°.2, is a mag. 7.5 globular cluster 30,000 l.y. away, visible in small telescopes and resolvable in 100 mm aperture, notably centrally condensed with finger-like chains of stars extending northwards.

Capricornus · Cap · Capricorni

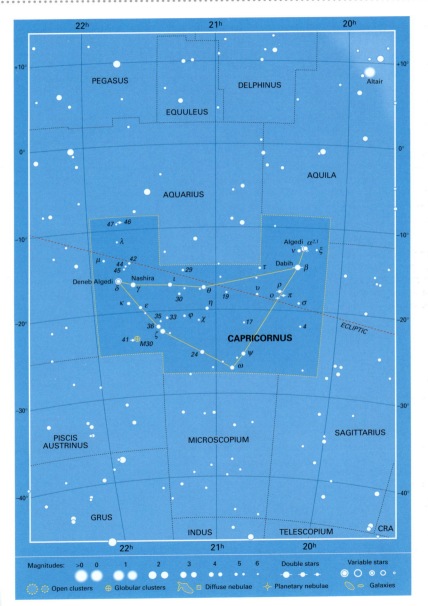

Carina – The Keel

This constellation was originally part of the extensive Argo Navis, the ship of the Argonauts, until that figure was subdivided into three parts in 1763 by the French celestial cartographer Nicolas Louis de Lacaille. The other two parts are Puppis and Vela; Carina is the smallest of the three. As a part of Argo Navis, Carina originated in ancient Greek times and is associated with the legend of Jason and the Argonauts and their quest for the Golden Fleece. Carina lies in the Milky Way, providing rich starfields and clusters for binoculars. The stars ι (iota) and ε (epsilon) Carinae, together with κ (kappa) and δ (delta) Velorum, form a shape known as the False Cross, sometimes confused with the real Southern Cross.

α (alpha) Carinae, 6h 24m −52°.7, (Canopus), mag. −0.62, the second-brightest star in the sky, is a white giant 313 l.y. away; the Hipparcos satellite found it to be variable by 0.1 mag. or so. It is named after the helmsman of the Greek King Menelaus, and appropriately enough is now used by spacecraft as a guide for navigation.

β (beta) Car, 9h 13m −69°.7, (Miaplacidus), mag. 1.7, is a blue-white star 111 l.y. away.

ε (epsilon) Car, 8h 23m −59°.5, mag. 1.9, is an orange giant star 630 l.y. away.

η (eta) Car, 10h 45m −59°.7, 7500 l.y. away, is a peculiar nova-like variable star embedded in the nebula NGC 3372 (see separate entry). In the past, η Carinae has fluctuated erratically in brightness, reaching a maximum of mag. −1 in 1843 when it was temporarily the second-brightest star in the sky; it subsequently settled at around 6th mag., but brightened to 5th mag. in 1998. The star is estimated to be over 100 times more massive and 4 million times brighter than the Sun, with an unseen companion orbiting it every 5½ years. The binary pair is surrounded by a shell of dust and gas thrown off in the 1843 outburst.

θ (theta) Car, 10h 43m −64°.4, mag. 2.7, is a blue-white star 440 l.y. away, a member of the sparkling cluster IC 2602 (see page 108).

ι (iota) Car, 9h 17m −59°.3, mag. 2.2, is a white supergiant 690 l.y. away.

υ (upsilon) Car, 9h 47m −65°.1, 1600 l.y. away, is a double star consisting of two blue-white giants of mags. 3.0 and 6.0, divisible in small telescopes.

l Car, 9h 45m −62°.5, a yellow supergiant 1500 l.y. away, is the brightest Cepheid whose variations are large enough to be obvious to the naked eye. It rises and falls between mags. 3.3 and 4.2 every 35.5 days.

R Car, 9h 32m −62°.8, 416 l.y. away, is a red giant variable star of Mira type that ranges between 4th and 10th mags. with a period of 309 days.

S Car, 10h 09m −61°.5, about 1300 l.y. away, is a red giant variable similar to nearby R Car, varying from 5th to 10th mag. over 150 days.

NGC 2516, 7h 58m −60°.9, is a naked-eye open cluster of some 80 stars, 1100 l.y. away, as large as the full Moon. It is a sparkling sight in binoculars, which show it to be cross-shaped. Its brightest member is a mag. 5.2 red giant.

NGC 3114, 10h 03m −60°.1, is a widely scattered open cluster the same apparent size as the full Moon, containing stars of 6th mag. and fainter, about 3000 l.y. away. It is best seen in binoculars and small telescopes with low power.

NGC 3372, 10h 44m −59°.9, is a celebrated diffuse nebula easily visible to the naked eye as a brilliant patch of the Milky Way four Moon diameters wide, surrounding the erratic variable star η (eta) Carinae. The nebula shines from the light of brilliant young stars born within it. Binoculars and small telescopes show jewelled star clusters and swirls of glowing gas alternating with ▶

Carina · Car · Carinae

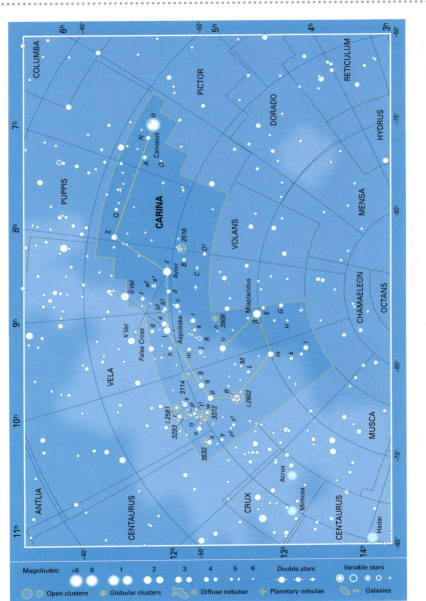

Magnitudes: >0 0 1 2 3 4 5 6   Double stars   Variable stars

Open clusters   Globular clusters   Diffuse nebulae   Planetary nebulae   Galaxies

dark lanes. Most famous is a dark notch, called the Keyhole because of its distinctive shape, silhouetted against the nebula's brightest central portion near η Carinae itself. The whole NGC 3372 nebula lies about 7500 l.y. from us, the same distance as η Carinae. (For a photograph of NGC 3372, Eta Carinae and the Keyhole see page 279.)

NGC 3532, 11h 06m −58°.7, 1350 l.y. away, is an outstanding open cluster, visible to the naked eye as a brighter patch nearly 1° wide among rich Milky Way starfields and glorious in binoculars. It contains 150 or so stars of 7th mag. and fainter,

including several orange giants, arranged in an elliptical shape with a star-free lane across its centre. The mag. 3.9 yellow-white supergiant x Carinae at the cluster's edge is not a member but a background object five times farther off.

IC 2602, 10h 43m −64°.4, is a large and brilliant open cluster containing a few dozen stars, popularly known as the Southern Pleiades, centred about 480 l.y. away. Its brightest members are visible to the naked eye, notably the blue-white star θ Carinae, mag. 2.7. The whole cluster appears twice as wide as the full Moon.

Cassiopeia

In Greek legend, Cassiopeia was the beautiful but boastful Queen of Ethiopia, wife of King Cepheus and mother of Andromeda. In the sky she is depicted sitting in a chair. The constellation is easily identifiable by the distinctive W-shape of its five brightest stars. Cassiopeia lies on the opposite side of the Pole Star from Ursa Major, in a rich part of the Milky Way.

Near the star κ (kappa) Cassiopeiae, at 0h 25.3m, +64° 09′, occurred the brilliant supernova outburst of 1572, which reached mag. −4. It is now known as Tycho's Star because it was observed by the great Danish astronomer Tycho Brahe. The remains of another supernova, which erupted around 1660 but which went unseen at the time, form the strongest radio source in the sky, Cassiopeia A; it lies at 23h 23.4m, +58° 50′, and is some 10,000 l.y. away.

α (alpha) Cassiopeiae, 0h 41m +56°.5, (Shedir, 'the breast'), mag. 2.2, is an orange giant star 229 l.y. away. It has a wide mag. 8.9 companion, which is unrelated.

β (beta) Cas, 0h 09m +59°.1, (Caph), mag. 2.3, is a white star 54 l.y. away.

γ (gamma) Cas, 0h 57m +60°.7, 613 l.y. away, is a remarkable blue-white variable star that rotates so rapidly that it is unstable, throwing off rings of gas from its equatorial region at irregular intervals. The ejections of gas cause it to vary unpredictably between mags. 3.0 and 1.6. Currently it hovers around mag. 2.2.

δ (delta) Cas, 1h 26m +60°.2, (Ruchbah, 'the knee'), mag. 2.7, is a blue-white star 99 l.y. away. It is an eclipsing binary of the Algol type that varies by about 0.1 mag. with the relatively long period of 2 years and 1 month.

ε (epsilon) Cas, 1h 54m +63°.7, mag. 3.3, is a blue-white star 442 l.y. away.

η (eta) Cas, 0h 49m +57°.8, 19 l.y. away, is a beautiful double star with yellow and red components of mags. 3.5 and 7.5, visible in small telescopes. They form a true binary with a period of 480 years.   ▶

Cassiopeia · Cas · Cassiopeiae

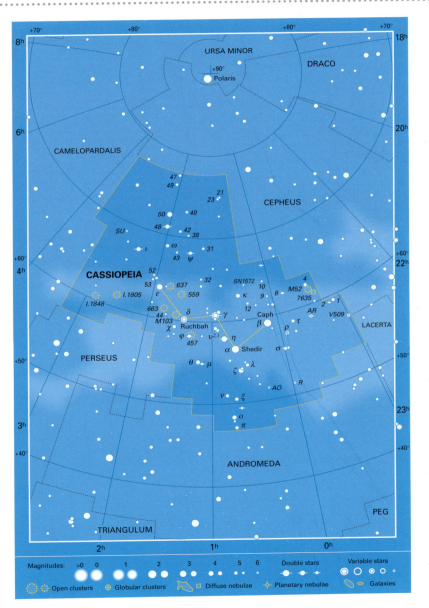

Magnitudes: >0 0   1   2   3   4   5   6   Double stars   Variable stars

Open clusters   Globular clusters   Diffuse nebulae   Planetary nebulae   Galaxies

ι (iota) Cas, 2h 29m +67°.4, 142 l.y. away, is a mag. 4.5 white star with a wide mag. 8.4 companion visible through a 60-mm telescope. With an aperture of 100 mm and high magnification, the brighter star is seen to have a closer mag. 6.9 yellow companion of its own, making this an impressive triple.

ρ (rho) Cas, 23h 54m +57°.5, is a yellow-white supergiant, one of the most luminous stars known, giving out as much light as half a million Suns. It is a semi-regular pulsating variable, ranging between mag. 4.1 and 6.2 every 320 days or so. Its distance is not known accurately, but is probably over 10,000 l.y.

σ (sigma) Cas, 23h 59m +55°.8, 1500 l.y. away, is a close pair of mags. 5.0 and 7.3 appearing green and blue, in striking contrast to the warmer hues of η Cas. An aperture of 75 mm and high power will split the pair.

ψ (psi) Cas, 1h 26m +68°.1, 193 l.y. away, is a mag. 4.7 orange giant with a wide 9th-mag. companion visible in a small telescope. High powers reveal that this companion is itself a close binary.

M52 (NGC 7654), 23h 24m +61°.6, is an open cluster of about 100 stars, 5200 l.y. away, visible as a misty patch in binoculars. It is somewhat kidney-shaped, with an 8th-mag. orange star embedded at one edge, like a poorer version of the Wild Duck Cluster (M11 in Scutum). M52 can be resolved into stars with 75 mm aperture.

M103 (NGC 581), 1h 33m +60°.7, is a small, elongated group of about 25 faint stars, 8200 l.y. away. What appears to be the brightest member, a double of 7th and 10th mags. near the cluster's northern tip, is in fact a foreground object.

NGC 457, 1h 19m +58°.3, is a loose open cluster of about 80 stars, 10,000 l.y. away, seemingly arranged in chains. It has been given various imaginative names inspired by its shape, such as the Dragonfly Cluster, the ET Cluster and the Owl Cluster. The mag. 5.0 white supergiant φ (phi) Cas on its southern outskirts is probably a true member.

NGC 663, 1h 46m +61°.2, is a prominent binocular cluster of about 80 stars appearing half the size of the full Moon, 8200 l.y. away.

Centaurus – The Centaur

A large and rich constellation representing a centaur, the mythical beast that was half man, half horse. Reputedly Centaurus depicts the scholarly centaur Chiron, the tutor of many Greek gods and heroes, who was raised to the sky after being accidentally struck by a poisoned arrow from Hercules.

A line from α (alpha) through β (beta) Centauri points to Crux, the Southern Cross (see the photograph on page 120). Currently α and β Centauri are about 4½° apart, but the rapid proper motion of α Cen is taking it towards β Cen, and about 4000 years from now the two will be little more than ½° (one Moon diameter) apart in our skies, making a stunning naked-eye pairing. Of particular

note in Centaurus is the closest star to the Sun, Proxima Centauri, an 11th-mag. red dwarf which is an outlying companion of α Centauri.

One of the strongest radio sources in the sky, Centaurus A, is associated with the unusual galaxy NGC 5128. Centaurus lies in a prominent part of the Milky Way and contains more naked-eye stars than any other constellation: 281 brighter than magnitude 6.5, according to the Hipparcos catalogue.

α (alpha) Centauri, 14h 40m −60°.8, (Rigil Kentaurus, abbreviated as Rigil Kent, 'foot of the centaur', or Toliman) lies 4.4 l.y. away. To the naked eye it shines at mag. −0.28, the third-

▶

Centaurus · Cen · Centauri

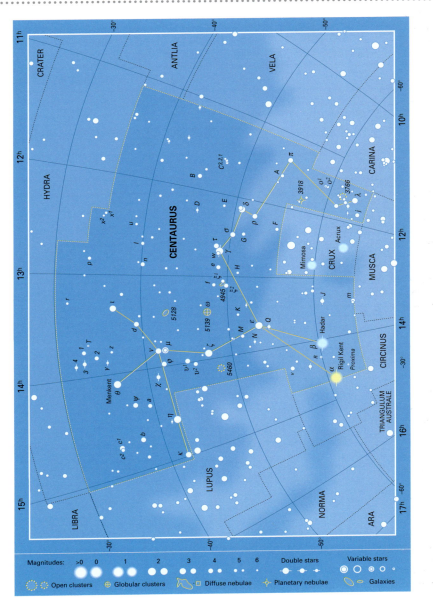

brightest star in the sky. But the smallest of telescopes reveals that it consists of twin yellow stars of mags. −0.01 and 1.35; the brighter of these is very similar to the Sun. They orbit each other every 80 years and are always divisible in amateur telescopes, although at their closest, around the years 2037–38, they will need 75 mm aperture. Also associated with α Centauri is an 11th-mag. red dwarf called Proxima Centauri, lying 2° away and therefore not even in the same telescopic field of view (see the finder chart below.) This star is estimated to take as long as a million years to orbit its two brilliant companions. At present, Proxima Centauri is about 0.2 l.y. closer to us than the two other members of α Centauri. Proxima Centauri is a flare star, suddenly brightening by as much as one magnitude for several minutes at a time.

β (beta) Cen, 14h 04m −60°.4, (Hadar or Agena), mag. 0.6, is a blue giant 525 l.y. away. It is in fact a very close double with a 4th-mag. companion, divisible only in larger apertures.

Finder chart for 11th-mag. Proxima Centauri, showing its proper motion over 200 years. Proxima lies 2° from Alpha Centauri , the bright star at upper left of the diagram. (Wil Tirion)

γ (gamma) Cen, 12h 42m −49°.0, 130 l.y. away, is a close double with blue-white components each of mag. 2.9, orbiting each other every 85 years. Together they shine as a star of mag. 2.2. As seen from Earth they are currently moving together, requiring 220 mm aperture to separate in 2005. At their closest, between 2010 and 2020, amateur telescopes will be unable to split them, but they will become divisible in 220 mm again by 2025, and in 150 mm from 2030.

3 Cen, 13h 52m −33°.0, 298 l.y. away, is a blue-white star of mag. 4.6 with a companion of mag. 6.1, forming a striking pair in small telescopes.

R Cen, 14h 17m −59°.9, is a red giant variable of Mira type, which varies between mags. 5.3 and 11.8 in about 18 months. It lies about 2100 l.y. away.

ω (omega) Cen (NGC 5139), 13h 27m −47°.5, is the largest and brightest globular cluster in the sky – so prominent that it was labelled as a star on early charts. It appears as a hazy star of mag. 3.7 to the naked eye, noticeably elliptical in shape and as large as the full Moon. It is inherently the most luminous of all globulars, with the light output of a million Suns. Small telescopes or even binoculars

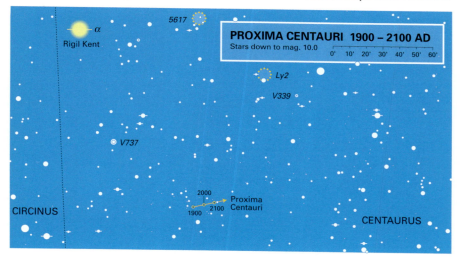

ω (omega) Centauri, the finest of all globular star clusters, appears noticeably elliptical in shape. It has a true diameter of about 150 light years. (NOAO/AURA/NSF)

begin to resolve its outer regions into stars, and it is a showpiece for all apertures. Its brilliance and large apparent size are due in part to its relative closeness, 17,000 l.y., which places it among the nearest globular clusters to us.

NGC 3766, 11h 36m −61°.6, is a naked-eye open cluster of about 100 stars of mag. 7 and fainter, resolvable in binoculars, 6300 l.y. away.

NGC 3918, 11h 50m −57°.2, is an 8th-mag. planetary nebula 2600 l.y. away, discovered in the 19th century by John Herschel and called by him the Blue Planetary. It is similar in appearance to

the planet Uranus, but three times the apparent diameter. Its central star, of 11th mag., should be detectable in modest amateur instruments.

NGC 5128, 13h 25m −43°.0, is a peculiar 7th-mag. galaxy, visually the brightest galaxy outside the Local Group, known to radio astronomers as Centaurus A. In long-exposure photographs such as the one on page 295 it appears as a giant elliptical galaxy with an encircling band of dust. It is thought to result from a merger between an elliptical and a spiral galaxy. Under good skies it is visible in binoculars as a rounded glow, but at least 100 mm aperture is necessary to trace its outline and the dark bisecting lane of dust. NGC 5128 is 12 million l.y. away.

NGC 5460, 14h 08m −48°.3, is a large, 6th-mag. open cluster of about 40 stars visible in binoculars or small telescopes. It lies 2500 l.y. away.

Cepheus

An ancient constellation representing the mythological King Cepheus of Ethiopia, the husband of Cassiopeia and father of Andromeda, who are themselves depicted by nearby constellations. Cepheus is replete with double and variable stars, including the celebrated δ (delta) Cephei, prototype of the Cepheid variables which are used as 'standard candles' for distance-finding in space. This star's fluctuations in light output were discovered in 1784 by the English amateur astronomer John Goodricke.

α (alpha) Cephei, 21h 19m +62°.6, (Alderamin), mag. 2.5, is a white star 49 l.y. away.

β (beta) Cep, 21h 29m +70°.6, (Alfirk, meaning 'flock', i.e. of sheep), 595 l.y. away, is both a double and a variable star. A small telescope shows that this blue giant, of mag. 3.2, has a mag. 7.9 companion. β Cephei is the prototype of a class of pulsating variable stars (also known as β Canis Majoris stars) with periods of a few hours and tiny brightness fluctuations. Over a period of 4.6 hours or so β Cephei varies by 0.1 mag., an amount indistinguishable to the naked eye but detectable by sensitive instruments.

γ (gamma) Cep, 23h 39m +77°.6, (Errai, 'the shepherd'), mag. 3.2, is an orange star 45 l.y. away.

δ (delta) Cep, 22h 29m +58°.4, 980 l.y. away, is a famous pulsating variable star, the prototype of the classic Cepheid variables. This yellow supergiant varies between mags. 3.5 and 4.4 in 5 days 9 hours, changing in size between about 40 and 46 times the Sun's diameter as it does so – see page 287 for a comparison chart. Less well known is

that δ Cephei is also an attractive double star for binoculars or the smallest telescopes, with a wide, bluish mag. 6.3 companion.

μ (mu) Cep, 21h 44m +58°.8, 2800 l.y. away, is a famous red star, called the Garnet Star by William Herschel because of its striking tint, which is notable in binoculars. μ Cephei is a red supergiant, a prominent example of a class of variable stars known as semi-regular variables. It varies between mags. 3.4 and 5.1 with a period of around 2 years.

ξ (xi) Cep, 22h 04m +64°.6, 102 l.y. away, is a double star of mags. 4.4 and 6.5 visible in small telescopes. The components are blue-white and yellow and form a true binary with an estimated orbital period of nearly 4000 years.

o (omicron) Cep, 23h 19m +68°.1, 211 l.y. away, is an orange giant of mag. 4.9 with a close mag. 7.1 companion for telescopes of 60 mm aperture and above. They orbit each other about every 1500 years.

T Cep, 21h 10m +68°.5, 685 l.y. away, is a red giant variable of the Mira type, about 500 times the diameter of the Sun, ranging between mags. 5.2 and 11.3 in around 13 months.

VV Cep, 21h 57m +63°.6, is an enormous red supergiant that varies semi-regularly between mags. 4.8 and 5.4. It is also an eclipsing binary with the unusually long period of 20.3 years, but the light dip during eclipse is too slight to be noticeable to the naked eye. Its estimated distance is more than 2000 l.y. and its diameter is probably over 1000 Suns, one of the largest stars known.

Cepheus · Cep · Cephei

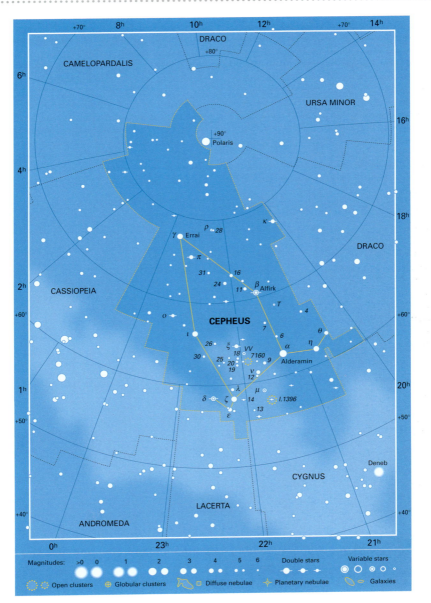

Cetus – The Whale

An ancient constellation depicting the sea monster that was about to devour Andromeda before she was rescued by Perseus. In the sky, Cetus is found basking on the banks of Eridanus, the River. The constellation is large but not prominent; nevertheless it contains several stars of particular interest, notably o (omicron) Ceti and τ (tau) Ceti.

One faint but famous star is UV Ceti, position 1h 38.8m, −17° 57′, which consists of a pair of 13th-mag. red dwarfs 8.7 l.y. away. One of these is the prototype of a class of erratic variables known as flare stars; these are red dwarfs that undergo sudden increases in light output lasting only a few minutes. The outbursts of the flare star component of UV Ceti can take it from its normal level of 13th mag. to as bright as 7th mag. ▶

Finder chart for the variable star Mira, also known as o (omicron) Ceti. The numbers against the surrounding stars are their magnitudes with the decimal points omitted, to prevent confusion with faint stars. These stars can be used to estimate the magnitude of Mira. (Wil Tirion)

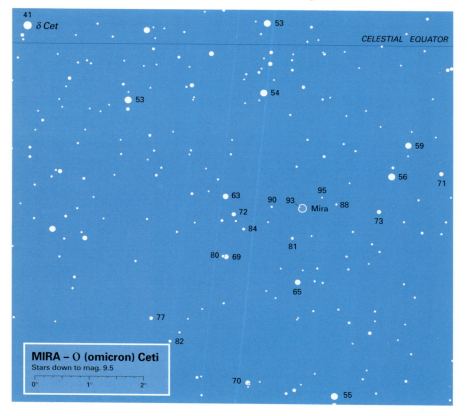

Cetus · Cet · Ceti

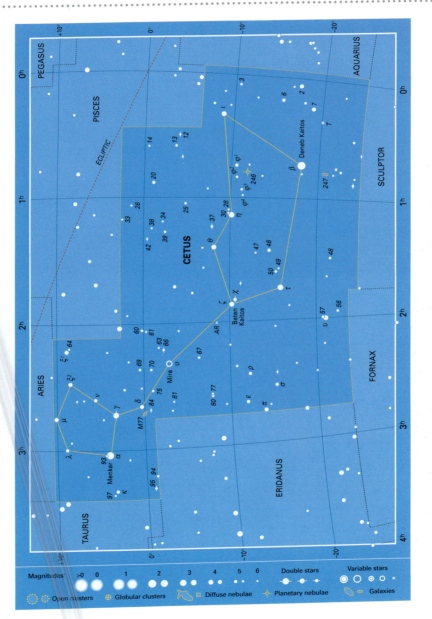

α (alpha) Ceti, 3h 02m +4°.1, (Menkar, 'nose'), mag. 2.5, is a red giant star 220 l.y. away. Binoculars show a wide mag. 5.6 blue-white apparent companion, 93 Ceti, which is actually unrelated to it, lying twice as far away.

β (beta) Cet, 0h 44m −18°.0, (Deneb Kaitos, 'tail of the whale', or Diphda), mag. 2.0, the brightest star of the constellation, is an orange giant 96 l.y. away.

γ (gamma) Cet, 2h 43m +3°.2, 82 l.y. away, is a close double star needing telescopes of at least 60 mm aperture and high power to split. The stars are of mags. 3.5 and 6.6, the colours yellow and bluish.

o (omicron) Cet, 2h 19m −3°.0, (Mira, 'the amazing one'), 420 l.y. away, is the prototype of a famous class of red giant long-period variable stars. Mira itself varies between about 3rd and 9th mags. (although it can become as bright as 2nd mag.) in an average of 332 days, changing in diameter from about 400 to 500 times the size of the Sun as it does so. Mira's light variations were first noted in 1596 by the Dutch astronomer David Fabricius, making it the first variable star (other than novae) to be discovered. The finder chart on page 116 shows various comparison stars down to mag 9.5 from which Mira's brightness can be estimated.

τ (tau) Cet, 1h 44m −15°.9, mag. 3.5, a yellow main-sequence star, is one of the nearest stars to us, lying 11.9 l.y. away. Its main claim to fame is that, of all the nearby single stars, it is the one most like the Sun, although we do not yet know whether it also has planets.

M77 (NGC 1068), 2h 43m −0°.0, is a small, softly glowing 9th-mag. face-on spiral galaxy with a 10th-mag. starlike nucleus. Apertures of 100 mm show the brighter patches in the spiral arms. M77 is the brightest example of a Seyfert galaxy, a close relative of the quasars, and it is a radio source. It lies roughly 50 million l.y. away. (See photograph on page 294.)

Chamaeleon – The Chameleon

A faint and unremarkable constellation between Carina and the south celestial pole, representing the colour-changing lizard. It was one of the constellations representing exotic animals introduced by the Dutch navigators Pieter Dirkszoon Keyser and Frederick de Houtman at the end of the 16th century.

α (alpha) Chamaeleontis, 8h 19m −76°.9, mag. 4.1, is a white star 63 l.y. away.

β (beta) Cha, 12h 18m −79°.3, mag. 4.2, is a blue-white star 271 l.y. away.

γ (gamma) Cha, 10h 35m −78°.6, mag. 4.1, is a red giant 413 l.y. away.

δ¹ δ² (delta¹ delta²) Cha, 10h 45m −80°.5, consists of a wide pair of unrelated stars, both clearly seen in binoculars: δ¹ Cha, mag. 5.5, is an orange giant 354 l.y. away and δ² Cha, mag. 4.4, is a blue star 364 l.y. away.

NGC 3195, 10h 09m −80°.9, is a faint planetary nebula of similar apparent size to the planet Jupiter, needing at least 100 mm aperture to be seen well.

Chamaeleon · Cha · Chamaeleontis

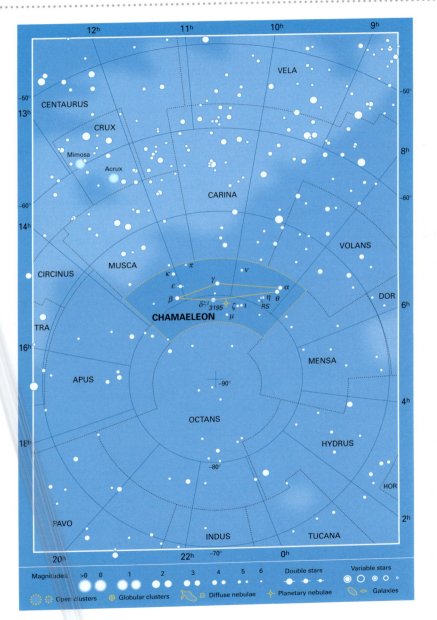

Magnitudes: >0 0 1 2 3 4 5 6   Double stars   Variable stars

Open clusters   Globular clusters   Diffuse nebulae   Planetary nebulae   Galaxies

Circinus – The Compasses

Another of the small and obscure southern constellations introduced in 1756 by the French astronomer Nicolas Louis de Lacaille. It represents a pair of dividing compasses as used by draughtsmen and surveyors, and is appropriately placed in the sky next to Norma, the Set Square. It is overshadowed by the brilliance of neighbouring Centaurus.

α (alpha) Circini, 14h 43m −65°.0, 53 l.y. away, is a white main-sequence star of mag. 3.2 with a companion of mag. 8.5 easily visible in small telescopes.

γ (gamma) Cir, 15h 23m −59°.3, 500 l.y. away, consists of a very close pair of blue and yellow stars of mags. 5.1 and 5.5, requiring an aperture of at least 150 mm and high magnification to see separately. Their orbital period is calculated to be 270 years.

Circinus is most easily found by reference to the prominent stars Alpha and Beta Centauri (seen left of centre in the photograph below), which point towards the familiar figure of Crux, the Southern Cross, at upper right. Alpha Circini is the star below and to the right of Alpha Centauri. Long-exposure photographs such as this one emphasize the darkness of the Coalsack Nebula in Crux against the star background of the Milky Way. (M. Bessell, R. Sutherland and M. Buxton, RSAA – Australian National University)

Circinus · Cir · Circini

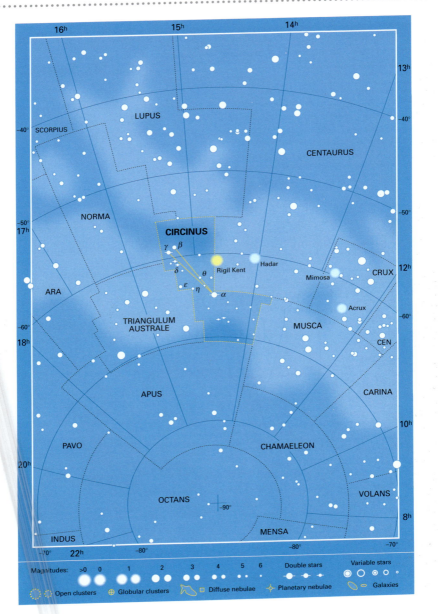

Magnitudes: >0   0   1   2   3   4   5   6   Double stars   Variable stars

Open clusters   Globular clusters   Diffuse nebulae   Planetary nebulae   Galaxies

Columba – The Dove

A constellation representing the dove sent out from Noah's Ark to find dry land after the Biblical Flood. The Dutchman Petrus Plancius formed it in 1592 from some stars adjacent to Canis Major that had not previously been part of any constellation. Columba is placed next to Puppis, the stern of the ship Argo, so it might alternatively be imagined as the dove that the Argonauts sent ahead to help them pass safely between the Clashing Rocks (the Symplegades) at the mouth of the Black Sea. Columba contains little of interest for amateur telescopes.

α (alpha) Columbae, 5h 40m −34°.1, (Phact, 'ring dove'), mag. 2.7, is a blue-white star 268 l.y. away.

β (beta) Col, 5h 51m −35°.8, (Wazn), mag. 3.1, is an orange giant 86 l.y. away.

NGC 1851, 5h 14m −40°.1, is a 7th-mag. globular cluster, visible in small telescopes but requiring moderate apertures to resolve its brightest stars. It lies 35,000 l.y. away.

Vanished constellations

Antinous, Felis, Globus Aerostaticus, Harpa Georgii, Machina Electrica, Officina Typographica, Quadrans Muralis, Robur Carolinum, Taurus Poniatovii, Telescopium Herschelii and Turdus Solitarius – these are all constellations which once graced the sky but which you will not find on any chart today. Where did they go?

During the golden age of celestial mapping, in the 17th and 18th and centuries, various astronomers tried to leave their mark on the sky by adding new constellations to those of the ancient Greeks. Constellations depicted on an atlas by one astronomer could be completely ignored by everyone else.

Some constellations were blatant attempts to flatter their monarchs or wealthy patrons. A 17th-century German astronomer, Julius Schiller, produced an atlas in which all the constellations were based on characters from the Bible – for example, the familiar constellations of the zodiac were changed to represent the 12 apostles. Such attempts to insert politics or religion into the skies did not succeed.

Over 100 different constellations were included in the immense *Uranographia* star atlas published by the German astronomer Johann Elert Bode in 1801, but during the following century common usage gave rise to the selection of 88 constellations that were officially adopted by the International Astronomical Union in 1922. Unlike the map of the Earth, which is continually affected by political changes, the map of the sky is now fixed.

Noctua, the night owl, perches on the tail of Hydra the water snake, on a colourful set of 19th-century constellation cards called Urania's Mirror, but has now flown from modern star charts. (Ian Ridpath)

Columba · Col · Columbae

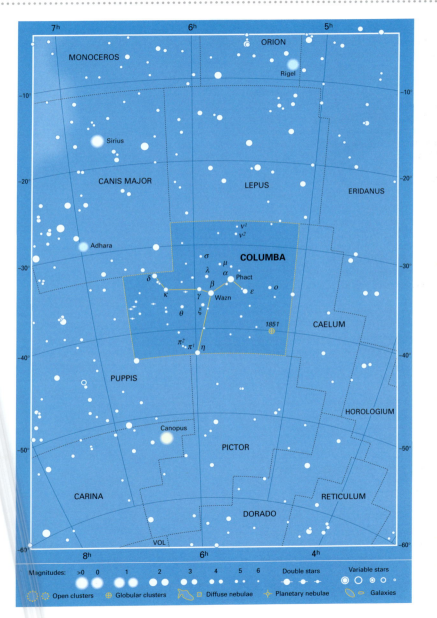

Magnitudes: >0 0 1 2 3 4 5 6   Double stars   Variable stars

Open clusters   Globular clusters   Diffuse nebulae   Planetary nebulae   Galaxies

Coma Berenices – Berenice's Hair

This faint constellation represents the flowing locks of Queen Berenice of Egypt, who cut off her hair in gratitude to the gods for the safe return of her husband Ptolemy III Euergetes from battle. Although the legend dates from Greek times, this group of stars was regarded as part of Leo until 1551 when the Dutch cartographer Gerardus Mercator made them into a separate constellation. The main part of the queen's severed tresses is represented by the extensive Coma Star Cluster (Melotte 111). Coma Berenices also contains another type of cluster – a cluster of galaxies. The Coma Cluster of galaxies lies about 280 million l.y. away, so its members are too faint for all but the largest amateur telescopes. But the constellation also contains some brighter galaxies, members of the nearer Virgo Cluster, the brightest of which are visible in amateur telescopes. The north pole of our Galaxy lies in Coma Berenices.

α (alpha) Comae Berenices, 13h 10m +17°.5, (Diadem), mag. 4.3, is a tight binary 47 l.y. away, consisting of twin yellow-white stars of mag. 5.1 that orbit each other every 26 years. Even at their widest, around the year 2010, they are at the limit of resolution of a 220-mm telescope.

β (beta) Com, 13h 12m +27°.9, mag. 4.2, the brightest star in the constellation, is a yellow main-sequence star 30 l.y. away.

γ (gamma) Com, 12h 27m +28°.3, mag. 4.4, is an orange giant 170 l.y. away, which appears to be a member of the Coma Star Cluster but is actually a foreground star.

24 Com, 12h 35m +18°.4, is a beautiful coloured double star for small telescopes, consisting of an orange giant of mag. 5.0, 610 l.y. away, and an unrelated blue-white companion of mag 6.6.

35 Com, 12h 53m +21°.2, 324 l.y. away, is a tight binary star with yellow and white components of

mags. 5.1 and 7.2 orbiting every 360 years and divisible in 150-mm apertures. Small telescopes show a wider 9th-mag. companion.

FS Com, 13h 06m +22°.6, 572 l.y. away, is a red giant that varies semi-regularly between mags. 5.3 and 6.1 every two months or so.

Coma Star Cluster (Melotte 111), 12h 25m +26°, is a scattered group of about 50 stars best seen in binoculars. The cluster's brightest members, of 5th mag., form a noticeable V-shape extending for several degrees south of γ (gamma) Com, which is not actually a member but a foreground star. The brightest true member seems to be 12 Com, mag. 4.8. The distance to the cluster's centre is 288 l.y.

M53 (NGC 5024), 13h 13m +18°.2, is an 8th-mag. globular cluster 56,000 l.y. away, visible in small telescopes as a rounded, hazy patch.

M64 (NGC 4826), 12h 57m +21°.7, is a famous spiral galaxy, called the Black Eye Galaxy because of a dark cloud of dust silhouetted against its nucleus. This dark dust lane shows up well in apertures above 150 mm; observers with smaller instruments must content themselves simply with locating this 9th-mag. galaxy some 20 million l.y. away, closer than the Virgo Cluster and not a member of it.

M85 (NGC 4382), 12h 25m +18°.2, is a 9th-mag. elliptical galaxy in the Virgo Cluster, 55 million l.y. away. Small telescopes show a brighter, starlike centre.

M88 (NGC 4501), 12h 32m +14°.4, is a 10th-mag. spiral galaxy in the Virgo Cluster, 55 million l.y. away. It is presented at an angle to us, so that it appears elliptical.

M99 (NGC 4254), 12h 19m +14°.6, is a 10th-mag. spiral galaxy 55 million l.y. away in the Virgo Cluster, presented face-on so that it appears almost circular.

▶

Coma Berenices · Com · Comae Berenices

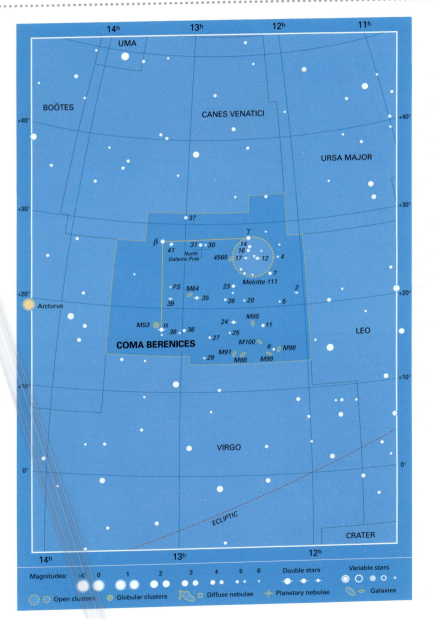

NGC 4565, a classically elegant spiral galaxy in Coma Berenices seen almost exactly edge-on. A dark lane of dust crosses its centre. NGC 4565 is estimated to be over 100,000 light-years in diameter, similar to our own Milky Way. (Bruce Hugo and Leslie Gaul/Adam Block/NOAO/AURA/NSF)

M100 (NGC 4321), 12h 23m +15°.8, is a 9th-mag. Virgo Cluster spiral seen face-on, similar to M99 but larger. The Hubble Space Telescope has measured its distance accurately at 52.5 million l.y.

NGC 4565, 12h 36m +26°.0, is a 10th-mag. spiral galaxy seen edge-on. It is the most famous of the edge-on spirals, and is pictured above. Apertures of 100 mm show its cigar-shaped body with a central bulge and starlike core, but larger instruments are needed to trace the dark band (actually a dust lane) that splits it lengthwise. NGC 4565 is not a member of the Virgo Cluster but only about half as far, around 30 million l.y. away.

Corona Australis – The Southern Crown

The southern counterpart of the Northern Crown (Corona Borealis). Corona Australis has been known since the time of the Greek astronomer Ptolemy in the 2nd century AD who visualized it not as a crown but as a wreath. In one legend it represents the crown placed in the sky by Bacchus when he rescued his dead mother from the Underworld; alternatively, it could simply have slipped from the head of the centaur Sagittarius, at whose feet it lies. Although faint, it is a distinctive figure, and is situated on the edge of the Milky Way.

α (alpha) Coronae Australis, 19h 09m −37°.9, mag. 4.1, is a blue-white main-sequence star 130 l.y. away.

β (beta) CrA, 19h 10m −39°.3, mag. 4.1, is an orange giant 510 l.y. away.

γ (gamma) CrA, 19h 06m −37°.1, 58 l.y. away, consists of a pair of near-identical yellow-white stars, mags. 4.9 and 5.0, orbiting every 122 years, forming a tight double for small telescopes. The stars were closest together during the 1990s, but since 2000 have become progressively easier to split with 100 mm aperture.

κ (kappa) CrA, 18h 33m −38°.6, is a pair of unrelated blue-white stars of mags. 5.7 and 6.3, distances about 1700 and 490 l.y., easily divisible in small telescopes.

λ (lambda) CrA, 18h 44m −38°.3, 202 l.y. away, is a mag. 5.1 blue-white star with a wide mag. 9.7 companion, visible in small telescopes.

NGC 6541, 18h 08m −43°.7, is a 7th-mag. globular cluster 22,000 l.y. away, visible in binoculars or small telescopes.

Corona Australis · CrA · Coronae Australis

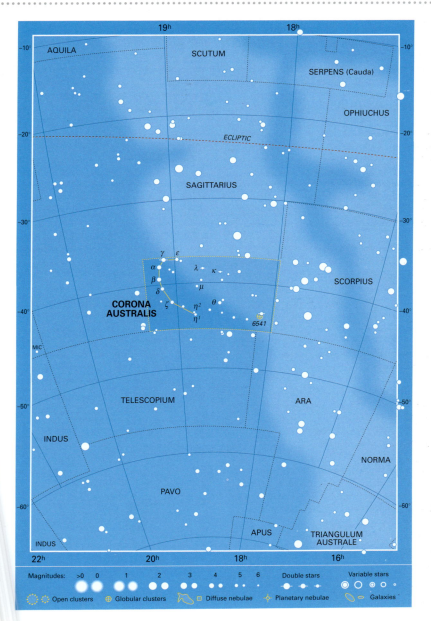

Corona Borealis – The Northern Crown

An ancient constellation, representing the jewelled crown worn by Ariadne when she married Bacchus and cast by him into the sky to mark the happy event. It consists of an arc of seven stars, all but one of 4th magnitude, the exception being Alphekka (a word derived from the Arabic name for the constellation) which is of 2nd magnitude. Alphekka is set in the crown like a central gemstone, as its alternative name Gemma implies. Corona Borealis contains a famous cluster of about 400 galaxies more than 1000 million light years away. Being so very distant, the galaxies are no brighter than 16th magnitude and are thus far beyond the reach of amateur telescopes.

α (alpha) Coronae Borealis, 15h 35m +26°.7, (Alphekka or Gemma), mag. 2.2, is a blue-white main-sequence star 75 l.y. distant. It is an eclipsing binary of the Algol type, but its variation every 17.4 days is only 0.1 mag., too slight to be noticeable to the naked eye.

ζ (zeta) CrB, 15h 39m +36°.6, 470 l.y. away, is a pair of blue-white stars, mags. 5.0 and 6.0, visible in small telescopes.

ν¹ ν² (nu¹ nu²) CrB, 16h 22m +33°.8, is a wide binocular pair of red and orange giants of mags. 5.2 and 5.4, both about 550 l.y. from us but moving in different directions, so they probably do not constitute a true binary.

σ (sigma) CrB, 16h 15m +33°.9, 71 l.y. away, is a pair of yellow stars for small telescopes, of mags. 5.6 and 6.6. They form a genuine binary with an estimated orbital period of about 900 years.

R CrB, 15h 49m +28°.2, is a remarkable yellow supergiant star lying within the arc of the Crown, halfway between the stars α (alpha) and ι (iota). It usually appears about 6th mag., but occasionally and unpredictably drops in a matter of weeks to as faint as mag. 15, from where it may take many months to regain its former brightness. Recent catastrophic declines in the star's brilliance were seen in 1983, 1995 and 1999, although less extreme fades are more frequent and can occur at any time. These sudden dips in the light of R Coronae Borealis are believed to be due to the accumulation of carbon particles (i.e. soot) in its atmosphere. R Coronae Borealis is estimated to lie over 7000 l.y. away.

S CrB, 15h 21m +31°.4, is a variable of Mira type, ranging from 6th to 14th mag. in just under a year.

T CrB, 16h 00m +25°.9, is another spectacular variable star, known as the Blaze Star, which performs in almost the opposite way to R Coronae Borealis. It is a recurrent nova, usually slumbering at around mag. 11 but which can suddenly and unpredictably brighten to mag. 2. Its last recorded outburst was in 1946, and the previous one was 80 years before that. It is not known when it may erupt again.

Corona Borealis · CrB · Coronae Borealis

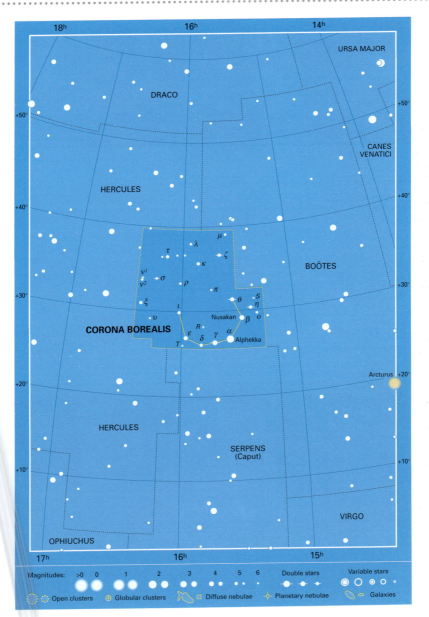

Corvus – The Crow

In Greek legend, Corvus is associated with the neighbouring constellations Crater, the Cup, and Hydra, the Water Snake. The crow is said to have been sent by Apollo to fetch water in a cup, but along the way it dallied to eat figs. When the crow returned to Apollo it carried the water snake in its claws, claiming that this creature had been blocking the spring and was the cause of its delay. Apollo, seeing through the lie, banished the the trio to the sky, where the Crow and the Cup lie on the back of Hydra. For its misdeed the crow was condemned to suffer from eternal thirst, which is why crows croak so harshly; in the sky, the cup is just out of the thirsty crow's reach. In another legend, a snow-white crow brought Apollo the bad news that his lover Coronis had been unfaithful to him. In his anger, Apollo turned the crow black. Apollo and crows are closely linked in legend, for during the war waged by the giants on the gods, Apollo

turned himself into a crow. The four brightest stars in Corvus, γ (gamma), β (beta), δ (delta) and ε (epsilon), form a quadrilateral shape somewhat reminiscent of the Keystone of Hercules.

α (alpha) Corvi, 12h 08m −24°.7, (Alchiba), mag. 4.0, is a white star 48 l.y. away.

β (beta) Crv, 12h 34m −23°.4, mag. 2.7, is a yellow giant star 140 l.y. away.

γ (gamma) Crv, 12h 16m −17°.5, (Gienah, 'wing'), mag. 2.6, the brightest star in the constellation, is a blue-white giant 165 l.y. away.

δ (delta) Crv, 12h 30m −16°.5, (Algorab, 'the raven'), is a wide double star for small telescopes. The brighter component, visible to the naked eye, is a mag. 2.9 blue-white star 88 l.y. away, which is accompanied by a 9th-mag. star often described as purplish in colour. ▶

Just over the northern border of Corvus into Virgo lies the Sombrero Galaxy, M104, a spiral galaxy with a bulging core and a dark central lane of dust. See page 260. (ESO)

Corvus · Crv · Corvi

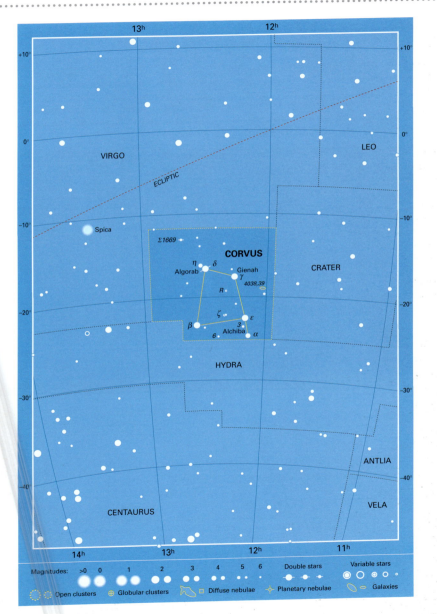

Magnitudes: >0 0 1 2 3 4 5 6   Double stars   Variable stars

Open clusters   ⊕ Globular clusters   □ Diffuse nebulae   ✧ Planetary nebulae   Galaxies

ε (epsilon) Crv, 12h 10m −22°.6, mag. 3.0, is an orange giant star 303 l.y. away.

Σ 1669 (Struve 1669), 12h 41m −13°.0, is a neat pair of white stars 280 l.y. away, appearing to the naked eye as a single star of mag. 5.2 but divisible by small telescopes into near-identical components of mags. 5.9 and 6.0.

NGC 4038–9, 12h 02m −18°.9, the Antennae, are a pair of spiral galaxies of 10th mag. that collided a few hundred million years ago. Streams of gas and stars thrown off in the collision, visible on photographs such as the one below, stretch for 250,000 l.y. or more and form the antennae that give the galaxies their popular name. The galaxies lie 63 million l.y. away.

NGC 4038–9, the peculiar pair of interacting galaxies known as the Antennae, lie in Corvus near the border with Crater. (M. Bessell, R. Sutherland and M. Buxton, RSAA – Australian National University)

Crater – The Cup

An ancient constellation representing the chalice of Apollo, associated in Greek legend with neighbouring Corvus and Hydra (see page 130). The stars of Crater are faint and the constellation contains no objects of particular interest.

α (alpha) Crateris, 11h 00m −18°.3, (Alkes, 'the cup'), mag. 4.1, is an orange giant star 174 l.y. away.

β (beta) Crt, 11h 12m −22°.8, mag. 4.5, is a blue-white star 266 l.y. away.

γ (gamma) Crt, 11h 25m −17°.7, mag. 4.1, is a white star 84 l.y. away. It has a mag. 9.6 companion visible in small telescopes.

δ (delta) Crt, 11h 19m −14°.8, mag. 3.6, the constellation's brightest star, is an orange giant lying 195 l.y. away.

Crater · Crt · Crateris

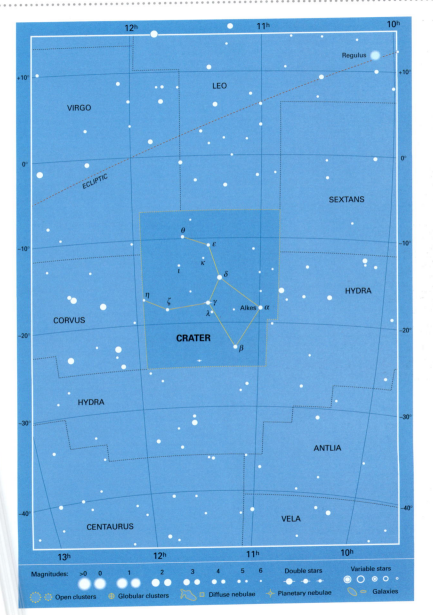

Crux – The Southern Cross

The smallest constellation in the sky, but one of the most celebrated and distinctive. Crux was visible from the Mediterranean area in ancient times, so its stars were known to Greek astronomers; the effects of precession have since carried it below the horizon from such northerly latitudes. The Greeks regarded it as part of Centaurus, but it was made a separate constellation by various seamen and astronomers in the 16th century. It can be useful for direction-finding at night, since its long axis, from γ (gamma) via α (alpha) Crucis, points towards the south celestial pole.

Crux lies in a dense and brilliant part of the Milky Way, and the famous dark nebula known as the Coalsack is particularly striking in silhouette against the starry background. α (alpha) Crucis is the most southerly first-magnitude star. α (alpha) and β (beta) Crucis are, by a small margin, the bluest of all first-magnitude stars.

α (alpha) Crucis, 12h 27m −63°.1, (Acrux), 321 l.y. away, appears to the naked eye as a bluish star of mag. 0.8, but a small telescope divides it into a sparkling double with components of mags. 1.3 and 1.8. There is also a wider 5th-mag. companion that can be seen with binoculars.

β (beta) Cru, 12h 48m −59°.7, (Mimosa), mag. 1.3, is a blue giant 353 l.y. away. It is a variable star of the β Cephei type, fluctuating by less than 0.1 mag. every 5 hours, too small to be noticeable to the eye.

γ (gamma) Cru, 12h 31m −57°.1, (Gacrux), mag. 1.6, is a red giant star 88 l.y. away. There is a very wide mag. 6.5 unrelated companion, three times as distant, visible in binoculars.

δ (delta) Cru, 12h 15m −58°.7, mag. 2.8, the faintest of the four main stars in the Cross, is a blue-white star 364 l.y. away.

ε (epsilon) Cru, 12h 21m −60°.4, mag. 3.6, is an orange giant 228 l.y. away.

ι (iota) Cru, 12h 46m −61°.0, 125 l.y. away, is an orange giant of mag. 4.7 with a mag. 9.5 companion visible in small telescopes.

μ (mu) Cru, 12h 55m −57°.2, is a wide pair of blue-white stars of mags. 4.0 and 5.1, divisible by the smallest telescopes or even good binoculars. They both lie about 370 l.y. away.

NGC 4755, 12h 54m −60°.3, the Jewel Box or κ (kappa) Crucis Cluster, is one of the finest open clusters in the sky, visible to the naked eye as a hazy 4th-mag. star. Binoculars resolve the brightest individual members, which are blue supergiants of 6th and 7th mag.; three of these form a chain across the cluster like a mini Orion's belt, with an 8th-mag. red supergiant next to the middle one. The star κ Crucis itself, of mag. 5.9, is the most southerly member of this chain. A small telescope brings at least 50 stars into view. John Herschel gave this cluster its popular name when he likened it to a piece of multicoloured jewellery. The distance of the Jewel Box is just under 5000 l.y.

The Coalsack Nebula is a dark, pear-shaped dust cloud silhouetted against the Milky Way, covering nearly 7° by 5° of sky and spilling over into neighbouring Centaurus and Musca. It lies an estimated 600 l.y. away. The Coalsack has no NGC or other identification number. For a photograph of the Coalsack, see page 120.

Crux · Cru · Crucis

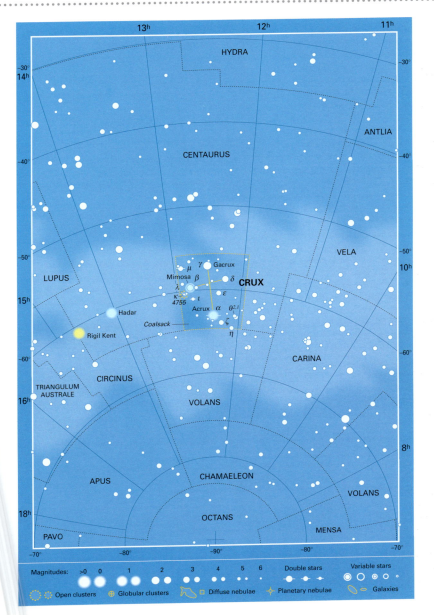

| 13ʰ | 12ʰ | 11ʰ |

HYDRA

-30°
14ʰ

ANTLIA

CENTAURUS

-40°

VELA

-50°
10ʰ

LUPUS

μ γ Gacrux
Mimosa β   δ   **CRUX**
λ
κ   ε
4755   ι
Acrux α θ^{2,1}
ζ
Hadar   η

Rigil Kent   Coalsack

15ʰ

CARINA

-60°

CIRCINUS

TRIANGULUM
AUSTRALE

VOLANS

16ʰ

8ʰ

CHAMAELEON

APUS

VOLANS

OCTANS   MENSA

18ʰ
PAVO

-70°   -80°   -90°   -80°   -70°

Magnitudes: >0   0   1   2   3   4   5   6   Double stars   Variable stars

○ ○ Open clusters   ⊕ Globular clusters   Diffuse nebulae   Planetary nebulae   Galaxies

Cygnus – The Swan

Cygnus represents a swan flying down the Milky Way. In Greek mythology, the swan was the guise in which the god Zeus visited Leda, wife of King Tyndareus of Sparta; the result of their union was Pollux, one of the heavenly twins. The flying swan's tail is marked by the star Deneb (α Cygni), its beak by Albireo (β Cygni), and its wings by δ (delta) and ε (epsilon) Cygni. These stars form a distinctive cross-shape, so the constellation is also referred to as the Northern Cross; it happens to be far larger than the more famous Southern Cross. Cygnus lies in a rich part of the Milky Way, which is split here by a dark lane of dust known as the Cygnus Rift or the Northern Coalsack. Deneb, the constellation's brightest star, forms one corner of the so-called Summer Triangle, completed by Altair and Vega.

Among the fascinating objects in Cygnus is an X-ray source called Cygnus X-1, thought to be a black hole orbiting a 9th-mag. blue supergiant star; it lies at 19h 58.4m, +35° 12′, near η (eta) Cygni. Near γ (gamma) Cygni, at 19h 59.5m, +40° 44′, is Cygnus A, a powerful radio source caused by two distant galaxies in collision. Long-exposure photographs of the region between ε (epsilon) Cygni and the border with Vulpecula reveal beautiful swirls of gas known as the Veil Nebula, the brightest part of which, NGC 6992, is detectable in amateur instruments (see page 138).

α (alpha) Cygni, 20h 41m +45°.3, (Deneb, 'tail'), mag. 1.2, is a blue-white supergiant star about 3200 l.y. away.

β (beta) Cyg, 19h 31m +28°.0, (Albireo), 386 l.y. away, is one of the sky's showpiece doubles. It consists of gloriously contrasting amber and blue-green stars, like a celestial traffic light. The brighter star, of mag. 3.1, is an orange giant, and its blue-green companion is mag. 5.1. They can be separated through good binoculars and are a beautiful sight in any amateur telescope.

γ (gamma) Cyg, 20h 22m +40°.3, (Sadr, 'breast'), mag. 2.2, is a yellow-white supergiant about 1500 l.y. away.

δ (delta) Cyg, 19h 45m +45°.1, 171 l.y. away, is a blue-white giant of mag. 2.9 with a close mag. 6.6 companion, visible in a telescope of 100 mm aperture or above at high magnification. The stars have an orbital period of nearly 800 years.

ε (epsilon) Cyg, 20h 46m +34°.0, (Gienah, 'wing'), mag. 2.5, is an orange giant 72 l.y. away.

μ (mu) Cyg, 21h 44m +28°.7, 73 l.y. away, is a pair of white stars of mags. 4.8 and 6.2 orbiting each other about every 790 years. They are currently closing slowly and should remain divisible in 100 mm apertures until about 2020, although 150 mm will probably be necessary when they are closest, between 2043 and 2050. A wide mag. 6.9 binocular companion is an unrelated background star.

o¹ (omicron¹) Cyg, 20h 14m +46°.7, also known as 31 Cygni, forms perhaps the most beautiful binocular double in the heavens with 30 Cygni. The stars are orange and turquoise, mags. 3.8 and 4.8, 1400 l.y. and 720 l.y. away, like a wider version of Albireo. A small telescope, or binoculars held steadily, shows a closer blue companion of mag. 7.0 to the brighter (orange giant) star.

χ (chi) Cyg, 19h 51m +32°.9, 350 l.y. away, is a red giant long-period variable of Mira type that varies every 400 days or so. At best it reaches mag. 3.3, brighter than any other star of its type except Mira itself, although R Hydrae can rival it. At its faintest χ Cyg drops to 14th mag. Its diameter is about 300 Suns. ▶

Cygnus · Cyg · Cygni

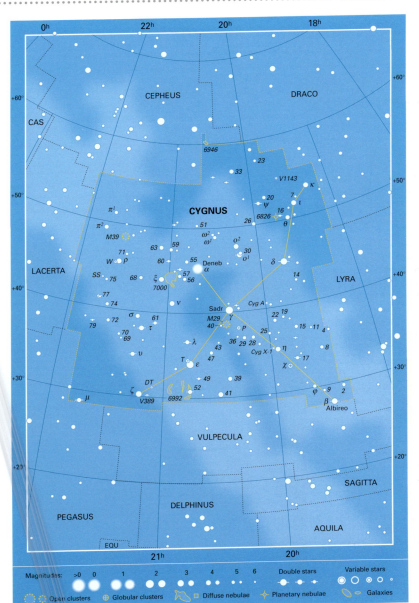

CYGNUS

CEPHEUS

DRACO

CAS

LACERTA

LYRA

SAGITTA

VULPECULA

PEGASUS

DELPHINUS

AQUILA

EQU

Magnitudes: >0 0 1 2 3 4 5 6   Double stars   Variable stars

○ Open clusters   ⊕ Globular clusters   Diffuse nebulae   ✦ Planetary nebulae   Galaxies

ψ (psi) Cyg, 19h 56m +52°.4, 289 l.y. away, is a pair of white stars of mags. 5.0 and 7.5 divisible in small to moderate apertures.

61 Cyg, 21h 07m +38°.7, 11.4 l.y. away, is a showpiece pair of orange dwarf stars of mags. 5.2 and 6.1, orbiting each other in about 680 years, divisible in a small telescope or even binoculars. In addition to being among the closest stars to Earth, 61 Cygni was the first star to have its parallax measured, by the German astronomer Friedrich Wilhelm Bessel in 1838.

P Cyg, 20h 18m +38°.0, is an erratically variable blue supergiant that normally resides around 5th mag., although in the year 1600 it reached a peak brightness of 3rd mag. Evidently the star is so large and luminous that it is close to instability. Its average brightness has increased gradually since the

18th century as it evolves into a red supergiant. Its distance is uncertain, but is probably several thousand light years.

W Cyg, 21h 36m +45°.4, 618 l.y. away, is a red giant that varies semi-regularly between 5th and 8th mags. with a rough period of 130 days.

M39 (NGC 7092), 21h 32m +48°.4, is a large, loose cluster of about 30 stars of 7th mag. and fainter, arranged in a triangle. It is visible in binoculars, and is even detectable with the naked eye under ideal conditions. It lies 950 l.y. away.

NGC 6826, 19h 45m +50°.5, is an 8th-mag. planetary nebula about 3200 l.y. away, known as the Blinking Planetary because it appears to blink on and off. It is visible as a pale blue disk in 75-mm telescopes, but 150 mm is needed to show it

The Veil Nebula: Drifting apart over thousands of years, the delicate traceries of the Veil Nebula are the tenuous remains of a star that shattered itself in a supernova explosion some 5000 years ago. Its brightest part, shown here, is NGC 6992, which can be glimpsed in binoculars under clear skies.
The arc of NGC 6992 extends across more than two Moon diameters of sky, equivalent to a true length of about 25 light years.
(Nigel Sharp, REU program/ AURA/NOAO/NSF)

The North America Nebula, NGC 7000, is a glowing cloud of gas shaped like the continent of North America, with a particularly distinctive Gulf of Mexico formed by an obscuring cloud of dark dust. It lies near the star ξ (xi) Cygni, an orange supergiant of mag. 3.7 seen at left. To the right is a smaller and fainter patch of nebulosity, IC 5070, known as the Pelican from its supposed resemblance to that bird. (Philip Perkins)

to advantage. At its centre is a 10th-mag. star. Looking alternately at this star and away again produces the 'blinking' effect. NGC 6826 lies less than 1° from the wide double star 16 Cygni, which consists of two 6th-mag. creamy-white stars 70 l.y. away.

NGC 6992, 20h 56m +31°.7, is the brightest part of the Veil Nebula, the remnant of a supernova explosion about 5000 years ago. Under ideal conditions NGC 6992 can be seen in binoculars as a faint arc. Another part of the nebula, NGC 6960, can be located in wide-angle telescopes with low power near the 4th-mag. star 52 Cyg, but the complete Veil Nebula, also known as the Cygnus Loop, is apparent only on long-exposure photographs, spanning nearly 3° of sky. Its distance is 1400 l.y.

NGC 7000, 20h 59m +44°.3, the North America Nebula, can be seen as a hook-shaped brightening in the Milky Way with the naked eye or binoculars in good skies. Despite its large size, 2° at its widest, the nebula can be difficult to detect because of its low surface brightness. Long-exposure photographs such as the one above clearly show its shape, like the continent of North America. The nebula is about 1500 l.y. away, half the distance to the star Deneb. The nebula is believed to be lit up by an extremely hot 6th-mag. star that lies within it.

Delphinus – The Dolphin

A constellation which originated in Greek times, celebrating the long-standing relationship between humans and these intelligent aquatic mammals. In legend, dolphins were the messengers of the sea-god Poseidon, who sent a dolphin to bring the sea nymph Amphitrite to his underwater palace where he made her his wife. In another story, dolphins were credited with saving the life of Arion, a musician and poet, who was attacked on a ship. According to this tale, Arion jumped overboard to escape his attackers and was carried on the back of a dolphin to Greece, where he later identified the robbers who were sentenced to death. In this legend, the nearby constellation Lyra represents Arion's lyre.

Delphinus has a distinctive shape, its four main stars forming a diamond known as Job's Coffin. Its two brightest stars are called Sualocin and Rotanev, which backwards read Nicolaus Venator, the Latinized form of the name Niccolò Cacciatore (1780–1841), who was assistant and successor to the Italian astronomer Giuseppe Piazzi at Palermo Observatory. These names first appeared in the Palermo Catalogue of 1814, and it is usually supposed that Cacciatore himself was responsible, although it is equally possible that Piazzi may have applied the names to honour his appointed successor.

Like the small neighbouring constellations Vulpecula and Sagitta, Delphinus lies in a rich area of the Milky Way and has become a favourite hunting-ground for novae.

α (alpha) Delphini, 20h 40m +15°.9, (Sualocin), mag. 3.8, is a blue-white main-sequence star 241 l.y. away.

β (beta) Del, 20h 38m +14°.6, (Rotanev), mag. 3.6, the constellation's brightest member, is a white star 97 l.y. away. It is a binary with an orbital period of 27 years, but the components are too close to be divided in all but the largest amateur telescopes.

γ (gamma) Del, 20h 47m +16°.1, 102 l.y. away, is a showpiece double star consisting of golden and yellow-white stars of mags. 4.3 and 5.1, neatly separated in a small telescope. In the same telescopic field of view, but about 25 l.y. more distant, lies a faint binary, Σ 2725 (Struve 2725), consisting of stars of mags. 7.5 and 8.3.

The naming of variable stars

In addition to the normal system of naming stars in a constellation (page 7), stars that vary in brightness have their own system of nomenclature. Stars that were already named when their variability was discovered, such as δ (delta) Cephei, β (beta) Persei or ο (omicron) Ceti, retain their existing designation. Other variable stars are denoted by a system of one or two capital letters or, where that is insufficient, by the letter V and a number. The sequence starts with the letters R to Z, which covers the first nine variables in a constellation. Then double letters are applied, from RR to RZ. Next the lettering runs from SS to SZ, and so on until ZZ is reached. Then the sequence goes from AA to AZ, BB to BZ, ending with QZ, at which point 334 variable stars have been named (the letter J is omitted). Further variables are designated V335, V336, and so on. Novae, too, are allocated variable-star designations, such as the nova that erupted in Delphinus in 1967, which became known as HR Delphini.

Delphinus · Del · Delphini

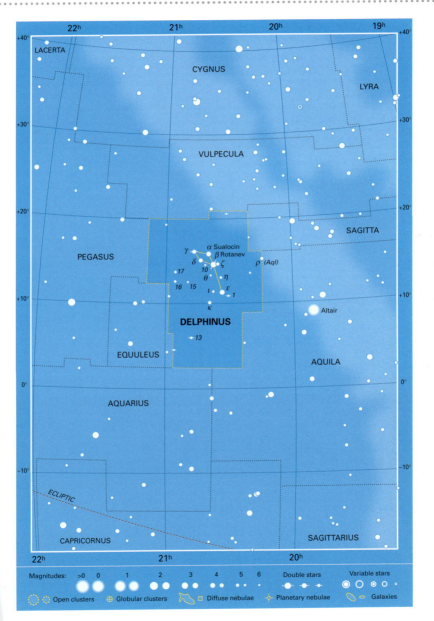

Dorado – The Goldfish

This constellation, also known as the Swordfish, was introduced at the end of the 16th century by the Dutch navigators Pieter Dirkszoon Keyser and Frederick de Houtman. Its most notable feature is the Large Magellanic Cloud (LMC), the larger of the two satellite galaxies that accompany our Milky Way. In 1987 the first supernova visible to the naked eye since 1604, Supernova 1987A, erupted in the LMC, at 5h 35m, −69°.3.

α (alpha) Doradus, 4h 34m −55°.0, mag. 3.3, is a blue-white star 176 l.y. away.

β (beta) Dor, 5h 34m −62°.5, a yellow-white supergiant 1040 l.y. away, is one of the brightest Cepheid variables, ranging from mag. 3.5 to 4.1 every 9 days 20 hours.

R Dor, 4h 37m −62°.1, 204 l.y. away, is a red giant that varies semi-regularly between mags. 4.8 and 6.6 with a period of around 11 months.

Large Magellanic Cloud (LMC), 5h 24m −69°, is a mini-galaxy 170,000 l.y. away, a satellite of the Milky Way, containing perhaps 10,000 million stars. To the naked eye it appears as a fuzzy elongated patch 6° in diameter, 12 times the apparent size of the Moon; its actual diameter is about 25,000 l.y. Binoculars and telescopes show individual stars, nebulae (notably the Tarantula Nebula, described below) and clusters.

NGC 2070, 5h 39m −69°.1, the Tarantula Nebula, is a looping cloud of hydrogen gas about 1000 l.y. in diameter in the Large Magellanic Cloud. To the naked eye the nebula appears as a fuzzy star, also known as 30 Doradus. The nebula's popular name, the Tarantula, comes from its spider-like shape. At the centre of the nebula is a cluster of supergiant stars, called R136, the light from which makes the nebula glow. The Tarantula is larger and brighter than any nebula in the Milky Way. If it were as close to us as the Orion Nebula, the Tarantula would fill the whole constellation of Orion, and would cast shadows on Earth.

The Large Magellanic Cloud: Loops of glowing gas can be seen among the star swarms. The pink knot of gas at left of centre is the Tarantula Nebula, NGC 2070. (Eckhard Slawik/ESA)

Dorado · Dor · Doradus

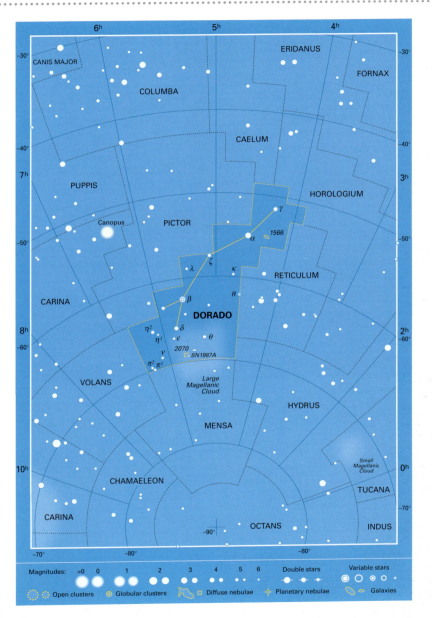

Draco – The Dragon

Dragons feature in many ancient legends, so it is not surprising to find such a monster in the sky. This one is said to be Ladon, the dragon slain by Hercules as a prelude to stealing the golden apples from the garden of the Hesperides. In the sky, one foot of Hercules rests upon the dragon's head, while the creature's body lies coiled around the north celestial pole. Although Draco is one of the largest and most ancient constellations it is indistinct, with no stars brighter than 2nd magnitude. Draco contains the north pole of the ecliptic, i.e. one of the two points 90° from the plane of the Earth's orbit, at 18h 00m, +66½°.

α (alpha) Draconis, 14h 04m +64°.4, (Thuban, 'serpent's head'), mag. 3.7, is a blue-white giant star 309 l.y. away. It was the pole star in about 2800 BC, but has lost that place to Polaris because of the effect of precession (see page 16).

β (beta) Dra, 17h 30m +52°.3, (Rastaban, 'serpent's head'), mag. 2.8, is a yellow giant 362 l.y. distant.

γ (gamma) Dra, 17h 57m +51°.5, (Etamin or Eltanin, 'the serpent'), mag. 2.2, is an orange giant 148 l.y. away, and the brightest star in the constellation. From observations of this star the English astronomer James Bradley discovered the effect known as the aberration of starlight in 1728.

μ (mu) Dra, 17h 05m +54°.5, (Alrakis), 88 l.y. away, is a close double star with matching cream-coloured components of mag. 5.6 and 5.7 which orbit every 670 years. The two stars are currently moving apart and becoming progressively easier to split in small apertures, although high magnification will be needed.

ν (nu) Dra, 17h 32m +55°.2, is a pair of identical white stars of mag. 4.9, easily visible in the smallest of telescopes and regarded as one of the finest binocular pairs. They lie 100 l.y. away.

ο (omicron) Dra, 18h 51m +59°.4, 322 l.y. away, is a mag. 4.6 orange giant star with a mag. 7.8 companion visible in small telescopes.

ψ (psi) Dra, 17h 42m +72°.1, 72 l.y. away, is a mag. 4.6 yellow-white star with a yellow mag. 5.8 companion visible in small telescopes or even binoculars.

16–17 Dra, 16h 36m +52°.9, is a wide pair of blue-white stars of mags. 5.1 and 5.5, 400 l.y. away, easily found in binoculars. Telescopes of 60 mm aperture with high magnification split the brighter star into a binary of mags. 5.4 and 6.5, making this a striking triple system.

39 Dra, 18h 24m +58°.6, 188 l.y away, is an impressive triple system. The two brightest members, at mags. 5.0 and 7.4, appear in binoculars as a wide blue-and-yellow pair. A telescope of 60 mm aperture with high magnification reveals that the brighter star has a closer companion of mag. 8.0.

40–41 Dra, 18h 00m +80°.0, is an easy pair of orange dwarf stars for small telescopes, mags. 5.7 and 6.1. They lie about 170 l.y. away.

NGC 6543, 17h 59m +66°.6, is a 9th-mag. planetary nebula 3500 l.y. away, one of the brightest such nebulae, showing in amateur telescopes as an irregular blue-green disk like an out-of-focus star. It is now known as the Cat's Eye Nebula from its appearance in Hubble Space Telescope photographs (see page 277).

Draco · Dra · Draconis

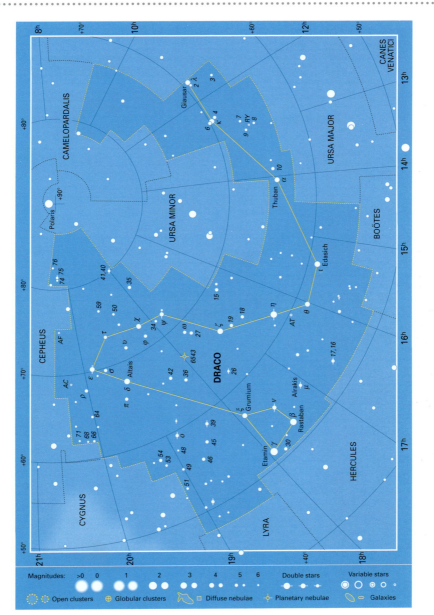

Magnitudes: >0 0 1 2 3 4 5 6   Double stars   Variable stars

Open clusters   Globular clusters   Diffuse nebulae   Planetary nebulae   Galaxies

Equuleus – The Little Horse

The second-smallest constellation in the sky, Equuleus seems to have originated with the Greek astronomer Ptolemy in the second century AD, as it appears for the first time among the 48 constellations listed in his book the *Almagest*. Only the head of the horse is shown, next to the much larger horse Pegasus, and there are no legends that identify it.

α (alpha) Equulei, 21h 16m +5°.2, (Kitalpha, 'the section of the horse'), mag. 3.9, is a yellow giant 186 l.y. away.

γ (gamma) Equ, 21h 10m +10°.1, is a mag. 4.7 white star 115 l.y. away. Through binoculars an apparent mag. 6.1 companion, 6 Equ, can be seen, but this is an unrelated background star.

1 Equ, 20h 59m +4°.3, also known as ε (epsilon) Equ, is a triple star 197 l.y. away. In small telescopes it appears as a white-and-yellow pair of mags. 5.4 and 7.4. The brighter component is also a close binary, of mags. 6.0 and 6.3; these stars orbit each other every 101 years. Currently they are closing together, and by 2015 will be too close to separate in amateur telescopes.

NGC 1300 in Eridanus (see page 148) is a classic example of a barred spiral galaxy with tightly wound arms, requiring quite large amateur telescopes to be seen. (José Alfonso López Aguerri, M. Prieto, C. Muñoz-Tuñón and A. M. Varela/Instituto de Astrofísica de Canarias)

Equuleus · Equ · Equulei

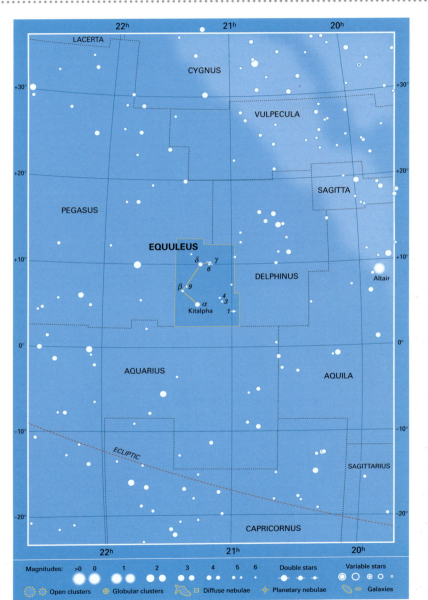

Eridanus – The River

An extensive constellation, the sixth-largest in the sky, but often overlooked because of its lack of any distinctive shape. It meanders from Taurus in the north to Hydrus in the south. In mythology, Eridanus was the river into which Phaethon fell after trying to drive the chariot of his father, Helios the Sun god. But it also supposedly represents a real river. Early mythologists identified it with the Nile, but later Greek writers said it was the Po in Italy.

Originally Eridanus included the stars of what is now Fornax and it stretched only as far as θ (theta) Eridani, which was given the name Achernar, from the Arabic meaning 'the river's end'. In more recent times Eridanus has been extended to nearly 60° south (below the horizon from Greece), and the title Achernar has been transferred to another star farther south. The star originally called Achernar is now known as Acamar, a name that comes from the same Arabic original as Achernar

The constellation contains several interesting galaxies, all too distant and too faint to be picked up easily in amateur telescopes. One celebrated example is NGC 1300, located at 3h 19.7m, −19° 25'; photographs such as the one on page 146 show that it is a beautiful 10th-mag. barred spiral. It lies 69 million l.y. away.

α (alpha) Eridani, 1h 38m −57°.2, (Achernar, 'the river's end'), mag. 0.5, is a blue-white main-sequence star 144 l.y. away.

β (beta) Eri, 5h 08m −5°.1, (Cursa, 'the footstool', referring to its position under the foot of Orion), mag. 2.8, is a blue-white star 89 l.y. away.

ε (epsilon) Eri, 3h 33m −9°.5, mag. 3.7, an orange main-sequence star 10.5 l.y. away, is among the most Sun-like of the nearby stars. It is orbited every 7 years by a planet of similar mass to Jupiter.

θ (theta) Eri, 2h 58m −40°.3, (Acamar), 161 l.y. away, is a striking pair of blue-white stars of mags. 3.2 and 4.3, divisible in small telescopes.

o² (omicron²) Eri, 4h 15m −7°.7, 16 l.y. away, also known as 40 Eridani, is a remarkable triple star. A small telescope shows that the mag. 4.4 orange primary, a star similar to the Sun, has a wide mag. 9.5 white dwarf companion, the most easily seen white dwarf in the sky. Small telescopes reveal that the white dwarf has an 11th-mag. companion which is a red dwarf, thereby completing a most interesting trio. The white dwarf and red dwarf orbit each other every 250 years, and will remain easy to split until the latter half of the 21st century.

32 Eri, 3h 54m −3°.0, 290 l.y. away, is a beautiful double star for small telescopes, consisting of a yellow giant of mag. 4.8 and a blue-green mag. 6.1 companion.

39 Eri, 4h 14m −10°.3, 206 l.y. away, is an orange giant of mag. 4.9 with an 8th-mag. companion divisible in small telescopes.

p Eri, 1h 40m −56°.2, 27 l.y. away, is a beautiful wide duo of orange stars, mags. 5.8 and 5.9, with an orbital period of about 500 years.

NGC 1535, 4h 14m −12°.7, is a small 9th-mag. planetary nebula about 2000 l.y. away. Small telescopes show it, but apertures of 150 mm are needed to appreciate its blue-grey disk.

Eridanus · Eri · Eridani

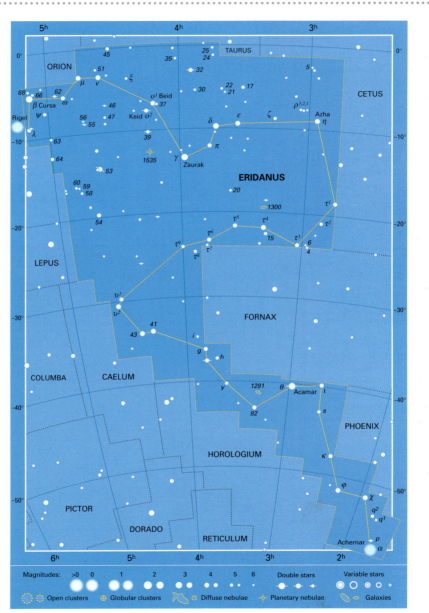

Magnitudes: >0 0 1 2 3 4 5 6   Double stars   Variable stars

Open clusters   Globular clusters   Diffuse nebulae   Planetary nebulae   Galaxies

Fornax – The Furnace

A barren constellation introduced in the 1750s by Nicolas Louis de Lacaille, originally under the name of Fornax Chemica, the Chemical Furnace. It contains a dwarf member of our Local Group of galaxies, called the Fornax Dwarf, some 450,000 l.y. from the Milky Way but too faint to see in amateur telescopes. Fornax also contains a compact cluster of galaxies about 60 million l.y. away, the brightest member of which is the 9th-mag. peculiar galaxy NGC 1316, also known as the radio source Fornax A, located at 3h 22.7m, −37° 12′. Another well-known member of the Fornax cluster is NGC 1365, pictured below.

α (alpha) Fornacis, 3h 12m −29°.0, 46 l.y. away, is a binary consisting of a yellow-white main-sequence star of mag. 3.9 with a deeper yellow mag. 6.5 companion of suspected variability. The pair orbit each other every 270 years or so and will remain divisible in small telescopes throughout the 21st century.

β (beta) For, 2h 49m −32°.4, mag. 4.5, is a yellow giant star 169 l.y. away.

NGC 1097, 2h 46m −30°.6, is a 9th-mag. barred spiral galaxy with a bright nucleus, visible in medium-sized telescopes. It lies about 50 million l.y. away.

NGC 1365, on the border of Fornax and Eridanus at 3h 33.6m, −36° 08′, is a striking barred spiral galaxy of 10th mag. with widely flung arms. It is a member of the Fornax cluster of galaxies, 60 million l.y. away. (Patrick Woudt, Univ. of Cape Town/South African Astronomical Observatory)

Fornax · For · Fornacis

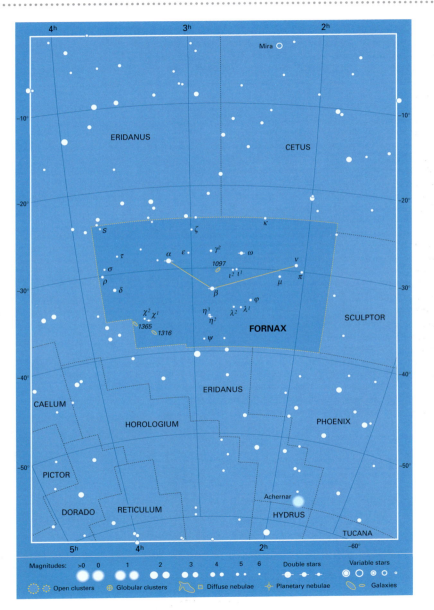

Gemini – The Twins

A constellation that dates from ancient times, representing a pair of twins. We know them as Castor and Pollux, members of the Argonauts' crew and of mixed parentage: both were sons of Queen Leda of Sparta, but by different fathers. Castor's father was her husband King Tyndareus, while the father of Pollux was the god Zeus. The twins were the protectors of mariners, appearing in ships' rigging as the electrical phenomenon now known as St Elmo's fire. In the sky, the stars Castor and Pollux provide a useful yardstick for measuring angular distances – they are exactly 4°.5 apart.

Gemini is a member of the zodiac, and the Sun passes through the constellation from late June to late July. Each year the Geminid meteors, one of the year's richest and brightest showers, radiate from a point near Castor, reaching a maximum around December 13–14, when up to 100 meteors per hour may be seen.

α (alpha) Geminorum, 7h 35m +31°.9, (Castor), 52 l.y. away, is an astounding multiple star, consisting of six separate components. To the naked eye Castor appears as a blue-white star of mag. 1.6, somewhat fainter than Pollux. A 60-mm telescope with high magnification splits Castor into two components of mags. 1.9 and 3.0, which orbit each other every 450 years. Separation of these stars is increasing, and they will become progressively easier to split throughout the 21st century, after which they will start to close up again. Both stars are spectroscopic binaries. Small telescopes also show a wide red dwarf companion to Castor; this is itself an eclipsing binary of Algol type, varying between mags. 9.3 and 9.8 in 19.5 hours, completing the six-star system.

β (beta) Gem, 7h 45m +28°.0, (Pollux), mag. 1.2, is the brightest star in the constellation. Some astronomers have speculated that Pollux, being labelled β Geminorum, was once fainter than Castor and has since brightened, or Castor has

faded. But the truth is that Johann Bayer, who allotted the Greek letters in 1603, did not distinguish carefully which star was the brighter, and so caused unnecessary confusion. Pollux is an orange giant 34 l.y. away.

γ (gamma) Gem, 6h 38m +16°.4, (Alhena), mag. 1.9, is a blue-white star 105 l.y. away.

δ (delta) Gem, 7h 20m +22°.0, (Wasat), 59 l.y. away, is a creamy-white star of mag. 3.5 with an orange dwarf companion of mag. 8.2. The brightness contrast makes the pair difficult in telescopes below about 75 mm aperture. Their estimated orbital period is over 1000 years.

ε (epsilon) Gem, 6h 44m +25°.1, mag. 3.1, is a yellow supergiant about 900 l.y. away. Binoculars, or a small telescope, reveal a wide companion of mag. 9.2.

ζ (zeta) Gem, 7h 04m +20°.6, 1200 l.y. away, is both a variable star and a binocular double. A yellow supergiant, it is a Cepheid variable, ►

NGC 2392, popularly known as the Eskimo or Clown Face Nebula, is a planetary nebula visible as a blue disk in amateur telescopes. See page 154. (Tom Tekach/Flynn Haase/NOAO/AURA/NSF)

Gemini · Gem · Geminorum

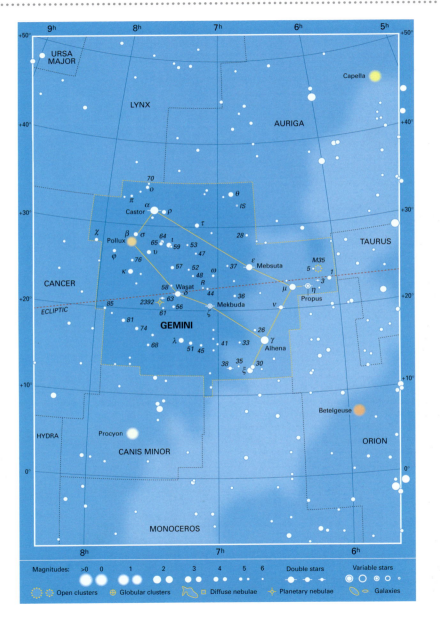

Magnitudes: >0 0 1 2 3 4 5 6   Double stars   Variable stars

Open clusters   ⊕ Globular clusters   Diffuse nebulae   Planetary nebulae   Galaxies

fluctuating between mags. 3.6 and 4.2 every 10.2 days. Binoculars or small telescopes reveal a wide mag. 7.6 companion, which is unrelated.

η (eta) Gem, 6h 15m +22°.5, 350 l.y. away, is another double–variable. A red giant star, it fluctuates in semi-regular manner between mags. 3.1 and 3.9 in about 233 days. It has a close 6th-mag. companion that orbits it every 500 years or so and requires a large telescope to distinguish it from the primary's glare.

κ (kappa) Gem, 7h 44m +24°.4, 143 l.y. away, is a mag. 3.6 yellow giant, with an 8th-mag. companion made difficult in small telescopes because of the extreme brightness difference.

ν (nu) Gem, 6h 29m +20°.2, mag. 4.1, is a blue giant 500 l.y. away with a wide 8th-mag. companion visible in binoculars or small telescopes.

38 Gem, 6h 55m +13°.2, 91 l.y. away, is a double star for small telescopes, with white and yellow components of mags. 4.8 and 7.8.

M35 (NGC 2168), 6h 09m +24°.3, is a large, 5th-mag. open cluster visible to the naked eye or through binoculars, noticeably elongated in shape. It consists of about 200 stars covering a similar area of sky as the Moon, and is 2800 l.y. away. Even a small telescope at low magnification will show the members of this outstanding cluster to be arranged in curving chains. Nearby in the sky, but actually about 10,000 l.y. farther off, is NGC 2158, a very rich open cluster that appears as a small, faint patch of light requiring at least 100 mm aperture to distinguish.

NGC 2392, 7h 29m +20°.9, is an 8th-mag. planetary nebula known as the Eskimo or Clown Face Nebula because it looks somewhat like a face surrounded by a fringe when seen through a large telescope. A small telescope shows it as a blue-green ellipse about the same apparent size as the disk of Saturn, with a central star of 10th mag. (see page 152 for a photograph). NGC 2392 lies 3000 l.y. away.

Grus – The Crane

One of the 12 constellations introduced at the end of the 16th century by the Dutch navigators Pieter Dirkszoon Keyser and Frederick de Houtman. It represents a water bird, the long-necked Crane, although it has also been depicted as a flamingo. The stars δ (delta) and μ (mu) Gruis are striking naked-eye doubles.

α (alpha) Gruis, 22h 08m −47°.0, (Alnair, 'the bright one'), mag. 1.7, is a blue-white star 101 l.y. away.

β (beta) Gru, 22h 43m −46°.9, is a red giant 170 l.y. away that varies between about mags. 2.0 and 2.3.

γ (gamma) Gru, 21h 54m −37°.4, mag. 3.0, is a blue giant 203 l.y. away.

δ¹ δ² (delta¹ delta²) Gru, 22h 29m −43°.5, is a naked-eye pairing of two unrelated stars: δ¹, mag. 4.0, is a yellow giant 296 l.y. away; δ² is a mag. 4.1 red giant 325 l.y. away.

μ¹ μ² (mu¹ mu²) Gru, 22h 16m −41°.3, is another naked-eye double of unrelated yellow giants that appear in the same line of sight by chance: μ¹ is of mag. 4.8, 262 l.y. away; μ² is of mag. 5.1, 240 l.y. away.

π¹ π² (pi¹ pi²) Gru, 22h 23m −45°.9, is a binocular duo of unrelated stars. π¹ is a deep-red semi-regular variable that ranges between mags. 5.4 and 6.7 every 150 days or so; it lies 500 l.y. away. π² is a white giant of mag. 5.6, 132 l.y. away.

Grus · Gru · Gruis

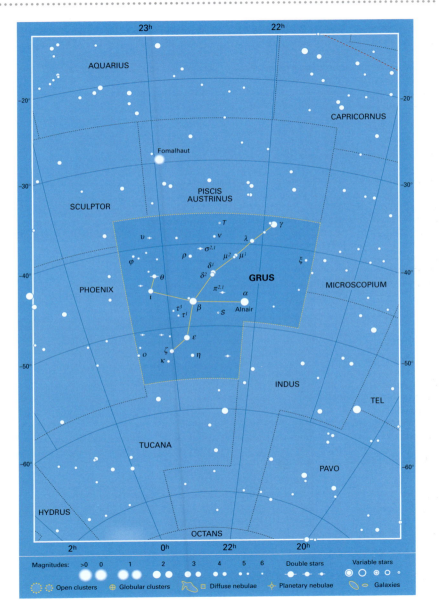

Hercules

Hercules represents the Greek mythological hero famous for his twelve labours. Originally, though, the constellation was visualized as an anonymous kneeling man, with one foot on the head of the celestial dragon, Draco, which adjoins to the north. Some legends identify the constellation with the ancient Sumerian superman, Gilgamesh. Despite being the fifth-largest constellation, Hercules is not prominent. But it is stocked with an abundance of double stars for users of small telescopes, plus one of the brightest and richest globular clusters, M13, which is easily found on one side of the so-called Keystone, a quadrilateral consisting of ε, ζ, η and π Herculis that marks the pelvis of Hercules.

α (alpha) Herculis, 17h 15m +14°.4, (Rasalgethi, 'the kneeler's head'), about 400 l.y. distant, is a red giant star some 400 times the Sun's diameter, making it one of the largest stars known. Like most red giants it is erratically variable, in this case fluctuat-

ing from about mag. 3 to mag. 4. It is actually a double star, with a mag. 5.4 blue-green companion visible in small telescopes. The estimated orbital period of the pair is 3600 years.

β (beta) Her, 16h 30m +21°.5, (Kornephoros, 'club-bearer'), mag. 2.8, the brightest star in the constellation, is a yellow giant 148 l.y. away.

γ (gamma) Her, 16h 22m +19°.2, mag. 3.8, is a white giant star 195 l.y. away, with a wide, unrelated 10th-mag. companion visible in small telescopes.

δ (delta) Her, 17h 15m +24°.8, mag. 3.1, is a blue-white star 78 l.y. away. Small telescopes show a nearby mag. 8.2 star which is physically unrelated.

ζ (zeta) Her, 16h 41m +31°.6, 35 l.y. away, is a mag. 2.9 yellow-white star with a close mag. 5.7 orange companion that orbits it in 34.5 years. The two stars were closest in 2001 but have since ▶

M13, the great globular cluster in Hercules, is a swarm of 300,000 stars appearing as a fuzzy ball in binoculars but which can be resolved by modest-sized amateur telescopes.
(Simon Tulloch and Daniel Folha, Isaac Newton Group of Telescopes, La Palma)

Hercules · Her · Herculis

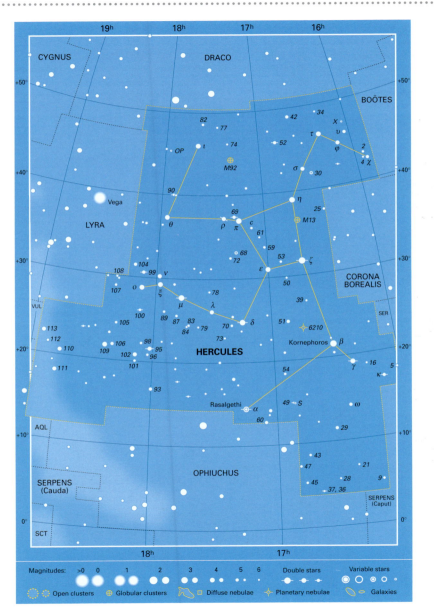

CYGNUS

DRACO

BOÖTES

19ʰ   18ʰ   17ʰ   16ʰ

+50°   +50°

82   77   42   34
χ
ν
OP   ι   74   τ   φ   2
90   52   4   χ
M92   σ   30
+40°   +40°

Vega
η   25
LYRA   69   M13
θ   ρ   π   c
61
68   59
72   ε   53   ζ
+30°   104   99   ν   50   +30°
108   ο   ξ   CORONA
107   78   39   BOREALIS
VUL   μ   λ   SER
100   89   87   83   70   51   6210
105   84   79   73   δ   Kornephoros   β
113   98   95   16   5
112   106   HERCULES   γ
110   109   102   96   54   κ
111   101
93   Rasalgethi   49   S   ω
+10°   α   29   +10°
AQL   60
43
47   21
OPHIUCHUS   45   28   9
SERPENS   37, 36
(Cauda)   SERPENS
(Caput)
0°   0°
SCT

18ʰ   17ʰ

Magnitudes: >0   0   1   2   3   4   5   6   Double stars   Variable stars

Open clusters   Globular clusters   Diffuse nebulae   Planetary nebulae   Galaxies

opened out, coming into the range of 220 mm apertures after 2010 and 150 mm apertures when widest around 2025. See page 282 for an orbit diagram.

κ (kappa) Her, 16h 08m +17°.0, is a mag. 5.0 yellow giant 388 l.y. away with an unrelated mag. 6.3 orange giant companion, 470 l.y. away, easily seen in small telescopes.

ρ (rho) Her, 17h 24m +37°.1, 402 l.y. away, is a pair of blue-white giants of mags. 4.5 and 5.5, visible in small telescopes.

30 Her, 16h 29m +41°.9, also known as g Her, is a red giant that varies semi-regularly between mags. 4.3 and 6.3 every 3 months or so. It lies 361 l.y. away.

68 Her, 17h 17m +33°.1, also known as u Her, 865 l.y. away, is an eclipsing binary of Beta Lyrae type varying between mag. 4.7 and 5.4 in just over 2 days.

95 Her, 18h 02m +21°.6, 470 l.y. away, is a double star for small telescopes, consisting of two giant stars of mags. 4.9 and 5.2, appearing silver and gold.

100 Her, 18h 08m +26°.1, is an easy duo for small telescopes consisting of identical blue-white stars of mag. 5.8, distances 165 and 230 l.y., like a pair of celestial cat's eyes.

M13 (NGC 6205), 16h 42m +36°.5, is a 6th-mag. globular cluster of 300,000 stars, the brightest of its kind in northern skies. It can be seen with the naked eye and is unmistakable in binoculars, spanning half the apparent width of the full Moon. The cluster lies 25,200 l.y. away and has a true diameter of over 100 l.y. Telescopes of 100 mm aperture resolve individual stars throughout the cluster, giving a mottled, sparkling effect.

M92 (NGC 6341), 17h 17m +43°.1, is a globular cluster only slightly inferior to its more famous neighbour, M13, which overshadows it. M92 is easily seen in binoculars as a fuzzy star. It is smaller and more condensed than M13, and needs a larger telescope to resolve its stars. It lies 29,000 l.y. away and has an estimated age of around 14 billion years, making it the oldest globular known.

NGC 6210, 16h 45m +23°.8, is a 9th-mag. planetary nebula which a telescope of 75 mm or larger shows as a blue-green ellipse. It is about 4000 l.y. away.

Horologium – The Pendulum Clock

One of the constellations representing mechanical instruments, in this case a pendulum clock used for timing observations, introduced in the 1750s by Nicolas Louis de Lacaille. As with so many of Lacaille's constellations, Horologium is faint and obscure.

α (alpha) Horologii, 4h 14m −42°.3, mag. 3.9, is an orange giant star 117 l.y. away.

β (beta) Hor, 2h 59m −64°.1, mag. 5.0, is a giant white star 314 l.y. away.

R Hor, 2h 54m −49°.9, is a red giant variable of the Mira type, ranging between extremes of mag. 4.7 and 14.3 in 13 months or so. It lies about 1000 l.y. away.

TW Hor, 3h 13m −57°.3, is a deep-red pulsating variable of semi-regular type, ranging between mag. 5.5 and 6.0 with an approximate period of 5 months. It lies about 1300 l.y. away.

NGC 1261, 3h 12m −55°.2, is an 8th-mag. globular cluster 44,000 l.y. away.

Horologium · Hor · Horologii

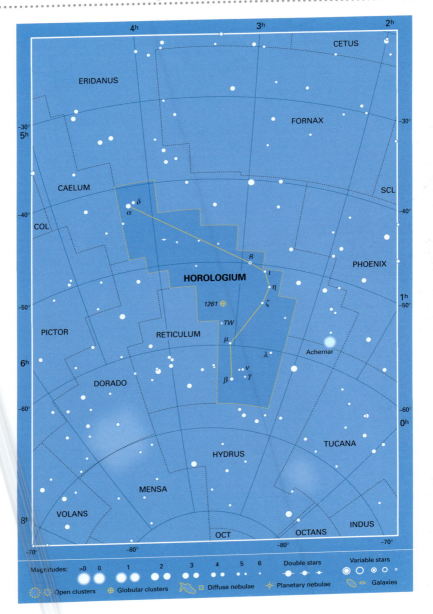

Magnitudes: >0 0 1 2 3 4 5 6   Double stars   Variable stars

Open clusters   Globular clusters   Diffuse nebulae   Planetary nebulae   Galaxies

Hydra – The Water Snake

The largest constellation in the sky, but by no means easy to identify because of its faintness. Apart from its brightest star, Alphard, which marks the heart of the Water Snake, Hydra's only readily recognizable feature is its head, an attractive group of six stars. Hydra winds its way from the head in the northern celestial hemisphere, on the borders of Cancer, to the tip of its tail, south of the celestial equator adjacent to Libra and Centaurus, a total length of over 100°.

In mythology, Hydra is usually identified with the multi-headed monster slain by Hercules. Another legend links it with the adjoining constellations of Corvus the Crow and Crater the Cup, which are found on its back. In this story the bird returned to the god Apollo with Hydra in its claws as an excuse for its aborted mission to fetch water in the cup.

α (alpha) Hydrae, 9h 28m −8°.7, (Alphard, 'the solitary one'), mag. 2.0, is an orange giant 177 l.y. away.

β (beta) Hya, 11h 53m −33°.9, mag. 4.3, is a blue-white star 365 l.y. away.

γ (gamma) Hya, 13h 19m −23°.2, mag. 3.0, is a yellow giant 132 l.y. away.

δ (delta) Hya, 8h 38m +5°.7, mag. 4.1, is a blue-white star 179 l.y. away.

ε (epsilon) Hya, 8h 47m +6°.4, 135 l.y. away, is a beautiful but difficult double star of contrasting colours, needing high power on a telescope of at least 75 mm aperture. The stars are yellow and blue, of mags. 3.4 and 6.7, and form a genuine binary with an estimated orbital period of nearly 1000 years.

▶

M83, a face-on barred spiral galaxy in Hydra, is a swirl of stars and gas sometimes known as the Southern Pinwheel. Our own Galaxy might look like this if we could see it from outside. See also page 162.
(Adam Block/NOAO/ AURA/NSF)

Hydra · Hya · Hydrae

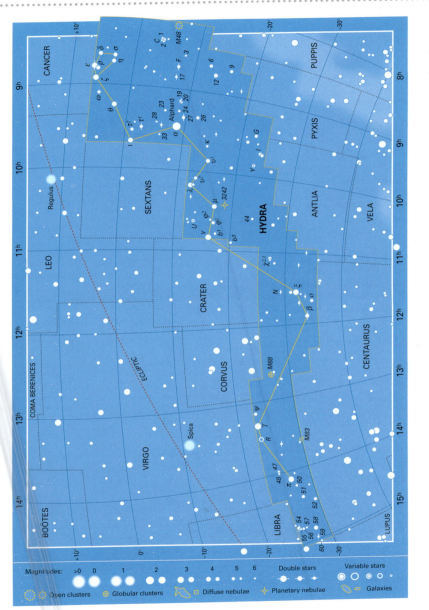

CANCER

LEO

BOÖTES

COMA BERENICES

VIRGO

SEXTANS

CRATER

CORVUS

LIBRA

HYDRA

ANTLIA

PYXIS

PUPPIS

VELA

CENTAURUS

LUPUS

Regulus

Spica

Alphard

M48

M68

M83

3242

Magnitudes: >0   0   1   2   3   4   5   6   Double stars   Variable stars

Open clusters   Globular clusters   Diffuse nebulae   Planetary nebulae   Galaxies

27 Hya, 9h 20m, −9°.6, mag. 4.8, is a white star 244 l.y. away with a wide mag. 7.0 companion visible in binoculars. The companion is 202 l.y. away and evidently unrelated. Small telescopes split this companion into components of mags. 7 and 11.

54 Hya, 14h 46m −25°.4, 99 l.y. away, is an easy double for small telescopes, consisting of yellow and purple stars of mags. 5.3 and 7.4.

R Hya, 13h 30m −23°.3, is a red giant variable star similar to Mira in Cetus that fluctuates between 4th and 10th mags. every 390 days. At its best it can reach mag. 3.5, making it one of the brightest Mira stars. Its distance is about 2000 l.y.

U Hya, 10h 38m −13°.4, 528 l.y. away, is a deep-red variable star that fluctuates semi-regularly between mags. 4.2 and 6.6 every 115 days.

M48 (NGC 2548), 8h 14m −5°.8, is a large open cluster of about 80 stars, 2000 l.y. away, just visible to the naked eye under clear skies and a fine sight in binoculars. It is somewhat triangular in shape, wider than the apparent size of the full Moon, and is well shown by small telescopes under low power.

M68 (NGC 4590), 12h 39m −26°.7, is an 8th-mag. globular cluster visible as a fuzzy star in binoculars and just resolved with apertures of 100 mm. It lies 31,000 l.y. away.

M83 (NGC 5236), 13h 37m −29°.9, is a large, face-on spiral galaxy of 8th mag., visible in a small telescope. It has a small, bright nucleus and signs of a central bar, similar to our own Galaxy. Its spiral arms can be traced with an aperture of 150 mm. (See photograph on page 160.) M83 has been the site of more known supernovae than any other Messier object, six in all. It is one of the brightest and closest galaxies outside the Local Group, about 15 million l.y. away. It is sometimes popularly termed the Southern Pinwheel.

NGC 3242, 10h 25m −18°.6, is a 9th-mag. planetary nebula of similar apparent size to the disk of Jupiter; it is popularly termed the Ghost of Jupiter. This often-overlooked object 2600 l.y. away is prominent enough to be picked up in small telescopes at low magnification as a blue-green disk, while larger instruments show a bright inner disk surrounded by a fainter halo.

Hydrus – The Lesser Water Snake

The Dutch navigators Pieter Dirkszoon Keyser and Frederick de Houtman introduced this constellation at the end of the 16th century as a smaller southern counterpart to the great Water Snake, Hydra. Lying between the two Magellanic Clouds, Hydrus almost bridges the gap between Eridanus and the south celestial pole. There is little to interest the casual observer.

α (alpha) Hydri, 1h 59m −61°.6, mag. 2.9, is a white main-sequence star 71 l.y. away.

β (beta) Hyi, 0h 26m −77°.3, mag. 2.8, the constellation's brightest member, is a yellow star 24 l.y. away.

γ (gamma) Hyi, 3h 47m −74°.2, mag. 3.2, is a red giant star 214 l.y. away.

π¹ π² (pi¹ pi²) Hyi, 2h 14m −67°.8, is a binocular pair of red and orange giants, unrelated: π¹ is mag. 5.6 and lies 740 l.y. away; π², mag. 5.7, is 468 l.y. distant.

Hydrus · Hyi · Hydri

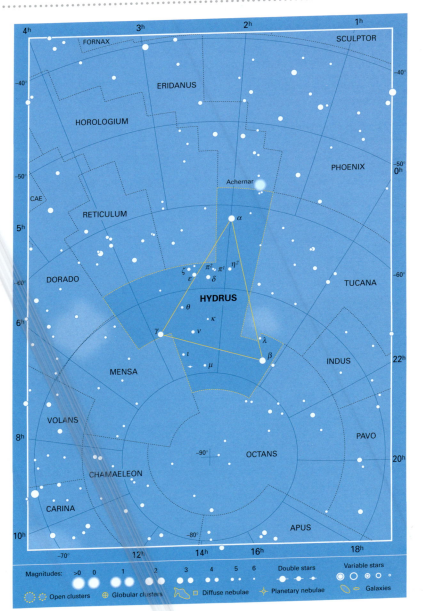

Magnitudes: >0 0 1 2 3 4 5 6   Double stars   Variable stars

Open clusters   Globular clusters   Diffuse nebulae   Planetary nebulae   Galaxies

Indus – The Indian

A constellation representing a native hunter, introduced at the end of the 16th century by the Dutch navigators Pieter Dirkszoon Keyser and Frederick de Houtman. On old star charts he was depicted holding aloft a spear as though in pursuit of prey, but it is not known whether he is supposed to be a native of the East Indies or the Americas. None of its stars is brighter than 3rd magnitude and none of them have names.

α (alpha) Indi, 20h 38m −47°.3, mag. 3.1, is an orange giant star 101 l.y. away.

β (beta) Ind, 20h 55m −58°.5, mag. 3.7, is an orange giant 600 l.y. away.

δ (delta) Ind, 21h 58m −55°.0, mag. 4.4, is a white star 185 l.y. away.

ε (epsilon) Ind, 22h 03m −56°.8, mag. 4.7, is an orange dwarf somewhat smaller and cooler than the Sun. At a distance of 11.8 l.y., it is one of the Sun's closest neighbours.

θ (theta) Ind, 21h 20m −53°.4, 97 l.y. away, is a pair of white stars of mags. 4.5 and 7.0, divisible in a small telescope.

T Ind, 21h 20m −45°.0, is a deep-red variable star ranging semi-regularly between 5th and 7th magnitudes in 11 months or so. It lies about 1900 l.y. away.

Between Indus and Hydrus lies the Small Magellanic Cloud, an irregularly shaped splash of stars which is actually a satellite of our own Galaxy. See page 248. (NOAO/AURA/NSF)

Indus · Ind · Indi

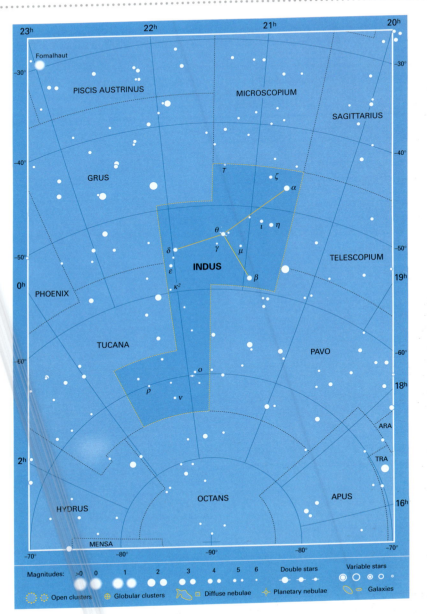

Magnitudes: >0   0   1   2   3   4   5   6   Double stars   Variable stars

○ ○ Open clusters   ⊕ Globular clusters   Diffuse nebulae   ✦ Planetary nebulae   Galaxies

Lacerta – The Lizard

An inconspicuous constellation sandwiched between Cygnus and Andromeda, introduced in 1687 by the Polish astronomer Johannes Hevelius (see box below). An alternative figure that previously occupied this area was Sceptrum, the Sceptre and Hand of Justice, created in 1679 by the Frenchman Augustin Royer to commemorate King Louis XIV. In 1787 the German Johann Elert Bode called this region Frederick's Glory in honour of King Frederick the Great of Prussia. Both these alternatives have been discarded.

The constellation's most celebrated object is BL Lacertae, location 22h 02.7m, +42° 17′, originally thought to be a peculiar 14th-magnitude variable star. It is the prototype of a group of objects, the BL Lac objects or Lacertids, believed to be giant elliptical galaxies with variable centres, lying far off in the Universe and related to quasars and other galaxies with active nuclei. Three bright novae appeared within the boundaries of Lacerta during the 20th century.

α (alpha) Lacertae, 22h 31m +50°.3, mag. 3.8, is a blue-white main-sequence star 102 l.y. away.

β (beta) Lac, 22h 24m +52°.2, mag. 4.4, is a yellow giant 170 l.y. away.

NGC 7243, 22h 15m +49°.9, is a scattered open cluster of similar apparent size to the full Moon suitable for small telescopes, consisting of a few dozen stars of 8th mag. and fainter, 2500 l.y. away.

Johannes Hevelius (1611–1687)

Johannes Hevelius of Danzig (now Gdansk, Poland) was one of the finest observers of his day. His masterwork was a catalogue of 1564 stars, called *Catalogus Stellarum Fixarum*, completed just before his death in 1687 and published posthumously in 1690. The catalogue was accompanied by a set of sky charts, *Firmamentum Sobiescianum*, on which Hevelius introduced seven constellations still in use today: Canes Venatici, Lacerta, Leo Minor, Lynx, Scutum, Sextans and Vulpecula. Another important cartographic product of Hevelius was his map of the Moon, published in 1647 in his book *Selenographia*. It was the first major Moon map, and introduced the first system of lunar nomenclature. He named lunar formations after features on Earth: for instance, the large, bright crater we know as Copernicus he called Etna, while another prominent crater, Tycho, was Mount Sinai and Mare Imbrium was the Mediterranean. Only a few of the names given by Hevelius remain, such as the lunar Alps and Apennines; his names have mostly been discarded in favour of the system introduced by the Italian astronomer Giovanni Battista Riccioli (1598–1671), who named the craters after famous philosophers and astronomers. Fittingly enough, the craters commemorating Hevelius and Riccioli are found close together on the Moon.

Lacerta · Lac · Lacertae

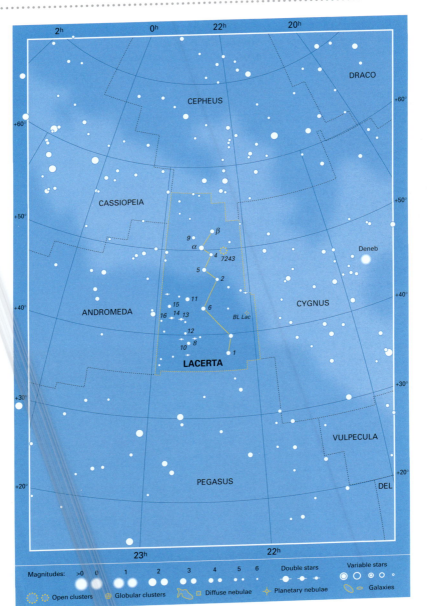

Leo – The Lion

One of the few constellations that looks like the figure it is supposed to represent – in this case, a crouching lion. The Lion's head is outlined by the so-called Sickle consisting of six stars from ε (epsilon) to α (alpha) Leonis; the Lion's body stretches out behind, its tail marked by β (beta) Leonis. Mythologically, this is the Lion reputedly slain by the hero Hercules as the first of his 12 labours. The Sun passes through the constellation from mid-August to mid-September.

Leo contains the third-nearest star to the Sun, CN Leonis (also called Wolf 359), a red dwarf 7.8 l.y. away. It is of magnitude 13.5, although it is a flare star and can occasionally brighten by up to a magnitude; it is located at 10h 56.5m, +7° 01′, near the border with Sextans. Leo contains numerous distant galaxies, the brightest of which are mentioned on page 170, plus three faint dwarf members of our Local Group, beyond the reach of amateur telescopes.

Every November, the Leonid meteors radiate from a point near γ (gamma) Leonis.

Usually the numbers are low, peaking at about 10 per hour on November 17–18, but the shower's activity increases dramatically at 33-year intervals when the parent comet, Tempel–Tuttle, returns to perihelion. High Leonid rates were last seen in 1999–2002.

α (alpha) Leonis, 10h 08m +12°.0, (Regulus, 'the little king'), mag. 1.4, is a blue-white main-sequence star 77 l.y. away. Binoculars or small telescopes will show a wide companion of mag. 7.7.

β (beta) Leo, 11h 49m +14°.6, (Denebola, 'the lion's tail'), mag. 2.1, is a blue-white star 36 l.y. away.

γ (gamma) Leo, 10h 20m +20°.0, (Algieba, 'the forehead'), 126 l.y. away, consists of a pair of golden-yellow giant stars of mags. 2.3 and 3.6, orbiting in about 500 years. They form an exceptionally handsome double in small telescopes, one of the finest in the sky. In binoculars, an unrelated mag. 4.8 yellowish foreground star, 40 Leonis, is visible nearby. ▶

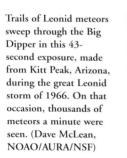

Trails of Leonid meteors sweep through the Big Dipper in this 43-second exposure, made from Kitt Peak, Arizona, during the great Leonid storm of 1966. On that occasion, thousands of meteors a minute were seen. (Dave McLean, NOAO/AURA/NSF)

Leo · Leo · Leonis

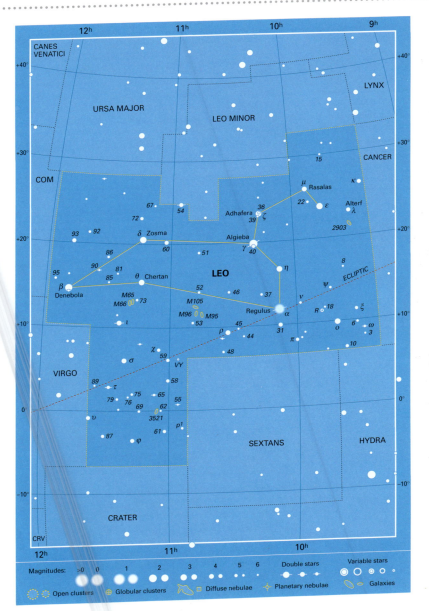

Magnitudes: >0   0   1   2   3   4   5   6   Double stars   Variable stars

Open clusters   ⊕ Globular clusters   Diffuse nebulae   Planetary nebulae   Galaxies

δ (delta) Leo, 11h 14m +20°.5, (Zosma), mag. 2.6, is a blue-white star 58 l.y. away.

ε (epsilon) Leo, 9h 46m +23°.8, mag. 3.0, is a yellow giant 251 l.y. away.

ζ (zeta) Leo, 10h 17m +23°.4, (Adhafera), mag. 3.4, is a giant white star 260 l.y. away. To the north of it, binoculars show 35 Leonis, an unrelated foreground star of mag. 6.0. To the south a wider third star, 39 Leonis, mag. 5.8 and also in the foreground, can be seen in binoculars, making this an optical triple.

ι (iota) Leo, 11h 24m +10°.5, 79 l.y. away, is a close and difficult double star. It appears to the naked eye as a yellow-white star of mag. 4.0, but actually consists of components of mags. 4.1 and 6.7 orbiting every 186 years. Currently the stars are moving apart; apertures of 100 mm should be sufficient to separate them until 2010 after which they become progressively easier, coming within range of all but the very smallest apertures when at their widest from 2053 to 2067.

τ (tau) Leo, 11h 28m +2°.9, 621 l.y. away, is a yellow giant of mag. 5.0 with an 8th-mag. companion visible in binoculars and small telescopes.

54 Leo, 10h 56m +24°.7, 289 l.y. away, is a double for small telescopes, consisting of blue-white components of mags. 4.5 and 6.3.

R Leo, 9h 48m +11°.4, is a red giant variable of Mira type, lying about 330 l.y. away. It appears strongly red when at maximum and is roughly 450 times larger than our Sun. R Leonis normally varies between 6th and 10th mags. with an average period of 310 days, but on occasion can become as bright as mag. 4.4.

M65, M66 (NGC 3623, NGC 3627), 11h 19m +13°.0, are a pair of spiral galaxies about 30 million l.y. away. At 9th mag. they can be detected in large binoculars under clear conditions, but at least 100 mm aperture at low power is required for their elongated shape and condensed centres to be clearly seen.

M95, M96 (NGC 3351, NGC 3368), 10h 44m +11°.7, 10h 47m +11°.8, are a pair of spiral galaxies of 10th and 9th mag. respectively, about 35 million l.y. away, visible as circular nebulosities in small telescopes. Larger apertures show that M95 has a central bar. About 1° away lies the smaller M105 (NGC 3379), 10h 48m +12°.6, a 9th-mag. elliptical galaxy at a similar distance.

Leo Minor – The Lesser Lion

Leo Minor lies between the larger and brighter constellations of Leo to the south and Ursa Major to the north. Johannes Hevelius, the Polish astronomer, introduced Leo Minor in 1687. There is little of interest in it. Surprisingly there is no star labelled α (alpha). This is the result of an error by the English astronomer Francis Baily, who assigned Greek letters to the stars of Leo Minor in 1845 but failed to letter the brightest star through an oversight.

β (beta) Leonis Minoris, 10h 28m +36°.7, mag. 4.2, is a yellow giant star 146 l.y. away.

46 LMi, 10h 53m +34°.2, mag. 3.8, the brightest star in the constellation, is an orange giant 98 l.y. away.

Leo Minor · LMi · Leonis Minoris

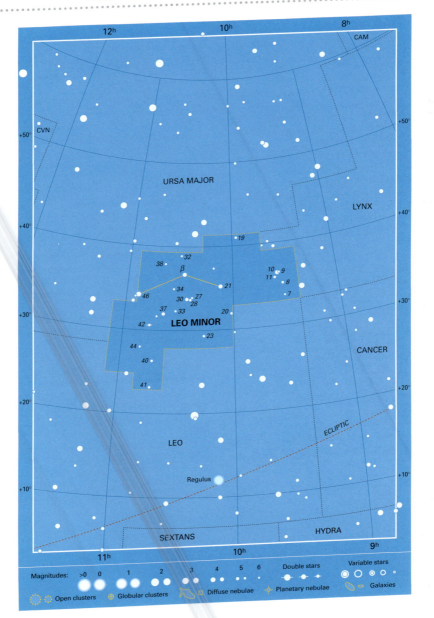

Lepus – The Hare

Lepus is a constellation known since ancient Greek times. It represents a hare, cunningly located at the feet of its hunter, Orion, and pursued endlessly across the sky by Canis Major, the hunter's dog. In one Greek legend, the inhabitants of the island of Leros began to breed hares but the population exploded and the island quickly became overrun with them. The hares destroyed the crops, reducing the inhabitants to starvation. After a concerted effort, the islanders drove the hares out of the island. They put the image of a hare among the stars as a reminder that one can easily end up with too much of a good thing.

The Hare is also associated in many legends with the Moon. For instance, the familiar figure of the man in the Moon is sometimes interpreted as a hare or rabbit, so perhaps Lepus is another incarnation of the lunar hare. Lepus is overshadowed by Orion's brilliance, but is not without interest for amateur observers.

α (alpha) Leporis, 5h 33m −17°.8, (Arneb, 'hare'), mag. 2.6, is a white supergiant star, about 1300 l.y. away.

β (beta) Lep, 5h 28m −20°.8, (Nihal), mag. 2.8, is a yellow giant star 159 l.y. away.

γ (gamma) Lep, 5h 44m −22°.5, 29 l.y. away, is an attractive binocular duo consisting of a yellow star of mag. 3.6 with an orange companion of mag. 6.2.

δ (delta) Lep, 5h 51m −20°.9, mag. 3.8, is a yellow giant 112 l.y. away.

ε (epsilon) Lep, 5h 05m −22°.4, mag. 3.2, is an orange giant 227 l.y. away.

κ (kappa) Lep, 5h 13m −12°.9, 560 l.y. away, is a mag. 4.4 blue-white star with a close mag. 7.4 companion, difficult to see in the smallest telescopes because of the magnitude contrast.

R Lep, 5h 00m −14°.8, 820 l.y. away, is an intensely red star known as Hind's Crimson Star after the English observer John Russell Hind, who described it in 1845 as 'like a drop of blood on a black field'. R Leporis is a Mira-type variable that ranges from mag. 5.5 at its brightest to as faint as 12th mag. in a period of around 430 days.

RX Lep, 5h 11m −11°.8, 447 l.y. away, is a red giant that varies semi-regularly between mags. 5.0 and 7.4 every 2 months or so.

M79 (NGC 1904), 5h 24m −24°.5, is a small but rich globular cluster 44,000 l.y. away, visible as a fuzzy 8th-mag. star in small telescopes. Nearby in the same low-power field is the multiple star Herschel 3752, consisting of a mag. 5.4 primary with two companions, a close one of mag. 6.6 and a wide one of mag. 9.1, all visible in small telescopes.

NGC 2017, 5h 39m −17°.8, is a small but remarkable star cluster, also known as the multiple star Herschel 3780. Modest amateur telescopes reveal a group of five well-spaced stars ranging from 6th to 10th mag. In addition, the brightest star has a mag. 7.9 companion that requires a telescope of at least 200 mm aperture to split, while an aperture of at least 100 mm shows that one of the 9th-mag. stars is a close double. There is also a 12th-mag. component which should be visible with 100 mm or upwards, so this is actually a group of at least eight stars. However, it is not a true cluster: the stars lie at a range of distances and are moving in different directions.

Lepus · Lep · Leporis

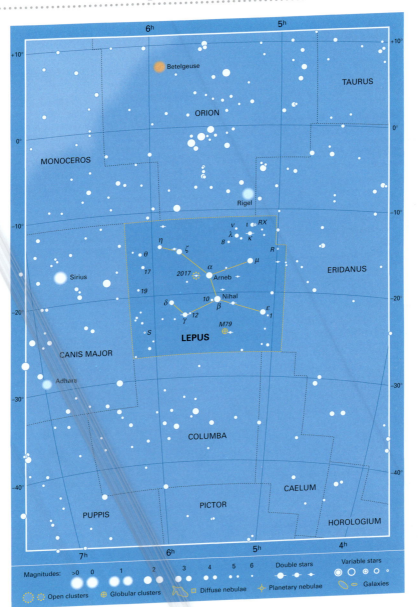

Libra – The Scales

A faint, easily overlooked constellation of the zodiac, through which the Sun passes during November. The ancient Greeks knew it as the Claws of the Scorpion, an extension of neighbouring Scorpius, and this old identification lives on in the Arabic-derived names Zubenelgenubi and Zubeneschamali ('southern claw' and 'northern claw', respectively) applied to the stars α (alpha) and β (beta) Librae.

The Romans made this region into a separate constellation during the time of Julius Caesar in the first century BC. Since then the Scales have come to be regarded as the symbol of justice, held aloft by the goddess of justice, Astraea, in the shape of the neighbouring figure of Virgo.

Libra once contained the September equinox, the point at which the Sun passes south of the celestial equator each year. Because of precession, this point moved into neighbouring Virgo around 730 BC, but the September equinox is still sometimes referred to as the First Point of Libra. Despite its relative faintness, Libra contains several stars of interest.

α (alpha) Librae, 14h 50m −16°.0, (Zubenelgenubi, 'the southern claw'), 77 l.y. away, is a wide binocular double consisting of a blue-white star of mag. 2.7 with a white companion of mag. 5.2.

β (beta) Lib, 15h 17m −9°.4, (Zubeneschamali, 'the northern claw'), mag. 2.6, the brightest in the constellation, is celebrated as one of the few bright stars to show a distinct greenish tinge. It lies 160 l.y. away.

γ (gamma) Lib, 15h 36m −14°.8, mag. 3.9, is an orange giant 152 l.y. away.

δ (delta) Lib, 15h 01m −8°.5, 304 l.y. away, is an eclipsing variable of the Algol type. It varies between mags. 4.9 and 5.9 in 2 days 8 hours.

ι (iota) Lib, 15h 12m −19°.8, is a multiple star 377 l.y. away. Its main blue-white component, of mag. 4.5, has a wide mag. 9.4 companion that is difficult to see in the smallest telescopes because of the brightness difference. An aperture of 75 mm or above with high magnification will split this fainter companion into two stars of 10th and 11th mags. The brightest component of ι Lib is itself a binary with a 23-year period, but too close for amateur telescopes. Binoculars show a mag. 6.1 star nearby called 25 Librae, which is a foreground object, 219 l.y. away.

μ (mu) Lib, 14h 49m −14°.1, 235 l.y. away, is a close double star consisting of components of mags. 5.7 and 6.8, divisible in a telescope of 75 mm aperture.

48 Lib, 15h 58m −14°.3, mag. 4.9, is a blue giant 513 l.y. away with an abnormally high speed of rotation that causes it to throw off rings of gas from its equator, as a result of which it varies irregularly by a few tenths of a magnitude in similar fashion to γ (gamma) Cassiopeiae and Pleione in Taurus. It also bears the variable-star designation FX Lib.

NGC 5897, 15h 17m −21°.0, is a large but loosely scattered 9th-mag. globular cluster 40,000 l.y. away, unspectacular in small instruments.

Libra · Lib · Librae

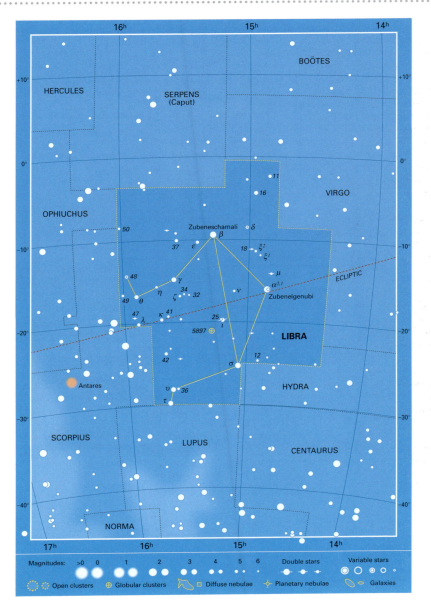

Lupus – The Wolf

Lupus is stocked with numerous interesting objects, although it is often overlooked in favour of its more spectacular neighbours Scorpius and Centaurus. The constellation was regarded by the Greeks and Romans as an unspecified wild animal, impaled on a pole by Centaurus the Centaur. Some mythologists said that Centaurus was about to sacrifice the animal on the altar, represented by nearby Ara. The constellation's identification with a wolf seems to have become common in Renaissance times. Lupus lies in the Milky Way and is rich in double stars. None of its stars is named.

α (alpha) Lupi, 14h 42m −47°.4, mag. 2.3, is a blue giant star 548 l.y. away.

β (beta) Lup, 14h 59m −43°.1, mag. 2.7, is a blue giant 524 l.y. away.

γ (gamma) Lup, 15h 35m −41°.2, mag. 2.8, is a blue-white star 570 l.y. away. It is a close binary with a 190-year orbital period, divisible only in apertures of 200 mm and above.

ε (epsilon) Lup, 15h 23m −44°.7, 504 l.y. away, is a blue-white star of mag. 3.4 with a wide mag. 8.8 companion visible in a small telescope. The primary is itself a close double, divisible only with large apertures.

η (eta) Lup, 16h 00m −38°.4, 493 l.y. away, is a double star consisting of a mag. 3.4 blue-white primary with a mag. 7.9 companion, not easy to see in a small telescope because of the magnitude contrast.

κ (kappa) Lup, 15h 12m −48°.7, 188 l.y. away, is an easy double star for small telescopes, consisting of blue-white components of mags. 3.9 and 5.7.

μ (mu) Lup, 15h 19m −47°.9, 291 l.y. away, is a multiple star. Small telescopes reveal a mag. 4.3 blue-white primary with a wide mag. 6.9 companion. But in telescopes of at least 100 mm, with high magnification, the primary itself is seen to be double, consisting of two near-identical stars of mags. 5.0 and 5.1.

ξ (xi) Lup, 15h 57m −34°.0, 200 l.y. away, is a neat pair of mag. 5.1 and 5.6 blue-white stars, well seen in a small telescope.

π (pi) Lup, 15h 05m −47°.1, 500 l.y. away, appears to the naked eye as mag. 3.9, but telescopes above 75 mm aperture show that it consists of two close blue-white stars of mags. 4.6 and 4.7.

GG Lup, 15h 19m −40°.8, 514 l.y., is an eclipsing binary of Algol type, ranging between mags. 5.6 and 6.1 with a period of 1.85 days.

NGC 5822, 15h 05m −54°.3, is a large, loose open cluster of about 150 faint stars, 2400 l.y. away, visible in binoculars or small telescopes.

NGC 5986, 15h 46m −37°.8, is an 8th-mag. globular cluster, 33,000 l.y. distant, visible as a rounded patch in a small telescope.

Lupus · Lup · Lupi

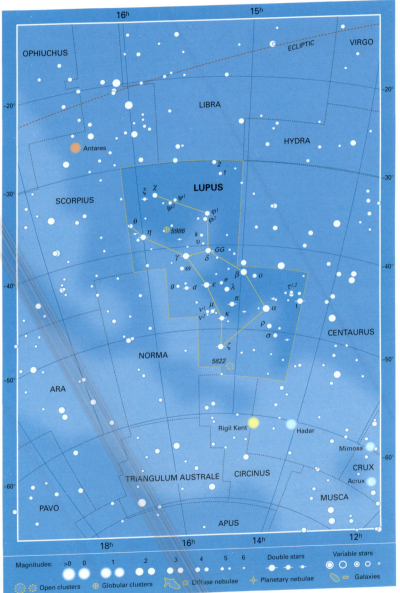

Lynx – The Lynx

A decidedly obscure constellation, despite its considerable size (larger than Gemini, for example), introduced in 1687 by the Polish astronomer Johannes Hevelius to fill the gap between the traditional figures of Ursa Major and Auriga. Hevelius named it Lynx because, he said, only the lynx-eyed would be able to see it – a reference to the fact that his own eyesight was exceptionally keen. Indeed, Hevelius continued to measure star positions with naked-eye instruments throughout his life, even though others had by then moved on to telescopes. Despite the constellation's faintness, owners of small telescopes will find many exquisite double stars within it.

α (alpha) Lyncis, 9h 21m +34°.4, mag. 3.1, is a red giant 222 l.y. away.

5 Lyn, 6h 27m +58°.4, 680 l.y. away, is an orange giant star of mag. 5.2 with a wide, unrelated mag. 7.9 companion, visible in a small telescope.

12 Lyn, 6h 46m +59°.4, 229 l.y. away, is a fascinating triple star. A small telescope will show a mag. 5.0 blue-white star with a fainter mag. 7.2 companion. Telescopes of 75 mm aperture and over reveal that the brighter component is itself a binary, of mags. 5.5 and 6.1, which orbit each other every 900 years.

15 Lyn, 6h 57m +58°.4, 170 l.y. away, is a close double star for telescopes of 150 mm aperture and above. The components are of mags. 4.7 and 5.8, the brighter star appearing a deep yellow colour.

19 Lyn, 7h 23m +55°.3, is an attractive triple star for small telescopes, with blue-white components of mags. 5.8 and 6.9. The very wide third star is of mag. 7.6. The trio lies about 500 l.y. away.

38 Lyn, 9h 19m +36°.8, 122 l.y. away, is a pair of mag. 3.9 and 6.3 blue-white stars, difficult in the smallest telescopes because of their closeness.

41 Lyn, 9h 29m +45°.6, 288 l.y. away, is actually over the border in Ursa Major (hence the designation '41 Lyncis' has now fallen out of use, but we retain it here for identification purposes). It is a yellow giant of mag. 5.4, and small telescopes reveal a wide companion of mag. 8.0. A 10th-mag. star nearby forms a triangle, making this an apparent triple.

NGC 2419, 7h 38m +38°.9, is an unusually remote globular cluster, of the type known as an intergalactic tramp. It is of 11th mag. and lies about 330,000 l.y. from the centre of our Galaxy, farther than either of the Magellanic Clouds.

Flamsteed numbers

Apart from α Lyncis, all the main stars in Lynx are referred to not by Greek letters but by so-called Flamsteed numbers. These numbers originate from a catalogue of 2935 stars, *Historia Coelestis Britannica*, compiled by the first Astronomer Royal of England, John Flamsteed (1646–1719), and published posthumously in 1725. In the catalogue, Flamsteed listed the stars in each constellation in order of right ascension. The numbers that are now known as Flamsteed numbers were not actually allocated by Flamsteed himself but were added later by the French astronomer Joseph Jérôme de Lalande (1732–1807). In a French edition of the catalogue published in 1783 Lalande inserted a column numbering the stars consecutively in each constellation in the order that Flamsteed had listed them.

Lynx · Lyn · Lyncis

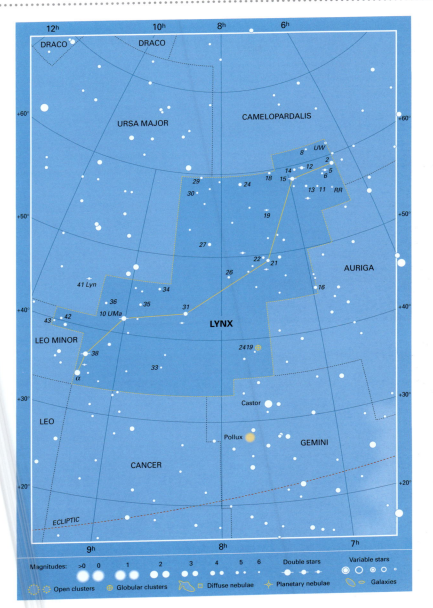

Magnitudes: >0   0   1   2   3   4   5   6   Double stars   Variable stars

Open clusters   ⊕ Globular clusters   Diffuse nebulae   Planetary nebulae   Galaxies

Lyra – The Lyre

A constellation dating from ancient times, representing the stringed instrument invented by Hermes and subsequently given by his half-brother Apollo to the great musician Orpheus. This constellation has also been visualized as an eagle or vulture. Although small, Lyra is bright and prominent. It contains the fifth-brightest star in the sky, Vega, which forms one corner of the northern Summer Triangle (Deneb in Cygnus and Altair in Aquila mark the other two corners). Because of precession, Vega will be the pole star between AD 13,000 and 14,000, although it will come no closer than 5°.7 to the pole. In a quite separate effect, our Sun's motion around the Galaxy is carrying us in the general direction of Vega at a velocity of 20 km/s relative to nearby stars. The Lyrid meteor shower emanates from this constellation each year, reaching a peak of about 10 per hour on April 21–22.

α (alpha) Lyrae, 18h 37m +38°.8, (Vega, 'the swooping eagle'), mag. 0.03, is a brilliant blue-white main-sequence star 25 l.y. away. It is the fifth-brightest star in the sky, and is surrounded by a disk of dust from which planets may be forming.

β (beta) Lyr, 18h 50m +33°.4, (Sheliak, 'the harp'), 882 l.y. away, is a remarkable multiple star. Small telescopes easily resolve it as a double star of cream and blue components. The fainter, blue star is of mag. 7.2, while the brighter star is an eclipsing binary that varies between mags. 3.3 and 4.4 in 12.9 days. β Lyrae is the prototype of a class of eclipsing variables in which the stars are so close together that gravity distorts them into egg-shapes, and hot gas spirals off them into space.

γ (gamma) Lyr, 18h 59m +32°.7, (Sulafat, 'the tortoise'), mag. 3.2, is a blue-white giant 635 l.y. away.

δ¹ δ² (delta¹ delta²) Lyr, 18h 54m +37°.0, is a wide naked-eye or binocular double consisting ▶

The four component stars of the Double Double, ε (epsilon) Lyrae, as seen through a telescope. See page 182 for a description. (Wil Tirion)

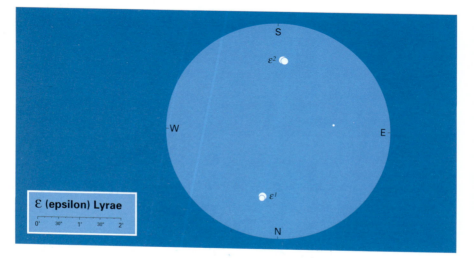

ε (epsilon) Lyrae

0'   30'   1'   30'   2'

Lyra · Lyr · Lyrae

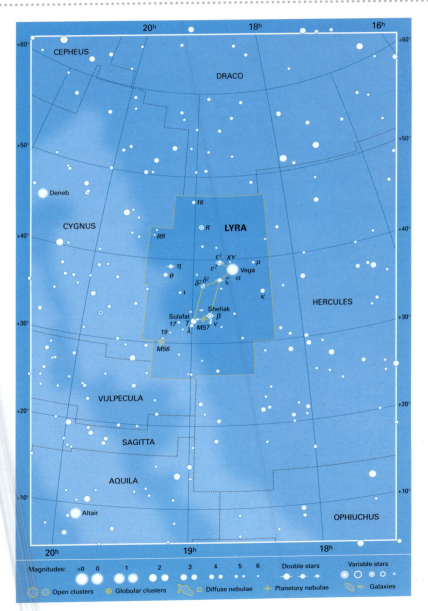

of two unrelated stars: δ^1, blue-white, mag. 5.6, 1080 l.y. away; and δ^2, a red giant 899 l.y. away, which varies erratically from mag. 4.2 to 4.3.

$\varepsilon^1 \varepsilon^2$ (epsilon[1] epsilon[2]) Lyr, 18h 44m +39°.7, 161 l.y. away, is a celebrated quadruple star known popularly as the Double Double. Binoculars or even keen eyesight separate it into two stars, ε^1 and ε^2, of mags. 4.7 and 4.6 respectively. But a telescope of 60 to 75 mm aperture and high magnification reveals that each star is itself double, the two pairs being oriented almost at right angles to each other (see diagram on page 180). The ε^1 pair has mags. of 5.0 and 6.1 and an orbital period of about 1750 years; the ε^2 pair, slightly closer together has mags. of 5.2 and 5.5, and a period of about 720 years. Quadruple stars are rare, and this is the finest of them.

ζ (zeta) Lyr, 18h 45m +37°.6, 152 l.y. away, is a double star, easily split in small telescopes or binoculars into components of mags. 4.4 and 5.7.

η (eta) Lyr, 19h 14m +39°.1, 1040 l.y. away, is a blue-white star of mag. 4.4 with a wide mag. 9.1 companion visible in a small telescope.

R Lyr, 18h 55m +43°.9, 350 l.y. away, is a red giant that varies semi-regularly between mags. 3.9 and 5.0 every 6 or 7 weeks.

RR Lyr, 19h 25m +42°.8, 745 l.y. away, is the prototype of an important class of variable stars used as 'standard candles' for indicating distances in space. RR Lyrae variables are often found in globular clusters and are thus known as cluster-type variables. Related to Cepheid variables, they are giant stars that pulsate in size, varying by about one magnitude usually in less than a day. RR Lyrae itself varies from mag. 7.1 to 8.1 in 13.6 hours.

M57 (NGC 6720), 18h 54m +33°.0, the Ring Nebula, is a famous 9th-mag. planetary nebula 2000 l.y. away, conveniently placed between β (beta) and γ (gamma) Lyrae. On photographs taken through large telescopes it looks like a celestial smoke ring, but in fact it is a cylinder seen end-on. A small telescope shows it as a noticeably elliptical misty disk, but a larger aperture is needed to see the central hole. It is one of the brightest planetary nebulae and appears larger in the sky than the planet Jupiter. Its true diameter is about one light year. (For a photograph see page 277.)

Mensa – The Table Mountain

The faintest of all the constellations, with no star brighter than magnitude 5.0. Mensa was introduced by the Frenchman Nicolas Louis de Lacaille to commemorate Table Mountain at the Cape of Good Hope from where he surveyed the southern skies in 1751–52. Part of the Large Magellanic Cloud strays from neighbouring Dorado over the border into Mensa, possibly reminding Lacaille of the cloud that frequently caps the real Table Mountain. Unfortunately, there is little else of interest here.

α (alpha) Mensae, 6h 10m −74°.8, mag. 5.1, is a yellow star similar to the Sun, 33 l.y. away.

β (beta) Men, 5h 03m −71°.3, mag. 5.3, is a yellow giant 642 l.y. away.

γ (gamma) Men, 5h 32m −76°.3, mag. 5.2, is an orange giant 101 l.y. away.

η (eta) Men, 4h 55m −74°.9, mag. 5.5, is an orange giant 712 l.y. away.

Mensa · Men · Mensae

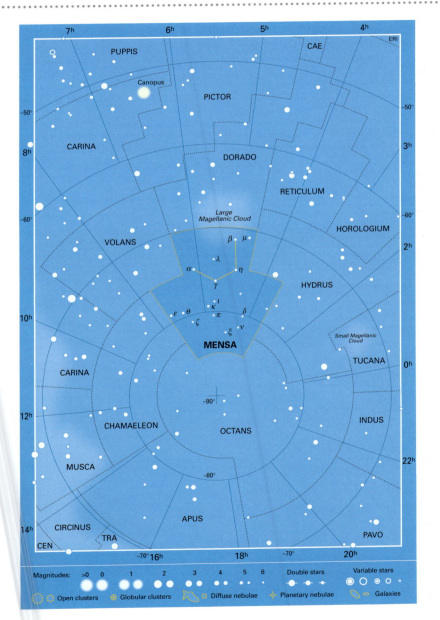

Microscopium – The Microscope

Another of the southern hemisphere constellations representing scientific instruments that were introduced in the 1750s by the Frenchman Nicolas Louis de Lacaille. The instrument in this case was an early form of compound microscope (i.e. one that uses more than one lens). As with so many of Lacaille's constellations, Microscopium is little more than a filler, encompassing a few faint stars between better-known figures.

α (alpha) Microscopii, 20h 50m −33°.8, mag. 4.9, is a yellow giant star 381 l.y. away. It has a 10th-mag. companion, visible in small telescopes.

γ (gamma) Mic, 21h 01m −32°.3, mag. 4.7, is a yellow giant 224 l.y. away.

ε (epsilon) Mic, 21h 18m −32°.2, mag. 4.7, is a blue-white main-sequence star 165 l.y. away.

The Rosette Nebula, NGC 2237, in Monoceros, perhaps the most beautiful nebula in the heavens, surrounds the star cluster NGC 2244. See page 186. (Nigel Sharp/NOAO/AURA/NSF)

Microscopium · Mic · Microscopii

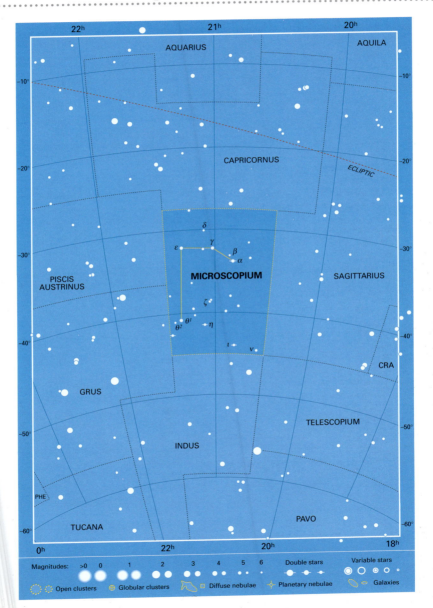

Monoceros – The Unicorn

A faint but fascinating constellation between Orion and Canis Minor, introduced by the Dutch theologian and astronomer Petrus Plancius in 1613, apparently because of several references to a unicorn in the Old Testament of the Bible. Its location in the Milky Way ensures that it is well stocked with nebulae and clusters.

Among the constellation's most celebrated features is Plaskett's Star, a mag. 6.1 spectroscopic binary named after the Canadian astronomer John Stanley Plaskett (1865–1941), who found in 1922 that it is the most massive pair of stars known; according to current data, it consists of two blue supergiants of masses 43 and 51 times that of the Sun, orbiting each other every 14.4 days. Plaskett's Star lies at 6h 37.4m, +6° 08′, near the open cluster NGC 2244, of which it may be an outlying member.

α (alpha) Monocerotis, 7h 41m −9°.6, mag. 3.9, is an orange giant star 144 l.y. away.

β (beta) Mon, 6h 29m −7°.0, 690 l.y. away, is rated as perhaps the finest triple star in the heavens. The smallest of telescopes should separate the three components, of mags. 4.6, 5.0 and 5.4, on a steady night. They form a curving arc of blue-white stars, the faintest two being the closest together.

δ (delta) Mon, 7h 12m −0°.5, mag. 4.2, is a blue-white star 375 l.y. away. It has a wide, unrelated naked-eye companion, 21 Mon, of mag. 5.5.

8 Mon, 6h 24m +4°.6, also known as ε (epsilon) Mon, is an easy double star for small telescopes, consisting of unrelated yellow and blue-white components of mags. 4.4 and 6.7, distances 128 and 79 l.y., in an attractive low-power field.

S Mon, 6h 41m +9°.9, also known as 15 Mon, is an intensely luminous blue-white star of mag. 4.7, situated 2600 l.y. away in the star cluster NGC 2264 (see page 188). It is a double star, with a close companion of mag. 7.6 visible in a small telescope. S Mon is slightly variable, fluctuating erratically by about 0.1 mag.

M50 (NGC 2323), 7h 03m −8°.3, is an open cluster of about 80 stars, half the apparent size of the full Moon, visible in binoculars and small telescopes. Apertures of 100 mm or so resolve it into a ragged patch of stars of 8th mag. and fainter, with a reddish star near its southern edge. M50 is 3300 l.y. away.

NGC 2232, 6h 27m −4°.7, is a scattered cluster of 20 stars for binoculars, containing the mag. 5.1 blue-white star 10 Mon. The cluster, which covers the same area of sky as the full Moon, lies 1200 l.y. away.

NGC 2237, NGC 2244, 6h 32m +4°.9, is a complex combination of a faint diffuse nebula, known as the Rosette Nebula, and a cluster of stars, all about 5000 l.y. away. Long-exposure photographs show the nebula as a pink loop, twice the apparent diameter of the full Moon. Visual observations with large amateur telescopes reveal only the brightest parts of the nebula. The associated cluster, NGC 2244, consists of stars that have been born from the Rosette Nebula's gas; it is just visible to the naked eye and is an easy binocular object. The six most prominent stars of the cluster form a rectangular shape, although the brightest of them, 12 Mon, mag. 5.9, is not a true member but an unrelated foreground star. The cluster is likely to be the only part of this celebrated object visible in a small telescope, but the pale outline of the nebula can just be made out in binoculars under clear, dark skies. (See picture on page 184.)

NGC 2261, 6h 39m +8°.7, Hubble's Variable Nebula, is a small, faint, fan-shaped nebula containing the remarkable variable star R Mon. Its erratic brightness fluctuations, from mag. 9.5 down to about 12th mag., may be caused by the pangs of its birth from the surrounding nebula. ▶

Monoceros · Mon · Monocerotis

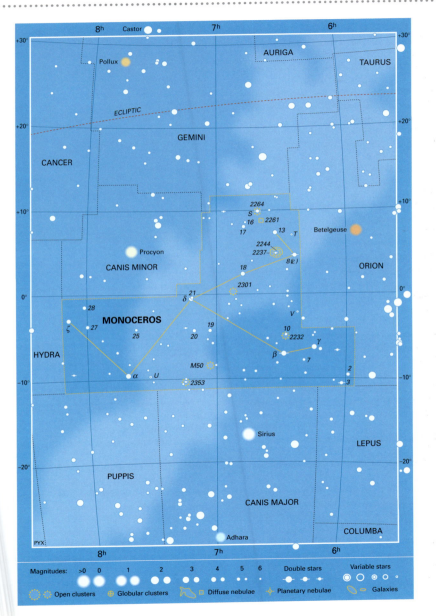

Magnitudes: >0   0   1   2   3   4   5   6   Double stars   Variable stars

Open clusters   Globular clusters   Diffuse nebulae   Planetary nebulae   Galaxies

This star and its nebula are open to study only by larger amateur telescopes; the star's distance is uncertain but it may be associated with the nearby NGC 2264 complex (see below), which would place it at about 2600 l.y.

NGC 2264, 6h 41m +9°.9, is another combination of star cluster and nebula. The cluster, visible in binoculars, has about 40 members, including the 5th-mag. S Mon (see page 186). The associated nebula, known as the Cone Nebula because of its tapered shape, shows up well only on photographs such as the one at the right and is beyond the reach of visual observation with amateur telescopes. NGC 2264 is 2600 l.y. away.

NGC 2301, 6h 52m +0°.5, is a binocular cluster of 80 or so stars of 8th mag. and fainter, the brightest of them arranged in a vertical chain. It lies 2500 l.y. away.

NGC 2353, 7h 15m −10°.3, is an open cluster for small telescopes, consisting of about 30 stars of 9th mag. and fainter seemingly arranged in a spiral pattern. It lies about 3900 l.y. away.

The Cone Nebula is a dark intrusion into the southern end of the star cluster NGC 2264, but is too faint to see visually. (Carlos and Crystal Acosta/Adam Block/NOAO/AURA/NSF)

Musca – The Fly

A small southern constellation lying at the foot of the Southern Cross. It is one of the 12 constellations introduced at the end of the 16th century by the Dutch navigators Pieter Dirkszoon Keyser and Frederick de Houtman. It was also widely known under the alternative name of Apis, the Bee, which is how it was shown on several old star atlases. There is little of note in Musca other than part of the dark Coalsack Nebula, which spills over the border from Crux.

α (alpha) Muscae, 12h 37m −69°.1, mag. 2.7, is a blue-white star 306 l.y. away.

β (beta) Mus, 12h 46m −68°.1, 311 l.y. away, is a close pair of stars of mags. 3.6 and 4.0, requiring 100 mm aperture and high magnification to split. The orbital period of the pair is 400 years or so.

δ (delta) Mus, 13h 02m −71°.5, mag. 3.6, is an orange giant 91 l.y. away.

θ (theta) Mus, 13h 08m −65°.3, is a double star of mags. 5.6 and 7.6 for small telescopes. The brighter star is a blue supergiant, while its companion is a Wolf–Rayet star, a rare type of very hot star; it is the second-brightest such star in the sky, γ (gamma) Velorum being the brightest of all.

NGC 4833, 13h 00m −70°.9, is a fairly large, 7th-mag. globular cluster 18,000 l.y. away, visible in binoculars and small telescopes and resolvable into stars with an aperture of 100 mm.

Musca · Mus · Muscae

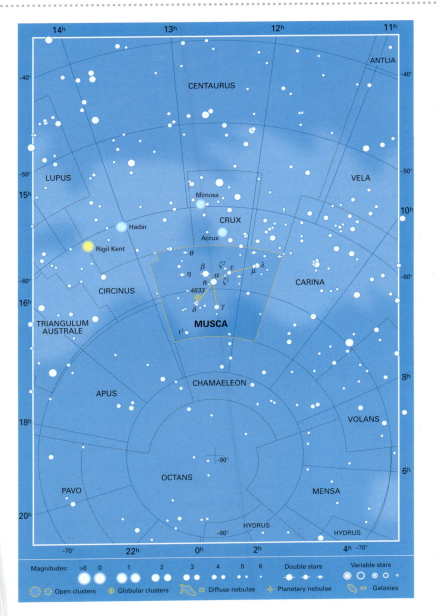

Norma – The Set Square

A superfluous constellation invented in the 1750s by Nicolas Louis de Lacaille, originally under the name Norma et Regula, the set square and ruler. Lacaille placed it next to the compasses (Circinus) and the southern triangle (Triangulum Australe), an earlier invention of Keyser and de Houtman which Lacaille visualized as a builder's level. The stars of Norma were previously part of Ara, Lupus and Scorpius, but since Lacaille's time the boundaries of Norma have been altered, so that the stars which he named α (alpha) and β (beta) Normae have been reabsorbed into Scorpius; in the chart on page 227 these two stars are labelled N and H Scorpii. Norma lies in a rich region of the Milky Way.

γ^2 (gamma²) Normae, 16h 20m −50°.2, mag. 4.0, is a yellow giant 128 l.y. away, the brightest star in the constellation. Next to it lies the far more distant yellow-white supergiant γ^1 (gamma¹) Normae, mag. 5.0, around 1500 l.y. away.

δ (delta) Nor, 16h 06m −45°.2, mag. 4.7, is a white star 123 l.y. away.

ε (epsilon) Nor, 16h 27m −47°.6, 400 l.y. away, is a double star with components of mags. 4.5 and 6.7 visible in small telescopes.

ι^1 (iota¹) Nor, 16h 04m −57°.8, 140 l.y. away, appears in small telescopes as a double star of mags. 4.6 and 8.1. In addition, the brighter star is itself a very close binary, divisible only in very large telescopes, with a 27-year orbital period.

NGC 6087, 16h 19m −57°.9, is a loose, large binocular cluster of about 40 stars, 3000 l.y. away, with chains of stars extending from it like a spider's legs. At the centre lies its brightest star, the Cepheid variable S Nor, which ranges from mag. 6.1 to 6.8 in 9.8 days.

At 15h 51.7m −51° 31′ in Norma lies the satisfyingly symmetrical planetary nebula known variously as Shapley 1 (Sp 1), PK 329+02.1 or RCW 100. At 13th mag., it requires fairly large apertures to be seen. The central star is 14th magnitude. (Anglo–Australian Telescope Board)

Norma · Nor · Normae

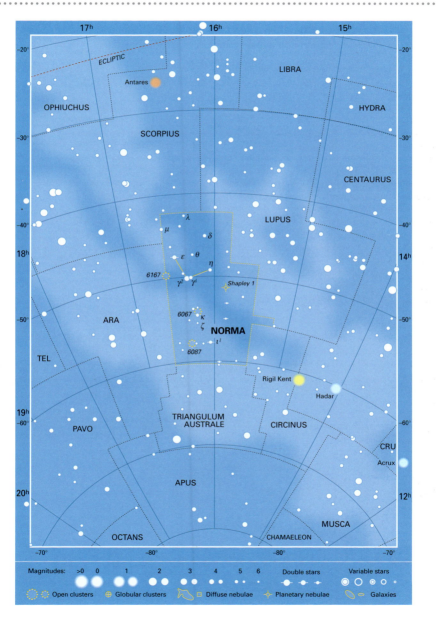

Magnitudes: >0   0   1   2   3   4   5   6   Double stars   Variable stars

⦿ Open clusters   ⊕ Globular clusters   ▱ Diffuse nebulae   ✦ Planetary nebulae   ⬭ Galaxies

Octans – The Octant

The constellation that contains the south pole of the sky. Despite this privileged position, Octans is faint and unremarkable. The south celestial pole forms an almost exact equilateral triangle with 5th-mag. τ (tau) and χ (chi) Octantis. There is no southern equivalent of Polaris, the north pole star; the nearest naked-eye star to the southern pole is 5th-mag. σ (sigma) Octantis. Currently this star lies about 1° from the pole, but the distance is increasing due to precession (see chart below); σ Octantis was closest to the pole, under ¾°, around 1860.

Octans commemorates the navigational instrument known as the octant, a forerunner of the sextant, invented in 1730 by the English instrument maker John Hadley (1682–1744). The octant consisted of an arc of 45°, i.e. an eighth of a circle, from which came its name. The constellation itself was introduced in the 1750s by Nicolas Louis de Lacaille, and its dullness is a memorial to his lack of imagination.

α (alpha) Octantis, 21h 05m −77°.0, mag. 5.1, is a spectroscopic binary consisting of white and yellow giants 148 l.y. away.

β (beta) Oct, 22h 46m −81°.3, mag. 4.1, is a white star 140 l.y. away.

δ (delta) Oct, 14h 27m −83°.7, mag. 4.3, is an orange giant 279 l.y. away.

ε (epsilon) Oct, 22h 20m −80°.4, also known as BO Oct, is a red giant that varies semi-regularly between mags. 4.6 and 5.3 with an approximate period of 8 weeks. It lies 268 l.y. away.

λ (lambda) Oct, 21h 51m −82°.7, 435 l.y. away, is a double star with yellow and white components of mags. 5.5 and 7.2, individually visible in small telescopes.

ν (nu) Oct, 21h 41m −77°.4, mag. 3.7, the brightest star in the constellation, is an orange giant 69 l.y. away.

σ (sigma) Oct, 21h 09m −89°.0, mag. 5.4, the nearest naked-eye star to the south celestial pole, is a white giant 270 l.y. away.

The movement of the south celestial pole over 800 years as a result of precession. (Wil Tirion)

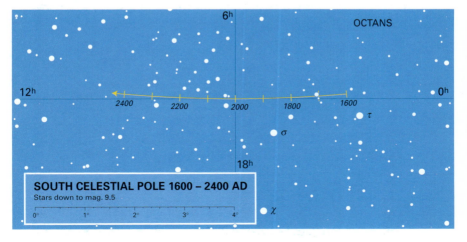

SOUTH CELESTIAL POLE 1600 – 2400 AD
Stars down to mag. 9.5

Octans · Oct · Octantis

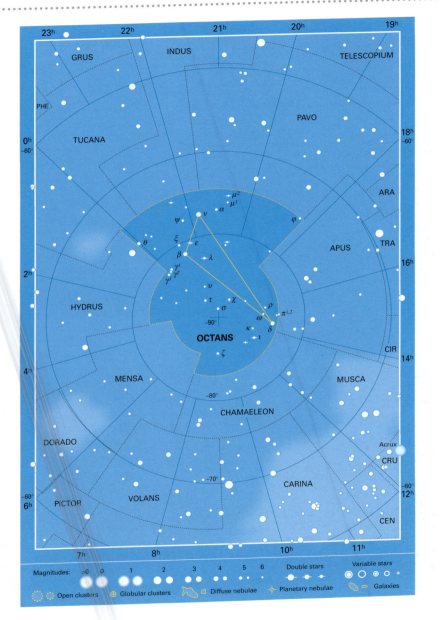

Ophiuchus – The Serpent Holder

An ancient constellation, representing a man encoiled by a serpent (the constellation Serpens). Ophiuchus is usually identified as Aesculapius, a mythical healer who was a forerunner of Hippocrates; his reputed powers included the ability to raise the dead. The serpent he holds is a symbol of this power, since snakes are seemingly reborn every year when they shed their skin. Perhaps the most celebrated star in Ophiuchus is Barnard's Star, a mag. 9.5 red dwarf 5.9 l.y. away, the second-closest star to the Sun. It lies at 17h 57.8m, +4° 42′, and is named after the American astronomer E. E. Barnard who found in 1916 that it has the greatest proper motion of any star, covering the apparent diameter of the Moon every 180 years.

The southernmost regions of Ophiuchus extend into rich starfields of the Milky Way, in the direction of the centre of the Galaxy; consequently the constellation is replete with star clusters. Ophiuchus was the site of the last supernova seen to erupt in our Galaxy, popularly called Kepler's Star, which appeared in 1604 at 17h 30.6m, −21° 29′, reaching mag. −3 at its brightest.

α (alpha) Ophiuchi, 17h 35m +12°.6, (Rasalhague, 'head of the serpent collector'), mag. 2.1, is a white main-sequence star 47 l.y. away.

β (beta) Oph, 17h 43m +4°.6, (Cebalrai, 'the shepherd's dog'), mag. 2.8, is an orange giant 82 l.y. away.

γ (gamma) Oph, 17h 48m +2°.7, mag. 3.7, is a blue-white main-sequence star 95 l.y. away.

δ (delta) Oph, 16h 14m −3°.7, (Yed Prior, 'the preceding star of the hand'), mag. 2.7, is a red giant 170 l.y. away.

ε (epsilon) Oph, 16h 18m −4°.7, (Yed Posterior, 'the following star of the hand'), mag. 3.2, is a yellow giant 108 l.y. away.

ζ (zeta) Oph, 16h 37m −10°.6, mag. 2.5, is a blue main-sequence star 458 l.y. away.

η (eta) Oph, 17h 10m −15°.7, (Sabik), mag. 2.4, is a blue-white main-sequence star 84 l.y. away.

ρ (rho) Oph, 16h 26m −23°.4, 400 l.y. away, is a striking multiple star for small instruments. The brightest component, of mag. 5.0, has a close companion of mag. 5.7 visible in a small telescope at high magnification; either side of this pair are wide binocular companions of mags. 6.7 and 7.3.

τ (tau) Oph, 18h 03m −8°.2, 170 l.y. away, is a close pair of cream-coloured stars, mags. 5.2 and 5.9, orbiting every 260 years and gradually closing; currently at least 75 mm aperture is required to separate them and 100 mm will be needed by the year 2025.

36 Oph, 17h 15m −26°.6, 20 l.y. away, is a pair of mag. 5.1 orange dwarf stars divisible with small apertures. Their calculated orbital period is nearly 500 years.

70 Oph, 18h 05m +2°.5, 16 l.y. away, is a celebrated double star, consisting of yellow and orange components of mags. 4.2 and 6.0 which orbit each other in a period of 88 years. They are easily divisible in the smallest apertures and will continue to be so throughout the first half of the 21st century, being at their widest around 2025. For a diagram showing how the positions and separations of the pair change throughout the 21st century, see page 282.

RS Oph, 17h 50m −6°.7, is a recurrent nova seen to have erupted six times, breaking the record it previously shared with T Pyxidis and the fainter U Scorpii. Normally around 12th mag., RS Oph flared up to naked-eye brightness in 1898, 1933, 1958, 1967, 1985 and 2006.

M10 (NGC 6254), 16h 57m −4°.1, is a 7th-mag. globular cluster visible in binoculars or a small ►

Ophiuchus · Oph · Ophiuchi

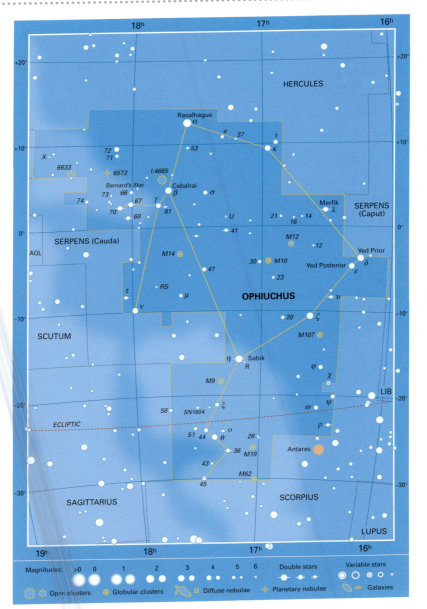

telescope. It is 14,000 l.y. away, somewhat closer than its neighbour M12 (see below). Individual stars in the cluster can be resolved with telescopes of 75 mm aperture.

M12 (NGC 6218), 16h 47m −1°.9, is a 7th-mag. globular cluster 18,000 l.y. away, visible in binoculars or a small telescope. In small apertures it appears slightly larger and less easy to resolve than its neighbour M10, and its stars are more loosely scattered. There are several other globular clusters in Ophiuchus worthy of attention, but M10 and M12 are the finest.

NGC 6572, 18h 12m +6°.8, is a planetary nebula of 9th mag., visible in apertures of 75 mm or more as a tiny blue-green ellipse. It lies 2000 l.y. away.

NGC 6633, 18h 28m +6°.6, is a scattered binocular cluster of about 30 stars of 8th mag. and fainter covering an area similar to that of the full Moon. It is 950 l.y. away.

IC 4665, 17h 46m +5°.7, is a loose and irregular open cluster of two dozen or so stars of 7th mag. and fainter, 1100 l.y. away, larger than the apparent size of the Moon and best seen in binoculars.

Orion – The Hunter

Without doubt the brightest and grandest constellation of all, crammed with objects of interest for all sizes of instrument. Orion's impressiveness stems in large measure from the fact that it contains an area of star formation in a nearby arm of our Galaxy, centred on the famous Orion Nebula. The Greek poet Homer described Orion as a giant hunter, armed with an unbreakable club of solid bronze. Legend tells that the boastful Orion was stung to death by a scorpion, and was placed in the sky so that he sets at the same time as his slayer, represented by the constellation Scorpius, rises.

In the sky, Orion is depicted brandishing his club and shield at the snorting Taurus, the Bull, while the hunter's dogs (the constellations Canis Major and Canis Minor) follow at his heels, in pursuit of the hare (Lepus). The Orion Nebula, M42, marks the hunter's sword, hanging from his belt. The belt itself is formed by a distinctive line of three bright stars, while the outline of his body is picked out by α (alpha), β (beta), γ (gamma) and κ (kappa) Orionis. Orion is one of the constellations in which the star labelled α is not the brightest; that honour goes to β Orionis, better known as Rigel. Each year the Orionid meteors, caused by dust from Halley's Comet,

radiate from a point near the border with Gemini. As many as 25 Orionid meteors per hour may be seen around October 22.

α (alpha) Orionis, 5h 55m +7°.4, (Betelgeuse, corrupted from an Arabic name referring to a hand), 427 l.y. away, is a red supergiant star about 500 times the size of the Sun, so large that it is unstable. It fluctuates erratically in size, changing in brightness as it does so from mag. 0.0 to 1.3, making it the most obviously variable of all first-magnitude stars; the average brightness is around mag. 0.5, fainter than Rigel.

β (beta) Ori, 5h 15m −8°.2, (Rigel, 'foot'), at mag. 0.2 the brightest star in Orion, is a blue-white supergiant 773 l.y. away; note its colour contrast with the ruddy hue of Betelgeuse. Rigel has a mag. 6.8 companion, difficult to see in small telescopes, particularly in poor seeing, because of glare from Rigel itself.

γ (gamma) Ori, 5h 25m +6°.3, (Bellatrix, 'the female warrior'), mag. 1.6, is a blue giant star 243 l.y. away.

δ (delta) Ori, 5h 32m −0°.3, (Mintaka, 'belt'), about 2000 l.y. away, is a complex multiple star. It is a blue giant which appears of mag. 2.2 to the   ▶

Orion · Ori · Orionis

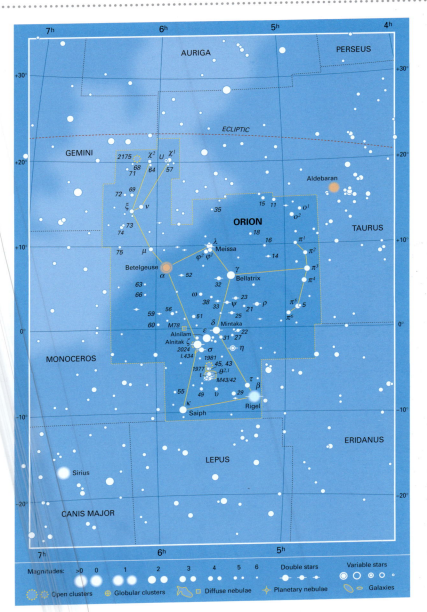

naked eye. Binoculars or small telescopes reveal a wide companion of mag. 6.9. The brighter star is also an eclipsing binary that varies by about 0.1 mag. every 5.7 days.

ε (epsilon) Ori, 5h 36m −1°.2, (Alnilam, 'the string of pearls'), mag. 1.7, is a blue supergiant about 1300 l.y. away.

ζ (zeta) Ori, 5h 41m −1°.9, (Alnitak, 'the girdle'), 820 l.y. away, is a blue supergiant that appears to the naked eye as mag. 1.7. But telescopes of 75 mm aperture and above reveal a close companion of mag. 3.9 that is estimated to orbit it every 1500 years. There is also a much wider 10th-mag. star.

η (eta) Ori, 5h 24m −2°.4, 900 l.y. away, is a complex multiple–variable. A telescope of at least 100 mm aperture at high magnification is needed to show that it consists of two close stars, of mags. 3.8 and 4.8. The brighter star is also an eclipsing binary, varying by 0.3 mag. every 8 days.

θ^1 (theta^1) Ori, 5h 35m −5°.4, about 1500 l.y. away, is a multiple star at the heart of the Orion Nebula, from which it has recently formed and which it now illuminates. This star is popularly known as the Trapezium, because a small telescope shows four stars here; but 100 mm aperture also reveals two others, of 11th mag. The four main stars of the Trapezium are of mags. 5.1, 6.7, 6.7 and 8.0. Nearby lies θ^2 (theta^2) Orionis, a binocular double of mags. 5.1 and 6.4.

ι (iota) Ori, 5h 35m −5°.9, 1300 l.y. away, is a double star on the southern edge of the Orion Nebula, divisible in a small telescope. Its components are of mags. 2.8 and 6.9. Also visible in the same field of view is a wider double of blue-white stars, Σ 747 (Struve 747), of mags. 4.8 and 5.7.

κ (kappa) Ori, 5h 48m −9°.7, (Saiph, 'sword'), mag. 2.1, is a blue supergiant 722 l.y. away.

λ (lambda) Ori, 5h 35m +9°.9, is a blue giant of mag. 3.5 with a mag. 5.6 companion visible in small telescopes under high magnification. The stars lie about 1060 l.y. away.

σ (sigma) Ori, 5h 39m −2°.6, 1150 l.y. away, is perhaps the most impressive of all Orion's stellar treasures. To the naked eye it appears as a blue-white star of mag. 3.8, but small telescopes reveal much more. On one side of the star are blue-white companions of mags. 6.8 and 6.6, the wider of which can be glimpsed in binoculars; it is an eclipsing binary with a range of about 0.1 mag. On the opposite side is a closer 9th-mag. companion, which is more difficult to see because of glare from the primary. The effect is like a planet with moons. To complete the picture, in the same telescopic field of view is a faint triple star called Σ 761 (Struve 761), consisting of a narrow triangle of 8th- and 9th-mag. stars. This is an extraordinarily rich and unexpected sight, to be returned to again and again.

U Ori, 5h 56m +20°.2, is a huge red giant variable of Mira type, many hundreds of times the diameter of the Sun, whose brightness ranges between 5th and 13th mags. in about 1 year.

M42, M43 (NGC 1976, NGC 1982), 5h 35m −5°.4, the Orion Nebula, is one of the greatest deep-sky wonders – a gigantic cloud of gas and dust, 1500 l.y. away and 20 l.y. in diameter, from which a star cluster is being born. Behind the visible part of the nebula, illuminated by the stars of the Trapezium (θ^1 Ori), radio and infrared astronomers have detected an even larger dark cloud in which more stars are forming. M42 covers an area greater than 1° × 1°, and is indisputably the finest diffuse nebula in the sky, clearly visible to the naked eye as a hazy cloud. Binoculars and small telescopes reveal some of the more prominent wreaths and swirls of gas, which become more complex and breathtaking with increasing aperture. Although colour photographs such as the one on page 268 depict the nebula as red and blue, to the eye it appears distinctly greenish; this is because the human eye has a different colour sensitivity to that of photographic film. A dark lane of dust separates M42 from M43, a smaller and rounder patch to the north that is centred on a 7th-mag. star. Although M43 has a separate catalogue number from M42, it is really part of the same huge gas cloud.

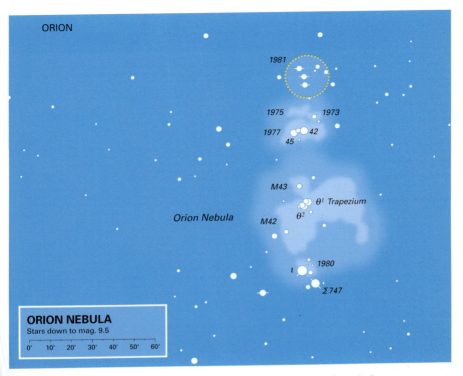

ORION

1981

1975   1973
1977
     45   42

M43
                    θ¹ Trapezium
Orion Nebula   M42   θ²

                    1980
              ι
                    Σ 747

ORION NEBULA
Stars down to mag. 9.5

0'   10'   20'   30'   40'   50'   60'

The region south of Orion's Belt known as the Sword of Orion stretches from the large open cluster NGC 1981 at the top to the double star ι (iota) Orionis at its southern tip. In between is the misty mass of the Orion Nebula. (Wil Tirion)

M78 (NGC 2068), 5h 47m +0°.0, is a small, elongated reflection nebula lying almost exactly on the celestial equator. Through small to moderate apertures it looks like a short-tailed comet, with a 10th-mag. double star at its head.

NGC 1977, 5h 36m −4°.9, 1500 l.y. away, is an elongated nebulosity just north of the Orion Nebula, centred on the mag. 4.6 blue giant star 42 Orionis, also known as c Orionis. This object would be more celebrated were it not so over-shadowed by M42.

NGC 1981, 5h 35m −4°.4, is a scattered cluster of about 20 stars of 6th mag. and fainter, 1300 l.y.

away, to the north of the nebulosity NGC 1977. Included in this cluster is the double star Σ 750 (Struve 750), a neat pair of 7th- and 8th-mag. components.

NGC 2024, 5h 41m −2°.4, is a mushroom-shaped cloud of gas about ½° wide surrounding the star ζ (zeta) Orionis. Running south from ζ Ori is a strip of nebulosity, IC 434, into which is indented the celebrated Horsehead Nebula, a dark cloud of obscuring dust shaped like a horse's head (see the photograph on page 270). Although long-exposure photographs show NGC 2024 and the Horsehead Nebula well, they are notoriously difficult to detect with amateur telescopes.

Pavo – The Peacock

A constellation introduced at the end of the 16th century by the Dutch navigators Pieter Dirkszoon Keyser and Frederick de Houtman. It is one of several celestial birds in this region, including Apus, Tucana, Grus and Phoenix. In Greek mythology the peacock was sacred to Hera, goddess of the heavens, from whose breast the Milky Way sprang. Hera set a creature with a hundred eyes called Argos to watch over a white heifer, into which she guessed her husband Zeus had turned one of his illicit lovers, the nymph Io. At the request of Zeus, Hermes slew the watchful Argos and released the heifer. Hera placed the hundred eyes of Argos on the peacock's tail.

α (alpha) Pavonis, 20h 26m −56°.7, (Peacock), mag. 1.9, is a blue-white star 183 l.y. away.

β (beta) Pav, 20h 45m −66°.2, mag. 3.4, is a white star 138 l.y. away.

δ (delta) Pav, 20h 09m −66°.2, mag. 3.6, is a yellow star 20 l.y. away.

η (eta) Pav, 17h 46m −64°.7, mag. 3.6, is an orange giant 371 l.y. away.

κ (kappa) Pav, 18h 57m −67°.2, 544 l.y. away, is one of the brightest Cepheid variables. It is a yellow-white supergiant, varying between mags. 3.9 and 4.8 in 9.1 days.

ξ (xi) Pav, 18h 23m −61°.5, 420 l.y. away, is a red giant of mag. 4.4 with a close companion of mag. 8.6, lost in the primary's glare in small telescopes.

SX Pav, 21h 29m −69°.5, 396 l.y. away, is a red giant that varies semi-regularly between mags. 5.3 and 6.0 every 7 weeks or so.

NGC 6744, 19h 10m −63°.9, is a 9th-mag. spiral galaxy for small telescopes, with a short central bar and widespread arms, as seen in the photograph below. It is one of the largest barred spirals, but its outer regions are faint and in modest apertures only the brightest central portion will be seen. It is about 30 million l.y. away.

NGC 6752, 19h 11m −60°.0, is a large 6th-mag. globular cluster, visible in binoculars and resolvable in 75-mm telescopes, covering half the apparent diameter of the Moon. A double star of 8th and 9th mags. at one edge is a foreground object. The cluster lies 15,000 l.y. away.

NGC 6744, a beautiful face-on spiral galaxy with a short central bar. Our own Milky Way, which is also thought to have a small central bar, might look much like this if seen from outside (M. Bessell, R. Sutherland and M. Buxton, RSAA – Australian National University)

Pavo · Pav · Pavonis

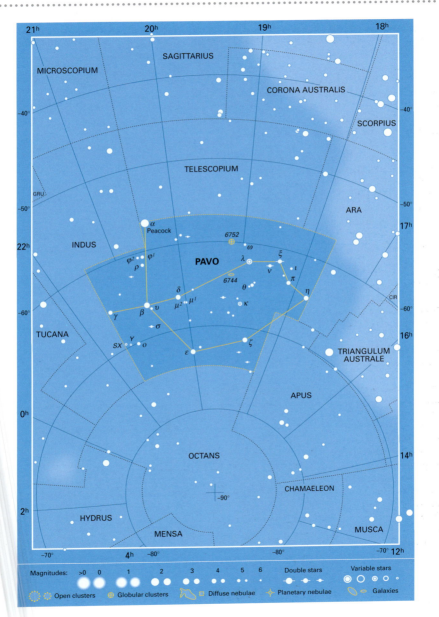

Pegasus

· ·

An ancient constellation representing the winged horse of Greek mythology, born from the blood of Medusa after she was slain by the hero Perseus, who lies nearby in the sky. Only the front half of the horse is shown. Its body is represented by the constellation's most famous feature, the Great Square, the corners of which are marked by four stars. One of these stars, once known as δ (delta) Pegasi, is now assigned to Andromeda. The Great Square of Pegasus is over 15° wide and 13° high, yet contains surprisingly few naked-eye stars for such a large area. The brightest of them are: υ (upsilon), mag. 4.4; τ (tau), mag. 4.6; ψ (psi), mag. 4.6; 56, mag. 4.8; φ (phi), mag. 5.1; 71, mag. 5.3; and 75, mag. 5.5.

α (alpha) Pegasi, 23h 05m +15°.2, (Markab, 'shoulder'), mag. 2.5, is a blue-white giant star 140 l.y. away.

β (beta) Peg, 23h 04m +28°.1, (Scheat, 'shin'), 199 l.y. away, is a red giant that varies from mag. 2.3 to 2.7 with no definite period.

γ (gamma) Peg, 0h 13m +15°.2, (Algenib, 'the side'), mag. 2.8, is a blue-white star 333 l.y. away. It is a pulsating variable of the β Cephei type, but its fluctuations every 3 hours 40 minutes are only 0.1 mag., too slight to be discernible with the naked eye.

ε (epsilon) Peg, 21h 44m +9°.9, (Enif, 'nose'), 670 l.y. away, is an orange supergiant of mag. 2.4. A small telescope, or even good binoculars, reveals a wide bluish mag. 8.4 companion star. Larger telescopes also show an 11th-mag. companion closer to ε Peg, making this an apparent triple system. ε Peg is catalogued as variable because of two

unexplained fluctuations: one night in November 1847 it was seen about a magnitude fainter than normal, while on a night in September 1972 it was seen at about magnitude 0.7 for four minutes before fading back to normal.

ζ (zeta) Peg, 22h 41m +10°.8, (Homam), mag. 3.4, is a blue-white star 209 l.y. away.

η (eta) Peg, 22h 43m +30°.2, (Matar), mag. 2.9, is a yellow giant 215 l.y. away.

π (pi) Peg, 22h 10m +33°.2, is a very wide binocular duo of white and yellow stars, both giants. They are of mags. 4.3 and 5.6, and lie 252 and 283 l.y. away respectively.

51 Peg, 22h 57m +20°.8, mag. 5.5, is a yellow main-sequence star 50 l.y. away, similar to the Sun. In 1995 it became the first star other than the Sun known to have a planet orbiting it; the planet's estimated mass is about half that of Jupiter.

M15 (NGC 7078), 21h 30m +12°.2, is an outstanding 6th-mag. globular cluster, 33,000 l.y. distant, at the limit of naked-eye visibility but easily seen in binoculars; a 6th-mag. star nearby is a sure guide to its location. A small telescope shows it as a glorious misty sight in an attractive field. Apertures of 150 mm or so resolve its outer regions into a mottled ground of sparkling stars, and larger telescopes show stars all the way to the bright and condensed core.

NGC 7331, 22h 37m +34°.4, is a 10th-mag. spiral galaxy seen nearly edge-on, visible under good conditions in apertures of 100 mm or so as an elongated smudge. It lies about 50 million l.y. away.

Pegasus · Peg · Pegasi

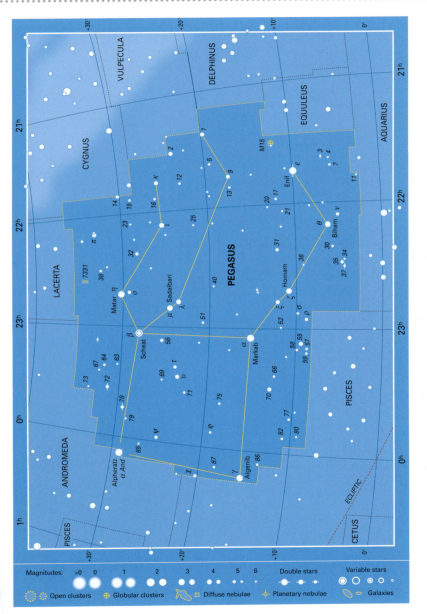

Perseus

Perseus was the hero of Greek mythology who rescued the chained maiden Andromeda from the clutches of the sea monster Cetus. Prior to that, Perseus had slain Medusa the Gorgon, whose head he is pictured holding in one hand. The Gorgon's head is marked by the winking star Algol, or β (beta) Persei, sometimes imagined as Medusa's evil eye.

Perseus lies in a rich part of the Milky Way and is well worth sweeping with binoculars; note, in particular, the Double Cluster, a sparkling pair of open clusters near the border with Cassiopeia. In 1901 Nova Persei flared up to mag. 0.2 at 3h 31.2m, +43° 54', throwing off a shell of gas that is now visible in large telescopes. NGC 1499, the California Nebula, so named because its shape resembles California, spans the apparent width of five full Moons north of 4th-mag. ξ (xi) Persei, an exceedingly hot blue giant or supergiant which illuminates it. Despite its considerable size the California Nebula is elusive visually, but shows up well on long-exposure photographs.

At 3h 19.8m, +41° 31', lies the radio source Perseus A, associated with the 12th-mag. peculiar galaxy NGC 1275, which is at the centre of the Perseus cluster of galaxies, 250 million l.y. away. Near γ (gamma) Persei lies the radiant of the Perseid meteors, the most glorious meteor shower of the year: around August 12–13 as many as 75 bright meteors can be seen flashing from Perseus each hour.

α (alpha) Persei, 3h 24m +49°.9, (Mirphak, 'elbow', or Algenib, 'the side'), mag. 1.8, is a yellow-white supergiant 592 l.y. away. Binoculars reveal a brilliant scattering of stars covering 3° in this region forming a loose cluster, Melotte 20. α Per itself seems to form the head of a snaking chain of stars within this cluster.

β (beta) Per, 3h 08m +41°.0, (Algol, 'the demon'), 93 l.y. away, is one of the most celebrated variable stars in the sky. It is the prototype of the eclipsing binary class of variables, in which two close stars periodically eclipse each other as they orbit their common centre of gravity. Algol's eclipses occur every 2.87 days, when the star's apparent brightness sinks from mag. 2.1 to 3.4 before returning to normal about 10 hours later.

γ (gamma) Per, 3h 05m +53°.5, mag. 2.9, is a yellow giant 256 l.y. away. It is an eclipsing binary with the unusually long period of 14.6 years, dimming by 0.3 mag. for 10 days. This star's variability was first detected in 1990.

δ (delta) Per, 3h 43m +47°.8, mag. 3.0, is a blue giant 528 l.y. away.

ε (epsilon) Per, 3h 58m +40°.0, 538 l.y. away, is a blue-white star of mag. 2.9 with an unrelated mag. 7.6 companion which is difficult to see through the smallest telescopes because of the brightness contrast.

ζ (zeta) Per, 3h 54m +31°.9, 980 l.y. away, is a blue supergiant of mag. 2.9 with a mag. 9.5 companion visible in a small telescope. ▶

M34 is an attractive open cluster for binoculars and small telescopes. Its brightest stars are of 8th magnitude. (Peter Wienerroither)

Perseus · Per · Persei

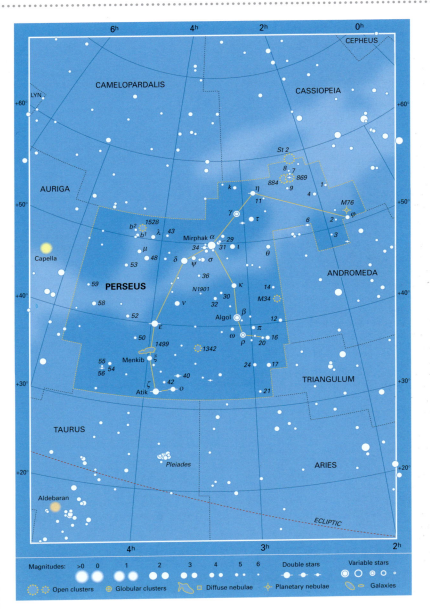

Magnitudes: >0 0 1 2 3 4 5 6   Double stars   Variable stars

○ Open clusters ⊕ Globular clusters ⌂ Diffuse nebulae ✦ Planetary nebulae ⬭ Galaxies η (eta) Per, 2h 51m +55°.9, about 1300 l.y. away, is an orange supergiant of mag. 3.8 with a mag. 8.5 blue companion that forms an attractive double for small telescopes. The field of view contains a sprinkling of background stars.

ρ (rho) Per, 3h 05m +38°.8, 325 l.y. away, is a red giant that varies between mags. 3.3 and 4.0 in semi-regular fashion every 7 weeks or so.

M34 (NGC 1039), 2h 42m +42°.8, is a bright open cluster at the limit of naked-eye visibility, containing about 60 stars splashed over an area larger than the apparent size of the full Moon. Binoculars resolve it into stars, and it is well seen in a small telescope, many of the stars seeming to form pairs. M34 lies about 1500 l.y. away.

M76 (NGC 650–1), 1h 42m +51°.6, the Little Dumbbell, is a planetary nebula, the faintest object on Charles Messier's famous list of deep-sky objects. At about magnitude 10 it is difficult to see, although it can be picked up in 100 mm apertures on a dark night. It is relatively large for a planetary nebula, similar in size to the Ring Nebula in Lyra, but smaller than its namesake the

Dumbbell Nebula in Vulpecula, the elongated shape of which it resembles. Each end of the Little Dumbbell has a separate NGC number. It lies about 3500 l.y. away.

NGC 869, NGC 884, 2h 19m +57°.2, 2h 22m +57°.1, the famous Double Cluster in Perseus, also known as h and χ (chi) Persei. They are two open star clusters visible to the naked eye and superb in binoculars, each covering an area equal to the full Moon. NGC 869 is the brighter and richer of the pair, containing an estimated 200 stars, while NGC 884 appears more scattered. They both lie about 7500 l.y. away and are relatively young, only a few million years old. Small telescopes have an advantage when observing these objects, for at low powers both clusters fit into the same field of view, which is not always the case with larger and more powerful telescopes. Most of the stars in the clusters are blue-white, but there are several red giants to be spotted in and around NGC 884. In binoculars, note a curving chain of stars leading northwards towards a large starry patch known as the cluster Stock 2 (abbreviated St 2). This whole area is a breathtaking sight in all apertures. (For a photograph of the Double Cluster, see page 274.)

Phoenix – The Phoenix

An inconspicuous constellation near the southern end of Eridanus, representing the mythical bird that was regularly reborn from its own ashes. It was introduced at the end of the 16th century by the Dutch navigators Pieter Dirkszoon Keyser and Frederick de Houtman in an area that had been known by the Arabs as the Boat, moored on the bank of the river Eridanus.

α (alpha) Phoenicis, 0h 26m −42°.3, (Ankaa), mag. 2.4, is an orange giant star 77 l.y. away.

β (beta) Phe, 1h 06m −46°.7, 185 l.y. away, appears to the naked eye as a yellow star of mag.

3.3. In fact, it is a close double with well-matched components of mags. 4.0 and 4.2, currently too close for resolution in small telescopes.

γ (gamma) Phe, 1h 28m −43°.6, mag. 3.4, is an orange giant 234 l.y. away.

ζ (zeta) Phe, 1h 08m −55°.2, 280 l.y. away, is a complex variable and multiple star. The main star is a blue-white eclipsing binary of the same type as Algol that rises and falls between mags. 3.9 and 4.4 every 1.67 days. It has a companion of 8th mag. visible in a small telescope. There is also a much closer 7th-mag. companion visible only in large apertures.

Phoenix · Phe · Phoenicis

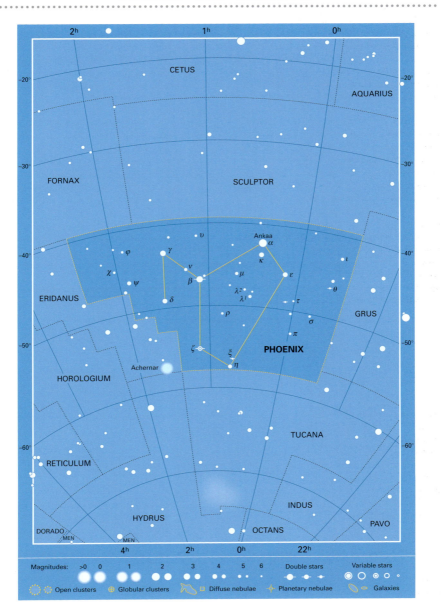

Pictor – The Painter's Easel

A faint constellation overshadowed by the neighbouring brilliant star Canopus in Carina on one side and the Large Magellanic Cloud in Dorado on the other. The constellation was invented in the 1750s by Nicolas Louis de Lacaille, who originally called it Equuleus Pictorius, which has since been shortened. At 5h 11.7m, −45° 01′ lies the mag. 8.9 red dwarf known as Kapteyn's Star, 12.8 l.y. away, named after the Dutch astronomer who discovered in 1897 that it has the second-largest proper motion of any known star (the record is held by Barnard's Star in Ophiuchus). Kapteyn's Star moves 1° in 415 years; see illustration below.

α (alpha) Pictoris, 6h 48m −61°.9, mag. 3.2, is a white star 99 l.y. away.

β (beta) Pic, 5h 47m −51°.1, mag. 3.9, is a blue-white main-sequence star 63 l.y. away. This star became famous in 1984 when astronomers photographed a disk of dust and gas around it, thought to be a planetary system in the process of formation. (See also page 307.)

γ (gamma) Pic, 5h 50m −56°.2, mag. 4.5, is an orange giant 174 l.y. away.

δ (delta) Pic, 6h 10m −55°.0, is a blue-white star about 1700 l.y. away. It is an eclipsing binary of the β (beta) Lyrae type, varying from mag. 4.7 to 4.9 every 1.67 days.

ι (iota) Pic, 4h 51m −53°.5, 120 l.y. away, is an easy double of mags. 5.6 and 6.4 for small telescopes.

Chart showing the proper motion of Kapteyn's Star over a period of 200 years, during which it crosses almost one Moon's width of sky. (Wil Tirion)

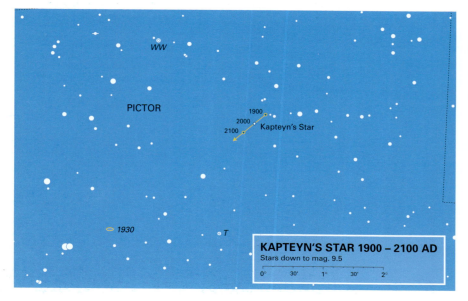

Pictor · Pic · Pictoris

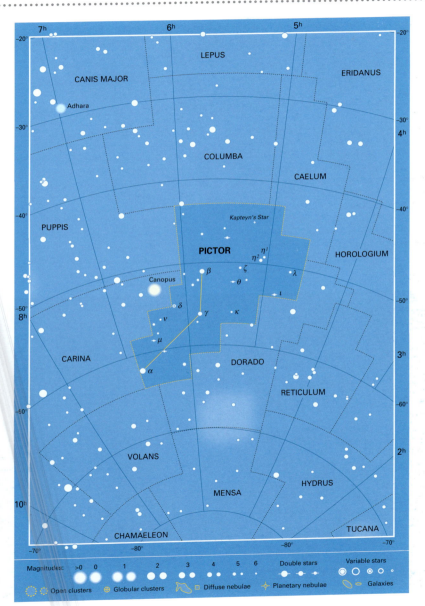

Pisces – The Fishes

An ancient constellation representing two fishes with their tails tied together by cords; the knot where the two cords join is marked by the star α (alpha) Piscium. One legend identifies the constellation with Aphrodite and her son Eros, who swam away from the attack of the monster Typhon in the guise of fishes.

The Sun is in Pisces from mid-March to late April, so the constellation contains the March (or *vernal*) equinox – the point at which the Sun crosses the celestial equator into the northern celestial hemisphere each year. This point originally lay in neighbouring Aries, but the effect of precession has now carried it into Pisces; eventually, in AD 2597, it will pass on into Aquarius. The constellation's most distinctive feature is a ring of seven stars called the Circlet, marking the body of one of the fish; clockwise from

north the seven stars are θ (theta), 7, γ (gamma), κ (kappa), λ (lambda), TX (or 19) and ι (iota) Piscium.

α (alpha) Piscium, 2h 02m +2°.8, (Alrescha, 'the cord'), 139 l.y. away, appears to the naked eye as a star of mag. 3.8, but in fact is a challenging double with an orbital period of over 900 years. Its components, of mags. 4.2 and 5.2, are gradually closing but will remain within range of 100-mm aperture telescopes for at least the first half of the 21st century. The brighter star is a spectroscopic binary, and the fainter one may be also. Their colour is bluish-white, although some observers see the brighter star as greenish. ▶

M74 in Pisces is a beautiful face-on spiral galaxy with loosely wound arms. See page 212. (Paul Vreeswijk and Nik Szymanek)

Pisces · Psc · Piscium

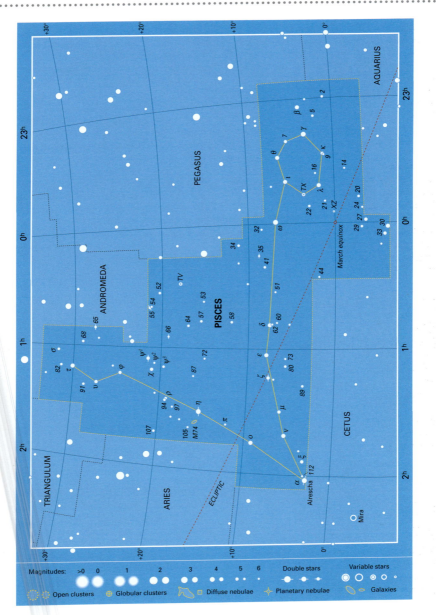

β (beta) Psc, 23h 04m +3°.6, mag. 4.5, is a blue-white star 493 l.y. away.

γ (gamma) Psc, 23h 17m +3°.3, mag. 3.7, is a yellow giant 131 l.y. away.

ζ (zeta) Psc, 1h 14m +7°.6, 148 l.y. away, is a wide double of mags. 5.2 and 6.4, divisible in the smallest telescopes.

η (eta) Psc, 1h 31m +15°.3, mag. 3.6, is the brightest star in the constellation. It is a yellow giant, 294 l.y. away.

κ (kappa) Psc, 23h 27m +1°.3, mag. 4.9, is a blue-white star 162 l.y. away. It forms a wide binocular double with 9 Piscium, mag. 6.3, actually a background star.

ρ (rho) Psc, 1h 26m +19°.2, mag. 5.3, is a white star 85 l.y. away that forms an easy binocular duo with the unrelated orange giant 94 Piscium, mag. 5.5, 307 l.y. away.

ψ¹ (psi¹) Psc, 1h 06m +21°.5, is a wide pair of blue-white stars of mags. 5.3 and 5.6 about 230 l.y. away, visible in small telescopes or even good binoculars.

TV Psc, 0h 28m +17°.9, 490 l.y. away, is a red giant that varies semi-regularly between mags. 4.7 and 5.4 every 7 weeks.

TX Psc, 23h 46m +3°.5, also known as 19 Psc, 760 l.y. away, is a deep-red irregular variable star in the Circlet of Pisces, visible with the naked eye or binoculars. It fluctuates between about mags. 4.8 and 5.2.

M74 (NGC 628), 1h 37m +15°.8, is a spiral galaxy of 9th mag., presented face-on to us. In dark conditions it can be glimpsed through a small telescope as a pale disk with a starlike nucleus and faint foreground stars dotted across it, but it needs an aperture of at least 150 mm to be well seen. M74 lies some 30 million l.y. away. (See the photograph on page 210.)

Piscis Austrinus – The Southern Fish

This constellation has been known since ancient times and is visualized as a fish lying on its back, drinking the stream of water flowing southwards from the urn of neighbouring Aquarius. It mouth is marked by the bright star Fomalhaut. This fish was said to be the parent of the two smaller zodiacal fishes, represented by Pisces.

α (alpha) Piscis Austrini, 22h 58m −29°.6, (Fomalhaut, 'the fish's mouth'), mag. 1.2, is a blue-white main-sequence star 25 l.y. away. It is surrounded by a disk of cool dust from which a planetary system may be forming.

β (beta) PsA, 22h 32m −32°.3, 148 l.y. away, is a wide double star consisting of a mag. 4.3 blue-white primary and a mag. 7.7 companion visible in small telescopes.

γ (gamma) PsA, 22h 53m −32°.9, 222 l.y. away, is a double star of mags. 4.5 and 8.0, made difficult to split in small telescopes by the magnitude contrast.

η (eta) PsA, 22h 01m −28°.5, 1000 l.y. away, is a close pair of blue-white stars of mags. 5.8 and 6.8, divisible with an aperture of 100 mm and high magnification.

Piscis Austrinus · PsA · Piscis Austrini

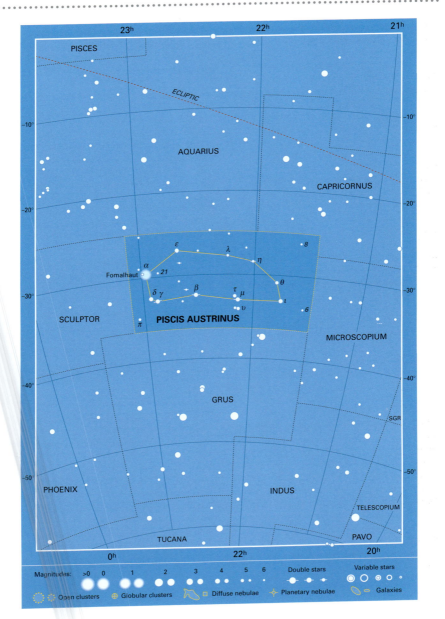

PISCES

23ʰ   22ʰ   21ʰ

ECLIPTIC

-10°

AQUARIUS

CAPRICORNUS

-20°

8

ε   λ

α   η

Fomalhaut   21   θ

-30°   δ γ   β   τ μ   ι

υ   6

π   **PISCIS AUSTRINUS**

SCULPTOR   MICROSCOPIUM

SGR

-40°   GRUS

-50°   INDUS

TELESCOPIUM

PHOENIX   PAVO

TUCANA

0ʰ   22ʰ   20ʰ

Magnitudes: >0 0 1 2 3 4 5 6   Double stars   Variable stars

Open clusters   Globular clusters   Diffuse nebulae   Planetary nebulae   Galaxies

Puppis – The Stern

This is the largest of the three sections into which the ancient constellation of Argo Navis, the ship of the Argonauts, was dismembered in 1763 by Nicolas Louis de Lacaille; the other sections are Carina and Vela. When Argo Navis was split up its stars retained their existing Greek letters, and it so happens that the labelling of the stars assigned to Puppis begins with ζ (zeta). Puppis lies in the Milky Way and contains rich starfields for sweeping with binoculars.

ζ (zeta) Puppis, 8h 04m −40°.0, (Naos, 'ship'), mag. 2.2, is a brilliant blue supergiant about 1400 l.y. away, the hottest (and hence bluest) of all naked-eye stars, with a surface temperature of about 40,000°C.

ξ (xi) Pup, 7h 49m −24°.9, mag. 3.3, is a yellow supergiant about 1350 l.y. away. Binoculars reveal a wide, unrelated mag. 5.3 yellow companion, 321 l.y. away.

π (pi) Pup, 7h 17m −37°.1, mag. 2.7, is an orange supergiant 1100 l.y. away.

ρ (rho) Pup, 8h 08m −24°.3, mag. 2.8, is a yellow-white star 63 l.y. away. It is a variable of the δ (delta) Scuti type, fluctuating by 0.2 mag. with a period of 3 hours 23 minutes.

k Pup, 7h 39m −26°.8, 454 l.y. away, is a striking double star with blue-white components of mags. 4.5 and 4.6 easily divisible in small telescopes.

L¹ L² Pup, 7h 13m −45°.2, is an optical double consisting of two unrelated and contrasting stars. L¹ is mag. 4.9, a blue-white star 182 l.y. away. L² is a red giant semi-regular variable, 198 l.y. away, that fluctuates between 3rd and 6th mags. every 140 days or so.

V Pup, 7h 58m −49°.2, is an eclipsing binary of the β (beta) Lyrae type, about 1200 l.y. away. It varies from mag. 4.4 to 4.9 with a period of 35 hours.

M46 (NGC 2437), 7h 42m −14°.8, is a 6th-mag. open cluster of about 100 faint stars of remarkably uniform brightness, most of them around 10th mag. With its neighbour M47 it is visible to the naked eye as a brighter knot in the Milky Way. In binoculars it appears as a smudgy patch two-thirds the size of the full Moon, while a small telescope shows it as a sprinkling of stardust. M46 lies 5200 l.y. away. On its northern edge lies the 10th-mag. planetary nebula NGC 2438. This is not a member of the cluster, but is a foreground object about 3000 l.y. from us.

M47 (NGC 2422), 7h 37m −14°.5, is a scattered naked-eye cluster of similar apparent size to the full Moon. It contains three dozen or so stars, the brightest being of mag. 5.7. M47 lies about 1500 l.y. away, less than one-third the distance of its richer neighbour M46.

M93 (NGC 2447), 7h 45m −23°.9, is a 6th-mag. binocular cluster, 3600 l.y. away, consisting of 80 stars of 8th mag. and fainter, arranged in a wedge-shape.

NGC 2451, 7h 45m −38°.0, is a large and bright open cluster of 40 stars 1050 l.y. away, well seen in binoculars, centred on the mag. 3.6 orange giant c Puppis.

NGC 2477, 7h 52m −38°.5, is a large 6th-mag. open cluster consisting of a swarm of faint stars, looking in binoculars like a loose globular, seemingly with arms. This excellent object would undoubtedly have featured on Messier's list had he lived farther south. It lies 4000 l.y. away.

Puppis · Pup · Puppis

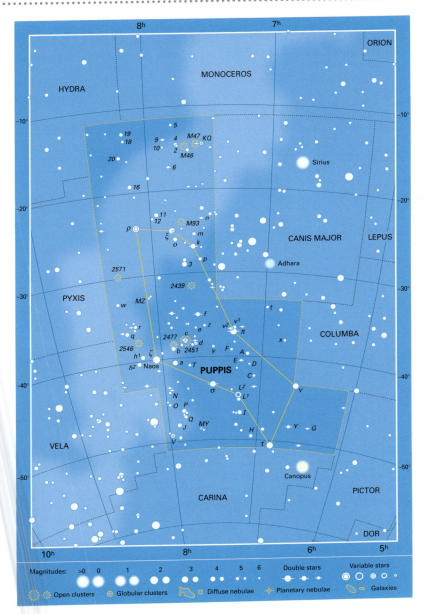

Magnitudes: >0   0   1   2   3   4   5   6   Double stars   Variable stars

Open clusters   Globular clusters   Diffuse nebulae   Planetary nebulae   Galaxies

Pyxis – The Compass

A small, faint constellation invented by Nicolas Louis de Lacaille in the 1750s, representing a magnetic compass as used by sailors. It lies near Puppis, the stern of the Argonauts' ship, and was formed from stars that Ptolemy had catalogued as being part of the mast of Argo; but that ship, of course, would not have had a magnetic compass, so Pyxis cannot really be considered a genuine part of the old Argo. This area has also been known as Malus, the mast of Argo, a suggestion made in 1844 by the English astronomer John Herschel, although it was not widely adopted. The German astronomer Johann Bode introduced an additional constellation here called Lochium Funis, the log and line, representing a device used for measuring distance travelled at sea, which he visualized as curving around the compass.

Pyxis contains no objects of particular interest to users of small telescopes, despite the fact that it lies in the Milky Way, and its brightest stars are only of 4th magnitude.

α (alpha) Pyxidis, 8h 44m −33°.2, mag. 3.7, is a blue giant star 845 l.y. away.

β (beta) Pyx, 8h 40m −35°.3, mag. 4.0, is a yellow giant 388 l.y. away.

γ (gamma) Pyx, 8h 51m −27°.7, mag. 4.0, is an orange giant 209 l.y. away.

T Pyx, 9h 05m −32°.4, is a recurrent nova that has undergone five recorded eruptions, in 1890, 1902, 1920, 1944 and 1966. Normally it is of mag. 14, but brightens to 6th or 7th magnitude. Further outbursts may be expected.

Nicolas Louis de Lacaille (1713–1762)

Lacaille, a French astronomer, was the first person to map the southern skies comprehensively, as a result of which he became known as the Father of Southern Astronomy. He directed an expedition of the French Academy of Sciences to the Cape of Good Hope in 1750–54, where he systematically surveyed the southern celestial hemisphere, listing nearly 10,000 stars. The accurate positions of 2000 of these, along with a star map, were published posthumously in 1763 under the title *Coelum Australe Stelliferum*. Lacaille is usually best remembered for the 14 new constellations he introduced, representing instruments used in science and the fine arts: Antlia, Caelum,

Circinus, Fornax, Horologium, Mensa, Microscopium, Norma, Octans, Pictor, Pyxis, Reticulum, Sculptor and Telescopium. Lacaille also dismantled one constellation, Robur Carolinum, Charles's Oak; this had been formed in 1678 by the English astronomer Edmond Halley from some of the stars of Argo Navis to commemorate the oak tree in which his patron, King Charles II, hid after his defeat by Oliver Cromwell at the Battle of Worcester. It is said that this inspired piece of flattery earned Halley his master's degree from Oxford by the king's express command. Lacaille, less impressed, uprooted the oak and returned its stars to Argo Navis.

Pyxis · Pyx · Pyxidis

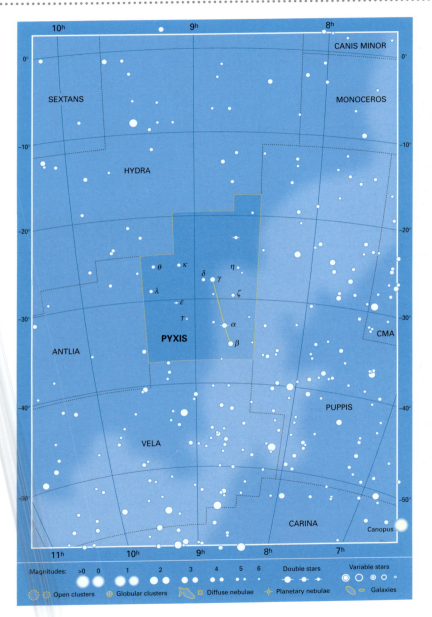

CANIS MINOR

SEXTANS

MONOCEROS

HYDRA

θ   κ   η
δ   γ
λ   ζ
ε
τ
α
PYXIS   β

ANTLIA

CMA

PUPPIS

VELA

CARINA

Canopus

Magnitudes: >0   0   1   2   3   4   5   6   Double stars   Variable stars

Open clusters   Globular clusters   Diffuse nebulae   Planetary nebulae   Galaxies

Reticulum – The Net

A constellation introduced in the 1750s by the French astronomer Nicolas Louis de Lacaille to commemorate a grid-like device in his telescope's eyepiece known as a reticle, which assisted him in measuring star positions during his surveys of the southern sky. The reticle was formed by silk threads and was diamond-shaped, like the constellation. Reticulum lies near the Large Magellanic Cloud, but is not prominent.

α (alpha) Reticuli, 4h 14m −62°.5, mag. 3.3, is a yellow giant star 163 l.y. away.

β (beta) Ret, 3h 44m −64°.8, mag. 3.8, is an orange star 100 l.y. away.

ζ^1 ζ^2 (zeta¹ zeta²) Ret, 3h 18m −62°.5, 39 l.y. away, is a wide naked-eye or binocular double of near-identical yellow main-sequence stars similar to the Sun, of mags. 5.5 and 5.2 respectively.

Across the border of Reticulum in neighbouring Dorado lies this attractive 10th-mag. spiral galaxy, NGC 1566. It is a type known as a Seyfert galaxy, with a bright, variable centre. It is the brightest member of a small cluster of over two dozen galaxies nearly 70 million l.y. away. (SAAO)

Reticulum · Ret · Reticuli

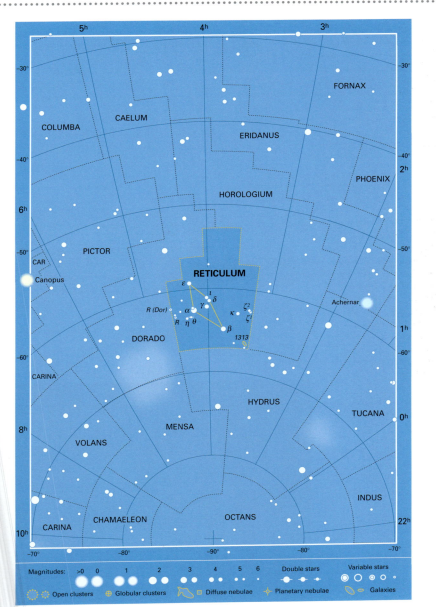

Magnitudes: >0   0   1   2   3   4   5   6   Double stars   Variable stars

Open clusters   Globular clusters   Diffuse nebulae   Planetary nebulae   Galaxies

Sagitta – The Arrow

Despite its diminutive size – it is the third-smallest constellation – this arrow-shaped group is distinctive enough to have been recognized by the ancient Greeks. In the sky, the Arrow seems to be flying between Cygnus the Swan and Aquila the Eagle; in one legend, the arrow was shot by Hercules, although it has also been seen as the arrow of Apollo or Eros, the god of love. Like its northerly neighbour Vulpecula, Sagitta lies in a rich part of the Milky Way.

α (alpha) Sagittae, 19h 40m +18°.0, mag. 4.4, is a yellow giant 473 l.y. away.

β (beta) Sge, 19h 41m +17°.5, mag. 4.4, is a yellow giant 467 l.y. away.

γ (gamma) Sge, 19h 59m +19°.5, mag. 3.5, the brightest star in the constellation, is an orange giant 274 l.y. away.

δ (delta) Sge, 19h 47m +18°.5, mag. 3.7, is a red giant 448 l.y. away.

ζ (zeta) Sge, 19h 49m +19°.1, 326 l.y. away, is a blue-white star of mag. 5.0 with a 9th-mag. companion, divisible in a small telescope.

S Sge, 19h 56m +16°.6, is a yellow supergiant Cepheid variable, ranging between mag. 5.2 and 6.0 in 8.4 days.

VZ Sge, 20h 00m +17°.5, 746 l.y. away, is a pulsating red giant that varies irregularly between mags. 5.3 and 5.6.

WZ Sge, 20h 08m +17°.7, is a so-called dwarf nova that flared up from 15th mag. to 7th or 8th mag. in 1913, 1946, 1978 and 2001; its location is worth checking in case of another outburst.

M71 (NGC 6838), 19h 54m +18°.6, is an 8th-mag. globular cluster 13,000 l.y. away, visible as a small, somewhat elongated misty patch in binoculars or a small telescope and resolvable with 100 mm aperture. Its stars are scattered and it lacks a central condensation, so it looks more like a dense open cluster than a typical globular.

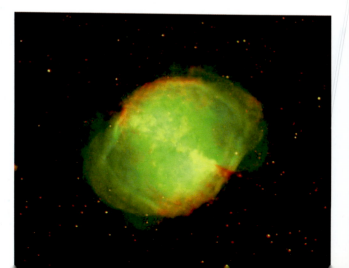

Just north of Sagitta's border, in neighbouring Vulpecula, lies the Dumbbell Nebula, M27, a shell of gas thrown off by a dying star. It is visible in binoculars and small telescopes. See page 262. (From The IAC Morphological Catalog of Northern Galactic Planetary Nebulae, by A. Manchado, M.A. Guerrero, L. Stanghellini and M. Serra-Ricart/IAC)

Sagitta · Sge · Sagittae

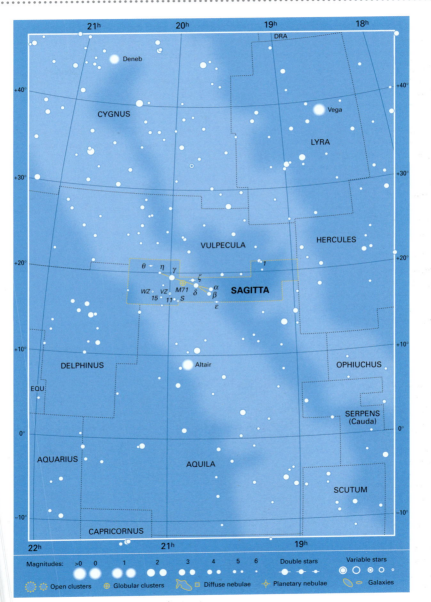

Sagittarius – The Archer

An ancient constellation depicting a centaur, a creature half man, half beast, with a raised bow and arrow. It is an older constellation than the other celestial centaur, Centaurus, and is different in character. Whereas Centaurus is identified as a scholarly, beneficent creature, Sagittarius is depicted with a threatening look, aiming his arrow at the heart of Scorpius, the Scorpion. The bow is marked by the stars λ (lambda), δ (delta) and ε (epsilon) Sagittarii, while γ (gamma) is the tip of the arrow. The shape outlined by the eight main stars of Sagittarius is popularly referred to as the Teapot, while λ (lambda), φ (phi), σ (sigma), τ (tau) and ζ (zeta) Sagittarii form a ladle shape known as the Milk Dipper – a suitable implement to dip into this rich region of the Milky Way.

The centre of our Galaxy lies in Sagittarius, so the Milky Way starfields are particularly rich here, as well as in neighbouring Scutum and Scorpius. The actual centre of the Galaxy is marked by a radio and infrared source known as Sagittarius A, at 17h 46.1m, −28° 51′. The main attraction of Sagittarius is its clusters and nebulae. Charles Messier catalogued a total of 15 objects in Sagittarius, more than in any other constellation; only a selection of them can be mentioned here. The Sun passes through the constellation from mid-December to mid-January, and thus lies in Sagittarius at the December solstice, its farthest point south of the equator.

α (alpha) Sagittarii, 19h 24m −40°.6, (Rukbat, 'knee', or Alrami, 'the archer'), mag. 4.0, is one of several instances in which the star labelled α in a constellation is not the brightest. It is a blue-white main-sequence star 170 l.y. away.

β¹ β² (beta¹ beta²) Sgr, 19h 23m −44°.5, (Arkab, from the Arabic for 'Achilles tendon'), is a pair of unrelated naked-eye stars. β¹ Sgr, a blue-white star of mag. 4.0, 378 l.y. away, has a mag. 7.2 companion visible in a small telescope. β² Sgr is a white star of mag. 4.3, 139 l.y. away. All three stars appear in the same line of sight by chance.

γ (gamma) Sgr, 18h 06m −30°.4, (Alnasl, 'the point', i.e. of the arrow), mag. 3.0, is an orange giant 96 l.y. away.

δ (delta) Sgr, 18h 21m −29°.8, (Kaus Media, 'middle of the bow'), mag. 2.7, is an orange giant 306 l.y. away.

ε (epsilon) Sgr, 18h 24m −34°.4, (Kaus Australis, 'southern part of the bow'), mag. 1.8, is the brightest star in Sagittarius. It is a blue-white giant 145 l.y. away.

λ (lambda) Sgr, 18h 28m −25°.4, (Kaus Borealis, 'northern part of the bow'), mag. 2.8, is an orange giant 77 l.y. away.

σ (sigma) Sgr, 18h 55m −26°.3, (Nunki), mag. 2.1, is a blue-white star 224 l.y. away.

W Sgr, 18h 05m −29°.6, is a yellow supergiant Cepheid variable ranging between mags. 4.3 and 5.1 with a period of 7.6 days. It lies about 2100 l.y. away.

X Sgr, 17h 48m −27°.8, is a yellow-white giant Cepheid variable ranging between mags. 4.2 and 4.9 in 7 days. It lies about 1100 l.y. away.

Y Sgr, 18h 21m −18°.9, is a yellow-white giant Cepheid that varies between mags. 5.3 and 6.2 in 5.8 days. It lies about 1300 l.y. away.

RR Sgr, 19h 56m −29°.2, is a red giant variable of Mira type, with a range from mag. 5.4 to 14.0 and a period of about 11 months. Its distance is too great to measure accurately.

RY Sgr, 19h 17m −33°.5, is the southern equivalent of R Coronae Borealis – a star like a reverse nova that normally shines at around 6th ▶

Sagittarius · Sgr · Sagittarii

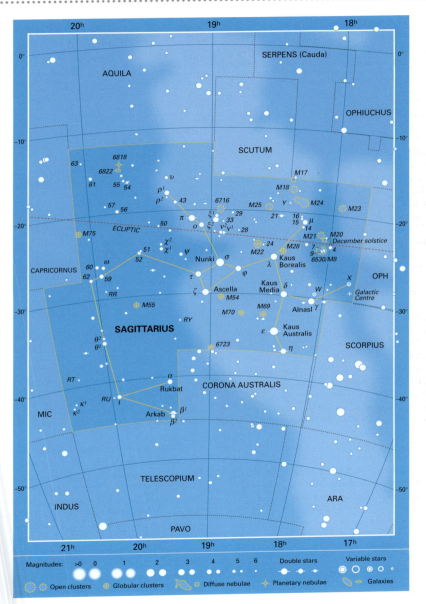

Among the Milky Way starfields of Sagittarius are two outstanding nebulae: M20, the Trifid Nebula (top), and M8, the Lagoon Nebula. The Trifid consists of a pink emission nebula and a blue reflection nebula. (Nik Szymanek)

mag., but which can suddenly and unpredictably drop to 14th mag.

M8 (NGC 6523), 18h 04m −24°.4, the Lagoon Nebula, is a famous gaseous nebula, visible to the naked eye, elongated in shape and encompassing the star cluster NGC 6530. M8 is a fine object for binoculars or telescopes, covering the area of three full Moons, with a dark rift down its centre. In the eastern half of the nebula is NGC 6530, a cluster of about 25 stars of 7th mag. and fainter, formed recently from the surrounding gas. The other (western) side of the nebula is dominated by two main stars, the brighter of which is the blue supergiant 9 Sgr, mag. 5.9. Photographs show the nebula as an intense red, but visually it appears milky-white. M8 is about 5000 l.y. away.

M17 (NGC 6618), 18h 21m −16°.2, the Omega, Horseshoe or Swan Nebula, is another gaseous nebula. Binoculars show it as a wedge-shaped object of similar apparent width to the full Moon, while in larger instruments it appears arch-shaped, variously likened to a Greek capital omega (Ω), a horseshoe or a swan, which accounts for its range of popular names. M17 lies 5000 l.y. away. About 1° south of it is M18 (NGC 6613), 4000 l.y. distant, a small, loose cluster of 20 stars of 9th mag. and fainter, unimpressive in binoculars.

M20 (NGC 6514), 18h 03m −23°.0, the Trifid Nebula, is a cloud of glowing gas far less impressive visually than photographically. Moderate-sized telescopes show it as only a diffuse patch of light centred on the double star HN 40, of 8th and 9th mags., which was evidently born from it and now illuminates it. The Trifid Nebula gets its name from three dark lanes of dust that trisect it, well shown on photographs but elusive in small apertures. It lies 5000 l.y. away, the same as M8.

M21 (NGC 6531), 18h 05m −22°.5, is a spider-like open cluster in the same low-power field of view as M20, containing about 70 stars of 7th mag. and fainter, 4000 l.y. away.

M22 (NGC 6656), 18h 36m −23°.9, is a large, rich 5th-mag. globular cluster, one of the finest in the entire heavens and ranked third only to ω (omega) Centauri and 47 Tucanae. Visible to the naked eye, M22 is an excellent binocular object and a fine sight in small telescopes, which reveal its noticeably elliptical outline. A telescope of 75 mm aperture will begin to resolve its outer regions, and larger apertures show its brightest stars to be reddish. Its nucleus is not as condensed as that of many other globulars. M22 lies 10,000 l.y. away. At the edge of the same binocular field is the smaller 7th-mag. globular M28 (NGC 6626).

M23 (NGC 6494), 17h 57m −19°.0, is a widely spread open cluster of fairly uniform appearance, just at the limit of resolution in binoculars. It is elongated in shape, consisting of a field of 10th- and 11th-mag. stars, some arranged in arcs. It lies 2100 l.y. away.

M24, 18h 18m −18°.5, is a rich and extensive Milky Way starfield south of M17 and M18, grainy and shimmering in binoculars. Some observers restrict the name M24 to a small cluster of faint stars in its northern half known also as NGC 6603, but this is not what Messier meant. The whole Milky Way star cloud that makes up M24 measures about 2° × 1° and is one of the most prominent parts of the Milky Way to the naked eye.

M25 (IC 4725), 18h 32m −19°.2, 2300 l.y. away, is a scattered cluster of about 30 stars, well seen in binoculars. The most prominent members form two bars across the cluster's centre. Its brightest star is U Sgr, a yellow supergiant Cepheid which varies from mag. 6.3 to 7.1 with a period of 6 days 18 hours.

M55 (NGC 6809), 19h 40m −31°.0, is a 6th-mag. globular cluster, nebulous-looking in binoculars with little central condensation. Small telescopes resolve individual stars and show a dark notch on one side. M55 lies 19,000 l.y. away.

M22: Easily visible as a misty patch through binoculars and small telescopes, the true nature of this huge globular cluster becomes apparent when viewed through larger apertures. (Nigel Sharp, REU program/NOAO/AURA/NSF)

Scorpius – The Scorpion

A resplendent constellation, lying in a rich area of the Milky Way and packed with exciting objects for users of small telescopes. In mythology, Scorpius was the scorpion whose sting killed Orion. In the sky Orion still flees from the scorpion, for Orion sets below the horizon as Scorpius rises.

Originally, in ancient Greek times and earlier, Scorpius was a much larger constellation, but in the first century BC the stars that comprised its claws were made into the separate constellation of Libra by the Romans. Despite the loss of its claws, Scorpius still bears a clear resemblance to the creature after which it is named, with a distinctive curve of stars forming its stinging tail. Its heart is marked by the bright star Antares, a name that can be translated either as 'rival of Mars' or 'like Mars', in reference to its strong red colour. North of β (beta) Scorpii, at 16h 19.9m, −15° 38′, lies the strongest X-ray source in the sky, Scorpius X-1. This has been identified with a 13th-magnitude spectroscopic binary some 9000 l.y. away consisting of a neutron star accreting matter from a companion.

A scattering of several hundred bright stars centred between about 400 and 500 l.y. from us extends from Scorpius via Lupus into Centaurus and Crux; this is known as the Scorpius–Centaurus (or Sco–Cen) association. Antares is a prominent member. The Sun passes briefly through Scorpius during the last week of November.

α (alpha) Scorpii, 16h 29m −26°.4, (Antares), 604 l.y. away, is a red supergiant 400 times the diameter of the Sun. It is a semi-regular variable, fluctuating between mags. 0.9 and 1.2 with an approximate period of 5 years. Antares has a mag. 5.4 blue companion that requires at least 75 mm aperture and the steadiest atmospheric conditions to be visible against the primary's glare. The orbital period of the companion around Antares is estimated to be over 1200 years.

β (beta) Sco, 16h 05m −19°.8, (Graffias, 'claws', or Acrab, 'scorpion') is a striking double star divisible in the smallest telescopes, consisting of unrelated blue-white main-sequence stars of mags. 2.6 and 4.9, distances 530 and about 1100 l.y.

δ (delta) Sco, 16h 00m −22°.6, (Dschubba, 'forehead'), is a blue-white star 402 l.y. away. Normally of mag. 2.3, in 2000 it began to brighten, apparently as a result of throwing off a shell of gas, reaching a maximum of around mag. 1.6 in 2002. It subsequently subsided to near-normal brightness but may surge again in future.

ε (epsilon) Sco, 16h 50m −34°.3, mag. 2.3, is an orange giant 65 l.y. away.

ζ¹ ζ² (zeta¹ zeta²) Sco, 16h 54m −42°.4, is a naked-eye double of unrelated stars, ζ² being a mag. 3.6 orange giant 151 l.y. away, and ζ¹ a blue supergiant that varies erratically between mags. 4.7 and 4.9; ζ¹ is probably an outlying member of the open cluster NGC 6231 (see page 229).

θ (theta) Sco, 17h 37m −43°.0, mag. 1.9, is a white giant 272 l.y. away with a mag. 5.3 companion visible in small telescopes.

λ (lambda) Sco, 17h 34m −37°.1, (Shaula, 'sting'), mag. 1.6, is a blue-white star 703 l.y. away.

μ¹ μ² (mu¹ mu²) Sco, 16h 52m −38°.0, is a naked-eye double of unrelated stars. μ¹, 822 l.y. away, is an eclipsing binary that varies from mag. 2.9 to 3.2 in 34 hours 43 minutes; μ² is a blue-white star of mag. 3.6, 517 l.y. away.

ν (nu) Sco, 16h 12m −19°.5, 437 l.y. away, is a quadruple star similar to the famous Double Double in Lyra. A small telescope, or even powerful binoculars, shows ν Sco as a wide double, with blue-white components of mags. 4.0 and 6.3. Telescopes of 75 mm and above reveal at high magnification that the fainter star is itself a close double of mags. 6.7 and 7.7. The brighter star is

▶

Scorpius · Sco · Scorpii

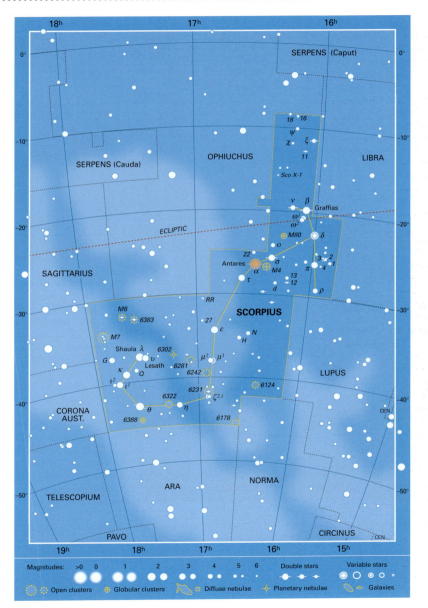

M6 and M7 are two glorious open clusters. Right: M6 is popularly known as the Butterfly Cluster because of its shape, although there is also a strong resemblance to the outline of a bird. Most of its stars are blue, with the exception of its brightest member, the orange giant BM Scorpii, seen at the left of the cluster. (Nigel Sharp, Mark Hanna, REU Program/NOAO/AURA/NSF)

Left: M7 is a large naked-eye cluster, seen against a backdrop of shimmering Milky Way starfields, unlike M6 to the north which has a much darker background. M7 is only just over half the distance of M6, so its individual members appear brighter than those of M6, and are scattered over a much wider area. (Nigel Sharp, REU program/NOAO/AURA/NSF)

an even closer double of mags. 4.3 and 5.4, requiring an aperture of 100 mm to divide.

ξ (xi) Sco, 16h 04m −11°.4, about 95 l.y. away, is a celebrated multiple star. A small telescope shows it as a white star of mag. 4.2 with a mag. 7.3 orange companion; also visible in the same field is a fainter and wider pair, Σ 1999 (Struve 1999), composed of mag. 7.4 and 8.0 stars that are gravitationally connected to ξ Sco. Therefore, at first sight, ξ Sco looks like another Double Double. But the brighter star is itself a close pair, consisting of yellow-white stars of mags. 4.8 and 5.1 orbiting each other with a period of 46 years. They were closest in 1996 and are currently moving apart; by 2007 they were divisible with 150 mm aperture and 100 mm should separate them by 2015.

ω^1 ω^2 (omega^1 omega^2) Sco, 16h 07m −20°.7, is a pair of unrelated stars distinguishable with the naked eye: ω^1, a blue-white main-sequence star of mag. 4.0, 424 l.y. away, and ω^2, a yellow giant of mag. 4.3, 265 l.y. away.

RR Sco, 16h 57m −30°.6, is a red giant variable of the Mira type, ranging between 5th and 12th mag. every 9 months or so. It lies about 1150 l.y. away.

M4 (NGC 6121), 16h 24m −26°.5, is a 6th-mag. globular cluster appearing almost as large as the full Moon. It looks like a woolly ball in binoculars, but is not as easy to spot as its magnitude would suggest because its light is spread over a large area. In 100-mm telescopes individual stars are resolved and there is a noticeable bar of stars running north–south across its centre. M4 is more loosely scattered than many globulars, and does not have a strong central condensation. It is the closest globular to us, 5600 l.y. away.

M6 (NGC 6405), 17h 40m −32°.2, is an impressive 4th-mag. open cluster of about 80 stars arranged in radiating chains, popularly called the Butterfly Cluster. Binoculars and small telescopes resolve the main stars which form the butterfly shape. The brightest of them, BM Sco, on one of the 'wings', is an orange giant semi-regular variable which ranges between 5th and 7th mags. every 27 months or so. M6 lies 1600 l.y. away. See the top photograph on the facing page.

M7 (NGC 6475), 17h 54m −34°.8, the most southerly object in the Messier catalogue, is a huge, scattered 3rd-mag. open cluster of 80 or so stars individually of 6th mag. and fainter, visible to the naked eye as a brighter knot in the Milky Way (see the photograph on the facing page). The apparent diameter is over twice that of the full Moon, and it is easily resolved in binoculars. With M6 at the edge of the same binocular field, this is an exceptionally rich sight. The central group of stars is arranged in an X-shape with scattered outliers that form triangular surroundings like a Christmas tree, set against the backdrop of a dense star cloud. An outstanding cluster and a classic for small apertures. M7 lies 950 l.y. away, just over half the distance of M6; the two clusters are not related.

M80 (NGC 6093), 16h 17m −23°.0, is a small, 7th-mag. globular cluster visible in binoculars or a small telescope, appearing like the fuzzy head of a comet. It lies 27,000 l.y. away.

NGC 6231, 16h 54m −41°.8, is a naked-eye open cluster of over 100 stars in a rich area of the Milky Way that is well worth sweeping with binoculars. The brightest stars of the group are of 6th mag. and give the impression of a mini-Pleiades in binoculars and small telescopes. The 5th-mag. blue supergiant ζ^1 (zeta^1) Sco (see page 226) is probably an outlying member of this cluster, which lies 6500 l.y. away. NGC 6231 is connected to a larger, scattered cluster of fainter stars visible in binoculars, known both as Trumpler 24 and Harvard 12, which lies 1° to the north. The chain of stars linking the two clusters delineates one of the spiral arms of our Galaxy.

NGC 6242, 16h 56m −39°.5, is a wedge-shaped open cluster for small telescopes containing about two dozen stars of 7th mag. and fainter. It lies about 3500 l.y. away.

NGC 6281, 17h 05m −37°.9, is an open cluster visible in small telescopes, consisting of over 50 stars of 8th mag. and fainter arranged in a rectangular shape, 1800 l.y. away.

Sculptor – The Sculptor

One of the faint and half-forgotten constellations introduced in the 1750s by Nicolas Louis de Lacaille to fill in the southern skies. It represents a sculptor's studio. Sculptor contains the south pole of our Galaxy, 90° from the plane of the Milky Way. In this direction we can look out into deep space, unobscured by stars or dust, and see many faint galaxies. Among these is a very faint member of our Local Group, the Sculptor Dwarf, detectable only on long-exposure photographs taken through large telescopes.

α (alpha) Sculptoris, 0h 59m −29°.4, mag. 4.3, is a blue-white giant 672 l.y. away.

β (beta) Scl, 23h 33m −37°.8, mag. 4.4, is a blue-white star 178 l.y. away.

γ (gamma) Scl, 23h 19m −32°.5, mag. 4.4, is an orange giant 179 l.y. away.

δ (delta) Scl, 23h 49m −28°.1, mag. 4.6, is a blue-white main-sequence star 143 l.y. away.

ε (epsilon) Scl, 1h 46m −25°.1, 89 l.y. away, is a binary of mags. 5.3 and 8.6, visible in small telescopes. The estimated orbital period is 1200 years.

κ¹ (kappa¹) Scl, 0h 09m −28°.0, 224 l.y. away, is a tight pair of white stars, of mags. 6.1 and 6.2, at the limit of resolution of a 75-mm telescope.

R Scl, 1h 27m −32°.5, is a deep-red semi-regular variable star that ranges from about mag. 5.8 to 7.7 with a period of about a year. It lies about 1500 l.y. away.

S Scl, 0h 15m −32°.0, is a red giant variable of Mira type, ranging from mag. 5.5 to 13.6 in around a year. It lies about 1500 l.y. away.

NGC 55, 0h 15m −39°.2, is an 8th-mag. spiral galaxy seen nearly edge-on, so it appears elongated. One half is more prominent that the other. It is similar in size and shape to NGC 253 (see below), although not quite as bright. Its distance is 6 million l.y.

NGC 253, 0h 48m −25°.3, is a 7th-mag. spiral galaxy seen nearly edge-on which gives it a cigar-shaped appearance, as seen in the photograph below. Nearly ½° long, it can be picked up in binoculars under dark skies but at least 100 mm aperture is required to distinguish the mottling caused by dust clouds in its spiral arms. NGC 253 lies 13 million l.y. away.

NGC 253, a spiral galaxy seen nearly edge-on and hence appearing elliptical. It has no central bulge, but its arms are a seething mass of stars and dust.
(Todd Boroson/ NOAO/AURA/NSF)

Sculptor · Scl · Sculptoris

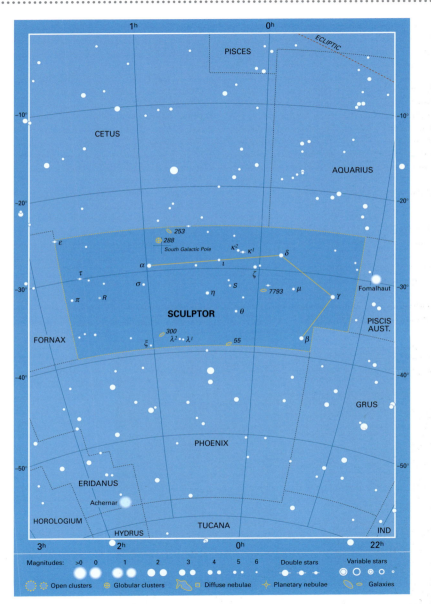

Scutum – The Shield

A faint constellation between Aquila and Serpens, introduced in 1684 by the Polish astronomer Johannes Hevelius under the title Scutum Sobiescianum, Sobieski's Shield, in honour of his patron, King John III Sobieski of Poland. Rich Milky Way star fields are the main attraction here, notably the Scutum star cloud in the northern half of the constellation, about 6° across and generally considered to be the brightest part of the Milky Way outside Sagittarius. The prominent open cluster M11 lies near a notch of dark nebulosity at the northern edge of the Scutum star cloud.

α (alpha) Scuti, 18h 35m –8°.2, mag. 3.8, is an orange giant 174 l.y. away.

δ (delta) Sct, 18h 42m –9°.1, 187 l.y. distant, is the prototype of a rare class of variable stars that pulsate in size every few hours, producing small-amplitude brightness changes. δ Scuti itself is a white giant that varies from mag. 4.6 to 4.8 with a period of 4 hours 39 minutes.

R Sct, 18h 48m –5°.7, is a pulsating orange super-giant about 1400 l.y. away that varies between mags. 4.2 and 8.6 every 5 months or so.

M11 (NGC 6705), 18h 51m –6°.3, the Wild Duck Cluster, is a showpiece open cluster of about 200 stars, half the apparent width of the full Moon. At 6th mag. it is at the limit of naked-eye visibility, but binoculars show it as a misty patch. In a telescope with a magnification of around ×100 it breaks up into a sparkling field of faint stardust. The cluster gets its popular name from the fact that its brightest members form a distinct fan-shape, resembling a flight of ducks, an effect that is noticeable visually through a telescope but which becomes lost on long-exposure photographs. An 8th-mag. star, slightly brighter than the rest, lies at the fan's apex, with a double star nearby. M11 is 6500 l.y. away.

M26 (NGC 6694), 18h 45m –9°.4, is an open cluster for small telescopes, of similar size to M11 but containing only about two dozen stars and hence much fainter. It lies about 5000 l.y. away.

Among the rich Milky Way starfields of Scutum lies M11, the Wild Duck cluster. In small instruments it appears to be shaped like a fan or arch, because of a lower density of bright stars towards one side, the right in this image. (Adam Block/NOAO/AURA/NSF)

Scutum · Sct · Scuti

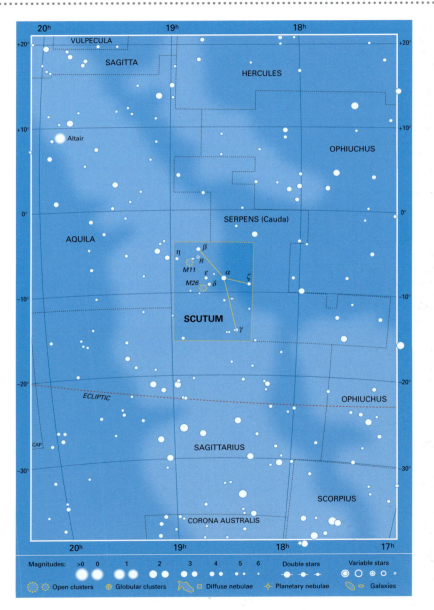

Serpens – The Serpent

An ancient constellation, representing a snake wound around the body of Ophiuchus. Serpens is actually split into two halves, one either side of Ophiuchus: Serpens Caput, the head, which is the larger and more prominent half; and Serpens Cauda, the tail. It is the only constellation to be split in two, but both halves count as one constellation.

α (alpha) Serpentis, 15h 44m +6°.4, (Unukalhai, 'the serpent's neck'), mag. 2.6, is an orange giant star 73 l.y. away.

β (beta) Ser, 15h 46m +15°.4, 153 l.y. distant, is a blue-white main-sequence star in the serpent's head of mag. 3.7, with a 10th-mag. companion visible in small telescopes. An unrelated mag. 6.7 background star, 29 Ser, is visible just north of it in binoculars.

γ (gamma) Ser, 15h 56m +15°.7, mag. 3.8, is a white main-sequence star 36 l.y. away.

δ (delta) Ser, 15h 35m +10°.5, 210 l.y. away, is a white star of mag. 4.2 with a close mag. 5.2 companion visible in a small telescope at high magnification.

η (eta) Ser, 18h 21m −2°.9, mag. 3.2, is an orange giant star 62 l.y. away.

θ (theta) Ser, 18h 56m +4°.2, (Alya), 132 l.y. distant, is an elegant pair of white stars of mags. 4.6 and 5.0, easily split in the smallest telescopes. ►

M16 and the surrounding Eagle Nebula in Serpens is a spectacular combination of star cluster and gas cloud. At the nebula's centre are dark fingers of dust and cooler gas that were made famous by the "pillars of creation" image taken by the Hubble Space Telescope. This photograph was taken with the 4-m telescope at Kitt Peak, Arizona. (Bill Schoening/NOAO/AURA/NSF)

Serpens · Ser · Serpentis

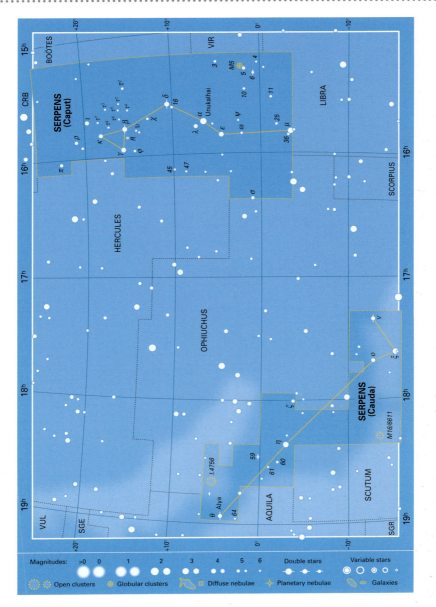

Magnitudes: >0 0 1 2 3 4 5 6   Double stars   Variable stars

○ Open clusters   ⊕ Globular clusters   ▷ Diffuse nebulae   ◇ Planetary nebulae   ⬭ Galaxies ν (nu) Ser, 17h 21m −12°.8, 193 l.y. away, is a blue-white star of mag. 4.3 with a wide mag. 8.3 companion visible in binoculars or small telescopes.

τ¹ (tau¹) Ser, 15h 26m +15°.4, 920 l.y. away, a red giant of mag. 5.2, is the brightest member of a loose scattering of eight stars of 6th mag. near β Ser, all visible in binoculars.

R Ser, 15h 51m +15°.1, is a red giant variable of Mira type, ranging between mags. 5.2 and 14.4 in approximately a year. It lies about 900 l.y. away.

M5 (NGC 5904), 15h 19m +2°.1, is a 6th-mag. globular cluster 26,000 l.y. away, visible in binoculars or small telescopes. It is rated as one of the finest globulars in the northern sky, second only to the famous M13 in Hercules. A telescope of 100 mm aperture reveals its brilliant, condensed centre and mottled outer regions with curving chains of stars. Close to M5 (but actually in the foreground) lies 5 Ser, a mag. 5.0 yellow-white star with a mag. 10 companion.

M16 (NGC 6611), 18h 19m −13°.8, is a hazy-looking open star cluster 8500 l.y. distant, of similar apparent size to the full Moon, embedded in the larger Eagle Nebula. The cluster is a grouping of about 60 stars of 8th mag. and fainter at the limit of resolution in binoculars. Small telescopes show that most of its members congregate in a V-shape in the northern half. The surrounding Eagle Nebula adds a touch of haziness to the cluster when seen in binoculars. The nebula is too faint to be seen well in amateur telescopes, but shows up beautifully on long-exposure photographs. It was the subject of a famous Hubble Space Telescope image taken in 1995 (see page 271).

IC 4756, 18h 39m +5°.4, is a scattered open cluster of 8th-mag. stars and fainter, about two Moon diameters wide, visible in binoculars. It lies 1300 l.y. away.

Sextans – The Sextant

A faint and insignificant constellation south of Leo, introduced in 1687 by the Polish astronomer Johannes Hevelius. It commemorates the instrument he used for measuring star positions. Hevelius continued to make naked-eye sightings of star positions with his sextant long after telescopes were available, and it is perhaps to demonstrate how good his eyesight was that he formed Sextans out of stars no brighter than mag. 4.5.

α (alpha) Sextantis, 10h 08m −0°.4, mag. 4.5, is a blue-white giant star 287 l.y. away.

β (beta) Sex, 10h 30m −0°.6, mag. 5.1, is a blue-white main-sequence star 345 l.y. away.

γ (gamma) Sex, 9h 53m −8°.1, mag. 5.1, is a blue-white main-sequence star 262 l.y. away.

δ (delta) Sex, 10h 30m −2°.7, mag. 5.2, is a blue-white main-sequence star 300 l.y. away.

17, 18 Sex, 10h 10m −8°.4, is a neat pairing of unrelated stars, mags. 5.9 and 5.6, distances 527 and 473 l.y., easily divisible in binoculars.

NGC 3115, 10h 05m −7°.7, is a 9th-mag. galaxy known as the Spindle Galaxy, some 30 million l.y. away. It is of the type known as a lenticular galaxy, with a disk of stars surrounding a central bulge but no spiral arms. Moderate-sized amateur telescopes show its elongated outline and brighter centre.

Sextans · Sex · Sextantis

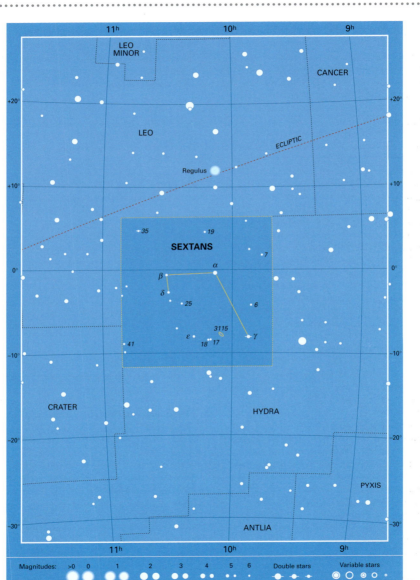

Magnitudes: >0 0 1 2 3 4 5 6   Double stars   Variable stars

Open clusters   ⊕ Globular clusters   Diffuse nebulae   ✦ Planetary nebulae   Galaxies

Taurus – The Bull

One of the most ancient constellations, recognized since the dawn of civilization. In Greek mythology, Taurus represents the animal disguise adopted by Zeus to carry off Princess Europa to Crete. Only the front half of the bull is depicted in the sky, its face being formed by the V-shaped cluster of stars known as the Hyades. Its glinting red eye is marked by the star Aldebaran, and its long horns are tipped by the stars β (beta) and ζ (zeta) Tauri. As well as the Hyades, Taurus contains another celebrated star cluster, the Pleiades or Seven Sisters. Taurus was the site of a supernova seen from Earth in AD 1054 that gave rise to the Crab Nebula, M1. At 4h 22.0m, +19° 32′, lies the faint Hind's Variable Nebula, NGC 1554–5, discovered in the 19th century by the English astronomer John Russell Hind; within this nebula lies the 10th-mag. star T Tauri, 576 l.y. away, prototype of a class of irregular variables that are stars still in the process of formation.

Each year, the Taurid meteors radiate from south of the Pleiades, reaching a maximum of about 10 per hour around November 4. The Sun passes through the constellation from mid-May to late June, and is in Taurus at the June solstice; precession carried the position of the June solstice into Taurus from Gemini at the end of 1989.

α (alpha) Tauri, 4h 36m +16°.5, (Aldebaran, 'the follower', i.e. of the Pleiades), is an orange giant irregular variable that fluctuates between about mags. 0.75 and 0.95. Although it appears to be part of the Hyades cluster, it is in fact an unrelated foreground star, 65 l.y. away.

β (beta) Tau, 5h 26m +28°.6, (Alnath or Elnath, 'the butting one'), mag. 1.7, is a blue-white giant 131 l.y. away.

ζ (zeta) Tau, 5h 38m +21°.1, 417 l.y. away, is a blue giant that is slightly variable, ranging erratically between about mags. 2.9 and 3.2.

θ¹ θ² (theta¹ theta²) Tau, 4h 29m +15°.9, is a naked-eye or binocular double in the Hyades cluster, consisting of yellow and white giants of mags. 3.8 and 3.4 respectively, distances 158 and 149 l.y. θ² is the brightest member of the Hyades.

κ¹ κ² (kappa¹ kappa²) Tau, 4h 25m +22°.3, are a pair of white stars of mags. 4.2 and 5.3 that form a naked-eye or binocular duo, 153 and 144 l.y. away respectively. Both are outlying members of the Hyades.

λ (lambda) Tau, 4h 01m +12°.5, 370 l.y. away, is an eclipsing binary of the Algol type, varying between mags. 3.4 and 3.9 with a period of 4 days.

σ¹ σ² (sigma¹ sigma²) Tau, 4h 39m +15°.8, is a wide binocular double of blue-white stars in the Hyades, mags. 5.1 and 4.7 and distances 152 and 159 l.y. respectively.

φ (phi) Tau, 4h 20m +27°.4, 342 l.y. away, is an optical double divisible in small telescopes, consisting of a mag. 5.0 orange giant and a white star of mag. 8.4.

χ (chi) Tau, 4h 23m +25°.6, 268 l.y. away, is a double star for small telescopes, with blue and gold components of mags. 5.4 and 7.6.

The Hyades, 4h 27m +16°, is a large and bright open cluster of about 200 stars covering over 5° of sky. The brightest members form a distinctive V-shape, easily visible to the naked eye. In Greek mythology the Hyades were the daughters of Atlas and Aethra, and half-sisters of the Pleiades. Because of its considerable size, the cluster is best studied with binoculars rather than a telescope. The bright star Aldebaran is not a member of the Hyades, but is superimposed on it by chance; the brightest true member is actually θ² (theta²) Tauri (see separate entry above). The centre of the cluster lies 150 l.y. away; the distance of the Hyades is important, for it marks the first step in our distance scale of the Galaxy.

▶

Taurus · Tau · Tauri

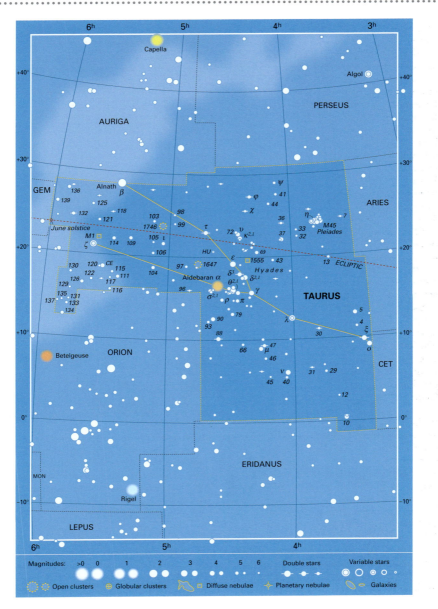

| Magnitudes: | >0 | 0 | 1 | 2 | 3 | 4 | 5 | 6 | Double stars | Variable stars |

○ Open clusters   ⊕ Globular clusters   ▢ Diffuse nebulae   ✦ Planetary nebulae   ⬭ Galaxies

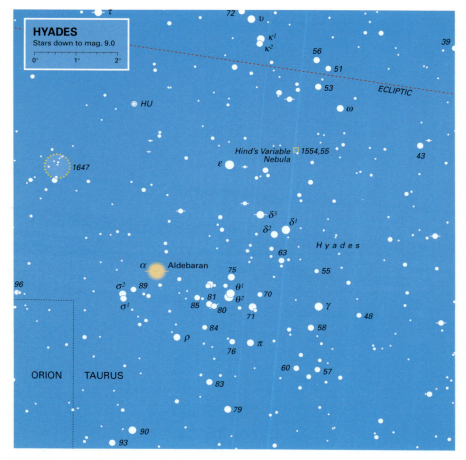

Detail chart of the Hyades cluster. (Wil Tirion)

M1 (NGC 1952), 5h 35m +22°.0, is the Crab
Nebula, the remains of a star that exploded as a
supernova. It can be glimpsed through binoculars
on clear, dark nights. Despite its fame, the Crab
Nebula is a disappointing object for small telescopes, appearing as an elliptical 8th-mag. wisp of
nebulosity several tines the apparent diameter of
the disk of Jupiter – in fact the Crab Nebula can
be missed because it is larger than expected. (For a
size comparison, see the picture on page 280.) At

the heart of the nebula, beyond the reach of
amateur telescopes, is a 16th-mag. object, the
remains of the star that exploded. This faint object
is now known to be a pulsar that spins 30 times a
second, emitting flashes at radio, optical and other
wavelengths as it does so. The Crab Nebula and
pulsar lie about 6500 l.y. away.

M45, 3h 47m +24°, the Pleiades, is the brightest
and most famous star cluster in the sky; it is popularly termed the Seven Sisters, after a group of
mythological nymphs, the daughters of Atlas and
Pleione. Approximately seven stars are visible to

the naked eye, arranged into a mini-dipper shape covering three full-Moon widths of sky; binoculars bring dozens more into view. About 100 stars belong to the cluster, which is centred 378 l.y. away. Unlike the stars of the Hyades, which are older and more evolved, the Pleiades formed within the last 50 million years and include many young blue giants. The brightest member is η (eta) Tauri (Alcyone), mag. 2.9. Other prominent members are 16 Tau (Celaeno), mag. 5.5; 17 Tau (Electra), mag. 3.7; 19 Tau (Taygeta), mag. 4.3; 20 Tau (Maia), mag. 3.9; 21 Tau (Asterope), mag.

5.8; 23 Tau (Merope), mag. 4.1; 27 Tau (Atlas), mag. 3.6; and BU Tau (Pleione), a so-called shell star that throws off rings of gas at irregular intervals, causing it to fluctuate unpredictably between mags. 4.8 and 5.5. The whole of the Pleiades cluster is embedded in a faint nebulosity which reflects the light of the hot blue stars. This nebula is noticeable on long-exposure photographs such as the one on the following page, and under very clear conditions its brightest part, around Merope, may be glimpsed in binoculars or small telescopes. This nebulosity was long thought to be the remains of the cloud from which the cluster formed, but now it seems more likely that it is an entirely separate cloud into which the stars have since drifted by chance. ▶

Detail chart of the Pleiades cluster and its surrounding nebulosity. (Wil Tirion)

M45, the Pleiades in Taurus, is the most glorious star cluster in the entire sky. Light from the hot, young stars is reflected from surrounding dust, producing a blue nebulosity that is brightest near Merope, bottom centre. The Moon has here been superimposed to the same scale for a size comparison. (Pleiades image Kevin Bays/NOAO/AURA/NSF.)

Telescopium – The Telescope

A constellation invented in the 1750s by the Frenchman Nicolas Louis de Lacaille to honour the most important of astronomical instruments, the telescope. Lacaille had in mind a specific instrument, the great refractor used by J. D. Cassini at Paris Observatory which, in common with other large refractors of the day, had an exceptionally long tube to combat chromatic aberration (false colour) of the image and was suspended from a mast. Lacaille's version of Telescopium originally extended northwards, including stars from Corona Australis, Sagittarius, Scorpius and Ophiuchus, but modern astronomers have cut off the top of the telescope's tube and supporting mast. As with so many of Lacaille's constellations, it is

faint and contrived, containing little to interest owners of small telescopes.

α (alpha) Telescopii, 18h 27m −46°.0, mag. 3.5, is a blue-white star 249 l.y. away.

$δ^1 δ^2$ (delta^1 delta^2) Tel, 18h 32m −45°.9, is a pair of blue-white stars of mags. 4.9 and 5.1, visible separately in binoculars. They are unrelated to each other, being 800 and 1120 l.y. from us respectively.

ε (epsilon) Tel, 18h 11m −46°.0, mag. 4.5, is a yellow giant 409 l.y. away.

ζ (zeta) Tel, 18h 29m −49°.1, mag. 4.1, is a yellow giant 127 l.y. away.

Telescopium · Tel · Telescopii

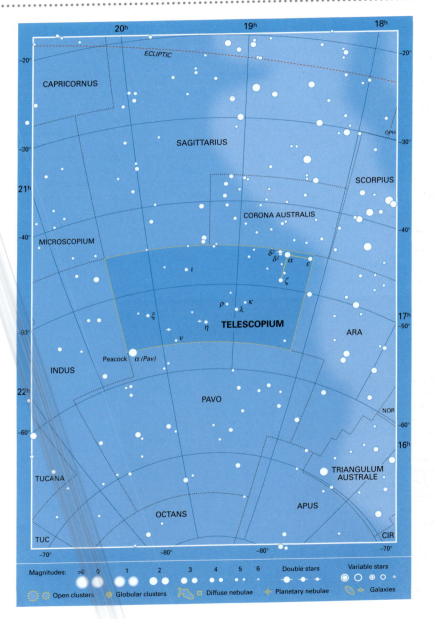

CAPRICORNUS

SAGITTARIUS

ECLIPTIC

CORONA AUSTRALIS

SCORPIUS

OPH

MICROSCOPIUM

δ^2 α ε
δ^1
ζ

ι

ρ κ
λ

ξ

TELESCOPIUM

η

ARA

ν

Peacock α (Pav)

INDUS

PAVO

NOR

TUCANA

TRIANGULUM
AUSTRALE

APUS

OCTANS

CIR

TUC

Magnitudes: >0   0   1   2   3   4   5   6   Double stars   Variable stars

Open clusters   Globular clusters   Diffuse nebulae   Planetary nebulae   Galaxies

Triangulum – The Triangle

A small but distinctive constellation lying between Andromeda and Aries, consisting of three main stars that form a shape like a thin capital delta; as a result, the Greeks referred to it as Deltoton. It has also been visualized as the Nile river delta and the island of Sicily. Its most important feature is the spiral galaxy M33, the third-largest member of our Local Group of galaxies, after the Andromeda Galaxy and our own Milky Way.

α (alpha) Trianguli, 1h 53m +29°.6, mag. 3.4, is a yellow-white star 64 l.y. away.

β (beta) Tri, 2h 10m +35°.0, mag. 3.0, the constellation's brightest member, is a white star 124 l.y. away.

γ (gamma) Tri, 2h 17m +33°.8, mag. 4.0, is a blue-white star 118 l.y. away.

6 Tri, 2h 12m +30°.3, 305 l.y. away, is a mag. 5.2 yellow giant with a close mag. 6.6 companion visible in a small telescope.

R Tri, 2h 37m +34°.3, is a red giant variable of Mira type, ranging from mag. 5.4 to 12.6 every 9 months or so. It lies about 1300 l.y. away.

M33 (NGC 598), 1h 34m +30°.7, is a spiral galaxy 2.7 million l.y. away in our Local Group, sometimes popularly termed the Pinwheel Galaxy. Presented almost face-on, it covers a larger area of sky than the full Moon. Despite its size and proximity M33 is not prominent visually because its light is spread over such a large area. M33 is best picked up on a dark night in binoculars or a small telescope using low power to enhance the contrast. Unlike most galaxies, it does not have a noticeably stellar nucleus. Quite large amateur telescopes are needed to trace the spiral arms.

M33, the Triangulum spiral galaxy, is a member of the Local Group and hence one of the closest galaxies to us, lying around 2.7 million light years away. (Adam Block/NOAO/AURA/NSF)

Triangulum · Tri · Trianguli

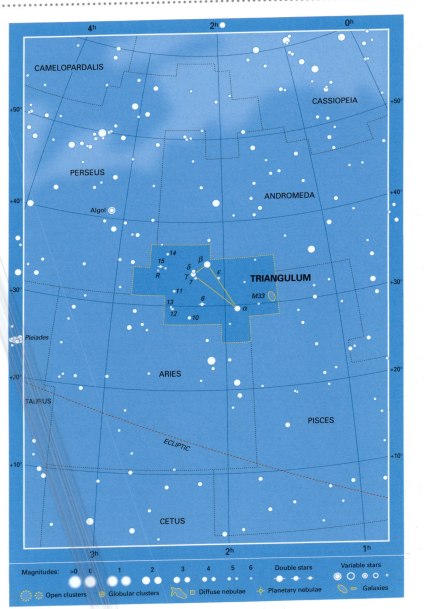

Magnitudes: >0 0 1 2 3 4 5 6 Double stars Variable stars

⊙ Open clusters ⊕ Globular clusters Diffuse nebulae Planetary nebulae Galaxies

Triangulum Australe – The Southern Triangle

A small but readily distinguishable constellation near α (alpha) Centauri, introduced at the end of the 16th century by the Dutch navigators Pieter Dirkszoon Keyser and Frederick de Houtman. The French astronomer Nicolas Louis de Lacaille visualized it as a surveyor's level with an attached plumbline and placed two of his own related inventions next to it, Circinus (the compasses) and Norma (the ruler and set square). Its three main stars are brighter than those of its northern equivalent, Triangulum, although the constellation itself is smaller.

α (alpha) Trianguli Australis, 16h 49m −69°.0, (Atria), mag. 1.9, is an orange giant star 415 l.y. away.

β (beta) TrA, 15h 55m −63°.4, mag. 2.8, is a white star 40 l.y. away.

γ (gamma) TrA, 15h 19m −68°.7, mag. 2.9, is a blue-white star 183 l.y. away.

NGC 6025, 16h 04m −60°.5, is a binocular cluster, elongated in shape, containing about 60 stars of 7th mag. and fainter, 2500 l.y. away.

Johann Bayer (1572–1625)

Johann Bayer was a German lawyer in Augsburg and an amateur astronomer who, in 1603, published the first star atlas that covered the entire sky, *Uranometria*. He based his maps of the northern heavens mainly on the observations made by the great Danish astronomer Tycho Brahe, while his information on the southern skies came from the work of the Dutch navigator Pieter Dirkszoon Keyser.

In addition to the 48 constellations known since ancient times, Bayer showed the 12 new constellations around the southern celestial pole invented by Keyser and his countryman Frederick de Houtman: Apus, Chamaeleon, Dorado, Grus, Hydrus, Indus, Musca, Pavo, Phoenix, Triangulum Australe, Tucana and Volans. Bayer's most important legacy to astronomers was his system of identifying stars by Greek letters. In each constellation the brightest stars were assigned letters of the Greek alphabet, usually, but not always, in approximate order of brightness (Gemini, Orion and Sagittarius are notable examples of constellations in which the star labelled α (alpha) is not the brightest).

Before Bayer's time, stars without proper names were identified by the cumbersome descriptions of the Greek astronomer Ptolemy such as 'in the left forearm of the advance twin', a reference to the 4th-magnitude star we now term θ (theta) Geminorum. Clearly, to make sense of such descriptions astronomers had to know their constellation figures well, and even then there was considerable room for confusion. The system of so-called Bayer letters was a vast improvement, and remains in use today.

Triangulum Australe · TrA · Trianguli Australis

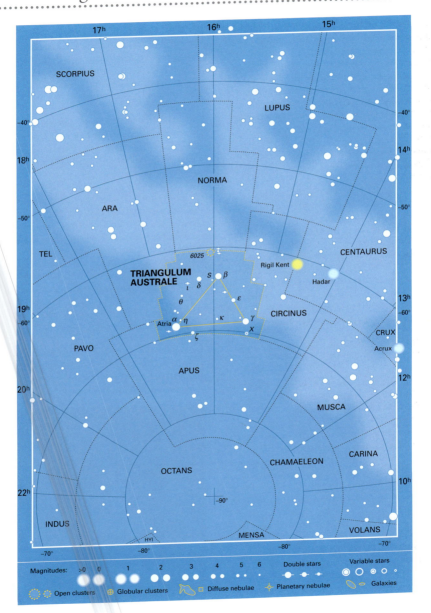

Tucana – The Toucan

A constellation near the south pole of the sky, introduced in the late 16th century by the Dutch navigators Pieter Dirkszoon Keyser and Frederick de Houtman. It represents a toucan, the South American bird with the large beak. Its most notable features are the Small Magellanic Cloud, actually a neighbouring mini-galaxy, and the globular cluster known as 47 Tucanae.

α (alpha) Tucanae, 22h 19m −60°.3, mag. 2.9, is an orange giant star 199 l.y. away.

β (beta) Tuc, 0h 32m −63°.0, is a complex multiple star. Binoculars or small telescopes show that it consists of two almost identical blue-white stars, β¹ and β², mags. 4.4 and 4.5; β² is itself a close binary with a period of 44 years, requiring an aperture larger than 200 mm to divide. Nearby lies a mag. 5.1 white star which is unlettered, although on some older charts and catalogues it was labelled β³. All three stars share the same proper motion through space, but their distances of 140, 172 and 152 l.y. suggest they are not truly connected.

γ (gamma) Tuc, 23h 17m −58°.2, mag. 4.0, is a white star 72 l.y. away.

δ (delta) Tuc, 22h 27m −65°.0, mag. 4.5, is a blue-white star 267 l.y. away with a 9th-mag. companion visible in small telescopes.

κ (kappa) Tuc, 1h 16m −68°.9, 67 l.y. away, is a double star consisting of components of mags. 5.1 and 7.3 visible in small telescopes. This pair moves through space with a wide mag. 7.2 star, itself a close binary with an orbital period of 85 years, just divisible in 150 mm aperture.

47 Tuc (NGC 104), 0h 24m −72°.1, is a prominent globular cluster the same apparent size as the full Moon, visible to the naked eye as a fuzzy 4th-mag. star; on early charts, it was actually catalogued as a star and given a stellar designation. Among globular clusters it is second only to

ω (omega) Centauri in size and brightness. Telescopes of 100 mm aperture begin to resolve 47 Tuc, and even binoculars show the brilliant blaze of its star-packed core. Its diameter is about 200 light years and it is among the closest globulars to us, 16,000 l.y. away.

NGC 362, 1h 03m −70°.8, is a 6th-mag. globular cluster visible in binoculars near the northern edge of the Small Magellanic Cloud, but not associated with it. NGC 362 actually lies 29,000 l.y. away, in our own Galaxy.

Small Magellanic Cloud (SMC), 0h 53m −73°, is a satellite galaxy of the Milky Way, as is its larger sibling, the Large Magellanic Cloud in Dorado. The Small Magellanic Cloud appears to the naked eye as a nebulous, tadpole-shaped patch 3½° across. Binoculars and small telescopes resolve star clusters and glowing gas clouds within it, although they are smaller and less impressive than those in the Large Magellanic Cloud. It lies about 200,000 l.y. away but is elongated along our line of sight. (See the photograph on page 164.)

47 Tucanae (NGC 104), one of the nearest and brightest globular clusters, is an excellent object for small instruments. (ESO)

Tucana · Tuc · Tucanae

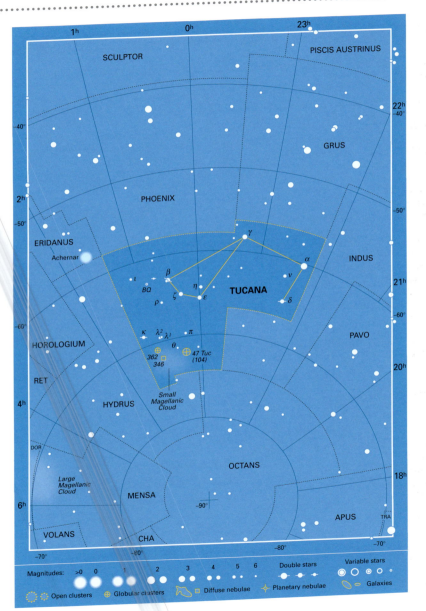

SCULPTOR

PISCIS AUSTRINUS

GRUS

PHOENIX

ERIDANUS

Achernar

INDUS

γ

α

β

ι

BQ

η

ν

ρ

ζ

ε

TUCANA

δ

κ

λ²

λ¹

π

θ

PAVO

HOROLOGIUM

362

346

47 Tuc
(104)

RET

Small
Magellanic
Cloud

HYDRUS

Large
Magellanic
Cloud

OCTANS

DOR

MENSA

−90°

APUS

TRA

VOLANS

CHA

Magnitudes: >0   0   1   2   3   4   5   6   Double stars   Variable stars

Open clusters   Globular clusters   Diffuse nebulae   Planetary nebulae   Galaxies

Ursa Major – The Great Bear

The third-largest constellation in the sky. Its central feature is the seven stars that make up the familiar shape variously called the Plough or the Big Dipper, the best-known of all star patterns, although why so many people, including the North American Indians, visualized this group as a bear remains a mystery. In Europe the pattern was seen as a wagon or chariot. Others, notably the Arabs, viewed the dipper shape not as a bear, but as a bier or coffin. In Greek mythology the bear represented Callisto, who was turned into a bear in punishment for her illicit love affair with Zeus.

The two end stars in the dipper's bowl, Merak and Dubhe, are known as the Pointers, since they indicate the direction of Polaris, the north pole star in neighbouring Ursa Minor. The curving handle of the Big Dipper points to the bright star Arcturus in Boötes. At 11h 03.3m, +35° 58′, lies the

mag. 7.5 red dwarf Lalande 21185, which is the Sun's fourth-closest stellar neighbour, 8.3 l.y. away. Its designation comes from its number in a catalogue drawn up by the 18th-century French astronomer Joseph Lalande.

With the exception of Alkaid and Dubhe, the stars of the Big Dipper are travelling together through space, along with a number of other stars in the region; together, these stars make up the so-called Ursa Major moving cluster. Ursa Major contains numerous galaxies, but only a few of them are easily visible in amateur telescopes.

α (alpha) Ursae Majoris, 11h 04m +61°.8, (Dubhe, 'the bear'), mag. 1.8, is a yellow-orange giant 124 l.y. away. It has a close mag. 4.8 companion that orbits it in 44 years. Usually the pair are too close to split in amateur telescopes but could be divisible with 250 mm when at their widest, in 2023–2026.

▶

Mizar and Alcor are a well-known naked-eye or binocular double in the handle of the Plough, but form an attractive multiple star when seen through a small telescope. (Wil Tirion)

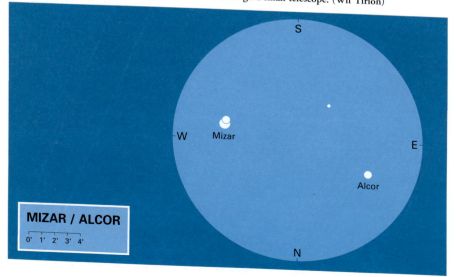

Ursa Major · UMa · Ursae Majoris

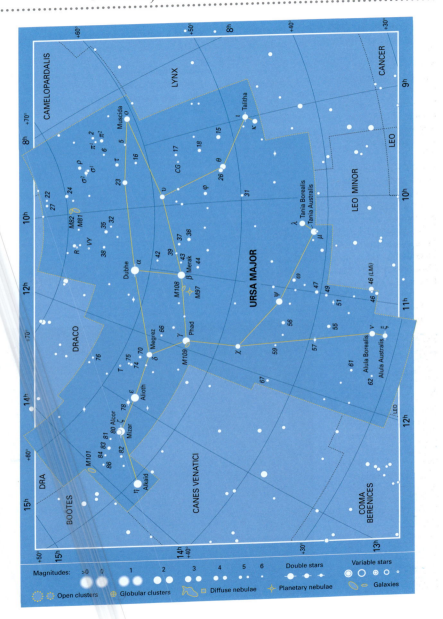

CAMELOPARDALIS

LYNX

CANCER

LEO

Muscida

Talitha

LEO MINOR

Tania Borealis
Tania Australis

M82
M81

VY
R

Dubhe

Merak
M108
M97

URSA MAJOR

Megrez
Phad
M109

DRACO

Mizar
Alcor
Alioth

M101

Alkaid

DRA

BOOTES

CANES VENATICI

COMA BERENICES

Alula Borealis
Alula Australis

Magnitudes: >0   0   1   2   3   4   5   6   Double stars   Variable stars

Open clusters   Globular clusters   Diffuse nebulae   Planetary nebulae   Galaxies

β (beta) UMa, 11h 02m +56°.4, (Merak, 'flank'), mag. 2.3, is a blue-white star 79 l.y. away.

γ (gamma) UMa, 11h 54m +53°.7, (Phad or Phecda, 'thigh'), mag. 2.4, is a blue-white star 84 l.y. away.

δ (delta) UMa, 12h 15m +57°.0, (Megrez, 'root of the tail'), mag. 3.3, is a blue-white star 81 l.y. away.

ε (epsilon) UMa, 12h 54m +56°.0, (Alioth), mag. 1.8, is a blue-white star with a peculiar spectrum, 81 l.y. away.

ζ (zeta) UMa, 13h 24m +54°.9, (Mizar), mag. 2.2, is a celebrated multiple star. Good eyesight, or binoculars, reveals a mag. 4.0 companion, Alcor. Mizar is 78 l.y. from Earth and Alcor 81 l.y. away, too far apart to be a genuine binary. However, a small telescope reveals that Mizar has another mag. 4.0 companion closer to it, which definitely is related (see the eyepiece view on page 250). This companion was first seen by the Italian astronomer Giovanni Riccioli in 1650, making Mizar the first double star to be discovered telescopically. Mizar itself was also the first star discovered to be a spectroscopic binary, by the American astronomer Edward C. Pickering in 1889. The companion of Mizar is another spectroscopic binary, as is Alcor, making this a highly complex group.

η (eta) UMa, 13h 48m +49°.3, (Alkaid or Benetnasch, both from the Arabic for 'leader of the mourners'), mag. 1.9, is a blue-white main-sequence star 101 l.y. away.

ξ (xi) UMa, 11h 18m +31°.5, 26 l.y. away, was the first binary star to have its orbit computed. Its two yellow components (both also spectroscopic binaries), of mags. 4.3 and 4.8, orbit each other with a period of 60 years. They are currently divisible in a 75-mm telescope and after 2015 will come within range of the smallest apertures, continuing to open out until 2035. For a diagram of the orbit, see page 282.

M81 (NGC 3031), 9h 56m +69°.1, is a beautiful 7th-mag. spiral galaxy, one of the brightest in the sky, visible in binoculars. A small telescope shows it as a roundish, softly glowing patch noticeably

M97, the Owl Nebula, gets its popular name from the two dark patches, like an owl's eyes, either side of the 16th-magnitude central star. This star, a white dwarf, originally ejected the gas that forms the nebula and the star's energy now makes the nebula glow. An aperture of at least 100 mm is needed to see the "eyes". Visually, the nebula appears grey rather than green. (NOAO/AURA/NSF)

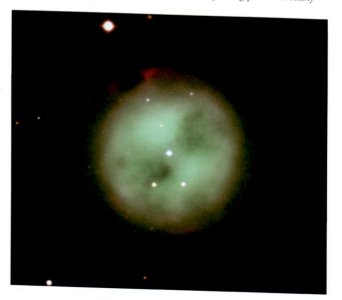

M101, a face-on spiral galaxy, displays an asymmetric shape in photographs. In amateur instruments only the core and traces of the spiral arms will be seen. (George Jacoby, Bruce Bohannan, Mark Hanna/NOAO/AURA/NSF)

brighter towards the centre. Being tilted at an angle to us it appears somewhat elliptical in outline, covering over half a Moon's width at its longest. In the same telescopic field of view ½° to the north is M82 (see separate entry below); the two galaxies are about 12 million l.y. from us. For a photograph of M81 see page 288.

M82 (NGC 3034), 9h 56m +69°.7, is a neighbour galaxy of M81, a quarter as bright and less than half its size but still visible in binoculars. In a small telescope it appears as an elongated blur and can actually seem more prominent than M81 because of its higher surface brightness. Detailed studies by professional astronomers have shown that M82 is an edge-on spiral galaxy mottled by dust clouds and experiencing a burst of star formation as a result of a recent interaction with M81.

M97 (NGC 3587), 11h 15m +55°.0, is an elusive 11th-mag. planetary nebula known as the Owl Nebula because of two dark patches like eyes that give it the appearance of an owl's face when seen

through a large telescope. In moderate apertures it appears as only a pale disk over three times the size of Jupiter, and will probably need an aperture of at least 75 mm to be seen at all. The Owl lies about 1300 l.y. away.

M101 (NGC 5457), 14h 03m +54°.3, is a spiral galaxy visible in binoculars as a pale, rounded smudge about half the apparent size of the full Moon; because of its large size it is less prominent than its quoted brightness of 8th mag. would suggest. Long-exposure photographs show it as a face-on galaxy with widely spread spiral arms, but these are not apparent in small telescopes which tend to show only the elliptical central region. M101 lies 22 million l.y. away.

Ursa Minor – The Little Bear

A constellation said to have been introduced in about 600 BC by the Greek astronomer Thales. Ursa Minor currently contains the north celestial pole, which lies within 1° of the conveniently placed 2nd-magnitude star popularly known as Polaris, α (alpha) Ursae Minoris. Precession will carry the pole closest to Polaris around AD 2100, when the two will be separated by just under ½°, after which it will start to move away again towards Cepheus, crossing the border in AD 2234 (see chart below).

Ursa Minor is also termed the Little Dipper because its seven brightest stars outline a shape like a smaller version of the Big Dipper in Ursa Major. The stars β (beta) and γ (gamma) Ursae Minoris (Kochab and Pherkad) in the Little Dipper's bowl are called the Guardians of the Pole.

α (alpha) Ursae Minoris, 2h 32m +89°.3, (Polaris), mag. 2.0, is a yellow-white supergiant 431 l.y. away. It is a Cepheid variable – in fact, the nearest Cepheid to us. Its pulsations diminished during the 20th century, stabilizing by the 1990s at a few hundredths of a magnitude. Polaris is also a double star, with a mag. 8.2 companion visible in a small telescope. Binoculars and small telescopes show a ring of 8th- to 11th-mag. stars some ¾° across, on which Polaris appears to be strung like some lustrous pearl on a necklace.

β (beta) UMi, 14h 51m +74°.1, (Kochab), mag. 2.1, is an orange giant 126 l.y. away.

γ (gamma) UMi, 15h 21m +71°.8, (Pherkad), mag. 3.0, is a blue-white giant star 480 l.y. away. The mag. 5.0 orange giant 11 UMi that appears near it, as seen by the naked eye or in binoculars, is unrelated, lying 390 l.y. away.

ε (epsilon) UMi, 16h 46m +82°.0, mag. 4.2, 347 l.y. away, is a yellow giant eclipsing binary that varies in a period of 39.5 days by under 0.1 mag., not discernible to the naked eye.

η (eta) UMi, 16h 18m +75°.8, mag. 5.0, is a white main-sequence star 97 l.y. away. A wide mag. 5.5 companion, 19 UMi, is an unrelated background star.

The movement of the north celestial pole over 800 years as a result of precession. (Wil Tirion)

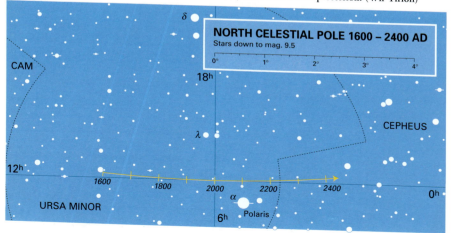

Ursa Minor · UMi · Ursae Minoris

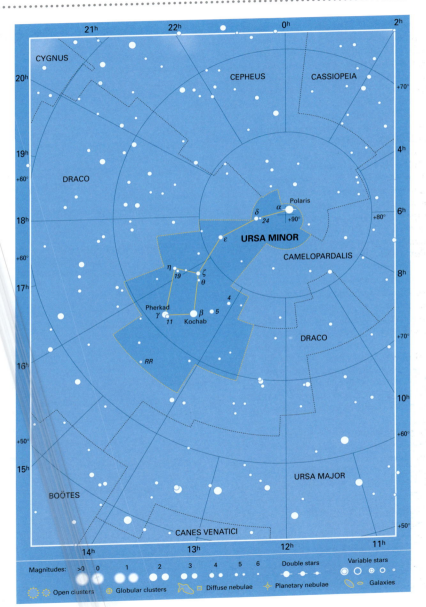

Vela – The Sails

Formerly part of the ancient constellation Argo Navis, the ship of Jason and the Argonauts, Vela was made into a separate constellation (along with Carina and Puppis) by the French astronomer Nicolas Louis de Lacaille in 1763. Vela represents the ship's sails while Carina is the keel and Puppis the stern. When Argo Navis was subdivided into these three parts, its stars were not given new Greek letters; as a result, the labelling of the stars in Vela begins with γ (gamma). In fact, Argo Navis was so large that astronomers ran out of Greek letters to label its stars and turned to Roman letters; many of these Roman-lettered stars have ended up in Vela.

The stars κ (kappa) and δ (delta) Velorum, in conjunction with ι (iota) and ε (epsilon) Carinae, form a shape known as the False Cross, sometimes mistaken for the real Southern Cross. Vela lies in a part of the Milky Way rich in faint nebulosity visible on long-exposure photographs. This nebulosity, named the Gum Nebula after the Australian astronomer Colin S. Gum who drew attention to it in 1952, is believed to be the remains of one or more supernovae that occurred long ago. Another remnant of a supernova in the constellation is the Vela Pulsar, which flashes 11 times per second, one of the few pulsars that can be seen flashing optically as well as at radio wavelengths.

γ (gamma) Velorum, 8h 10m −47°.3, is an interesting multiple star. Binoculars or small telescopes divide it into two blue-white components of mags. 1.8 and 4.3. The brighter of these is the brightest known example of a Wolf–Rayet type, a rare class of stars with very hot surfaces which seem to be ejecting gas. It is 840 l.y. away, while the fainter component is estimated to lie 1600 l.y. away and hence is unrelated. There are also two wider companions of 8th and 9th mags., distances unknown.

δ (delta) Vel, 8h 45m −54°.7, mag. 1.9, is a blue-white main-sequence star 80 l.y. away with a mag.

5.1 companion requiring apertures of 100 mm to be detected. The brighter star is an eclipsing binary which dips to mag. 2.3 for a few hours every 45 days.

κ (kappa) Vel, 9h 22m −55°.0, mag. 2.5, is a blue-white star 539 l.y. away.

λ (lambda) Vel, 9h 08m −43°.4, mag. 2.2, is an orange supergiant, irregularly variable (by less than 0.2 mag.), 573 l.y. away.

H Vel, 8h 56m −52°.7, 376 l.y. away, is a neat double of mags. 4.8 and 7.4, difficult in the smallest telescopes because of the magnitude contrast.

NGC 2547, 8h 11m −49°.3, 1400 l.y. away, is an open cluster of about 80 stars of mag. 6.5 and fainter, just visible to the naked eye and best seen in binoculars.

NGC 3132, 10h 08m −40°.5, is a relatively large and bright planetary nebula of 8th mag., known as the Eight-Burst Nebula. Through a small telescope it appears larger than Jupiter, with a central star of 10th mag. It lies 2600 l.y. away.

NGC 3228, 10h 22m −51°.7, is an open cluster of about 15 faint stars for binoculars and small telescopes, 1600 l.y. away.

IC 2391, 8h 40m −53°.1, is a large naked-eye cluster of 50 stars, 500 l.y. away, scattered around the mag. 3.6 blue-white star ο (omicron) Vel, a small-amplitude variable of β Cephei type. About 1° from it is the binocular cluster NGC 2669.

IC 2395, 8h 41m −48°.2, is a binocular cluster of 40 stars, 3100 l.y. away. A mag. 5.5 star which seems to be the brightest member is probably a foreground star. Also visible ½° to the south is the 8th-mag. open cluster NGC 2670.

Vela · Vel · Velorum

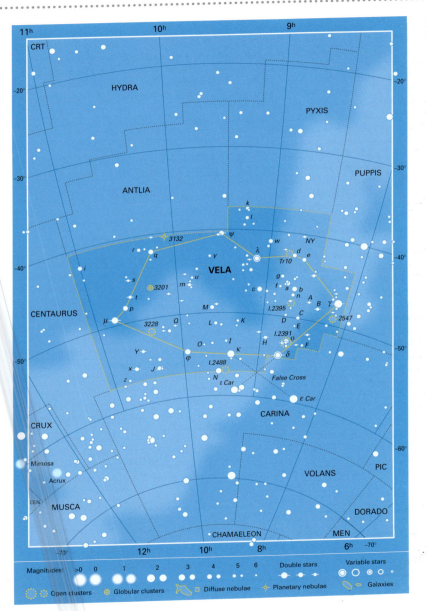

Magnitudes: >0   0   1   2   3   4   5   6   Double stars   Variable stars

Open clusters   Globular clusters   Diffuse nebulae   Planetary nebulae   Galaxies

Virgo – The Virgin

The second-largest constellation in the sky (only Hydra is bigger), and the largest in the zodiac. Virgo is usually identified as Dike, the goddess of justice, the scales of justice being represented by neighbouring Libra. But another legend sees her as Demeter, the corn goddess, and in the sky she is pictured holding an ear of wheat (the star Spica). The Sun passes through the constellation from mid-September to early November, and thus is within Virgo's boundaries at the time of the September equinox each year, when the Sun moves south of the celestial equator.

Virgo contains the nearest major cluster of galaxies to us, which spills over into neighbouring Coma Berenices; the area is sometimes known as 'the realm of the galaxies'. The Virgo Cluster lies 55 million l.y. away and contains about 3000 members, several dozen of which are visible in apertures of 150 mm or so, although they appear as little more than hazy patches; some of the brightest members are mentioned below. Another famous feature in Virgo, unrelated to the Virgo Cluster of galaxies, is the optically brightest quasar, 3C 273, located at 12h 29.1m, +2° 03′. It appears as a 13th-mag. blue star and is estimated to lie about 3000 million l.y. away.

α (alpha) Virginis, 13h 25m −11°.2, (Spica, 'ear of wheat'), mag. 1.0, is a blue-white main-sequence star 262 l.y. away. It is a spectroscopic binary, tidally distorted by its companion so that it varies slightly with a period of 4 days as it rotates, although only by 0.1 mag.

β (beta) Vir, 11h 51m +1°.8, (Zavijava), mag. 3.6, is a yellow-white main-sequence star 36 l.y. away.

γ (gamma) Vir, 12h 42m −1°.4, (Porrima), 39 l.y. away, is a celebrated double star. Together, the stars shine as mag. 2.7. But a small telescope reveals γ Vir to consist of a matching pair of white stars, each of mag. 3.5. They orbit each other every 169

years and were last closest in 2005, when a 250-mm telescope was needed to split them. Now moving apart rapidly, they become divisible in 100 mm by 2010 and in 60 mm after 2012, remaining within range of small telescopes for the rest of the 21st century. See diagram page 282.

δ (delta) Vir, 12h 56m +3°.4, mag. 3.4, is a red giant 202 l.y. away.

ε (epsilon) Vir, 13h 02m +11°.0, (Vindemiatrix, 'grape gatherer'), mag. 2.8, is a yellow giant 102 l.y. away.

θ (theta) Vir, 13h 10m −5°.5, mag. 4.4, is a blue-white star 415 l.y. away with a 9th-mag. companion visible in a small telescope.

τ (tau) Vir, 14h 02m +1°.5, mag. 4.3, a blue-white star 218 l.y. away, forms a wide optical double for small telescopes with a 9th-mag. companion.

φ (phi) Vir, 14h 28m −2°.2, 135 l.y. away, is a yellow giant of mag. 4.8 with a 9th-mag. companion, difficult to see in the smallest telescopes because of the brightness contrast.

M49 (NGC 4472), 12h 30m +8°.0, is an 8th-mag. elliptical galaxy visible as a rounded glow in a 75-mm telescope under low power. It is one of the largest and brightest members of the Virgo Cluster of galaxies.

M58 (NGC 4579), 12h 38m +11°.8, is a 10th-mag. barred spiral galaxy with a noticeably brighter core.

M59 (NGC 4621), 12h 42m +11°.6, is a 10th-mag. elliptical galaxy with a starlike nucleus, lying about a quarter of the way from M60 to M58.

M60 (NGC 4649), 12h 44m +11°.5, is a 9th-mag. elliptical galaxy, one of the most prominent members of the Virgo Cluster, detectable in 75 mm aperture.

▶

Virgo · Vir · Virginis

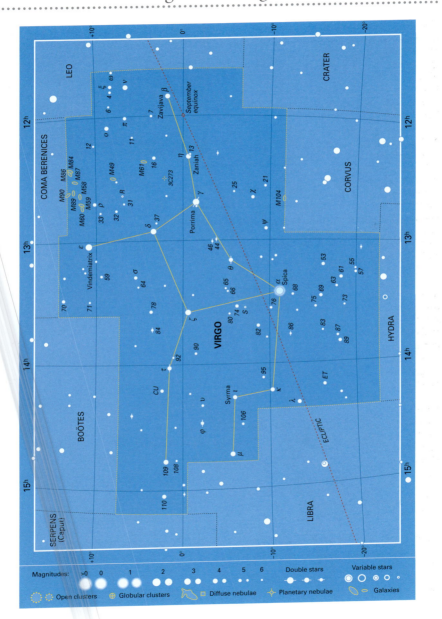

M84 (NGC 4374), 12h 25m +12°.9, and M86 (NGC 4406), 12h 26m +12°.9, are a pair of 9th-mag. elliptical galaxies appearing in the same telescopic field as fuzzy patches with noticeably brighter cores. M86 is slightly the larger of the two and noticeably elongated, whereas M84 appears round.

M87 (NGC 4486), 12h 31m +12°.4, is a celebrated giant elliptical galaxy. It is also a strong radio source, known as Virgo A, and an X-ray source. Photographs taken through large telescopes show a jet of matter emerging from M87 (see right for an example). In amateur telescopes, M87 appears as a rounded, 9th-mag. glow with a noticeable nucleus.

M90 (NGC 4569), 12h 37m +13°.2, is a large 9th-mag. spiral galaxy, tilted at an angle to us so that it appears elongated.

M104 (NGC 4594), 12h 40m −11°.6, is an 8th-mag. spiral galaxy seen edge-on so that it appears elongated. It is popularly known as the Sombrero because its appearance on long-exposure photographs has been likened to that of a Mexican hat

M87, a giant elliptical galaxy in the Virgo cluster, has a jet of gas extending from its central core. (Adam Block/NOAO/AURA/NSF)

(see page 130). However, with its bulging nucleus ringed by tightly coiled spiral arms, its appearance is more reminiscent of Saturn. Apertures of 150 mm reveal a dark lane of dust along its rim, silhouetted against the brighter arms and nucleus. The Sombrero is not in the Virgo Cluster but somewhat closer, about 30 million l.y. away.

Volans – The Flying Fish

This figure was invented at the end of the 16th century by the Dutch navigators Pieter Dirkszoon Keyser and Frederick de Houtman. It represents the type of fish found in tropical waters that can leap out of the water and glide through the air on wings. None of its stars is particularly bright, but there are two fine double stars for small telescopes.

α (alpha) Volantis, 9h 02m −66°.4, mag. 4.0, is a blue-white star 124 l.y. away.

β (beta) Vol, 8h 26m −66°.1, mag. 3.8, is an orange giant 108 l.y. away.

γ (gamma) Vol, 7h 09m −70°.5, 142 l.y. away, is a pair of gold and cream stars of mags. 3.8 and 5.7, beautiful in a small telescope.

δ (delta) Vol, 7h 17m −68°.0, mag. 4.0, is a yellow-white giant 660 l.y. away.

ε (epsilon) Vol, 8h 08m −68°.6, 642 l.y. away, is a mag. 4.4 blue-white star with an 8th-mag. companion visible in a small telescope.

Volans · Vol · Volantis

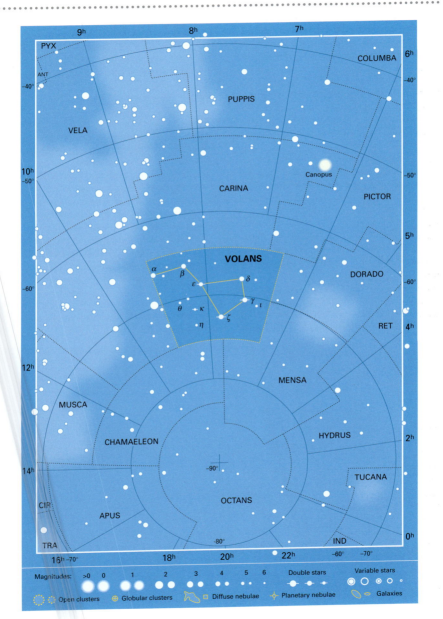

Vulpecula – The Fox

A faint constellation at the head of Cygnus. It was originated in 1687 by the Polish astronomer Johannes Hevelius, who called it Vulpecula cum Anser, the Fox and Goose. Since then the goose has fled, leaving the fox on its own. The first pulsar, or flashing radio source, was discovered in Vulpecula in 1967 by radio astronomers at Cambridge, England. It lies about 1½° north of the notable grouping called Brocchi's Cluster.

α (alpha) Vulpeculae, 19h 29m +24°.7, mag. 4.4, is a red giant 297 l.y. away. An unrelated mag. 5.8 orange giant, 8 Vul, 484 l.y. away, is seen nearby in binoculars.

T Vul, 20h 51m +28°.3, is a yellow-white supergiant Cepheid variable that ranges between mags. 5.4 and 6.1 every 4.4 days. It lies about 1700 l.y. away.

M27 (NGC 6853), 20h 00m +22°.7, the Dumbbell Nebula, is a large and bright planetary nebula, reputedly the most conspicuous of its kind, visible in binoculars as an elliptical misty glow. Its dumbbell shape is better seen through telescopes, which also reveal its greenish tinge. M27 is of 8th mag. and spans about one-quarter the apparent diameter of the full Moon. M27 is about 1400 l.y. away. (For a photograph see page 220.)

Brocchi's Cluster (Collinder 399), 19h 25m +20°.2, is a striking binocular group of stars on the border with Sagitta, popularly known as the Coathanger because of its distinctive shape. An almost straight line of six stars extends for three Moon diameters; from the centre of this line emerges a curve of four more stars, forming the Coathanger's hook. The brightest member of the group, in the hook, is 4 Vul, mag. 5.1. Distances of the individual stars range from just over 200 l.y. to more than 1000 l.y., and all have different motions through space, so this is not a true cluster but a chance alignment.

The stars of Brocchi's Cluster form the shape of a coathanger. (Wil Tirion)

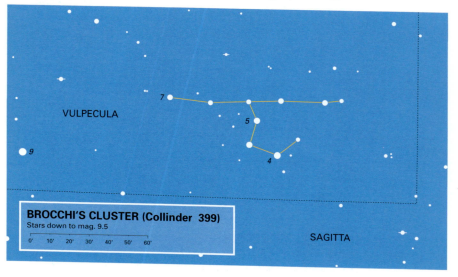

Vulpecula · Vul · Vulpeculae

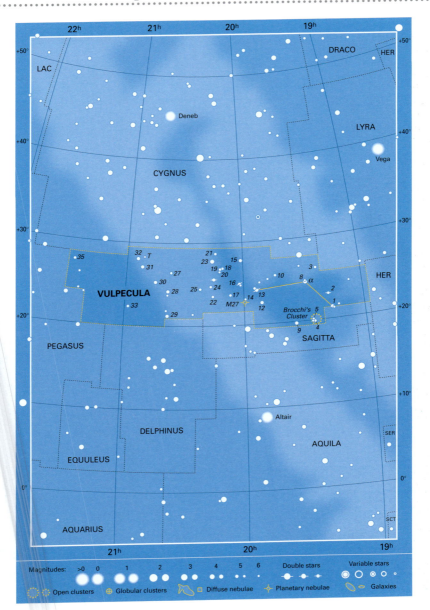

Magnitudes: >0 0 1 2 3 4 5 6   Double stars   Variable stars

Open clusters   Globular clusters   Diffuse nebulae   Planetary nebulae   Galaxies

SECTION II

The Pleiades star cluster in Taurus hovers above a winter landscape in this composite image. (Robin Scagell)

Stars and nebulae

Stars are balls of gas made incandescent by energy from nuclear reactions deep in their interiors. They come in a wide range of sizes and brightnesses, from faint dwarfs a hundredth of the Sun's diameter to dazzling supergiants hundreds of times larger than the Sun. They range in temperature from intensely hot blue-white specimens with surface temperatures of more than 20,000°C to cool red stars with surfaces at around 3000°C. The Sun, which is a medium-temperature yellow star (surface temperature 5800°C) turns out to be pretty average in all respects.

Stars are born from massive clouds of gas and dust within our Galaxy. An interstellar gas cloud is termed a *nebula* (plural: *nebulae*), from the Latin for 'cloud'. A nebula is not uniformly distributed in space, but contains denser knots – the seeds of future stars. If the knot is dense enough it begins to contract under the inward pull of its own gravity.

As it gets smaller and denser it heats up, until the temperature and pressure at the centre of the shrinking blob become so great that nuclear reactions begin. The gas blob has switched on to become a true star, generating its own heat and light for millions or, more usually, billions of years.

Several star-spawning clouds are well within reach of observation by amateurs. Most famous is the Orion Nebula, marking the sword in the constellation of Orion the Hunter. This nebula is visible as a hazy green glow to the naked eye; binoculars show it more clearly, while on photographs it appears complex and colourful (see next page).

Embedded within the Orion Nebula is a star called θ^1 (theta[1]) Orionis, recently born from the surrounding gas. Small telescopes divide this star into four components which form a group known as the Trapezium. Energy emitted by the brightest of these four stars makes the surrounding nebula shine.

Behind the bright, visible part of the cloud is an even larger, still-dark area where stars are being born at this moment. The Orion Nebula is estimated to contain enough matter to produce hundreds of stars: it is a star cluster in the making.

The Orion Nebula is by no means unique in our own Galaxy, and there are plenty of similar nebulae in other galaxies, too. One such example is the Tarantula Nebula in the southern constellation Dorado, which dwarfs the Orion Nebula. The Tarantula is part of a small nearby galaxy called the Large Magellanic Cloud.

Star clusters and associations

One celebrated group of stars that has come into being recently is the Pleiades cluster, popularly known as the Seven Sisters, in the constellation Taurus, the Bull. At least five members of the Pleiades can be distinguished by normal eyesight; binoculars and small telescopes bring dozens more members into view. The whole cluster is estimated to contain about a hundred stars. The brightest and youngest of these formed no more than 2 million years ago, making them extremely youthful by astronomical standards.

The Pleiades is an example of a type of cluster referred to as an *open cluster* or *galactic cluster*. About a thousand such clusters are known to astronomers, and the most prominent of them are listed in this book. Not far from the Pleiades in Taurus is a larger and older open cluster, the Hyades, which is estimated to be about 500 million years old. Being older than the Pleiades, the stars have had more time to drift apart. Eventually, most open clusters disperse completely. The Sun was probably a member of such a cluster when it was born 4600 million years ago.

Much larger than open clusters are *stellar associations*, vast scatterings of young stars hundreds of light years across. It is no coinci-

dence that most of the bright stars in Orion lie at similar distances from us, for they are members of such an association, centred on the Orion Nebula about 1500 light years away. Three times closer to us is the extensive Scorpius–Centaurus association, which extends across 60° or more of sky from Scorpius via Lupus into Centaurus and Crux. Antares is the brightest member; other prominent members are β (beta) Centauri, α (alpha) and β (beta) Crucis, and the open cluster IC 2602 in Carina. Associations arise from particularly large clouds of gas and dust in the spiral arms of our Galaxy.

An altogether different type of cluster, containing much older stars, is a *globular cluster*; these are described on page 291.

Star sizes and lifetimes

Nebulae are composed of a 10:1 mixture of hydrogen and helium, the primary constituents of the Universe, so, naturally enough, stars have this same composition. Stars get their energy from nuclear reactions which transform hydrogen into helium. In the reactions, four hydrogen atoms are crushed together to make one atom of helium; an uncontrolled version of the same reaction occurs in a hydrogen bomb.

There are certain limits on the size of a star. A gas blob with less than about 8 per

Ghostly, glowing swirls of the Orion Nebula, M42, a cradle of star formation. At its heart is the multiple star θ¹ (theta¹) Orionis, also known as the Trapezium (see inset); this lies near the tip of the dark intrusion known as the Fish's Mouth. North of M42 is the smaller, rounded knot of M43, actually part of the same great gas cloud. Farther north is the fainter smudge of NGC 1977 and, at top, the scattered cluster NGC 1981. South of M42 is ι (iota) Orionis and the wide double Struve 747. (Ryan Steinberg and Family/Adam Block/NOAO/AURA/NSF. Inset: Jim Rada/Adam Block/NOAO/AURA/NSF)

cent of the Sun's mass (equivalent to about 80 times the mass of Jupiter, the largest planet in the Solar System) cannot become a true star, because conditions in its interior will never reach the extremes necessary for nuclear reactions to begin.

Below this threshold, the gas blob would become a *brown dwarf*, a not-quite star that shines feebly from energy released during its contraction. Smaller still, below about 1 per cent the Sun's mass, the gas blob would be regarded as a planet. In other words, if gaseous Jupiter had possessed at least 10 times its current mass it would have been not a planet but a brown dwarf, and with a mass over 80 times its current value it would have been a small star, in which case our Sun would have had a faint companion.

At the other end of the scale, the largest stars have masses of about a hundred times that of the Sun. It was once thought that stars more massive than this would produce so much energy that they would literally disintegrate, but this may not be true in all cases. A few stars are known that seem to have masses greater than a hundred Suns, one example being η (eta) Carinae in the southern constellation Carina; this star has varied erratically in brightness in the past, as though on the verge of instability.

A star's most vital statistic is its mass, for this factor affects everything else about it: its temperature, its brightness and its lifetime. The stars with the least mass are, not surprisingly, the coolest; they are known as *red dwarfs*. A typical red dwarf such as Barnard's Star, the second-closest star to the Sun, has a mass about a tenth that of the Sun and glows a dull red with a surface temperature of about 3000°C. Even though Barnard's Star is only six light years away, it is too faint to be seen with the naked eye.

Surprisingly enough, stars with the lowest mass live the longest. Their nuclear fires burn so slowly that they can survive for as much as a million million years, a hundred times as long as the Sun. The Sun itself, which by definition is of one solar mass, has

The Horsehead Nebula in Orion, a dark cloud of cooler gas and dust seen in silhouette against a bright background of glowing hydrogen, looks like an interstellar chess piece. (Nigel Sharp/ NOAO/AURA/NSF)

a surface temperature of 5800°C, and is expected to live for about 10,000 million years. It is currently in the prime of its life.

Moving up the weight scale, a star such as Sirius, which is twice the Sun's mass, can live for only about 1000 million years, a tenth of the Sun's age. The surface temperature of Sirius is a blue-white 11,000°C. Larger and hotter still, the star Spica in the constellation Virgo has a mass of about 11 Suns and a surface temperature of around 24,000°C. The lifetime of this intensely hot, highly luminous star is less than 1 per cent of the lifetime of the Sun.

Star temperatures and colours

A star's colour is a direct indicator of its temperature. The most precise way to measure a star's temperature is to study the spectrum of its light, which is done by splitting up the light in a device called a spectroscope.

Stars are classified into a sequence of so-called *spectral types* according to their temperature, as shown in the table on page 273. The bluest and hottest stars are categorized as spectral types O and B. Stars of type O are rare and none is close enough to us to appear really bright. However, B-type stars are more common; prominent examples are α (alpha) and β (beta) Crucis, β (beta) Centauri and Spica; these are in fact the bluest of the first-magnitude stars.

Then come the cooler blue-white A-type stars, which include Sirius, followed by stars of F type, which appear white or yellow-white; Procyon is an example. G-type stars are yellow; they include the Sun, α (alpha) Centauri and τ (tau) Ceti. Cooler still are K-type stars, such as ε (epsilon) Eridani, which have orange hues. Coolest of all are stars with an M-type spectrum, examples being Antares and Betelgeuse which are the reddest first-magnitude stars. Red dwarfs also have M-type spectra but none of them are bright enough to be visible to the naked eye.

Each spectral type is subdivided into ten steps from 0 to 9; on this more precise scale, the Sun ranks as a G2 star. The seemingly haphazard lettering sequence used for spectral types is the result of a previous classification scheme which was rearranged and shortened to produce the present system. The sequence of stellar spectral types can be remembered by the mnemonic: 'Oh Be A Fine Girl, Kiss Me'.

Star colours are necessarily subjective, given the individual characteristics of different people's eyes and the varying conditions under which stars are viewed. For example, astronomers define Vega, of spectral type A0, as pure white, yet to most eyes it has a distinctly bluish cast, as do the components of Castor, also of type A. At the other end of

Columns of cooler hydrogen gas and dust up to one light year long protrude into the Eagle Nebula, M16, in Serpens. Ultraviolet light flooding from hot, young stars off the top of the picture evaporates gas from the surfaces of the columns, leaving behind denser knots where new stars are forming. In this image from the Hubble Space Telescope, hydrogen gas is depicted as green rather than the usual pink. (Jeff Hester and Paul Scowen, Arizona State University/NASA)

the scale, few so-called red giant or super-giant stars appear truly red, but more a deep orange or tan colour. The first-magnitude stars on the charts in this book are coloured according to their spectral types rather than how they actually appear to the eye.

An apparent paradox is that our Sun, whose light is usually thought of as white, is classified as a yellow star. In fact, what makes the daytime Sun appear white is its over-powering brilliance. If we could see it from a distance, so it was much fainter, it would indeed appear yellowish. It turns out that a star of truly white appearance to the eye has a spectral type of around F0, similar to that of Canopus, 2000°C hotter than the Sun.

The star colours described in the constel-lation notes in this book are an indication of how stars appear to an observer, although the real colours are subtle and your own visual impressions may well disagree. Indeed, you will find that the apparent intensity of the coloration varies from night to night with

NGC 2070 in the Large Magellanic Cloud is popularly known as the Tarantula Nebula because of its spidery shape. At its heart is an open cluster, R 136, containing some of the hottest and most massive stars known. Such massive stars have short lifetimes and are likely to die in supernova explosions. (ESO)

STELLAR SPECTRAL TYPES

Type	Assigned colour	Temperature range (°C)	Examples
O	Blue	40,000–25,000	ζ Puppis (supergiant)
B	Blue	25,000–11,000	Spica (main sequence) Regulus (main sequence) Rigel (supergiant)
A	Blue-white	11,000–7500	Vega (main sequence) Sirius (main sequence) Deneb (supergiant)
F	White	7500–6000	Canopus (supergiant) Procyon (subgiant) Polaris (supergiant)
G	Yellow	6000–5000	Sun (main sequence) α Centauri (main sequence) τ Ceti (main sequence) Capella (giant)
K	Orange	5000–3500	ε Eridani (main sequence) Arcturus (giant) Aldebaran (giant)
M	Red	3500–3000	Barnard's Star (main sequence) Antares (supergiant) Betelgeuse (supergiant)

changing atmospheric conditions. For faint stars, you will be unlikely to see any colour at all without optical aid.

When the spectral type of stars is plotted against their actual luminosity (absolute magnitude), all stars that are in stable, hydrogen-burning middle age are found to lie in a well-defined band across the graph known as the *main sequence*. Such a plot of stellar brightness against spectral type is known as a Hertzsprung–Russell diagram, after the Danish astronomer Ejnar Hertzsprung and the American Henry Norris Russell who jointly devised it in 1911–13. An example is shown on page 275.

A star's position along the main sequence is fixed by its mass, with the least massive stars at the bottom and the most massive stars at the top. The Sun, as befits its middle-of-the-road nature, lies about halfway along the main sequence.

Although most stars lie on the main sequence, a number of particularly bright stars lie above and to the right of it, while a few faint stars lie below and to the left of it. These stars are all in late stages of evolution. We can best understand what is happening to them by following the future evolution predicted for the Sun.

Evolving stars

As mentioned earlier, the Sun formed about 4600 million years ago and is now about halfway through its expected lifespan. In a few thousand million years, though, it will start to run out of hydrogen at its core. In search of more hydrogen to use as fuel, the nuclear reactions inside the Sun will start to move outwards, releasing more energy. Eventually, when they are surrounded by a

The Double Cluster in Perseus, NGC 869 and 884, is a pair of open clusters in a spiral arm of our Galaxy. NGC 884, at left, contains several red giants, suggesting that it is the more evolved of the two. (Leland Wehland/Flynn Haase/ NOAO/AURA/NSF)

shell of burning hydrogen, even the helium atoms in the Sun's core will enter into nuclear reactions of their own, fusing together to form carbon atoms.

With all this extra energy being given off, the Sun will become much brighter than it is today and will start to swell alarmingly in size. But as the Sun's outer layers expand they will also cool, becoming redder in colour, and the Sun will turn into a *red giant*, similar to the bright stars Aldebaran and Arcturus. At its largest, the red giant Sun will grow to at least a hundred times its present

diameter, engulfing Mercury, Venus and perhaps even the Earth within its outer layers. Needless to say, all life on our planet will long since have become extinct.

On the Hertzsprung–Russell diagram, the Sun's increase in brightness will move it upwards, off the main sequence, and its change in spectral type will in addition move it to the right. Stars at the top end of the main sequence, which are far more massive

In the Hertzsprung–Russell diagram, right, the true brightness of stars (their absolute magnitude) is plotted against their temperature (spectral type). Stars of different types fall in different areas of the diagram. The band running from top left to bottom right is the main sequence; the Sun falls roughly halfway along it. Giants and supergiants lie above the main sequence, while white dwarfs are below and to the left of it. (Wil Tirion)

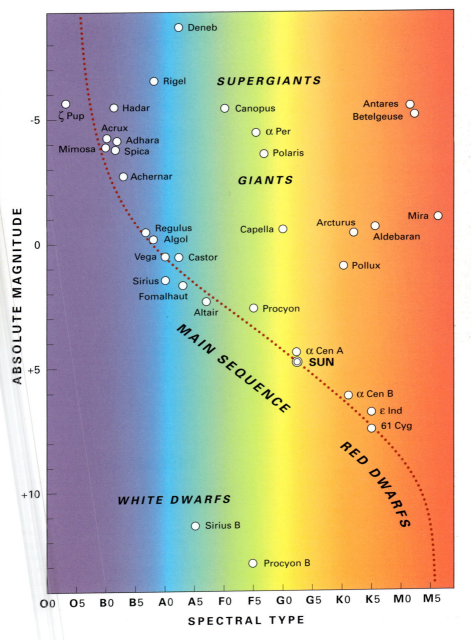

SUPERGIANTS

GIANTS

MAIN SEQUENCE

RED DWARFS

WHITE DWARFS

Deneb
Rigel
ζ Pup
Hadar
Acrux
Adhara
Mimosa
Spica
Achernar
Canopus
α Per
Polaris
Antares
Betelgeuse
Mira
Arcturus
Aldebaran
Capella
Regulus
Algol
Vega
Castor
Pollux
Sirius
Fomalhaut
Altair
Procyon
α Cen A
SUN
α Cen B
ε Ind
61 Cyg
Sirius B
Procyon B

ABSOLUTE MAGNITUDE

-5
0
+5
+10

SPECTRAL TYPE

O0 O5 B0 B5 A0 A5 F0 F5 G0 G5 K0 K5 M0 M5

STELLAR LUMINOSITY CLASSES

Ia0	Exceptionally bright supergiant
Ia	Bright supergiant
Iab	Less bright supergiant
Ib	Supergiant
II	Bright giant
III	Giant
IV	Subgiant
V	Main sequence
VI or sd	Subdwarf

than the Sun, become so big and bright at this stage of their evolution that they are referred to not as mere giants but as *supergiants*. Prominent examples of red supergiants are Betelgeuse and Antares, both of which are hundreds of times larger than the Sun. Other stars which have not yet evolved enough to become red in colour but which are nevertheless firmly in the supergiant bracket are Rigel, Deneb and Polaris.

To distinguish whether a star is, say, a giant or supergiant, or lies on the main sequence, astronomers assign stars a luminosity class (see the table above) in addition to the spectral type. For example, a G-type main-sequence star such as the Sun is classified GV, whereas a G-type giant such as Capella is GIII and the G-type supergiant Sadalmelik (Alpha Aquarii) is GIb.

As an aside, it should be noted that main-sequence stars are commonly referred to as dwarfs, even though the most massive of them may be several times larger in diameter than the Sun. Hence, although the Sun is in most ways an average star, in astronomical terminology it is classified as a dwarf.

Taken together, the spectral type and luminosity class define the main properties of a star as it exists at present. But those properties change as the star ages. Stars spend only a few per cent of their total lifetime in the red giant phase, which in the case of stars like the Sun amounts to no more than a few hundred million years. A red giant is a star that has grown old and is about to die.

Star death

Once a red giant has swollen beyond a certain size its distended outer layers drift off into space, forming a stellar smoke ring known rather confusingly as a *planetary nebula*, even though it has nothing to do with planets. The name was first used in 1785 by William Herschel, because they looked like the small, rounded disks of planets as seen through his telescope.

Probably the best-known of all planetary nebulae is the Ring Nebula in Lyra (M57), although it is not the easiest to see. Much larger is the Dumbbell Nebula, M27, in Vulpecula, which can be picked up in binoculars on a clear, dark night. Two small but bright planetary nebulae for amateur telescopes are NGC 6826 in Cygnus and NGC 7662 in Andromeda.

At the centre of a planetary nebula, the core of the former red giant is exposed as a small, intensely hot star. Once the surrounding gases of the planetary nebula have dispersed, usually after a few thousand years, the central star remains as a so-called *white dwarf*.

A white dwarf is only about the diameter of the Earth, but contains most of the matter of the original star; only about 10 per cent of the star's mass is lost in the planetary nebula stage. White dwarfs are therefore exceptionally dense bodies. A teaspoonful of white dwarf material would have a mass of thousands of kilograms. Over thousands of millions of years, white dwarfs slowly cool off and fade into oblivion.

NGC 6543, the Cat's Eye Nebula in Draco, consists of overlapping loops of ejected gas. In this image from the Hubble Space Telescope, different colours represent gas at different temperatures. (Bruce Balick, U. of Washington/NASA)

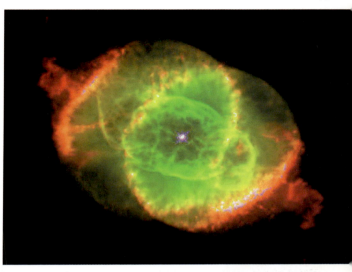

Below: M57, the Ring Nebula in Lyra, is actually a cylinder of gas ejected by the central star; it appears ring-like because we are looking at the cylinder end-on. (Adam Block/NOAO/ AURA/NSF)

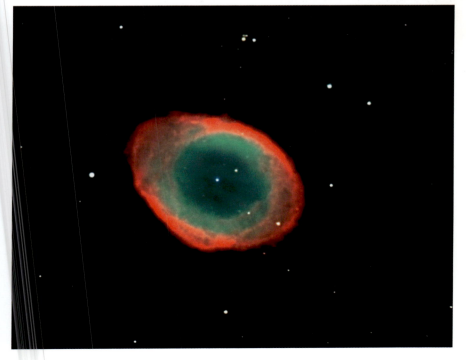

Being so small, white dwarfs are very faint. Not one is visible to the naked eye. Both the nearby bright stars Sirius and Procyon have white dwarf companions, but Procyon's companion is too close to its parent to be distinguishable in amateur telescopes, and the companion of Sirius can be glimpsed only under the most favourable conditions. The easiest white dwarf to see is a companion of the star o^2 (omicron^2) Eridani (also known as 40 Eridani); a small telescope will show it. Of added interest is a fainter third member of this system, a red dwarf, which is also visible in amateur telescopes.

Our Sun, it seems, is destined to go through the stage of being a planetary nebula before fading away as a white dwarf. But stars with several times the Sun's mass, towards the top end of the main sequence, suffer a far more spectacular end. As we have seen, they first become dazzling supergiants rather

Main picture, right: The η (eta) Carinae Nebula, NGC 3372, a large cloud of glowing hydrogen gas visible to the naked eye in the southern hemisphere, containing clusters of hot young stars. The nebula is named after η Carinae itself, a massive star that lies in the brightest central part, just above the V-shaped dark lane. (NOAO/AURA/NSF)

Inset, right: The area around η (eta) Carinae, left of centre, which is cocooned in a reddish cloud of gas thrown off in past outbursts. To the right of Eta Carinae is the bulbous Keyhole Nebula, shaped like a figure of eight, which appears slightly darker than the background nebulosity. η Carinae is a massive, unstable star that could erupt as a brilliant supernova within the next 10,000 years. (M. Bessell, R. Sutherland and M. Buxton, RSAA – Australian National University)

The Eskimo Nebula, NGC 2392 in Gemini, photographed with unprecedented clarity by the Hubble Space Telescope, gets its name from its resemblance to a face surrounded by a fur parka. In reality, the 'parka' is a disk of material thrown off the central star during its red giant phase, while the Eskimo's 'face' is a bubble of gas being blown into space by the intensely hot central star. (Andrew Fruchter, STScI/NASA/ESA)

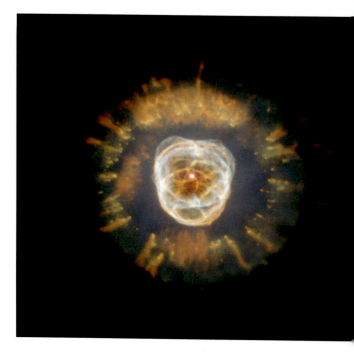

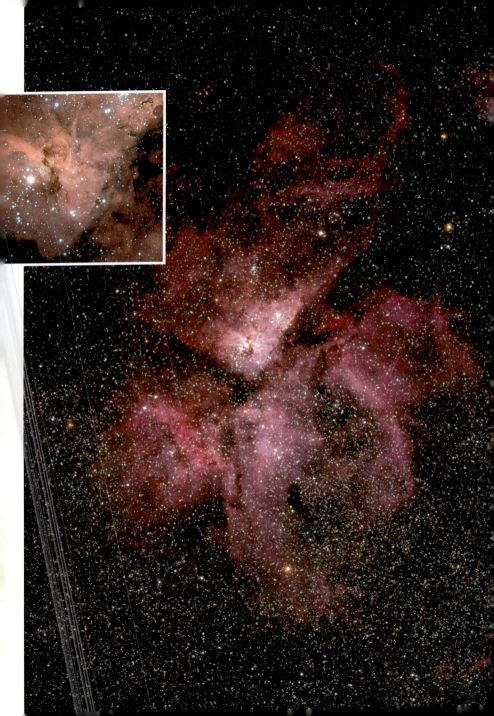

than mere giants. They do not get a chance to reach the planetary nebula stage. So massive are they that the nuclear reactions at their centres continue in runaway fashion until the star becomes unstable and explodes. Such an explosion is known as a *supernova*.

Supernovae and their remnants

In a supernova eruption a star's brightness increases millions of times, so that for a few days the star can rival the brilliance of an entire galaxy. The shattered outer layers of the star are thrown off into space at speeds of around 5000 km per second. In AD 1054 astronomers on Earth saw a star erupt as a supernova in the constellation Taurus. The star became brighter than Venus, and was visible in daylight for three weeks. It finally faded from naked-eye view more than a year after it had first appeared.

The Crab Nebula, M1, the remains of a star that exploded as a supernova, with the planet Jupiter superimposed for size comparison. The blue colour of the nebula comes from electrons spiralling in its magnetic field, while the red flecks are hydrogen gas. The Crab Pulsar is the lowermost of the two stars near the nebula's centre; the other star is an unrelated foreground object. (Crab Nebula image: Laird Thompson, University of Hawaii/CFHT)

At the site of that explosion lies one of the most famous objects in the heavens: the Crab Nebula, the shattered remains of the star that erupted. The Crab Nebula is visible as a smudgy patch in amateur telescopes, but is best seen on long-exposure photographs taken with large instruments. Over the next 50,000 years or so the gases of the Crab Nebula will disperse into space, forming delicate traceries like those of the Veil Nebula in Cygnus (see page 138), itself the remains of a former supernova.

The last supernova observed in our Galaxy was in 1604. This star, in the constellation Ophiuchus, reached a maximum magnitude of around −3, brighter than Jupiter. It was studied by the German astronomer Johannes Kepler, and is often known as Kepler's Star.

Hundreds of supernovae in other galaxies have been seen telescopically since then, but only one has become bright enough to be visible to the naked eye. That was Supernova 1987A, which erupted in our neighbouring galaxy the Large Magellanic Cloud. It was first spotted in 1987 on February 24 and rose to a maximum magnitude of 2.9 in late May, eventually fading from naked-eye view by the end of the year.

Another supernova in our Galaxy is long overdue. When it comes, it should be a spectacular sight. Many astronomers dream of seeing it outshining the other stars in the sky, dazzling the eye and casting shadows.

Supernova 1987A (the very bright star at lower right) exploded in 1987 in the Large Magellanic Cloud, near the Tarantula Nebula (left). The supernova was visible to the naked eye from the southern hemisphere for several months. (ESO)

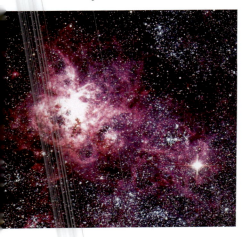

A star might not be entirely destroyed in a supernova explosion. Sometimes the central core of the exploded star is left as an object even smaller and denser than a white dwarf, termed a *neutron star*. In such an object, the protons and electrons of the star's atoms have been crushed by the tremendous forces of the supernova so that they combine to form the particles known as neutrons. A typical neutron star is a mere 20 km in diameter, but contains as much mass as one or two Suns.

Being so minute, neutron stars can spin very rapidly without flying apart. Each time they spin we receive a flash of radiation like a lighthouse beam. Astronomers have detected radio pulses from well over a thousand such sources, which they term *pulsars*; one lies at the centre of the Crab Nebula. The Crab Pulsar flashes 30 times per second; others pulse hundreds of times a second, while the slowest takes over 10 seconds. Most neutron stars are too faint to be seen optically, but the pulsar in the Crab Nebula has been seen flashing in step with the radio pulses.

Black holes

If the core of the exploded star has a mass of more than three Suns, then even a neutron star is not the end for it. Instead, it becomes something still more bizarre: a *black hole*. No force can shore up a dead star weighing more than three solar masses against the inward pull of its own gravity. It continues to shrink, becoming ever smaller and denser until its gravity becomes so great that nothing can escape from it, not even its own light. It has dug its own grave – a black hole.

Since a black hole is by definition invisible, it is of only academic interest to amateur observers. However, professional astronomers have detected X-ray emissions from various sources which they believe are caused by hot gas plunging into the bottomless pits of black holes. The best-known candidate for a black hole, Cygnus X-1, orbits a 9th-magnitude star in the neck of Cygnus, the Swan.

Double and multiple stars

To the naked eye, stars appear as solitary, isolated objects. But the great majority of them actually have one or more companion stars, too faint or too close to be seen separately with the naked eye but which can be distinguished telescopically. Many attractive double and multiple stars are within the range of binoculars and small telescopes, and the best are described in the constellation notes in this book.

There are two sorts of double star. In one type, the two stars are not truly associated but happen to lie in the same line of sight by chance; in this arrangement, termed an *optical double*, one star may be many times farther from us than the other. Such doubles are comparatively rare. In most cases, the two stars are physically linked by gravity, forming a genuine *binary* system. The two stars in a binary orbit their mutual centre of

gravity, which can take decades, centuries, or even millennia, depending how far apart they are. There are also triple, quadruple and even larger families of stars, and in such cases the orbits can become very complicated.

The closest star to the Sun, α (alpha) Centauri, is a triple system – a bright binary accompanied by a much fainter red dwarf known as Proxima. Another celebrated multiple star is the so-called Double Double, ε (epsilon) Lyrae. Binoculars show it to be a wide double, but modest-sized amateur telescopes reveal that each of these stars is itself double, making a quadruple system.

Orbits of four fast-moving binaries: 70 Ophiuchi (period 88 years), Zeta Herculis (34.5 years), Xi Ursae Majoris (60 years) and Gamma Virginis (169 years). (Ian Ridpath/Wil Tirion)

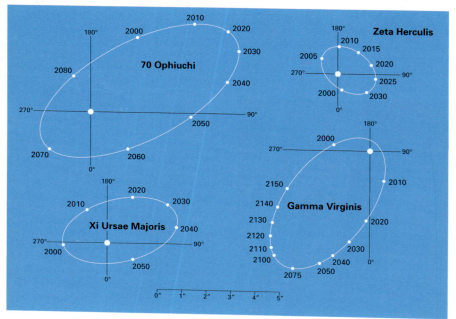

Three parameters describe the appearance of a double star: the brightnesses of the individual components, their separation and their relative orientation, known as position angle (PA). Separation is usually given in seconds (") of arc, although minutes (') may be used for wider pairs. Position angle is more tricky to understand. It is the direction of the fainter star relative to the brighter one, measured in degrees counterclockwise from north (0°) via east (90°), south (180°) and west (270°). The east–west line (90°–270°) can be established by allowing objects to drift through the field of view as the Earth rotates. The diagram below shows the view through the eyepiece of an inverting telescope, with north at the bottom and east at the right. A double star with a position angle of 150° is illustrated.

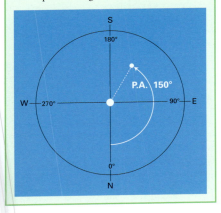

Even more remarkable is Castor, a system of six stars all linked by gravity. Amateur telescopes show that Castor consists of two bright blue-white stars close together, with a fainter third star some way off. Professional observations have revealed that each of these three stars is itself a *spectroscopic binary*. In a spectroscopic binary the two stars are too close together to be seen individually in any telescope, but analysis of the light from the star reveals the companion's presence. The two brightest stars of Castor take nearly 500

years to orbit each other, whereas their spectroscopic companions whirl around them in only a few days. Sometimes the members of a binary system eclipse each other as seen from Earth. Such *eclipsing binaries* are dealt with in the section on variable stars.

Observing double stars

For amateurs, the attraction of observing double stars lies in separating (or 'splitting') close doubles and in comparing their brightnesses and colours. Some pairs display a beautiful colour contrast, as with the yellow and blue-green components of Albireo, β (beta) Cygni. A similar pair with contrasting colours but smaller separation is γ (gamma) Andromedae. For a pair with almost identical colours look at 61 Cygni. Star colours are subtle, but can become more noticeable if you slightly defocus the telescope, or tap it gently to make the image vibrate.

The closer together two stars are, the larger the aperture of telescope needed to split them. A table giving the resolutions of various apertures can be found on page 392, but this not the whole story since the relative brightness of the two components also affects their observability. If one star is much fainter than the other it will be swamped by the primary star's light, and so will be more difficult to see than a companion that is of similar brightness to the main star.

Another factor to take into account is that the separation of binary pairs with relatively short orbital periods can change markedly over a few years as the stars orbit each other. The changing positions of four fast-moving binaries is shown in the diagram on page 282.

The notes in this book on objects of interest give guidance as to the likely aperture needed to split various double stars. But there can be no hard-and-fast rules. So much depends on the observer's eyesight, the quality of telescope and the observing conditions. The only way to find out for sure is to look yourself.

Variable stars

Certain stars change in brightness over time, and are known as *variable stars*. Amateur astronomers can make valuable observations of such stars. The observer estimates the brightness of the variable by comparing it with nearby stars of known constant magnitude, and the observations are plotted on a graph to form what is known as a *light curve*, illustrating how the star's brightness varies with time. Such a graph can reveal much about the nature of the star under study. Light curves of three famous variables are shown on the facing page.

As might be expected, the usual reason that a star appears to vary is because of actual changes in its light output, but that is not the only possible explanation. In some cases the star is a member of a binary system in which one star periodically eclipses the other. For this to happen, the stars' orbits must be oriented virtually edge-on to us. The first such *eclipsing binary* to be noticed, and still the most famous, is Algol in the constellation Perseus; its variability was discovered in the 1660s by Geminiano Montanari of Italy.

Eclipsing variables

Algol consists of a blue-white main-sequence star, from which most of the light comes, orbited by a fainter orange subgiant. Every 2.87 days Algol's brightness drops from magnitude 2.1 to 3.4 in five hours as the fainter star obscures the brighter one, returning to normal after another five hours as the star reemerges. Compare it at maximum with α (alpha) Persei, magnitude 1.8, and at minimum with δ (delta) Persei, magnitude 3.0 (see the chart on page 286). There is also a secondary minimum half an orbit later when the brighter star passes in front of the fainter one, but the drop in light is too small for the eye to notice. Most variable-star observers start their careers by following the changes in

Algol's brightness; predictions of its eclipses are issued by astronomical societies and in astronomy magazines.

An extreme form of eclipsing binary is β (beta) Lyrae, in which the stars are so close together that they have been distorted into elongated shapes by each other's gravity. Beta Lyrae varies between magnitudes 3.3 and 4.4 every 12.9 days. Its brightness continually changes even outside of eclipses as the elongated stars move around their orbits. Compare it with nearby γ (gamma) Lyrae, constant at magnitude 3.2, and κ (kappa) Lyrae, magnitude 4.3.

Pulsating variables

Of the stars that vary intrinsically in brightness, most do so because of physical changes in their size. These are known as *pulsating variables* (not to be confused with pulsars). Of particular importance to astronomers are the so-called *Cepheid variables*, named after their prototype δ (delta) Cephei.

Cepheid variables are yellow supergiant stars that go through one cycle of pulsations in periods ranging from about 2 to 40 days, varying in brightness by up to one magnitude as they do so. δ Cephei itself ranges between magnitudes 3.5 and 4.4 every 5.4 days, and is thus an easy object for amateur observation. Good comparison stars are ε (epsilon) Cephei, magnitude 4.2, and ζ (zeta) Cephei, magnitude 3.4 (see the chart on page 287). Other bright Cepheids for easy amateur observation are η (eta) Aquilae (magnitude range 3.5 to 4.4, period 7.2 days), ζ (zeta) Geminorum (3.6 to 4.2, 10.2 days) and, in the southern hemisphere, l Carinae (3.3 to 4.2, 35.5 days).

The importance of Cepheid variables is that their period of pulsation is directly related to their absolute magnitude: the brighter the Cepheid, the longer it takes to

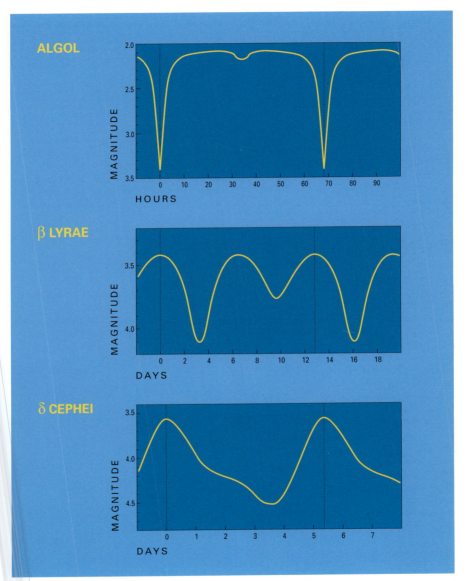

ALGOL

β LYRAE

δ CEPHEI

Light curves of three well-known variable stars: Algol, β (beta) Lyrae and δ (delta) Cephei. Their brightness rises and falls in a predictable fashion over the course of a few days. Note that the rise to maximum of δ Cephei is quicker than its subsequent decline. The small secondary minimum of Algol midway between the main fades is undetectable to the naked eye. (Wil Tirion)

complete one cycle of variation. Astronomers therefore have an easy way of finding these stars' absolute magnitude, simply by observing their period of fluctuation. When the absolute magnitude is compared with the apparent magnitude, the star's distance can easily be computed. Cepheid variables thus make important distance indicators within our own Galaxy and to other galaxies.

Another important class of pulsating stars are the *RR Lyrae variables*. These are old blue stars frequently found in globular clusters, and they vary by about 0.5 to 1.5 magnitudes in less than a day. Their prototype, RR Lyrae itself, varies from magnitude 7.1 to 8.1 and back in 0.57 days. Stars of this type all have similar absolute magnitudes, which makes them valuable distance indicators.

Minor types of pulsating variables include β (beta) Cephei stars and δ (delta) Scuti stars, both of which have short periods of only a few hours and ranges of variation too small to be noticeable to the naked eye.

Each type of variable falls in a specific area on the Hertzsprung–Russell diagram, and represents stars of different mass at various stages of their evolution. Variability of one kind or another seems to be an inevitable consequence of the ageing process of all stars – including, one day, our own Sun.

Long-period variables

Red giants and red supergiants are old stars that frequently prove to be variable. They pulsate, but not with anything like the same regularity as the types of stars mentioned above. The most abundant type of variables known are the Mira stars, also termed *long-period variables*, which have periods ranging from about three months to two years and amplitudes of several magnitudes. This is the type of variable our Sun is expected to evolve into, billions of years from now.

Their prototype is Mira, o (omicron) Ceti, in the constellation Cetus, the Whale, a red giant which ranges between about 3rd and 9th magnitude every 11 months or so, although the exact period and amplitude differ slightly from cycle to cycle. A finder chart is given on page 116. Another promi-

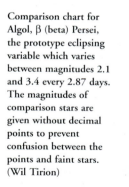

Comparison chart for Algol, β (beta) Persei, the prototype eclipsing variable which varies between magnitudes 2.1 and 3.4 every 2.87 days. The magnitudes of comparison stars are given without decimal points to prevent confusion between the points and faint stars. (Wil Tirion)

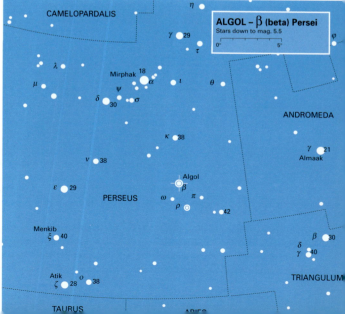

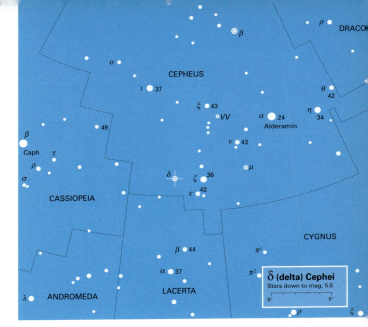

Comparison chart for δ (delta) Cephei, the prototype Cepheid variable which varies between magnitudes 3.5 and 4.4 every 5.4 days. The magnitudes of comparison stars are given without decimal points to prevent confusion between the points and faint stars. (Wil Tirion)

DRACO

CEPHEUS

CASSIOPEIA

Caph

ANDROMEDA

LACERTA

CYGNUS

δ (delta) Cephei
Stars down to mag. 5.5

0°   5°

Alderamin

nent Mira-type variable is χ (chi) Cygni, in the neck of Cygnus, the Swan.

More erratic are the *semi-regular variables*, typically with periods of about 100 days and amplitudes of 1 or 2 magnitudes. Finally, the *irregular variables* have little or no discernible pattern at all to their fluctuations. All these stars are red giants and red supergiants that have reached a stage of instability, oscillating in size and brightness. Prominent examples of semi-regular and irregular variables are Antares, Betelgeuse, α (alpha) Herculis and μ (mu) Cephei.

Novae

Most spectacular of all variable stars are the *novae*, which suddenly and unexpectedly erupt by perhaps 10 magnitudes (10,000 times) or more, sometimes becoming visible to the naked eye where no star appeared before. Their name comes from the Latin meaning 'new', for they were once thought to be genuinely new stars. Now we know that they are merely old, faint stars under-

going a temporary outburst. Despite their name, they are not related to supernovae, which are massive stars that explode for different reasons, as explained on page 280.

According to current theory, novae are close binary stars, one member being a white dwarf. Gas spilling from the companion star onto the white dwarf is thrown off in an eruption. The star does not disrupt itself in a nova outburst. In fact, some novae have undergone more than one recorded outburst, notably RS Ophiuchi and T Pyxidis, and perhaps all novae recur, given time.

A nova rises to maximum brightness in a few days. Amateur astronomers are often the first to spot such eruptions and to notify professional observatories. After a few days or weeks at maximum comes a slow decline over several months, as the nova slowly sinks back to its previous obscurity, sometimes punctuated by minor additional outbursts. Following the progress of a nova is one of the most fascinating aspects of variable star observation. Prominent naked-eye novae occur only about once a decade, but many fainter ones are visible through binoculars.

M81, a near-perfect spiral galaxy in Ursa Major, is tipped at an angle to our line of sight and so appears foreshortened along one axis. (Nigel Sharp/NOAO/AURA/NSF)

The Milky Way, galaxies and the Universe

Our Sun and all the stars visible in the night sky are members of a vast aggregation of stars known as the Galaxy (given a capital G to distinguish it from any other galaxy). Our Galaxy is spiral in shape, with arms composed of stars and nebulae winding outwards from a central bulge of stars. It is about 100,000 light years in diameter; the Sun lies in a spiral arm some 30,000 light years from the Galaxy's centre. Astronomers estimate that the Galaxy contains at least 250,000 million stars.

Most of the stars in the Galaxy lie in a disk about 2000 light years thick. Seen from our position within the Galaxy, this disk of stars appears as a faint, hazy band crossing the sky on clear, dark nights. We call this band the Milky Way, and the name Milky Way is often used for our entire Galaxy. The star fields of the Milky Way are particularly dense in the region of Sagittarius, which is the direction of the Galaxy's centre. Note that the plane of the Milky Way is tilted at 63° with respect to the celestial equator. This results from a combination of the tilt of the Earth's axis, and the fact that the plane of the Earth's orbit around the Sun is tilted with respect to the plane of the Galaxy.

M3 in Canes Venatici, visible with binoculars and small telescopes, is one of the brightest and richest of the globular clusters that surround our Galaxy in a halo. Globular clusters contain some of the oldest stars in the Galaxy. (Maureen Van den Berg, Univ. Leiden/Nik Szymanek/ING)

M51, the beautiful Whirlpool Galaxy in Canes Venatici, and its small companion galaxy NGC 5195. This companion has apparently twisted the outstretched spiral arm of M51 during a recent encounter, and it now lies behind the arm. (Javier Méndez/ING and Nik Szymanek/SPA)

Globular clusters

Dotted around our Galaxy in a spherical halo are more than a hundred ball-shaped conglomerations of stars known as *globular clusters*. These each contain from a hundred thousand to several million stars, all bound together by gravity. Several globular clusters are visible with the naked eye or binoculars. The brightest are ω (omega) Centauri and 47 Tucanae, both in the southern hemisphere; in the northern hemisphere the best example is M13 in Hercules.

To the naked eye and in binoculars, these objects appear as softly glowing patches of light. Moderate-sized telescopes start to resolve some of the individual red giant stars, giving the clusters a speckled appearance. Globular clusters formed early in the history of the Galaxy and contain some of the most ancient stars known, 10,000 million years or more old, over twice the age of the Sun.

The Local Group

Our Galaxy has two small and irregularly shaped companion galaxies called the Magellanic Clouds. To the naked eye they appear like detached portions of the Milky Way, in the southern constellations Dorado and Tucana. The Large Magellanic Cloud contains about one-tenth the number of stars in our Galaxy and lies about 170,000 light years away. The Small Magellanic Cloud has only about a fifth as many stars as the Large Magellanic Cloud, and lies somewhat farther off, about 200,000 light years. Both Clouds contain numerous star clusters and bright

Galaxies are classified according to their shape: elliptical, type E; spiral, type S; barred spiral, type SB; and irregular. It was once thought that galaxies evolved from one type into another as they aged, but this is not so. (Wil Tirion)

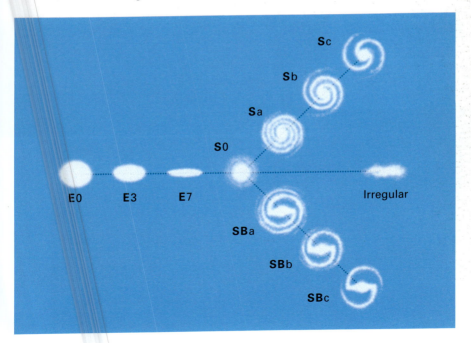

nebulae, and are rich territories for sweeping with instruments of all sizes. One can only imagine the magnificent view of our Galaxy that any astronomers living in the Magellanic Clouds would have.

Countless galaxies are dotted like islands throughout the Universe as far as the largest telescopes can see. Most galaxies are members of clusters containing anything from a dozen to many thousands of galaxies. Our own Milky Way is the second-largest member of a small cluster of 40 or so galaxies known as the Local Group.

The largest galaxy in the Local Group is visible to the naked eye as a fuzzy, elongated patch in the constellation Andromeda. The Andromeda Galaxy, also commonly known as M31, is estimated to contain about twice

Right: NGC 5850 is an 11th-mag. barred spiral in the Virgo Cluster. Its arms are wound tightly around the central bar, forming the shape of a Greek letter theta (θ). (Jeff and Paul Neumann/Adam Block/NOAO/AURA/NSF)

Below: NGC 4013 in Ursa Major is a spiral galaxy seen edge-on, crossed by a dark lane of dust in its central plane. (Blair Savage and Chris Howk, U. Wisconsin/Nigel Sharp, NOAO/WIYN/NSF)

Above: M87 is a massive elliptical galaxy in the Virgo Cluster, surrounded by a swarm of hundreds of globular clusters, visible here as hazy dots. (NOAO/AURA/NSF)

Right: M82 in Ursa Major is an edge-on spiral galaxy undergoing an immense burst of star formation. (Nigel Sharp/ NOAO/AURA/NSF)

as many stars as our own Galaxy, and to be about 25 per cent greater in diameter. It lies about 2.5 million light years away.

Long-exposure photographs reveal that the Andromeda Galaxy is a spiral, but tilted so that we see it almost edge-on. Amateur telescopes show that the Andromeda Galaxy has two small companion galaxies, M32 and M110, its equivalent of the Magellanic Clouds, although several additional fainter ones are visible through large telescopes.

The only other member of the Local Group within easy reach of amateur instruments is M33 in Triangulum, another spiral galaxy, somewhat farther from us than the Andromeda Galaxy and containing considerably fewer stars. M33 can be picked up in binoculars under clear, dark skies.

The nearest rich cluster of galaxies to the Local Group lies in the constellation of Virgo, part of it spilling over into neighbouring Coma Berenices. Of the Virgo Cluster's 3000 or so known members, dozens are within the reach of amateur telescopes.

Types of galaxy

Astronomers classify galaxies into three main types: elliptical, spiral and barred spiral (see the diagram on page 291). *Elliptical galaxies* range in shape from virtually spherical, designated E0, to flattened lens shapes, designated E7. They include both the largest and the smallest galaxies in the Universe. Supergiant ellipticals composed of up to 10 million million stars are the most luminous galaxies known. An example is M87 in the Virgo Cluster. At the other end of the scale, dwarf ellipticals resemble large globular clusters. Dwarf ellipticals may be the most abundant

type of galaxy in the Universe, but their faintness makes them difficult to see.

Spiral galaxies (type S), such as the great Andromeda Galaxy, M31, have arms winding out from a central bulge. There are usually two arms, but sometimes more. In *barred spirals* (type SB), such as NGC 1300 in Eridanus, the arms emerge from the ends of a bar of stars and gas that runs across the galaxy's centre. Most of the galaxies we see in the Universe are large, bright spirals.

Spiral and barred spiral galaxies are subdivided according to how tightly their arms are wrapped around the galaxy's core: types Sa and SBa have the tightest-wound arms, while types Sc and SBc have the loosest-wound arms. The Andromeda Galaxy is type

M77 in Cetus is the most prominent example of a Seyfert galaxy, a type of spiral with an unusually bright and active nucleus. (ING Archive/Nik Szymanek)

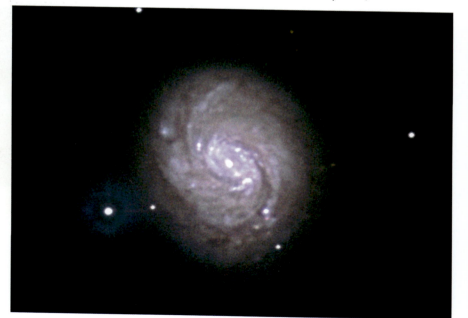

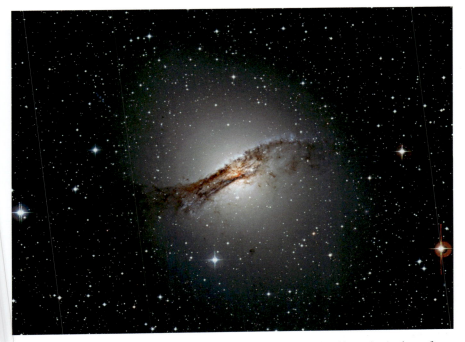

NGC 5128, also known as Centaurus A, is a supergiant elliptical galaxy with a prominent dust band. Elliptical galaxies do not normally contain dust, so NGC 5128 is thought to result from the merger of an elliptical galaxy with a spiral. (ESO)

Sb. Until recently, our own Galaxy was thought to fall midway between Sb and Sc, but it is now generally classified as a barred spiral, although the bar is only short.

In addition to these three main types there are certain galaxies classified as *irregular*; the two Magellanic Clouds are usually reckoned to fall into this class, although there is some semblance of spiral structure in the Large Magellanic Cloud.

Being faint, fuzzy objects, galaxies are best seen where skies are clear and dark, away from city haze and stray light. Low magnification is best, to increase the contrast of the galaxy against the sky background. Through a telescope you should see the nucleus of a galaxy as a starlike point surrounded by the misty halo of the rest of the galaxy. Do not expect to see prominent spiral arms, as on a long-exposure photograph, except through larger apertures at dark sites. Galaxies present themselves to us at all angles, so even spirals can seem to be elliptical in shape when viewed edge-on.

Peculiar galaxies

Strange things are going on within some galaxies. For example, certain galaxies give off vast amounts of energy as radio waves; these *radio galaxies* include the supergiant ellipticals M87 in Virgo and NGC 5128 (pictured above) in Centaurus. NGC 5128, in particular, looks like an elliptical galaxy that has been caught merging with a spiral. Some spiral galaxies have unusually bright nuclei. These are termed *Seyfert galaxies*, after the American astronomer Carl Seyfert, who was the first to draw attention to them, in 1943. M77 in Cetus (see the photograph on page 294) is the brightest Seyfert galaxy.

Most peculiar of all are the objects known as *quasars*, which emit as much energy as hundreds of normal galaxies from an area less than a light year in diameter. Despite their exceptional nature, quasars are not at all exciting visually, which is why they were overlooked until 1963. The brightest quasar, 3C 273, appears as an unimposing 13th-magnitude star in Virgo.

Observations with the Hubble Space Telescope have shown that quasars are actually the highly luminous centres of galaxies far off in the Universe. Radio galaxies, Seyferts and quasars are all now known to be related and are collectively termed *active galaxies*. Their central powerhouse is thought to be a massive black hole that gobbles up stars and gas from the surrounding galaxy, and its activity can be boosted by infalling gas when two galaxies collide. Most galaxies may have experienced such activity at their centres early in their evolution.

The expanding Universe

In 1929 the American astronomer Edwin Hubble made the most significant of all discoveries in cosmology: the galaxies are moving apart from one another, as though the Universe is expanding like a balloon being inflated. However, clusters of galaxies such as the Local Group do not expand – they are held together by their mutual gravitational attraction.

Hubble's discovery that the Universe is expanding came from a study of the spectrum of each galaxy's light. This revealed that the light from the galaxies was being lengthened

The redshift in the light from a distant galaxy is measured by the change in position of lines in its spectrum. Here, the change in position is shown in the visual window, the range of wavelengths to which the human eye is sensitive. All light from the galaxy is shifted by the same amount, so while some of the galaxy's light moves out of sight beyond the red end of the visual window, other light moves into the visible window from the ultraviolet. (Wil Tirion)

VISUAL WINDOW

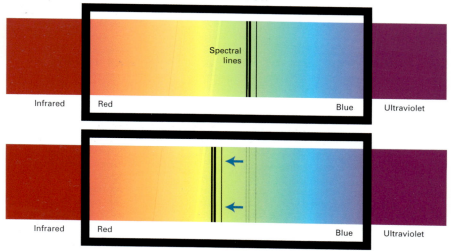

Infrared   Red   Blue   Ultraviolet

Spectral lines

Infrared   Red   Blue   Ultraviolet

in wavelength as a result of high-speed recession (this is called the Doppler effect). Such a lengthening of wavelength is called a *redshift*, because the light from the galaxy is moved towards the red (longer-wavelength) end of the spectrum.

Hubble found that the amount of redshift in a galaxy's light becomes greater with distance. Therefore, by measuring the red-shift of a galaxy astronomers can tell how far away it is. Quasars, for instance, exhibit such enormous redshifts that they must be the most distant objects visible in the Universe, over 10,000 million light years away.

Since the Universe is expanding, it is logical to conclude that it was once smaller and more densely packed than it is now. According to the most widely accepted theory, the entire Universe was originally a compressed, superdense blob which, for some unknown reason, exploded in a cata-

Stephan's Quintet in Pegasus is a group of five galaxies: NGC 7317 (top left), NGC 7318A and B (centre), NGC 7319 (bottom right) and NGC 7320 (lower left). However, NGC 7320 has a lower redshift than the others and also appears larger, which suggests it is a foreground object and not a true member of the cluster at all. (Nigel Sharp/NOAO/AURA/NSF)

clysm known as the Big Bang. The galaxies are the fragments from that explosion, still flying outwards as the space between them expands.

As far as anyone can tell at present, the Universe will continue to expand for ever. According to the best current estimates the Big Bang took place 13,700 million years ago; that is the age of the Universe as we know it. It is impossible to tell what, if anything, happened before the Big Bang.

The Sun

Our Sun is a glowing sphere of hydrogen and helium gas 1.4 million km in diameter, 109 times the diameter of the Earth and 745 times as massive as all the planets put together. The Sun is vital to all life on Earth because it provides the heat and light that makes our planet habitable. To astronomers, the Sun is important because it is the only star that we can observe in close-up. Studying the Sun tells us a lot that we could not otherwise know about stars in general.

Whereas most celestial objects pose problems for observers because they are faint, the Sun presents entirely the opposite dilemma: it is so bright that it is dangerous to look at. **It cannot be emphasized too strongly that anyone glancing for an instant at the Sun through any form of optical instrument, be it binoculars or telescope, risks instant blindness.** Even staring with the naked eye at the Sun for a few seconds can permanently damage your sight. There is a

The Sun on 19 May 2000, during the rise to solar maximum showing several sunspot groups, each large enough to swallow the Earth many times over. Note the effect of limb darkening, against which brighter faculae may be seen. (Mees Solar Observatory, University of Hawaii)

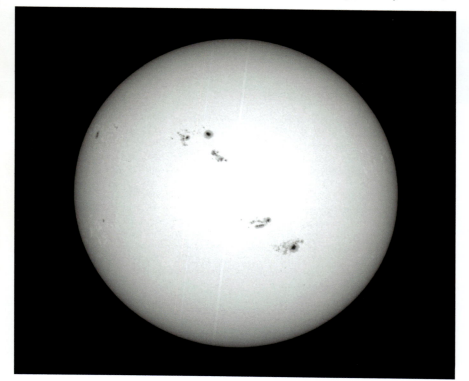

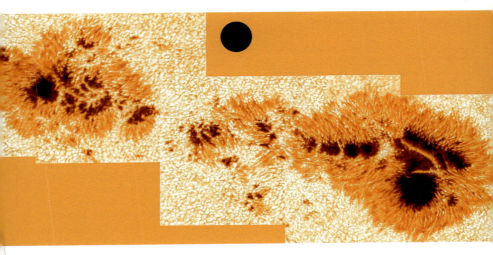

A complex group of sunspots some 200,000 km long as it appeared on 4 September 1998. The black circle shows the Earth to the same scale. Filamentary structure in the outer penumbra of the spots gives them a sunflower-like appearance. Note also the granulated appearance of the surrounding solar photosphere. (Kiepenheuer-Institut für Sonnenphysik)

safe and easy way to observe the Sun, and that is by projecting its image onto a white surface such as a screen or sheet of card (see box on page 302).

Some telescopes come equipped with dark Sun filters to place behind the eyepiece, but these should never be used because the focused light and heat of the Sun can crack them, with inevitably disastrous results. Safe filters for telescopic solar observation do exist, made either of glass or plastic film with a metallic coating. These filters fit over the front of the telescope tube, reducing the amount of incoming light and heat to safe levels. Filters made from a thin plastic film called Mylar give a bluish image, whereas other types give yellow or orange images.

A telescopic view of the Sun, seen either by projection or through a safe filter, displays the brilliant solar surface, the *photosphere* ('sphere of light'), consisting of seething gases at a temperature of 5500°C. Although intensely hot by terrestrial standards, this is cool by comparison with the Sun's core, where the energy-generating nuclear reactions take place; there, the temperature is calculated to be about 15 million °C.

Seen at high magnification, the photosphere exhibits a mottled effect termed *granu-lation*, caused by cells of hot gas bubbling up in the photosphere like water boiling in a pan. Granules range from about 300 km to 1500 km in diameter.

Look carefully at a projected image of the Sun, and you will notice that the edges of the Sun appear fainter than the centre of the disk, an effect known as *limb darkening*. This is caused by the fact that the gases of the photosphere are somewhat transparent, so that at the centre of the disk we are looking more deeply into the Sun's hotter and brighter interior than at the limbs.

Brighter patches on the photosphere known as *faculae* may be visible against the limb darkening. Faculae are areas of higher-temperature gas. More prominent are dark markings known as *sunspots*, patches of cooler gas that come and go on the photosphere.

Sunspots and solar rotation

Sunspots arise where magnetic lines of force burst through the photosphere from within the Sun. The presence of a strong magnetic field blocks the outward flow of heat from inside the Sun, producing the cooler spot. Sunspots have a dark centre known as the *umbra*, of temperature about 4000°C, surrounded by a brighter *penumbra* at about 5000°C. The temperature of a sunspot's umbra is similar to that of the surface of a red giant star such as Aldebaran, so a spot would glow quite brightly if it could be seen in isolation; in practice, sunspots appear dark by contrast with the brilliance of the surrounding photosphere.

Sunspots range in size from small pores no bigger than a large granule to enormous, complex patches many times larger than the Earth. Spots of that size are visible to the naked eye when the Sun is dimmed by the atmosphere, shortly after sunrise or before sunset, or through special solar filters.

A major sunspot takes about a week to develop to full size, then slowly dies away again over the next fortnight or so. The largest sunspots tend to form in groups long enough to span the best part of the distance from the Earth to the Moon. Spot groups can persist for one or two solar rotations (a month or two).

As the Sun rotates, new spots are brought into view at one limb while others disappear around the opposite limb. By observing the progress of spots as they are carried across the Sun's face, we can measure the rotation period of the Sun.

Being gaseous and not solid, the Sun does not rotate at the same rate at all latitudes. It spins most quickly at its equator, in 25 days; this slows to about 28 days at latitude 45°; and near the poles it is slowest of all, 34 days. The average figure usually quoted, 25.38 days, refers to the rotation rate at latitude 17°. These rotation periods are relative to a fixed external point. Since the Earth is not fixed but is orbiting the Sun, a spot takes

SUN DATA

Diameter	1,392,000 km
Mass	1.99×10^{30} kg
Mean density (water = 1)	1.41
Volume (Earth = 1)	1,304,000
Apparent magnitude	−26.8
Absolute magnitude	+4.82
Axial rotation period (average)	25.38 d
Axial inclination	7°.25
Mean distance from Earth	149,600,000 km

about two days longer than this to rotate once with respect to the Earth.

Usually, a spot group contains two main components, aligned east–west. The spot that leads across the disk as the Sun rotates is termed the p (preceding) spot, and is usually larger than its follower, the f spot. The p and f spots have opposite magnetic polarities, like the ends of a horseshoe magnet. The horseshoe is completed by invisible lines of force looping between the spots.

Flares, CMEs and aurorae

Sometimes the intense magnetic field lines in a complex sunspot group become entangled, releasing a sudden flash of energy known as a *flare* that may last from a few minutes to an hour. Atomic particles are spewed out into space by the eruption of a flare. These particles reach Earth about a day later where they cause effects in the upper atmosphere such as radio interference and the ethereal displays known as *aurorae*.

In an aurora, the sky glows with patches of green and red light that can take the form of folded drapery or arches, shimmering and changing shape for hours on end. Aurorae occur near the Earth's magnetic poles and extend to lower latitudes only at times of extreme solar activity, so they are seldom visible outside far northerly or southerly latitudes.

Until the 1970s, flares were the only known cause of aurorae, but it is now realized that another form of activity called

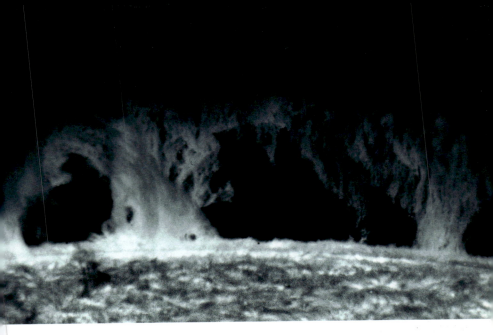

coronal mass ejections (CMEs) actually has a greater effect. CMEs are huge bubbles of hot gas thrown off from the Sun, sometimes at the same time as a flare but often without flares. The existence of CMEs was not recognized earlier because they can be detected only from space. They are now monitored routinely by spacecraft.

The solar cycle

The number of sunspots on view, along with other forms of solar activity, waxes and wanes in a cycle lasting 11 years on average, although the length of individual cycles has been as short as 8 years and as long as 16 years. At times of minimum activity the Sun may be spotless for days on end, whereas at solar maximum over a hundred spots may be visible at any one time.

However, the level of activity varies considerably from cycle to cycle; the average number of sunspots visible at maximum has ranged from 40 to 180, and even when the Sun is supposedly quiet some large spots and

Solar prominences extending 65,000 km into space look like enormous burning trees at the edge of the Sun. This photograph was taken at the wavelength of light emitted by hydrogen gas. (Big Bear Solar Observatory)

flares can break out. Solar activity is notoriously unpredictable, which adds to its fascination for observers.

A few general rules can be deduced, however. The first spots of each new cycle appear at latitudes of about 30–35° north and south of the Sun's equator. As the cycle progresses, spots tend to form closer to the equator. Sunspot numbers build up to a peak, then start to decay again.

As minimum approaches, the last spots of the cycle are found at latitudes between 5° and 10° north and south of the equator. At the same time – that is, around solar minimum – the first spots of the next cycle are starting to appear at higher latitudes. Sunspots are seldom found on the Sun's equator, and spots at solar latitudes greater than 40° are exceedingly rare.

The Sun's outer layers

Above the photosphere is a tenuous layer of gas known as the *chromosphere*, about 10,000 km deep. So faint is the chromosphere that it is normally invisible except with special instruments. It can, however, be seen for a few seconds at a total eclipse, when it appears as a pinkish crescent just before and after the Moon completely covers the face of the Sun. This pinkish colour is caused by light from hydrogen gas, and gives rise to the layer's name, which means 'colour sphere'.

Also visible around the edge of the Sun at total eclipses are huge tufts or loops of gas known as *prominences,* which extend from the chromosphere into space. They have the same characteristic rosy-pink colour as the chromosphere, caused by emission from hydrogen.

Like so many features of the Sun, prominences are controlled by magnetic fields. So-called *quiescent prominences* extend for 100,000 km or more across the Sun, often forming graceful arches tens of thousands of kilometres high. When seen silhouetted against the brighter background of the Sun's disk they are termed *filaments*. Quiescent prominences can last for months.

At the other end of the scale are *eruptive prominences*, with lifetimes of only a few hours. They are actually flares seen at the limb of the Sun, ejecting material into space at speeds of up to 1000 km per second. All forms of solar activity – sunspots, flares and prominences – follow the 11-year solar cycle.

Observing the Sun

Projecting the Sun's image is the recommended method of observation for all beginners. A small refractor is ideal for this purpose. If you have a reflector larger than 100 mm, stop down the aperture or heat may damage the optics. Take great care when aiming the telescope. Cover the main lens or mirror and the finder to ensure that no light accidentally enters your eyes. Squint along the tube or line up the telescope on its own shadow (do *not* look through the telescope).

Regular observers use a lightweight solar observing box attached to the eyepiece, into which the Sun's image is projected. Counting individual sunspots and sunspot groups to build up a record of changing solar activity is one of the main purposes of solar observation.

You may also wish to make a sketch of the Sun's appearance. A circle of 6 inches (150 mm) diameter is the standard size for solar disk drawings. Divide the circle into smaller squares 1 cm or so across so that the positions of sunspots can be accurately copied onto a chart.

In a projected image, north is at the top and west at the left for an observer in the northern hemisphere, but the other way round in the southern hemisphere. To find the exact orientation at any time, watch sunspots drift from east to west as the Earth turns.

To observe the Sun safely, project its image onto a white surface. Never look directly at the Sun through any form of optical instrument without a specialized solar filter. (ESO)

The corona and solar wind

The Sun's crowning glory is its *corona*, a faint halo of gas that comes into view only when the brilliant photosphere is blotted out at a total solar eclipse. The corona is composed of exceptionally rarefied gas at a temperature of 1 to 2 million °C. Petal-like streamers of coronal gas extend from the Sun's equatorial zone, while shorter, more delicate plumes fan out from the polar regions. The shape of the corona changes during the solar cycle: at solar maximum, when there are more active areas on the Sun, the corona appears more rounded than at solar minimum.

Gas from the corona is continually flowing away from the Sun out into the Solar System, forming what is known as the *solar wind*.

The spectacular corona of the Sun springs into view at total solar eclipses. This was its appearance at the eclipse of 21 June 2001, near the time of solar maximum, photographed from Zambia. (John Walker)

Atomic particles of the solar wind are detected streaming past the Earth at a speed of about 400 km per second. The most obvious effect of the solar wind is to push comet tails away from the Sun.

The solar wind extends outwards beyond the orbit of the most distant planet, finally merging with the thin gas between the stars. In a sense, therefore, all the planets of the Solar System can be said to lie within the outer reaches of the Sun's corona.

The Solar System

In one sense our Sun is unusual, for it is not accompanied by another star, as are most stars, but has a family of eight major planets, various moons and countless smaller lumps of debris. This retinue of bodies, all held captive by the Sun's gravity, is called the Solar System.

All the objects in the Solar System shine by reflecting the light from the Sun. Several of the planets when at their brightest can equal or outshine the brightest stars. All the planets orbit the Sun in approximately the same flat plane, so they are always to be found near the ecliptic. A bright 'star' that disturbs a familiar constellation pattern along the ecliptic is therefore almost certainly a planet (although it could, just possibly, be a nova).

Planetary orbits

As seen from above the Sun's north pole, the planets orbit the Sun in an anticlockwise direction. Their orbits are slightly elliptical in shape, so that each planet's distance from the Sun varies somewhat during one orbit. The closest point of a body's orbit to the Sun is known as the *perihelion*; the farthest point is the *aphelion*.

In order of distance from the Sun, the eight major planets are: Mercury, Venus, Earth, Mars, Jupiter, Saturn, Uranus and Neptune. The four inner planets are rocky and relatively small. Then come four giants composed mostly of gas and liquid.

Between the orbits of Mars and Jupiter lies a belt of rocky bodies known as the minor planets or asteroids; some asteroids stray outside this belt across the paths of the planets, creating an impact hazard. At the outer limits of the Solar System is an assortment of small, frozen bodies including Pluto, once regarded as the ninth planet but downgraded to the status of a dwarf planet in 2006.

Venus has the most circular orbit of all the planets; its distance from the Sun varies by less than 1.4% (the Earth's distance varies by 3.4%). The planet with the most elliptical orbit is Mercury, which is over 50% farther from the Sun at aphelion than when at perihelion. Some of the asteroids have orbits that are more elliptical than this, while comets have highly distended orbits that can take them from the innermost part of the Solar System out to way beyond Neptune.

The basic unit of distance in the Solar System is the *astronomical unit*, the average distance of the Earth from the Sun; it is equivalent to 149,597,870 km. Light takes 499 seconds (8.3 minutes) to cross this gulf, so we on Earth see the Sun as it actually appeared 8.3 minutes ago. Although large compared with everyday distances on Earth, the astronomical unit is insignificant in comparison with a light year, the unit used to express distances between stars. There are 63,240 astronomical units in a light year.

How long a planet takes to orbit the Sun depends on its distance: the closest planets orbit the quickest, and the farthest orbit the slowest. The orbital periods of the planets are usually expressed in terms of Earth days and years; they range from 88 days for Mercury to 165 years for Neptune. These values are known technically as *sidereal periods*, and are measured with respect to a fixed point such as the distant stars.

Aspects of the planets

As the two inner planets, Mercury and Venus, move along their orbits they periodically pass between us and the Sun; when that happens, they are said to be at *inferior conjunction*. They are then closest to the Earth, although this fact is of little use to observers since they are lost in the Sun's glare and their illuminated hemispheres are turned away from us.

Above left: The sizes of the planets to scale, compared with a section of the Sun. Above right:
The orbits of the planets to scale. (Wil Tirion)

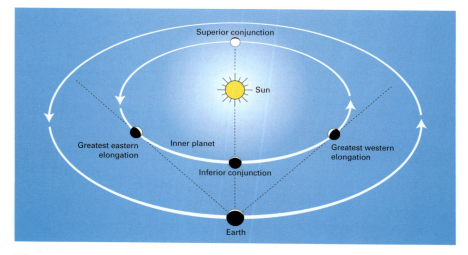

When Venus or Mercury lies directly between the Earth and the Sun it is said to be at inferior conjunction; on the far side of the Sun it is at superior conjunction. Maximum angular separation from the Sun is termed greatest elongation. (Wil Tirion)

The orbits of Mercury and Venus are tilted by 7° and 3°.4 respectively to the orbit of the Earth, sufficient to ensure that they usually pass above or below the disk of the Sun at inferior conjunction. But occasionally they do cross the face of the Sun as seen from Earth, an event termed a *transit*. When in transit, the planet appears as a tiny dark dot like a small sunspot against the glaring solar surface. Transits of Mercury are more common than those of Venus: the next are due in

2016, 2019, 2032 and 2039, whereas the transit of Venus in 2012 is the last one for over a century.

When Mercury or Venus lie on the far side of the Sun from us they are said to be at *superior conjunction*. However, when Mars or any of the planets beyond it lie on the far side of the Sun they are simply said to be at conjunction – being farther from the Sun than we are, outer planets can never come between Earth and the Sun, so there is no ambiguity about which sort of conjunction is

Transit: Multiple images of Mercury at the transit of 8 November 2006 create a dotted line across the face of the Sun in this composite view from the Solar and Heliospheric Observatory (SOHO) spacecraft. (ESA/NASA)

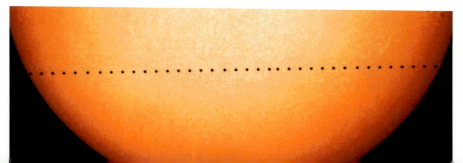

meant. Planets at conjunction are invisible in the Sun's glare.

The best time to view the two inner planets is when they are at their maximum angular separation from the Sun, known as *greatest elongation*. At greatest elongation Venus appears almost exactly half-phase; in the case of Mercury, though, the phase can vary noticeably from 50 per cent as a result of the planet's elliptical orbit. When at eastern elongation, planets set after the Sun in the evening sky; at western elongation, they rise before the Sun in the morning.

The time between one greatest eastern elongation of Mercury and the next, or one greatest western elongation and the next, is 116 days. With Venus, greatest western elongations or greatest eastern elongations recur every 584 days, although Venus is so prominent that it can be adequately observed well away from greatest elongation.

Incidentally, the interval between one given aspect of a planet and the next – be it conjunction, elongation or whatever – is known as its *synodic period*. This differs from the sidereal period because our observation platform, the Earth, is constantly moving in orbit around the Sun.

The best opportunities to see Mars and the other outer planets is when they are directly opposite the Sun in the sky; this is termed *opposition* (Mercury and Venus, being between the Earth and the Sun, cannot come to opposition). At opposition, a planet appears due south for northern hemisphere observers (due north for observers in the southern hemisphere) at midnight local time, or 1 a.m. if daylight-saving time is in operation. Opposition is the best time to observe the outer planets for this is when they lie closest to the Earth and hence appear at their biggest and brightest.

Other Solar Systems?

Planets are thought to be born from a disk of gas and dust left over after the formation of a star, a process that happened some 4.6 billion years ago around our Sun. Several stars are known to have such disks around them, including Vega, Fomalhaut and β (beta) Pictoris, so in these cases we may well be catching the process of planet formation in action. Astronomers have also detected signs of fully formed planetary systems, in most cases from the slight wobble in position of a star as a large planet orbits it. The first star with a planet detected in this way was 51 Pegasi, in 1995. Four years later, not just one but three planets were found around υ (upsilon) Andromedae, the first multi-planet system known.

Other techniques have since confirmed the existence of extrasolar planets, such as tiny dips in a star's light as a planet crosses in front of it and the detection of a star's light reflected from the surface of a planet. With large telescopes of the future, it may be possible to obtain direct images of planets around other stars.

A disk of dust around β (beta) Pictoris, photographed by the Hubble Space Telescope and depicted in false colour, presents persuasive evidence of planet formation. Beta Pictoris itself is obscured by the black circle at the centre. The dust disk is aligned almost edge-on to us, and is larger than the orbit of Neptune around the Sun. (NASA)

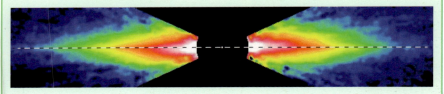

The Moon

The Moon, the Earth's natural satellite and nearest celestial neighbour, is an object of perennial fascination for observers. Despite its small size – 3475 km in diameter, roughly a quarter that of the Earth – it is so close to us, on average 384,400 km, that even the unaided eye can pick out the major markings that create the familiar 'man in the Moon' pattern, while ordinary binoculars reveal a wealth of detail on its cratered surface. Some of the most interesting objects to look out for with small instruments are described in the notes on pages 319–327.

The Moon undergoes the most obvious changes in appearance of any celestial body, termed its phases. In the course of a month we see it change shape from a thin crescent to fully illuminated and back again, a result of its orbital motion around us which affects how much of its sunlit side we can see.

When the Moon is in line with the Sun, all its sunlit side is turned away from us and the Moon is said to be *new*. A day or so later the Moon emerges as a thin crescent low in the evening sky. At this stage its night side can be seen faintly illuminated by light reflected from the Earth, a phenomenon known as *earthshine* or, more popularly, 'the old Moon in the young Moon's arms'.

Lunar phases: The Moon goes through a cycle of phases as it orbits the Earth and we see differing proportions of its illuminated side. (Wil Tirion)

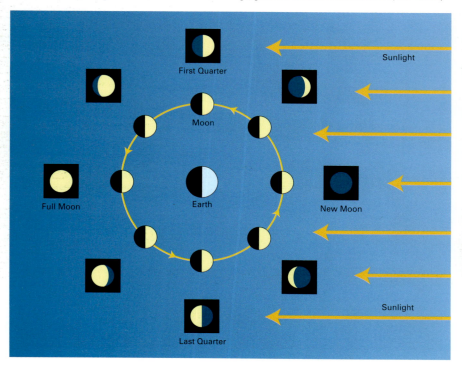

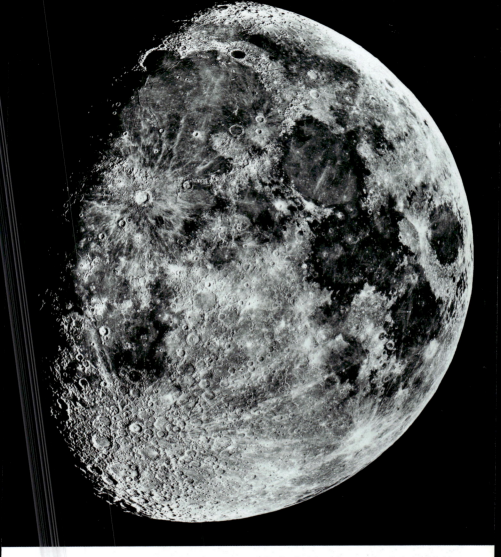

The Moon at gibbous phase, 10 days after new. Dark lowland plains (the maria), relatively devoid of craters, contrast with bright, rugged highlands. The large mare towards the top is Mare Imbrium, with the horseshoe-shaped bay Sinus Iridum on its shore. South of Mare Imbrium is the prominent rayed crater Copernicus. Most of the features in this photograph can be picked out with small telescopes or even binoculars, if firmly mounted. (Lick Observatory)

After a week we see the Moon half-lit, a phase termed first quarter because the Moon is a quarter of the way around its orbit. The Moon then fills out, passing through the gibbous phase to become full, approximately 15 days after new Moon. At full the Moon lies on the opposite side of the sky from the Sun and rises around sunset. The phases then repeat in reverse order, reaching last quarter a week or so after full and passing through a crescent back to new Moon. As the Moon's phase increases towards full it is said to be *waxing*, and when the phases are decreasing it is said to be *waning*.

Motions of the Moon

One complete cycle of lunar phases takes 29.5 days, an interval called a *synodic month* or a *lunation*. However, there is a second type of lunar month, called a *sidereal month*, which lasts 27.3 days; this is the time the Moon takes to complete one orbit of the Earth relative to a fixed point such as a dis-

Perigee and apogee: The Moon appears noticeably larger when it is at its closest to Earth (left) than when it is at its farthest.

MOON DATA	
Diameter	3475 km
Mass (Earth = 1)	0.012
Mean density (water = 1)	3.35
Volume (Earth = 1)	0.02
Apparent magnitude (full)	−12.7
Axial rotation period (sidereal)	27.32 d
Orbital period (sidereal)	27.32 d
Orbital period (synodic)	29.53 d
Mean distance from Earth	384,400 km
Orbital eccentricity	0.055

tant star. The two differ because the Earth is on the move around the Sun, so the Moon must complete rather more than one orbit to return to the same phase as seen from Earth.

Since the Moon's orbit is somewhat elliptical, its distance from Earth changes during the month. When at its nearest to Earth, a point called *perigee*, it appears as much as 12% larger than when at its farthest, *apogee*.

The Moon spins on its axis in 27.3 days, the same as its orbital period. Such an arrangement is known as a *captured rotation* and comes about because of the effect of the Earth's gravity. With a captured rotation, the Moon keeps the same face turned towards us at all times – so whenever we look at the Moon we always see the same features.

In practice, though, we can see slightly more than half the Moon's surface because of an effect termed *libration*. The Moon's equator is tilted at about 6½° to the plane of its orbit, so that at times we can see as much as 6½° over the Moon's north or south pole; this is known as *libration in latitude*.

In addition, the Moon's speed of motion along its elliptical orbit changes rhythmically as it approaches and recedes from the Earth, while its axial rotation remains uniform. The Moon therefore seems to rock slightly to west and east as it orbits the Earth, so that we can peer up to 7¾° or so around each limb; this is known as *libration in longitude*. The net effect of these librations is that we can see 59 per cent of the Moon's surface at one time or another.

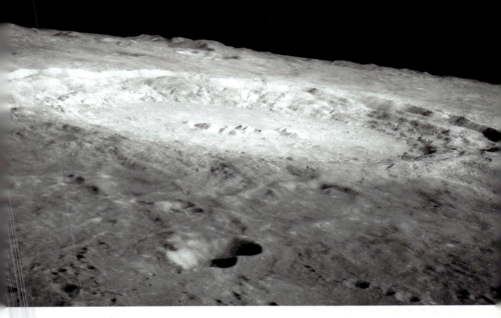

The lunar surface

The line dividing the lit and unlit portions of the Moon is known as the *terminator*. An astronaut standing on the terminator would see the Sun either rising or setting. Objects near the terminator are thrown into sharp relief by the low angle of illumination; with no atmosphere to soften the shadows, craters and mountains appear particularly rugged. As the Sun rises higher over the moonscape, details become more washed out, but at the same time the difference in contrast between the bright highlands and the dark lowland plains becomes more noticeable.

Near full Moon many individual formations are difficult to pick out. An exception is those craters that have bright ray systems, apparently made of pulverized rock thrown out from the crater during its formation; the rays become more prominent under high illumination. Notable examples of rayed craters are Copernicus, 93 km in diameter, and Aristarchus, 40 km across, the brightest area on the Moon. Most magnificent of all is Tycho, 85 km across, with rays that stretch for over 1000 km.

An oblique view of the rayed crater Copernicus, taken from orbit by the Apollo 12 astronauts in 1969, demonstrates the relative shallowness of such large formations. The keyhole-shaped feature in the foreground is Fauth. (NASA)

With the exception of a few small areas near the poles, each spot on the Moon is subjected to two weeks of unbroken daylight, during which surface temperatures reach more than 100°C, i.e. higher than the boiling point of water, followed by a two-week night when temperatures plummet to −170°C or less. At the poles, though, some crater floors remain permanently shaded from the Sun so temperatures never rise above freezing. Here, ice deposited by cometary impacts could exist beneath the surface.

After looking at the brilliant full Moon it comes as a surprise to realize that the lunar surface rocks are actually dark grey in colour; on average, the Moon's surface reflects only 12 per cent of the light that hits it. If the Moon were, for instance, covered in clouds like those of Venus, it would be over five times brighter.

Seas, mountains and craters

Formations on the Moon bear a variety of curious names. The dark lowland plains are termed *maria* (singular: mare), Latin for 'seas', because the first observers imagined them to be stretches of water; the name persists, even though it has been clear for centuries that the Moon possesses neither air nor liquid water.

Thus we have, for instance, Oceanus Procellarum (Ocean of Storms), Mare Imbrium (Sea of Rains) and Mare Tranquillitatis (Sea of Tranquillity). Less prominent lowlands are termed bays (Sinus), marshes (Palus) or lakes (Lacus). The mare areas were formed by giant impacts and were subsequently flooded, not by water but by lava – so perhaps the old names are not so inappropriate after all.

Mountains on the Moon are named after terrestrial ranges; hence we have the lunar

Mare Humorum, a lowland plain filled with solidified lava that has wrinkled in places. The large, partially flooded crater on its northern shore is Gassendi, noted for the complex clefts on its floor. (European Southern Observatory)

Apollo 12 made a precision landing in November 1969 along-side the Surveyor 3 probe that had arrived 2½ years earlier. Here, astronaut Pete Conrad prepares to remove part of the Surveyor's camera, which was brought back to Earth. In the back-ground is the lunar module. (NASA)

Alps (Montes Alpes) and the lunar Apennines (Montes Apenninus). The craters have been named after philosophers and scientists of the past, although it is true to say that the selection has been somewhat arbitrary.

The term 'crater' is rather misleading as it conjures up the vision of a deep, circular bowl. A better term for the largest craters is walled plains. For example, the 150-km-diameter Ptolemaeus, near the Moon's centre is noticeably hexagonal in outline, as is the 115-km Purbach farther south. These distorted shapes presumably arose from stresses in the lunar crust.

Many large craters have terraced walls, caused by slumping, and central peaks, caused by rebound of the crater floor after the impact of the meteorite that formed them. Outstanding examples of craters that show both terracing and central peaks are Theophilus, Arzachel and Copernicus.

There is a near-continuous range of sizes from the largest craters to the smallest maria.

Most crater-like in appearance of the maria is Mare Crisium, a basin some 500 km across, twice the width of the largest craters. Some craters have been flooded with dark lava which has left them with mare-like floors; a notable example is Plato, 100 km wide, on the northern shore of Mare Imbrium.

Near Plato is a huge half-crater called Sinus Iridum (Bay of Rainbows), 250 km across, which bridges the gap between craters and maria. It opens into Mare Imbrium and only a few low ridges, visible under oblique sunlight, remain where its seaward wall was overrun by the advancing lava. The wall of Sinus Iridum that still stands forms an arcuate range called the Montes Jura (Jura Mountains), 4.5 km high. Sunrise on the Montes Jura, 10 days after new Moon, is one of the most impressive sights for lunar observers (see the photograph on page 309).

Controversy over the origin of the lunar features started almost immediately after Galileo turned his first telescope towards the

Moon in 1609. One school of thought held that they were caused by volcanic action; the opposition believed the craters and maria to have been blasted out by impacts of meteorites and asteroids. It was not until the late 1960s, when space probes and astronauts first reached the Moon, that the controversy was finally resolved in favour of the impact theory, although it is accepted that there has also been a certain amount of subsequent volcanic action.

Space-probe exploration

In 1964 and 1965, three American probes called Ranger 7, 8 and 9 zoomed towards the Moon, sending back a stream of photographs showing features down to a metre across, a hundred times smaller than Earth-based telescopes could see. They revealed that even the apparently smoothest parts of the Moon's surface were pitted with small craters caused by aeons of meteorite bombardment. Landing sites for the manned missions which were then being planned would have to be chosen with particular care, to prevent the landing craft from toppling into a crater or hitting a boulder.

This initial cursory examination by the Rangers was followed by a two-pronged attack: the Surveyors, a series of craft which soft-landed automatically (the Rangers had simply crashed), and the Lunar Orbiters which, as their name implies, photographed the Moon from close orbit.

Between 1966 and 1968, these two series of probes revolutionized our knowledge of the Moon, paving the way for the manned Apollo landings. The Surveyors showed that the Moon's surface rocks had been eroded by micrometeorites into a compacted topsoil, known as the *regolith*, which fortunately was firm enough to bear the weight of astronauts and their spacecraft. Lunar Orbiter photographs allowed astronomers to compile their most detailed maps of the near and far sides of the Moon.

The Moon's far side, permanently turned away from the Earth, had first been glimpsed by Luna 3, a Soviet probe, in October 1959. Although poor by modern standards, its

Tsiolkovsky, a 185-km-diameter crater on the far side of the Moon with a dark floor and a prominent central peak, photographed by Lunar Orbiter 3 in 1967. Five Lunar Orbiters were launched in all, photographing the entire Moon in detail and mapping potential landing sites for Apollo astronauts. Lunar Orbiter pictures were transmitted to Earth in strips and so appear banded. (NASA)

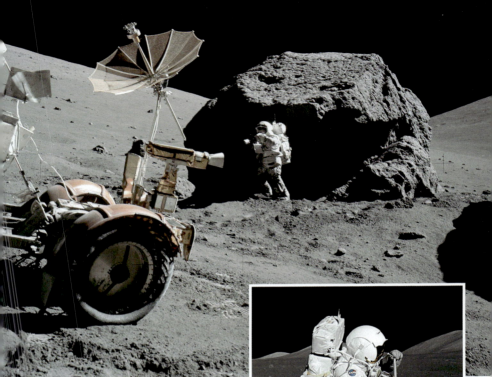

On the Apollo 17 mission in December 1972, the last of the Apollo Moon landings, astronauts Eugene Cernan and Harrison Schmitt spent three days exploring southeastern Mare Serenitatis.

Above: Schmitt is dwarfed by a rock that has rolled downhill. In the foreground is the electric Moon car, the lunar rover. (NASA)
Right: Schmitt scoops up pebbles from the lunar soil with a rake. (NASA)

photographs did at least reveal the main difference between the two hemispheres of the Moon: there are scarcely any mare areas on the Moon's far side. Instead, heavily cratered bright uplands dominate the scene. This asymmetry arises because the Moon's crust is some 15 km thicker on the far side.

Large lowland basins like Mare Imbrium do exist on the far side of the Moon, but they have not been flooded by dark lava. Volcanic lavas from the Moon's interior found it easier to leak out through the thinner crust of the Earth-facing hemisphere. The most prominent dark area on the Moon's far side is not a true mare at all, but a deep crater called Tsiolkovsky, 185 km in diameter, three-quarters the size of Sinus Iridum on the visible hemisphere.

The Apollo missions

Once the Lunar Orbiter probes had spied out potential landing sites, the stage was set for astronauts to follow. On 20 July 1969, the Apollo 11 lunar module called Eagle carried Neil Armstrong and Edwin Aldrin to the first manned lunar landing, in the south-western Sea of Tranquillity. The two astronauts spent two hours exploring the Moon's surface, setting up experiments and collecting samples for geologists to study. For the first time, humans had touched another world in space.

By the time Apollo 17 concluded the series of manned landings in December 1972, astronauts had brought back to Earth over 380 kg of Moon samples, most of which remains stored at NASA's Johnson Space Center in Houston, Texas. When divided into the overall cost of Apollo, one kilogram of Moon rocks is worth $100 million. In addition to the Apollo samples, three Soviet automatic lunar probes have returned with a few hundred grams of Moon soil.

What have we learned from these precious specimens? The most astounding fact about the Moon rocks is their immense age. The Apollo 11 samples, for instance, proved to have an age of 3700 million years, older than virtually any rocks on Earth – yet the site from which they came, Mare Tranquillitatis, is one of the youngest areas on the Moon. The youngest of all the rocks brought back came from the Apollo 12 site in Oceanus Procellarum; they are 3200 million years old.

As expected, the lunar maria turned out to be covered with lava flows similar in composition to volcanic basalt on Earth. They do not resemble a rugged lava field on Earth because, over the thousands of millions of years since the lavas were laid down, the sandblasting effect of micrometeorites has eroded the surface rocks to form a layer of soil, the regolith, several metres deep.

By contrast, the highlands, sampled by later Apollo missions, consist of a paler rock called anorthosite, rare on Earth. Rocks from the highlands proved older than those from the maria, mostly dating back 4000 million years or more. Their jumbled, fragmented nature bears witness to the violent bombardment from meteorites which the Moon suffered early in its history.

Tycho, 85 km wide, in the Moon's southern highlands, is the youngest large crater on the Moon, with an estimated age of around 300 million years. Bright rays, thrown out in the impact that created it, extend across the visible face of the Moon. Terraces on its inner slopes, also seen on other large impact craters, are caused by slumping. This photograph was taken by Lunar Orbiter 5 in 1967. (NASA)

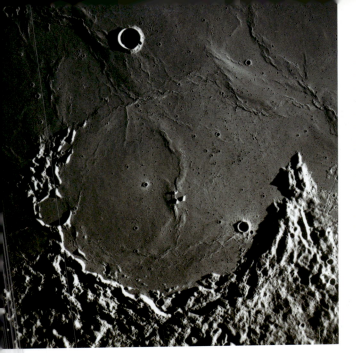

Letronne, a crater
flooded by lava on the
southern shore of
Oceanus Procellarum.
One wall has been
destroyed, although
parts of its central peak
remain. The low angle
of illumination throws
the wrinkles of solidified
lava into sharp relief.
This photograph was
taken from orbit during
the Apollo 16 mission in
1972. (NASA)

Origin and evolution of the Moon

At the time of Apollo there were three main
theories of the Moon's origin – that it split
from our planet shortly after its formation,
that it was once a separate body that was
captured by the Earth's gravity, or that the
Earth and Moon formed side by side, much
as they are now – but all had drawbacks.

Following the Apollo landings, a fourth
proposal emerged, usually termed the Giant
Impact theory, which combined aspects of
the others. According to this now widely
accepted view, a stray body the size of Mars
struck the young Earth a glancing blow,
spraying debris into orbit around the Earth
where it coalesced into the Moon.

Precise dating of lunar samples suggests
that this collision happened about 4.5 billion
years ago, some 50 million years after the
Earth formed. By then, iron had sunk to the
Earth's centre, producing a core, so that the
material thrown off the outer layers in the
collision was predominantly rocky.

While many details of the Moon's origin
remain obscure, we now have a much clearer
picture of its subsequent history. Heat
released by its rapid accumulation in orbit
around the Earth (a process termed *accretion*)
melted its outer layers. A scum of less dense
rock formed a primitive crust which was
then battered for several hundred million
years by the infall of other debris left over
from the Solar System's formation. Similar
scars from this mopping-up operation can
also be seen on other rocky bodies in the
Solar System, notably lunar-like Mercury.

This heavy bombardment created the
Moon's jumbled highlands and carved out
the mare basins, in the process removing
much of the crust on one hemisphere – the
side that ended up facing the Earth when the
Moon's rotation became tidally locked.

About 4000 million years ago, the storm
of meteoric debris abated. Then, slowly,
molten lava began to seep out from inside
the Moon, solidifying to form the dark lowland maria. So-called *wrinkle ridges* of solidi-

fied lava, hundreds of kilometres long but only a few hundred metres high, are visible through binoculars and small telescopes when the maria are under low illumination. In particular, look out for the Serpentine Ridge in eastern Mare Serenitatis when the Moon is five to six days old, or six days past full. Mare Tranquillitatis and Mare Imbrium also have prominent wrinkle ridges. In fact, one 'crater' on Mare Tranquillitatis, called Lamont, consists of nothing more than low ridges of solidified lava.

In places, particularly in western Oceanus Procellarum, a number of blister-like domes can be found near the crater Marius, produced by the upwelling of molten lava. The largest lunar dome, or rather a complex of domes, is Rümker, 70 km wide, farther north on Oceanus Procellarum. Volcanic cones like Vesuvius are absent on the Moon, evidently because the lunar lavas were too runny to build up into mountains.

Further evidence of geological activity is provided by valleys of various kinds. One obvious example, Vallis Alpes (the Alpine Valley), slices through the lunar Alps near Plato. The Alpine Valley seems to be a result of crustal faults, as do some narrower grooves known as *rilles*. The crater Hyginus near the Moon's centre lies in the middle of a long, rimless cleft along which smaller craters have been formed by subsidence. Some lunar faults have produced shallow cliffs, as in the case of the Rupes Recta (popularly termed the Straight Wall), which stretches for 120 km down the eastern edge of Mare Nubium.

Another type of rille, called a *sinuous rille*, snakes over mare surfaces like a meandering river. Apollo 15 landed at the edge of one of these sinuous rilles, called Hadley Rille. Such winding rilles were not formed by running water but are probably collapsed tunnels through which lava streams once flowed.

By 1000 million years ago the volcanic outpourings had ceased, leaving the Moon cold and dead. Since then it has remained virtually unchanged, save for the arrival of an occasional meteorite to punch a new crater in its surface. For instance, the rayed crater Copernicus was formed roughly 1000 million years ago; Tycho was blasted out about 300 million years ago.

Meandering near the foothills of the Apennine Mountains at the eastern rim of Mare Imbrium, Rima Hadley (or Hadley Rille) is a dried-up lava channel that was visited by the Apollo 15 astronauts in 1971. (NASA)

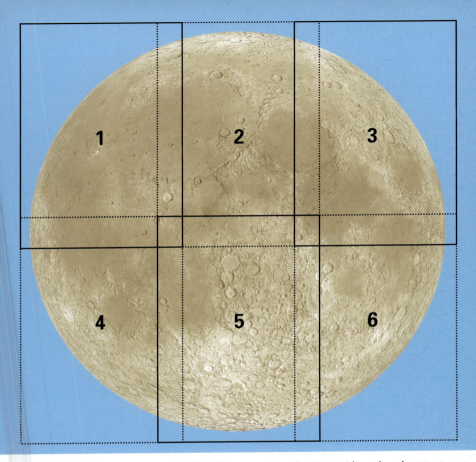

Key to the Moon maps on pages 328–339. These maps show the Moon with north at the top, as it appears to the naked eye and in binoculars. Through an astronomical telescope, south will be at the top, so telescope users must invert the maps. West is at the left, as on Earth, although in the rest of the sky west is in the opposite direction, towards the western horizon.

Moon map 1

Aristarchus Brilliant young crater 40 km in diameter with multiple terracing on its inner walls. The brightest area on the Moon, and the centre of a major ray system. Dark bands are visible on its inner walls under high illumination. Aristarchus has been the location of numerous red glows known as transient lunar phenomena (TLPs), possibly caused by outgassing from the surface. Mountains to the north exhibit fantastic sculpturing.

Copernicus Diameter 93 km. One of the most magnificent craters on the Moon. Centre of a major ray system. Terraced walls and numerous hummocky central peaks. Rays from Copernicus are splashed for more than 600 km across the Mare Imbrium and Oceanus Procellarum.

Encke Low-walled crater 28 km in diameter covered by rays from nearby Kepler. Brilliant under high illumination.

Euler   Small, sharp crater, 28 km across, in southwestern Mare Imbrium. Centre of a minor ray system.

Fauth   Keyhole-shaped crater south of Copernicus, nearly 2 km deep. Striking under low illumination.

Harpalus   Crater 39 km in diameter on Mare Frigoris, bright under high illumination. The smaller crater Foucault, 23 km in diameter, lies between it and Sinus Iridum.

Herodotus   Companion to Aristarchus, similar in size (diameter 35 km) but different in structure – Herodotus has a dark, lava-flooded floor and it is not a ray centre. The W-shaped Vallis Schröteri (Schröter's Valley), 150 km long, starts at a craterlet outside the northern wall of Herodotus.

Hevelius   Large, bright crater 115 km in diameter on western shore of Oceanus Procellarum, with clefts crossing the floor. The smaller, sharper crater Cavalerius (diameter 60 km) adjoins to the north.

Kepler   Major ray centre in Oceanus Procellarum. Brilliant crater, 31 km in diameter, with central peak and heavily terraced walls.

Mairan   Prominent crater in highlands west of Sinus Iridum. Diameter 40 km.

Marius   Dark, flat-floored ring 41 km in diameter on Oceanus Procellarum, notable because it lies on a wrinkle ridge. There are many dome-like structures in this area where lava has bubbled up through the surface.

Oceanus Procellarum   Vast dark plain with no clear-cut borders extending from Mare Imbrium southwards to Mare Humorum. Oceanus Procellarum has a maximum width of about 2000 km and occupies an area of more than two million square km. It is dotted with numerous craters and bright rays.

Prinz   U-shaped formation 52 km in diameter, remains of a half-destroyed crater flooded by lava

Copernicus, a large, bright ray crater on Oceanus Procellarum, is one of the most impressive sights on the lunar surface. (**Consolidated Lunar Atlas**)

from Oceanus Procellarum. Notable because of sinuous rilles to the north.

Pythagoras   Magnificent large crater 128 km in diameter with terraced walls rising nearly 5 km and prominent central peak, near the northwestern limb of the Moon.

Reiner   Sharp crater 30 km in diameter west of Kepler in Oceanus Procellarum. Particularly notable is a tadpole-shaped splash of brighter material on the dark plain to the west and north.

Reinhold   Prominent crater 42 km in diameter southwest of Copernicus, with terraced walls. A smaller, lower ring to the northeast is Reinhold B.

Rümker   Remarkable formation on northwestern Oceanus Procellarum, visible only under low illumination. Rümker is an irregular, lumpy dome 70 km wide.

Sinus Iridum   Beautiful large (diameter 250 km) bay on the Mare Imbrium. Its seaward wall has been broken down by invading lava and is reduced to a few low wrinkle ridges. Its remaining walls, known as Montes Jura (the Jura Mountains), are brilliantly illuminated by the morning Sun. The deep, 38-km-diameter crater on the northern rim is Bianchini.

Moon map 2

Agrippa   Oval-shaped crater 46 km in diameter with central peak, forming a neat pair with Godin.

Anaxagoras   Crater 51 km in diameter near the lunar north pole, centre of an extensive ray system.

Archimedes   Distinctive, flooded ring 83 km in diameter in eastern Mare Imbrium, notable for its almost perfectly flat floor. Apollo 15 landed south-east of here, at the foot of the Montes Apenninus, in 1971.

Aristillus   Prominent crater 55 km in diameter in eastern Mare Imbrium with terraced walls, numerous surrounding ridges and a complex central peak 900 m high. Under high illumination it is seen to be surrounded by a faint ray system. Forms a pair with Autolycus to the south.

Aristoteles   Magnificent, partially lava-flooded crater 87 km in diameter, touching the smaller crater Mitchell to the east. Numerous ridges radiate from its outer walls. Makes a pair with Eudoxus to the south.

Aristillus (top right), Autolycus and the flooded Archimedes form a fascinating group on the eastern Mare Imbrium. (Consolidated Lunar Atlas)

Autolycus   Prominent crater 39 km in diameter, south of Aristillus. It is the centre of a faint ray system, seen under high illumination.

Cassini   Flooded ring of unusual appearance with partially destroyed walls, 56 km in diameter. Contains a bowl-shaped crater, Cassini A, 15 km wide.

Eratosthenes   Prominent, deep crater on the edge of Sinus Aestuum at the southern end of Montes Apenninus (the Apennine Mountains). Terraced walls and craterlet on central peak. Its diameter is 58 km.

Eudoxus   Rugged crater 67 km in diameter with small central peak and terraced walls. South of Aristoteles.

Godin   Smaller but deeper companion to Agrippa; 35 km in diameter with central peak, bright walls and faint ray system.

Hyginus   Rimless crater 9 km in diameter, centre of a cleft or rille 220 km long, visible in small telescopes, evidently formed by collapse of the surface. To the east is another cleft, Rima Ariadaeus.

Lambert   Crater 30 km in diameter in Mare Imbrium, with central craterlet. Situated on a wrinkle ridge. Under low illumination a larger 'ghost' ring, Lambert R, is seen to the south.

Linné   Bright spot on Mare Serenitatis, best seen under high illumination. At its centre is a small, young crater 2.4 km in diameter.

Manilius   Bright crater 39 km in diameter in Mare Vaporum, with terraced walls and central peak. Develops a ray system as illumination increases, as does its neighbour Menelaus (diameter 27 km) on the rim of Mare Serenitatis.

Mare Imbrium   Enormous circular plain 1150 km in diameter, dominating this section. Bounded by the Montes Alpes, Caucasus, Apenninus and Carpatus, but open on the southwest to Oceanus Procellarum. Mare Imbrium has a double structure: traces of a smaller inner ring are visible, marked by a few isolated mountains and wrinkle ridges. Note the different shades of lava on its surface. Isolated mountains protruding from its dark floor include Pico and Piton, plus the ranges known as Montes Recti, Spitzbergen and Teneriffe.

Mare Serenitatis   A major rounded lunar sea 660 × 600 km, bounded on the northwest by Montes Caucasus and on the southwest by Montes Haemus. A bright ray from Tycho crosses the dark lava plain, passing through the crater Bessel, 16 km in diameter. Under high illumination, Mare Serenitatis is seen to be rimmed with darker lava. Note also a major wrinkle ridge (the Serpentine Ridge) on the east side. Apollo 17 landed at the southeastern edge of Mare Serenitatis in 1972.

Plato   Unmistakable large, dark-floored crater in the highlands north of Mare Imbrium, 101 km in diameter; prominent under all conditions of illumination. Tiny craterlets pockmark its flat floor. Temporary obscurations of the surface, presumed to be caused by outgassing, have been observed in this area. Landslips appear to have detached part of the inner western wall.

Pytheas   Small (diameter 20 km) but deep and prominent crater on Mare Imbrium, rhomboidal in outline. Becomes brilliant under high illumination.

Stadius   'Ghost' ring to the east of Copernicus, outlined only by a few ridges and craterlets and visible only under low illumination. It is 69 km in diameter.

Timocharis   Bright crater 34 km in diameter on Mare Imbrium, with terraced walls and distinctive central crater. Faint ray centre.

Triesnecker   Crater 26 km in diameter with a surrounding system of clefts.

Vallis Alpes (Alpine Valley)   Flat-floored valley 180 km long through the lunar Alps, connecting Mare Imbrium with Mare Frigoris.

Moon map 3

Atlas   Large crater, 87 km in diameter, with terraced walls and complex floor. A ruined ring abuts to the northwest. Atlas and Hercules form one of the many crater pairs in this region.

Burckhardt   Complex crater 57 km across, overlapping older formations (Burckhardt E and F) on either side.

Bürg   Prominent crater despite its moderate size (diameter 40 km). Central peak. Lies in the centre of Lacus Mortis. Note nearby rilles.

Cleomedes   Large, irregular-shaped crater 126 km in diameter with partially flooded floor, to north of Mare Crisium. West wall is interrupted by 43-km-diameter crater Tralles.

Endymion   Large, dark-floored enclosure 125 km in diameter, with walls up to 4900 m high.

Franklin   Crater 56 km in diameter. Forms a pair with the 40-km-diameter Cepheus to the northwest.

Geminus   Prominent crater 86 km in diameter with central peak. Bright rays emanate from two smaller craters nearby, Messala B and Geminus C.

Hercules   Flat-floored enclosure 67 km in diameter containing sharp, bright bowl crater Hercules G.

Le Monnier   Old and flooded crater with its western wall washed away by lava from Mare Serenitatis. Diameter 61 km.

Mare Crisium   Unmistakable dark lowland plain ringed by high mountains like an oversized crater, 420 × 550 km. Main feature on its flat, lava-flooded floor is the crater Picard, 23 km across, with smaller crater Peirce to its north.

Posidonius, complex and partly ruined, lies east of Mare Serenitatis near a prominent wrinkle ridge, the Serpentine Ridge. (Consolidated Lunar Atlas)

Mare Tranquillitatis   An irregular-shaped lowland, 540 × 780 km. Wrinkle ridges attest to numerous lava flows over the plain. The main crater on the mare is the distorted Arago, on the western side, 26 km in diameter. Apollo 11 made the first manned lunar landing in southwest Mare Tranquillitatis in 1969.

Plinius   Distinctive crater 42 km in diameter with complex central peak combined with a central craterlet. Stands between Mare Serenitatis and Mare Tranquillitatis, along with Dawes to the northeast, 18 km in diameter.

Posidonius   Large (diameter 100 km) partially flooded and ruined crater on the northeast shore of Mare Serenitatis. Its floor contains a curving ridge, several rilles and a small bowl crater. The ruined structure Chacornac, 51 km in diameter, abuts to the southeast.

Proclus   Small (28 km wide) but brilliant crater on the western edge of Mare Crisium. High illumination shows it to be the centre of a fan-shaped ray system.

Taruntius   Low-walled crater in northwestern Mare Fecunditatis, 56 km in diameter, with concentric inner ring. Crater Cameron (formerly Taruntius C) interrupts the northwestern wall. Centre of a faint ray system.

Thales   Bright ray crater 32 km in diameter, northeast of Mare Frigoris.

Moon map 4

Bullialdus   Handsome crater in Mare Nubium with terraced walls and complex central peak. Diameter 59 km. Two smaller craters, Bullialdus A and B, form a chain extending south.

Flamsteed   Modest (diameter 21 km) crater on Oceanus Procellarum with a much larger ring of eroded hills to its north, Flamsteed P, which appears bright against the mare background at full Moon.

Gassendi   Large, 110-km-diameter, partially flooded ring on northern border of Mare Humorum. Complex internal pattern of clefts, ridges and hillocks. A rich area for transient lunar phenomena (TLPs). Deeper crater Gassendi A interrupts the north wall, with the smaller Gassendi B lying farther north.

Grimaldi   Vast, 220-km-diameter, dark-floored enclosure at the western limb of the Moon with broad, crater-strewn walls. Nearer the limb is a smaller dark patch, marking the floor of Riccioli, 140 km in diameter.

Hainzel   Curious keyhole-shaped formation, composed of three craters fused together; the two smaller ones are Hainzel A and C.

Hippalus   Lava-flooded bay 58 km in diameter on the shores of Mare Humorum, in an area with many rilles.

Lansberg   Prominent crater 40 km in diameter with massive walls and a central peak, on Oceanus Procellarum. Apollo 12 landed southeast of Lansberg in 1969.

Schickard, the large formation at upper left, lies north of the lava-filled plateau Wargentin. Note the oddly shaped Hainzel and Schiller at upper and lower right. (Consolidated Lunar Atlas)

Letronne Large bay, 120 km wide, on the south side of Oceanus Procellarum. Its seaward-facing wall has evidently been washed away by invading dark lava.

Mare Humorum Rounded lowland plain 370 km across with Gassendi on its northern rim. Ringed by clefts and wrinkle ridges. On the south it invades the rings Doppelmayer and Lee, although Vitello escapes destruction. On the east is the ringed bay Hippalus, associated with much surface faulting.

Schickard Major dark-floored enclosure 227 km across. South of Schickard are the overlapping craters Nasmyth (diameter 77 km) and Phocylides (114 km). Adjoining it to the southwest is the extraordinary plateau Wargentin, 84 km wide, evidently a crater filled to the brim with solidified lava.

Schiller Curious footprint-shaped enclosure, 165 × 65 km.

Sirsalis and Sirsalis A Twin craters 42 and 49 km wide near a 280-km-long cleft, Rima Sirsalis, which stretches towards 130-km Darwin.

Moon map 5

Abulfeda Prominent smooth-floored crater with sculptured inner walls, 65 km in diameter. Apollo 16 landed in the highlands north of here in 1972.

Albategnius Large (diameter 136 km) walled enclosure with central peak. The prominent crater Klein, 44 km in diameter, breaks its southwest rim.

Aliacensis Prominent crater with irregular outline, 80 km in diameter. Forms a pair with the slightly smaller crater Werner.

Alpetragius Bowl-shaped crater 3900 m deep on outer slopes of Alphonsus, with large central dome. Diameter 40 km.

Alphonsus Large enclosure 118 km in diameter with complex walls and a ridge running through its centre. Numerous craterlets and clefts cover the floor; several dark patches are visible under high illumination. Alphonsus has been the site of

reported obscurations, possibly caused by the release of gas from the surface.

Arzachel Magnificent crater 96 km in diameter with terraced walls and prominent central peak. To its east is a noticeable crater 31 km in diameter with central peak, like a smaller version of Alpetragius, called Parrot C.

Barocius Large formation southeast of Maurolycus, diameter 82 km. Its northeast wall is broken by Barocius B. To the southwest is Clairaut, 75 km in diameter, between Barocius and Cuvier.

Birt Sharp, bright crater 17 km in diameter on eastern Mare Nubium. Telescopes reveal a smaller crater (diameter 7 km), Birt A, on the east wall, and under low illumination a rille to the west.

Blancanus Crater 110 km in diameter, south of Clavius.

Clavius   Magnificent walled plain 225 km in diameter. Note the distinctive arc of smaller craters across its convex floor. Its south wall is interrupted by the 50-km crater Rutherfurd, and its northeast wall by 52-km Porter.

Delambre   Prominent crater 53 km in diameter with irregular interior, southwest of Mare Tranquillitatis.

Deslandres   Huge, low and eroded formation 235 km in diameter, southeast of Mare Nubium. The partially ruined ring Lexell, diameter 63 km, opens onto its southern side, and the prominent crater Hell (diameter 33 km) lies on its western floor.

Fra Mauro   Largest member, 94 km wide, of an old, eroded crater group north of Mare Nubium, also including Bonpland (diameter 60 km), Parry (47 km) and Guericke (60 km). Apollo 14 landed just north of Fra Mauro in 1971.

Heraclitus   Curious elongated formation 90 km long with central ridge, south of Stöfler. Its southern end is rounded off by the crater Heraclitus D. Between Heraclitus and Stöfler is the crater Licetus, diameter 75 km. Touching Heraclitus to the east is Cuvier, also 75 km in diameter.

Clavius is a magnificent formation in the Moon's southern uplands with an arc of smaller craters crossing its floor. (Consolidated Lunar Atlas)

Herschel   Deep (3900 m) crater with elongated central peak, north of Ptolemaeus; diameter 41 km. Farther north is the slightly smaller Spörer, a partially filled ring.

Hipparchus   Large, eroded enclosure 150 km in diameter north of Albategnius. Its central 'peak' is actually a small ruined crater. On its northeastern floor is Horrocks, 31 km in diameter and 2800 m deep. Between Hipparchus and Albategnius lies the crater Halley (diameter 36 km), east of which is Hind, 29 km wide and 2800 m deep.

Longomontanus   Large walled plain in the rugged southern uplands of the Moon. Diameter 145 km. A ridge to the east forms a crescent-shaped enclosure known as Longomontanus Z.

Maginus   Major walled plain 185 km in diameter north of Clavius. Convex floor with small peaks in centre. Southwest wall is interrupted by smaller crater, Maginus C.

Mare Nubium   Irregular dark lowland plain, covered with numerous wrinkle ridges and ghost craters. On its southern shore is the flooded crater Pitatus, and in the southwest are the dark-floored pair Campanus and Mercator (48 km and 47 km in diameter). Its most celebrated feature is a 120-km-long fault on the eastern side called the Rupes Recta, or Straight Wall, between the craters Birt and Thebit. The Rupes Recta appears to run north–south through the remains of an old flooded crater of which only the eastern half remains. At the southern end of the Rupes Recta are the Stag's Horn Mountains, apparently the remains of a flooded crater.

Maurolycus   Distinctive crater, 114 km wide, with twin central peak. Its walls rise to 5000 m. It partially obliterates a smaller, unnamed formation to the north.

Moretus   Crater with a central peak in the jumbled uplands southeast of Clavius. Diameter 114 km. Closer to the south pole are the craters Short (diameter 71 km) and Newton (diameter 79 km), heavily foreshortened.

Pitatus   Large, dark-floored ring 105 km across on the southern shore of Mare Nubium. Invading lava from Mare Nubium has partly destroyed the crater's walls and left only the vestige of a central peak. Note the rilles around its inner walls. A smaller, similarly flooded ring adjoining it to the east is Hesiodus.

Ptolemaeus   Vast walled plain 153 km in diameter, hexagonal in shape. Its ancient floor is heavily pockmarked with smaller craters, the most prominent being Ptolemaeus A.

Purbach   Battered but still prominent large crater, 115 km in diameter. Its floor contains ridges, and its north wall is interrupted by the oval crater Purbach G, while its south wall intrudes into Regiomontanus.

Regiomontanus   Flooded crater, 124 km across. Its central peak has a summit craterlet. Forms a pair with Purbach, both noticeably hexagonal in outline.

Scheiner   Crater 110 km in diameter southwest of Clavius. The largest of three craterlets on its floor is Scheiner A.

Stöfler   Large, flat-floored formation 126 km wide, west of Maurolycus. Its eastern wall is destroyed by the intrusion of several craters, the largest being Faraday, diameter 69 km. The southern wall of Faraday is disturbed by Faraday C, which itself intrudes into Stöfler P.

Thebit   Fascinating triple crater on southeastern Mare Nubium. The main crater, 55 km in diameter, is broken by the 20-km Thebit A, which in turn is broken by the still-smaller Thebit L.

Tycho   Magnificent crater in the Moon's southern uplands, 85 km in diameter. Prominent at all angles of illumination, and brilliant under high lighting. Massively terraced walls rising up to 4500 m, imposing central peak and rough floor. Tycho is the major ray crater on the Moon. Rays from Tycho extend for 1500 km or more in all directions. Note the dark 'collar' around Tycho under high illumination. Tycho is the youngest of the Moon's major features, some 300 million years old.

Walter   Large crater 128 km in diameter, considerably modified by landslips on the inner walls and by several interior craterlets. Appears almost square in outline.

Werner   Prominent crater 70 km in diameter with walls 4200 m high, notably sharper and more rounded than neighbouring craters. The floor of Werner is dotted with several hills.

Moon map 6

Capella   Prominent crater north of Mare Nectaris, 45 km in diameter, deformed by a surface fault. Large central peak. Isidorus, 42 km in diameter, adjoins it to the west.

Catharina   One of a curving trio of craters around western Mare Nectaris. Diameter 104 km. A faint ring, Catharina P, covers much of its northern floor.

Cyrillus   Crater 95 km in diameter, with complex terraced walls, multiple central peak and rugged floor. Overlapped by Theophilus.

Fracastorius   Horseshoe-shaped bay 124 km in diameter on the southern shore of Mare Nectaris. Dark lava has breached its northern wall and flooded its interior. The crater Fracastorius D distorts its western wall.

Janssen   Vast, irregular enclosure, 180 × 240 km across, heavily bombarded. In the north it is interrupted by Fabricius, 78 km wide, which has a central peak. On the west wall is a smaller (diameter 34 km) sharp crater, Lockyer. Southeast of Janssen are the twin craters Steinheil and Watt (67 km and 66 km in diameter respectively). Farther north of Fabricius is Metius, diameter 88 km.

Langrenus   Magnificent bright-walled plain on eastern Mare Fecunditatis with terraced walls, outer ridges and a complex central peak. Its diameter is 133 km and it is a ray centre. Northwest of it, on Mare Fecunditatis, is a trio of smaller craters called Langrenus F, B and K in order of decreasing size. South of Langrenus is the large, flooded formation Vendelinus, 155 km across.

Mädler   Prominent crater (diameter 28 km) on northwest Mare Nectaris, with a central ridge.

Mare Fecunditatis   Irregularly shaped 820 × 660 km dark lowland area, connecting with Mare Tranquillitatis. On its western border it invades several craters, notably Gutenberg (diameter 71 km) and Goclenius (diameter 55 × 75 km). Note the numerous clefts in this area.

Mare Nectaris   Rounded lowland plain 350 km wide, bordered by several large craters, notably Theophilus, Cyrillus, Catharina and Fracastorius. An outer mountain ring, Rupes Altai (the Altai Scarp), surrounds Mare Nectaris.

Messier and Messier A   Elliptical pair of craters on Mare Fecunditatis, prominent despite their small sizes, 11 km and 13 km. Two bright rays extend from the western member, Messier A. Both craters appear brilliant under high illumination. The pair may be the result of a glancing impact.

Palitzsch   A crater and valley on the eastern side of Petavius. The crater Palitzsch itself, 41 km wide, is at the southern end of the valley, Vallis Palitzsch, which is 110 km long.

Petavius   Magnificent walled enclosure 177 km in diameter. A prominent rille runs across the floor from the massive, complex central peak to the terraced walls, which appear double in parts. Ridges radiate from its outer walls. West of Petavius is Wrottesley, 57 km in diameter, and with a central peak.

Piccolomini   Beautiful crater on Rupes Altai (the Altai Scarp). Diameter 89 km, with a broad central peak and terraced walls.

Snellius   Eroded crater 83 km in diameter which straddles the shallow Vallis Snellius, running northwest towards Borda and southeast past Adams.

Theophilus   Imposing crater 110 km in diameter on the northwestern rim of Mare Nectaris, with a massive 2200-m central mountain. Terraced walls rise over 5000 m above the floor, with many external ridges.

Vallis Rheita (Rheita Valley)   Crater chain northeast of Janssen and Fabricius. It can be traced for a total length of about 500 km. The crater Rheita itself, 70 km in diameter and with a small central peak, lies at the northern end of the valley.

The curving crater chain of Theophilus (top), Cyrillus and Catharina on the western shore of Mare Nectaris is a distinctive feature of this section of the Moon. (Consolidated Lunar Atlas)

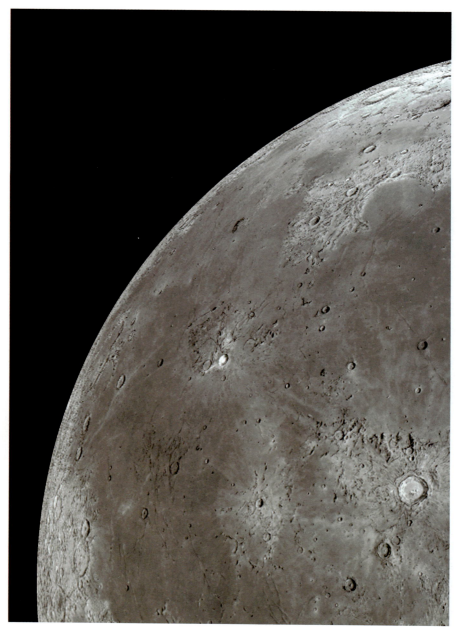

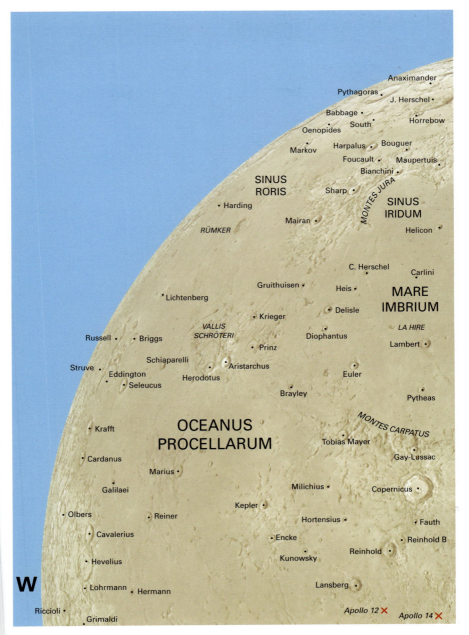

Anaximander

Pythagoras •

J. Herschel •

Babbage •

South •

Horrebow •

Oenopides

Harpalus •

Bouguer

Markov •

Foucault •

Maupertuis •

Bianchini •

SINUS
RORIS

Sharp •

MONTES JURA

SINUS
IRIDUM

• Harding

Mairan •

Helicon •

RÜMKER

C. Herschel •

Carlini •

Gruithuisen •

Heis •

MARE
IMBRIUM

• Lichtenberg

• Delisle

• Krieger

Diophantus •

LA HIRE

VALLIS
SCHRÖTERI

Russell •

• Briggs

• Prinz

Lambert •

Schiaparelli

• Aristarchus

Struve •

Herodotus •

Euler •

Eddington

• Seleucus

Brayley •

Pytheas •

• Krafft

OCEANUS
PROCELLARUM

MONTES CARPATUS

• Cardanus

Tobias Mayer •

Gay-Lussac •

Marius •

Galilaei •

Milichius •

Copernicus •

• Olbers

• Reiner

Kepler •

Hortensius •

• Fauth

• Cavalerius

• Encke

Reinhold B •

• Hevelius

Kunowsky •

Reinhold •

W

• Lohrmann   • Hermann

Lansberg •

Riccioli •

Apollo 12 ✗   Apollo 14 ✗

• Grimaldi

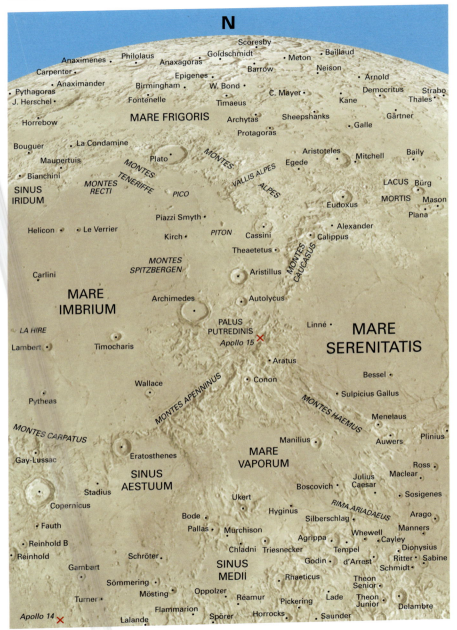

N

Scoresby

Anaximenes •   Philolaus •   Goldschmidt   • Meton   • Baillaud
Carpenter •   Anaxagoras   Barrow   Neison •
•   Anaximander   Epigenes •   • Arnold
• Pythagoras   Birmingham •   W. Bond •   C. Mayer •   Democritus   Strabo
J. Herschel •   Fontenelle   Timaeus   Kane   Thales •

Horrebow   MARE FRIGORIS   Archytas   Sheepshanks   Gärtner
                               Protagoras   • Galle

Bouguer   • La Condamine   Aristoteles   Mitchell   Baily
  Maupertuis   Plato   MONTES   Egede
• Bianchini   MONTES   VALLIS ALPES   LACUS   Bürg
SINUS   MONTES   TENERIFFE   ALPES   MORTIS   Mason
IRIDUM   RECTI   PICO   Eudoxus   Plana

           Piazzi Smyth •
Helicon •   • Le Verrier   PITON   Cassini   • Alexander
          Kirch •   • Calippus
                        Theaetetus •   MONTES
          MONTES   CAUCASUS
Carlini   SPITZBERGEN   Aristillus
•
    MARE   Archimedes   • Autolycus
  IMBRIUM   •
                   PALUS   Linné •   MARE
↖ LA HIRE   PUTREDINIS   SERENITATIS
Lambert •   Timocharis   Apollo 15 ✕
                           • Aratus
        Wallace   • Conon   Bessel •
                               • Sulpicius Gallus
Pytheas   MONTES APENNINUS   MONTES HAEMUS   Menelaus
•
MONTES CARPATUS   Manilius   Auwers   Plinius
Gay-Lussac   Eratosthenes   MARE   Ross •
                     VAPORUM   Julius   Maclear •
      Stadius   SINUS   Boscovich •   Caesar
      AESTUUM   Ukert   • Sosigenes
Copernicus   Hyginus   RIMA ARIADAEUS   Arago
            Bode •   Silberschlag •   Manners
• Fauth   Pallas •   Murchison   Whewell   • Cayley
• Reinhold B   Agrippa •   • Dionysius
• Reinhold   Schröter •   Chladni   Triesnecker   Tempel   Ritter •   Sabine
   Gambart   SINUS   Godin •   d'Arrest   Schmidt •
      Sömmering •   MEDII   Rhaeticus •   Theon
                                       Senior •
Turner •   Mösting •   Oppolzer •   Lade   Theon   Delambre
         Flammarion   Réamur   Pickering   Junior   •
Apollo 14 ✕   Lalande   Spörer   Horrocks •   • Saunder

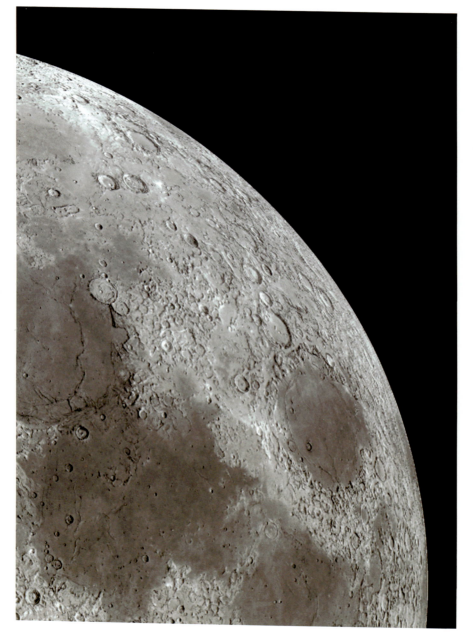

Democritus
Strabo
Thales
Gärtner   de la Rue
MARE HUMBOLDTIANUM

MARE FRIGORIS
Endymion

Baily

Hercules   Atlas
Mercurius
LACUS   Bürg
Chevallier
Zeno
MORTIS   Mason
Carrington
Shuckburgh
Schumacher
Plana   Williams   Oersted
Hooke
Grove   Cepheus
Franklin
Messala

LACUS SOMNIORUM
Maury   Berzelius   Bernoulli   Gauss
Daniell   Geminus   Berosus
Hall   Hahn
G. Bond   Burckhardt
Posidonius   Kirchhoff   Newcomb
Chacornac   Debes
MONTES   Tralles   Delmotte
Le Monnier   TAURUS   Cleomedes
MARE   Römer   Eimmart   Plutarch
SERENITATIS
MARE
Bessel   Macrobius   ANGUIS
Littrow
✕ Apollo 17   Hill   Tisserand
Maraldi   Carmichael   Peirce
Dawes   Vitruvius   MARE
Franz   Proclus   CRISIUM   Alhazen
PALUS   Yerkes
Auwers   Plinius   SOMNI   Picard   Hansen
Jansen   Lyell   Glaisher
Ross   Lick   Condorcet
Maclear   Auzout
MARE   Cauchy   da Vinci
Sosigenes   Sinas   Shapley
TRANQUILLITATIS   Firmicus   MARE
Arago   Lawrence   UNDARUM
Manners   Lamont   Daly
Dionysius   Taruntius   Apollonius   Dubyago
Ritter   Maskelyne
Sabine   Secchi   MARE
Schmidt   ✕ Apollo 11   MARE   SPUMANS
Censorinus   FECUNDITATIS
Delambre   Messier A • • Messier   Webb   Maclaurin
Hypatia

MARE MARGINIS

MARE SMYTHII

E

W

OCEANUS PROCELLARUM

Kunowsky

Reinhold

Hevelius

Lansberg

Lohrmann Hermann

Apollo 12 ✕

Apollo 14 ✕

Riccioli

Grimaldi

Damoiseau

Flamsteed

Fra Mauro

Bonpland

Euclides

MONTES RIPHAEUS

MARE COGNITUM

Letronne

Hansteen

Herigonius

Rocca

Sirsalis

Sirsalis A Billy

Gassendi B

Darney

Fontana

Gassendi A

Opelt

Crüger

Zupus

Gassendi

Lubiniezky

Darwin

de Vico

Agatharchides

Bulialdus

MARE ORIENTALE

Mersenius

Loewy

Bulialdus A
Bulialdus B

Prosper Henry

Paul Henry

MARE HUMORUM

König

Eichstädt

Liebig

Hippalus

Kies

Byrgius

Cavendish

Campanus

de Gasparis

Doppelmayer

Mercator

Palmieri

Vieta

Lee Vitello

PALUS EPIDEMIARUM

Fourier

Ramsden

Cichus

Lagrange

Elger

Capuanus

Piazzi

Clausius

Lacroix

Haidinger

Lehmann

Drebbel

A C

Epimenides

Hainzel

Mee

Lagalla

Schickard

Inghirami

Nöggerath

Wargentin

Nasmyth

Bayer

Phocylides

Schiller

Rost

Pingré

Segner

Zucchius

Bettinus

Bailly

Kircher

Reinhold

Schröter

Chladni　Triesnecker　Agrippa　Tempel　Whewell　Cayley　Dionysius

Gambart

Godin　d'Arrest　Ritter　Schmidt　Sabine

SINUS
MEDII

Sömmering

Rhaeticus

Theon
Senior

Turner

Mösting　Oppolzer

Réaumur

Lade　Theon
Junior

Delambre

Flammarion

Spörer　Horrocks

Saunder

Apollo 14 ✕

Lalande

Pickering

Taylor

Fra Mauro

Herschel　Gyldén　Hipparchus

Alfraganus

Bonpland　Parry

Ptolemaeus　Müller　Hind

Apollo 16　Zöllner
✕

Palisa

Halley

Andĕl　Dollond

Kant

MARE
COGNITUM

Guericke

Davy

Albategnius

Ritchey　Descartes

Klein

Alphonsus

Burnham

Abulfeda　Cyrillus

Darney

Lassell

Parrot　Vogel

Tacitus

Opelt

Alpetragius

Argelander　Almanon

Catharina

Lubiniezky

MARE
NUBIUM

Arzachel

Airy

Geber

Bullialdus

Thebit

Donati
Faye

Abenezra

Bullialdus A

Nicollet

Delaunay

Azophi　Sacrobosco

Fermat

Bullialdus B

Birt

La Caille

Playfair

König

RUPES RECTA

Purbach

Blanchinus

Pons

RUPES ALTAI

Kies

Apianus

Pontanus

Mercator

Hesiodus　Pitatus

Regiomontanus

Werner

Wilkins

Weiss

Aliacensis

Poisson

Zagut　Lindenau

Cichus

Hell

Walter

Goodacre

Gauricus

Deslandres

Gemma
Frisius

Celsius　Rabbi Levi

Capuanus

Wurzelbauer

Lexell　Nonius

Kaiser

Riccius

Ball

Fernelius

Haidinger

Heinsius　Sasserides

Miller

Buch　Büsching

Epimenides

Orontius

Stöfler

Wilhelm

Huggins　Nasireddin

Maurolycus

Nicolai

Lagalla

Tycho　Pictet　Saussure

Faraday

Montanari　Brown

Proctor

Barocius

Spallanzani

Street

Licetus

Clairaut

Breislak

Dove

Longomontanus

Heraclitus

Ideler

Pitiscus

Bayer

Maginus

Cuvier

Baco

Vlacq

Schiller

Hommel

Rost

Porter　Deluc　Lilius

Asclepi

Rosenberger

Jacobi

Tannerus

Nearch

Segner

Clavius

Kinau

Hagecius

Zucchius

Bettinus　Scheiner

Zach

Mutus

Bailly　Kircher

Blancanus　Gruemberger　Cysatus

Pentland

Manzinus

Helmholtz

Wilson

Klaproth

Curtius

Boussingault

Casatus　Short

Moretus　Simpelius

Boguslawsky

Newton

Schomberger

Rutherfurd

Rost

S

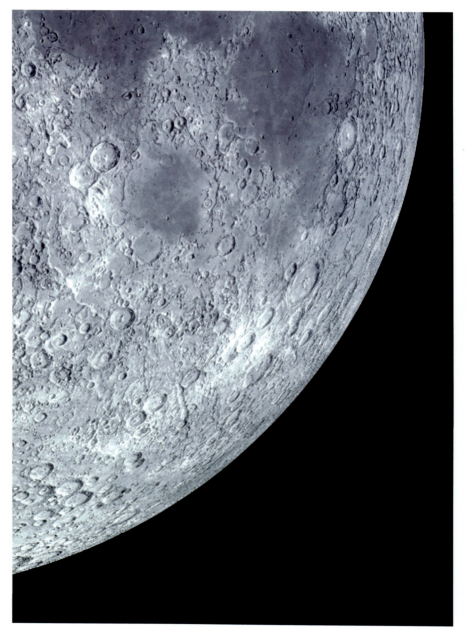

Dionysius
Ritter
Sabine
Maskelyne
MARE
TRANQUILLITATIS
Secchi
Apollonius
Dubyago
MARE SMYTHII
E
Schmidt
✗ Apollo 11
Censorinus
MARE
FECUNDITATIS
MARE
SPUMANS
Webb
Maclaurin
Messier A
Messier
Delambre
Hypatia
Taylor
Alfraganus
Torricelli
Langrenus F
Kästner
Capella
Isidorus
Gutenberg
Langrenus
La Pérouse
Zöllner
Goclenius
Kant
Theophilus
Mädler
Gaudibert
Kapteyn
Daguerre
Magelhaens
Magelhaens A
Bellot
Crozier
Lohse
Ansgarius
Cyrillus
Colombo A
Colombo
McClure
Lamé
Behaim
Tacitus
MARE
NECTARIS
Bohnenberger
Vendelinus
Beaumont
Rosse
Cook
Catharina
Monge
Holden
Balmer
Fracastorius
Santbech
Fermat
Polybius
Wrottesley
RUPES ALTAI
Borda
Petavius
Phillips
Humboldt
Pons
Palitzsch
Weinek
Snellius
Hase
Legendre
Wilkins
Rothmann
Piccolomini
Reichenbach
Adams
Zagut
Neander
Stevinus
Lindenau
Stiborius
VALLIS RHEITA
Rabbi Levi
Furnerius
Riccius
Rheita
Wöhler
Brenner
Fraunhofer
Marinus
Metius
Young
Nicolai
Fabricius
Oken
Vega
Spallanzani
Lockyer
Peirescius
Dove
Janssen
Pitiscus
Steinheil
Watt
Brisbane
MARE AUSTRALE
Vlacq
Hommel
Biela
Nearch
Rosenberger
Hanno
Hagecius
Pontécoulant
Helmholtz
Boussingault

Eclipses of the Sun and Moon

Occasionally the Sun, Moon and Earth line up exactly to cause an eclipse of either the Sun or the Moon. The Sun is eclipsed when the Moon passes directly between it and the Earth; the Moon's shadow falls on part of the Earth, and from within the shadow part or all of the Sun is obscured from view. Lunar eclipses occur when the Moon is on the opposite side of the Earth to the Sun; the Moon can then enter the Earth's shadow and be darkened.

If the Moon orbited the Earth in the same plane that the Earth orbits the Sun, a solar eclipse would occur at each new Moon and a lunar eclipse at each full Moon. But the Moon's orbit is inclined at 5° to that of the Earth, just enough to ensure that the alignment of the three bodies is seldom exact. Only on those occasions when the Moon crosses the Earth's orbit at the time of new or full Moon does an eclipse occur.

Each year at least two solar eclipses are visible somewhere on Earth, and there can be as many as five, while there can be up to three eclipses of the Moon. The maximum number of eclipses possible in one year, both solar and lunar, is seven. Whereas a lunar eclipse is visible from anywhere on Earth that the Moon is above the horizon, an eclipse of the Sun can be seen only from within the narrow band along which the Moon's shadow passes. Hence, from any one place, lunar eclipses are about twice as frequent as solar ones.

Scientifically, total eclipses of the Sun are by far the more important. At a total solar

Eclipses: When the Moon passes in front of the Sun as seen from the Earth, a solar eclipse occurs. When the Moon enters the Earth's shadow, a lunar eclipse results. (Wil Tirion)

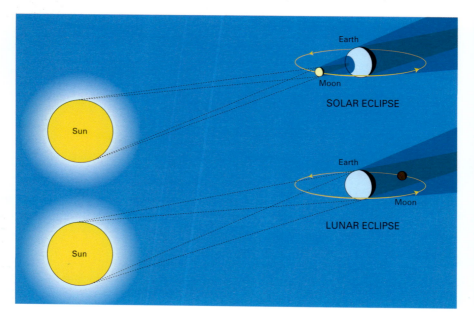

eclipse the Moon completely blots out the brilliant disk of the Sun, allowing astronomers to observe the Sun's faint outer halo of gas, the corona. To see the Sun totally eclipsed we must be in the darkest central portion of the Moon's shadow, the umbra, as it sweeps over the Earth. The band of totality is usually no more than a few hundred kilometres wide, but outside this is a much wider area that experiences a partial eclipse.

Astronomers travel across the globe for the few precious moments that totality affords. The longest that a total eclipse of the Sun can last in theory is just over 7½ minutes, but in practice the usual duration is 2–4 minutes. Total solar eclipses demonstrate one of the most extraordinary coincidences in nature: the Sun and Moon appear virtually the same size in the sky. This results from the fact that the Moon, despite being 400 times smaller than the Sun, is also 400 times closer.

Sometimes, though, when the Moon is at its farthest from us in its elliptical orbit, it appears slightly too small to cover the Sun completely, and a ring of bright sunlight remains visible around the Moon's obscuring disk. Such an event is termed an *annular* eclipse (from the Latin word 'annulus' meaning a ring, not because they occur yearly). Partial and annular eclipses are of curiosity value only; they have none of the scientific importance of a total eclipse.

Safe ways to watch solar eclipses

Suitable filters for looking at the Sun with the naked eye are now produced commercially, so there is no excuse for risking your eyesight by using unsafe materials. One popular type of filter specifically intended for solar observation is made of aluminized plastic film, known by the trade name Mylar, while a second type consists of a thicker, black plastic. Mylar filters give a bluish image but black polymer filters give a more natural-looking orange image. These types of filter are often mounted in cardboard to make simple lightweight eclipse-watching glasses, as shown in the photograph.

A welder's glass of shade 13 or 14 makes a safe solar filter for naked-eye observing. Two or three layers of heavily fogged black-and-white photographic negative film are also safe, because the silver in the film absorbs the Sun's heat as well as its light. Unsuitable materials include sunglasses, neutral-density photographic filters, colour film and compact discs (CDs); although these and other materials dim the light from the Sun, the Sun's heat will still get through to damage your eyes.

A simple arrangement not involving filters is to make a pinhole in a piece of card and allow the Sun's light to shine through this hole onto a

Eclipses can be watched safely using goggles with specially designed filters. Ordinary sunglasses are completely inadequate. (ESO)

white surface. You are in fact using a pinhole camera to observe the Sun. Drawbacks with this arrangement are that the image so formed is small and faint and requires strong sunlight, undimmed by clouds, to work successfully.

For more detailed information see http://sunearth.gsfc.nasa.gov/eclipse/SEhelp/safety2.html

If you prefer to use a telescope, the safest method is to project the Sun's image onto a white surface (see the box on page 302).

The 'diamond ring' effect, plus pink prominences visible against the pearly light of the Sun's inner corona, at the end of the total solar eclipse of 21 June 2001, viewed from Zambia. For a view of the full corona at the same eclipse, see page 303. (John Walker)

Progress of a solar eclipse

A solar eclipse gets underway at *first contact*, when the edge of the Moon begins its progress across the face of the Sun. Totality is still 1½ hours away. The partial phases of the eclipse can be observed by looking at the Sun through a special filter (see the box on page 341), or by projecting the Sun's image through binoculars or a telescope onto a white surface. When you do this, compare the jet-black outline of the Moon with the umbra of sunspots. This will confirm that sunspots are not totally black but appear somewhat brownish in colour.

Not until about 20 minutes before totality, when the Sun's disk is over two-thirds covered, does the sky start to darken noticeably. An eerie half-light covers the landscape; animals act as though night is falling. Totality itself rushes up as the last crescent sliver of sunlight is blotted out by the Moon.

In the final seconds, chinks of sunlight peep between the mountains at the Moon's rugged edge, producing *Baily's beads*, named after the English astronomer Francis Baily who described them at the eclipse of 1836. Often one bead shines brighter than the others, giving the appearance of a dazzling diamond in a ring.

Then, second contact: the Moon completely covers the Sun, and the pearl-coloured corona springs into view. Now it is safe to watch without eye protection.

Feather-like plumes and streamers of the corona extend from the polar and equatorial regions of the Sun for several solar diameters. The shape of the corona changes during the solar cycle, being more rounded near solar maximum. Pinkish-red prominences can be seen looping out from the Sun's chromosphere around the dark outline of the Moon. Bright stars are visible in the darkened sky.

All too soon, the beautiful spectacle is over. The diamond ring flashes out at third contact, signalling the end of totality. At fourth contact, the Moon moves completely clear of the Sun. The eclipse is over.

Lunar eclipses

Eclipses of the Moon are far less spectacular than solar ones, although they last longer. The Moon takes several hours to move completely through the dark inner part of the Earth's shadow, the umbra. The outer part of the shadow, the penumbra, is so light that it produces little noticeable darkening of the Moon's surface.

A total lunar eclipse can last up to 1¾ hours. Even when totally eclipsed the Moon rarely disappears because light is scattered into the Earth's shadow by the Earth's atmosphere, becoming reddened in the process.

In the early stages of the eclipse the shadow appears dark grey by contrast with the brighter lunar surface, but as the eclipse progresses and more of the Moon is covered the shadow seems to lighten and turn orange or coppery in colour. Binoculars are ideal for observing these colourful effects.

The appearance of the Moon during totality can vary markedly from one eclipse to another. The darkest lunar eclipses occur when the Earth's atmosphere is unusually cloudy or dusty (as after a volcanic eruption). Although an interesting natural spectacle, a lunar eclipse is of little scientific importance.

Eclipsed Moon: Unusual colour effects were seen at the very dark total lunar eclipse of 9 December 1992, in which most of the Moon became almost invisible to the naked eye, apart from a brighter crescent with a bluish tinge. (Eric Hutton)

Mercury

Mercury is a disappointing object for observers. Small telescopes show its changing phase as it orbits the Sun every 88 days, but little else is visible because the planet is small, it is usually viewed close to the horizon where seeing is bad and its surface markings are of low contrast. Most observers must therefore be content with simply catching a glimpse of this elusive object during one of its periodic excursions into the evening or morning sky.

Being the innermost planet, Mercury keeps closest to the Sun; hence would-be observers are restricted to the handful of times each year when it is at or near its maximum angular separation from the Sun, known as *greatest elongation*. Since Mercury's orbit is markedly elliptical, taking it between 46 and 70 million km from the Sun, the separation between the two at greatest elongation varies from nearly 28° to less than 18°. At greatest elongation, a magnification of 250 times is needed to show Mercury the same size as the full Moon appears to the naked eye.

Circumstances dictate that there are two favourable times to look for Mercury each year. From mid-northern latitudes, the planet is most easily seen when setting after the Sun (eastern elongation) in March and April, and when rising before the Sun (western elongation) in September and October. For those at mid-southern latitudes the best times are mornings in March and April and evenings in September and October.

Even when it is best placed, a low, clear horizon will be needed to see it; binoculars help to pick the planet out of the twilight glow, for Mercury can never be seen against a truly dark sky. With all these complications, it is little wonder that many town dwellers have never seen the planet. Nevertheless it is worth looking for, because at its best it can become almost as bright as Sirius.

Rarely, Mercury can be seen as a tiny black dot passing in front of the Sun, an event termed a *transit*. Transits of Mercury in the first half of this century take place on 9 May 2016, 11 November 2019, 13 November 2032, 7 November 2039 and 7 May 2049.

Mercury's rotation

The difficulty in observing Mercury led to a long-standing misconception about the time it takes to rotate on its axis. Towards the end of the 19th century, the Italian astronomer Giovanni Schiaparelli proposed that the planet spins on its axis in 88 days, the same time as it takes to orbit the Sun. It would therefore keep one face turned permanently towards the Sun, as the Moon does to the Earth. In the 1920s a respected planetary observer, Eugène Antoniadi, compiled a map based on an assumed 88-day rotation which seemed to settle the matter once and for all.

Then, in 1965, came a surprise. Astronomers at Arecibo Radio Observatory in

MERCURY DATA

Diameter	4879 km
Mass (Earth = 1)	0.06
Mean density (water = 1)	5,43
Volume (Earth = 1)	0.06
Axial rotation period (sidereal)	58.65 d
Orbital period (sidereal)	87.97 d
Orbital period (synodic)	115.88 d
Axial inclination	0°.0
Mean distance from Sun	57.91×10^6 km
Orbital eccentricity	0.206
Orbital inclination	7°.0
Number of moons	0

Mercury's lunar-like landscape, photographed by the American space probe Mariner 10 in March 1974. The bright ray crater just above centre is called Kuiper, 62 km across, shown in more detail in the inset. It intrudes onto a crater twice its size, called Murasaki. (USGS)

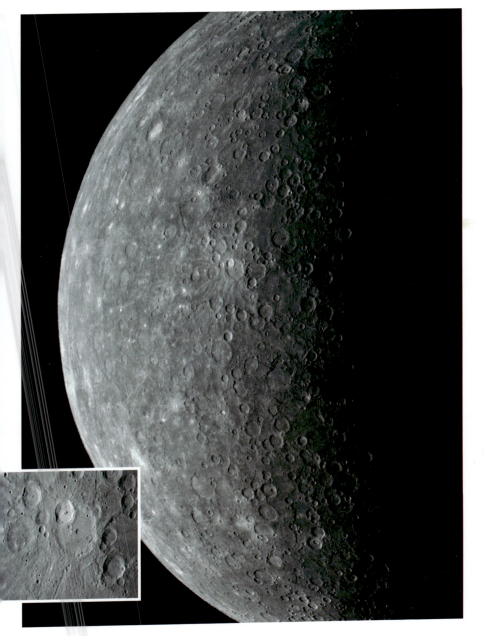

Puerto Rico bounced radio waves off the planet. From the change in frequency of the reflected radio waves, they deduced that Mercury spins once every 59 days, two-thirds of the time it takes to orbit the Sun.

A rotation period that is such a large fraction of the planet's orbital period has some odd consequences. The Sun does rise and set on Mercury, but it does so very slowly. For the Sun to go once around the sky as seen from the planet's surface – say, from one noon to the next – takes 176 Earth days, during which time Mercury orbits the Sun twice, spinning three times on its axis.

As seen from Mercury the Sun would appear two and a half times larger than it does from Earth. Lethal doses of high-energy solar radiation blast Mercury's daytime side. The Sun's intense heat roasts the surface rocks to over 400°C at noon on the equator, hot enough to melt tin and lead. Yet, without an atmosphere to hold in the heat, the planet's surface drops to a frigid −180°C during the long night.

With a diameter of 4879 km, Mercury is only 40 per cent larger than our Moon and smaller than every other major planet in the Solar System. Given that Mercury is rocky, airless and waterless like the Moon, it is no surprise that it strongly resembles our Moon in appearance.

The surface of Mercury

Our first close-up views of Mercury came in 1974 when the space probe Mariner 10 flew past the planet, photographing a surface heavily pockmarked with craters of all sizes that look almost identical to their lunar counterparts. There are deep, young craters, eroded ancient craters, craters with terraced walls, central peaks and bright rays.

Many of the features on Mercury have been named after artists, composers and writers. For instance, we now find memorials to Bach, Mozart, Van Gogh, Shakespeare and Chekhov on Mercury. Its largest crater, 640 km across, is named Beethoven.

At first glance it is difficult to distinguish between a picture of Mercury and one of the Moon. Craters on both bodies have been formed in the same way, by the impact of asteroids, meteorites and comets early in the history of the Solar System.

One noticeable difference on Mercury is that material ejected from the impacts has not travelled as far as around lunar craters, because Mercury has a stronger surface gravity – over twice that of the Moon, although still only 38 per cent of the Earth's. Another result of the higher gravity on Mercury is that craters tend to be shallower for a given diameter than on the Moon.

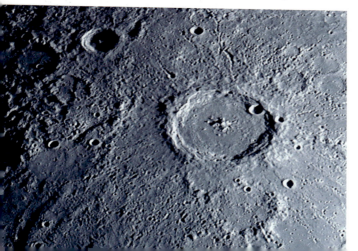

Verdi, a crater 160 km in diameter on Mercury, has similar characteristics to many lunar craters: terraced walls, a complex central peak and a surrounding blanket of secondary craters. The shadow-filled crater at upper left is Martial, 50 km wide. (NASA/JPL/Mark Robinson)

Santa Maria Rupes, a surface fold on Mercury of the type known as a lobate scarp, runs nearly vertically for 200 km through this picture from Mariner 10. It cuts across old craters and intercrater plains, evidence that Mercury has shrunk slightly in size since these features were formed. (NASA/JPL/ Mark Robinson)

Scarps, plains and basins

Meandering cliffs called *lobate scarps*, several hundred kilometres long and a kilometre or so high, are a feature of Mercury's surface unlike anything on the Moon. These features are believed to have been caused by a shrinking of the planet as its core cooled early in its history, leading to compression and faulting in the crustal rocks.

The surface rocks of Mercury are slightly darker in tone than those of the Moon, reflecting a mere 11 per cent of the sunlight hitting them, compared with an average 12 per cent for the Moon; overall, Mercury in fact has the darkest surface of any planet in the Solar System, although the lunar maria are darker than Mercury.

Between many of the large craters in the highlands of Mercury are areas peppered only by small craters. These areas, termed the *intercrater plains*, have no real counterpart on the Moon. They clearly pre-date the large craters, but whether they were formed by volcanic action or are deposits of ejecta from large impacts is uncertain. Future Mercury orbiters should resolve the question.

Other areas of particular interest for closer study are deep craters near the poles whose interiors are permanently shaded from the Sun, thereby preserving in deep freeze any gas that has seeped out from within the planet or ice deposited by cometary impacts.

Of all the features seen by Mariner 10, the most prominent is an enormous bull's-eye structure, partly hidden by shadow, named the Caloris Basin. It is 1300 km across, larger than Mare Imbrium on the Moon and fully one-quarter the diameter of Mercury.

The Caloris Basin contains several concentric rings of mountains and is surrounded by radial ridges and grooves. Its interior, and much of the low-lying land around it, has been flooded by molten rock. Whether this is lava from inside the planet that oozed out after the impact, or rock melted by the heat of the impact, remains uncertain.

Geological activity died out on Mercury over 3000 million years ago, as it did on the Moon. Since then, little has changed except for the random arrival of a stray meteorite.

Despite its outward resemblance to the Moon, inwardly Mercury is believed to be more like the Earth. Mercury has a relatively large mass for its small diameter, implying that it has a large iron core three-quarters of its own diameter. A core that size would be as big as the Moon.

One explanation for such a disproportionately large core is that Mercury was originally much bigger, but had most of its rocky outer layers blasted off in a collision or collisions with one or more asteroid-sized bodies, possibly being knocked into its current elliptical orbit in the process. In its own way, Mercury turns out to be a fascinating world containing many clues to the origin and development of the Solar System.

Venus

Many people have seen Venus without realizing it. The planet appears as the brilliant evening or morning 'star', the most prominent object in the twilight, outshining every genuine star with its cold white light. So striking is Venus when at its best that it is frequently reported as a hovering UFO.

Venus orbits the Sun at a distance of 108 million km and can approach closer to Earth than any other planet, within 40 million km.

With a diameter of 12,100 km, only 5 per cent smaller than the Earth, it is almost a twin of our own planet in size. The main

The clouds of Venus circulate around the planet every 4 days, spiralling from equator to pole and creating V- or Y-shaped patterns that are most prominent in ultraviolet light, as in this image from the Pioneer Venus orbiter. (NASA/Ames)

VENUS DATA

Diameter	12,104 km
Mass (Earth = 1)	0.82
Mean density (water = 1)	5.24
Volume (Earth = 1)	0.86
Axial rotation period (sidereal)	243.02 d
Orbital period (sidereal)	224.70 d
Orbital period (synodic)	583.92 d
Axial inclination	177°.4
Mean distance from Sun	108.2×10^6 km
Orbital eccentricity	0.007
Orbital inclination	3°.4
Number of moons	0

reason for the brilliance of Venus in the sky is not its size or proximity but its cloak of unbroken clouds that reflect two-thirds of the light hitting them. While making Venus so prominent, these clouds also conceal its surface from observers.

As with Mercury, visibility of Venus is restricted to the evening or morning sky but it can be seen over a much wider arc of its orbit than Mercury. Its elongations from the Sun are greater than Mercury's, up to 47°, and at best it can be observed for several hours after sunset or before sunrise. Transits of Venus across the face of the Sun are even rarer than those of Mercury,

Phases of Venus: At full phase Venus is farthest from the Earth and only about 10 arc seconds across; when at half phase (dichotomy) the apparent diameter has grown to 24 arc seconds and by the time of greatest brilliancy it is nearly 40 arc seconds across. (Wil Tirion)

occurring in pairs over a century apart. In the 21st century the dates are 2004 and 2012, while the next pair will not happen until 2117 and 2125.

Observing Venus

Through a telescope, Venus appears like a white billiard ball that exhibits a cycle of phases as it orbits the Sun. At half phase, around the time of greatest elongation, it appears half the size of Jupiter; a magnification of 75 times will then show it the same size as the Moon appears to the naked eye. As Venus approaches the Earth its apparent size grows to equal or exceed that of Jupiter.

Seen from Earth, Venus goes through one cycle of phases (say, from one superior conjunction to the next) in 584 days This, its synodic period, is two and a half times longer than it takes to orbit the Sun (the sidereal period). The two intervals are very different because the Earth and Venus move rapidly relative to each other in their respective orbits around the Sun.

When it is a crescent, Venus is close enough to the Earth for its phase to be picked out in modest binoculars; some people even claim to have seen Venus as a crescent with the naked eye. The planet appears most brilliant when about 27 per cent of its disk is illuminated as seen from Earth, this being the most favourable combination of distance and phase.

Venus can reach a maximum magnitude of −4.7, nearly seven times brighter than the next most prominent planet, Jupiter. At such times, Venus is best observed telescopically against a twilight sky to reduce dazzle.

Only the vaguest markings can be made out in the clouds through telescopes, usually dusky shadings shaped like a sideways V or Y. The clouds often appear brighter at the poles, with a surrounding darker collar. These polar brightenings are termed *cusp caps*.

Observers draw the disk of Venus to a standard diameter of 50 mm, and estimate the brightness of features on a scale ranging from extremely bright to unusually dark. Observing forms are issued by the relevant sections of the main astronomical societies. Different societies use different scales for making intensity estimates.

The terminator of Venus (the edge of the illuminated portion) can appear irregular, including extensions to or blunting of the cusps, due not so much to differences in the height of the clouds as to differences in brightness. These effects are caused by the corkscrew circulation of clouds around Venus from its equator to its pole.

One curiosity is that the observed time of half phase, known as *dichotomy*, does not coincide with its predicted date. This is termed the *phase anomaly* or *Schröter effect* after a German astronomer, Johann Schröter, who discovered it in the late 18th century. Dichotomy at eastern (evening) elongations, when the planet's phase is decreasing, or waning, is usually a few days early, while dichotomy at western (morning) elongations,

when the phase is increasing, is correspondingly late. It is usually attributed to the fact that the clouds near the terminator are darker than the rest of the disk.

An even odder phenomenon is the *ashen light*, an apparent brightening of the night side of the crescent Venus when seen against a dark sky. To observe the ashen light reliably the illuminated portion of the planet must be blocked out, otherwise any reports will probably be spurious. The reality of the ashen light remains controversial, but if it exists it may be due to scattering of sunlight or electrical effects in the atmosphere.

Large meteorites can penetrate the thick atmosphere of Venus to produce impact craters. In the foreground is Howe, 37 km wide, surrounded by a blanket of bright ejecta. This image, created from Magellan radar data, has been coloured to match the hues recorded by Soviet Venus landers. (NASA)

Beneath the clouds

Unable to see the planet's surface because of the enveloping clouds, astronomers could only guess at the rotation period of Venus until the 1960s – and they guessed incorrectly. As with Mercury, radar observations provided the surprising truth. It turns out that Venus rotates on its axis from east to west, the opposite direction from the Earth and other planets, and it does so very slowly: once every 243 days, longer than the 225 days the planet takes to orbit the Sun. Its clouds, though, rotate every four days, also retrograde (east to west), a result of high-speed winds in the upper atmosphere.

Before space probes arrived there, no one came close to anticipating the uniquely hostile conditions on Venus. First to experience them was a Soviet probe, Venera 4, which parachuted down through the clouds in October 1967. It found that Venus' atmosphere is made almost entirely of unbreathable carbon dioxide gas, but the intense heat and crushing pressure destroyed it long before it could reach the surface.

Later probes, better reinforced, reached the surface intact, registering temperatures of 460°C on both the day and night sides and

Maat Mons, a volcano on Venus 8 km high, in a view reconstructed from Magellan radar imagery. Lava flows extend across the plains in the foreground, where an impact crater can also be seen. The vertical scale has been exaggerated tenfold, making the terrain seem much rougher than it is in reality. (NASA)

an atmospheric pressure over 90 times that on Earth. Why should Venus be so hot – hotter even than the day side of Mercury, despite the fact that its clouds reflect over three-quarters of the incoming sunlight?

The answer lies in the *greenhouse effect*, which works far more effectively on Venus than on Earth. About 1 per cent of the incoming sunlight penetrates to the planet's surface, so that it is as gloomy there as on a heavily overcast day on Earth. That incoming sunlight is absorbed by the surface and is re-radiated at longer wavelengths, in the infrared. Although the carbon dioxide of the atmosphere is transparent to visible light, it traps infrared; since infrared is heat energy, the temperature of the atmosphere rises.

An additional contribution to the greenhouse effect comes from the clouds themselves. These are made not of water vapour, as are the clouds of Earth, but of sulphuric acid of 80 per cent concentration, stronger than in a car battery. Sulphuric acid is another absorber of infrared. Taken together, the carbon dioxide atmosphere, the sulphuric acid clouds and a trace of water vapour turn Venus into a perfect trap for solar heat.

The uppermost layer of sulphuric acid clouds, the one which we view through telescopes, starts about 65 km above the planet's surface and is a few kilometres thick. Around 55 km altitude is a thin haze layer apparently consisting of sulphuric acid particles, which give the clouds their yellow tinge.

The densest cloud layer of all is at about 50 km altitude, and from this layer falls a corrosive rain of sulphuric acid. Below the clouds, the gloom is broken by flashes of lightning. Despite its heavenly name, Venus turns out to be an incarnation of hell.

The surface of Venus

Although the clouds of Venus mask its surface from view, astronomers have nevertheless been able to map the planet's features by radar, which penetrates the clouds. Detailed maps of the entire planet have been made by spacecraft, notably NASA's Magellan probe that went into orbit around Venus in 1990.

Venus is mostly rolling plains, but there are three main continental areas. One, called Ishtar Terra, the size of the United States, has a mountain range, Maxwell Montes, which towers 12 km above the mean surface level, higher than Mount Everest on Earth. The largest continental area of all, Aphrodite Terra, the size of South America, is cut by a system of rift valleys that extends for thousands of kilometres.

Magellan's radar spotted impact craters ranging in size from over 100 km across down to 3 km, demonstrating that large meteorites can get through the dense atmosphere without burning up. Most exciting of all were volcanic mountains with fresh-looking lava flows on their flanks, notably Maat Mons, at 8½ km high the second-highest peak on the planet, which lies near the equator in Aphrodite Terra. Evidently Venus is still an active planet, with highlands formed by volcanic action.

Other types of volcanic feature on Venus include flattened, pancake-like domes, thought to be formed by the outpouring of sticky lava, and ringlike formations of cracks and ridges termed coronae, hundreds of kilometres across, apparently caused by subsidence after upwelling of magma from below.

Photographs from Soviet lander probes resting on the planet's surface show a rocky wasteland bathed in a sulphurous glow. Chemical analyses made by these probes confirm that the surface rocks of Venus are similar in composition to volcanic basalts on Earth. Venus is a tantalizing vision of what the Earth might have been had it been born closer to the Sun – and a terrifying demonstration of what it might yet become if the greenhouse effect were to take hold here.

Under its clouds, Venus is bathed in a sulphurous yellow glow, as photographed by the Russian Venera 13 probe which landed there in 1982. Part of the spacecraft is visible at the bottom. (Brown University/Russian Academy of Sciences)

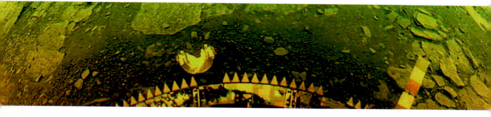

Mars

Mars is distinguishable by its intense reddish or orange hue, stronger than the colour of any star and the cause of its association with the god of war. Potentially it is the most exciting planet of all to observe, although not the easiest. It is a rocky world about half the size of the Earth with a day about 40 minutes longer than our own. Its year lasts nearly twice as long as ours, 687 Earth days, during which it undergoes seasonal changes, including melting of its polar caps and variations in the size and shape of its surface markings. Its atmosphere is so thin that we can usually see straight through to the surface, but occasionally white clouds or dust storms interrupt our view. Studies of the red planet are all the more important because one day humans will walk on its surface.

Mars in 1997, photographed by the Hubble Space Telescope. The dark feature at the centre is Syrtis Major. South of it is the lowland basin Hellas, filled with frost and clouds. At right, white clouds also lie around Elysium Mons, a volcano. (Steve Lee/Jim Bell/Mike Wolff/NASA)

Observing Mars

As with all the outer planets, the best time to observe Mars is near opposition. Because the orbit of Mars lies beyond that of the Earth it does not go through a cycle of phases like the inner planets, although when it is at an elongation of around 90° from the Sun it displays a distinctly gibbous phase, like the Moon a couple of days from full.

Mars comes to opposition every 26 months but some oppositions are much more favourable than others because its orbit is markedly elliptical, taking it between 207 and 249 million km from the Sun. When oppositions occur at perihelion, as in 2003 and 2018, Mars can come as close as 56 million km to us and we get our best views of the planet.

At such times Mars shines like a brilliant red star at magnitude −2.9, rivalling Jupiter, and a magnification of ×75 will show the planet the same size as the full Moon to the naked eye. (Incidentally, the date of closest approach may differ by a week or more from

MARS DATA	
Diameter (equatorial)	6792 km
Mass (Earth = 1)	0.11
Mean density (water = 1)	3.94
Volume (Earth = 1)	0.15
Axial rotation period (sidereal)	24.62 h
Orbital period (sidereal)	686.98 d
Orbital period (synodic)	779.94 d
Axial inclination	25°.2
Mean distance from Sun	227.9×10^6 km
Orbital eccentricity	0.093
Orbital inclination	1°.9
Number of moons	2

the date of opposition because of the eccentricity of the planet's orbit.)

But at aphelic oppositions, as in 2012 and 2027, Mars is 100 million km from Earth, almost twice the distance of the closest approaches, and it appears unimpressive even in powerful telescopes. Hence astronomers do not waste their chances of observing Mars when it is at its closest.

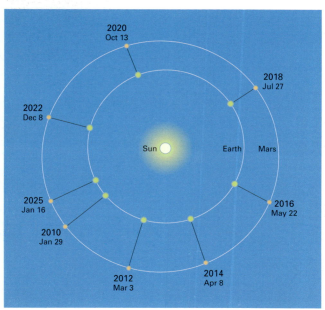

Oppositions of Mars over a 15-year period. The actual distances on each occasion shown are: 2010, 99.4 million km; 2012, 100.9 million km; 2014, 92.9 million km; 2016, 76.2 million km; 2018, 57.7 million km; 2020, 62.6 million km; 2022, 82.3 million km; 2025, 96.2 million km. (Wil Tirion)

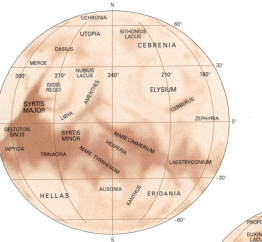

Albedo markings on Mars, as mapped from Earth. North is at the top. (Wil Tirion)

Left: Mars from longitude 300° to 180°. Note the dark wedge-shaped Syrtis Major just north of the equator and the bright Hellas basin in the southern hemisphere.

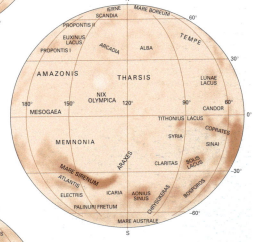

Right: Mars from longitude 180° to 60°. The white spot of Nix Olympica in the northern hemisphere is actually a large volcanic mountain better known as Olympus Mons.
NASA's Spirit rover landed in 2004 at roughly longitude 175° and latitude 15°south.

Left: Mars from longitude 60° to 300°. This face of the planet is crossed by the elongated feature called Sinus Sabaeus, which stretches westwards from Syrtis Major and ends in the clawlike Sinus Meridiani. NASA's Opportunity rover landed in 2004 at the western end of Sinus Meridiani at approximately longitude 354° and latitude 2°S.

Through a telescope, the most obvious features on Mars are the white polar caps, which stand out in stark contrast to its ochre-coloured deserts. The caps shrink noticeably during summer in each hemisphere, leaving detached 'islands'. The southern cap shrinks more than the northern one because the southern hemisphere of Mars is tilted towards the Sun at perihelic oppositions, and so gets warmer than the northern hemisphere, which leans sunwards at aphelic oppositions.

The dark markings, once thought to be vegetation, are now known to be areas of rock and dust. These markings change in appearance from year to year as winds blow the dust around, so any map of Mars can be only an approximation of the planet's true appearance. Such markings are termed *albedo features* as they are simply differences in surface brightness and do not necessarily correspond to actual physical features.

The most prominent dark albedo feature is a large triangular area named Syrtis Major. This should be visible in a modest amateur telescope when it is on the Earth-facing side, as should a bright circular lowland to the south of it called Hellas.

Sometimes, yellow clouds appear on the planet, particularly in the areas of Hellas and Solis Lacus. These clouds are in fact dust storms which, with the increased temperatures around the time of perihelion, can be whipped up by high winds to envelop the entire planet and obscure its features.

Different parts of the surface will be seen as the planet rotates, turning through nearly 15° every hour. Since Mars rotates slightly more slowly than the Earth, the same features will be on view just over half an hour later each night.

Drawings of Mars are usually made with a disk size of 50 mm, the same as Venus. As well as making drawings, observers estimate the brightness of features on a scale of 0 to 10 from the white polar caps to the blackness of the sky. Report forms are issued by amateur astronomy organizations.

Dust storm on Mars in 2001, observed by the Hubble Space Telescope. In June the atmosphere was mostly clear, apart from some water-ice clouds around the north polar region and at lower left. But a storm was brewing in the Hellas basin (lower right) and by August the planet's surface was almost entirely obscured (second image). The dark spot at upper right is the peak of the volcano Olympus Mons. Mars is gibbous in the image at right because our viewing angle has changed. (James Bell/Michael Wolff/STScI/AURA)

The illusory canals

The temptation to assume too many similarities between Mars and the Earth led early astronomers astray. The dark areas, which range in colour from brown to grey-green, were termed seas and lakes in the belief that they really were filled with water, while the orange areas were named after places on Earth – there is an Arabia, Libya, Syria and Sinai on Mars.

By the end of the 19th century it was realized that there were no oceans on Mars after all, but in their place arose a much more intriguing explanation for the dark areas: that they were covered with primitive vegetation, such as moss or lichen. In support of this view, observers noted that when the polar caps melted in the Martian summer, the surface markings became larger and darker; this was interpreted as vegetation growing in the milder, wetter conditions.

The most extreme proponent of the life-on-Mars idea was an American astronomer,

Clouds of ice crystals over Olympus Mons (top left) and the chain of three volcanoes of the Tharsis Bulge: Ascraeus Mons (top), Pavonis Mons (middle) and Arsia Mons, in a mosaic of images from the Mars Global Surveyor orbiter. These clouds are visible from Earth. The cracked terrain at lower right is the Valles Marineris fault complex. (NASA/JPL/MSSS)

Percival Lowell. His ideas were inspired by an Italian observer, Giovanni Schiaparelli, who in 1877 reported seeing long, straight lines that appeared to criss-cross the planet's surface. Schiaparelli called these lines *canali*, a word which in Italian means 'channels'; but inevitably it was translated as 'canals', implying that they were artificial.

For Lowell, the canals were evidence of an advanced civilization clinging to existence on an arid planet, reliant on the canals to bring meltwater from the polar caps to irrigate their crops at the equator. His beliefs gave rise to a whole generation of science-fiction

stories, including the famous *War of the Worlds* by H. G. Wells.

Most other astronomers failed to see the canals, or in their place could detect only broad, irregular smudges. It is now clear that Lowell's canals were illusory, testimony to the fallibility of human observers straining at, or past, the limits of vision.

Space-probe exploration of Mars

Mars is currently the subject of a vigorous programme of exploration by space probes, leading to a sample-return mission and an eventual human landing. The first close-up pictures of the planet were sent back in July 1965 by NASA's Mariner 4 probe as it swept past at a distance of 10,000 km. It photographed craters on Mars, looking like more eroded versions of those on the Moon. Since then, a succession of probes has examined the planet in increasing detail, both from orbit and by landing on the surface.

Mars turns out to be a planet of two contrasting halves. The northern hemisphere is the lower and smoother of the two, flooded by lava from volcanoes. The youngest eruptions occurred within the past few hundred million years. The southern hemisphere is higher and has been heavily cratered by meteorite impacts, giving it a broad similarity to the lunar highlands.

Among the major formations on Mars is a chain of three volcanic mountains atop a highland area known as the Tharsis Bulge

which straddles the equator; these volcanoes are named Arsia Mons, Pavonis Mons and Ascraeus Mons ('Mons' means mountain). Other types of Martian landforms and the names given to them include lowland plains (Planitia), highland plateaus (Planum), valleys (Vallis), canyons (Chasma), and eroded craters (Patera).

Northwest of the chain of Tharsis volcanoes is an even bigger individual volcanic mountain, Olympus Mons, visible from Earth as a white ring and originally named Nix Olympica ('the snows of Olympus'). Olympus Mons, 600 km wide and 25 km high, is the largest volcano in the Solar System, larger even than the volcanic islands of Hawaii on Earth. The whole Tharsis area is noted for the frequent appearance of white clouds, often described as being shaped like a letter W. The presence of mountains explains the preference of clouds for this region.

An immense system of canyons, up to 500 km wide and 4 km deep, extends eastwards from the Tharsis Bulge. This massive rift in the surface of Mars, the Valles Marineris (Mariner Valleys, named in the plural because of their multiplicity), not merely dwarfs the Earth's Grand Canyon, but at 4000 km long could span the entire United States. Valles Marineris is visible from Earth as a feature called Coprates; it is prominent because dark dust collects on its floor.

In the southern hemisphere are two large impact basins, Hellas and Argyre. Argyre, 900 km in diameter, is similar in size to the Moon's Mare Imbrium, while Hellas is

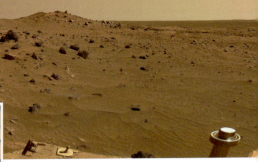

Above: The rocky red surface of Mars inside the crater Gusev as seen by the Spirit rover in 2006. Spirit's wheel tracks, visible on the left, have churned up bright underlying material, thought to consist of salty minerals created by water. Many dark, porous volcanic rocks can be seen around the rover. Among them is a smoother, lighter one (inset, foreground) which may be an iron meteorite. (NASA/JPL/Cornell)

nearly three times larger, equivalent in size to Oceanus Procellarum. Unlike the lunar maria, however, Argyre and Hellas are filled with light-coloured dust. Many of the dust storms that periodically obscure the surface of Mars after perihelion start in Hellas.

Much of the surface of Mars consists of dusty red deserts liberally scattered with rocks of all sizes, thrown out by meteorite impacts. The rusty redness of the soil is due to iron oxide. Mars may be the richest source of iron ore in the Solar System. Even the sky is pink, a result of fine particles of dust suspended in the wispy atmosphere.

Astronauts who land on Mars will need to wear spacesuits to explore the surface, as they did on the Moon, because the atmosphere is unbreathable and temperatures are sub-zero. About 95 per cent of the atmosphere consists of carbon dioxide, the remainder being mostly nitrogen and argon with a trace of water vapour. The average atmospheric pressure is a mere 6 millibars (600 pascals), equivalent to the pressure 35 km above the Earth's surface. Surface temperatures can reach 20°C on a summer's afternoon, but the temperature of

the atmosphere drops rapidly with height to well below freezing. At the poles, surface temperatures are about −130°C.

Each polar cap has a permanent core, consisting of water ice a few metres thick, augmented each winter by carbon dioxide. Carbon dioxide freezes out of the atmosphere to produce a thin polar 'hood' of frost that can extend more than halfway to the equator. During each Martian year the atmospheric pressure changes by 25 per cent or more as carbon dioxide evaporates from one polar cap with the coming of spring, migrates to the opposite hemisphere and then freezes out again as winter arrives at the other pole. Such atmospheric motions may help set off the dust storms that sweep across Mars.

Water on Mars

Although the Lowellian canals are not in evidence, space probes in orbit and on the surface have found convincing signs that water once flowed on Mars. Sinuous channels, looking like dried-up river beds, snake across parts of the planet's surface, and some of the lowlands appear to have been inundated by flash floods.

Direct evidence for past water on Mars has been found by NASA's two Mars Exploration Rovers, Spirit and Opportunity, which landed on the planet in January 2004. Spirit touched down in an impact crater called Gusev (see photograph below), thought to have been the site of a former lake, while Opportunity descended in Meridiani Planum, on the western edge of the albedo feature Sinus Meridiani. Both craft found minerals in the surface rocks which indicated that liquid water had once been present.

Mars is not short of water today, although it is in frozen form because because the atmospheric pressure is too low for it to exist as a liquid. Apart from traces of water vapour in the atmosphere, most of the water on Mars is in the polar caps and in a subsurface permafrost layer polewards of about 30° latitude north and south.

If watercourses and lakes really did exist on Mars in the past, the atmosphere must then have been denser – and a denser atmosphere would keep the planet warmer. Perhaps enough gas gushed out of the volcanoes to change the climate temporarily. Alternatively, subsurface ice could have been melted by volcanic heating or meteorite impacts. Either way, life might have had a chance to arise on Mars at some time in the past, and microscopic organisms such as bacteria might still cling to existence underneath the red sands of the planet.

Looking for life on Mars

The first search for Martian life was carried out in 1976 by two American space probes called Viking. Each probe came in two halves: a lander and an orbiter. The Viking 1 lander touched down on a lowland plain called Chryse in the northern hemisphere, over which water appears to have flowed during the wet times on Mars. The second lander descended on the opposite side of the planet in an area known as Utopia, which is encroached upon by the outer fringes of the north polar cap during winter.

The landers carried colour cameras as well as instruments to analyse the soil and the atmosphere. Each Viking lander, like those

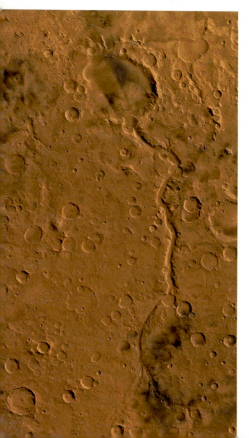

Ma'adim Vallis, over 800 km long, leads northwards into a crater called Gusev, 165 km wide. at the top of this Viking image. NASA's Spirit rover landed in Gusev in January 2004. Water may once have flowed through Ma'adim Vallis, creating a lake within Gusev. Dark areas on the crater floor are where wind has swept away light dust to reveal underlying rock. (USGS)

Phobos (lower right) and Deimos, the moons of Mars, are thought to be captured asteroids. Here they are compared with the asteroid Gaspra, top, all at the same scale and under similar lighting conditions. Gaspra was photographed by the Galileo probe, Phobos and Deimos by the Viking orbiter. (NASA)

that have landed subsequently, found itself on a rock-strewn desert without any visible signs of life – no plants, insects or animal tracks. A mechanical arm on each Viking picked up samples of the soil and tipped them into an on-board biological laboratory which set to work in search of Martian microorganisms. Neither Viking found life in the soil of Mars, despite exhaustive tests.

That is not to say that Mars is completely sterile; maybe life exists in places that the Vikings were unable to sample, such as deeper underground or inside rocks. Alternatively, perhaps life once got started but then died out when the climate changed; there may be fossil life, rather than current life, to be found on Mars. Future probes will examine such possibilities.

One final puzzle from the pre-space-probe era has now been explained: what causes the seasonal changes in the dark areas if there is no vegetation on Mars? Wind-blown dust provides the answer. Orbiting probes have recorded many examples of changes in surface markings caused by light and dark dust being blown by seasonal winds. Syrtis Major, for example, is a gently sloping area of dark volcanic rock which periodically becomes partly covered by paler dust and is later swept clear again. Dust blown by the winds

on Mars, which can reach 200 km per hour, is also a powerful erosive agent, sandblasting the surface rocks.

The moons of Mars

No discussion of Mars would be complete without reference to its two tiny moons, Phobos and Deimos, discovered in 1877 and both beyond the range of normal amateur telescopes. Space probe photographs show that they are are cratered chunks of rock shaped like lumpy potatoes. Phobos, larger and closer to Mars, measures about 27 × 18 km; Deimos is about 15 × 10 km.

Phobos lies closer than any other moon to its parent – a mere 6000 km above the surface of Mars, at which distance it orbits Mars three times a day. Probably Phobos and Deimos are former asteroids which strayed too close to Mars and were captured by the planet's gravity. They will make a fascinating sight in the sky for the first astronauts to set foot on Mars, the planet of red, frozen deserts which was so nearly suitable for life of its own.

• Charts showing the positions of Mars over a five-year period can be found at www.collins.co.uk/starsandplanets

Jupiter

Jupiter is the king of the planets, and the most fascinating of all to study with small instruments. Humble binoculars reveal the planet's cream-coloured disk and four main moons, called the Galilean satellites after the Italian scientist Galileo Galilei who discovered them in 1610. Some people with exceptionally acute vision can see the Galilean satellites with the naked eye as faint starlike points either side of the planet.

A small telescope brings into view the main features of Jupiter's disk: dark belts parallel to the equator, along with an eye-shaped mark-ing in the southern hemisphere known as the Great Red Spot. This seems to have been first observed in 1831, and a similar feature was seen as early as 1664. Careful study of these features reveals that Jupiter's rotation period varies with latitude, averaging 9 hours

Jupiter as seen by the Cassini space probe in 2000. Light-coloured zones of cloud alternate with darker belts. In the southern hemisphere is the swirling Great Red Spot, with white ovals to the south of it. (NASA/University of Arizona)

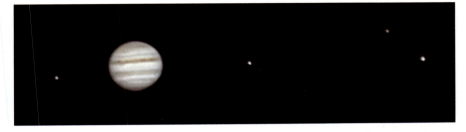

50 minutes in the bright equatorial zone (System I, the fastest rotation of any planet in the Solar System) and about 5 minutes longer at higher latitudes, called System II. Hence the equatorial zone gains one rotation on the regions to the north and south every 48 days. In addition, the Great Red Spot drifts slightly in relation to its surroundings.

These effects demonstrate that the visible surface of Jupiter is not solid. We are looking at clouds, constantly seething and swirling, changing in colour and shape. Jupiter never appears the same twice. That is its attraction.

Jupiter is easy to spot with the naked eye, looking like a bright cream-coloured star. It comes to opposition every 13 months and can appear as bright as magnitude −2.9 at the closest oppositions, when it is within 600 million km of us. At such times, a magnification of only 40 times will show it as large as the full Moon appears to the naked eye.

Even well away from opposition Jupiter still outshines every star in the sky. Its bright-ness results from its highly reflective clouds and its imposing size – it is the largest planet in the Solar System.

Examination of Jupiter's outline gives added confirmation that it is not a solid planet: Jupiter has a bulging midriff. At the equator it is nearly 143,000 km across, but from pole to pole it measures some 9000 km less. A line of 11 Earths would be needed to equal Jupiter's equatorial width. Even though Jupiter is composed largely of the lightest elements in the Universe, hydrogen and helium, its bulk is such that its mass is two and a half times as much as all the other planets put together.

Observing Jupiter

Observers draw Jupiter on pre-printed blank outlines with an equatorial diameter of 64 mm and a polar diameter of 60 mm; forms are issued by amateur astronomy societies or can be drawn on a computer. After sketching in the main features, details can be added starting at the leading limb, where the planet's rotation of 6° every 10 minutes rapidly carries the features out of sight. Intensities can be estimated on a scale from 0 to 10 (European observers rate 0 as the brightest and 10 the blackest, but in the US the scale runs the

JUPITER DATA	
Diameter (equatorial)	142,984 km
Mass (Earth = 1)	317.83
Mean density (water = 1)	1.33
Volume (Earth = 1)	1321
Axial rotation period (sidereal)	9.84 h
Orbital period (sidereal)	11.86 y
Orbital period (synodic)	398.88 d
Axial inclination	3°.1
Mean distance from Sun	778.4 × 10⁶ km
Orbital eccentricity	0.048
Orbital inclination	1°.3
Number of moons	60+

other way). By continuing to watch Jupiter as it rotates, the observer can build up a strip chart of the entire planet.

Most valuable of all are timings of the passage of various spots across the central meridian, the imaginary line running north–south down the centre of the planet's visible disk. Repeated timings will establish the rotation rate of spots, and reveal any drift in their longitude caused by winds in Jupiter's atmosphere. Even in this age of space probes and space telescopes, long-term series of such observations are useful.

Because Jupiter's cloud features are so impermanent and mobile, it is impossible to give more than a generalized description of the planet's appearance. Its disk is crossed by alternating bright and dark bands, termed

zones and belts respectively, named according to their latitude: equatorial, tropical, temperate, or polar. The main belts and zones, along with their names and abbreviations, are shown on the diagram below.

Frozen ammonia crystals form high, cold clouds in the bright zones, where gas ascends; the darker belts, where the gases descend, are lower and warmer (although 'warm' is only a relative term, for the temperature of the cloud tops is around −150°C). The colours of the belts can vary from yellow and brown

The main belts and zones in the clouds of Jupiter. This outline has a diameter of 64 mm and a depth of 60 mm, the size used for making disk drawings of the planet. (Wil Tirion)

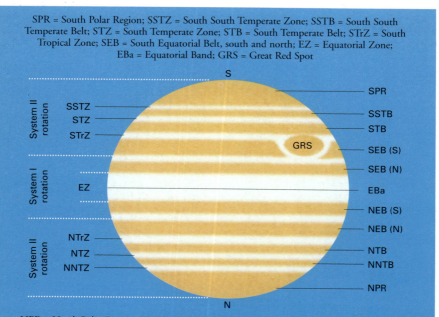

SPR = South Polar Region; SSTZ = South South Temperate Zone; SSTB = South South Temperate Belt; STZ = South Temperate Zone; STB = South Temperate Belt; STrZ = South Tropical Zone; SEB = South Equatorial Belt, south and north; EZ = Equatorial Zone; EBa = Equatorial Band; GRS = Great Red Spot

System II rotation

System I rotation

System II rotation

S

SSTZ
STZ
STrZ

EZ

NTrZ
NTZ
NNTZ

N

SPR
SSTB
STB
GRS
SEB (S)
SEB (N)
EBa
NEB (S)
NEB (N)
NTB
NNTB
NPR

NPR = North Polar Region; NNTZ = North North Temperate Zone; NNTB = North North Temperate Belt; NTZ = North Temperate Zone; NTB = North Temperate Belt; NTrZ = North Tropical Zone; NEB = North Equatorial Belt, north and south; EZ = Equatorial Zone. System I and System II are the rotation periods of the planet's equatorial regions and higher latitudes, respectively.

to orange, red or even purple as a result of complex chemicals in the atmosphere of Jupiter, sulphur being one of the prominent colourants.

High-speed winds of up to 500 km per hour whip the edges of the zones and belts into turbulent eddies, giving them a scalloped appearance. The weather on Jupiter is unpredictable. Dark and light spots can suddenly erupt in the clouds, lasting for weeks or even decades before fading away. One of the main roles of amateur observers is to track these storms as they erupt and circulate around the planet.

The Great Red Spot

Of all the markings on Jupiter, the most famous, and by far the longest-lived, is the Great Red Spot, centred at about latitude 22° south. It certainly is great: 14,000 km wide and as much as 40,000 km long, enough to swallow three Earths. But it is not always red: most often it is pinkish, and sometimes it can fade to a colourless grey. Its colour is believed to be due either to red phosphorus or sulphur.

Even now its nature is not fully understood, but it appears to be an upwardly spiralling column of gas similar to a hurricane on Earth, its top spreading out about 8 km above

Dark stains in Jupiter's clouds south of the Great Red Spot mark the sites where fragments of Comet Shoemaker–Levy 9 impacted the planet in July 1994. This photograph was taken by the Hubble Space Telescope. (STScI/NASA)

the surrounding cloud deck. Jupiter's other, smaller spots, including a series of long-lived white ovals, are believed to be similar swirling storm systems. As if to emphasize the storminess of the planet, the Voyagers and the more recent Galileo probe photographed massive flashes of lightning on Jupiter's night side, far larger than in any thunderstorm on Earth.

In 2005 a mini red spot, about half the width of its older relative, formed at latitude 34° south from the merger of three large white oval clouds in the South Temperate Belt. The increased size of the merged ovals is thought to have created a sufficient disturbance to dredge up reddish material from deeper in the atmosphere. Here we may be seeing a re-enactment of the process by which the Great Red Spot itself originally formed. No one knows how long this mini red spot may last.

The key to Jupiter's meteorology is the fact that it gives off twice as much heat as it receives from the Sun. The planet was hot when it formed, and still retains some of that

heat today. This internal store of heat drives the complex cloud systems of Jupiter, keeping the Great Red Spot and its smaller relatives alive far longer than any storms can persist on Earth.

Interestingly, Jupiter has virtually the same chemical composition as the Sun: mostly hydrogen and helium. There is thought to be a rocky core about twice the size of the Earth at Jupiter's centre, but no space probe could ever land on it. Beneath the wispy high-altitude clouds of frozen ammonia are complex chemicals that give the dark belts their colour.

Deeper still, temperatures are similar to those on Earth and clouds of water vapour condense. About 1000 km below the visible cloud tops, temperatures and pressures have increased to the point where hydrogen is compressed into a liquid. Jupiter's liquid hydrogen seas are about 20,000 km deep. Below, under the crushing pressure of 3 million Earth atmospheres, hydrogen is compressed into a superdense state with the properties of a metal; such a substance is known as metallic hydrogen.

Convection within the hot metallic hydrogen interior of Jupiter is thought to be responsible for the planet's intense magnetic field, 10 times stronger than the Earth's and extending out for 100 times Jupiter's radius into space. If the magnetosphere around Jupiter were visible to the naked eye to us on Earth, it would appear over twice the size of the full Moon.

Family portrait of Jupiter's four largest satellites as seen by the Galileo space probe, to scale. From left: the sulphurous surface of volcanic Io; icy, cracked Europa; dark markings and bright craters on Ganymede; and battered Callisto, with the Valhalla impact basin at centre. (NASA)

Cometary impact

One of the most remarkable events in the history of planetary observation took place in 1994 when Comet Shoemaker–Levy 9 collided with Jupiter. The comet had been captured into orbit around the planet some time in the 1920s but was not discovered until 1993 by when it had broken into over 20 pieces. These crashed into Jupiter during the week of 16–22 July 1994, leaving dark markings in its clouds that were visible from Earth through small telescopes.

Over the ensuing months, the dark patches spread out into a band around Jupiter that took over a year to fade away. Crater chains on Jupiter's moons Callisto and Ganymede suggest that they, too, have been struck by fragments of disintegrated comets in the past.

Jupiter's moons and rings

Jupiter possesses a fascinating collection of over 60 satellites, like a mini Solar System. With the simplest optical aid the four largest, known as the Galilean satellites, can be seen performing a merry dance around Jupiter, changing position from night to night – sometimes out of sight behind the planet, sometimes transiting across its face and sometimes being eclipsed in its shadow.

The closest to Jupiter of the Galilean satellites is Io, 3643 km in diameter (slightly larger than our own Moon), orbiting every 42½ hours. Io is the most volcanically active body in the Solar System. The Voyager 1 probe in 1979 photographed eight volcanoes erupting simultaneously on it. Hundreds of other volcanic vents were visible, although not actually erupting. Those volcanoes erupt not just molten rock (lava) as on Earth but also sulphur which solidifies to form the garish red, orange and yellow of Io's surface.

Io is molten because it is caught in a gravitational tug of war between Jupiter and the other Galilean satellites; their opposing pulls release tidal energy that melts Io's interior. Io recycles its interior onto its surface, endlessly turning itself inside out. Some of the sulphur escapes and showers onto the innermost moon of Jupiter, Amalthea, giving it an orange coating. Amalthea is an irregularly shaped lump of rock only about 200 km in diameter, too faint to be seen in amateur telescopes.

Within the orbit of Amalthea is a faint ring of dust, extending inwards to a mere 30,000 km above Jupiter's cloud tops. This tenuous ring of Jupiter is believed to result from the break-up of one or more tiny moons.

Moving outwards past Io we come to Europa, smallest of the Galilean satellites with a diameter of 3122 km. Europa is encased in a white shell of ice, veined with fine cracks probably produced by tidal forces. Underneath its fractured icy crust, Europa may have an ocean of liquid water.

Next in line from Jupiter is Ganymede, the largest and brightest of the satellites; what's more, at 5262 km in diameter it is the largest moon in the Solar System, larger even than the planet Mercury. Ganymede and the fourth of the Galilean satellites, Callisto, 4821 km in diameter, are both balls of rock and ice, rather like giant muddy snowballs.

Callisto is saturated with impact craters, the largest 300 km in diameter and called Valhalla; it is similar to the large basins on the Moon and Mercury, surrounded by wave-like ridges. Ganymede is also cratered by impacts, but less heavily than Callisto, and exhibits a strange grooving on much of its surface, apparently formed by faulting and stressing of the moon's icy surface layers. Bright spots on Ganymede and Callisto mark places where recent impacts have exposed fresh ice.

The rest of Jupiter's moons are small and insignificant. Most of them – particularly the outermost ones, which move in retrograde orbits – were probably passing bodies that were captured by Jupiter's gravity.
• Charts showing the positions of Jupiter over a five-year period can be found at www.collins.co.uk/starsandplanets

Blowing its top – a volcano called Loki erupts at the limb of Jupiter's moon Io, sending clouds of sulphur 150 km into space, as photographed by the Voyager 1 probe in 1979. The volcanoes of Io are named after fire gods. (USGS)

Saturn

Bright rings girdle Saturn's equator, making it the most beautiful of the planets. Those distinctive rings can be spotted clearly in a small telescope; good binoculars, mounted steadily, will show the small outline of the planet elongated into an ellipse by the rings. Mounted binoculars should also pick out Saturn's largest moon, Titan, which orbits the planet every 16 days.

Saturn's rings can reflect more light than the body of the planet itself, so that at its best Saturn appears as a bright yellowish star of magnitude −0.3, outshone only by Sirius and Canopus. Without the rings, Saturn would be less than half as bright, no more than magnitude 0.7.

Strange to say, from time to time Saturn really can appear to be without rings. The reason is the tilt of the planet's axis. As Saturn orbits the Sun, the rings are presented to us at an angle that varies from 27° to 0°. So thin are the rings that when they are edge-on (which happens about every 15 years, as in 2009 and 2025) they disappear from view in even the largest telescopes on Earth. The brightness of Saturn therefore depends not only on its distance from us, but also on the aspect of the rings.

The ringed planet orbits the Sun every 29½ years at an average distance of 1430 million km, 9½ times farther than the Earth. Being so slow-moving, Saturn returns to opposition about two weeks later each year. At a typical

Saturn photographed by Voyager 2 in 1981; note the Cassini Division and subtle detail in the rings. Three moons, Tethys, Dione and Rhea, are visible as tiny dots beneath the planet, with the shadow of Tethys on the clouds. (USGS)

opposition, a magnification of 90 times will show the globe of Saturn as large as the full Moon viewed with the naked eye.

In many ways, Saturn is a smaller version of Jupiter. Its equatorial diameter is second only to that of Jupiter; its rotation period is second-fastest to that of Jupiter; and, like Jupiter, it is composed mostly of hydrogen and helium. In one way, though, Saturn is unique among the planets: its average density is a mere 70 per cent that of water. This remarkable fact comes about because the planet's mass is less than a third that of Jupiter, so its gravity is less and hence its central regions are not compressed as densely.

Saturn's low density is apparent from its outline, which is even more squashed than that of Jupiter. Saturn's pole-to-pole diameter is fully 10 per cent smaller than its equatorial diameter, against 6 per cent for Jupiter.

Observing Saturn

Through a telescope Saturn appears as a tranquil, ochre-coloured disk, darker at the poles and with some dusky horizontal bands. The pattern of belts and zones is much the same as on Jupiter (see diagram on page 364). In addition, Saturn throws its shadow onto the rings, and the rings throw their shadow onto the globe of the planet, creating the impression of a dark equatorial belt.

Pleasing views of Saturn and its rings can be obtained with small telescopes, but serious study requires at least 200 mm aperture. When drawing Saturn, observers use a range of pre-printed blank forms to match the changing tilt of the rings. On such blanks the polar diameter of Saturn is 50 mm, the equatorial diameter 55 mm and the diameter of the rings 126 mm. As with Jupiter, the main features are sketched in quickly and detail added before it rotates out of view.

Observers can estimate the intensities of various features; in Europe, the scale runs from 1 (the brightest part of the rings) to 10 (black sky), whereas the US scale runs the

SATURN DATA	
Diameter (equatorial)	120,536 km
Mass (Earth = 1)	95.16
Mean density (water = 1)	0.69
Volume (Earth = 1)	764
Axial rotation period (sidereal)	10.23 h
Orbital period (sidereal)	29.45 y
Orbital period (synodic)	378.09 d
Axial inclination	26°.73
Mean distance from Sun	1426.7×10^6 km
Orbital eccentricity	0.054
Orbital inclination	2°.5
Number of moons	55+

opposite way, from 0 (black sky) to 8 (brightest part of the rings). Markings in the clouds can be timed as they cross the planet's central meridian, in the same way as with Jupiter.

There are none of the swirling, multi-coloured storm clouds that make Jupiter's globe so interesting, and no equivalent of the Great Red Spot. However, every 30 years or so a large white spot erupts in Saturn's northern hemisphere. Evidently, these white spots are storm clouds produced by solar heating, as they occur when the planet's north pole is tilted at its maximum towards the Sun. Such an outbreak occurred in 1990 and lasted a few months, with a succession of smaller spots appearing over the next few years.

White spots apart, this is not to say that Saturn lacks activity in its atmosphere; it is just that the cloud patterns are usually concealed by high-altitude haze. Low-contrast cloud swirls resembling those on Jupiter have been recorded by space probes.

The meteorology of Saturn and Jupiter is similar, for they both have internal sources of heat. Like Jupiter, Saturn radiates twice as much heat as it receives from the Sun, a legacy of its birth. However, since Saturn is farther from the Sun, its clouds are about 30°C colder than on Jupiter and form lower in the atmosphere. Tracking of cloud systems has revealed gales blowing at up to 1800 km per hour on Saturn, over three times faster than the winds of Jupiter.

8°

16°

24°

Rings of Saturn

Inevitably, much of the interest in Saturn lies in its magnificent rings. As seen from Earth, they look like a continuous disk encircling the planet, but appearances are deceptive. The Dutch scientist Christiaan Huygens in 1655 was the first to realize that the rings are not solid, but consist of a swarm of tiny particles in orbit around Saturn.

The central part of the rings, known as Ring B, is the widest and brightest. It is separated from the outer, fainter Ring A by a 5000-km-wide gap called Cassini's Division, visible with a 75-mm telescope. Extending inwards from Ring B towards the planet is the faintest ring of all, the transparent Ring C, also known as the crêpe ring.

A narrow gap called Encke's Division can be seen in the outer part of Ring A, while observers using large telescopes under good conditions have reported apparent ripples within the rings, a sign that the density of ring material varies from place to place.

But even the best telescopic views did not prepare astronomers for the astounding wealth of detail that has been revealed by space probes – firstly the two Voyager craft that flew past Saturn in 1980 and 1981, and then Cassini which began orbiting the planet in 2004. Under the close-up scrutiny of these probes, the rings break up into thousands of narrow ringlets and gaps, like the ridges and grooves of a gramophone record.

Some ringlets are not perfectly circular, but are elliptical in shape. Even Cassini's Division is not empty, but contains thread-like ringlets. An outer ring, called the F Ring, first shown by the Voyager probes, is distorted by the gravitational pull of satellites orbiting close to it, giving it a twisted appearance like strands of rope.

Saturn's rings are presented to us at a range of angles from 0° to a maximum of 27° as it orbits the Sun, so a range of printed blanks is used for drawing the planet. (Wil Tirion)

Saturn's rings are extraordinarily thin in relation to their 275,000 km diameter, no more than 100 m thick. On the same ratio of thickness to diameter, a CD or DVD disk would be about 5 km in diameter.

The particles that make up the rings come in a wide range of sizes, from dust specks to lumps the size of a house or larger. Their composition is mostly frozen water, possibly mixed with dust, resembling loosely compacted snowballs.

Saturn's rings could have originated from material that was prevented from forming into a moon by the overpowering force of Saturn's gravity. Alternatively, they may be the remains of a former moon that strayed too close to the planet and broke up, or a moon that was broken up by the impact of a comet. In fact, the rings may be replenished from time to time by icy material from impacting comets.

In some places, fine dust overlays the rings, producing transient darker features known as *spokes*. Spoke-like features were first reported by ground-based observers, but it took space probes to establish their reality.

Saturn's moons

In recent years, a host of small moons of Saturn have been discovered by space probes and Earth-based observations, bringing the known total to over 50 and climbing. The small innermost moons are intimately associated with the rings. One, Pan, orbits in Encke's Division in Ring A. Another, Atlas, patrols the outer edge of Ring A. Two of the moons, Prometheus and Pandora, orbit either side of the F Ring, shepherding its particles.

Slightly farther out from Saturn, Janus and Epimetheus move along the same orbit, which initially confused astronomers who first spotted them from Earth in 1966. Orbit-sharing is common among Saturn's moons. Tethys, a satellite visible from Earth, has two small siblings, Telesto and Calypso, moving on the same path. Dione, visible from Earth, shares its orbit with tiny Helene, another Voyager discovery.

The gravitational effect of some of these satellites helps maintain the gaps in Saturn's rings. For instance, the gravitational tug of Mimas pulls particles out of the Cassini Division. Mimas itself, like most of Saturn's moons, is a dirty snowball of frozen water and rock. It sports a remarkable crater 135 km wide, larger than the crater Copernicus on the Moon and fully a third of its own 400-km diameter. The impact that caused this grotesque feature, called Herschel, must have nearly shattered Mimas.

Iapetus, Saturn's third-largest moon, is another strange body: one side is five times darker than the other. This harlequin effect is probably caused by dust knocked off a more distant moon, Phoebe, which is the darkest of Saturn's moons. The dark dust from Phoebe falls inwards to be swept up by Iapetus, coating its leading face while bright ice on its trailing side remains exposed.

The largest of Saturn's moons, Titan, 5150 km in diameter, deserves to be considered a planet in its own right. Bigger than Mercury (but slightly smaller than Jupiter's main moon Ganymede), it is the only moon to have a substantial atmosphere – in fact, the atmospheric pressure on the surface of Titan is 50 per cent greater than at sea level on Earth. But being so far from the Sun, Titan's surface temperature is very low, about −180°C.

Titan's atmosphere is 90 per cent nitrogen, with methane making up most of the rest.

Mimas, one of the smaller moons of Saturn, sports a huge crater with a central peak, formed by a major impact. The crater is called Herschel, after William Herschel, the astronomer who discovered Mimas in 1789. The rest of the moon's surface is saturated with smaller craters. This photograph was taken by the Cassini spacecraft in 2005. (NASA/JPL/Space Science Institute)

Clouds of orange smog blanket its surface from view at visual wavelengths, but it has been possible to map most of Titan at infra-red wavelengths and by radar. In January 2005 the Huygens probe parachuted down to the surface of Titan, landing on an area covered with frozen water and dotted with icy pebbles. It is thought that methane rain falls on Titan from time to time.

• Charts showing the positions of Saturn over a five-year period can be found at www.collins.co.uk/starsandplanets

Ring C   Ring B   Ring A

Cassini Division   Encke Division   Ring F

Saturn's rings as seen by the Cassini probe. From left are the faint Ring C; Ring B (the brightest section); the Cassini Division, with faint ringlets within it; Ring A with the narrow Encke Division towards its rim; and the thin F Ring outermost. (NASA/JPL/Space Science Institute)

Uranus, Neptune and beyond

Uranus should in theory be visible to the naked eye: at its brightest it is of magnitude 5.5. But it is so insignificant that it was never noticed by ancient astronomers, for whom the Solar System stopped at Saturn. Uranus was not discovered until March 1781, when William Herschel spotted it through his telescope during a systematic survey of the skies.

Once its position is known, Uranus can easily be followed in binoculars as it moves against the background stars. There is a certain fascination in seeing the blue-green disk of this distant planet through a telescope, but even with large apertures Uranus displays no detail.

Uranus is one of the four 'gas giants' of the outer Solar System, the others being Jupiter, Saturn and Neptune. Uranus has an equatorial diameter less than half that of Saturn but four times larger than the Earth. It lies 2900 million km from the Sun, 19 times farther than the Earth. Seasons pass slowly on Uranus, for the planet takes 84 years to

The green, featureless disk of Uranus, with its encircling rings, photographed by Voyager 2 in 1986. The brightest ring is the outermost one, the Epsilon ring. Background stars and moons can also be seen. (Erich Karkoschka/NASA)

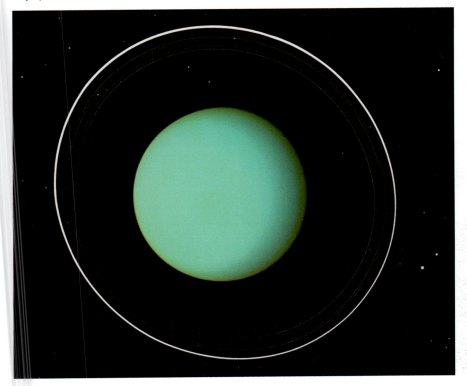

complete one orbit, and they are extreme, for Uranus appears to have been knocked over onto its side: the planet's axial tilt is 98°, meaning that its axis of rotation lies almost in the plane of its orbit.

As a result, every 42 years one of the poles of Uranus is pointing towards the Sun, while its opposite pole is in darkness for decades. In between times the planet's equatorial region faces sunwards. During each 84-year orbit the Sun can appear overhead at every latitude on Uranus, something that never happens on any other planet. No one knows why Uranus should be lying on its side in this unique way; perhaps it suffered a collision with another large body long ago.

Uranus is celebrated for another reason: it was the second planet discovered to have rings. In 1977, astronomers watched as Uranus passed in front of a star. Unexpectedly, they noticed that the star winked on and off a number of times before and after it was obscured by the disk of Uranus, from which they deduced that Uranus was encircled by nine faint rings. The existence of these rings was confirmed by the Voyager 2 space probe which flew past the planet in January 1986. Since then the rings have been photographed from Earth at infrared wavelengths and the known number has increased to 13.

The rings are narrow, mostly only a few kilometres wide, separated by broad gaps. They lie between 12,000 and 72,000 km

NEPTUNE DATA

Diameter (equatorial)	49,528 km
Mass (Earth = 1)	17.15
Mean density (water = 1)	1.64
Volume (Earth = 1)	58
Axial rotation period (sidereal)	16.11 h
Orbital period (sidereal)	164.8 y
Orbital period (synodic)	367.49 d
Axial inclination	28°.33
Mean distance from Sun	4498.3×10^6 km
Orbital eccentricity	0.009
Orbital inclination	1°.8
Number of moons	13

above the cloud tops of Uranus, and are composed of dust and other debris from tiny moonlets that orbit among them.

In addition to the rings, Uranus has five large moons visible from Earth: Miranda, Ariel, Umbriel, Titania and Oberon, ranging in diameter from 500 to 1500 km. Eleven smaller moons were discovered by Voyager 2 and other, more distant ones have since been discovered from Earth. The inner moons, like the rings, move in nearly circular orbits around Uranus's crazily tilted equator, while the outer ones have elliptical and inclined orbits, suggesting they have been captured since the planet's formation.

Even to the close-up gaze of Voyager, the gaseous surface of the planet itself was disappointingly bland, with scarcely any cloud features. In structure, Uranus is believed to have a rocky core surrounded by a mantle of ice, topped by an atmosphere of hydrogen and helium with about 2 per cent methane, which gives the planet its greenish colour.

Neptune, the outermost giant

Neptune, the outermost major planet of the Solar System, is in some ways a twin of Uranus. It is slightly smaller and shows the same featureless disk through amateur telescopes, with a stronger blue-green tinge because there is more methane in the atmos-

URANUS DATA

Diameter (equatorial)	51,118 km
Mass (Earth = 1)	14.54
Mean density (water = 1)	1.27
Volume (Earth = 1)	63
Axial rotation period (sidereal)	17.24 h
Orbital period (sidereal)	84.02 y
Orbital period (synodic)	369.66 d
Axial inclination	97°.77
Mean distance from Sun	2871.0×10^6 km
Orbital eccentricity	0.047
Orbital inclination	0°.8
Number of moons	27

The icy blue of Neptune's clouds is disturbed by the Great Dark Spot, an anticyclone the size of the Earth, fringed with white methane cirrus. This photograph was taken by the Voyager 2 probe in August 1989. (NASA)

phere above its clouds. Magnitude 7.8 at its brightest, Neptune is far too faint to be seen with the naked eye, but can be followed in binoculars when one knows where to look.

Unlike the accidental discovery of Uranus, Neptune's existence was predicted in advance. Astronomers found that Uranus was not keeping to its expected course, and some suspected that it was being pulled by the gravity of an as-yet-unseen planet. In France, mathematician Urbain Le Verrier calculated the new planet's position in 1846, beating the Englishman John Couch Adams who had been working on the same problem. In September that year, astronomers at the Berlin Observatory found Neptune close to Le Verrier's predicted position.

Neptune crawls around the Sun in 165 years at an average distance of 4500 million km, 30 times farther away than the Earth. Being so distant from the Sun, it is very cold and dark. Unlike bland Uranus, Neptune has markings in its clouds more reminiscent of

Jupiter. One such feature called the Great Dark Spot, similar in nature to Jupiter's Great Red Spot, was revealed by the cameras of Voyager 2 when it reached Neptune in August 1989. This spot gradually drifted towards the planet's equator and had disappeared by the time the Hubble Space Telescope looked at Neptune in 1994, although similar spots have appeared since.

As with the other giant planets, Neptune's moons are as interesting as the planet itself. The largest of its 13 known satellites, Triton, is 2700 km in diameter, over three-quarters the size of our own Moon. It has one of the coldest known surfaces in the Solar System, −235°C, and is covered with frozen nitrogen and methane. Geysers of nitrogen or methane gas spout from beneath the surface, leaving dark streaks on the bright ice.

Triton is in a retrograde (east to west) orbit around Neptune which suggests that it was captured. Tidal forces from Neptune mean that Triton's orbit is gradually shrinking, so that the moon will spiral closer to the planet until it is broken up in the distant future. A shattered Triton will form a far more substantial set of rings around Neptune than the faint, narrow ones that currently encircle it. The most prominent of Neptune's rings are named Galle, Le Verrier, Lassell, Arago and Adams, after those involved in the discovery and early study of the planet.

Trans-Neptunian objects

Beyond Neptune lies a swarm of icy bodies known collectively as trans-Neptunian objects (TNOs). The first of these was discovered in 1930 by Clyde Tombaugh at the Lowell Observatory in Arizona as part of a search for a new planet, and was named Pluto. Pluto was regarded as the ninth planet of the Solar System until 2006, when the International Astronomical Union reclassified it as a *dwarf planet*.

Pluto is far smaller than any of the eight major planets, being under 2400 km in diameter, smaller than Neptune's largest moon, Triton. Even less planet-like is Pluto's eccentric orbit which crosses the path of Neptune, as happened between February 1979 and February 1999; no other major planet crosses another's orbit, although many asteroids do.

During the 1990s astronomers began to discover many other trans-Neptunian objects; over a thousand are now known. One of these, Eris, discovered in 2005, is larger than Pluto. Eris and Pluto are both now classified as dwarf planets, a category which also includes the largest member of the asteroid belt, Ceres. Possibly more dwarf planets will be added to the list as further large TNOs are discovered.

Pluto orbits the Sun every 248 years at an average distance nearly 40 times that of the Earth. At 15th magnitude, it is difficult to spot, let alone study. Eris, even farther and fainter, takes over 500 years to complete one orbit.

Pluto has three known moons and Eris has one. By far the largest of them is Pluto's main moon, Charon, discovered in 1978, which is half Pluto's size. Charon orbits Pluto every 6.4 days, the same time that the planet takes to spin on its axis. Charon therefore hangs over one spot on the surface of Pluto, visible permanently from one hemisphere of the planet but invisible from the other. In close-up, Pluto's surface probably looks much like that of Triton.

Pluto's largest moon, Charon, is shown above and below the planet in these two images taken three days apart. (Gemini Observatory)

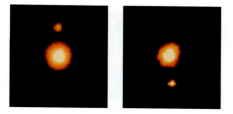

Comets and meteors

Comets are insubstantial bodies, loosely knit assemblages of frozen gas and dust that loop around the Sun on highly elongated orbits. They return to the inner Solar System at intervals ranging from a few years to many thousands of years, becoming visible to us on Earth as ghostly, glowing apparitions for a few weeks or months before receding back into distant obscurity.

When far from the Sun, a comet shines only by reflecting sunlight. At that stage it is small – usually no more than a few kilometres across – and faint. Approaching the Sun, the comet warms up, turning its icy surface into gas. Under the influence of the Sun's radiance the gases of the comet begin to fluoresce, in similar fashion to the gas in a neon tube, thereby considerably increasing the comet's brightness.

Halley's Comet pursues an elliptical path around the Sun, steeply inclined to the orbits of the planets. It travels from between the orbits of Mercury and Venus out to beyond Neptune and back again every 76 years. (Wil Tirion)

Gas and dust released from the warming comet produce a halo or *coma* 100,000 km or so in diameter. At the centre of the coma is the *nucleus*, the only solid part of the comet, consisting of a 'dirty snowball' of ice, dust and perhaps some rock. In a large comet the nucleus may be a few tens of kilometres across, but most are only a kilometre or so wide. Well over a thousand million comet nuclei would be needed to equal the mass of the Earth.

Not all comets develop tails, but many do. A typical tail stretches for 1°–2° (two to four Moon diameters) but in exceptional cases can be much longer. Comets are brightest – and their tails longest – near perihelion, so they are usually most prominent shortly after sunset or before sunrise when they are inevitably low down in the twilight.

One part of a comet's tail consists of gas blown away from the comet's head by the solar wind of atomic particles streaming from the Sun. The other part of the tail is made up of dust particles liberated from the head. The gas tail appears bluish in colour because of the fluorescing of the gas molecules,

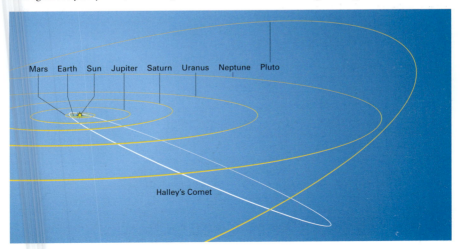

Mars   Earth   Sun   Jupiter   Saturn   Uranus   Neptune   Pluto

Halley's Comet

whereas the dust tail is yellowish because it shines by reflecting sunlight.

Comet tails always point away from the Sun. Gas tails are mostly straight but dust tails tend to fan out more as the dust particles lag behind the comet. Some comets seem to have an *anti-tail* pointing towards the Sun, but this is a perspective effect resulting from the curving dust tail being seen from an unusual angle.

A comet's tail can extend for 100 million km or so, farther than the distance from the Earth to the Sun, as did the gas and dust tails of of Comet Hale–Bopp in 1997. Yet, for all its glorious appearance, the tail is less dense than a laboratory vacuum – stars shine through it undimmed. The tail of a comet gives it the appearance of speeding across the sky, but actually its movement against the stars is barely noticeable during the course of a night.

Being so large and diffuse, comets are best observed with binoculars and wide-field telescopes. Draw the comet in negative with a soft pencil on white paper. Record the shape of the coma, its central condensation and any tail. Plot the brightest background stars

Comet Hale–Bopp seen over Stonehenge in April 1997. Cassiopeia is at upper right and the Pleiades at upper left. The comet previously appeared some 4200 years ago, about the time that Stonehenge was built. (Paul Sutherland)

so that the dimensions of the coma and tail can later be measured from a star atlas.

Comet magnitudes are difficult to estimate. One way is to defocus your binoculars or telescope and compare the image of the comet with that of nearby stars. This technique works well only with brighter, condensed comets. For more diffuse comets, fix the in-focus image of the coma in your mind before defocusing your instrument, and compare this image with the defocused images of nearby stars.

Each year's batch of comets is a mixture of known specimens returning to the Sun and completely new discoveries. Dozens may be visible through an amateur telescope each year, and several can come within the range of binoculars, but only occasionally does one become bright enough to be prominent to the naked eye. Over 2500 comets have well-known orbits, and more are being discovered all the time. Dedicated amateur astronomers sweep the skies to discover new ones; each new comet is given its discoverer's name.

Comets with the longest orbital periods – more than a few centuries – are thought to come from an unseen swarm of thousands of millions of comets, the Oort Cloud, that envelops the Solar System at its dim outer edges, about a light year from the Sun. The gravitational influence of passing stars nudges comets from this cloud into new orbits that bring them in towards the Sun.

An inner comet cloud, termed the Kuiper Belt, lies just beyond the orbit of Neptune. Most so-called *periodic comets*, which have orbital periods of a few hundred years or less and have been observed on more than one return, are thought to come from the Kuiper Belt rather than the Oort Cloud.

The comet of shortest known period is Encke's Comet, which orbits the Sun every 3.3 years. It is so old that it has lost most of its gas and dust, and is too faint to see with the naked eye. Most famous of all is Halley's Comet, named after the English astronomer

Edmond Halley, who calculated its orbit in 1705. Halley's Comet returns every 76 years or so, and last appeared in 1985–6. Its orbit takes it from 88 million km from the Sun (between the orbits of Mercury and Venus) out to 5300 million km (beyond Neptune).

Meteors and meteor showers

Dust lost from a comet disperses into space. The Earth and other planets are continually sweeping up cometary dust. When a particle of cometary dust comes whizzing into the atmosphere, it burns up by friction at a height of about 100 km, producing a streak of light known as a shooting star or meteor. The whole event is over quite literally in a flash, usually lasting less than a second. On

Members of a meteor shower appear to diverge from a small area of sky termed the radiant. This diagram shows the radiant of the Lyrid meteors, which lies in the constellation Lyra, near the bright star Vega. (Wil Tirion)

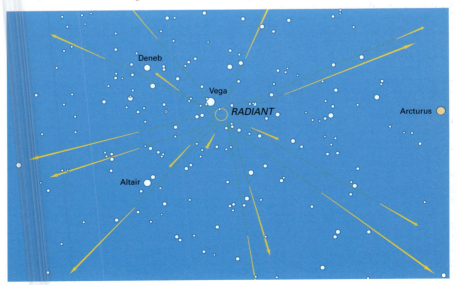

any clear night, a few meteors are visible each hour as particles of dust dash at random to their deaths in the atmosphere.

Such random meteors are termed *sporadic*. Occasionally, though, the Earth crosses the orbit of a comet and encounters a dense swarm of dust. This gives rise to a so-called meteor shower, in which meteors may be visible coming from one direction in the sky at the rate of dozens per hour.

The area of sky from which the meteors seem to come is known as the *radiant*. However, this is not the best point to look at, since the meteors are approaching head-on from this direction and so their trails are shortest; the longest trails will be seen up to 90° from the radiant.

A meteor shower is named for the constellation in which the radiant lies. For instance, the Perseids, an abundant shower of bright meteors which the Earth encounters each August, seem to radiate from Perseus; the Geminids from Gemini; and so on. One historical oddity concerns the Quadrantids, which come from an area in Boötes that was once part of the now-defunct constellation of Quadrans Muralis, the wall quadrant.

The strength of a meteor shower is measured by its *zenithal hourly rate* (ZHR), which is the number of meteors that an individual observer would see if the radiant were directly overhead in a dark sky. Since the radiant is seldom, if ever, at the zenith, the number of meteors actually seen per hour will be less than the theoretical ZHR. In addition, bright moonlight and sky glow from artificial lights will wash out the fainter meteors, again reducing the observed ZHR.

Amateur astronomers make valuable observations of meteor showers, counting the number of meteors visible with the naked eye and estimating their brightness. Comfort is essential for a meteor watch, which may last several hours: wrap up warmly and recline in a deckchair or on a sunbed.

Typical meteors are of magnitude +2 or +3, but some are brighter than the brightest stars and the occasional spectacular example, termed a *fireball*, can cast shadows. Some meteors seem to split up as they fall, and some leave a train of glowing gas which takes several seconds to fade. The table shows the main meteor showers visible each year. The ZHR is only a guide, and can vary considerably from year to year.

One extreme case is the Leonids, normally a modest shower, which bursts into life at 33-year intervals when its parent comet, Tempel–Tuttle, returns to perihelion. An intense storm of Leonids was seen over the United States in 1966 with as many as 100,000 in an hour, like celestial snowflakes, while rates of up to 4000 an hour were seen in 1999, 2001 and 2002.

MAJOR METEOR SHOWERS

Shower	Limits of activity	Date of maximum	Maximum rate (ZHR)
Quadrantids	January 1–6	January 3–4	100
Lyrids	April 19–25	April 21–22	10
Eta Aquarids	May 1–10	May 5	35
Delta Aquarids	July 15–August 15	July 28–29	20
Perseids	July 23–August 20	August 12–13	80
Orionids	October 16–27	October 20–22	25
Taurids	October 20–November 30	November 4	10
Leonids	November 15–20	November 17–18	10
Geminids	December 7–15	December 13–14	100

Asteroids and meteorites

Between Mars and Jupiter orbits a belt of rubble known as the asteroids or minor planets. Their existence was unknown until 1801, when the Italian astronomer Giuseppe Piazzi discovered Ceres, the largest of them, although astronomers had previously speculated that an unknown planet might exist in the suspiciously wide gap that separates Mars and Jupiter.

Well over 100,000 asteroids are now known, and there are estimated to be at least a million of them of 1 km diameter or larger in the asteroid belt. However, even if all the asteroids were rolled together, they would make a body less than half the size of the Moon. The asteroids are not, as was once suggested, the remnants of a former planet that was disrupted; they are merely the leftovers from the formation of the other planets, although many asteroids have been broken into smaller pieces by collisions.

Ceres itself is 940 km in diameter and takes 4.6 years to orbit the Sun. In 2006 the International Astronomical Union included Ceres in a new category of objects called *dwarf planets* on account of its size and the fact that it is rounded in shape. Ceres is composed of dark rock and, despite its size, is not the brightest asteroid. That honour goes to Vesta, 530 km in diameter, which is composed of paler rock; at times it is just visible to the naked eye. Ceres, Vesta, Pallas and several other asteroids are bright enough to be followed in binoculars as they move from night to night against the background stars. If you are uncertain which is the asteroid, draw the star field and look again the following night.

Our first close-up view of an asteroid came in 1991 when the space probe Galileo, on its way to Jupiter, flew past the asteroid Gaspra, showing it to be an irregularly shaped, rocky body about 17 km long, pitted with impact craters. Gaspra resembles the moons of Mars, Phobos and Deimos, thus strengthening the suspicion that those moons are captured asteroids (see photograph on page 361). Asteroids can have their own moons, as was confirmed in 1993 when Galileo flew past asteroid Ida, 55 km long, photographing a tiny companion, now named Dactyl.

More recently, extraordinary views of the highly eroded surface of the irregularly shaped asteroid Itokawa, 500 m long, were obtained by the Japanese probe Hayabusa (see photograph below). The probe also took samples of the asteroid for return to Earth.

Ninety-five per cent of asteroids orbit in the main belt between Mars and Jupiter, but there are some notable exceptions. One group of asteroids, known as the Trojans, moves along the same orbit as Jupiter. Most

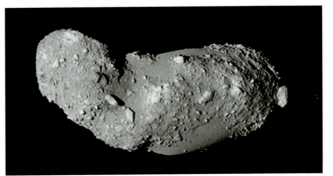

Asteroid Itokawa, seen from the Hayabusa spacecraft in 2005, resembles a pile of rubble, as though it was formed from the fragments of a former asteroid that was broken apart by a collision. (JAXA)

significant from our point of view are the near-Earth asteroids, which have orbits that bring them close to or even across the path of the Earth. Some of these objects may be the nuclei of extinct comets.

Asteroids of this type must have hit the Earth in the past, and others may do so in future, with devastating effect. Searching for such potentially hazardous asteroids is now a major international project.

Meteorites and meteorite craters

Objects that do reach the surface of the Earth are termed meteorites. Most meteorites are believed to be chips off asteroids, but a few rare specimens have compositions that show they come from the Moon and Mars.

Over 10,000 meteorites are estimated to land on Earth each year, but only about a dozen are actually picked up; the rest fall in uninhabited areas or into the sea. Most meteorites observed to fall are of the stony kind, and if not recovered immediately they soon weather away – or at least they do under normal conditions. But in Antarctica, scientists have found large numbers of ancient meteorites, including many rare types, preserved in pristine condition by the natural deep-freeze of the ice cap. Another rich source is the deserts of Earth, where the arid conditions preserve the meteorites.

Stony meteorites are usually termed *chondrites*, because they contain mineral-rich blobs known as chondrules. The small percentage of stones without chondrules are called *achondrites*. The most interesting class of stony meteorite is the *carbonaceous chondrites*; these have a high carbon content, and are believed to be among the most primitive rocks in existence, virtually unchanged since the formation of the Solar System. Some carbonaceous chondrites may be fragments of comets.

A small intermediate group of meteorites is the stony-irons, roughly half-and-half iron and rock. But the other main group of

meteorites apart from the chondrites is the irons. These contain 90 per cent iron and about 10 per cent nickel.

The largest known meteorite, the Hoba West meteorite, is an iron, and weighs about 60 tonnes. It must have hit the Earth at a relatively slow speed, for it did not dig a crater and did not break up. It lies where it fell in ancient times, near Grootfontein in Namibia. By contrast, the largest stony meteorite weighs 1.7 tonnes, and is one of a group of meteorites that fell near the city of Jilin, China, in 1976.

One particularly large meteorite, estimated to have weighed a quarter of a million tonnes, crashed into the Arizona desert about 25,000 years ago, digging out the now-famous Meteor Crater, 1.2 km in diameter. (Strictly, it should be called Meteorite Crater, but the old name is too firmly entrenched to change now.) Most of the meteorite was destroyed on impact, but enough fragments remain scattered around the crater to show that the meteorite was made of iron.

Over 150 meteorite impact sites are now known on Earth, including one 170 km in diameter at Chicxulub in Mexico which was formed 65 million years ago, at the time when the dinosaurs died out on Earth.

Meteor Crater, 1.2 km across and nearly 200 m deep, was formed by the impact of an iron meteorite in the Arizona desert about 50,000 years ago. Most of the meteorite was vaporized in the heat of the impact. (Ian Ridpath)

Astronomical instruments and observing

Binoculars and telescopes serve two main purposes: they collect more light than the human eye, and they magnify objects. In astronomy, the first of these two aspects is paramount. Astronomers seek large telescopes not because they magnify more, but because their increased light-gathering power brings fainter objects into view and allows finer details to be distinguished.

Telescopes come in two main types: refractors, which collect light through a main lens (known as the *object glass* or *objective*); and reflectors, which use a mirror. All the smallest telescopes are of the refracting type. Astronomical telescopes have interchangeable eyepieces to give different magnifications. Binoculars are a modified form of refractor in which the light path is folded by prisms to make them shorter and more portable.

Telescopes that combine lenses and mirrors are now very popular; these are known as *catadioptric* systems, and are best thought of as a modified form of reflector. Each type of instrument is dealt with in turn below.

Binoculars

The first optical equipment that almost every astronomer acquires is a pair of binoculars. Indeed, they are virtually indispensable for any observer, even those who own a substantial telescope. The advantages of binoculars are that they are portable, have a wide field of view and are relatively inexpensive.

Binoculars usually have a central focusing wheel that allows you to home in rapidly on objects of interest. One eyepiece should be individually adjustable to allow for differences in vision between your eyes. Avoid binoculars that can be focused only by adjusting each eyepiece separately as these are cumbersome to use. Zoom binoculars with a variable range of magnifications are made, but for best optical quality it is advisable to choose binoculars of fixed magnification.

Most binoculars used for astronomy incorporate what are known as Porro prisms to fold the light as shown in the diagram below. An alternative design uses so-called roof

Binoculars can be adjusted to suit the observer's eyes, using the following steps:

1. Alter the separation between the eyepieces by pivoting the two halves of the binocular around the central bar.

2. Turn the central focusing wheel until the image you see through the non-adjustable eyepiece is in focus.

3. Then turn the individually adjustable eyepiece to bring that eye into focus. Note the setting for future reference.

4. Turning the central wheel will then bring both eyepieces into focus at once.

Light emerges

Focus wheel

Eyepiece

Prisms

Objective lens

Light enters

prisms to provide a straight-through light path. While these are more compact they have smaller apertures and hence are less suitable for astronomy.

Binoculars bear markings consisting of two figures, such as these: 8 × 30, 8 × 40, 7 × 50, 10 × 50. In each case, the first figure is the magnification, and the second figure is the aperture (in millimetres) of the front lenses which gather the light. A magnification of 8 times, for example, means that the object appears 8 times larger than to the naked eye and hence 8 times closer.

There is a double price to be paid for magnification, though, and it applies to optical instruments of all kinds. Firstly, when an image is enlarged it becomes dimmer because the light is spread out over a larger area. So the greater the magnification, the more light is required to maintain an acceptably bright image. That can be obtained only with a larger collecting area – in other words, a wider aperture.

Secondly, as the magnification applied to a particular instrument goes up, its field of view shrinks. To get a satisfactory field of view and an acceptably bright image in bin-oculars you should look for a ratio of at least 1:5 between the magnification and aperture.

Another factor to consider is that binoculars with powers greater than about ×10 are difficult to hold steady, because the image vibrates with each tremble of the hand; powerful binoculars need to be mounted on a stand, but this negates their portability.

Image-stabilizing binoculars are now made which use either microprocessors, gyros or a mechanical suspension system to compensate for hand tremors, but they are heavier and cost more than normal binoculars; an additional disadvantage of the first two varieties is that they require batteries.

Good binoculars have fields of view of 3°–6° (six to ten times the apparent diameter of the Moon) and give breathtaking wide-angle views of the heavens that telescopes cannot match. For comparison, the typical field of view of a telescope with a low-power eyepiece is about 1°.

Binoculars are ideal for scanning constellations and the Milky Way; observing variable stars, star clusters, nebulae and large galaxies; and comets, asteroids, the Moon and lunar eclipses – but *never* turn them on the Sun.

Choosing a telescope

Which telescope is best for you depends on the type of observing you intend to do, as well as your budget. Many amateurs start with small refractors of 50–60 mm (2–2.4 inches) aperture. These are sufficient to show details on the Moon and planets, to find the brighter galaxies and planetary nebulae, and to separate many well-known double stars. They are particularly suitable for projecting the image of the Sun, which is so bright that large apertures are unnecessary (but heed the safety precautions on page 302 and never look directly at the Sun through any form of optical equipment without an approved filter). Refractors are preferable for solar observing since the Sun's concentrated heat and light can damage a reflector's secondary mirror.

For larger sizes, the cost advantage of a simple Newtonian reflector usually outweighs all other considerations. Newtonians in the 150 mm (6 inch) to 250 mm (10 inch) range are commonly used by amateurs. Their only real drawback is that periodically the mirror needs its reflective coating renewed, although each coating should last many years.

If you intend to specialize in areas such as planetary observation or close double stars, the slightly better definition of a refractor may be worth the additional expense. If compactness and portability are the governing factors, then catadioptric telescopes have the advantage.

Whichever type of telescope you eventually decide on, remember that the bigger the aperture the more you will see, so get the largest aperture you can afford.

Refracting telescopes, also known simply as refractors, collect light through a lens and focus it to an eyepiece at the end of a long, narrow tube. Almost all telescopes with apertures smaller than 100 mm are refractors. In each of these diagrams, D is the telescope's aperture and F is the focal length of the main lens or mirror.

Reflecting telescopes, or reflectors, bounce light off a concave main mirror onto a secondary mirror near the entrance to the tube, which diverts the light into the eyepiece. In the Newtonian design shown here, the most common type used by amateurs, the eyepiece is in the side of the tube.

Catadioptric telescopes such as the popular Schmidt–Cassegrain design shown here have a thin lens at the front of the tube to improve the telescope's field of view. After passing through the lens the incoming light bounces off the main mirror onto a secondary and then back through a hole in the main mirror where the eyepiece is placed. (Wil Tirion)

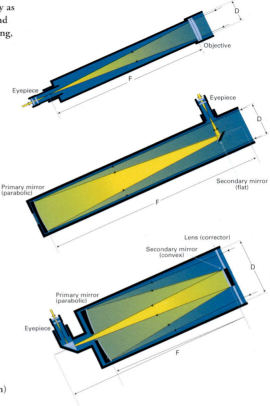

Telescopes for beginners

A small telescope – one with an aperture of 50–60 mm (2–2.4 inches) – can cost several times more than a pair of binoculars, with little gain in light grasp. What telescopes do offer over binoculars is higher magnification and a mounting for support. Unfortunately, in some mass-produced telescopes the mounting is not as steady as might be wished, and the image can vibrate for several seconds each time the telescope is moved.

As a selling point, some small telescopes offer eyepieces with impressively high powers of over ×200. But such high magnifications

applied to a small telescope produce images so faint that little can be seen, and are therefore a complete waste.

As a good general rule, the maximum usable magnification on a telescope is ×20 for each 10 mm of aperture (×50 per inch). These pitfalls aside, there are many serviceable small telescopes available which will bring into view a wide selection of the celestial sights mentioned in this book.

The smallest telescopes are all refractors (top diagram above), which collect and focus light with a lens. For more ambitious observers, a telescope with an aperture of 75 mm (3 inches) aperture is the minimum required to begin serious work. Telescopes greater than 75 mm in aperture are usually of the reflecting type, because size for size they are cheaper to make than refractors. Popular sizes of reflectors are 150 mm (6 inch) and 220 mm (8½ inch) aperture, which should bring into view virtually all the targets for observation listed in this book.

Reflectors used by amateurs are usually built to the design invented in 1668 by Isaac Newton. In the Newtonian reflector, light collected by the concave main mirror is bounced back up the tube to a smaller secondary mirror, which diverts the light into an eyepiece at the side of the tube (centre diagram on previous page). Inevitably, the secondary mirror blocks some of the incoming light from the main mirror, but this shadowing effect of the secondary is not significant and does not adversely affect the image. An extreme form of Newtonian is the *rich-field telescope* or RFT, which uses a mirror of very short focal length and a low-power eyepiece to give a field of view of around 3°, not as good as binoculars but suitable for general stargazing.

Another design of reflecting telescope is the Cassegrain, in which the light is reflected back from the secondary through a hole bored in the main mirror where the eyepiece or other detectors can be mounted. Large professional telescopes commonly use the Cassegrain design or variants of it.

In *catadioptric* systems, which combine lenses and mirrors, the incoming light passes through a thin glass plate at the front of the telescope before falling onto the main mirror and being reflected as in a Cassegrain. The most commonly encountered variant in amateur astronomy is known as a Schmidt–Cassegrain telescope or SCT (bottom diagram on previous page, and at right).

The advantage of catadioptric designs is that, because the light path is folded back within the tube, the overall length of the telescope is much shorter than in a conventional reflector. The consequent saving in weight and space, allied with increased port-

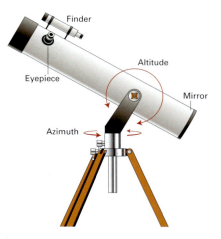

A Newtonian reflector on an altazimuth mount, the simplest form of support for a telescope. The telescope is held in a cradle which allows it to rock up and down (in altitude) and swivel from side to side (in azimuth). (Wil Tirion)

A Schmidt–Cassegrain telescope on an altazimuth mount. In equatorial versions the base is tilted so that the arms of the fork holding the telescope tube point at the celestial pole. (Wil Tirion)

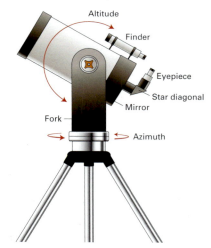

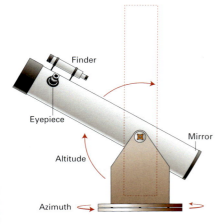

The Dobsonian is a popular type of altazimuth mounting for reflectors of all sizes where low-power viewing is all that is required. (Wil Tirion)

ability, compensates for the higher cost of a catadioptric telescope. Catadioptrics are particularly popular for astronomical imaging because cameras can be mounted behind the main mirror without unbalancing them.

As for cost, remember that a telescope is a precision optical instrument, and so you must expect to pay at least as much as you would for any similar instrument such as a good-quality camera.

Telescope mountings

A telescope requires a mounting on which it can be supported and swivelled to point at various places in the sky. The quality of the mounting is just as important as the quality of the optics, for even the best telescope cannot be expected to show much if it is shaking all the time, or if you have difficulty steering it to track objects as the Earth rotates. Sturdiness and smoothness of movement are all-important in a telescope mounting.

The simplest form of telescope mounting is the *altazimuth* (see diagrams on the facing page). This has two axes, one horizontal and one vertical, which allow the telescope to be

pivoted up and down (in altitude) and to pan from side to side (in azimuth). In an altazimuth mount, the telescope is usually held in a fork on top of a tripod, although in the case of small, lightweight telescopes the 'fork' can be reduced to a single arm.

Unless a refractor is mounted on a very tall tripod, the eyepiece will be too low down to look through comfortably when the tele-scope is pointed upwards. A common solution is to insert a *star diagonal* at the eyepiece end. Star diagonals use a mirror or prism to turn the light through 90° so that the observer can look downwards into the eyepiece, which is a more convenient observing position. For Newtonian reflectors, short tripods suffice since the eyepiece is near the top of the tube, and so is normally quite accessible from a standing position.

Convenient additions to an altazimuth mount are small knobs, known as slow-motion controls, which can be turned to move the telescope slightly in each axis. This

In a German-type equatorial mounting, one axis (termed the polar axis) is set up so that it is par-allel to the Earth's axis and thus points towards the celestial pole; the other axis (the declination axis) is at right angles to it. (Wil Tirion)

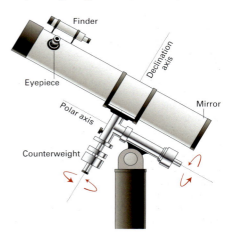

is useful both for centring an object in the field of view, and for tracking it as the Earth spins. When high powers are in use, the Earth's rotation can carry an object out of the telescope's field of view in a remarkably short time.

A popular version of the altazimuth for large Newtonian reflectors is the *Dobsonian* mount, named after the American amateur John Dobson who devised it. In a Dobsonian, the telescope tube is made of lightweight material so that its centre of gravity lies near the mirror end. The tube is supported at its lower (mirror) end by a wooden box with a Formica base that swings around in azimuth on pads made of Teflon, the slippery plastic material used in non-stick frying pans. Formica glides smoothly on Teflon, making a simple yet steady bearing. The tube pivots up and down in altitude on a shaft supported by more Teflon pads (see the diagram at the top of the previous page).

Despite its deceptive simplicity, the Dobsonian has proved a very effective mounting. Cheapness and portability have ensured its widespread adoption by observers requiring wide-angle, low-power views of the heavens that do not involve precise tracking.

Best of all for tracking objects accurately as the Earth turns is an *equatorial* mount. In this, one axis, called the polar axis, is aligned so that it points directly at the celestial pole (either north or south, depending which hemisphere the observer is in). The sky appears to rotate around the celestial pole, so simply turning the polar axis will keep an object in view. A second axis at right angles to the first, called the declination axis, allows the telescope to pivot up and down (i.e. in declination).

There are several varieties of equatorial mounting, the most usual being the German type in which the telescope is counterbalanced by weights on the declination axis. In fork mountings as used by catadioptric telescopes the arms of the fork point towards the celestial pole, and the telescope tube pivots between them on the declination axis.

Which way round?

An astronomical telescope produces an image that is inverted top to bottom and reversed left to right by comparison with the naked-eye or binocular view. A 90° star diagonal, used on some telescopes to make observing more convenient, flips the image upright again but leaves it reversed left to right as in a mirror. These different orientations must be taken into account when trying to match up the view through a telescope with a star chart or a map of the Moon.

The Moon as seen with the naked eye or through binoculars

The Moon as seen through an astronomical telescope: upside down and reversed left to right

The Moon as seen through a 90° star diagonal: upright but still reversed left to right

Equatorial mounts are usually fitted with a small motor that slowly turns the equatorial axis at exactly the same speed as the Earth rotates. Once the telescope is pointed at a celestial object and the drive motor is running, the object will remain fixed firmly in the field of view for as long as the observer wishes, essential for high-power observing or photography. Experience soon demonstrates the desirability of a stationary image if you are trying to split a faint double star or make a drawing of a planet.

To help with locating objects, a smaller sighting telescope called a *finder* is usually mounted on the side of the main tube. Simple finders for small telescopes consist of a red dot from a light-emitting diode (LED) which reflects off a small glass window; the telescope is lined up by superimposing the dot on the required star. For larger telescopes, small low-power refractors are used as finders. Cross-wires in its eyepiece like the telescopic sights of a rifle, or sometimes a concentric series of faintly illuminated rings, allow the user to centre the target.

Computer-controlled telescopes are now widely available that will automatically align themselves on the sky and then point to any required object, selected from a list of many thousands whose positions are programmed into a handset. Such GOTO telescopes, as they are commonly termed, can also be controlled by a home computer with suitable software. Unlike traditional telescopes the altazimuth mounts of GOTO telescopes are motorized for tracking objects, although the accuracy is not as good as with an equatorial mounting.

Through the telescope

A few words need to be said about what you can expect to see with telescopes of different sizes, and why. Anyone looking through an astronomical telescope for the first time is usually surprised to find that the image is upside down. There is a simple practical reason for this: to turn the image the right way up, an extra lens would have to be inserted in the eyepiece.

Every time light passes through a lens or is reflected off a mirror, some light is lost. Celestial objects are usually so faint that any loss of light is undesirable. For astronomical purposes it does not really matter which way up the image appears, so the extra lens is left out and the image remains inverted. So-called terrestrial eyepieces or erecting prisms will turn the image the right way round for everyday viewing if required.

When you make an observation you should record the date, the time, the size of the instrument, the magnification and the sky conditions. Astronomers record dates in the form year/month/day. Times of astronomical events are usually given in Universal Time (UT), which is the same as GMT (Greenwich Mean Time). If you are in a different time zone from Greenwich and prefer to use your

The eye and observing

The human eye is an optical instrument in its own right which forms an image upon its rear surface, the retina. At night, the retina becomes much more sensitive to light, a process known as *dark adaptation*, but the increased sensitivity builds up only slowly. Hence, when going outdoors at night from a brightly lit room you should allow time for your eyes to adjust before beginning to observe.

The main change in sensitivity comes in the first ten minutes, but dark adaptation continues to improve for half an hour or more. Green and blue light rapidly destroys dark adaptation but red light does not, so when observers need to see to read or write at night they use a red light such as a torch with a red filter.

Images on the retina are sensed by two types of nerve endings, termed rods and cones on account of their shape. The central part of the retina consists only of cones, whereas rods are predominant in the outer regions. Rods are far more light-sensitive than cones. As a result, it is easier to see faint objects if you look slightly to one side of them so that the image falls on the rods in the outer regions of the retina. This technique is known as *averted vision*. Tapping the telescope so that the image gently vibrates is another way to make elusive objects easier to see.

local time (e.g. Eastern Standard Time for the eastern seaboard of the USA) then be sure to note which time system you are using. Also remember to allow for the hour's difference when summer time (daylight saving time) is in operation.

Incidentally, your eyes need time to become accustomed to the dark before you can hope to see the faintest objects; when you go out at night allow at least 10 minutes for your eyes to become dark adapted. A useful trick when trying to glimpse faint objects is to use *averted vision* – that is, to look to the side of the object under study so that its light falls on the outer, more sensitive part of the retina.

Eyepieces and magnification

Unlike binoculars and spyglass telescopes, which have fixed eyepieces, the eyepieces in astronomical telescopes are interchangeable, offering a range of magnifications to suit the object under study. For instance, a star cluster or galaxy will require low magnification; planets are best viewed with medium magni-

The 8-m Gemini North reflector in Hawaii is one of the most powerful telescopes in the world. A series of exposures were taken as the dome was turned and combined to give the appearance of transparency. (Peter Michaud & Kirk Pu`uohau-Pummill/Gemini Observatory)

fication; and to split a close double star you will need your highest powers.

The magnification of an eyepiece depends on two factors: its own focal length and the focal length of the telescope. To work out the magnification of an eyepiece in a particular telescope requires no more than a little straightforward arithmetic: you simply divide the focal length of the telescope by the focal length of the eyepiece. The result tells you the power of that eyepiece.

You will soon realize that the shorter the focal length of the eyepiece, the higher its magnification. Eyepieces have their focal length marked on them in millimetres; a typical range of focal lengths is 6 mm to 40 mm. An additional lens, called a *Barlow lens*, can be inserted in the drawtube to increase the magnification of any eyepiece (usually doubling it), thereby offering a wider range of powers from a given set of eyepieces.

Manufacturers often describe their telescopes in terms of *focal ratio*, such as *f*/6 or *f*/8. The focal ratio is the focal length of the lens or mirror divided by its aperture. If you don't know the focal length of your telescope you can easily find out by multiplying its aperture by the focal ratio stated by the manufacturers. For instance, a 100-mm telescope with a focal ratio of *f*/6 has a focal length of 600 mm; if its focal ratio is *f*/8, its focal length is longer, at 800 mm. For a 150-mm telescope of *f*/6 or *f*/8, the focal length would be 900 mm or 1200 mm respectively.

Now, assume that you have an eyepiece of focal length 20 mm. In a telescope of 600 mm focal length it will give a magnification of 600 divided by 20, which is 30 times, usually expressed as ×30. That is quite a low power for astronomical purposes. In a telescope of 1200 mm focal length, the same eyepiece will give a magnification of ×60. An eyepiece of half the focal length, 10 mm, will give twice the magnification. Note that the aperture of the telescope is irrelevant in these calculations; the focal length is the sole figure governing magnification.

The most popular type of eyepiece for general use is the Plössl, named after its inventor, the Austrian optician Simon Plössl. Various other designs are used for wide-field views of the deep sky. Different designs of eyepiece have different fields of view, even though they may be of the same focal length.

A field of view is sometimes stated on the eyepiece itself, and is usually between about 30° and 80°, but this is the *apparent field of view* – it is not the field of view you will actually see, for the final result also depends on the focal length of the telescope. To find the true field of view for an eyepiece, divide the apparent field by the magnification it produces. For example, an eyepiece with 50° apparent field of view that magnifies 40 times will give a true field of 1¼°, just over twice the apparent diameter of the full Moon.

An easy way to measure your telescope's field of view is to time a star near the celestial equator as it crosses the field. The Earth rotates through 0.25 minutes of arc in 1 second of time so if the star takes 60 seconds to cross, then the field is 60 × 0.25 = 15 arc minutes wide.

Another feature of eyepieces to consider is their *eye relief*. This is, in effect, how close you have to place your eye to the eyepiece to see the entire field of view. Good eye relief means that you do not have to cram your eye right up against the eyepiece, so those who need to wear glasses while observing should choose eyepieces with good eye relief. Incidentally, if you are short- or long-sighted you do not need to wear glasses for observing because you can adjust the focus of the telescope or binoculars to compensate.

Light grasp and resolution

Where a telescope's aperture becomes crucial is in the matters of light grasp and resolution of detail. All other things being equal, a larger aperture shows fainter stars and finer detail than a smaller aperture, but exactly how faint the stars are and how fine the detail is depends on atmospheric conditions, optical quality and the observer's eyesight. Practical experience shows that the faintest stars likely to be visible through amateur telescopes of various apertures are as given in the table below.

TELESCOPIC LIMITING MAGNITUDES	
Aperture	Limiting magnitude
50 mm (2 inches)	11.2
60 mm (2.4 inches)	11.6
75 mm (3 inches)	12.1
100 mm (4 inches)	12.7
150 mm (6 inches)	13.6
220 mm (8.5 inches)	14.4

TELESCOPIC LIMITS OF RESOLUTION

Aperture		Limit of resolution (seconds of arc)
50 mm	(2 inches)	2.3
60 mm	(2.4 inches)	1.9
75 mm	(3 inches)	1.5
100 mm	(4 inches)	1.1
150 mm	(6 inches)	0.8
220 mm	(8.5 inches)	0.5

The resolution, or resolving power, of a telescope is expressed in seconds of arc (″). One second of arc is a very small quantity, equivalent to the size a coin would appear when several kilometres away. A telescope's resolution governs the detail that one can see on the Moon or planets, and the closeness of double stars that can be separated. The theoretical limits of resolution for telescopes of various apertures are shown in the table above. Under exceptional conditions, the limits of magnitude and resolution tabulated here may be surpassed; but in many cases, particularly when observing from cities, they will not be achieved.

Transparency and seeing

Finally, we come to the atmosphere itself. Professional observatories are sited on high mountain tops to get above as much of the atmosphere as possible, but most amateurs are stuck with conditions in their own back yard, all too often including urban haze and glare from streetlights. There are two aspects of the atmosphere to take into account: its clarity and its steadiness.

Atmospheric clarity is known to astronomers as the *transparency*. A good index of atmospheric transparency is the magnitude of the faintest stars that can be seen overhead by the naked eye. The zenithal limiting magnitude should always be noted when observing meteors, because it affects the hourly rates. Transparency needs to be at its best when you are looking for faint objects, particularly nebulae, galaxies and comets.

On the other hand, the steadiness of the atmosphere, termed the *seeing*, is paramount for planetary and double star observation. Turbulence in the atmosphere produces a boiling effect of the image, drastically reducing the resolution. Hot air rising from neighbouring buildings can be a particularly annoying localized form of turbulence. Good transparency and good seeing do not always go hand in hand. On a crystal-clear night after a rainstorm the seeing can be particularly atrocious, whereas slightly misty nights, when the clarity is low, can be the steadiest.

Seeing is estimated on a five-point scale: 1, perfect; 2, good; 3, moderate; 4, poor; 5, very bad. This is sometimes known as the Antoniadi scale after the astronomer who devised it, Eugène Antoniadi. If a close double star cannot be clearly split on a night of indifferent seeing, examine it again on a better night. Transparency and seeing share one characteristic: they are always poorest closest to the horizon, so to get the brightest, steadiest image objects should be observed when they are as high in the sky as possible.

A useful addition to the modern astronomer's armoury is one of the special filters designed to enhance the visibility of faint objects such as nebulae, galaxies and comets. Such filters screw into the barrel of the eyepiece and come in two main types: one type, called Light Pollution Reduction or LPR filters, blocks out light pollution, thereby increasing the contrast of objects against the night sky; more extreme types, called nebula filters, block out all wavelengths except those which nebulae and comets emit most strongly.

Finally, one important but often overlooked part of an astronomer's equipment is warm clothing. Even on a seemingly mild night a tracksuit and training shoes make a practical outfit, while in the depths of winter you will need to dress like a mountaineer, with a quilted jacket, thick trousers, a hat, thermal socks and boots.

INDEX

Entries in this Index are listed in strict alphabetical order. All named stars of mag. 2.0 and brighter are included. Star designations such as α (alpha) Centauri and η (eta) Carinae will be found under the relevant constellations. Page numbers in **bold type** refer to photographs or illustrations.